THE OPEN DOOR

WINGS OF
THE MORNING

BERYL MATTHEWS

THE OPEN DOOR

WINGS OF THE MORNING

BCA

This edition published 2003
By BCA
By arrangement with Penguin Books Ltd
An imprint of the Penguin Group

CN115062

Set in Monotype Dante by Intype London Ltd
Printed in Germany by GGP Media, Pössneck

CONTENTS

THE OPEN DOOR

' . . . behold, I have set before thee an open door, and
no man can shut it: . . .'

Revelation 3:8

I

Bermondsey, London. September 1913

The door across the street opened and Rose caught a glimpse inside the house; the walls had colourful paper on them and the furniture gleamed from continual polishing. She let out a ragged sigh. How she longed to be clean! She continued to gaze at the posh houses and felt anger rise inside her. Why did some people live in comfort and ease, and others, like herself, in squalor?

She was a seething mass of questions. Her whole life she'd been asking, Why? Her search for knowledge was like a living thing inside her, never giving her any peace. Everyone kept telling her she was only a child and shouldn't bother with things nobody could understand, and it was useless asking questions at home because all it ever got her was a clip round the ear. School was different, though. She smiled when she thought about it. She might be only eleven but she was clever, her teacher said so. She soaked up knowledge, but was never satisfied – Miss Gardner had to push her out when the bell rang. 'Rose,' she'd say, taking from her whatever book she was reading, 'go home, child.'

'Can I take it with me?' she would plead. 'I'll take good care of it, Miss.'

But the answer was always the same, it was not allowed, so she would try to sneak into a bookshop without anyone seeing. If she was lucky, she could huddle in a corner and read for half an hour or so, but if she was spotted she was thrown out. Today she'd hardly set foot inside the door before she was marched out again.

It made her so cross. Just because she was shabby, they thought she was up to no good – but she wasn't and she'd fight anyone who said she was. All she wanted to do was look at the books: there were rows and rows of them in there and it was like heaven to her.

Her dark, resentful eyes swept over a well-dressed couple. The man waved a hand angrily and shouted at her to go away, but she ignored him. The only difference between her and them was that they had money and she didn't.

She looked down at her worn frock and ground her teeth. One day things would be different.

'What are you up to?' a stern voice asked.

'Nothing,' she replied, looking the policeman straight in the eyes. 'They needn't worry over there, I'm not dangerous,' she said, cheekily, and saw surprise in his eyes: she knew how to speak properly – every day she listened to her teacher and copied her.

'What are you doing round here?'

'Just looking. You can't arrest me for that, can you?' Again her gaze was direct; she had learnt early that it was a weakness to show fear.

'Where do you live?' he persisted.

'Over there.' She pointed across the river. 'Garrett Street.'

He stroked his chin thoughtfully. 'I'd better walk you back.'

Her laugh was scornful. 'You new around here?

Someone should've told you that the coppers have to come down our street in threes.'

'Oh, and why is that?'

'Because our filthy, rat-infested hovels are full of bullies who don't want the police to know what they're up to. They must be a couple of hundred years old and should have been pulled down long ago.'

'Well, you'd better be getting home. Your folks will be worried about you.'

She gave him a pitying look and lapsed back into the London twang. 'What makes you think they care tuppence about me?'

His smile was tinged with sadness. 'What's your name?'

'Emily Rose, but everybody calls me Rose, when they're being polite.'

'And what do they call you when they're being rude?'

'"That black-eyed bitch," among other things.' Her eyes flashed like jet, defying him to laugh.

There was a shout from across the street. 'Constable, send her away. She belongs round the docks with the others of her kind. This is a respectable area.'

The policeman raised his hand in acknowledgement, and turned to the girl beside him. 'You'd better go.'

'What's he talking about?' she demanded.

'He . . . um . . . thinks you're older than you are.'

'Older?' It took a few moments for his meaning to sink in, then she started across the road with a growl, but the policeman caught her and held her back.

'Oh, no, you don't.'

Rose tore herself free and glared at him. 'He's calling me a tart! You should have let me at him – he deserves a thrashing for that.'

'Do your duty, constable,' the man called, from a safe distance.

'It's all right, sir, she's only a child.'

The man laughed. 'Is that what she's telling you?'

Rose swore and started across the road again, but the policeman held on to her.

'Let me go!' she demanded. 'He's calling me a liar now.'

'Well, to be honest, you don't look like a child,' he said, slackening his grip slightly. 'And with your black hair and foreign looks, you're already a pretty girl.'

'Even with the dirt?' she sneered.

'Your clothes have seen better days, but you're clean enough.'

At that Rose felt a little better and smoothed down her frock. At least her efforts to stay clean had not been in vain.

'Off you go, Rose, and don't come here again, will you?'

'I got as much right as anyone else to go where I want. That man might own a big fancy house but he don't own the street.'

'That's true, but you're not welcome in this part of town.'

She glowered. 'Well, some day I'm gonna change that.'

As she turned away she heard him mutter, 'Poor little sod.'

Rose spun back, flushed with anger. 'Keep your pity, Mister, because one day I'm going to be living like them over there – you see if I'm not!' Then, fists clenched in determination, she turned and ran across the bridge.

*

'Rose! Where've you been? Come and get the kids their tea.'

She stopped, one foot on the stairs. She had been about to make her getaway to an empty space somewhere. She'd found a whole page of a newspaper today and wanted to read it. It was a rare prize, so her visit to posher parts had been worth while.

'Rose!'

She sighed, folded the paper carefully, then slipped it into her pocket. It would have to wait until later.

In the scullery it was bedlam. 'Quiet!' she yelled.

The noise stopped instantly and six pairs of eyes, ranging from blue to hazel, turned in her direction. She stared at the children, defying them to speak, then said, 'Sit at the table.'

They scrambled on to the chairs, but eight-year-old Bob scowled. He was a bully, just like his father, but he knew better than to try to beat Rose.

Her mother put a large bowl of dripping on the table and a loaf of bread. 'When they've had their tea, put them to bed.'

'Why me?' she protested. 'Why can't Flo take a turn?'

'Because you're the oldest.'

Rose began to cut thick slices of bread and spread them with dripping. It was useless arguing. It never got her anywhere because her mother was too worn out with trying to look after them all. She cast her a worried glance. She was having another baby. Where the blazes were they going to put it? The house was already full to bursting.

A little hand came out and tried to take a slice. She slapped it away and made the mistake of looking at their expectant faces. The scene tugged at her heart – six little urchins with grubby faces and empty bellies. She tried to be hard, she really did, because turning off her emotions was the only way she could stand this hell, but this wasn't right!

Diving down to the bottom of the dripping bowl, she scraped out some of the rich dark jelly and spread a little on each slice of bread, then handed it round and watched the kids eat like wolves – except the youngest, Annie, who was too small to manage the big chunk of bread.

Rose squatted beside her and started to break it into smaller pieces. 'Come on, Annie,' she coaxed, 'eat it.'

'I'll have it if she don't want it.' Bob made a grab for it, but Rose was too quick for him.

'Leave it alone, you greedy pig,' she scolded, then turned back to Annie. She didn't like the look of her: the child's face was so white that her skin looked almost transparent. Annie was the only one of her brothers and sisters Rose worried about: at two, she couldn't talk properly, or walk, and Rose doubted that she would live very long.

'Mum?' Rose went to stand next to her mother, who was at the stove, stirring a pot. 'What you cooking?'

'Scrag-end of beef with dumplings.'

It smelt delicious and Rose's stomach grumbled. 'Can I have some of the gravy for Annie?'

'This is for your dad.'

'I know, but Annie's sick and she needs proper food. It isn't right he gets a dinner at night and everyone else gets next to nothing.'

'I do the best I can, but you know how the old man gets into a rage if he doesn't have his meat and gravy.'

Rose bit back angry words and glanced at her mother's rounded stomach. 'Why do you keep having kids?' she asked, her lip curling with distaste.

'Because that's the way it is. We have to accept our lot in life.'

Why? Rose wanted to shout, but knew she'd be wasting her breath. She took another quick look at Annie, who had eaten a little of her bread. 'What about that gravy, Mum?'

'All right, then, just a little.' Her mother ladled some into a plate. 'Annie does look sick. It's not that I don't care,' she protested, 'but your dad must come first. We'd be in a right pickle without him.'

Rose took the plate and said nothing. As far as she could make out, he never did anything for them. He drank too much and got nasty with a few pints inside him.

She soaked the rest of Annie's bread in the gravy and was relieved when the little girl ate it. Then she swept her sister up in her arms. 'Come on, let's get you into bed. I'll try and get you an apple tomorrow, shall I?' she whispered. 'Our secret, eh?'

Rose spat on the flat iron and watched it sizzle.

'What's she doing that for?'

She kept her head down and concentrated on her ironing. She hated the way he never spoke to her directly.

'Answer your dad,' her mother said sharply.

'It's the school prize-giving tomorrow.' Rose ironed carefully around a patch on the skirt of her frock.

'Ha! Thinks she gonna win somefing, does she?'

'Yes, I do.' She put the iron back on the stove, picked

up another and spat on it. She wasn't ashamed of being clever, and that probably made him madder because he couldn't even write his name.

'How did you ever have a kid like that?' he yelled at her mother now. 'Look at her, she's like a bleeding cuckoo in the nest.'

'She likes learning,' her mother defended Rose weakly. 'There's no shame in that.'

Rose shut out the talk: it was best not to listen to his ranting. She put down the iron, held up the frock and examined it critically. It was too old to do much with, but at least it was clean and pressed.

'Look at her, putting on airs and graces. She thinks she's too good for us.'

I might have to live in this place, Rose declared silently, but inside I'm different. She sighed.

Her father pushed his chair back from the table. 'Where's your purse, Marj? I need some beer money.'

'I haven't got any. I spent the last on your dinner tonight.'

'I don't believe you, woman. Give me your purse.'

Marj pulled it out of the pocket of her pinny. He snatched it and tipped out the contents on to the table. 'A penny!' he bellowed. 'How am I going to have a night out with that?'

'It's all I've got.'

With a snarl, he pocketed the coin and stormed out of the house.

'Oh, Mum,' Rose muttered, 'how you going to get by?'

'I don't let him know everything. I've got a few pennies put aside and I'll get some oxtail tomorrow and give you all a treat for your tea. You're right about Annie, she's looking peaky, but so are you all.' She sat down heavily. 'I haven't being paying much notice just lately – this baby's draining me.'

'I'm not going to get married and have squalling babies when I'm grown-up,' Rose declared.

Her mother gave a rare smile. 'That won't be easy, my girl, because you're going to be quite a beauty. The men are going to chase after you in packs.'

'They'll be wasting their time,' Rose said confidently. Then something occurred to her. 'Mum, why am I so dark?'

'Well . . .' her mother seemed to be searching for words ' . . . you take after my mother's side of the family, I expect. We've got Italian blood and it's come through in you.'

'What were they like?'

'I don't know. I never knew any of them.' Marj hauled herself to her feet. 'I'm going to have a rest.'

As their mother left the scullery Flo wandered in. 'Anything to eat?' she asked.

'Only bread and dripping.' Rose pushed the bowl towards her sister. Let the lazy devil do it herself.

Flo grumbled a bit, then sat down and started to eat.

'Flo?'

'What?'

'Can I wear the good boots tomorrow?'

'No, they're mine.' Flo spread more dripping on her bread.

'Oh, go on,' Rose pleaded. 'It's the school prize-giving and I want to look nice. You can wear mine for a day, can't you?'

'They've got holes in. What if it rains?'

'It won't rain. Anyway, I've put some thick cardboard in them.'

'I dunno.'

'I'll get you an apple tomorrow if you let me have them.' Rose was sure she could bribe her sister.

'Where you gonna get that from?' Flo was suddenly interested.

'That's my secret.'

'How many can you get?'

'Two or three.' She hoped.

Flo considered. 'I'll let you wear them for two apples,' she said.

'Don't be greedy!'

'Oh, all right.'

At nine o'clock that evening Rose crept out of the house and ran across the bridge. As she made her way round to the back of the big houses, she shivered in the fading light. Then she pulled herself together and told herself sternly that she needn't be frightened about taking a few apples from these people because they already had more than they could eat. However, that didn't ease her conscience, which was surprising: you didn't find much honesty in Garrett Street.

She reached the garden where she'd seen the fruit trees; they'd been loaded with apples the other week and she hoped they still were. She took a deep breath, pulled herself to the top of the wall and peered into the deepening gloom but could not see if the fruit was still there. She'd have to go over and take a closer look. Hoping the owners didn't have a dog, she jumped down from the wall and crept towards the tree. The apples were still there.

She grasped a low branch, pulled herself up, careful to keep the trunk between herself and the house, she removed three large apples, hesitated, then took another. They'd never miss it.

She shoved the fruit into the bag she'd brought with her, scrambled down and ran for the wall. She scaled it rapidly and then, her heart beating wildly, she ran back across the bridge and headed for the alley behind the row of shops at the top of her street. It was dark now but she knew how to get to her secret hiding place. The cobbler's yard was full of junk piled up against a wall, and she heaved aside an old mattress to reveal a small, sturdy cupboard. She put the apples inside then replaced the mattress, making sure it covered the cupboard. They would be safe in there from man or rodent until tomorrow. Then Rose ran into Garrett Street and laughed as she remembered the man who had insulted her today: she hoped it had been his apples she'd pinched.

2

Rose wished they'd get on with it.

She tried not to fidget or kick off Flo's boots because she might not be able to get them on again, and she didn't want to go barefoot to collect her prize.

She was going to win, she kept telling herself. She was always top of her class – but was she top of the school? Doubt crept in and she looked down at the floor to hide her expression: she didn't like people to see what she was thinking. Then her head came up again. Of course she was good enough to come first.

Her gaze locked on the prize and her heart nearly burst with yearning. She wanted it so much!

The Head, Mr Spencer, stood up and banged on the table for quiet. A couple of small prizes were presented, but Rose wasn't interested in them; there was only one thing on that table she wanted.

'And now we come to the top award,' the Head said, looking around the room. 'This is a special prize for the pupil who did best in all subjects.'

Rose was almost afraid to breathe. He was droning on about excellence, or some such thing, but her ears were tuned for only one thing: her name.

'And the winner is . . . Emily Rose Webster.'

The long-held breath whooshed out of her lungs.

'Emily,' the Head actually smiled, 'come and receive your prize.'

She was on her feet immediately, the pinching boots forgotten in her excitement.

'Well done, Emily. I want you to come and see me at the close of school today.' He held out the prize.

Her hands closed eagerly around the beautiful Bible. This was the best thing she had ever had in her life, a treasure beyond her wildest dreams. It was black, real leather, she was sure, with gold lettering, and it was just the right size to fit into the large patch pocket on her dress. She could keep it with her all the time.

'I hope you're going to read it,' he said, smiling again.

'Oh, I will, sir. I've already learned quite a lot of it. Miss Gardner lets me read it at break-time.'

'That's right, Mr Spencer,' Miss Gardner told him from her seat on the platform, 'I've never met a girl with such a thirst for knowledge.'

Rose looked at her teacher with affection. Miss Gardner was quite young, around twenty-three, Rose thought. She had grey eyes, shiny brown hair, and always looked so clean and tidy. She was a good teacher and answered Rose's questions patiently.

The Head smiled at Rose again. 'Don't you go and play during the free time?'

'No, sir, I'd rather read.' She had no interest in games; all she needed was between the covers of books.

For the rest of the day the precious Bible was never out of her sight, and at the end of lessons, Miss Gardner gave her a bag to put it in. 'That will keep it clean.'

'Thank you, Miss.'

Miss Gardner looked at the clock. 'You'd better go and see the Head now.'

Rose made her way along the corridor. On reaching

the door marked 'Mr Spencer', she knocked and waited. She was a little worried because you were only called to his office when you'd done something wrong.

'Come,' he called.

She stood in front of the desk, wondering what he could want with her.

'Emily, you've done remarkably well this year and shown a love of learning that is unusual . . .' He hesitated and looked at her closely. 'We have decided to offer you the chance of a free place at the secondary school.'

The big school! Her eyes opened wide. 'Thank you, sir –'

He held up his hand to stop her. 'You must ask your family first, because although they won't have to pay the fees, they will have other expenses. It will mean new clothes, and books.'

Her spirits sank. Then she rallied. This was her chance – she couldn't let it go. 'I'll ask them, sir, but I'm sure everything will be all right.'

He nodded gravely. 'You must let me have your decision by tomorrow morning. The place will be given to someone else if you are unable to take it.'

'You won't have to do that, sir.' She spoke with a confidence she wasn't feeling.

'I hope you're right. Now, off you go, and see me first thing in the morning.'

She hurried away, her mind in turmoil. The chances of her taking up this place at the big school were slim, but she *had* to try.

'Did you win?' her mother asked, as she walked into the scullery.

'Yes.' She held out the book. 'Isn't it lovely? The Head's signed it.'

'Very nice, Rosie.' Her mother put plates on to the scrubbed wooden table. 'Something to be proud of, eh?'

Rose nodded. Today had been the best day of her life. Suddenly she became aware that the room was silent. A quick look told her that the children were already sitting at the table, waiting expectantly for their tea.

'What a lovely book,' Nancy whispered.

'Have you got clean hands?' Rose asked the timid seven-year-old, who was gazing at her with big blue eyes.

Nancy held them out for inspection and Rose placed the book in front of her, knowing it would be quite safe with Nancy. Then she turned back to her mother. 'Something smells good.'

'I got a nice bit of oxtail cheap – the butcher was about to close.'

Rose helped to dish up the food then sat next to Annie and started to feed her. Their mum had done well today – there was even some potato in it. When she saw how much Annie was enjoying it, Rose spooned some potato from her plate on to the little girl's.

'Rose!' her mother scolded. 'You need that just as much as she does.'

'I'm fine, Mum, you know I get the free dinner at school.'

'What did you have today?'

'Bowl of pea soup, chunk of bread, semolina pudding. It's much the same every day.'

Marj looked at her daughter intently. 'Does it shame you that you have to have the dinner provided for the poor kids?'

Rose shook her head. 'I don't care what other people think. If they want to make fun of us because we're poor, it's up to them.'

'You've a strange way of thinking. I can't make head nor tail of you sometimes.'

With a shrug and a grin Rose turned back to Annie. 'You eat that all up,' she coaxed, 'and then you can have our secret.'

Annie giggled and obediently swallowed her food.

Flo rushed in, late as usual, and quickly cleared her plate. Then she looked at Rose. 'You get it?'

'Of course, top prize,' she said, her dark eyes glinting with devilment.

'You know I didn't mean that.' Flo kicked the leg of her chair impatiently.

'Oh, I thought you did,' Rose teased.

'I know all about it, silly! I was in the hall when you got it, wasn't I? We're sick of hearing how clever you are. Our teacher's been bleating about it all day, and I got fed up and told her you was wearing my boots.'

Rose tried to keep a straight face. 'And did you tell her what you were charging me?'

Flo laughed. 'Not likely, 'cos she started to tell the class what an example the Webster girls were, one clever, the other generous and kind, and I wasn't going to do nothing to change her mind.'

'I'll bet you weren't,' Rose muttered.

'So, did you get them?' Flo persisted.

Rose picked up the bag she had collected from its hiding place on her way home from school, took out an apple and gave it to her sister, who disappeared to eat it in peace.

'You got any more?' Bob eyed the bag greedily.

She took out another and carefully cut it into identical pieces, then handed them round.

'Flo got a whole one,' the boy complained.

'She let me wear her boots today and that was her reward, but,' she flashed him a stern look, 'if you don't want your piece I'm sure one of the others will eat it.'

He snatched it up and headed for the door.

She heard her mother sigh. 'That boy doesn't know when to be grateful.'

Because he's the image of his dad, Rose thought. 'All the others are enjoying it, aren't you?' she asked, glancing around the table at the children who nodded, their mouths full of apple. 'And you won't mind if I give Annie a whole one, will you?'

'No,' they all said together.

'She looks poorly,' Will said quietly. He was only six, but he seemed to understand about other people's troubles.

She cut an apple into small pieces for Annie.

'Where did you get them from?' her mother asked.

'I went scrumping.' She held out the last apple. 'This one's for you.'

'Oh, you shouldn't have done that. I wouldn't like to see you get into trouble with the law. We get enough of that with your dad – and, anyway,' she waved aside the apple, 'you should keep it for yourself.'

'No, you need it more than I do, and I can have a bit of Annie's. I don't think she'll eat it all.'

Her mother nodded. 'She don't look good, does she?'

'Can't we get a doctor to look at her?'

'I wish we could, but where are we going to get the money from? Doctors don't come cheap.'

Neither do posh schools, Rose thought, with a sinking heart. She turned back to Annie, and was pleased to see she'd eaten more than half of her apple. 'Was it nice?' she asked, wiping the sticky fingers with a rag.

Annie pushed the rest of the fruit towards Rose. 'You,' she said, quite clearly.

'Sure you've had enough?'

''Nough.' Her pale face was showing a bit of colour.

'Goodness,' Marj said, surprised, 'she's trying to talk.'

Rose popped the remains of the apple into her mouth and picked up Annie. 'And at her age she should be running around.'

'Some kids are more forward than others. She's like you, a thinker.'

'Hmm, don't know how you can tell that,' Rose said, as Annie laid her head on her shoulder.

'She's the same as you when you were born. You didn't say much at first, but your eyes were always alert and following what was going on, taking everything in.'

Rose laughed loudly. 'I can't imagine me being quiet.'

'Well,' her mother grinned, 'it didn't last long. As soon as you could talk you never stopped asking questions.'

'I have a job getting answers, though, don't I?' Rose couldn't help pointing out.

'That's because you're asking the wrong people. We don't know nothing around here,' her mother said, resignedly.

'I must have got my brains from someone and they didn't come from Dad.'

Her mother looked at the apple in her hand and said nothing.

'You make sure you eat that,' Rose said sternly. 'Don't go giving it to the old man.'

'I won't. He wouldn't appreciate it anyway – it hasn't got hops in it.' She pulled a comical face, and Rose laughed. It was good to see her mother relax.

Rose stood up and brushed back her hair. He must have finished his dinner by now. She braced herself and walked into the scullery.

'Rosie came top of the school today,' her mother said, unable to hide her pride.

'Humph!' was the only response from the man sitting at the table.

'Yes,' Marj continued undeterred, 'and they've given her a Bible.'

That caught his attention. 'Where is it? Might be able to get a few pennies for it.'

Rose's heart leaped in alarm. Thank goodness she'd hidden it.

'Who do we know who'd pay good money for a Bible or any other book? Not many around here can even read,' her mother pointed out.

'Why couldn't they have given her something we could flog?' Without waiting for an answer, he got to his feet. 'I'm off down the pub.'

'But you haven't got any money,' her mother said.

'Yes, I have.'

'Then you'd better give me some for food.'

He counted out a few pennies, careful not to let them see just how much he had.

A glimmer of hope grew inside Rose. Where he'd got the money from she didn't know or care, but he was in a better mood tonight. This was her chance.

'I've been offered a free place in the big school,' she blurted out. 'I'll be able to learn to type and get a job in an office afterwards.'

'No!' The refusal was instant.

'But, Dad – '

'I said no.' He turned to her mother. 'Her and her high and mighty ideas! How does she think we're going to pay for her to go to a posh school?'

'We might be – '

'Don't be daft, woman,' he cut in. 'You won't get a farthing from me. I don't even have to have her under my roof, you know that, Marj.'

He stormed out and her mother sat down with a stricken look on her face.

Rose felt her dreams tumble like the walls of Jericho. 'Why does he hate me?'

'He doesn't – '

'Come on, Mum, you know he does, and what did he mean about not having to keep me?'

'Don't take any notice of that. You know he talks a lot of rubbish when he's had a few pints.'

Rose eyed her mother. She was hiding something. 'He was dead sober when he said it, Mum.'

Her mother fiddled with the teapot.

Rose didn't like this. She could usually talk openly with her mother and she'd never considered her secretive. What was this all about? 'Tell me why he said he didn't have to keep me, Mum.'

'Well . . .' Marj lowered her head, then drew in a shaky

breath and looked up at her daughter. 'I suppose you're old enough to know, and it's better I tell you than someone else. You're not his child. I was expecting when I met him and he took me in.' She looked at Rose imploringly. 'I didn't have no choice. It was that or the workhouse.'

So she was a bastard. Shame and fury raged through Rose. 'Who is my father?' she asked, after a long pause.

'I can't tell you.' A tear trickled down her mother's cheek. 'I'm so sorry, Rosie.'

'Don't upset yourself, Mum, I'm strong enough to survive anything,' Rose said gently.

'I know you are, but I hate to hurt you.'

'It's not your fault.' Rose couldn't believe she was talking so calmly when she was boiling with rage inside, but she didn't want to distress her mother any further.

'I was taken advantage of, then turned out. I was innocent and too trusting.' Marj wiped her eyes on her pinny.

'Tell me who he is,' Rose said, 'and I'll go and teach him a lesson.'

'That's what I'm afraid of. You've got his quick temper.'

'And his looks?' Now she understood why she was so different.

Marj Webster nodded.

'I see. Was he tall?'

'A giant of a man.' Her mother clasped and unclasped her hands. 'More than six foot.'

'Does he still live in London?' Rose asked, even though she knew her mother didn't want to say any more.

'How do you know he comes from London?'

'Because you've never been anywhere else, have you?'

'You've got a mind like a razor.' Her mother sighed.

'A bit like him?' Rose asked, but that was all the information she was going to get because her mother had closed her mouth tightly. Still, she'd found out quite a lot.

'About that school . . .' Her mother blew her nose.

'I know – it's impossible.' That admission nearly tore Rose apart.

'If I had any money I'd see you went, but I can't do it on my own, not even if I took in more washing.'

'You're not to do that! You're working yourself to death as it is, Mum.'

'But you've worked so hard for this chance.' Her mother was on the verge of tears.

'There'll be other chances.'

But inside Rose was screaming at the injustice of it all. No one was going to know that, though.

3

'Come.'

Rose turned the door handle, stepped into Mr Spencer's office and waited for him to finish what he was doing.

'What did your family say?' he asked.

'Can't take it, sir.' She spoke clearly, but it was an effort to keep her voice steady.

'Is there no way?' he asked kindly.

'Only if I don't have to have new clothes.'

'I'm afraid you have to be dressed the same as the other pupils. It's a rule of the school.'

'Would they give me time?' Rose was grasping at any straw. 'I might be able to get a weekend job and buy the things bit by bit.'

'No, Emily. You wouldn't be allowed to do that.'

'No, of course not, sir.' She had already known it wouldn't be possible, but she'd had to try, hadn't she? Had to make one last effort not to let this chance slip away, but it was hopeless and she felt bereaved.

'I'm sorry you can't take the place because you deserved this opportunity.' He stood up, turned his back to her and gazed out of the window.

When he didn't say anything for some time, Rose began to fidget: she didn't want to miss her lessons. Should she go? But he hadn't dismissed her. 'Can I go, sir? Class will have started.'

He turned back to her. 'I'm afraid you'll have to leave, Emily.'

'Begging your pardon, sir?'

'You will have to leave,' he repeated.

'Leave?' The word came out in a strangled squeak.

Mr Spencer nodded. 'I'm sorry. I know how much you like school.'

Like it? It was her whole world. 'But why?'

'We can't teach you any more here.'

'Yes, you can! I've got lots to learn. I don't know nearly enough . . .' She ground to a halt as her voice wavered.

'Emily.' He came and sat on the edge of the desk in front of her. 'You're always the first with your hand up, you know all the answers and you're way ahead of the others.'

'It doesn't matter. Don't make me leave, sir. I'll sit at the back of the class. I won't answer any questions. I don't mind doing the same lessons again.' She stopped to take a breath. 'Don't make me leave,' she whispered, her voice breaking. 'I'm only eleven.'

He straightened up and said briskly, 'The decision has been taken.'

Rose struggled to pull herself together. She had been making an exhibition of herself, she saw. She would never lower herself to behave like that again. Whatever disappointments she had to face in the future, she would *never* beg for anything again.

'When do you want me to go?'

'At once.'

The two words sliced through her like a knife and she opened her mouth to ask if she could stay until the end of term, but closed it again. No more pleading.

'You might as well have your dinner before you leave.'

Semolina pudding would choke her today, she thought, and her stomach heaved. What was she going to do? No more books, no more learning.

'You may go now.'

'Goodbye, sir.'

'Rose!' Miss Gardner was hurrying towards her. 'What are you doing in here? I've been looking for you everywhere.'

Rose was in a small classroom where they taught the six-year-olds, huddled on one of the tiny seats, her knees sticking up above the desk. It had been the first quiet place she had seen after leaving Mr Spencer's office, and she had slunk in to lick her wounds like an injured animal.

'Have you had your dinner?'

Rose looked up blankly and shook her head.

'Well, don't bother. We'll go into the park and you can share my sandwiches. I want to talk to you.'

Rose unwound herself from the small bench and stood up.

'Come along. Let's find a seat in the sun.'

It was a lovely day. Rose turned her face to the sun's warmth and closed her eyes, feeling bewildered and numb. Then she opened them and watched her teacher spread out a cloth on the seat. 'There we are, plenty for both of us.'

The food looked delicious, but Rose wasn't sure she could eat anything today. It was the worst kind of night-mare and something she had not thought to face for two or three years.

She knew some children left at twelve or thirteen, but

she had always hoped she would be able to find a way to stay on.

'Try to eat, Rose,' Miss Gardner said. 'I know you've had a shock, but there might be something we can do about it.'

'I don't see how. My dad won't hear of it.'

'I guessed this might happen. What are you going to do, Rose?'

She shrugged and bit into a sandwich. She had decided she was hungry after all. She made sure she swallowed before she spoke. 'Suppose I'll get a job.'

'Hmm. Children as young as you shouldn't have to work.'

'I don't have no choice.'

'You do not have a choice,' her teacher corrected, 'no double negatives, remember?'

'Sorry, Miss Gardner, I forgot.' Rose's eyes filled with tears, and she fought for control. 'I'm going to forget everything, aren't I?'

'Not if I can help it.' She handed Rose a banana. 'My intended is a teacher at the secondary school – '

'You getting married?' Rose interrupted, looking at her teacher with fresh eyes. She'd thought she had more sense than that.

Miss Gardner nodded. 'Some time, but we haven't decided when. Now, as I was saying, he would be willing to take you for lessons on a Sunday afternoon.'

'Oh.' Rose didn't know what else to say – she was having a job taking all this in. Why would a stranger want to teach her?

'So, what do you think, Rose? Would you like Mr Trenchard to help you?'

She nodded wordlessly, and tears welled in her eyes again. Lessons!

'Could you get away from your family for a couple of hours, or do you have to look after the children?'

'Sunday's all right,' Rose told her, excited now that the offer had finally sunk in. Then her expression clouded. 'But I can't afford to pay anything.'

'He doesn't want payment. I've told him all about you and he'll teach you for nothing, as long as you're willing to work hard.'

'Oh, I will, I will!' she cried, leaping to her feet. 'He won't be sorry, you'll see.'

Miss Gardner laughed at her joy. 'That's what I told him. Would you be able to start this Sunday at three o'clock?'

'Yes, please. Where?'

'At my house.' Miss Gardner took out a piece of paper and wrote down her address. 'That's where I live. Do you know the street?'

'I think so. It's on the other side of the park, isn't it?'

'That's right. You'll need to take the number five bus and it will drop you right at my door.'

'I can walk.' It was less than ten minutes on the bus and she was used to walking everywhere.

'No, Rose, it's a long way. Here.' Miss Gardner opened her purse and gave her a penny. 'Take that for your fare.'

'I couldn't, not after everything you're doing for me.'

'Of course you can.' Miss Gardner tucked the coin into Rose's pocket. 'Mr Trenchard will be waiting for you on Sunday. Try not to be late.'

'I won't.' Nothing in this world was going to keep her away from her lessons.

'There's one more sandwich left and you'd better take it with you.'

Rose accepted the packet and slipped it into her pocket with the banana – an unheard-of luxury. After that exciting news she was hungry enough now to eat it all herself, but she would save it for Annie.

As wonderful as the thought of the Sunday lessons was, it still hurt to know that she couldn't go to school any more. Still, she had been given a chance to carry on learning and that was something to be grateful for. A couple of hours a week was better than nothing, and Mr Trenchard must be good if he taught at the big school. She pushed away her gloom and began to wonder what exciting things he was going to show her.

She wandered along for a while, deep in thought, until she found herself in front of a church, its door wide open. She didn't want to go home so she decided to go in and read her Bible, which she had kept with her since she'd been given it. She settled on one of the pews, gazed around for some moments, then opened it.

'Are you lost?' A man in a flowing black coat came and sat beside her.

'No.' She smiled. 'I saw the door open and thought I'd come in and read for a while.'

He glanced at the book in her hands. 'Where did you get that?'

'It's mine,' she told him, wondering why everyone jumped to the conclusion that she was dishonest. Being poor didn't mean you were a thief. 'Look, it's got my name in it, see? I won it for coming top of the school.'

'And why aren't you at school today?'

'Because they've made me leave. I had the chance of

a free place at the secondary school, but I couldn't take it because we're too poor. The Head said they couldn't teach me any more and I had to go.'

'How old are you?' the man asked.

'Eleven.' Rose looked at him carefully. Perhaps he could answer some of her questions? 'Why do some people have so much and others, like me, can't even afford a few new clothes to go to another school? It doesn't seem right,' she said.

'There have always been the poor and the rich.' He pointed to the Bible she was clutching. 'If you read that you'll see it's so.'

'I have read it,' she told him indignantly.

He gave a smile of disbelief. 'Right through?'

'Yes, every single word, and I've started on it for the second time, but it only makes me want to ask more questions. I still can't understand why some people are rich and others poor.'

'It's just the way things are. We have to accept our lot in life.'

Rose snorted. She was sick and tired of hearing that. She held out the Bible. 'Show me where it says that in here. I've never seen it, and look at this.' She flicked over the pages until she found the place she wanted. '"God is love." If that's true, it doesn't make sense that some people don't know where the next meal is coming from, does it? If you love someone you don't try to hurt them, do you?'

He patted her hand. 'You're too young to understand these things yet. You'll know more when you get older.'

'Well, you're older,' she said rudely, 'so why can't you tell me?'

'We're not here to question the wisdom of God.'

'Why not?' She turned the pages again, looking for a well-known passage. When she'd found it she held it out. 'It says here, "Come now, and let us reason together, saith the Lord." I know what "reason" means – I looked it up in the dictionary at school. Why can't I ask questions?'

He stood up, clearly having had enough of her. 'You don't know what you're saying, child. God has His own purpose for each of us and we must be satisfied with that.'

She looked at him suspiciously. He didn't seem to have the answer to anything. 'Are you a priest?'

'No, I'm the verger.'

'What's that?'

'I take care of the church and assist at services.' Before she could ask anything else, he turned and hurried back to his duties.

She watched him walk away, disappointed that he hadn't been able to answer her questions. But that was nothing new, was it?

On the way home she decided not to tell anyone about the Sunday lessons, and that she would wait until her mother was alone before she told her that the school had turned her out.

Annie held out her arms as Rose walked into the scullery. She stooped down to her, ignoring the others sitting at the table. 'Hello, Toots, you're looking better today.' She dived into her pocket and brought out the sandwich. 'Want a bit of cheese?' She was rewarded with a smile, and started to break off small pieces to pop them into the little girl's mouth. When that was finished, she took out the banana and peeled it.

'Where'd you get that?' Bob demanded.

'My teacher gave it to me, and it's for Annie.'

'She had the cheese so why can't we have the banana?'

'Because there isn't enough to go round and she needs it more than you.'

'You're mean,' he whined.

Suddenly there was a thump on the table. Rose turned to see Annie pulling herself upright on her chair, gripping the table for support. Her face was red with fury and she was looking at her brother with loathing. 'Not mean,' she said clearly, lifting an accusing finger at Bob. 'Wosie good. You mean.'

Everyone burst out laughing, except Bob, who stood up so suddenly that his chair went flying.

'Who taught *her* to talk? Haven't we got enough to put up with with one bossy girl?' Then he stormed out of the room.

'Ugh.' Annie screwed up her face and plonked down on to her chair. 'Bad boy.'

'There! I told you she was like you, Rose.' Her mother wiped tears of laughter from her eyes. 'That put the boy in his place.'

'At last I've got someone to stick up for me,' Rose joked.

Then there was a tug at her sleeve and she looked down at Annie. 'Bed.' She held up her arms. 'Tired, Wosie.'

Rose picked her up, the little girl laid her head on her shoulder and was instantly asleep. 'All that talk has tired her out, but it's good to see her showing some sign of life.'

'It is, and if she gets her strength, I think she's going to be a force to be reckoned with.' Her mother was clearly delighted at this turn of events.

Rose hoisted the sleeping child higher on to her shoulder. 'I'd better put her to bed, or else she might tell *me* off.'

She left the scullery with the welcome sound of her mother's laughter in her ears.

Right, that was the last of the little ones in bed. Now she'd go down and see if there was any tea left in the pot.

Flo was there with her mother and the old man – she refused to think of him as her father now. Her sister smirked when Rose walked into the scullery. 'Rose has been kicked out of school,' she said with relish.

'What?' Her mother was shocked.

'I was going to tell you later.' Rose looked at her sister accusingly. 'Can't keep your mouth shut, can you?'

'Didn't know it was a secret,' Flo protested.

'What's going on?' the old man demanded.

Rose sighed. 'They said that as I couldn't take the free place at the big school, I'd have to leave because they couldn't teach me any more.'

'Oh, Rosie,' her mother moaned. 'What a terrible thing to happen to you.'

'What's terrible about it, woman? She can get a job now and pay for her keep. It's time she did something useful. Tell her to go down the Labour tomorrow.'

'That's what I'm going to do.' And why don't *you* try it? Rose thought.

He grunted and stood up. 'About time.' Then he left for the pub.

'Why didn't you tell me?' her mother said.

'I was going to when you were alone, but Big Mouth here' – she glared at her sister – 'had to blurt it out, didn't she?'

'I don't know what all the fuss is about. You've only been turned out because you're too clever for us,' her sister muttered, then stormed out of the scullery.

'Don't go into service, Rose,' her mother said.

'I might not have any choice. There can't be much else for me to do.'

'You mustn't!' Marj's mouth had set in a straight line.

Rose was taken aback. 'I'll try not to.'

'I won't have you being a skivvy for someone else, and I need you here anyway. You've got a brain, you deserve better.'

'I'll see what they've got at the Exchange tomorrow.'

Rose couldn't help wondering why her mother was so agitated. She'd been in service when she'd been young, hadn't she? Was that where she'd got into trouble? Yes, that was probably it, she thought angrily. Some man had got her pregnant and her employers had dismissed her.

Injustice made Rose angry, but she controlled herself. Her mother must have suffered so much and she didn't want to add to her burdens by exploding in rage. But she would not let anything like that happen to her.

4

'Next!' The man looked up briefly as Rose came and stood before him. 'Sit.'

She boiled. Who did he think she was? A dog?

'Name.'

'Emily Rose Webster.' She had to hold her temper in check as she needed a job. If she got cheeky he would throw her out, because there were plenty of others he could choose from. The Labour Exchange was packed.

'Age?'

'Fourteen,' she lied, without a blink.

'Can you read and write?'

She looked him straight in the eyes. 'Of course I can, and I'm good at numbers too.'

He scribbled on a form, then handed it to her. 'Go there.'

'When?'

'Now.'

'What is it?'

'Factory. They make metal cans and things.'

Her mouth was open to ask another question when he shouted, 'Next!'

She pushed her way out through the heaving mass of people, stood on the pavement and grinned reluctantly. What a daft conversation that had been. Still, he hadn't doubted her when she'd said she was fourteen. Being tall had its advantages.

The factory was as crowded as the Labour Exchange had been.

A boy took her form and showed her into a long corridor lined with chairs, filled with hopefuls looking for work. 'Wait here.'

Damn. She groaned under her breath. That man must be sending everyone down here. What a waste of time. She had waited three hours at the Labour and it looked like she'd have another two or three hours of hanging around. If only she could be at school. A sensation of something between despair and anger swept through her, but she pushed it away.

She leaned against the wall and studied the others. They were all young – boys and girls – and some evidently didn't know what a wash flannel looked like. Poverty hung around every one of them, as if they had labels around their necks, while desperation and need were imprinted on each forlorn face. Again, the words *This isn't right* filled her mind.

Nearly two hours later she was still there but several chairs were empty now. So was her stomach, which rumbled in protest. She was going to miss her school dinner – even the semolina. Try as she might, she couldn't keep the picture of her beloved classroom out of her mind, and her vision blurred.

'That's her, Mr Baker, sir.'

Rose looked up to see the boy standing in front of her with a man of about forty, she reckoned.

'Miss Webster, come with me.'

He turned immediately and strode along the corridor, leaving her to trot after him. He opened a door at the end of the passage and as they stepped through it the noise stopped her dead. Rows and rows of machines were thumping away, men were hammering, and down at the end she could see benches filled with youngsters who were packing huge boxes. And by the look of them she needn't have lied about her age – if they were fourteen she'd eat her boots.

She covered her ears.

The man in front of her didn't slacken his pace and was soon disappearing through another door. Finally he stopped in a small office. The quiet was a blessed relief.

'What are they making in there?' she gasped.

'Tin cans.' Mr Baker sat behind a desk and looked her over critically. 'Sit down, please.'

She did as ordered.

'Your form says you can read and write?'

'Yes, sir.' She added the 'sir' because he looked as if he expected it.

'And you know how to add?'

'Yes, sir.'

'Six twelves?' he threw at her.

'Seventy-two, sir.'

He raised his eyebrows at her quick response. 'You know your tables?'

'All of them.' Her dark eyes shone with pride. 'Would you like me to recite them for you?'

'I don't think that will be necessary.' His expression remained the same but his lips twitched at the corners. 'I need someone who can add correctly.'

'Oh, I can do that.' Rose smiled, showing a row of perfect teeth. This sounded promising.

'And you are fourteen?'

'Yes, sir.' It was getting easier all the time.

36

'Very well . . . er . . .' He looked at the form again. 'Emily.'

'Rose. Everybody calls me Rose.'

He nodded. 'You can start tomorrow at seven o'clock.'

'Do I have to work in that racket?' she asked boldly.

'Yes, but you'll soon get used to it, and if you prove yourself good at figures, I might consider moving you on to something else.'

'Fair enough. I'll bring something to stuff in my ears.'

He seemed to be having real trouble with trying not to smile. 'You'll work from seven to six, Monday to Friday, and seven to one on Saturday. The pay is six shillings a week.'

'Thank you, sir.' It wasn't much, but at least she'd got a job.

He stood up. 'Come with me, and I'll show you the way out.'

When they went back through the factory, she stuck her fingers in her ears and rushed through the workshop as quickly as she could.

By way of celebration she decided to walk home and spend her fare money on a nice piece of cod in batter for Annie.

'How'd you get on?' her mother asked, as Rose walked into the scullery.

'I got a job and I start tomorrow.'

'What kind of a job?'

'It's in a factory and the noise is awful, but the boss said he'd move me later if I can add up well.'

Her mother smiled in relief. 'That sounds fine. Did you tell them you were only eleven?'

'No.' She grinned. 'I said I was fourteen, but I'm not sure he believed me. He probably didn't care. He just wanted someone who could add up.'

'Well, you won't have any trouble with that. I've never known anyone so quick at reckoning.'

Rose looked around. 'Where's Annie?'

'Still in bed. Hasn't been too bright today.'

'Oh?' Rose tore up the stairs and rushed to Annie's bed. 'What's up, Toots?' she asked.

'Tired, Wosie.' She yawned and held out her arms.

Back in the scullery a few minutes later, with Annie, Rose asked, 'How long's she been like this?'

'Most of the day. She won't eat anything.'

Rose sat down, holding the child firmly on her lap. Then she opened the bag and put the fish on to a plate. 'You got something I can give her with this, Mum? I couldn't afford the chips as well.'

Her mother dished up a spoonful of mashed potato. 'How's that?'

'Fine, thanks.' Then she fed Annie, coaxing her to take every mouthful, until the plate was empty.

'Well, I'll be blowed,' her mother exclaimed. 'You can get her to do anything.'

'Not me.' She grinned at the little girl. 'It was the fish, wasn't it?'

'Yum, yum,' was the little girl's reply.

'Why wouldn't you eat your dinner today?' Rose asked her.

Annie screwed up her little face. 'Ugh, bread.'

'The little minx,' her mother murmured, 'I think she'd rather starve than eat something she doesn't want.'

38

'She's got a stubborn streak, all right, but I think she's ill.' Rose brushed Annie's hair away from her face, which was alarmingly white. 'We're all sick of bread, Annie, but we have to eat it.' She tickled the little girl's tummy. 'It fills us up in there.'

Annie giggled and struggled to get down. Once on the floor she grabbed a chair, pulled herself upright and took a couple of wobbly steps. Then she sat down and beamed at Rose. 'Walk now, showed you.'

'There's a clever girl,' Rose and her mother said, encouragingly.

'Clever, like Wosie.'

'Don't you turn out too clever or you'll get thrown out of school, like me.' Rose heard the bitterness in her voice.

'How much they going to pay you?' her mother asked, changing the subject.

'Six shillings a week.'

'Don't tell the old man how much, will you?'

'No fear. I'm going to keep a shilling for myself and give the rest to you.'

'I'll see it all goes on food and clothes. I'm sorry you've had to go out to work, but a bit of extra money'll be a big help,' her mother admitted.

Rose knew that, and was glad, but she wished the knot of resentment inside her would go away.

When she came into the scullery after putting the kids to bed, the old man said, 'Has she got a job, then?'

'Yes, and she starts tomorrow,' Marj told him.

'How much they paying her?'

'Five shillings a week.' Marj didn't hesitate.

Rose hid a smile. Her mother was almost as good a liar as she was.

'What? That's robbery.'

'I was lucky to get anything.' Rose glared at the man, who was clutching his knife and fork, waiting for his dinner. 'It was like a madhouse down at the Labour Exchange, and I only got this because I'm good at adding up.'

'She can give me her pay packet at the end of each week.' He started to eat the dinner Marj had put in front of him.

Oh, no, she wouldn't! She wasn't going to work like a slave and give him the money to drink. 'I'm giving it to Mum for my keep. You said it was time I paid my way.' She spoke boldly, expecting to receive the back of his hand, but to her surprise he didn't move.

He scraped his plate clean, stood up, reached for her mother's purse and tipped it upside down. It was empty. 'You've never got any money, woman,' he complained.

'I've got eight kids and you to feed, not forgetting the rent.'

'Well.' He looked smug. 'We'll soon have a bit more when she gets her money.'

'And all of it will go on decent food and warm clothes for the children. Winter's on the way, you know,' his wife told him.

He scowled and went out without another word.

Rose left the house and walked until she had calmed down. The very idea that that man might get his hands on her wages! As she wandered along the riverbank, she picked up a stone and threw it into the water, then watched the ripples as they spread outwards. Everyone kept telling her she was just a child, but she didn't feel like one. In fact, she knew she'd never been like the other children – all she'd ever wanted was to learn.

Something deep inside was telling her that knowledge was the only way to improve her lot. She didn't know why she felt like that, but something drove her all the time, and one day she would find the answers she was looking for.

5

Rose shoved the wadding into her ears, picked up a pencil and started counting, writing the tally neatly in the book. She gritted her teeth in concentration. It was like being in the depths of hell, but the boss had said he'd find her something else to do if she proved her adding was good, so she was determined not to make any mistakes.

The time passed at snail's pace and the noise made her feel sick. To have been wrenched out of the classroom into this was almost more than she could bear.

She continued writing. The only way to get through it was to shut everything out and concentrate on what she was being paid to do. So, using every bit of stubbornness she possessed – which was a considerable amount – she blocked out her surroundings. When someone tapped her on the shoulder she jumped. It was the foreman who had shown her what to do when she'd arrived and his mouth was moving, but she was so dazed she didn't understand what he was saying.

He grinned and pulled the stuffing out of her ears. 'Time for dinner.'

She looked around and saw that a lot of the men had already stopped work. As the last of the noisy machines was turned off, she rolled her eyes in relief.

'Give me your book and go to the canteen, Rose.' He handed her back the wadding. 'You'll need that this afternoon.'

'How do you stand this every day?' she asked, rubbing her temple.

'You'll get used to it.'

'Never!'

He opened the book. 'It's unusual for Mr Baker to give this job to someone so young, but you've got a neat hand. Let's hope the figures are right.'

'They are,' she said stoutly. 'You won't find one mistake, and you can show it to the boss because I don't want to do this job any longer than I have to.' Then a horrible thought struck her. She had been thrown out of school because she was too good, so if she was too good at this job would the boss refuse to move her to something better?

The foreman put the book into his pocket. 'Off you go now or there won't be anything left for you.'

Rose queued up for her dinner. It was only broth and a chunk of bread, but it was free for the youngsters. She found herself a seat in the corner, away from everyone else. She needed a few quiet moments, and was surprised everyone else didn't feel the same after working in that awful noise all morning.

A crushing feeling of despair swamped her, but she fought it with all her might. It wouldn't help her. She tried to replace despair with gratitude, but it was difficult. The only beacon of hope was her Sunday lessons.

The rest of the day was agony as the metal was pounded into tin cans, and Rose had just about reached screaming point when it was time to knock off. As soon as she was outside the building, she headed for the park and ran and ran, putting as much distance as possible between her and the hated factory.

43

When she got home the scullery was empty, except for her mother.

'I've saved your tea,' she said. 'Sit down and tell me what your first day was like.'

At the mention of the factory, Rose froze, unable to move or speak as the horror of the day surfaced. Misery swamped her, and tears poured down her cheeks.

'Oh, Rosie!' Her mother reached out to comfort her, but Rose stepped back. Sympathy would only make things worse – and it had. She sobbed uncontrollably.

Suddenly there was a cry of anguish and someone grabbed her leg. 'Don't cwy, Wosie, don't cwy.'

Rose brushed away the tears and saw Annie wrapped around her leg, her little face contorted with distress. Forgetting her own unhappiness, she picked the child up. 'It's all right, Toots.'

'Not all wight. Wosie *never* cwy.'

'I'm silly today.'

Annie gave her a disbelieving look. 'You not silly.'

Rose sighed. What she had told Annie was true – she had been acting like a baby, and she would make sure she never did it again. 'Don't you believe it. And what are you doing still up? I never saw you when I came in.'

'Under table.'

'Hiding, were you?'

Annie nodded and ran her small hand over Rose's face. 'Not cwy no more?'

'Never, I promise.' And that was one promise she would do her best to keep. 'Why aren't you in bed like all the others?'

'Wait for you.'

'Oh?' Rose gave her mother a questioning look.

'She'd only let Will near her and he's too young to put her to bed.'

'What about Flo?'

'Annie screamed the place down when she tried to pick her up.'

'You mustn't do that, Toots,' she scolded gently. 'You must let Flo put you to bed at night because I'm going to be coming in too late to do it.'

'Why you late?'

'I have to go to work now.'

Annie seemed to chew that over for a while, then she nodded. 'You come see me when you get home?'

'I promise.' Then Rose glanced at her mother. 'That was a long sentence, even if it did take a lot of thought and effort.'

'Yes, she's coming on. Must be all those treats you bring her.'

'Oh, I almost forgot. I didn't catch the bus home so I got this.' She produced a small orange and Annie shrieked with delight.

'What that?'

'Shush.' Rose put her finger to her lips. 'Don't want to wake the others up, do we?'

Annie shook her head vigorously. 'Not Bob, he eat it all.'

The orange was split between Annie, Rose and her mother, but the little girl had the lion's share.

As Rose had only worked for half of the week, she received three shillings in wages. She handed it all over to her mother but was given sixpence back.

'I'm not taking everything. You must have something for yourself,' Marj said.

Rose returned twopence. 'This will be enough for me, but when I've worked a full week I'll keep a shilling.'

Her mother took it reluctantly. 'What are you going to do with your pocket money?'

She lifted up her foot to show the holes in her boots. 'I'm going to save up for a pair of shoes.'

At last it was Sunday, and she could go for her lesson.

Rose got on the bus and fidgeted all the way, anxious not to miss her stop. They were there in no time. She made sure her frock wasn't too crumpled and smoothed her thick mop of black hair with a lick on her hands, then opened the gate and walked up the path.

'Hello, Rose.' Miss Gardner greeted her with a smile. 'Come in.'

She stepped inside the house. Everything was lovely and clean, and she was glad she'd had a good wash before she came. It was not grand, like the big houses across the river, but it was a whole lot better than the place she lived in, and it looked positively empty.

'I like your house, Miss.'

Miss Gardner looked pleased. 'Thank you. I inherited it from my father and I've worked hard to make it pleasant and comfortable.'

'It's certainly that,' Rose remarked, with genuine admiration. Fancy owning your own house. If she ever lived in a place like this, she'd be happy.

'Mr Trenchard's waiting for you.'

Rose fished in the pocket of her frock. She pulled out the penny Miss Gardner had given her and handed it to

46

her. 'I didn't need this. I've got a job now, but thank you very much for lending it to me.'

The teacher looked doubtful. 'Are you sure you have enough for your fare home?'

Rose showed her the coins she had left after paying for her bus ride. 'I've still got this.'

'All right.' Miss Gardner took back the penny and studied Rose thoughtfully. 'You didn't have to return it. You could have kept it.'

'Oh, no!' Rose was horrified. 'I couldn't have done that when I had enough to pay for myself. It wouldn't have been right.'

'Ah, so this is Rose.'

A tall man with spectacles propped on the end of his nose came out of another room. Rose liked the look of him.

'Are you ready to start the lesson?'

'Yes, please, sir.' She followed him into the front room.

A large table over by the window was covered with books and Rose gasped with delight, then ran over to it. Oh, they were beautiful. Her hands ran over them lovingly and she turned to Mr Trenchard. 'These all yours?'

He nodded. 'Sit down, and we'll have a look at them, shall we?'

Still smiling, she sat, then turned her large dark eyes on him expectantly.

'What I want to do this afternoon is find out what you know, and then I'll be able to plan a course of study for you. If you're as bright as Miss Gardner says, I'll teach the same subjects you would have taken at the secondary school, and after a while I'll set you some exams.' He paused, took off his spectacles and polished them. 'Would you like that?'

She nodded eagerly. 'Yes, please, sir. I'll work very hard and I learn quick.'

He poured them a cup of tea from a pot standing on a small table, and handed the plate of biscuits to her. They were whole ones, she saw with pleasure, not the broken ones they had to buy because they were cheap. Then he opened one of the books.

For the next two hours Rose answered questions, did exercises and read aloud for Mr Trenchard. She also subjected him to a constant flow of questions, and was overjoyed when he answered all of them in a way she could understand. He was indeed a good teacher.

Finally he closed the books, and smiled at her. 'Well, Rose, I can see you're eager to learn and have an inquiring mind.'

She pulled a face. Oh dear, had she overdone the questions? 'Everyone gets fed up with me, but I can't help it because I've always been like this. It's a bit of a nuisance at times.'

'You mustn't think like that. You have a thirst for knowledge and it's a rare gift.'

'Do you think so?' Rose had never heard her questions referred to as a gift before: where she came from she was looked upon as an oddity.

'Yes, it is, and I'll see if I can assuage your need for knowledge.'

'Assuage?' she repeated. 'What does that mean?'

He opened a large dictionary, found the right place and pushed it towards her. 'What does that say?'

She read it carefully. 'To satisfy,' she told him, then grinned. 'It's a good word. I'd not heard it before.' She fingered the large book. 'Will you teach me lots of new words?'

'If you keep coming I'll try to teach you everything I know.'

Her eyes opened wide. 'You will?'

He nodded again. 'I think you should learn Latin.'

'Latin!' Rose sat bolt upright. 'Only those in the posh schools learn that.'

'Rose,' he leaned forward earnestly, 'I believe you have a lot of potential, and Latin could be useful to you in later years.'

'Then I'll learn it,' she told him confidently. She had met Mr Trenchard this afternoon for the first time, but already she trusted his judgement.

'Good, we'll start next week.' He took a watch out of his waistcoat pocket, flicked it open, then closed it and slipped it back. 'That's enough for today. Come at the same time next Sunday.'

'Has two hours gone already?' she asked, sorry the lesson was at an end.

'I'm afraid so.'

'I wish they went that quick at the factory.'

'How are you getting on there?' he asked kindly.

Her bottom lip trembled, but she remembered her promise to Annie and herself, and banished the tears. 'I hate it. They shouldn't have made me leave school. I wouldn't have minded doing all the lessons again.'

'It's a great shame, Rose, but we'll see that you still get a good education. However, as you will only be having two hours a week tuition, it will take longer and you will need determination.'

He used long words, but she knew what that one meant. 'I got plenty of that. You'll see.'

He looked at her thoughtfully. 'Yes, I do believe you have. I've written out some exercises for you to do during the week.'

Rose took the paper from him and started to read it eagerly. 'I can do this.'

'I'm sure you can.' He handed her a little notebook, a pencil and a rubber. 'I want you to write the answers in this book – in your best handwriting – and bring it back next week.'

'How much is the book and stuff?'

'Nothing, you may take them,' Mr Trenchard told her.

'Oh, no,' Rose said, scandalized at the suggestion. 'I can pay, look.' She pulled the coins out of her pocket. 'Is there enough here?'

'More than enough, child, but you need not.'

'I want to,' she told him firmly. 'You're being very kind by giving me these lessons, and I wouldn't be happy letting you spend any of your own money on me. It wouldn't be right.' She pushed a penny towards him.

He pushed it back. 'That's too much.'

'You take what's right then.' She laid out the money for him to see.

He slid a farthing from among the coins on the table, but Rose was not having that, and gave him another. 'These things cost more than a farthing – I know because I've seen them in the shops. You mustn't spend your money on me, Mr Trenchard, it isn't right.'

'You use that word a lot,' he said, sitting back, folding his arms and looking at her intently.

'What word?' Rose frowned.

'"Right". Tell me what you mean.'

She reached for the dictionary. 'Shall we look it up?'

'No.' He took the book from her and closed it. 'I want you to explain what the word means to you, what you are thinking when you use it.'

Rose clasped her hands in her lap and stared into space. 'Well . . . when something isn't right, then it shouldn't be happening.' She fidgeted and gave him an appealing glance.

'Go on.'

'I'm not used to being asked what I think.'

'I don't suppose you are.'

Rose arranged the books in a neat row on the table while she sorted out in her mind what she wanted to say. Then she sat back. 'It isn't right when some people have so much and others have to live in the dirt. It shouldn't be like that and something ought to be done about it. It isn't right for me to take money from you or Miss Gardner when I have some of my own . . .' She tailed off, hoping that was enough explaining.

'And why do you feel like that?' he coaxed.

'Well, you and Miss live a whole lot better than me, but you work hard for your pay and you're not as rich as those who live across the river.'

'And would you take money from them?' he probed.

'No, I would not,' Rose exclaimed indignantly. 'I don't want charity from the likes of them.'

'But you wanted the free place at school.'

'That was different. I'd worked hard for it.' She could not understand why he was asking all these questions.

'So you think you have to earn the good things in life?'

'How else am I going to get them?' She leaned forward, and spoke with passion: 'But I'm not just talking about me, sir. I think I've got enough brains to make a difference to my life if I work at it hard enough, but what about those who don't know how to escape? That's what I mean by something being not right. There should be some help for them, but there's nothing.' She ground to a halt and glanced at him anxiously.

'So, what are you going to do about it?'

'Me?' she squeaked. 'What can I do? I'm nobody.'

Mr Trenchard's face was alight with pleasure, and she couldn't help wondering what he found so interesting about this talk. She was babbling away like an ignorant kid.

'Don't think one person can't make a difference because they can. One voice raised against injustice can have a dramatic effect.'

Rose pulled a face, not quite believing him. 'It would be a bit like a "voice crying in the wilderness",' she quoted.

He nodded. 'I agree, but think about the difference that single voice made.'

She remembered when she had tossed a stone into the river, and smiled broadly. She was beginning to understand where his questions were leading. 'When I threw a stone into the water it sent out ripples that kept going in ever-widening circles.'

'Exactly!' He leaned forward. 'One small pebble, but the splash it made kept reaching out and changing the surface of the water.'

Now she'd got it.

'Each one of us can make a difference in this world. It

might be in just a small way, but it could open the path for bigger things. Take Miss Gardner, for instance. There are very few women teachers, but she persevered until she was given her post. Her actions might make it easier for other women to go into the profession.'

'She's a good teacher,' Rose said, with affection, 'got ever so much patience. Without her help I wouldn't have won the Bible.'

'Do you like reading the Bible?'

'Oh, yes, it's my favourite book.' She pulled it out of her pocket. 'I keep it with me all the time. It's safer than leaving it at home.'

'And do you understand it?'

She laughed. 'No. But that doesn't matter because I love trying to work out what it all means.'

At that moment the door opened and Miss Gardner came into the room. 'John, we will be late for the service if we don't leave soon.'

Rose leaped to her feet. 'Oh, I'm so sorry. I've kept you talking way past time.'

'Don't worry about it,' Mr Trenchard assured her. 'It's been a very enlightening discussion.'

'Enlightening?'

'Hmm. Revealing. You have opened the door of your mind just a crack for me, and now I have an idea of the way you think and feel. It will help me to prepare lessons that you will find interesting and helpful for your mission in life.'

'I don't have a mission in life – except to get out of the slums, of course,' she told him, feeling rather self-conscious. He was saying some strange things.

'I think you do, but you just don't know what it is yet.

Now, off you go, and come at the same time next week.'

'I will, sir, and I'll have all my exercises done.'

Rose ran across the road to wait for her bus, her head buzzing with all the things they'd talked about.

Two pairs of eyes watched her as she waited at the bus stop, already reading the exercise paper.

'What do you think, John?'

He slipped his arm around Grace's shoulder. 'She's everything you said and more. She has a remarkable mind and it would be criminal for her to stay where she is. She couldn't have had a worse start in life, but she doesn't belong in Garrett Street.'

'I agree with you, but I think she already knows that, and believes education is the way forward for her.'

'And she's right. She has a wisdom far beyond her years, but that hasn't come as a result of education. It's something she was born with.' He removed his spectacles and frowned.

'What is it?' Grace asked him.

'I don't know, really. It's just that there's something familiar about her.'

'Such as?'

He studied the girl across the road. 'The directness of her gaze, the way she carries herself, the pride and determination in those great dark eyes . . .' He tailed off, then shrugged. 'I can't pin it down, but I feel sure I've met someone like her before.'

6

At the end of another dreadful week, Rose walked into the scullery and found the place almost as noisy as the factory. 'What's going on?' she bellowed.

Flo was nowhere to be seen. Bob was tormenting a screaming Annie. Nancy was cowering in the corner, frightened of her own shadow. Will was trying to pull Bob off Annie. Bert and Charlie were on all fours, pretending to be dogs and 'barking'.

Rose grabbed Bob's collar and pulled him away from Annie, which added to the racket as he yelled at the top of his voice. 'Quiet!' she thundered. 'Where's Flo?'

'Up-up stairs,' Nancy whispered.

'Mum's having another kid.' Bob lashed out at Rose in an effort to get away from her.

'So you all thought you'd run riot, did you?'

'We weren't doing no 'arm,' Bob argued.

Rose glared at him. 'And hurting a little girl isn't doing any harm?'

'Wosie . . . fwightened,' Annie wailed. 'Nasty boy.'

'All right, Toots, I'm here now.' Rose picked her up and turned to the rest of them. 'Nancy, stop whimpering.'

'Sorry, Rosie,' the seven-year-old whispered, 'but I'm scared of all that shouting.'

'I know, but you've got to be brave because Mum's going to need your help with the new baby.'

'Oh.' Nancy's face lit up. Nancy loved babies, though

what she saw in them was a mystery to Rose. 'And you' – she peered under the table at Bert and Charlie, aged four and three respectively – 'what do you think you were playing at?'

'Dogs,' they answered, and scuttled out of her reach.

'Well, pick something quieter next time,' she told them briskly.

'Rose!' Flo rushed into the scullery. 'Thank goodness you're home. Mum's having a bad time and the baby won't come.'

'Who's with her?'

'Mrs Jenks and Mrs Peters.'

Rose handed Annie to her sister and went up the stairs.

Her mother's hair was spread across the pillow in soaking wet strands, and she was gasping in pain. 'Is there anything I can do?' Rose asked Mrs Jenks.

'No, love, we just have to wait. The kid's in no hurry to come into this world.'

And who could blame it? Rose thought bitterly. There wasn't much waiting for it. 'How much longer do you think it will be?'

'Another hour or so.' Mrs Jenks seemed unconcerned.

Rose winced visibly as another spasm caught her mother, then went back downstairs where, mercifully it was now quiet.

'Is it going to be long?' Flo was close to tears.

'Mrs Jenks thinks another hour or so.'

'It's awful, isn't it? I don't want any kids.' Flo was shaking.

'I'm sure I don't! Where's the old man?' Rose asked.

'Dad? He poked his nose in, but when he knew the baby was coming, he disappeared quick.'

Rose wasn't surprised.

Two hours later they heard the squalling of a new baby, and Rose sighed with relief. It sounded healthy enough and she only hoped her mother was all right. Although she hated the thought of another mouth to feed, she was glad it was all over.

Mrs Jenks came into the scullery. 'That's done then. You have another brother.'

No one looked enthusiastic about that.

'How's Mum?' Rose asked.

'Tired, and she's going to need a lot of rest, but she's come through it pretty well.'

'We'd better go and see her. Come on, Flo.' Rose stopped at the door and glared menacingly at the other children. 'I don't want to hear a peep out of any of you.'

When they came into the room their mother looked exhausted but managed a weak smile.

'I'm going to need your help,' she told both of them, 'because I'll be laid up for a while.'

They nodded.

'Do you want to see the baby?'

Without a word they walked over to a drawer that had been turned into a cot and gazed at the tiny bundle. Rose was overcome with guilt: it was wrong to resent this little thing – he hadn't asked to be born. But the thought of another child in the house was almost too much for her. They were already sleeping three to a bed.

'He's so tiny,' Flo said in awe.

'Yes, but he's got a good pair of lungs on him. He'll be all right. I'm going to call him David.' Their mother struggled to sit up. 'Flo, you look after the others while

Rose goes shopping. There isn't much food in the house. Rose, there's some money in the top drawer over there. The rent collector's coming tonight and there's enough to pay off what's owing. The rest I want you to spend on food.'

Rose rummaged through the drawer and came up blank. 'There's nothing here.'

'But there must be.' Her mother became agitated. 'Have another look. I put it right at the back so your father wouldn't find it.'

After another thorough search, she turned to her mother. 'I'm sorry, but it isn't here.'

'He's found it,' her mother cried. 'What are we going to do? I promised the rent man the money tonight.'

Rose was furious and dismayed at the same time. Of all the thoughtless, selfish men in this world, the old man must take the biscuit. 'At least I got paid today.'

'That'll be enough for some food, but what about the rent?'

'I'll get the money.' Rose lifted her head in determination, but inside she was trembling with fear. She knew what she had to do.

Her mother lay back. 'Oh, Rosie, what would I do without you?'

'Find a better hiding place?' Rose joked.

Once the shopping was done, Rose started to cook a meal for them all. The old man wouldn't get any favours tonight. He'd have to eat the same as everyone else. She had managed to get a large ham bone and some vegetables from the market. It would make a nourishing soup, which would last a couple of days, with luck. A suet pudding was boiling away too – that would fill them up.

'Rose?' Flo's bottom lip trembled. 'Are we going to get chucked out?'

'Not if we can get the money back.'

'How are we going to do that? I don't think I'd have the nerve to ask him.'

'I don't fancy it either, but we'll have to.' Rose squared her shoulders, trying to give the impression that it was nothing to her, but she'd seen the old man in a rage many times and it wasn't something to look forward to.

'He'll flatten you!' Bob said, with relish.

'Well, if he does you'll be sleeping in the gutter tonight.' She was pleased to see he didn't like *that* idea.

'Wosie!' Annie crawled out from under the table, pulled herself upright and tottered towards her sister. 'Eat.'

'I don't know how you understand her. She talks so funny,' Nancy said, helping the little girl on to her chair.

'You have to listen carefully.' Rose sliced the bread and put a large piece in front of Annie. 'Dinner won't be long, Toots.'

As if that was a signal, the rest of the kids sat down. They ate the ham soup with enthusiasm and wiped the bowls clean with chunks of bread. While they were tucking into the suet pudding, Rose took a plate of soup up to her mother, and was pleased when she ate everything, and then had a helping of pudding.

They were just finishing their meal when the old man arrived, smelling of booze. 'What's for dinner?' he demanded, pulling Will out of his chair and sitting in it, holding a knife and fork at the ready.

'Dad, don't you want to see the new baby?' Flo asked hesitantly.

'They all look the same.' And without looking up, he dived into the food.

'Mum's had a bad time.' Rose was going to make sure he knew.

'Rubbish, she's strong as an 'orse. Got any more of that puddin'?' He scraped his plate clean and held it out.

'It's all gone.' He grunted and stood up, ready to walk out. Rose took a deep breath and positioned herself in the doorway. 'I need the money you took out of Mum's drawer.'

'You got paid today,' he snarled.

'That's all gone on food. You took the rent and the week's food money.'

His face turned purple with rage and he lashed out, catching her a stinging blow on the side of her head. 'Don't you give me no lip! It's none of your bloody business. Out of my way!'

She straightened to her full height, pleased to see she was now eye to eye with him, and stood her ground. 'We'll end up in the workhouse if you don't stop drinking and gambling – '

She saw the blow coming and didn't flinch, although the force of it made her head swim and her vision go cloudy. 'They'll turn us out for sure if we don't pay today.'

With a growl of rage he tried to push her out of the way but she was too strong for him, and the blows he rained on her were futile. He had done his worst and she would not budge.

'Wosie!' Annie screamed, clambering over to grab her father's ankle. 'Don't hurt Wosie!'

He lifted his foot and tried to shake her off.

'Flo! Take Annie away,' Rose ordered her sister, not taking her eyes off the old man – she mustn't show a sign of weakness or fear.

When the little girl was safely out of the way she held out her hand. 'The money.' Her dark gaze was unwavering.

He hit her again.

'Leave her alone!'

Through the haze of pain she recognized Bob's voice with a jolt of astonishment. Why was he defending her?

The old man pushed him roughly away and tried to get past Rose, but she wouldn't move. He was not in a strong position now because even the kids were ganging up on him. They were all lined up beside Rose.

He took a shilling out of his pocket and placed it in her outstretched hand. She snorted. 'And the rest.'

'I ain't got no more.'

'Dig deeper. I want every penny you took.'

He licked his lips, but then, with a snarl of fury, he took out more coins and thrust them at her. Rose did a quick calculation. It wouldn't be enough to clear all of the outstanding debt, but it would satisfy the rent man for another week. Anyway, it was no use trying to squeeze any more out of him because he'd probably spent it.

'Now get out of my house,' he shouted. 'Go and sleep in the gutter where you belong.'

Her fingers closed around the money and she stepped aside. He rushed out past her, uttering a stream of abuse, but she didn't care. She had won.

Only then did she allow herself to shake and feel the pain.

'Oh, Rose.' Flo rushed over and started to dab the blood off her lip. 'Sit down and let me clean your poor face.'

'Don't fuss.' Nevertheless she allowed Flo to tend her because it gave her a chance to calm down. Her action had been born of desperation and, although she hadn't shown it, she had been frightened and very aware that she was still only a child. But she couldn't have seen them evicted, not when they had a newborn baby and her mother was weak.

Annie held on to her skirt and looked up at her with frightened eyes. 'Hurt?' she asked tremulously.

Rose stroked her hair. 'I'm all right.'

'There, that's stopped bleeding now,' Flo muttered, 'but you're going to have a black eye.'

'It'll heal – and we got the money, didn't we?' She tried to smile at her sister. 'Ouch!'

'Yes, Rose, but you took a beating getting it.'

'He won't touch me again,' she vowed. Then she saw that she was surrounded by all of the youngsters. She had never known them to be so quiet, except Annie, who had begun to sob. She lifted her up and cradled her on her lap. 'Shush, Toots, it's all over now.'

'You're hurt bad.' Will's eyes brimmed over with tears, and Bob edged closer for a better look.

'Thanks for standing up for me, Bob,' she said. 'It was brave of you.'

He studied her carefully, then his usual surly expression came back. 'I still don't like you, but you was tryin' to help us.'

'Rosie!' Her mother was calling from upstairs.

'Oh, dear, she heard the row.' Flo wrung her hands.

'She could hardly miss it. I'd better go up.' Rose touched her face carefully. 'How do I look?'

'Terrible.'

With a helpless shrug, she went up the stairs.

'What was going – ' Her mother stopped when she saw her. 'Oh, Rosie, your poor face.'

'I made him give me the money back – or, at least, as much as he still had.'

'Is there enough for the rent man?' her mother asked anxiously.

'Almost. We'll be a bit short, but I think it's enough to keep him quiet for the time being.'

Her mother closed her eyes. 'Thank God!' Then she opened them and studied her daughter with new respect. 'You're having to grow up fast, aren't you?'

Flo poked her head around the door. 'You should have seen Rosie stand up to Dad,' she said in awe. 'When he hit her she didn't move, she just stood there, refusing to let him go until he'd handed over the money. He's – he's told her to get out.'

'Flo, don't bother Mum with that now,' Rose told her sharply.

Their mother, weakened by the long, painful birth, began to cry silently, then made an effort to pull herself together. 'You're not to take any notice of that. I won't have you turned out on the street.'

They left her to rest and went back downstairs.

'You're not going to leave us, are you?' Nancy asked, her face as white as a sheet.

'No fear.' Rose tried to smile, but her lip was too badly swollen, and the split opened again.

Flo handed her a cloth to wipe away the trickle of blood.

The rent collector came on time. 'Your ma in?'

'She's in bed. Had another baby today.'

'She promised to pay me tonight.'

Rose held out the money. 'I got most of it.'

'Hmm.' He checked his book. 'This'll still leave you a bit behind.'

'How much?'

'Four and sixpence.'

'You'll have it all next week.' Rose spoke with confidence, and hoped he believed her.

He studied her battered face. 'You look as if you've had a beating.'

'I'm all right.' She lifted her chin proudly. 'You'll get your money next week and that's a promise.'

'Same time next week, then.'

It was impossible to sleep. Rose held the damp cloth over her swollen left eye, and her lip hurt too.

She heard the door open and looked up to see the old man standing there. 'You still here? Thought I told you to get out.' His speech was slurred.

'You did, but I'm not going.' The expected cuff around the ear never came.

'You're a nasty piece of work,' he snarled. 'I should have made Marj get rid of you when you was born. I knew you was nothing but trouble.'

She watched him lurch out of the door and breathed

a shuddering sigh of relief. Alone again, hopelessness and anger overwhelmed her.

There *had* to be more to life than dirt, hunger and beatings.

7

'Are you going out, Rose?' Flo put the last of the plates away.

'Yes.' She slipped the exercise book into her pocket. Thank heavens it was Sunday – she couldn't wait for her lesson. 'Why?'

'Would you take Annie with you?'

'Oh, I don't know that I can.'

'Oh, please,' her sister begged. 'I've not had time to go and see my friends for ages.'

Rose knew this was true because since she'd had to go out to work Flo had been good about helping with the little ones. 'I suppose I could.' She looked around the scullery. 'Where are the others?'

'Bob's out, Nancy and Will are with Mum and the baby, Bert and Charlie are next door, so that just leaves Annie.'

The little girl was sitting on her chair and looking expectantly from one to the other. 'Be good, Wosie,' she promised.

Rose sighed inwardly. There was nothing for it: if Miss Gardner didn't want her little sister there, she'd have to miss her lesson this week. It was a crushing thought.

'All right, you go and meet your friends.'

'Hooray! Thanks.' Flo was out of the house like a shot.

'Want a ride on a bus?' she asked the little girl.

Miss Gardner gasped when she opened the door.

'I've come to tell you I can't have my lesson today,' Rose said quickly. She hadn't realized how horrified her teacher would be to see Annie with her.

Miss Gardner pulled her in and closed the door. 'What's this all about, Rose?'

'I've got to look after my sister because Mum's just had another baby, and – '

'That's not what I meant. I'll be happy to look after the little girl while you have your lesson. I'm distressed about the condition of your face.'

'Oh, that.' Rose hadn't given her bruises and cut lip a thought.

'Wosie hurt,' Annie told the woman, her little face serious.

'I can see that, sweetheart.'

'Dad hit.'

'It's nothing.' Rose was glad Annie couldn't say much yet or she'd be spilling out the whole story to Miss Gardner.

Miss Gardner turned Rose's face towards the light. 'Do you feel well enough to have your lesson?'

'Oh, yes. It's just I thought you might not like me bringing Annie.'

The little girl looked worried. 'Me good.'

'I'm sure you are.' Miss Gardner reached out and took her from Rose, then stood her on the floor.

Annie tottered and grabbed hold of the nearest skirt.

'Her walking isn't too good,' Rose said.

At that remark, Annie's face puckered with outrage. She reached up and took Miss Gardner's hand. 'I walk.'

Rose smiled, or as much as her sore lip would allow. 'She's stubborn too.'

'Like Wosie,' Annie said, looking up at the tall lady with something like a touch of pride.

Miss Gardner laughed and led her away, careful to let her go at her own pace. 'Would you like a lesson, too?' she asked her.

Annie nodded so hard she nearly fell over.

'Rose?' She turned and saw Mr Trenchard studying her intently. 'Are you ready to start?'

'Yes, please.' She followed him into the front room and sat down, eager to study. She was glad she hadn't had to give up her lesson: the thought of it had kept her going all through the long, noisy week.

'May I see your homework?'

She handed it over and watched as he checked everything carefully. 'Excellent,' he told her, after a while. 'I've set you more difficult exercises this time.'

'I'll enjoy that, sir. I like something to puzzle over.'

'Good.'

The time flew by, as it always did when Rose was surrounded by books and had someone with her to answer her questions. She was sure she was going to learn much more like this than she would in a classroom with other children. And Mr Trenchard was starting her on Latin today. It was all so exciting.

When the door opened and Miss Gardner came in carrying a tray, with Annie holding on to her skirt, Rose looked at the clock in surprise.

Miss Gardner put down the tray, sat Annie on a chair and gave her a cup of milk. 'John, this is Annie.'

Then she said something so quietly that Rose couldn't hear it.

Mr Trenchard nodded and stooped down to the little girl. 'Hello, Annie.'

The little girl cast Rose a glance to see if it was all right for her to speak to him. When her sister nodded, she smiled at him, milk all around her mouth.

He watched as she drained the cup and put it carefully back on to the table. Then he wiped away the milk with a napkin and asked, 'Will you let me have a look inside your mouth, Annie?'

Rose started in alarm.

However, Annie didn't seem at all put out by the strange request and opened it.

Mr Trenchard slipped his finger under her tongue and peered inside. Then he smiled, ruffled her hair and stood up. 'I think you're right, Grace,' he said. 'I'll go and see if Edward's in.'

As he walked out, Rose asked, agitated, 'What's the matter? Where's he going?'

'We think there's something wrong with Annie's mouth and that's why she has difficulty speaking. I don't believe she's backward, Rose, it's just that it's an effort for her to form the words so she doesn't bother.'

'Oh.' Rose was relieved. 'I'm so pleased you don't think she's short of brains, but what about her walking?'

'That's probably due to lack of nourishing food,' Miss Gardner told her gently.

'We do our best,' Rose said. 'All the other kids are strong enough, but Annie's always been a bit sickly. Why do you think she can't talk properly?'

'We're not sure, but Mr Trenchard's brother is a doctor and he only lives next door. He'll be able to tell us.'

At the word 'doctor' Rose's heartbeat accelerated. 'We can't afford doctors.'

'Don't worry,' Miss Gardner soothed her. 'This won't cost you anything.'

The door opened and a man strode in carrying a small black bag. He was older than Mr Trenchard, but they were obviously brothers.

'Hello, little one,' he said kindly, as he pulled up a chair and sat beside the wide-eyed Annie. Then he opened the bag and took out a flat thing. 'Will you let me have a look in your mouth?'

Clearly Annie was not too sure about this. She shot Rose a frightened look. 'Wosie?'

'It's all right, Toots.' She sat beside her little sister and took her hand. 'He's a doctor and he wants to see why you can't talk properly.'

Annie cast the big man beside her a quick glance, her eyes lingering on the implement he held in his hand, then turned back to Rose. 'Hurt?'

'No.'

Annie gave a little sigh, faced the doctor and opened her mouth.

The examination didn't take long. When the doctor had finished, Annie muttered, 'Ugh,' picked up her cup and looked into it hopefully. Finding it empty, she put it back on the table. Miss Gardner hurried to pour some more milk and was rewarded with a sweet smile. Rose noticed how the grown-ups in the room looked at the little girl with affection, and began to understand why she herself took so much trouble with her sister. She was a little charmer.

'How old is she?' the doctor asked.

'Two and a half.'

He looked across at his brother. 'You were right, and it's time it was dealt with.'

'What's wrong with her?' Rose couldn't hide her anxiety.

'It isn't serious but it should be put right, or it will be an impediment in her life and that would be a shame.' He smiled at Annie. 'She's a lovely child but she's tongue-tied.'

'What's that mean?'

'It's a restricted mobility of the tongue because of an abnormality of tissue connecting it to the floor of the mouth.' He rattled off the medical explanation.

Rose had to let that sink in for a few moments. 'You mean she can't move her tongue enough to get the words out?'

'Yes.'

Annie couldn't go through life like that – it wouldn't be right. 'Can anything be done about it?'

'It's a simple operation and if you'd like to bring her to the hospital next Wednesday at ten I'll put it right for her.'

'Hospital?' Rose fingered the few coins in her pocket. 'How much will it cost?'

'I take a few charity cases and I'm prepared to make Annie one of them.'

'Charity', of course, was a dirty word to Rose, but pride wouldn't get Annie's trouble sorted out. 'Give me the address.'

71

He handed her a card.

'Thank you. We'll be there. How long will it take?'

'Not long, but as she's rather frail I'll want to keep her overnight. I'll make special arrangements for you to stay with her, if you would like to?'

'Thank you.' Her insides knotted in apprehension as she realized she'd have to take time off from the factory. She hadn't been there long – would the boss let her miss work, or would he sack her on the spot? She hated the job, but work was hard to come by, and the money made a difference to her mother.

She stooped down in front of Annie. 'Next week the doctor's going to put your tongue right so you'll be able to talk properly.'

Annie looked doubtful.

'But you mustn't be afraid because I'm going to stay with you all the time.'

The little girl looked at the tall doctor. 'Hurt?'

'No,' he laughed, 'you won't feel a thing.'

Annie seemed satisfied with that, but as he turned away, she caught hold of his coat. 'Wosie hurt.'

'I know. I'm just going to have a look at her too.'

'Tank you.'

'Who hit you?' he asked, as he examined Rose's face.

'Dad. Ugh, nasty,' Annie informed him.

'Annie!' Rose scolded.

'Did,' the little one protested.

'I know, but you don't have to tell everyone.' Rose raised her eyebrows at the doctor. 'You sure it's a good idea to free her tongue?'

Everyone laughed, including Annie.

The doctor smoothed some ointment on to her lip. 'Why did he do this?'

'Took lent.'

'Annie!'

'You took the rent?' he asked, puzzled.

'No, of course not.' Rose knew she'd have to explain now that her blabbermouth sister had aroused their interest. 'He took the money Mum had put aside for the rent collector. I had to get it back,' she added simply.

'Did you succeed?'

'Yes, but he didn't like it.'

'Hmm. I can see that.' He patted something on to her bruised eye, then handed her a small jar. 'Put some of that on night and morning. It'll help to reduce the swelling.'

'How much?'

'Nothing.'

'You don't have to treat *me* like a charity case,' Rose told him indignantly. 'I can afford to pay for a bit of salve.'

'Such pride.' The doctor looked at his brother, who nodded in agreement. Then he sat beside her. 'I realize you have a tough life, Rose, and you need to be strong, but don't be too proud to accept help when it's offered. Some of us do care what happens to you, you know.'

Rose felt ashamed of her outburst. 'I'm sorry.'

He gave an understanding smile. 'You must learn to take as well as give. The two go hand in hand.'

Rose knew that he was right: she loved to give, but pride reared its head when her role was reversed. 'I'll try.'

Annie, clearly fed up with being left out, wriggled across the chairs until she was sitting on the doctor's lap.

Rose couldn't believe her eyes. She'd never seen her sister behave like that – and to have the nerve to sit on the man's lap . . . Good Lord, he must be furious. She reached out for her and the little girl came willingly.

'Wosie cwy, no cool, 'ate din,' she informed everyone.

The doctor frowned at Rose. 'I'm afraid I didn't understand that.'

'She means I was upset because I had to leave school, and I hate the noisy factory, and . . .' she glared down at her sister ' . . . I think she's not having that operation.'

Dr Trenchard stood up, chuckling. 'She's got character.'

'A bit too much of it,' Rose muttered darkly. Here she was, trying to keep her life and feelings to herself, and this bundle of mischief had told everyone their business. And she couldn't even talk properly! What on earth was she going to be like when she could get her tongue round the words?

Rose knocked on the boss's door and sent up a silent prayer that she wasn't about to lose her job.

'Come.'

She went in, feeling rather like Daniel entering the lion's den.

'Yes?' Mr Baker asked abruptly, then stared. 'What happened to your face?'

'Ran into a door,' she lied.

He snorted in disbelief. 'More like somebody's fist, by the look of it.'

Rose saw little point in trying to deny it. He knew where she came from. He didn't seem to be in a very good mood. Oh, hell, she thought, but pitched in anyway. 'I need Wednesday and Thursday off, please, sir.'

'Why?'

'My sister – she's only two and a half – has to have an operation and she'll be scared if I don't stay with her.'

'What's the matter with her?' he asked sharply.

'She's tongue-tied, sir, can't speak properly. They've got to – '

'I know what it means.' He sat back and looked her up and down. 'Operations are expensive, how are you going to pay for it?'

'I'm not, sir. The doctor's doing it as a charity case.'

'Who is he?'

'Dr Trenchard.'

'I know him. He's a good man. How did you come to know him?'

Rose bit back the retort that it was none of his business, but after a moment's hesitation, she decided to tell him the truth – after all, her job might depend upon this interview. 'His brother is giving me lessons every Sunday afternoon. He's a teacher at the secondary school.'

Mr Baker looked interested. 'And why is he doing that?'

'I won a scholarship but couldn't take up the place because we couldn't afford the new clothes. My school made me leave because they couldn't teach me any more.'

'How old are you really?'

That had torn it. Now she was definitely going to lose her job. 'Well, I'm not fourteen,' she hedged.

'I've been aware of that from the beginning.' He sat up straight. 'How old are you?'

75

'Nearly twelve, sir.' That sounded a bit better than eleven, she comforted herself.

'Good grief!' He was startled. 'And they made you leave school?'

Rose nodded. It still hurt. 'Are you going to sack me?'

He shook his head and she breathed a sigh of relief.

'If you can't go to school, then someone must employ you. Your work is good and you appear to be very bright,' he told her.

'Top of the school, I was,' she said, with pride.

'And what is Mr Trenchard teaching you?'

'Reading, writing, arithmetic, history and Latin.'

'Latin!' Now he was astonished. 'What good is that going to do you?'

'Don't know, sir, but it's fun and he said it might be useful later on.'

Mr Baker's gaze ran over her again, thoughtfully this time. Then he nodded. 'Very well. You may have leave this week, but don't make a habit of it.'

'I won't, sir, and thank you.' She couldn't believe it. He'd given her the time off, he knew her real age *and* he hadn't sacked her.

8

August 1914

It was too hot to sleep. Rose slid carefully out of the bed she shared with Flo, picked up her books and made her way downstairs. The scullery was a little cooler, but not much. The night was humid and stifling, and the heat only made their living conditions even more unbearable. It encouraged vermin, she thought, with a shudder, as she put her books on the old wooden table. At least that was clean – it was scrubbed every day.

After the bank holiday, Mr Trenchard was going to set her an exam, so as she couldn't sleep, she might as well study. First, though, she would read a bit more of her Bible. She had reached the Book of Revelation, and found it most puzzling of all.

She lit a candle rather than the smelly oil lamp, and settled down to read.

Some time later, she picked up her pencil and underlined a sentence, then sat back, deep in thought.

What did that mean? ' . . . behold, I have set before thee an open door, and no man can shut it: . . .' The thought of an open door was exciting, but there didn't seem to be an open door anywhere in her life. Every turn she made seemed to lead to a dead end and there was no escape. She had a job she hated, she was still locked in poverty, and as far as she could see only her mind was free. No one could cage that. She could weave wonderful dreams and wander where she pleased, was free to explore others' thoughts and ideas through their writings.

She chewed the end of her pencil. Was that what the passage meant? When all other doors appeared closed, was the door of your mind the one that 'no man can shut'?

But if she believed that, it would surely be like accepting that things like poverty couldn't be changed? She rejected that idea. There must be a way of opening those closed doors and stepping through into a better life. And she wasn't talking about dying – oh, no, the improvement in life had to take place here, or what was the struggle for?

She threw down the pencil and stood up to get herself a cup of water. Even that was warm.

'Can I have a drink, Rosie?'

She spun round. 'Annie, I didn't hear you come down.'

Annie grinned. 'I haven't got any shoes on.'

Rose poured her some water and handed it to her. 'Can't you sleep?'

'Too hot.' Annie drank the water and put the empty cup on the table. 'What you doing?' she asked.

'I couldn't sleep either so I thought I'd do some reading.'

Annie nodded, yawned and trotted back to bed.

Rose watched her go. What a difference in less than a year. After the operation she'd begun to speak properly and now she could talk the hind legs off a donkey. Her health and confidence had improved and she was like any normal three-year-old, under everyone's feet.

Rose rinsed the cups and decided she'd better get down to some serious studying, but before she could sit down, the old man lurched in.

Drunk again, she saw, and turned away in disgust. Since their run-in over the rent, he'd stayed out of her way as much as possible.

She jumped when she felt a hand slip round her waist. She turned quickly, sending the old man staggering across the scullery.

'What do you think you're up to?' she demanded, hands on hips.

'Don't be like that, Rosie.' He held on to the table to steady himself. 'I was just trying to be friendly.'

'Friendly?' she blazed. 'When have you ever been friendly to me?'

He came towards her, a crafty look on his face. 'If you give me a chance, I'll show you how nice I can be.'

'You're disgusting!'

'What's disgusting about it?' He leered. 'Come on, Rosie, I'll teach you things you can't learn from no books. You're turning into quite a beauty, and someone's going to get you before long.'

He reached out, clearly intending to run his hands over her again, but she slapped them off her. 'Get away from me.' She had her back to the sink and he'd blocked her only escape route. She was frightened.

'Come on.' He got within touching distance again. 'You're not my flesh and blood, so there's no harm in it.'

This was unbelievable. He'd hit and insulted her all her life, and all of a sudden he wanted to touch her.

'You think you're better than us, don't you?' He swayed drunkenly. 'But let me tell you, girl, you're in the dirt and some day you'll see there's no way out. We takes what little pleasure there is in this life – '

'Not with me, you don't!'

'You was born a bastard and yer only fit for one thing,' he shouted.

Rose felt like strangling him.

He smirked, and then, with surprising agility, made a lunge for her.

She sidestepped and he fell against the stove.

'Stand still, you slippery bitch.'

She clenched her fists and lifted them. 'You take one more step towards me and I'll knock your teeth down your throat.'

He saw evidently that she meant what she said, and stepped back. He forced a laugh. 'You're too serious for a young'un, girl. I was playing a joke on you.'

'I didn't see the funny side of it.'

Thank heaven it was Sunday. That set-to with the old man last night had unsettled her, but she could forget it for a couple of hours while she had her lesson. Rose sighed as she looked around Miss Gardner's pleasant front room, a haven of peace. She picked up a newspaper and sat in one of the comfortable chairs, at once absorbed in what she was reading.

'Don't frown like that, Rose.' Mr Trenchard walked into the room.

Rose looked up from the paper. 'Hello, sir.'

'What's making you scowl so?'

'Do you think there's going to be a war?'

'It looks very likely. But tell me what you've gleaned from the paper.'

'Well.' Rose leaned forward. 'There was a short report last month about some Archduke and his wife being killed in a place called Bosnia – '

'And what do you think that has to do with us?'

'It's complicated, but it seems that Austria is about to declare war on Serbia, with Germany's support, and if Germany threatens France, we will go to war with them.' She watched Mr Trenchard polish his spectacles. 'Have I got that right?'

'Yes. That's exactly the situation.'

Rose frowned at the newspaper again. 'I find it hard to understand why we should have to fight. I hope it never happens.'

A week later that was still Rose's hope when she took some of the children out for a treat. It was a scorching August bank holiday and she wanted to get out of their cramped little house. She sat under a huge tree and watched them. Annie was chattering happily to another little girl she'd just met, Will and Charlie were chasing pigeons and Nancy was sitting quietly beside her on the grass.

'This is a nice place,' Nancy said. 'Thank you for bringing us, Rosie.'

She turned and smiled. 'Better than Garrett Street, isn't it?'

'Oh, yes. What's this place called?'

'Green Park,' Rose told her. 'As it's so hot I thought it would be nice to come somewhere with lots of nice shady trees.'

'Feels cooler here,' Nancy agreed.

'Rosie!' Charlie and Will skidded to a halt in front of

her. 'There's a shop across the road selling lemonade.'

'And you'd like some, I suppose?' She stood up.

They nodded eagerly, then looked doubtful. 'Only if you've got enough money.'

'I think I can manage that, and we'll see if they've got some buns too.'

'Wow!' said Charlie. 'This is the best day we've ever had.'

Rose was glad she'd thought of this treat. She'd tried to get all the kids to come with her, but Flo was with her friends, Bob had vanished, as usual, and Bert wasn't feeling well. Still, she'd take the other three a bun too. After buying herself some new shoes, she'd been saving up for a winter coat, but in this heat winter seemed a long way off and it wouldn't do any harm to spend a little of the money.

When they'd enjoyed the lemonade and buns, they went back into the park for another hour and then, reluctantly, made their way to the bus stop for the homeward journey.

There was a lot of noise, with people talking excitedly, so Rose looked towards the newspaper seller. Her heart raced with alarm.

'What does that say?' Will asked.

The news placard read, 'WAR INEVITABLE.'

For four months the recruitment campaign raged, using any means to get the young men into the army. They flocked to join up. There were many reasons why the boys and men enlisted – excitement, patriotism, fear of what others might say if they didn't, and many because they couldn't get any other work.

The children found it all very interesting as one man after another from their street joined up.

'You going in the army?' Bob asked his father, jumping up and down with excitement. 'Jack's dad's just come home for Christmas and he looks smashing in his uniform.'

'That's all right for your mate's dad but I'm not fit enough to fight.'

Bob eyed him suspiciously. 'What's wrong with you?'

'I got a bad back.' He gave his son a sharp clip round the ear. 'Anyway, it's none of your bloody business. You're too young to understand.'

Bob ran out of the scullery, straight into Flo.

'Have you heard?' Flo cried. 'The Germans have shelled Hartlepool, Scarborough and Whitby. There's loads of people dead.'

There was silence around the table as they all tried to take in this piece of distressing news.

'Oh, my.' Their mother sighed. 'It'll be our turn next, you see if I'm not right.'

'Don't be daft, woman,' her husband told her scathingly. 'Their guns can't reach London.'

'No, but they've got Zeppelins.'

Nancy whimpered. 'What will we do if they drop bombs on us?'

'It might not come to that,' Rose said soothingly. 'We don't know what's going to happen, do we?'

Nancy gave a tremulous smile, clearly trying to be brave.

The old man's chair scraped back and he stood up. 'You're all talking a lot of nonsense. The war won't last long.'

Marj Webster shook her head sadly. 'Everyone said it would all be over by Christmas, but it isn't, is it?'

'I'm off down the pub, then. I'm not staying here to listen to your doom and gloom.' With that, he stormed out of the house.

'Things could get rough, couldn't they?' Rose said to her mother quietly.

'Yes, though you probably know more about it than I do, Rosie, with all your reading. What does Mr Trenchard think?'

'Well, he says it won't be the quick war everyone was expecting, and now the Germans have started to attack the ordinary people . . .' She tailed off.

Her mother looked out at the crowded back-to-back houses and frowned. 'If they drops bombs on a place like this it'll be terrible.'

Rose gave a humourless laugh. 'If it wasn't for the people living here I'd tell the Germans to come and destroy it. It would be one way of getting rid of this slum.'

'You really do hate living like this, don't you, Rosie?'

'I've never made a secret of it, Mum.'

'I know, and perhaps one day you'll get out of here, but for the moment we must get through this war as best we can.'

Rose nodded. The months or years ahead were going to be a hard struggle for everyone.

9

June 1916

Mr Trenchard removed his spectacles, polished them, then laid them on the table. 'I'm afraid this will be our last session, Rose.'

'Last?' She tried to hide her shock. It was a terrible blow to hear that he was going to stop her Sunday visits. However, she couldn't expect him to bother with her for ever, and he had been teaching her for almost three years now. 'I'm sorry about that, Mr Trenchard, but I do understand. It's been good of you to keep up the lessons for so long, and I've enjoyed every minute of them,' she assured him. 'You've opened up a whole new world to me.'

'Rose, you're only fourteen and I'd be happy to teach you for many years to come, but I'm afraid I have received my conscription papers.'

She was horrified. They'd been at war for nearly two years and she was aware that there was now compulsory conscription, but she had never thought that he would be called upon. 'But you're a teacher and needed at home,' she blurted out.

'Women are taking on men's work now, as you know.' He sighed. 'It's ironic that it's taken this dreadful war for a woman's worth to be recognized.'

That was true enough, Rose thought. She herself had

been promoted, and the factory was working continual shifts to turn out all that was needed for the war effort. 'Isn't there an age limit, sir?' she asked, looking frantically for a reason to keep him from getting killed.

'Forty-five.'

'Oh.' Mr Trenchard was nowhere near that old. 'Are you going into the army?'

'The navy.'

That was a relief. It was dangerous in the navy, of course, as the sinking of the *Lusitania* last year had shown, but at least he wouldn't be going into the trenches. The losses there had been horrific.

'Grace and I will be getting married next Saturday, Rose, and we'd like you to come to the wedding.'

'Oh, thank you, sir, I'd like that.'

'I think it's time you called me John, don't you?'

'I don't think – '

He smiled at the look of doubt on her face. 'This war is changing many old attitudes, Rose, and I would like to think we have become friends.'

She realized that what he'd said was true, they had become friends, but more than that: he had been her teacher, guide and someone she had been able to confide in. She was going to miss him dreadfully. She had talked to him openly and honestly, telling him things she would normally have kept to herself.

He understood her volatile nature, and she respected his intelligence and genuine kindness – but now she was going to lose him. It had had to come, of course, she knew that, but not like this.

She would pray for him every day, and if there *was* a God He would not let this good man die.

'I want you to do something for me while I'm away, Rose.'

'Anything,' she answered immediately.

'Will you visit Grace regularly?'

'Of course I will.' She swallowed hard, trying to keep tears at bay, although she felt as if her foundations had been torn away.

John patted her hand. 'That will be a great comfort to us, and I shall be able to picture you both sitting here, surrounded by books.'

Oh, Lord, she was going to cry.

'Don't grieve for me, Rose,' he told her gently. 'I've set out a programme of reading and study for you, and when I return I shall expect you to have completed it.'

She took the books and sniffed loudly, as a tear ran down her cheek.

He waited while she composed herself. 'I don't want you to neglect your studies,' he told her sternly. 'You have a fine mind, but you will never reach your full potential unless you continue to work. I was in the process of preparing some examinations for you to tackle, but they will have to wait for a while.'

'What kind of examinations?' she asked wistfully.

'Secondary standard.'

'What?' Her eyes opened wide in surprise. 'Do you think I'd be good enough?'

'With a bit of extra coaching, I think you might be. That's why I don't want you to stop studying.'

Rose sat up straight 'When the war's over will you still teach me?'

'Of course. I shall look forward to taking up where

we've left off, and discovering how much you've learned while I've been away.'

She smiled. 'I'll see if I can surprise you, then.'

He tipped back his head and laughed. 'You have continually surprised me, Rose, from the moment we met.'

They were both laughing when the door opened and Grace came in with Annie – the little girl was a frequent visitor now.

'How lovely to see two such happy faces.' Grace beamed.

It was only when Rose looked into her eyes that she saw how worried Grace was about John going into the navy, and she vowed to help them as much as she could. She would never be able to repay them for what they had done for her. John had become the pivot of her life, opening doors in her mind and giving her a wider view of the world.

'I was so happy to hear about your marriage,' she said brightly to Grace.

'Thank you.' Grace put the tray of tea and biscuits on the table. 'I hope you're coming to the wedding?'

'You couldn't keep me away. I'll buy a new frock, so you won't be ashamed of me.'

'We'd never be ashamed of you,' Grace and John said together.

Annie clambered on to a chair and slid across until she was sitting on John's lap. Then she turned her large eyes to him. 'Can I come to your wedding, please?'

'We shall be very upset if you don't,' he told her seriously.

'Can I have a new frock too?' she squeaked excitedly.

'Hmm. I think you should have new shoes, too. You've

88

got holes in the bottom of those.' Rose could see them plainly as her sister waved her feet about in excitement.

Annie lifted up a foot and showed it to John. 'They've got holes and they're too small.'

He tutted. 'Then you must definitely have new ones.'

Annie glanced uncertainly at Rose. 'Don't worry, Toots, I think I can manage it.' There went her winter coat again, she thought philosophically. She had never been able to get one as something else was always more pressing.

Grace stooped down in front of Annie, who had got off John's lap now and was sitting on a chair waiting patiently for her milk. 'Will you be my flower-girl, Annie?'

'What's that?'

'Well, you stand behind me during the wedding and hold my flowers for me.'

Annie thought about it for a few moments, then nodded. 'I can do that.'

'Good. That's settled, then.'

Rose studied John and Grace. They had been walking out for a long time and she wondered why it had taken them so long to decide to get married. After all, John was a kind person, not a bit like their old man. 'Is it because of the war that you're getting married?' she asked, knowing it was a cheeky question, but she'd come to know them so well.

'We've always intended to wed,' John told her, not seeming to mind the question, 'but it was frowned upon for married women to work, and Grace had had such a struggle to get a job as a teacher that she didn't want to give it up.'

'But things are changing, aren't they?' Rose asked. 'Lots of married women are working for the war effort now.'

'Yes.' Grace poured Annie some more milk. 'Women are going to have a lot more freedom now, and that's a good thing, don't you think?'

Rose nodded. 'Yes, that's one door open, but we are still restricted.' She thought of herself now as a woman. She turned to John. 'Do you think we will ever get the vote?'

'After the war, the pressure on the government to extend the franchise to women will be immense, and I don't think they will be able to evade the issue much longer.'

'The Suffragettes won't let them, will they?' Rose grinned at the thought.

'Don't get involved with the suffrage movement, Rose,' John told her, as if he had read her mind. 'You wait your time. There will be many things for you to do when you've finished your education.'

'Such as?'

'I'm not sure yet, but one day you will see exactly where your destiny lies.'

Another week done, thank goodness. Rose slumped into a chair and rubbed her temple.

'Headache?' her mother asked.

'Hmm, a bit, but it'll soon go.' She emptied her pay packet on to the table, counted out eighteen shillings and gave them to her mother.

'Rose, you must keep more for yourself. You're working like a slave at that factory.'

'Everyone is, but you need it more than I do.'

Her mother gave her back two shillings. 'You must think of yourself more.'

'But I do,' she protested.

'No, you don't, my girl. I know how badly you need a winter coat, but each time you've saved enough together, you spend it on me or the children, and it isn't right.'

Rose grinned when she heard her mother use that phrase, remembering the first Sunday lesson she'd had. John had asked her what she was going to do about injustice and had pointed out that one person could make a difference.

'Why don't you get yourself a coat from the tallyman?'

That brought Rose out of her reverie. 'You know I won't have anything unless I can afford to pay for it,' she reminded her mother. The old man's theft of the rent money had made a deep impression on her. Now she had an aversion to debt of any kind.

'Jobs are secure now,' her mother pointed out. 'You'd be able to afford it all right.'

'No,' she said, emphatically. 'I'll wait until I can pay for it.'

'But that could take some time, and you're going to need it soon.'

Rose dismissed the idea with a shrug.

'There.' Her mother gave up and poured her a cup of tea. 'You drink that, it will soon clear the headache.'

'The cure-all brew.' Rose laughed.

'Don't mock it. There's a lot of truth in some of these old wives' remedies.'

Rose didn't argue. Her mother was a great believer in that kind of thing.

'Better?' Marj asked.

She nodded, and it was true: the niggling pain had almost gone.

'Rosie.' Annie ran into the scullery. 'Is it time to get ready yet?'

'We've got plenty of time,' she told the impatient child. 'The wedding isn't until four.'

'Oh.' Annie stood on tiptoe to look at the clock on the shelf. It took her some time to work out where the big and little hands were. 'It's one o'clock now?' she asked hesitantly.

'Very good,' her mother praised her.

Although Annie was now five, she was small for her age, and still lagged a little behind the others, but she was improving all the time, and Rose hoped she would soon catch up.

'We're going out soon, Toots, and I want you to put your clean knickers in a bag.'

'Why?' Annie looked puzzled.

'Because we're going to the public baths,' she told her.

'What for?'

'To have a bath, silly. We can't wear our new frocks without being clean, can we?'

As she reached out to pick up her empty cup, Rose noticed a letter on the table. 'What's that?' she asked, her heart beginning to thump uncomfortably. The only other time they'd had a letter delivered to them was when they'd been up to their eyes in debt.

Before her mother could answer, the old man came in. Since the start of the war, he'd been forced to take work in a munitions factory and he'd never stopped complaining about it. Rose, however, had been glad to see him do something useful for a change.

'There's a letter for you.' Marj held it out to him.

'Well, read it for me,' he said irritably.

Marj opened the envelope.

'What does it say?'

'It's your conscription papers. You're to report for the army next Wednesday.'

'What?' He snatched it out of her hands and thrust it at Rose. 'She read it wrong.'

After a quick glance, Rose handed it back. 'That's what it says.'

'But I can't!' he bellowed. 'I'm not fit enough. I told them – my back – '

'They don't agree,' Rose told him. 'They've passed you fit for duty.'

He turned pale and, for the first time in her life, Rose felt a stirring of pity for him. She'd never like him, of course, but what chance had he ever had in life? He'd been born in the slums and hadn't had enough education to better himself, so was it any wonder he'd accepted that this kind of life was all he was ever going to get? Now he was about to be dragged out of the only environment he'd ever known into heaven knows what.

'Mr Trenchard has got his papers as well.' Rose needed to offer some comfort – she wouldn't wish the trenches on her worst enemy.

'Is it him what's been learning you all this time?'

'Yes.'

'Knows what's what, does he?'

'Yes, he's very clever.'

'And they've called him up?'

Rose nodded sadly.

He stared gloomily out of the window at the grimy street. 'They must be desperate 'cos they're scraping the bottom of the barrel if they want the likes of me.'

'You mustn't think like that, Tom,' Marj admonished. 'You'll make as good a soldier as anyone else.'

His usual cockiness was restored. 'You're right, Marj, and it's no use grousing about it. I'll go down the boozer and see if any of the others are going, as well.'

They watched him head across the street. It was a wonder there wasn't a permanent groove in the road between their house and the pub, Rose thought.

She looked at her mother. Since she'd had David, she hadn't become pregnant again and looked years younger. She was an attractive woman again.

'I'm thinking of getting a job. Mrs Jenks down the road has offered to look after the kids.' Marj looked at Rose. 'What do you think?'

'With the old man away and the children growing up, it will give you a real change – and extra cash.' Rose was delighted at the idea.

'Yes, and I'll get twenty-five shillings a week from the army, paid straight to me.' Marj frowned at the letter sitting on the table. 'I don't know how he'll cope with it.'

'It's tough for everyone.' Rose paused. She'd never told her mother about the time the old man had tried to mess with her. Some things in life were best left unsaid. 'It's funny, you know, I always call him "the old man", but he can't be forty-five yet or he wouldn't have been called-up.'

'He's only thirty-nine,' her mother told her, 'but the kind of life we lead ages you.'

Rose knew this was true – and another thing that

wasn't right. No one's life should be blighted like this. But the politicians were paying more attention to the working classes now – if only because they needed them, Rose thought cynically.

'Hello, Rose.' The woman behind the counter handed her a towel and a bar of soap. 'You can have your usual room.'

'Can my sister come in with me?'

'Of course.' The attendant leaned over the counter to look at the child. 'And what's your name?'

'Annie.' She beamed. 'We're going to a wedding and I'm going to hold the flowers, so we've got to be clean.' She held up the bag she was clutching. 'I've got my clean knickers with me.'

Rose dragged her away before she could tell the woman their entire family history.

'You been here before, Rosie?' Annie asked, trotting along the corridor, trying to peer into the rooms as they went past.

'I come every week.' Her sister's curiosity was insatiable, Rose marvelled. Not like hers, of course – she was only interested in books and learning: Annie wanted to know what was going on around her, what other people were doing. Rose couldn't care less what other people thought and did.

They reached the allotted room and she opened the door. Annie rushed in and peered over the edge of the bath. 'Oooh, it's big.' Her eyes were wide.

Rose couldn't help laughing at the expression on her little face. 'You can come in with me, then you'll be safe.'

It turned out to be more of a playtime than a bath, with Annie squealing in delight, but Rose finally managed to give them both a good scrub and wash their hair. They came out of the baths pink and glowing.

Grace didn't wear the traditional white dress, but Rose thought she looked beautiful. Her frock was of the palest blue, with a heart-shaped neckline and long sleeves. The material was so flimsy that it swirled around her ankles as she walked. Her hat's small brim was surrounded with white flowers and her shoes were also white. To add to the charming picture, Grace was clearly delighted to be marrying the man she loved. John looked distinguished and proud in his new dark grey suit. His brother, Dr Edward Trenchard, was the best man, and because Grace's father was dead, another friend of theirs, Harold, they called him, was giving the bride away. Rose had not met him before, but he looked a kindly man.

Annie took her duty very seriously, looking at her big sister from time to time for a nod of approval. After the ceremony they all went back to Grace's house. It was a small gathering of only ten people, and Rose made herself useful by handing round the sandwiches and tea. It was a happy occasion, for John and Grace were well liked, but she couldn't help feeling sad because John had to report to the navy in a few days.

Rose had just come back from the kitchen with another plate of sandwiches when she heard Annie giggle, and spun round to see what the little rascal was doing. 'Oh, no,' she groaned, 'I can't trust her for one minute at a time.'

Grace laughed and stopped her from dashing across

the room to retrieve the little girl. 'Leave her – Edward won't mind. He's become fond of her since he did the operation on her tongue.'

Rose fidgeted. 'I'm not sure it was such a good idea,' she muttered. 'You ought to hear the things she tells people! And look at her now! She's getting too big to sit on anyone's lap, and why is it always the men?'

'Perhaps she doesn't get the chance at home,' Grace said softly.

'You're right. I've never seen her dad playing with any of them, let alone cuddling them.'

Grace gave her a strange look, then glanced at Annie. 'She's an affectionate child, and I suspect you might be the only one to show her any love – she adores you.'

'Mum loves all of us, I'm sure, but she's just too busy trying to make ends meet to be able to spend any time on us. It's not her fault,' Rose said stoutly.

'Of course it isn't. It must be hard bringing up nine children.' Grace looked across at Annie again and started to chuckle. 'Look at her, the poor little thing's fallen asleep on Edward's lap. She's tired out after all the excitement.'

'I'd better take her home.'

It was an hour later when they finally left the party. Rose had to carry Annie from the bus stop because she was too exhausted to walk. It had been difficult not to cry when she'd said goodbye to John. She was going to miss him so much, and he would be in her prayers every night. She hoped that God would be listening to her.

'You awake, darling?' John kissed his new wife gently.

'Hmm.' Grace wrapped her arms around him and

98

yawned sleepily. 'It was a lovely wedding, wasn't it?'

'Yes, it went very well.' He paused. 'We should have done this a long time ago, Grace.'

She pulled herself upright, now wide awake. 'I'm sorry I've made you wait so long, but there never seemed to be any hurry. Now we have such a short time together.'

He stroked her hair. 'You make it sound as if I'm not coming back,' he chided. 'You never know, they might give me an office job.'

'Oh, do you think they would?' she asked eagerly.

'Well, of course my eyesight's not perfect, and they seemed very interested in my qualifications.'

'Oh, John! That would be wonderful.'

'We'll have to wait and see, but whatever happens, you mustn't worry about me.' He grinned down at her. 'I'm going to be perfectly safe because Rose has promised to pray for me, and I don't think even the Almighty would ignore her.'

Laughter shook Grace. 'At fourteen she's turning into quite a formidable young woman, isn't she?'

'She certainly is. On the outside she appears distant, unemotional and controlled, and that is the way she wants the world to see her, but you've only to watch her with Annie to see she has a softer side.'

'She's had a hard life and believes she'll only survive by being tough.' Grace laid her head on his chest. 'I hope she doesn't have to take too many knocks and disappointments or that loving spark might he buried beneath anger and resentment.'

'She has a strong will and plenty of determination, and I think she'll be all right. Don't let her stop studying, will you?'

'I won't, but I don't think anything in this world would stop her. She has a voracious appetite for knowledge.'

'I still can't believe she comes from Garrett Street.'

'She must be a real misfit there.' Then Grace started to laugh. 'Didn't Annie looked a picture today in her pink dress?'

John chuckled. 'She told me and Edward that Rose had taken her to the public baths, and described it all in great detail. Rose would have been horrified.'

'It's lovely the affection between them, but have you noticed how different they are? Annie's fair and delicate, and Rose is dark and strong.' Grace frowned. 'You'd never believe they came from the same family.'

'I noticed that especially today when Annie was sleeping on Edward's lap. The little girl is loving, outgoing and trusting, but Rose is quite the opposite. She keeps a tight hold on herself and does not give her trust easily.'

'She trusts you.' Grace smiled affectionately at her husband.

John nodded. 'I do believe she does, and I'm honoured.' Then he slid Grace down in the bed, and they abandoned all talk.

Later, as he was drifting into sleep he awoke with a start. 'Oh, good Lord!' He shook Grace. 'Wake up, darling.'

'What is it?' she said, alarmed.

'I've just remembered who Rose reminds me of.'

'Who?' she asked, puzzled.

'I must be imagining it.' He spoke almost to himself. 'Grace, I've never heard her speak about her father, have you?'

'Now you mention it, I don't think so. But just today

she talked about Annie's father, as if the man had nothing to do with her.'

'She's the eldest, isn't she?'

'Yes.'

'Then perhaps the man her mother married isn't Rose's father?'

Grace shrugged. 'I suppose so, but what are you getting at? Who does she remind you of?'

'Well, I might be mistaken, but she's the image of him.'

'In what way?'

'The dark eyes, for a start, but that isn't all, she has the same blue-black hair.'

'That isn't much to go on.'

'Agreed, but all his characteristics are there – the proud way she holds her head, the directness of her gaze, even the way she moves, and her intelligence. There are too many similarities to dismiss.'

'Who is it?' Grace asked excitedly.

He bent his head and whispered in her ear.

'But – but – ' she stuttered. 'Good heavens! I've met him and you're right, she's the image of him, especially now she's older. But we must be mistaken, he's – ' She came to an abrupt halt.

'I know what you're thinking, but I'm convinced I'm right. When I first met her I felt as if I'd seen her before, but she came from Garrett Street, and that clouded my judgement. Now she's older the resemblance is evident. She must have something to do with that family.' He rolled over and groaned into the pillow. 'Damn it! I *wish* I wasn't going away. I'd love to look into this further.'

Rose stood on the platform with her mother and watched

the men boarding the train. It was a sad scene. Some were already in uniform, but the majority were conscripts trying to put a brave face on things in an effort to comfort their weeping women.

She could see Grace hugging John, and wondered if she should go over to them, but quickly decided against it. She had said goodbye and this moment was for husband and wife. Swallowing a lump in her throat, she looked away, but it seemed as if everyone else on the platform was crying. Even her mother was wiping away a tear as she watched the old man get on to the train. However, he was with a group of his drinking friends and seemed happy enough, which was hardly surprising as they had been drinking since breakfast.

Rose shook her head sadly: they were in for a shock when they sobered up and found themselves in an army camp with the sergeant shouting orders at them.

As the train pulled out of the station, everyone was waving and calling, but Rose watched in silence, wondering how many of the men would come back. She cast a quick glance at her mother and saw that although she wasn't crying her expression was grim.

'He'll be all right, Mum. If anyone can dodge trouble, it'll be him,' she joked. 'After all, he's had plenty of practice.'

'I expect you're right.' Marj sighed and looked around the platform at the silent women now making their way back to their homes.

Rose edged her towards the exit. She had to get back to work.

'Thank you for coming. I couldn't have faced it without you,' Marj said.

Rose pulled a face. 'I don't think he knew we were here.'

'But someone from the family had to see him off to war. He's frightened, you see, and drinking was the only way he could get over it. I just hope the army has a good supply of beer.'

As they walked out of the station, Grace was waiting for them. Her eyes were red but she managed a smile. 'Hello, Rose.'

Rose turned to her mother. 'This is Mrs Trenchard, Mum.'

Grace held out her hand. 'I'm pleased to meet you, Mrs Webster.'

'I'm ever so grateful to you and your husband for helping Rose carry on with her lessons,' her mother said. 'It near broke her heart when she had to leave school.'

'Oh, John has loved teaching her.' Grace smiled. 'You have a remarkable daughter, Mrs Webster.'

Marj nodded. 'Yes, she's always been bright.'

Rose shuffled uncomfortably from foot to foot. She wished they wouldn't talk about her. 'Annie hasn't stopped going on about the wedding,' she blurted out.

'A real chatter-box she is now.' Marj laughed.

'She's a delightful little girl,' Grace told her.

At that moment a woman walked past them sobbing loudly, and Grace gave her a compassionate glance. 'Such a terrible war, isn't it? I expect all your children will miss their father.'

'I suppose so, though they never saw much of him.'

'How many children do you and your husband have, Mrs Webster?'

'Eight,' Marj answered automatically. 'Oh, and Rose, of course, that makes nine.'

'My goodness, you have your hands full.'

'You can say that, all right.'

Grace turned to Rose. 'Will you visit me this Sunday? I expect I shall be feeling rather lonely.'

'Of course. I'll come at the usual time.'

'That would be lovely, thank you. And now perhaps you would both like to come to the tea-room with me. I don't feel like going home just yet.'

'I've got to get back to work,' Rose told her, looking anxiously at the clock above the station entrance.

'What a shame. Would you join me, Mrs Webster?'

'Er . . .'

'Go on, Mum,' Rose urged. 'It'll do you good.'

'That's settled, then,' Grace said, not giving Marj Webster a chance to refuse.

Rose said goodbye and hurried away. Her mother had looked a bit doubtful, but Grace would soon put her at her ease, and if Marj was thinking of going out to work, then she'd have to get used to mixing with other people again.

Rose had had more than her allotted time off work, and broke into a trot, thinking about the conversation they'd had outside the station. Her mother had nearly told Grace that she was not one of the old man's kids, but she didn't think Grace had noticed the slip.

II

December 1916

Rose shivered and pulled her coat around her. She'd go through the park tonight: there were some nice little shops on the other side, and she wanted to find something to give the children this Christmas. She opened the rickety old gate, and smiled to herself. To call this a park was giving it a grandeur it didn't deserve, but it was a bit of green space and everyone used it. There were trees and rough areas of tangled bushes and gorse, but the middle had been cleared. In the winter the youngsters played football and in the summer people walked about or sat in the sun.

Rose shivered again as a gust of biting wind whipped at her. She'd never get a new coat at this rate, she thought, stuffing her hands into her pockets. This one was too small and threadbare, but she couldn't see the kids with nothing to look forward to this festive season. She remembered her own disappointment when she'd been told repeatedly that Father Christmas had had his sleigh stolen and hadn't been able to deliver the presents.

She paused briefly by a group of carol singers. There were about ten of them swinging lanterns and singing at the top of their voices, and another four blowing trumpets. They had collected quite a crowd around them who were also joining in.

Her spirits were high and she was looking forward to Christmas. The old man wouldn't be home – they didn't have the faintest idea where he was, and as he couldn't write there hadn't been any letters from him. Her mum was working so they had more money coming in and, best of all, she'd just heard that John had been given a job at headquarters and would not be going to sea. She couldn't remember when she had felt so happy.

She threw a farthing into the collection tin and hurried on, eager to get her shopping done and out of the bitter wind.

The shops were in view when someone grabbed her from behind and dragged her across the grass into a clump of bushes.

Rose was stunned by the suddenness of the attack. The park was full of people and it had not entered her head that it might be unsafe.

He was pulling her further into the shrubbery. She could feel the branches scratching her face and legs. Terrified, she began to lash out at her assailant and shout as loudly as she could, but all that got her was a slap round the head that nearly knocked her out. Then a large hand was clamped across her mouth.

'Quiet, bitch,' he growled, 'or I'll kill you.'

There was something about his voice that turned her blood to ice. He sounded frenzied, excited and out of control.

She kicked, and heard him grunt as she made contact with his shins. Feeling his grip slacken, she wrenched herself free and started to run, but she hadn't taken more than a couple of steps before he caught her by the hair. She squealed in pain.

When he hit her this time, her head reeled. As she staggered, he threw her to the ground with force, knocking the breath out of her body. She could hear her clothes being torn, but she was incapable of defending herself. Then, with a demented laugh, he was on her.

She didn't know how long she lay there after he'd gone. She was oblivious to the cold; all she could feel was pain.

After a while she became conscious of her surroundings, and the sheer horror of what had happened galvanized her into action, but as she sat up dizziness and sickness overwhelmed her. Amid her distress one thing was clear – she was hurt and needed help.

With a tremendous effort, she pulled herself upright, and wrapped the coat around her torn clothes. She wasn't going to let strangers see her shame. The first few steps were excruciatingly painful, but she held her head high and walked out of the bushes towards the gate.

There were no tears, she was beyond that, just an empty void inside her. She had to find somewhere to clean herself up. But where could she go?

She was nowhere near the public baths, and she couldn't get on a bus in this state. Home was on the other side of the park and, anyway, she couldn't go in like this. The disgusting things that maniac had done to her made her feel dirty and ashamed.

She reached the street and held on to a fence for support. It was an effort to focus on anything so she took a few deep breaths of the cold air and her head cleared a little. That was better. Now, where was she?

Of course, there were the shops she'd been making

for – at the top of Miss Gardner's road. She'd be safe there.

Ten minutes later she was knocking at the door.

'Rose, what a lovely surpr—' A look of horror crossed Grace's face. 'Oh, my dear.'

It was only when she was inside, and felt the warmth and safety of the house, that Rose began to shake. She looked down at the floor and, in a detached way, noticed the blood on her legs and shoes.

'Come with me.' Grace gently led her upstairs and sat her on a stool while she filled the bath with water.

When Grace tried to remove her coat Rose shook her head, stood up and stepped away. 'I understand, Rose,' she told her. 'I'll leave you to see to yourself. Just call me if you need anything.' Then she turned and left, closing the door behind her.

Rose eased herself into the warm water, laid her head back and gave a ragged sigh of relief as her mind shut down. She was vaguely aware that Grace came in, picked up her clothes, and left again.

The water was lovely, she didn't ever want to get out . . .

'Rose?' There was a quick knock on the door and Grace came in again. 'You must get out now, the water will be cold.' She held a large towel.

Obediently Rose stepped out and wrapped the towel around her. It didn't seem as if she'd been in the bath more than a few seconds.

'Edward's here. Will you let him have a look at you?'

She shrugged. She felt detached from reality, but a glimmer of common sense made itself heard. She needed the help of a doctor.

'Come in, Edward,' Grace called, and when he appeared, she said anxiously, 'She hasn't spoken since she arrived.'

'Will you let me have a look at you?' Dr Trenchard brushed the wet hair away from Rose's face, and when she didn't protest, he gently removed the towel.

Rose turned her head and began to study the bathroom. Not only did it have a bath, but a toilet and washbasin as well. Such luxury! The wallpaper was pretty, with little flowers scattered over it. She began to count them, one, two, three . . .

'Where did this happen?' Dr Trenchard asked, as he wrapped her in the towel again.

'Hmm?'

He repeated the question.

'In the park.'

'I'll call the police.' He looked furious.

That catapulted Rose out of her stupor. 'No!' Her voice rang out with force. 'I came to you because I didn't know what else to do, but I won't have anyone else knowing my shame.'

'*Your* shame?' The doctor made her sit on the stool, then he squatted in front of her and took her limp hands in his. 'You haven't done anything to be ashamed of, Rose. This wasn't your fault.'

She wanted to believe him, she really did, but she couldn't. 'I *feel* ashamed.'

'The man who assaulted you should feel shame, not you.'

When she didn't speak, he continued, 'Can you describe him?'

'A soldier.'

'You saw him clearly?'

'No, I felt his uniform.' Rose remembered the rough material under her hands as she'd tried to get away from him.

'Didn't anyone come to help you? There must have been other people about?'

'There were lots, but no one heard me because of the carol singers.'

He squeezed her hands. 'You must let me tell the police. This man is vicious.'

'No!' Rose was adamant.

'She's right, Edward,' Grace interrupted. 'She can't identify him. All she knows is that he was a soldier, and there are hundreds of them around. If you call in the police it will only cause Rose more pain.'

Dr Trenchard sighed wearily. 'You're right, but I don't like to think of him getting away with such a violent attack.'

Rose remembered something the soldier had said, then shook her head. 'I don't think he will get away with anything because he said he was being sent back to the trenches and was going to have some fun before he died.'

Edward Trenchard looked ready to explode. 'Fun! If I could get my hands on him he'd never be able to do this again. I'd see to that!'

'Calm down, Edward,' Grace urged. 'Getting angry will not help Rose.'

He shook his head, then turned back to the girl. 'You know that what's happened to you could have serious consequences?' he asked gently.

She looked at him blankly.

'When is your monthly cycle due?'

'In a few days, I think.'

'At least that might eliminate the danger of pregnancy.' He stood up. 'Grace, will you give her some towels to use?'

'Of course.'

'Now, Rose, I want you to come and see me in two days' time, but if the bleeding doesn't stop within the next few hours, I want you to contact me at once. Is that clear?' he added sternly.

She nodded, deciding that she would never speak of this again, or let a man touch her like that *ever*.

'I've cleaned your clothes as best I could, and mended them.' Grace put them on the edge of the bath. 'I've also given you some of my underclothes.' Then she left the room with the doctor.

Rose retched as she put on her clothes. Then she put on the coat and pulled it tightly around her. The money in the pocket jingled and she was surprised it was still there – but, of course, he hadn't wanted money.

The full horror of what he *had* wanted rushed into her mind, and she retched again. If he hadn't caught hold of her hair she would have escaped. Her hands probed her tender scalp and, with a moan, she started to search the room. In a small cupboard she found a pair of scissors and hacked away at her hair, arranging the black tresses in a neat pile. Then she left the bathroom.

Grace and Dr Trenchard were in deep conversation when she came downstairs. They stopped talking when she appeared, and although they must have noticed her mutilated hair, they said nothing.

'Thank you very much for your help,' she said politely,

her voice devoid of expression. 'I'm sorry to have caused you this trouble, but I didn't know what else to do.'

'You did the right thing, Rose.' Grace reached out and took her hand. 'We're relieved you came to us.'

She pulled away and turned towards the door.

'Where are you going?' the doctor asked.

'I came to buy presents for the family, and if I don't hurry the shops will be closed.'

'Leave it for another day,' he said firmly. 'I'll take you home now.'

The only emotion Rose felt was anger, and now it erupted. 'I don't need you to fuss over me! I'm not a child. I'm quite capable of doing a bit of shopping.'

Edward Trenchard sighed. 'You have just been subjected to a vicious attack.'

Rose looked at him, remembering all he'd done for Annie, and felt ashamed of her outburst. 'You're right,' she said quietly, 'it is going to be hard, but you must let me do it in my own way and in my own time. I'm grateful for your kindness, but you can't help me come to terms with this horror. It isn't only my body that has been violated, something deep inside me has been badly injured . . .' She paused. 'But I'm buggered if I'm going to let it crush me!'

'If anyone can make a complete recovery, it's you.' Grace gave her an encouraging smile. 'You're not a weakling, physically or mentally, and we have great faith in you.'

Rose was glad someone had, because at that moment she felt as if her life was ruined and all her dreams for the future counted for nothing.

'Let me come shopping with you,' Grace said, 'I need

a few things myself, and then I'll see you safely on to the bus.'

Rose considered this for a moment, then nodded, and heard the doctor sigh in relief.

Later that night, Rose sat in the scullery surrounded by her beloved books, but this time they did not give her the comfort she needed. When she'd arrived home she'd told her mother that she had fallen over and hit her head on a lamp-post, and Dr Trenchard had cut her hair so he could examine her head properly. Much to her relief, this explanation had been accepted without question, and her mother had made a neater job of her hair, levelling off the ragged edges. Grace had done well with mending and cleaning her clothes, so apart from some cuts and bruises on her face and legs, nothing else was visible. The tearing hurt inside her was evident only to Rose.

She opened the Bible and read some favourite passages, but at this moment, it was almost impossible to believe in God. Then she found a passage that said, 'God is of purer eyes than to behold evil.' She concentrated hard, trying to get some sense into her befuddled brain. What had happened to her was evil, of that there was no doubt, and the passage seemed to imply that evil did not come from God and, therefore, must come only from mankind. That was an interesting idea, but it didn't ease her distress.

She got up and made herself a cup of tea, wincing at the pain and stiffness in her body, then sat down again. Thank goodness the bleeding had almost stopped. It had worried her.

She closed her books and stood up. She must try to get some rest.

★

Rose watched the children opening their presents and smiled at the cries of pleasure. With Grace's help she had done well with the shopping. David, the youngest, had a stuffed bear, Annie a pretty doll in a pink frock, Charlie and Bert had identical trains, Will was looking at a picture book, Nancy had a sewing kit, Bob a model of one of the latest cars, Flo a warm pair of gloves, and she'd found a pretty scarf for her mother.

Annie came running over, all excited. 'Thank you for my dolly, Rosie. She's got a pink dress, just like the one I had for the wedding. Where's your present?'

Rose laughed. 'I didn't buy myself anything, Toots.'

The little girl frowned, laid her doll carefully in Rose's lap, and ran up the stairs. She was soon back and held out a drawing. 'I made this at Sunday School. I was going to put it on the wall by my bed, but you must have it. It isn't right you've got nothing,' she told her, very seriously.

'Thank you.' Rose took the picture and looked at it carefully. It was a rather good attempt at a Christmas scene of shepherds on a hill with the sheep. 'That's lovely, Annie,' she said. 'It'll be the first thing I see when I wake up in the mornings.'

Annie glowed with pride, picked up her doll and hurried off to show it to her friends.

When the children had all disappeared, Rose and her mother sat and had a quiet cup of tea.

'You're looking better,' her mother remarked. 'You were quite shaken up by that fall you had.'

'I'm fine, now,' was all she said, then changed the subject. 'Have you any idea where the old man is?'

'I think he's in France, but I don't know for sure. I thought he might get leave for Christmas – there seem to be plenty of soldiers who have. I wish he'd get someone else to write a letter for him.'

Rose flinched inwardly at the mention of soldiers.

'Hey, guess what?' Bob erupted into the scullery. 'That Amy from number nineteen has just joined the army!'

'Don't be daft,' Rose reprimanded. 'Girls can't do that.'

'Yes, they can. Jim, her brother, told me. She joined up this week.'

'Bob's right,' her mother interrupted. 'They've formed the Women's Army Auxiliary Corps – WAAC, for short. They started taking recruits this month.'

Rose was immediately interested. 'How do you know, Mum?'

'The posters are everywhere – haven't you seen them? They're plastered all over the Labour Exchange. You have a look after Christmas.'

Rose nodded thoughtfully.

Rose stood in front of the poster, chewing her lip. She'd been looking at it for the last two months, ever since she'd heard about it at Christmas. Should she chance it? She was sick and tired of the factory job, and the desire to do something different was overwhelming. Her body had healed after the attack, but her mind was a different matter: some days and nights were dark when despair flooded her. With a shudder of revulsion, she made up her mind. Since John had gone she'd felt as if she'd been drifting helplessly, which made it difficult to study. Even worse, ever since the attack, she'd felt as if she had a banner hanging over her with the words 'I've been raped' written on it in large red letters. If she didn't do something to pull herself together she would never finish the work

John had left for her. She would be letting him down, and herself, and she could not allow that to happen.

Bad as this experience was, she would get over it in time. Just as the anger and disappointment of being told to leave school at eleven had faded, so would the horror of the rape. This, too, will pass, she thought. It could only ruin her life if she let it. It was up to her.

She pushed aside the lethargy that had weighed her down lately and turned her attention back to the poster. There was no need to read it again, she knew it by heart, but she looked at it anyway.

'Women Urgently Wanted for the WAAC – Women's Army Auxiliary Corps. Work at home and abroad with the forces. Good Wages, Quarters, Uniform, Rations.'

'You thinking of joining?'

Rose looked at the young girl standing next to her. 'Yes. Are you?'

'I'm in service and anything must be better than that.' She looked up at Rose and smiled. 'What about you?'

'I'm in a factory.'

'Ugh, not much better, then?' She held out her hand. 'I'm Hilda.'

'Rose.'

'Let's go in together,' Hilda said excitedly, taking her arm. 'You're very pretty, Rose, you'd look lovely in the uniform.'

That remark gave her confidence: Hilda hadn't questioned her age, so she might get away with it.

An hour later Rose was hurrying back to the factory, feeling more alive than she had since the attack. She and Hilda had been accepted and, much to her relief, there hadn't been any problem with her age. She had stood tall and lied convincingly, and they'd accepted her explanation that she didn't have a birth certificate. The question of a reference was trickier and she'd assured them that she would get one. She would have to write it herself, of course. And if the thought of deceiving them like that worried her, Rose wasn't going to let it stop her. This was her chance to do something different, and she was determined to make the most of it.

Rose broke into a trot. She'd been sent out on an errand for the boss and had taken much longer than she should have done. He wasn't going to be happy when she told him she was leaving. And that posed another problem. She couldn't tell him she had joined the WAAC, because he knew she was too young. She sped through the door and along to his office. Time to lie again.

Luckily he was on his own and she took a deep breath. 'I'm leaving, Mr Baker.'

He didn't look surprised, but he didn't look pleased, either. 'Where are you going?'

'Nowhere, sir, I'm needed at home.' Her gaze was direct. She mustn't appear ill at ease because that might raise his suspicions.

He threw down his pencil and stood up. 'Can't your mother get someone else to help? I don't want to lose you, Rose, especially when we're so busy.'

'It can't be helped. She's having a job to cope with nine children and go out to work.'

'She could give up *her* job,' he suggested hopefully.

'Wouldn't make sense for her to do that because she earns more than me.'

'Hmm, I could give you a rise, I suppose.'

This was getting difficult. Rose didn't want him looking into things too far: he'd soon find out she was telling a pack of lies. 'I must leave, sir, it's all arranged.'

'Very well,' he said, scowling. 'You may go at the end of the week.'

'Thank you.' She turned to make a hasty exit, wondering why lying made her uncomfortable when others thought nothing of it. It must be her conscience, she decided. At times it could be a blasted nuisance.

Later that night, Rose sat in the scullery, elbows on the table, chin propped in her hands. Her mother couldn't understand why she was joining the WAAC. Perhaps I should have told her about the rape, Rose thought fleetingly, but it was too late now. Anyway, she was still ashamed that it had happened to her, and believed that somehow it had been her fault.

'Rose? Can't you sleep again?' Annie trotted into the scullery, a look of concern on her face.

'I'm not tired, Toots,' she replied, with a smile. 'What are you doing up?'

'Can't sleep either. It's cold up there.'

'Come and sit over here.' Rose put a chair in front of the black-leaded range. 'Are you feeling all right?' Although the little girl had improved, she was still delicate and Rose couldn't help worrying about her.

Annie gazed at her big sister, her eyes sad. 'Are you going away, Rosie?'

She nodded. 'How did you know?'

'I heard you talking to Mum, and she was sad.'

'I'm joining the WAAC, but you mustn't tell anyone.'

Annie's bottom lip trembled. 'You will come back, won't you?'

Rose reached out and pulled the child towards her. 'You mustn't be upset. I'll have leave sometimes, and I'll come straight home, I promise.'

'Is that tea I can smell?' Their mother came into the room.

'Can't you sleep, either?' Rose asked.

'No. I've been thinking over what you told me earlier, and I've got over the shock now. It'll give you a chance to see a bit more of life. We'll miss you, but you have my blessing, and we won't tell a soul where you've gone. The WAAC won't find out you're under age from us.'

12

September 1917

The last seven months had been heaven. Rose walked along the country lane with a smile of contentment on her face as she took in the beautiful scenery and breathed the fresh air. How clean and vibrant everything was on this lovely warm September day, and how far away Bermondsey and its squalor seemed. She wouldn't care if she never saw the place again. A shudder rippled through her as she remembered the small, overcrowded house. The bedrooms were the worst and, no matter how careful she and her mother were, the bugs soon returned. It made her feel sick to see them crawling up the walls, and the whole street was alive with rats and mice.

She stopped and gazed at a large oak tree. It was just beginning to show the golden shades of autumn as a gentle breeze rustled its leaves. Life had changed for her beyond her wildest dreams. From the moment she'd arrived at the camp, she had loved the life, and when she'd first seen the sparkling polished floors and pristine sheets, she had felt as if she'd stepped into another world. And as for the food, well, she'd never had so much in her life.

Rose spotted a blackberry bush and leaned across the hedge to pick a couple of berries. She popped them into her mouth and sighed with pleasure as the sharp juice trickled over her tongue. How Annie would love to taste these.

The thought of the little girl still living in those squalid conditions made her feel guilty, but she sent most of her pay home to help her mother and knew that things were a bit easier for them now. With so many mouths to feed, though, money was still in short supply.

She sampled a few more berries, then resumed her walk. She did this at every spare moment, no matter what the weather, because she loved the green, open spaces. There were parks in London, of course, but they were nothing like the fields of corn and rolling hills of the Sussex countryside.

Hilda, the girl she'd met in the recruitment office, had come down here with her, and she'd found herself a boyfriend. But Rose didn't want that: she was happy to wander around on her own, and she had brought her books with her so she could keep up with her studies.

Hilda had been put into the stores to work, but Rose had been learning to type and yesterday she had passed all of the tests. That meant she would get twenty-three shillings a week. The WAAC were teaching her skills that would be useful in the future. She sighed and lifted her face to the sun. For the first time in her life, she was content. She would stay here until the war ended, then decide what to do with her life. This was a time to enjoy.

'Hello, Rose.' Two soldiers fell into step beside her.

She smiled at them. Jim and Fred were harmless enough, and over the last few months she'd realized that not all men in uniform were rapists. In fact, the vast majority were gentlemen and took 'No' with good grace.

'Coming to the dance tonight?' Jim asked.

'I might.'

'Oh, you must,' Fred pleaded. 'We're going back to France in two days' time.'

Suddenly Jim dashed into a field, picked a handful of flowers and hurried back. Then he sank on to one knee in front of her. 'Rosie, will you marry me?'

'Get up, you fool,' she told him, laughing at his antics. 'You want to be careful who you say that to because some girl might accept you, and where would you be then?'

'In France.' He grinned, got to his feet and tucked a flower into her buttonhole. 'But if you won't marry me, at least come to the dance.'

'All right, but you two must promise to behave your-selves.' Jim and Fred had been joking, but Rose hadn't missed the anxiety in their eyes. Returning to France was not something to look forward to.

'We always do,' they protested together, scandalized. Then they broke into broad grins and chuckled.

'We behave ourselves with you,' Jim told her, 'because you're strong enough to flatten us if we didn't.'

Rose said nothing, but was pleased by that remark. During the last few months, she had filled out, due to the regular food and exercise, and although she was always surrounded by eager men, not one took liberties with her.

She waved them goodbye, promised to be at the dance and went towards her quarters.

'Rose!' Hilda was running towards her, and skidded to a sudden halt. 'Have you heard?'

'What?'

'We're being sent to France next week.' The girl hopped from foot to foot. 'Isn't it exciting?'

'France? You sure?' Rose couldn't believe she was hearing this.

'Positive! There have been recruits arriving from other parts of the country all day.'

Rose wanted to shout for joy. This was what she had been praying for. The WAAC had started sending women overseas a few months ago, and she desperately wanted to go.

'We've got three days' leave, starting from tomorrow, then we come back and sail for France almost immediately. We've really got something to celebrate at the dance tonight, Rose.' Hilda grinned.

'Webster!'

Rose watched the officer striding towards her.

'You're wanted in the office, immediately.'

It was an order, and she had learned early on that it was wise to respond smartly, so she saluted and sped off. It was probably something to do with the posting to France, she thought, and was eager to hear more.

One look at the Commander's face told Rose it was serious. She stood to attention and waited, her heart hammering, wondering what she had done.

'It has come to my attention that you have only just turned fifteen.'

As Rose heard that, her hopes and dreams crumbled into dust at her feet.

'Is this true?'

What was the point of lying? 'Yes, ma'am.'

'Why do you girls think you can get away with it?

We're bound to find out in the end, you know.' The officer shook her head in disgust.

Yes, Rose thought, seething with fury, but how did they find out?

'You are dismissed with immediate effect. Hand in your uniform. You will be given your train fare home.'

Once again she was standing in front of someone, being dismissed. The pain was as intense as it had been the first time.

'You may go, Webster.'

Rose turned smartly and left. With a growl of fury, she erupted out of the main doors.

'What was that all about?' Hilda wanted to know, looking anxiously at her.

'I've been dismissed.' Rose spoke through clenched teeth, trying to control her rage. 'I'm under age and someone's told them.'

'I had no idea,' Hilda gasped. 'You look more than twenty.'

'Well, I'm not. I'm only fifteen. And when I find out who did this, I'll tear them apart with my bare hands.' She had to leave all this behind, and her chance to go to another country had gone. That thought nearly brought tears to her eyes. Bermondsey had been bad enough before this, but now she knew that there was something different – something better – it would be unbearable.

'Who do you think told on you?'

'I don't know.' Then Rose looked up and saw her. Amy, from Garrett Street, with a satisfied smirk on her face. Rose went cold with loathing.

Amy came over to her, flanked by two of her friends. 'Not so high-and-mighty now, are you?' she sneered.

Rose gave the three a contemptuous glance. 'I might have guessed it was you,' she said to Amy. 'Are you too afraid to face me on your own?'

'I'm not daft, Rose Webster. Your family's got a violent streak running through it. I've seen you after your old man's had a go at you, and I'm sure you're all the same.'

'Really?' Rose's fingers itched to wrap themselves around the girl's neck, so she clamped them to her hips, and stood with her feet apart.

'I know you want to hit me,' Amy taunted, 'so why don't you try it? We'd love to give you a beating.'

Rose stared at each girl in turn. 'It'll be a pleasure! I can take on the three of you and win.' She was considerably taller than them and had the satisfaction of seeing Amy's friends take a step back. Then she moved forward.

'Rose, don't!' Hilda placed a hand on her arm. 'It's not worth it.'

'Oh, I don't know. If they're caught in a fight, I might be able to get them dismissed as well.'

All three girls went a sickly colour. 'You'd like that, wouldn't you?' Amy said. 'You're a bully, Rose Webster!'

'Of course I am. Look where I came from.' Then she dropped her aggressive stance. The trio of cowards had lost the urge to fight, and the battle was won.

She turned and strode away.

Rose looked out of the train window with unseeing eyes. Just a few short hours ago she had been so happy and now she was devastated.

The rhythmic clatter of the train began to have a soothing effect upon her, and the bitter anger inside her eased. The last few months had been wonderful, but she had lied to get what she wanted, and that never paid. This disappointment was of her own making: she was bound to have been found out sooner or later. Oh, how she wished it had been later! The train pulled into the station, she picked up her bag, opened the door and stepped on to the platform. The noise, smoke and grime of Bermondsey hit her and it was only with extreme determination that she held back the tears.

The sight that met Rose when she walked into the scullery at home made her heart miss a beat. Her mother was sitting at the table, her face grim, and all the children were clustered around her. 'Mum, what's the matter?'

'Oh, Rosie, thank God you're home.' Marj pushed a telegram towards her.

'Missing presumed dead,' the telegram said. Rose thought she should feel something, but she couldn't pretend she had any affection for the old man. What a selfish, hard-hearted bitch she was turning into! However, her mother was upset, and she cared about her, so she sat down and gave a faint smile. 'It only says missing – that doesn't mean he's dead.'

'Well, why would they frighten us by sending a telegram like that?' her mother asked. 'What do they mean by missing?'

'That they can't find him.'

Marj mulled this over for a few moments. 'Do you mean he might have buggered off?'

'It's possible, but he might just have got separated from his company.'

'I never thought of that. But if he's done a runner and they catch him, they'll shoot him.'

'I doubt he's done that, Mum, he wouldn't risk a firing

squad. Don't believe anything until you get a notice from the army. He'll quite likely turn up like the bad penny – as usual.'

'You're right.' Her mother looked at the children. 'We won't believe he's been killed until we hear something definite. It's no good trying to cross our bridges before we get to them.'

They all nodded and drifted away to whatever they'd been doing before the telegram had arrived.

'Rosie.' Annie sat on the chair next to her and put her arms as far round her sister as they would go. 'I didn't know you were coming home today.'

'Neither did I, Toots. They've thrown me out of the WAAC.'

Her mother looked appalled. 'Why did they do that?'

'Bit of bad luck, Mum. That Amy turned up and told them I was only fifteen.'

The stream of bad language that came from her mother's lips made Rose clap her hands over Annie's ears. Then she started to laugh. 'That's just what I thought, but I didn't say it.'

'Well, I hope you gave her a good hiding.'

Rose took her hands away from the little girl's ears. 'No, but I felt like it.'

'What stopped you?' her mother asked.

'I suppose I knew I was in the wrong because I *had* lied about my age.'

For the first time since it had happened, Rose could see the funny side of it. 'She brought two friends with her.'

'I'm sorry this has happened,' her mother told her. 'You were so happy.'

'I know, but I've had a smashing time over the last few months, and I'll always be grateful for that.'

'What a sad day.' Marj poured them a cup of tea. 'The old man reported missing, and you dismissed.'

Rose sipped her tea and said nothing.

'What you going to do now?' Annie asked. 'Are you going back to the factory?'

'I don't think so. I lied to Mr Baker when I left.' She sat the child on her lap. 'So you see, Annie, it never pays to tell fibs because they come back to haunt you.'

'Like ghosts?' Annie giggled.

'Nasty ones!' Rose pulled a fierce face and tickled her sister, who jumped off her lap, squealing.

'What are you going to do?' her mother asked, changing the subject.

'I don't know. It's all come as a shock and I haven't had time to think about it.' Sadness swept through Rose. 'We were going to France,' she said quietly.

Her mother patted her hand. 'Never mind, when this war's over you'll be able to go over there yourself. Things will be different, you'll see.'

Rose's gaze swept around the scullery and she shuddered. She certainly hoped her mother was right, because nothing much had changed here while she'd been away. The oilcloth on the floor had even more holes in it, there was still the nauseating smell of too many people crowded into a small space, and an added feature was a piece of brown paper stuck over a broken window. Rose was dreading what she might find upstairs.

'Rosie?' Annie sat on the bed and pulled her hand.

'What?'

'Will you take me to see Auntie Grace? I haven't seen her since you went away, and I've got a lot to tell her.'

'Isn't she still at your school, then?' Rose asked in surprise.

'No. She's been moved to the big school. They haven't got enough teachers,' Annie said. 'But the new teacher is nice.'

'Good.' Four years ago the secondary school would never have considered taking on Grace.

'Rosie?' Annie tugged her arm. 'When can we go?'

'This afternoon.' And for that she received a tight hug and a wet kiss.

'Uncle John!' Annie squealed, and threw herself at the sailor.

'Rose,' Grace kissed her cheek, 'are you on leave?'

'No, they dismissed me when they found out I was only fifteen.' She tried to sound amused.

'How did that happen?' Grace took Rose's coat and hung it over the banister.

'They were shipping in a lot of new people because we were going to France, but one of them knew me and told them.' Rose shrugged. 'It was my own fault. I took a chance joining up and got caught.'

'Did you enjoy yourself?' John asked.

'I had a lovely time. It was a glimpse of another world. Everything was spotless, the food was regular and it was a treat to wear decent clothes.'

'And how did you get on with the discipline?' he asked perceptively.

'Ah, now, that was hard,' Rose admitted. 'I don't like

129

people bossing me around, but I thought it was worth putting up with it.'

He smiled in amusement. 'I can't imagine you taking orders meekly.'

'It wasn't easy.' She looked at him thoughtfully: the uniform suited him. 'When did you get home?'

'This morning.'

'Oh, we wouldn't have come if we'd known. You'll want to have a quiet time with Grace.' She took Annie's hand. 'Come on, Toots, we'll come back another time.'

'No, don't go.' John sat Annie at the table. 'Join us for tea, and you can tell me how you're getting on with your studying.'

'You sure?'

'We're both pleased to see you.' John handed round the bread and butter. 'What are you going to do now?'

'I'll have to get a job, but I don't want to go back into a factory. I learned to type in the WAAC.'

'Did you? That might be useful.' John drank his tea and gazed into space, then he smiled. 'Grace, would you look after Annie for an hour or so?'

'What are we doing here?' Rose asked in awe, as they walked along a corridor of Grove School in Southwark.

'I want to see someone.' John stopped outside a room and grasped the doorknob.

'But it's Sunday. No one will be here.'

'He'll be here,' John answered confidently, as he knocked on the door and opened it.

It was the most untidy place Rose had ever seen, and that was saying something. Papers and files were piled on the desk, stacked on the floor and spilling off every chair in the room, and in the middle of the chaos was an elderly man. He looked up distractedly when they came in, then hauled himself to his feet. His untidy hair was grey and thinning at the front. He had removed his jacket and rolled up the sleeves of a creased white shirt. Rose smiled inside. This was the man who'd given Grace away, but that day he'd been tidy and wearing a suit. Then he smiled and his face lit up, the clear grey eyes sparkling.

'John! How good to see you.'

'Hello, Harold.' John eyed the room with amusement. 'How did you end up in a place like this?'

'Damned war. Just because I'm too old to join up they expect me to run this place single-handed *and* teach a class.' He dropped a pile of papers into the wastepaper basket. 'I wanted to retire, you know, but they wouldn't let me. I should have stayed at the University of London, but I thought this might be easier for the duration of the war.'

'That was naïve of you, Harold,' John observed.

'I know that now, but it's a good school, John. There are two hundred boys and a few are bright enough to go on to university.' Harold waved a hand impatiently at the piles of paperwork. 'But I can't keep up with it all.'

'Why don't you get some help?'

'Do you think I haven't bloody well tried –' He stopped suddenly and looked at Rose. 'I beg your pardon, miss.'

She grinned. 'I've heard a lot worse.'

'This is Rose,' John introduced. 'You saw her at our wedding. Rose, this is Professor Harold Steadman.'

'Pleased to meet you again, Professor.'

Harold Steadman studied her briefly, then turned to John. 'You've brought her here for a reason?'

'She needs a job and doesn't want to go back into a factory.'

Rose started. Was John trying to get her a job? Excitement rushed through her. She cleared two chairs of papers so that they could all sit down. This might take some time, and she wasn't going to budge until it was settled.

John told Harold the whole story then sat back, waiting for his response.

The silence was long and unnerving for Rose, and she couldn't hold her tongue any longer. If there was a chance of working here, she wanted it. 'I can type as well,' she said.

'You'll have to work any hours I say and I'll pay you one pound ten shillings a week.' He gave her another searching look. 'You can start tomorrow.'

'Thank you, sir. What will I have to do?' Rose always liked to know what was expected of her.

'Type letters, lecture notes, run around after me, and get this office into some kind of order.' He screwed up another piece of paper and tossed it into the basket, which was now overflowing. 'Do you think you can do that?'

'Yes, sir.'

John got to his feet. 'Good. Now can I show Rose the library?'

'Of course.' The Professor was already at work again.

As soon as they'd closed the door, she let out a squeal of delight. 'I can't believe he's given me a job! Oh, thank you, John, I'm so excited.' Tears of joy filled her eyes. 'I'm glad they threw me out of the WAAC now.'

He laughed. 'Don't get too excited. That cussed old

132

man will work you like a slave, but it'll be worth it because' – he opened another door – 'you'll have access to all of this.'

Rose rushed into the middle of the room and turned slowly. She had never seen so many books before. 'Will I be able to come in here?'

'Yes, when the pupils aren't using it.'

'Oh, it's like paradise.'

'Darling, I'm so happy for Rose, but I'm also a little worried.'

'Why?' John took Grace into his arms and settled back on the pillow with a sigh of contentment.

'Isn't the man you think might have something to do with Rose connected to the school?'

'Yes, he's on the Board of Education, but it's unlikely she'll come across him. I don't think he ever goes there.' He started to chuckle. 'He's in for a shock if he does see her – she's grown even more like him over the last few months. From the way Harold was looking at her today, I think he noticed it, too, but he didn't say anything.'

Grace snuggled down. 'I hope she'll be all right. If he does see her and she turns out to be related to him, he could make things difficult for her. He's not a very nice man.'

'We needn't worry about Rose. She can look after herself.'

13

March 1918

Rose had been in her new job six months, and although John had been right about the professor working her hard, she didn't mind. It had taken her a couple of months to wade through all his papers and get them into some kind of order, but he needed watching constantly. He was the most disorganized man she had ever come across. As soon as he went to take a class, she set to and filed everything he had left lying about. He could never find anything and was always calling, 'Rose!' It was hard work but how could she feel anything but joy when she had access to all those books?

She bent down to put the heavy volume back on to the lower shelf, and nearly dropped it when a voice behind her said, 'What have you been reading?'

'Plato.'

'How did you get on with him?' Harold Steadman asked.

'Hard going,' she admitted.

A slight smile tugged at the corners of his mouth. 'Why don't you try something easier?'

'What's the point of that? I won't learn anything that way.'

'I've been watching you carefully over the last six months, Rose, and John is right, you have a fine mind.

However, I believe your reading is too eclectic, you need to make a choice now and study a specific subject.'

She chewed her lip thoughtfully. 'Such as?'

'What are you most interested in?' Harold Steadman leaned against the bookcase and folded his arms.

'I've been considering politics – you know, social reform and things like that.'

He shook his head. 'I can't see you as a politician, you're far too quick-tempered. You'd be rolling up your sleeves and fighting with them.'

Rose burst out laughing. 'I'm not that bad.'

'Perhaps not,' he grinned, 'but you're a determined young woman with firm opinions.'

'Is that a bad thing?' she asked.

'Not at all, but you need to channel your thoughts and decide what you're going to do with your life.'

'I miss John,' she told him, running her hand lovingly over a row of books. 'I've read everything he told me to and now I'm not sure what to do.'

Harold reached out and patted her shoulder. 'Would you let me help you until he comes home?'

Rose nodded eagerly. She'd been tempted to ask his advice on quite a few occasions, but he was always so busy.

'All right. You know I specialize in law, so what do you think about making that your goal in life? It would give you a sound platform to help bring about some of those reforms you were talking about.'

'Law!' she exclaimed in surprise. 'I never thought about that. Could a woman go into that profession?'

'I believe so. Things are opening up. However, if you decide to take this on, you must be aware that you will have to fight hard to be recognized as worthy of it.'

'I don't mind that.' She straightened up. 'I like a good fight.'

He tipped his head back and roared with laughter. 'The first time you get into court, I want to be there.'

'Are you sure I can do this, sir?' She looked at him doubtfully.

He nodded, then took two books from the shelves. 'I want you to start with these. They'll give you an idea of the different branches of the law and help you choose one you would like to study. I will then give you the same lessons the boys here receive.'

Rose looked at the books in her hand and trembled with anticipation. She must write to John and tell him.

The next few weeks passed in a blur for Rose, and it didn't take her long to make her choice. She would become a solicitor. In that job she would be well placed to help ordinary people. Now when she wasn't working, she was studying hard, absorbed in her subject. The more she learned about the law, the more she saw that it would be the right thing for her to do. She remembered the stone thrown into water sending out ripples. Perhaps now she might be able to make a few ripples of her own.

She was hurrying back from the library after finishing her work for the day, when she turned a corner and ran full pelt into someone. Rose gasped as the breath was knocked out of her. 'I'm so sorry.'

'Well, what have we here?'

His accent was posh, and she looked up. The young man standing in front of her was about twenty, she reckoned, and she took an instant dislike to him. He was tall, reasonably good-looking, but his light brown eyes held a sly look. He was not someone to be trusted.

As she tried to walk past him he caught hold of her arm. His grip was painful. 'Let go of me!'

'Oh, she has a temper.' He smirked. 'I like a bit of fire in a woman.' Then he dragged her into a room, kicked the door shut and leaned against it, holding her in an intimate embrace.

Visions of the last time she had been attacked like this came vividly to mind, and her knee came up hard. He let out a yelp of pain and released her. With a mighty push she shoved him away from the door and ran into the corridor.

'You bitch!'

She ignored him and began to walk away. A hand touched her shoulder and she spun round, eyes flashing.

'Are you all right?' Harold asked.

'You should be asking *me* that.' The young man came out of the room, his face contorted with pain. 'She nearly crippled me.'

'Up to your old tricks again, Andrew?' Harold Steadman snapped.

'She threw herself at me.' The boy ran an insolent gaze over Rose. 'A man would have to be half dead to resist such a beauty.'

Rose couldn't ignore that. She thrust her books at the professor and started to roll up her sleeves. 'I can soon see to that.' She stepped forward. When he backed away she sneered, 'Coward!'

'Who is she?' Andrew asked, putting the professor between them for safety.

'Rose Webster. She works for me.'

'Well you can sack her for attacking me.'

'I was defending myself!' Rose exploded. Who did he think he was, giving orders like that? 'Women need protecting from lechers like you.'

'I was only having a bit of fun,' he complained.

'Really? Well, I wasn't enjoying it,' she said scornfully.

'You're not supposed to,' he said smartly. 'Women are supposed to submit to a man's will.'

That did it! She stepped forward menacingly.

'Stop her, Steadman,' the boy yelled in fear. 'She's mad and violent.'

'Then I suggest you get out of here, Andrew, while you still can,' Harold told him softly, 'because I would love to see her give you the thrashing you deserve.'

Andrew went red with fury. 'You forget who you're talking to. You'll both be sacked when I tell my father about this.' He turned on his heel and hurried away.

Harold Steadman watched him silently, a frown puckering his brow, then he turned and stared at Rose, tipping his head to one side as he examined her intently.

She shuffled uncomfortably. 'Will you lose your job?' She was appalled at the idea.

'No. The boy is all bluster.'

Rose faced him, hands on her hips. 'Tell me the truth. Can he have you dismissed?'

'He might try, but his father would not be able to replace me at the moment. I am only here because they couldn't find anyone else, and I would never have taken the job if they hadn't been desperate.'

'He would be able to dismiss you when the men come back.'

'Rose,' he laughed, 'I retire next year, anyway.'

Rose sighed with relief. She would have hated to cause him trouble. 'I'm sorry to have lost my temper, but I wasn't going to let him get away with treating me like that.'

'You were quite right to defend yourself, and it's about time someone put that young man in his place.'

'Who is he, anyway?' she asked, falling into step beside the professor.

'Sir George Gresham's son.'

'Is he the Gresham the library's named after?'

'No, that was his father.' Harold Steadman stopped and looked at her intently. 'Do you know Sir George?'

'Me!' She grinned. 'What would a girl from Garrett Street be doing knowing the nobility?'

He stroked his chin thoughtfully. 'Keep out of his way, Rose.'

'Huh! If he's anything like his son, I don't want to know him.'

'Is there any news about the old man?' Rose asked her mother later that evening as they cleared up after giving the children their supper.

'I've asked, but all they say is he's missing.'

'I expect there are thousands like that,' Rose said sadly. 'It's going to take a lot of sorting out when the war ends.'

'I wonder how much longer it's going on? When it started everyone said it would be over in a few months, but it's almost four years now.'

Could it be that long? Rose had been so caught up in her studies that she hadn't taken much notice of the news.

'Are you still enjoying it at the school?' her mother asked, taking some cups out of the cupboard.

'Yes, it's wonderful . . .' she hesitated ' . . . except I nearly got the professor the sack today.'

'Why was that?' Her mother filled the teapot.

'Some boy tried to assault me and Professor Steadman stuck up for me.'

'I hope you gave the lad what for.' Her mother frowned. 'Who was he, one of the pupils?'

'No. He was the son of one of the school's benefactors – ' A cup crashed to the floor, interrupting her.

'What was his name?'

Rose was startled by the note of panic in her mother's voice. 'Andrew Gresham.'

'He didn't touch you, did he?' her mother demanded.

'No, Mum. Don't take on so.'

Her mother let out a ragged sigh, and sat down. 'You mustn't have anything to do with him.'

'I don't intend to – but why are you in such a state?'

Before her mother could answer, the door burst open and Bob tore into the scullery. He was twelve now and not quite as surly, but Rose still found him the least likeable of her brothers and sisters.

'Have you heard?' Bob hopped from foot to foot in excitement. 'Amy's been thrown out of the WAAC for stealing.'

'How do you know?' Rose asked.

'Her brother's just told me. He said she was in real trouble.'

'Stop jumping about, Bob, and tell me about it quick.' Rose grabbed a chair and made him sit in it.

'She was in France and she kept sneaking into the

men's camp. I always knew she were a tart,' he stated gleefully.

'Get on with the story, and keep your opinions to yourself,' Rose scolded.

He pouted. 'Well, she stayed at night with the men, and when they was asleep she picked their pockets. She was stealing food, too, and selling it.'

'Silly girl.' Marj looked at her silent daughter.

'I didn't think she'd be so daft.' Rose shook her head in disbelief. 'She had a good life in the WAAC. Why go and throw it all away?'

'There's no accounting for folks. They do foolish things sometimes,' her mother opined.

Bob jumped up and tore out again.

Her mother bent down and started to pick up the broken pieces of cup, and Rose helped her. 'You were going to tell me why I should stay away from Andrew Gresham,' she reminded her mother.

'Just stay away from him.'

'That won't do, Mum. You know I always have to know why. How do you know him?'

Marj Webster poured them both a cup of tea. She was silent for a moment, then looked up with troubled eyes. 'Andrew Gresham is your half-brother.'

Rose was about to take a sip of tea but the cup clattered back into the saucer. 'That means – that means – ' She couldn't get the words out.

'That means Sir George Gresham is your father.'

'Bloody hell, Mum,' she exclaimed. 'Are you sure?'

'Of course I'm sure!' her mother exclaimed. 'Do you think I had so many men that I wouldn't know who'd fathered you?'

'Oh, I didn't mean that,' she said hastily, 'but it's a bit of a shock.'

'I know that, and I think it's time I told you the whole story.'

They took a gulp of tea to calm their nerves, then Marj Webster began.

'I was in service for Sir George and his wife. I was only sixteen and as innocent as a newborn babe. Lady Gresham was a spiteful creature – '

'Her son must take after her, then,' Rose muttered.

'Don't interrupt, Rose,' her mother reproved her. 'It's going to be hard enough for me to tell this story.'

'I won't say another word.'

'As I was saying, it wasn't a happy household and we were all pleased when her ladyship went away for a few weeks to the country.' Marj fiddled with the empty cup. 'It was then the master took notice of me. He was tall and handsome, and I felt sorry for him. We could all hear the rows they had. Well, one night I had to take him up a drink and he kept me talking for quite a while. He was lonely, you see, and I didn't see no harm in it.'

So the crafty old devil had waited until his wife was out of the way, Rose thought.

'Then he kissed me, just on the cheek, but things got out of hand, and I didn't know what to do.' Marj took a deep breath. 'He was the master, you see, and I'd never been one to disobey.'

Rose clenched her fists.

'When I found out I was pregnant, I went to the master and told him, but he said it was useless to accuse him of being the father because he would deny it, and everyone would believe him, not some servant, out for what she could get.' Her mother poured herself another cup of tea with shaking hands.

'What happened then?' Rose asked gently.

'They turned me out. I had nowhere to go and I was afraid I'd end up in the workhouse. It was then I met the old man. He was working in a shop and I'd seen him a few times.' She looked at her daughter. 'He wasn't a bad man, then, the drink hadn't got to him. Well, he saw how distressed I was and I told him I was in trouble. He'd just rented this house and said he'd take me in. I was that relieved, Rose. We got on well enough and I married him before you was born.'

'Did you ever tell him who my father was?'

Marj shook her head vigorously. 'No fear. He'd have tried to make some gain out of it, and I didn't want anything to do with the Greshams again.'

'When did he start to drink?'

'Oh, he'd always liked a pint, but he started drinking seriously just after Flo was born. He was impossible after that.'

'You stayed with him, though, Mum.'

She shrugged helplessly. 'What else could I do? There was nowhere to go. If I'd walked out, I'd have lost my kids, and I do love you all.'

'I know,' Rose told her. 'You've always done your best for us.'

'I've tried.' Marj sat back and sighed wearily. 'I'm glad I've told you at last. It's a weight off my mind, but you can understand why I want you to stay away from the Greshams. If Sir George sees you, he'll recognize you because you're the image of him.'

'His son can't take after him, then, because we don't look like brother and sister.'

'No, he's like his mother.' She looked at her daughter pleadingly. 'If you do run across Sir George at the school, I'd like you to keep quiet about me.'

'You don't want me to admit to being his daughter?'

'You must make up your own mind. But I don't want that man stepping back into our lives. He treated me without a thought for what would happen to me, and I've never forgiven him for that.'

'I won't say anything.'

'Thanks, Rose. I wish I'd had as much sense as you have. Then I wouldn't have got into such trouble.'

'And I wouldn't have been born.'

The worry left her mother's face and she smiled. 'That's one thing I've never regretted – having you. Now I'm exhausted, so I think I'll go and have a nap.'

Rose watched her mother walk out of the scullery and ground her teeth. If she did come face to face with him, she'd break his neck!

14

Rose was busy typing lecture notes the next day when a man stormed into the professor's office.

'Steadman, what's all this I hear about my son being attacked, and you taking the other's part?'

Rose looked up from her typing. The man was well over six feet tall, his black hair was sprinkled with grey and his dark eyes were blazing. The arrogance of rank and privilege was evident in his stance. There was no mistaking who he was.

The professor was silent. He didn't stand up, but sat back and folded his arms.

Rose was getting used to Harold Steadman, and he was showing this man that he did not consider him worthy of respect.

'Send for this person,' Sir George raised his voice, 'and I'll have him expelled. I will have you removed too if you show me any more insolence, sir.'

'You cannot do that to either of us,' Harold informed him calmly. 'You cannot run the school without me, and the young woman isn't a pupil here.'

'Woman! What are you talking about? Are you telling me a female attacked my son?' Sir George looked incredulous.

'Your son was making unwelcome advances and she defended herself. If she hadn't been able to fend him off, I should have had to thrash him myself.'

'How dare you?' Sir George was incandescent with rage. 'And tell me what you mean by "unwelcome advances".'

Rose's mouth curled in disgust. Unwelcome advances?

'He was trying to rape her,' Harold Steadman told him plainly.

'Rubbish! Where is this female?' he bellowed.

Rose was on her feet. 'Here.'

Sir George spun round. 'Well? What have you to say for yourself.'

Rose stepped forward until she was standing within two feet of him. 'Your son dragged me into another room and tried to molest me. I made sure he couldn't,' she told him succinctly, and then turned back to her desk. When he grabbed hold of her arm, she gave him a contemptuous glance. 'Let go of me or I'll do the same to you.'

'Why you insolent . . .' He raised his hand, but she stared at him defiantly, looking into eyes identical to hers.

'You don't frighten me. I've been thrashed before.' She shook herself free of his grip. 'It's the sign of a weak man.'

He let her go, but couldn't tear his eyes off her face. Suddenly he was disconcerted. 'Who are you?'

'None of your business!'

'Don't be too sure!' he bellowed. 'You've got the likeness of a Gresham. What's your mother's name?'

'You wouldn't remember it. You took advantage of an innocent girl, then abandoned her.'

'Why are you so sure it was me? I had a younger brother.'

Rose had moved closer to him. The anger she felt for what her mother had suffered at his hands would not be denied. This was one confrontation that was long overdue and she was eager to let the man know what she thought of him. 'It was you, all right. My mother doesn't lie.'

'You forget who I am,' he growled, his face dark with fury.

'I know exactly who you are. You are an arrogant, selfish bastard.'

'*You* are the bastard here,' he snarled.

'And whose fault is that?' She raised her eyebrows.

'I don't have to explain myself to the likes of you.'

'Oh, dear me, I forgot!' she smiled. 'You're the great Sir George Gresham, and as such can do whatever you like to people without having to answer for your crimes.'

At her tone he took a step back. The fury left his face, to be replaced with something akin to respect. 'You've a sharp tongue, girl.'

'Really? I must have inherited it from somewhere.'

The corners of his mouth twitched. 'I can see now why my son was frightened.'

'Your son is a spoilt coward, who thinks he has the right to harass any female he comes across. But I don't suppose he's had a very good example to follow.'

'Hmm.' Sir George didn't seem to hear the insult, but reached out and took hold of her chin, then turned her face to the light so he could see it better. 'You are certainly no coward. Perhaps I should have kept you – *if* you're mine.'

She wrenched herself free.

'What's your name?' His tone was coaxing now.

'Rose. That's all you need to know.'

'Don't be so quick to dismiss me, girl. I could help you.'

That was too much for Rose. 'If you try to come anywhere near us, you'll regret the day you were born.'

'You can't stop me, girl,' he told her, with absolute confidence.

'Oh, yes I can.' Rose held his gaze unwaveringly. 'If you dismiss the professor or me, or try to interfere in my mother's life, then I will blacken your name and ruin your son.'

'And how do you propose to do that?' he asked with irony.

'You will see headlines in all the papers.' Her hand swept across an imaginary newspaper. '"Gresham's Son molests Sister."'

'I will deny you are anything to do with me, and I will be the one they believe. I will denounce you as a fraud who is trying to blackmail me.'

'Not when I explain that I wouldn't touch you or your money.'

'Don't be ridiculous.' He roared with laughter. 'No one would believe that!'

'Don't be too sure, *Father*.' She grimaced. 'One photograph of me will wipe away any doubt. No one could mistake whose child I am. Take a good look.' She turned him so that they were both looking into a mirror on the wall.

'Coincidence. Unless you tell me who your mother is, I cannot verify your claim.'

'I'm not making any claim.' Her eyes swept over him in contempt.

'I don't believe you. No one in your position could resist making money from such a situation.'

Rose heard the slap and saw his head jerk back before she realized what she had done. Expecting him to retaliate, she stood her ground, head up, but he just stared at her in disbelief. His eyes bored into hers as if he was trying to get inside her mind, then he stepped back.

'I have misjudged you.' He spoke softly, as if he couldn't believe it.

'You have! I wouldn't touch a penny of your money. I will never forgive you for the way you treated my mother, and I don't want to see you again.'

He was silent for a while, then nodded. 'As you wish.' He turned and strode out of the room.

Rose took a couple of deep breaths as the door closed. Thank God that was over.

Then she heard a muffled sound and turned towards the professor's table – she had forgotten he was still in the room. He was sitting in his chair, shaking with suppressed laughter, and his eyes were running with the effort of keeping quiet. Someone else was there too. John Trenchard was leaning against the wall, polishing his spectacles and grinning.

'John! I didn't hear you come in.'

The professor roared with laughter. 'I don't suppose you did, Rose. Your whole attention was focused on Sir George.'

She pulled a face, and John chuckled.

'I came in at just the right time. I'd have hated to have missed that.' John put on his spectacles and leaned forward to whisper in her ear: 'I knew you'd put him in his place when you met him.'

She frowned. 'You knew who my real father was?'

'I guessed, Rose. There was always something about you that seemed familiar, but it was only as you got older that I recognized the connection.'

Harold Steadman got to his feet and took her hands. 'Rose, I'm proud of you. That was the first time I've ever seen anyone get the better of Sir George.'

'Oh, I'm not so sure I did.' She felt uncertain.

'You did. I know him well and that's the first time I've ever seen him back away from a fight.' Harold Steadman smiled warmly. 'I think you impressed him.'

'Good Lord, I hope not!' she exclaimed in alarm. 'I don't want him taking any interest in me.'

'That might be a forlorn hope. I don't think you've seen the last of him,' John told her gently.

'But I hit him!'

'That wouldn't have worried him – quite the reverse, in fact.' The professor sat on the edge of his table. 'He likes someone with spirit.'

She groaned. 'I wish I'd known that. I'd have stayed icy calm.'

The two men roared with laughter.

They spent the next hour discussing her decision to study law. John approved the choice of career, and in the tea-room across the street, the two men mapped out a course for her.

'Rose must become a full-time student.' John stirred his tea thoughtfully. 'How can that be arranged, Harold?'

She listened to them scheming, and would have laughed if she hadn't ached with longing to do what they were suggesting. They were talking about the impossible, though.

'We've got some general exams in September,' Harold said eagerly. 'Rose is more than capable of passing them, so I'll sit her at the back of the class and let her take them too.'

'That won't be allowed.' She couldn't stay silent any longer. 'Wouldn't it be better if I stayed in your office, Professor, and did them there?'

'No, no.' Harold Steadman waved dismissively. 'You must be with everyone else, under supervision.'

'I won't cheat!' she told them indignantly.

'Of course you won't,' John said.

She listened for another ten minutes, then sighed wearily. 'You're wasting your time. I'll not be allowed to take the exams.'

The men looked at her as if they had forgotten she was there. 'Yes, you will,' they said together, then returned to the discussion.

Harold Steadman continued, 'Then when I've got the results, I'll put in an application for her to go to the London University – '

'Just a minute!' Rose thumped the table, making the cups rattle. 'If I can pass those exams, where is this leading?'

'I'll get you enrolled at the university, so you can study law.'

'It's the only way,' John told her. 'If you try to do it on your own, it will take you a lifetime to qualify, but only about another three years if you do it full-time.'

'But – but –' she stuttered. 'You're weaving fairy stories.' She started to count on her fingers. 'One, there will be objections if I take the same exams as the real pupils at the school. Two, the university will never agree to let me enrol. Three, I'm never going to be able to afford the money.' She sighed sadly. 'I can't be out of work for three years.'

The professor mimicked her actions and started to count on his own fingers. 'One, I will say that you are my private student and I want you to take these exams. Two, the university will accept you when they see your excellent results. Three, you can work for me at the weekends,' he told her. 'That should give you enough to survive on.'

'But you'll be retiring at the end of the war,' she reminded him.

'That's true, but I intend to write a book, and I'll need a lot of help with that. You're nimble on the typewriter,' he added.

'I'd be happy to help you, but I couldn't take any money from you.'

'Stop letting your heart rule your head, Rose.' He patted her hand affectionately. 'I need a typist, you need money, and I can afford to pay you.'

'But –'

Harold Steadman held up his hand. 'No more buts. Do you want this chance or not?'

Rose screwed her napkin up in excitement. What a daft question. 'You know I do.'

The men winked at each other. 'You leave everything to us,' Harold told her.

Rose looked at them and slowly shook her head. She knew they wanted to help her, but she mustn't get her hopes up too much. What they were suggesting just couldn't come true. She stood up. If she listened to this much longer she might begin to believe it. 'I'm going back to work.'

They hardly seemed to notice her leaving.

The next week passed without another mention of the exams, and she tried to dismiss the idea from her mind as another lost opportunity – another closed door. However, her determination to succeed made her intensify her studying. It was a heavy load. Working all day for the professor and reading long into the night was taking its toll. Not to mention the travelling between Bermondsey and Southwark every day.

'Rose.' Harold Steadman looked over her shoulder. 'I want you to study here for two hours every afternoon, and then go to bed at a reasonable hour. If you carry on like this, then by the time you sit the exams you'll be too tired to think clearly.'

She gaped at him in astonishment.

'Close your mouth and study. I've sung your praises to everyone and I expect you to pass with high marks. Once I've got proof of your academic excellence, I'll go to the university and give you a glowing reference.' He looked smug. 'I should be able to convince them to let you enrol as a student.'

'I still think you're dreaming, Professor.' She didn't dare believe it was possible.

'Have a little faith in me,' he joked. 'There's a dearth of students at the moment, but when the war ends it might be more difficult to have you admitted. There will be young men coming back to continue their studies.'

But there would also be many who would not, she thought sadly.

Some time later that afternoon, absorbed in study, she didn't hear the door open.

'Will you leave us alone, Professor Steadman.' It wasn't a question, it was a demand, but spoken kindly.

Rose looked up and the breath caught in her throat. The lady was a good age, and leaning heavily on an ebony stick with an ivory lion's head handle. She was an imposing figure. Her hair was white, her eyes were dark, and shone with intelligence and alertness. Rose got to her feet and was subjected to a thorough scrutiny. Then the lady nodded, as if satisfied.

'Get me a chair. I'm too old to be standing like this.'

Rose hurried to obey, and waited until she was settled. She didn't have to ask who she was.

'Sit down, or I'll get a crick in my neck.'

The lady spoke with such authority that it seemed natural to obey without question, but that put Rose on her guard. She was not going to be intimidated by any member of the Gresham family. And this was undoubtedly a Gresham.

The lady did not prevaricate. 'You attacked my grandson.'

Rose braced herself. 'Yes.'

'Good for you. About time somebody put him in his place.'

That wasn't what she'd expected.

'Don't look so surprised. I hear you also took on my son.' Her eyes crinkled at the corners.

'It was time somebody put *him* in his place,' Rose said,

and nearly fell off her chair when the old lady chuckled.

'You are certainly my granddaughter. George told me you are the image of me when I was young, and he's right.'

'He told you about me?'

'When he came home with a clear handprint across his face, I demanded to know what he'd been doing. Had to threaten to cut him out of my will before he told me.'

'Bet that frightened him.' Rose tried to smother a grin.

'Indeed.' She put her head to one side. 'This is quite incredible. It is like looking at myself as a young girl.'

'If I'm so like you, then why didn't your grandson notice it?' Rose asked.

'Because he takes after his mother, not the Gresham side of the family. All he thinks about is gambling and chasing girls. You're a beauty and that's all he would have noticed. Did your mother work for us?'

The change of tactic took Rose by surprise. 'Yes.'

'What happened?'

'Your son seduced her and when she became pregnant he threw her out.' Rose gave her the plain facts.

Lady Gresham gazed into space as if trying to bring something to mind. 'Was her name Potter?'

What a memory this lady had. Rose kept her mouth shut.

'I can see by your silence that I am right. I remember the incident well. I questioned my son and he denied having interfered with Miss Potter. Knowing my son as I do, I was doubtful that he was telling the truth, and I told him she was not to be dismissed. I went away for a few months and when I returned I was told that Potter had left of her own accord.'

'That's a lie!' Rose leaped to her feet. 'She was turned out with nowhere to go but the workhouse.'

'I know now that that is what happened. I would like to see your mother.'

'No!'

'You have inherited my pride,' Lady Gresham told her, with a wry smile, 'but be careful, it can be uncomfortable to live with.'

'I manage.'

'What are you studying?' Lady Gresham reached out for the book on Rose's desk. 'Law?'

'Is there something wrong with that?' she asked defensively.

'Not at all. My father was a barrister.' She put the book down. 'Which branch of the law are you intending to pursue?'

'I'm going to be a solicitor.'

The lady nodded. 'I'll make you a monthly advance – '

'I won't take anything from the Greshams.' Rose stood in front of the lady, feet apart, hands on hips, her gaze unflinching.

After what seemed an age, Lady Gresham sighed, then nodded. 'I would like to know how you are getting along, though. Will you keep in touch with me?'

'No.'

Lady Gresham appeared to age in front of her as she grasped her stick and stood up. 'If you change your mind – '

'I won't!'

Without another word, Lady Gresham left the room.

15

'How did you get on with the exams?' her mother asked, as soon as Rose walked into the house.

Rose sat down and rubbed her temple. 'All right, I think, but it was hard.'

Her mother placed the cure-all cup of tea in front of her. 'Will you have to take them again if you don't do well enough?'

'No, this is the only chance I'll get. How the professor got away with it this time, I'll never know.'

'From what you've told me, it seems as if he's running the school single handed until the war ends. I expect he can do much as he pleases.'

Rose nodded. 'That's why he's been rushing me, I expect. Once things are back to normal, he won't be able to bend the rules.'

'Don't look so worried.' Her mother patted her hand. 'What happens next?'

'When my results come through, and if they're good enough, the professor will go to the university and try to persuade them to let me enrol.' Rose fidgeted with her cup, then looked up. 'I don't believe he can do this for me, Mum. I'm going to have to be very, *very* good.'

'The professor wouldn't have put you through all this and raised your hopes if he had any doubts.'

'I suppose you're right.' Rose drank her tea. 'Anyway, it's done now, and all we have to do is wait and hope for the best. Even if nothing comes of it, I'll still have learned a lot by trying.'

'Er . . . have you seen any more of the Greshams?' her mother asked hesitantly.

'Not a sign. I don't think they'll come near me again.' She hesitated for a moment. 'But I couldn't help liking the old lady. When I refused to take her money, she asked me to keep in touch.'

'And will you?'

'No.' Rose didn't miss the look of relief on her mother's face.

Annie burst into the room. 'A boy on a bike just gave me this.' She held out a telegram.

'Shall I open it, Mum?' Rose asked gently, knowing what it was. Marj Webster shook her head, opened the message, read it in silence, then folded it again and placed it behind the clock on the mantelpiece. She blew her nose and turned to face them. 'It's been confirmed. Your dad's dead.'

Although she had known what the telegram would say, Rose was still shocked. It had been happening to thousands of families, of course, but this was someone close to them and it felt different. She thought back over the last four years. A generation of young men slaughtered. What a waste.

Annie tugged at her arm. 'Shall I go and tell Mrs Jenks?'

'Good idea, Toots.' Rose watched her little sister run out and realized that she didn't seem upset but, then, why should she? Her father had never given her so much as a passing glance. She searched her mind for something to say, but everything she thought of sounded hollow and insincere.

'Mum . . .'

'You don't have to say anything. I'll be all right when I've got over the shock. I can't believe he won't be coming back, shouting and stinking of beer.'

'No, it'll be strange,' Rose admitted. And a surge of pity rippled through her. 'He never had much of a life, did he?'

Tears ran down Marj's face. 'He was a swine at times, Rose, but he was good to me till the drink got to him. But what else did he have?'

His family, Rose thought, but didn't say it. It had probably been the constant struggle to feed a growing family that had driven him to the pub every night.

'He didn't deserve to die like that,' her mother added softly.

'None of them did, Mum.' Rose sighed. The futility of war filled her mind. Would the sacrifice of all those men help those who had survived, or would everything go back to the way it had been? And if it did, what had it all been about?

Annie returned with their next-door neighbour, who was staggering under the weight of David. Mrs Jenks handed him to Rose. 'Put him to bed. He's sick.'

He was wrapped in an old blanket. Rose pulled it aside. 'What's wrong with him?' Her voice wavered.

'I think he's got the influenza,' Mrs Jenks said, matter-of-factly. 'This epidemic's bad.'

'Should I take him to a doctor?'

'Waste of time and money. They're all rushed off their feet, and there's nothing they can do.'

'I'll help you.' Annie peered at her brother in concern.

'No – and don't you come too close. I don't want you catching it.' Rose stepped away from her sister.

While she was making David as comfortable as possible, she heard someone come up the stairs, coughing. Bert came into the room, crawled on to his bed and scrambled under the blanket with all his clothes on.

'Not you too?' Rose exclaimed, hurrying over to him.

'I feel rotten,' he rasped.

'Get undressed, Bert. You'll be more comfortable.' But her words were ignored – he was already asleep. She removed his boots and left him in peace; she could undress him later.

Rose's mother hurried into the room. 'Oh, dear God. I was praying this would miss us.'

'Not much chance of that,' Rose told her. 'We're crammed together in these houses and any epidemic's going to sweep through here.'

The next three days were agony as Rose watched her two young brothers suffer. She felt so helpless, as influenza raged through the slum dwellings and news of deaths filtered through to them all the time. She was trying to change Bert's soiled bed without disturbing him when she heard her mother give an anguished cry.

'What is it?' She rushed to her mother, who was staring down at the child in the bed.

'David's dead,' Marj cried, and fell into Rose's arms.

'I only went to get him a drink of water. I wasn't away for more than a minute . . .'

Rose closed the little boy's eyes and pulled a blanket over his face, fighting to keep her own tears at bay. Only five years old, and what kind of a life had he had?

She led her distraught mother to a chair and made her sit down. 'I'll go and get the undertaker.'

'No!' Marj clutched at her daughter's arm and looked anxiously at Bert. 'You send Flo. I need you here.'

'All right, Mum.' Rose hurried downstairs, sent her sister on the errand, and told eleven-year-old Will to make their mother a cup of tea. Then she went back upstairs.

The undertaker was so busy that it was around nine o'clock that evening before he managed to come. Then, with that distressing business dealt with, Rose ordered her mother to get some rest. She was too upset and weary to argue, and once Rose knew she was asleep, she settled herself in a chair beside Bert to watch him through the night. The signs weren't good, and she felt sure that he wouldn't live much longer.

She was right: at about five o'clock the next morning Bert died. It was only then, in the quiet hours before anyone else was awake, that she allowed herself to weep.

For the next two days Rose and her mother scrubbed the place out with carbolic, praying that this was the end of the sickness in their house. They had just finished when Nancy and Will developed colds.

'Oh, Rosie,' her mother moaned, 'I don't think I can bear to lose any more of them.'

Rose had hardly slept for days and was exhausted, but

her mother was distraught with grief. She reached out to her in an effort to comfort her. 'Nancy and Will aren't as bad, Mum. They'll be all right. Why don't you lie down? I'll watch them.'

Her mother left the cramped bedroom and Rose could hear her sobbing all the way down the stairs. She felt herself start to crumble inside, but she shook herself and straightened up. This was no time to fall apart. At least Annie hadn't caught it. Although her little sister's health and strength had improved markedly over the years, she still looked fragile. The mortality rate was high in Garrett Street: the epidemic was taking a terrible toll.

Rose went to look at Nancy, gave her a drink, wiped her face, then sat on the edge of the bed and gazed around the room. It was dingy and crowded with beds, but it was clean. Lord, how she hated this street. She got up and walked over to the window to look out at the crowded back-to-back houses, the piles of rubbish everywhere.

'Rosie?' someone croaked.

Rose spun round and saw Flo holding on to the door. 'I don't feel well and Mum said I was to sleep in here.'

'Get into this bed.' Rose rushed to her sister and helped her undress. Flo was no sooner under the blanket than she was asleep.

Rose dropped her head into her hands. How many more?

'Rosie.' Annie was standing by the door. 'Auntie Grace is downstairs. She wants to see you.'

'Don't come in here, Annie,' she said. 'And Grace shouldn't be here.' She ran down the stairs, her heart thudding. Suppose something had happened to

John. She erupted into the scullery. 'Is John all right?'

Grace stopped her conversation with Marj. 'Of course, Rose.'

'Thank God for that!' She sank on to a chair. 'You should have sent a message, not come here. We've already lost two of the children.' She cast a quick glance at her mother and was frightened to see that she was coming down with a cold too. She suspected that her mother was still on her feet only because of her worry about her children.

'That's why I'm here.' Grace turned back to Marj. 'Have you enough money for the funerals?'

A tear trickled down Marj's face, but she pulled herself together. 'I've got a penny insurance on all of them. I take it out as soon as they're born. It isn't much, but it pays for a funeral.' She blew her nose. 'Thank you for asking.'

'What about your husband?' Grace asked gently.

'Oh, the army took care of that. He's been buried somewhere in France.'

Grace nodded, then smiled at Annie. 'And how are you, little one?'

'I'm not little now, I'm seven years old,' Annie said importantly.

'That old!' Grace raised her hands in mock-surprise. 'I remember you when you were no bigger than a doll.'

Annie giggled.

It was lovely to hear laughter again, Rose thought. Since the sickness had struck them, the house had been hushed, shrouded in grief.

'I wondered if you'd like Annie to come and stay with me until everyone's well again.'

'What a kind thought,' Rose exclaimed. With Annie

163

away from the house, at least she wouldn't have to worry about her.

'No!' Annie's lips set in a firm line. 'I'd like to stay with Auntie Grace, but I'm not going to leave you and Mum. The funerals are tomorrow and you'll need me. I can make the tea and do all sorts of other things.'

'Of course, she must stay here then.' Grace smiled at the little girl. 'You can visit me some other time.'

Who would believe it was early October? Rose pulled up her coat collar, then put her hand through her mother's arm. David and Bert were being buried together, and it couldn't be a worse day for the funeral. It was dark and grey, with a thick mist of rain drenching everyone standing at the graveside. It was a sparse gathering, with only herself, her mother and Bob. Most of the others were ill and she had flatly refused to let Annie come in this dreadful weather. She had got round her by saying that they would all need a hot drink when they got back, and Annie had reluctantly agreed to stay behind and see to it.

Rose felt her mother shiver and squeezed her arm, as the vicar droned on, mouthing the beautiful words of the Bible without an ounce of feeling . . .

'Such a poor send-off,' Marj Webster murmured.

'I know, Mum. But the neighbours would have come if they hadn't been nursing their own families.'

'As if we haven't had enough to put up with over the last four years. God must think we're very wicked to send this disaster on us.'

'It's got nothing to do with Him,' Rose stated with conviction.

The vicar came to the end of the service, and Rose

breathed a sigh of relief. Her mother needed to be home by the fire, not standing around this bleak muddy hole in the ground. Rose had never believed that you were born, lived, died, and that was all there was to it. There had to be something else, and she hoped her brothers had gone to a better place.

'Where does all the trouble come from then?' her mother asked, as they walked out of the churchyard.

'I don't know, Mum. I'm still looking for the answers to about a million questions.'

'Only a million?' Her mother gave a faint smile, the first Rose had seen for some time.

'Yes. I've managed to whittle them down a bit,' she joked.

It was a month before Rose was back at work. Will, Nancy and Flo recovered from the influenza and no one else caught it, thank goodness.

Rose paced the office, waiting anxiously for Professor Steadman to come and tell her the result of her exam. There hadn't been time to wonder about it, but now she wanted desperately to know.

She stood up and walked over to the window. The pupils were hurrying along, books clutched in their hands, and the longing that filled her was almost more than she could bear. Her hand shook as she pushed the thick hair away from her face. Her life had been a series of disappointments, and the dream she had had last night was a vivid illustration of how she felt. She had been running down a long passage, but the door in front of her seemed to get further and further away, no matter how fast she ran. She had gritted her teeth and finally reached it, but when she'd turned the handle, the door had been locked.

She pressed her forehead against the cold window. What a dreadful few weeks it had been.

'Rose.'

She turned at the sound of the professor's voice. She had been lost in thought and had not heard him come into the room. She waited for him to speak.

'I've had your results.' A broad smile of pleasure lit his face. 'And you have received higher marks than any of the other candidates.'

She gasped and held on to the desk.

'I've just been to the university and shown them the results. They were impressed, especially when I explained that you have studied in your spare time – under my guidance, of course.'

She took a deep breath. If he didn't tell her soon, she'd scream.

'However . . .'

Please just tell me!

' . . . as you are a female, they took a lot of convincing, but I have won them round. You start next October.'

Her head came up sharply and her black eyes locked on to his. 'Would you repeat that, please?' The voice didn't sound like hers.

'You can study law there full-time.'

She groped for a chair and sank on to it. 'I can't believe it! How did you persuade them to agree?'

'I prodded their political aspirations by reminding them how much women have done in this war, and that it was almost certain the government would soon give them the vote.'

'I bet they weren't too keen on that idea.' She was beginning to come out of her shock, and realize what a gift she had been given.

The professor smiled broadly. 'No, but I swayed them with the argument that it would not harm their reputations if they took in more women students. It would show them as progressive thinkers.'

Then Rose laughed. 'Good heavens, you're a crafty old devil, aren't you?'

'Have you only just found out?' He rubbed his hands together gleefully. 'I'm proud of you, Rose.'

She felt like shouting for joy. 'I don't know how to thank you, Professor.'

'You work hard and pass all the exams. That's all the thanks I need. And I think it's time you called me Harold, don't you?'

In a rare show of affection, she went up to him and kissed his leathery cheek. 'Thanks, Harold. I won't let you down.'

'Don't let yourself down. It isn't going to be easy. You'll have to face many challenges. You might encounter hostility from other students and some of the lecturers.' Harold studied her intently. 'But the only way they can get rid of you is to find a reason to expel you, so hold on to your temper and your tongue.'

'I'll try.'

'You'll have to do better than that. You will have to learn not to rise to provocation, however infuriating.'

She lifted her head and grinned. 'I'll be as docile as a sleeping kitten.'

'That I would like to see!'

'Now, now, Harold, where's your faith?' Rose chided.

'I want this so badly that you can be sure I won't do anything to jeopardize my chances.'

Suddenly the door burst open and three boys tumbled into the room, shouting, 'It's over! *The war's over!*'

16

April 1919

'Uncle John! Uncle John!'

Rose watched Annie hurl herself into John's arms. He staggered back with the impact of her exuberant greeting.

'He's home for good,' Grace said, her face glowing with excitement as she hung Rose's coat over the banisters.

'Oh, I'm so pleased!' Rose turned to greet him, but found that her sister had dragged him into the front room.

'Ooooh, aren't you tall?' Annie's voice was full of admiration.

'Now what's she up to?' Rose wondered.

'She's just met Bill, by the sound of things,' Grace told her.

'Who's Bill?'

'Someone John met while he was in the navy.' Grace lowered her voice. 'He's had a terrible time. His ship was sunk and he spent four days in a small boat. Only two of the men were alive when they were finally rescued.'

Rose shuddered. So many young men had seen and experienced things they would never forget.

'He doesn't get on with his father, poor boy, so we've given him the back bedroom until he can find somewhere of his own.'

Rose opened her mouth to speak, when she heard Annie again.

'How tall are you?'

An educated, soft voice answered, 'Six feet four.'

'Cor! My sister's nearly as tall as you.'

Rose groaned. But Grace looked up at her. 'You *are* taller than the average woman and you're only sixteen.'

'Nearly seventeen, and I hope I stop growing soon,' she muttered, as they walked into the front room.

'Rose!' John hurried to her side and kissed her cheek. 'Congratulations. When do you start at the university?'

'Six months' time.' She grinned. 'Did Grace tell you how Harold forced them to let me enrol?'

John's face was alight with amusement. 'He's a crafty old devil.'

'That's what I told him!' Rose chuckled.

'John,' Grace interrupted, 'introduce Rose to Bill.'

'Oh, I'm sorry. I was so pleased to see my *protégée* again that I've quite forgotten my manners.' He drew her forward. 'Rose, this is Bill . . . Bill, this is Rose.'

She found herself looking into the kindest, gentlest eyes she had ever seen. He was also rather handsome, but deep lines of strain were etched into his face, making it difficult to assess his age. If you disregarded the lines, she reckoned he couldn't be more than in his late twenties.

'Hello, Rose.' He shook her hand politely. 'I've heard a great deal about you.'

'Has my sister been blabbing again?' She glared at Annie accusingly.

'I haven't said anything, honest.' Annie tipped her head back to look up at Bill, giggled, then sidled up to her sister. 'He's tall enough for you too.'

'Annie! I wish you'd watch your tongue. I've a good mind to ask Edward to stitch it down again.'

Annie laughed, then rushed out to the kitchen to help Grace with the tea.

Bill looked puzzled, so John started to explain about how Annie had been born tongue-tied, but he hadn't got far with the story when the child came back with a plate of bread and butter. She put it carefully on to the table, knelt on the chair beside Bill and delighted in telling him the whole story.

'What a good thing you had the operation,' Bill told her.

This sent Annie off into peals of giggles. 'Rosie doesn't think so.'

When Bill laughed, the strain left his face, and Rose caught a glimpse of just how good-looking he really was. He had dark brown hair, perfectly proportioned features, and his mouth was full and gentle, as were his grey-green eyes. If they hadn't held such a tortured look, they would have been beautiful, she thought, as she studied him from beneath lowered lashes. He had a strange effect upon her, which she had not experienced before, and she didn't like it. It frightened her.

Tea was lively and she didn't have time to dwell on imaginary fears – for that was all they were. Her over-active imagination was playing tricks with her again. Not all men were brutes, and this one was no threat to her.

Rose helped Grace clear up afterwards. When she went back into the front room, she stood stock still in horror. Annie was sitting next to Bill, leaning on his arm, and eyeing his knees with a 'dare I?' look on her face. Rose knew what her sister was thinking: he looked big and strong enough for her to sit on. Rose couldn't understand it: Annie was like a kitten, always looking for warmth and comfort.

'Annie!' she said sharply.

The child sighed, slipped off her chair and came to Rose. 'I don't think he'd mind,' she said, quietly this time. 'He's a nice man.'

'You're too big, Annie. And why do you always want to sit on a man's lap?'

'I like men.'

Oh, my God! Rose thought. We could be in for trouble when she grows up. She stooped and straightened her sister's dress. 'Well, you mustn't do it any more, Toots. It was all right when you were a baby, but you're getting to be a big girl now.'

'I am so,' Annie agreed reluctantly.

'Who wants to go to the pictures?' John asked.

'Me! Me!' Annie rushed over to John and grabbed his hand. 'What's on?'

'Buster Keaton.'

'Rosie? Can we go, please?' she pleaded.

'All right, but you be good now, Annie.'

'I'm always good,' she declared with conviction, and let Grace help her with her coat.

There was still a chilly wind blowing as they made their way to the local fleapit, as it was affectionately known, but Annie seemed oblivious to the weather. She was chattering nineteen to the dozen to John and Bill.

'What a difference in her,' Grace remarked, as they walked along behind them.

'Yes. When she was two I didn't think she'd see her third birthday, but she's surprised us all.'

'She doesn't miss much that's going on around her,' Grace observed.

'I know that to my cost.' Rose pulled a face. 'I have to be careful what I say and do.'

Grace laughed quietly. 'She's very perceptive – especially where you're concerned. She loves you so much.'

A lot of people were waiting to see the film, so they had to queue for a while. A young man limped along the line playing a violin and Rose's heart ached for him. Once out of the forces, so many were reduced to begging, especially if they were injured, as this one clearly was.

As the man approached them, Rose dipped into her pocket and found a shilling. When she gave it to him he bowed. 'Thank you, miss, and God bless you.'

Bill and John gave him something too. Then the queue started to move and they were soon inside.

'Where's the music coming from?' Annie knelt on her seat to get a better view.

'Down the front.' Rose pointed to the man playing the piano.

'Oh . . .' She stood up then, wobbling alarmingly, to see past the large woman in front of her.

Before Rose could steady her, Bill caught Annie and held her securely.

Annie grinned at Rose. 'I like that music.'

With one smooth movement, Bill lifted Annie off her seat and put her into his. 'She'll be able to see better there.' He sat down next to Rose and eased his long legs into the tiny space. He was a giant, she thought uncomfortably, and leaned as far away from him as she could.

It was a funny film and even Rose forgot her reserve,

laughing until the tears streamed down her face. When it was over, they went back to Grace and John's for a hot drink.

'Are you going to live at the university,' John wanted to know, 'or will you travel there each day?'

'It's difficult to study in our house, so they've given me a room in the staff quarters. I'll go home at the weekends.'

'Why can't you live with the other students?' Annie piped up.

'Because they're all boys,' Rose explained. 'I can't stay in the same place as them.'

'What? Like at home? We have all the boys in one room, and us girls in another.'

'That's right.' Annie seemed satisfied with that explanation, so Rose turned back to John. The thought of him being home again made her yearn for their Sunday talks once more, but it was asking a lot of him when he probably only wanted to rest and be with his wife again.

She hesitated, then drew a deep breath. 'Now you're home for good, would you be able to spare an hour or two for me? I wouldn't expect our usual Sunday lessons, but I'd love to talk to you.' She added hastily, 'You don't have to agree if you don't want to.'

'I'd like that very much, but I didn't think you'd want to now you're going to study full-time.'

'My Latin's not as good as it should be, and there are other things I'd like to learn.'

'Such as?'

'I've been reading about some of the old philosophers, and I'd like to discuss them with you.'

John leaned forward eagerly. 'How did you get on with them?'

Rose pulled a face. 'Blooming hard going. Some of their ideas take a bit of understanding.'

'Would next Sunday be all right for you? We could make it a regular thing, if you like.'

'Oh, John, I'll look forward to it.' Rose could have hugged him, but she didn't, of course. At times like this she wished she was more like Annie – outgoing and demonstrative. Then she noticed Annie stifling a yawn and stood up. 'We'd better be getting back. Thanks for a lovely afternoon.'

Bill unwound himself from the chair. 'I'll see you home.'

'You don't have to do that. We'll be all right on our own.' The last thing she wanted was this disturbing man with her. 'It's cold out there. You stay in the warm.'

'I've known it colder,' he said simply, then picked up her coat to help her on with it.

Grace had buttoned up Annie and the little girl was already holding Bill's hand, looking up at him trustingly. Rose felt backed into a corner: if she protested too much she would seem childish. Anyway, she had Annie with her, so he was unlikely to try anything. Then she looked into his kind eyes. She really must stop believing that all men were the same.

As soon as they crossed the road the bus came and Bill carried Annie upstairs. Rose couldn't help being amused, because as soon as he sat down Annie curled up on his lap and fell asleep. She had finally got her wish.

The conductor came for the fares and she fished in her pocket, but Bill was already paying. She held out the money to him, but he gave it a contemptuous glance, settled Annie more comfortably and ignored her. She fumed: if he thought she was going to let him pay for them, he had another think coming.

Knowing he had his hands full with the sleeping Annie, she slipped the money into his pocket. This produced a resigned sigh. 'I'm not going to let you pay our fare,' she told him firmly.

He spoke then. 'Why not? Do you think it will make you beholden to me?'

'I can afford to pay.' She felt put out by the edge of sarcasm in his voice. 'And, anyway, I don't know you. You might be broke, for all I know.'

'I'm not.' He turned his head and stared at her intently.

His direct gaze made her uncomfortable, and she wished fervently that the journey was over. It wasn't like her to allow anyone to get under her skin in the way this tall man had. She was experiencing emotions she didn't understand, and hoped she would never see him again.

The bus started to slow for their stop and she shook Annie. 'Wake up! Here we are.'

When they were on the pavement, Rose pointed across the road. 'You can get the bus back from there.'

'I'll see you to your door,' he said, taking Annie's hand and starting to walk along the road.

'There's no need for that.' She grabbed his arm to stop him. 'We'll be all right from here, but thank you for coming with us.'

This little speech produced another deep sigh from him.

'Rosie's right.' Annie stood on tiptoe and looked up

at him. 'It isn't safe to come down our street. You look like a toff and they might rob you.'

He stooped down to her. 'What about you and your sister? Will you be safe?'

'Oh, yes. They'd never touch one of their own.'

'I'd kill them if they did,' Rose muttered.

A twitch of his lips showed her that Bill was amused. 'I think I'll still come with you,' he said.

It was her turn to sigh.

'Oh, well.' Annie took hold of his hand again, and gave him an admiring smile. 'I expect they'll think twice before they jump on you. It would take six of them to hold you down.'

'Oh, at least.' There was a hint of laughter in his voice.

Rose saw little point in arguing. She had the strong feeling that this quiet man was made of steel.

When they reached the house, Bill said a polite goodnight, turned and walked away, whistling a lively tune. He was halfway up the road before Rose tore her gaze away from him. Infuriating man!

Bill strode up the dreadful street, feeling as if he was being watched, but the dark shadows and threatening atmosphere didn't frighten him. This he could handle. It was the sea with its inky depths that made his blood run cold. The sight of his shipmates dying before his eyes still tortured him, disturbing his nights, until he was almost afraid to sleep. When he did drift off, the memory of that terrible time played over and over in his dreams. It was like a demented picture running non-stop, making him experience all over again the rage and helplessness he had felt. He didn't know why he had survived, but for the first time he was glad that he had.

He launched into another popular song, whistling easily and in perfect tune. He had felt happy today. The little girl was a delight – so open and loving – and her untainted affection had soothed his wounded soul. As he'd sat in that small boat, watching each man die, the true values in life had become crystal clear. Annie had got it right, but her sister was another matter. He had sensed anger in her when they had walked down Garrett Street. She hadn't wanted him there, hadn't wanted him to see the squalor.

The bus arrived and he hopped on. When he reached into his pocket for a penny to pay his fare, his fingers closed around the money Rose had insisted on giving him. There had been a fierce pride shining in her dark eyes.

Rose Webster was an intriguing mystery, and he didn't know what to make of her. She was breathtakingly beautiful, and her intelligence was obvious, but she gave away little of her feelings. However, he had seen tonight that she loved to laugh and she had enjoyed the film. Yet when he'd seen her home, she had been prickly and guarded.

She lived in a horrible area and obviously hated it, but there was more to it than that, he was sure. He'd love to know what kind of a life she'd had to make her so defensive.

17

October 1919

'You all right, Mum?' Rose could see she had been crying.

Marj took a letter from behind the clock and handed it to Rose. 'This was waiting for me when I got up this morning. Bob's run away to sea.'

Rose read the note. 'The idiot – he's only fourteen. Why'd he do a stupid thing like that?'

'Wants to get out of this dump, he says.' Her mother wiped away a tear. 'When I lay my hands on him he won't sit down for a week.'

Rose sighed. 'Well, there's no point me going after him. He says here he was sailing at first light, so he'll be long gone by now.'

Her mother started to lay the table for the children's breakfast.

'Shall I do that while you get ready for work?' Rose took a plate out of her mother's hand then noticed it was shaking.

'I haven't got a job any more. We've all been dismissed,' said her mother.

'But that isn't right!' Rose exploded. 'The women are still needed. There are so few men around now that they're not going to be able to fill the jobs. A lot of those coming home aren't even out of the forces yet.'

Marj shrugged. 'But that's what they've done. They don't want us any more.'

'It didn't take them long to forget what the women have done during the war, did it?' Rose muttered bitterly. 'Less than a year into the peace and they want them out of the way.'

Marj gave her daughter a wan smile. 'We were needed for a while, but now the men want everything back the way it was.'

'I know, and a lot of women are going to find it hard to go back to the old ways.'

Her mother nodded. 'If it hadn't been for the women, we wouldn't have survived. No one at the factory wanted to leave. We all enjoyed the friendship and the extra cash.'

At the mention of money, Rose frowned. 'What are you going to do, Mum? Prices have almost doubled recently.'

'Oh, I'll manage. Don't you fret.' Marj looked shifty and shoved a piece of paper out of sight.

Rose guessed what it was and whipped it out from under a plate. As she looked at it, her heart nearly broke. It was a reckoning of income and expenses, and the two didn't come close. Visions of their existence before the war came to her with awful clarity. The struggle to pay the rent, the constant hunger . . .

Her mother took the paper from her. 'We'll be all right. You never know, I might get another job.'

Rose knew the chances of that were slim. 'Don't you get a war widow's pension?'

'Yes, but it's only a few shillings.' A look of sadness crossed her face. 'Flo's got a good job in the shop, though, and she might be able to give me a bit.'

Rose thought about her sister, and knew that she had always been selfish. Although she was only sixteen, she was already walking out, and had started saving to get married. 'You still won't have enough.'

Rose could have wept. Her dreams were crumbling again. She took a deep breath, knowing what she had to do. 'I won't go to the university. I'll get a job instead.' Her voice was husky with distress.

'No! I can't have you doing that. I'd never forgive myself if I held you back.' She gave her daughter a proud smile. 'You're going to make something of yourself. You've got the brains and guts to get out of the slums, and I want to see you do it.'

'But, Mum – '

Marj held up her hand. 'I won't hear a word about you giving it all up. You've worked hard for it.'

'I've got a bit put by. You can have that.'

Her mother shook her head again. 'You'll need it.'

'Well, then, I'll be working for Harold on Saturdays so you can have that money. It won't be much, but it'll help.'

'I won't take it, my girl.' Her mother was adamant. 'You've got three years of study in front of you, and you're going to need every penny you can find. How are you going to be a success if you don't eat?'

Rose couldn't argue with that.

'I'll take in a lodger,' her mother declared.

'What?' Rose was startled. 'Where are you going to put him?'

'With Bob gone and you living at the university during the week, that only leaves six of us. Seven when you come home at weekends. I could use the top two rooms for us and turn the downstairs room into a nice little let.'

'Do you think you'll be able to get a lodger?' Rose looked around and pulled a face.

'It's cleaner than most, and there'll be a lot of men about with nowhere to live.'

The thought of her mother taking a stranger into the house made Rose feel uneasy. 'You be careful who you choose, won't you?'

'I'm not daft, Rosie.'

By the time Rose left to start her first term, the room was ready. They had scrubbed, polished, then put into it the best bits of furniture. It didn't look too bad, she had to admit, and her mother was hopeful of finding a lodger.

She arrived at the university feeling somewhat apprehensive. This was a big step for her and the problems at home had made her wonder yet again if she was doing the right thing. And was she good enough to take on such a challenge?

'How are you feeling, Rose?' Harold asked, when he met her in the corridor.

'Excited, and nervous. What are you doing here?'

'I've come to wish you luck – and you needn't worry, there will be two other girls as well. They've put you all together.' He chuckled. 'If the boys cause you any trouble, you'll be able to support each other.'

'What are they like, these other girls?'

'Middle class, but that needn't bother you.' A grin spread across his face. 'You're brighter than they are.'

'I hope you're right.'

'Don't go thinking this is a mistake, because it isn't,'

he told her. 'I've every faith in you. You've earned the right to become a student here.'

The word *student* brought on a surge of excitement and the doubts dropped away. She could do this.

'Who are you?'

Rose continued to put away her few belongings, and ignored the strident voice behind her.

'Answer me! Are you the maid?'

The insult made her turn slowly, her dark eyes flashing, but she was outwardly icy calm. She found herself looking down at a short, dumpy blonde with a petulant expression.

'Well?'

'If you're starting here today, then we're sharing a room.' Rose enjoyed telling her that, and fought to stop herself laughing at the look of horror on the other girl's face.

'It's insulting enough being put in this inferior accommodation, but I'm not sharing a room with *you*.'

'We're here because they haven't got any proper facilities for women yet, and they certainly can't put us in with the men. You'd better go and see if they can make other arrangements for you, because I'm staying.' Rose had known she would come across some rudeness and prejudice, so she had started as she meant to go on. No one was going to get the better of her.

As the blonde stormed out, she pushed aside another girl who was just coming into the room. Rose caught her as she stumbled. She was about five feet two, with ordinary brown hair but very nice clear blue eyes. They went a long way towards making her attractive.

She looked at Rose nervously. 'Who was that?'

'A disagreeable girl who doesn't like the idea of sharing a room.'

'Oh dear.' The newcomer glanced around the room and grimaced. 'Bit cramped, isn't it?'

Was it? It looked positively luxurious to Rose. 'I understand that, as we're the only females, they didn't know where to put us. Do you mind sharing?'

'Oh, no. I wouldn't like to be on my own, not with the place full of boys.' She eyed Rose up and down. 'Would you mind if I stayed close to you?'

'Of course not.' Rose was pleased. She had been chosen as a protector already, and she had only just arrived. 'You needn't be nervous of the boys.'

'Oh, I'm always nervous. People frighten me, you see, and I don't know what I'm doing here.' There was an edge of panic in her voice.

'Why are you then?'

'My mother's a sympathizer of the suffrage movement, and has insisted I train for a career. She chose law for me.'

'And how do you feel about that?' Rose was interested in the girl, especially as her mother was involved with the suffrage movement. That indicated a family keen on social reform.

'I like the idea, but I'm not sure I can do it.' She fiddled with her dress.

'I'm sure you can. We'll do it together.' She held out her hand. 'I'm Rose.'

'Harriet.' She gave Rose a rather damp handshake. 'I'm so glad you're here. Can we be friends?'

'Of course. Now, why don't you claim the bed next to

mine and leave the one by the draughty window for her ladyship?'

Harriet giggled. 'Do you think she'll mind?'

'She will, but I'll sort her out if she causes trouble.'

They were both laughing when the blonde came back. 'It seems we're stuck with each other! This is all that's available at the moment.' She threw her case on to Harriet's bed.

'That's taken,' Rose informed her.

'I can have this one, if I want it.' She turned up her nose and sniffed.

Rose resisted the temptation to wipe the haughty look from her face. 'No, you can't. First to come gets the pick.'

'But I was here before her.' She pointed rudely at Harriet.

Harriet started to edge towards the other bed, but Rose put a hand on her shoulder and stopped her. 'But you left again. You didn't want to share a room, you said.'

'It seems I have no choice, unless I want to stay in the same building as the boys.' She snatched up her bag and stormed over to the window.

It was silly to fight, Rose thought. They were going to have to get on with each other. 'We're going to be seeing a lot of each other, so I suggest we try to be civil. I'm Rose, and this is Harriet. What's your name?'

'I'm Miss Bretton.'

'I'm not going to call you Miss Bretton,' Rose told her firmly. 'Haven't you got a Christian name?'

'Angelina, but everyone calls me Angel.'

Rose smothered a laugh. She had never met anyone

less like an angel. 'What are you going to study, *Angelina*?'

'Law, of course. My father's a barrister.'

And mine's a Sir, Rose thought, with a degree of amusement.

'Where do you live?' Harriet asked Angelina shyly.

'Park Lane. What about you?'

'Kensington.' Harriet glanced at Rose.

'I come from Bermondsey.'

'*Bermondsey*?' Angelina looked appalled. 'How did you manage to get a place here?'

'Professor Steadman helped me. He and another teacher have been coaching me.'

Angelina's expression told Rose that she doubted she could read or write, but Rose didn't care. Let people think what they wanted to – she'd show them all in the end.

Rose rubbed her temple and closed her eyes. She was so very weary, but nothing would keep her away from her regular Sunday visit to Grace and John. She had so much to discuss with John and he was giving her the much-needed tuition in Latin. Anyway, Annie would be upset if she couldn't come here once a week. Rose knew that her little sister missed her and looked forward to her coming home every Friday night.

'Do you feel up to this today?' John came in and sat beside her.

Rose opened her eyes and smiled. 'I've been looking forward to it all week.'

The time flew by, as it always did when she was with John. He was the only person with whom she felt she could let down her guard, and she poured out her hopes, fears and the difficulties she had encountered in the first week at the university. They spent the first hour catching up on what she had been reading, and then discussing any subject that came to mind. She soon forgot her tiredness.

They were in the middle of one of their usual arguments when Annie came in with a plate of biscuits for their break. Then Grace joined them and asked how she had got on at the university.

Rose told them about Harriet and the snobbish Angelina, and they were all in fits of laughter when the door opened and Bill came in. She hadn't realized he was still staying with Grace and John.

'I'll be off, now,' he told John and Grace. 'Thank you for your hospitality. I've enjoyed my time with you. Good company, regular food and rest were just what I needed.'

John shook his hand, and Grace hugged him. 'There's a room here for you whenever you want it, Bill,' Grace told him.

Rose gaped. He was in uniform, but it wasn't an ordinary seaman's outfit. She was mesmerized by the decoration on his lapels and the hat tucked beneath his arm.

Annie got off her chair and gazed up at him in wonder. 'Ooh, don't you look lovely?'

With a chuckle, he stooped and kissed the top of her head. 'Thank you, Annie. So do you.'

'Are you going away?' she asked.

'Yes, sweetheart, I am, but I'll come and see you when I'm on leave.'

'You promise?'

He held his hand over his heart. 'I promise.'

187

'Are you going on a boat?' Annie persisted, holding his hand tightly.

Bill nodded again, his expression tightening. Then he turned to Rose. 'John told me about your brother. I'll see if I can find out where he is.'

Her mouth was still open and she hadn't heard what he had said. 'What kind of a uniform is that?' she blurted out.

'He's a captain,' John told her.

Now Rose understood why he had felt responsible for all those men when his ship had been sunk. And he was going back to sea again. That took guts. She was sorry she had been so sharp with him.

With a genuine smile, she held out her hand. 'Good luck.'

He ignored her hand, leaned forward and kissed her cheek. 'I hope your dreams come true.' He turned on his heel and left.

18

Bill stood on the dock at Portsmouth, his mood as bleak as the weather. He didn't want to go back to sea, but knew that this was something he had to do. His gaze swept over the ship in front of him, but he couldn't appreciate the trim lines, the gleaming paintwork, the impressive array of guns. Thank God they would only be used for practice now. HMS *Grenadier* was the most recent battleship to come into service, and the navy had paid him a great honour by giving him command of her, but he felt no affection for her. How could he? She was a stranger to him. Not like his other command – a battered old cruiser that had felt like a living entity . . .

'Sir!'

Bill snapped back to the present.

'I'm Able Seaman Smithy, sir, your steward.' The sailor picked up Bill's bag. 'She's a fine ship, sir.'

'Yes, very impressive.' He tried to dredge up some enthusiasm, but there was nothing inside him except fear at facing the sea again.

'The crew's all ready and waiting, sir.'

Bill lifted his head and straightened his shoulders. It was time to lay a few ghosts.

As he stepped on to the deck, the welcoming party saluted smartly, and just for a moment – a brief flash – the faces of the men changed. Instead of the fresh-faced eager recruits, he was seeing the other crew, whom he had watched die. Many had been his friends, and in the long sleepless nights, he could still hear their cries as he had searched for them in the inky dark as their ship had disappeared beneath the sea. Gradually all sounds had ceased and the silence had been worse than the noise and confusion. He remembered looking over the side of the little boat into the churning depths. The deathly quiet and vast emptiness of the ocean had nearly unmanned him, but he had held on to his composure by telling himself that this couldn't be the only lifeboat to have been launched successfully. He had jumped overboard at the last moment, and if it hadn't been for the willing hands pulling him into the boat, he would now be with his friends at the bottom of the ocean.

Sweat broke out on his upper lip as the pictures played over and over in his mind.

'Welcome aboard, sir. I'm Petty Officer Stevens.'

'Are you familiar with the ship?' he asked, once more in control, and ready to face the task ahead of him.

'Yes, sir. I've been here a week.'

Bill nodded. 'Come with me. I'll inspect my cabin and then you can give me a guided tour.'

'We're all proud to have a hero of Jutland as our captain, sir.' Stevens nearly bowed.

'There aren't any heroes,' he told the young man, rather sharply, 'just ordinary men who did the best they could.'

'Yes, sir. I'm sure you're right, sir. I was too young to join in the fighting, sir.'

'Be grateful you were.' Bill smiled to soften his rejection of the boy's praise. 'It was damned dangerous.'

190

Stevens relaxed a little, then smiled back. 'So I've heard.'

His tour of the ship was thorough and Bill was impressed, but the vessel still seemed soulless to him.

The time for sailing came and Bill stood on the bridge, his attention focused on getting the ship safely out of harbour and on to the high seas, where she belonged. As she was new, they were going to spend two weeks cruising and testing all the equipment. Then they would be given their sailing orders. He was already aware it was to be an exercise in diplomacy, showing the flag, but he didn't know the countries they would visit.

Once they were well away from land, Bill stood with his feet apart, felt the ship roll beneath him, and was surprised to find himself enjoying the sensation.

He began to relax, and his mind drifted back to when the petty officer had called him a hero. What a joke! But he wasn't laughing. He had survived Jutland, and put it out of his mind, as horrendous as the battle had been. The thing that haunted him was when they had been steaming to catch up with a convoy and escort it home. They had never reached it. That day the North Atlantic had claimed many lives and blighted many more. However, Bill was determined not to be one of the damaged ones, like some of the poor devils he had seen who had returned from the trenches, mutilated in body and mind.

He left the bridge and walked to the stern of the ship, watching the churning sea as they sped through the dark waters. Then he made himself gaze down into the depths, as he had done in the lifeboat, and he remembered the friends who had sunk beneath the waves, never to return.

Gradually the burden of guilt lifted. He had done everything he could to save his men. It hadn't been his fault that the enemy had been waiting for them, or that rescue had been so long in arriving. He saw at last that he wasn't responsible for their deaths. It had been the bloody war.

He knew then that he had done the right thing in coming back to sea. Only by facing his fears and guilt would he be able to exorcize them. When he returned home this time he would be a whole man. And maybe he would see Rose again.

A slight smile touched his lips as he thought of the dark-eyed beauty. She was touchy, defensive and proud, and she would be difficult to handle. The grin spread. His calm approach to life infuriated her but she had a lot of growing up to do and he had patience. He already knew he wanted to be part of her life, but he wasn't sure how he would achieve that. At times she appeared completely self-contained, not needing anyone, but he knew that was only the image she presented to others. Her love for her family and her friendship with John and Grace told another story. But it would be a challenge to find the girl beneath the carapace she showed the world.

When Rose arrived home the following Friday evening, her mother was sitting in the scullery talking to a stranger. 'This is Mr Pearce, Rose. He's come about the room.'

Rose studied the man, who was scrambling to his feet. He was in his forties, she guessed, though it was hard to tell: so many boys had gone to war and come back old men. He was of average height and stocky build, but he looked clean and respectable. 'Have you seen the room, Mr Pearce?' she asked politely.

'Yes, and it would suit very well.' He paused, looking slightly uncomfortable. 'That's if you'd take me, of course.'

Rose sat down, and saw that Mr Pearce didn't take his seat until both she and her mother had done so. He was polite, which was another thing in his favour.

'Were you in the army?' She handed him the sugar for his tea.

'Yes, I was just under the conscription age limit.'

'That was a pity.'

He smiled, but not with his eyes. 'That's what I thought when I found myself up to my knees in mud.'

Rose's answering smile was sympathetic. 'And why do you need lodgings?'

'My home is in Kent, but I've managed to find a clerical post at the commercial docks.'

Rose's suspicious nature showed itself. 'If you've got such a good position, why do you want to live here?' she asked. 'Garrett Street's a rough place.'

'Oh, I'm not worried about that.' This time his eyes shone with amusement. 'I grew up in Lambeth, so I'll feel quite at home.'

'Maybe so,' she persisted, 'but you could surely afford something better.'

'I'll be earning a respectable wage, but I need to send money home each week. My old mother is living with my sister in Kent and I have to help support them. My sister lost her young man in the war and she won't marry now.'

That explained why he had come to them for a room.

He seemed to be a man who cared for his family, and what he said about his sister remaining unwed rang true. There were many more women than men now, and a lot would remain single. That meant women would need careers.

Rose caught her mother's questioning look, and gave a slight nod. He would do.

On Monday Rose returned to the university. Mr Pearce had moved in immediately, seeming delighted with the arrangement. He had paid her mother two weeks in advance.

'Ah, you're back,' Angelina said, as she came into their room. There was a strange look on her face, as if she was bursting with curiosity. 'Someone's been asking for you.'

'Oh?'

'Sir George Gresham.' Angelina delivered the name as if she was talking about the Archangel Gabriel.

Rose almost laughed. If only she knew. 'Really?'

'Yes.' Angelina looked at her speculatively. 'What would he want with you?'

Rose shrugged. 'Who knows?'

'He's waiting for you in the library.'

Rose continued to collect her papers for the first class of the day.

'Did you hear me?' Angelina persisted. 'He wants to see you.'

'Well, he'll have to wait. I'm not going to be late for my class.'

'Wait?' Angelina squeaked. 'You don't keep someone like Sir George waiting!'

'Why not?'

'Because – because you don't,' the girl stuttered.

'Then it will be a new experience for him, won't it?' Rose gave a grim smile and left the room.

Angelina fell into step beside her. 'Are you frightened of *anyone*?'

'I don't think so. Should I be?'

'Most people are careful around Sir George Gresham. He's a powerful man.'

Rose came to a sudden halt. 'Rank doesn't impress me. He was born the same way as us, and it's what a person is that brings respect, or otherwise. From what I've seen of Sir George, there's little to respect about him.'

'You're a strange one, Rose.' There was a note of grudging admiration in Angelina's voice. 'You come from the slums, but you don't seem ashamed of it, and you have strong views about life and justice and equality.'

'Not all the people who live in squalor and poverty are idiots.' Rose glared at her. 'They have feelings, hopes, fears and dreams, just like anyone else, but most of them drift into apathy because of their constant struggle to stay alive. They're exploited as cheap labour, and considered only half human by the affluent classes. They're locked in a cage, and there doesn't seem to be a way of escape.' She started to walk again.

'But you're going to get out, aren't you?'

'I'm picking at the bars, and education will free me.' Rose reached the room, opened the door, and walked in to take her seat.

Harriet was already there, tucked into a corner at the back of the lecture room. Rose walked up to her, took her arm and towed her further down. They were now about six rows from the front. The seats were arranged in a semicircle and it was rather like a theatre.

'I was all right there,' Harriet whispered.

'No, you weren't.' Rose smiled encouragingly. 'You'll hear better down here. This is going to be interesting. It's about famous court cases.'

The lecturer walked in, stopped and looked at the students. His eyes rested on the three girls. 'You can't sit there. Move to the back,' he ordered.

Rose stood up at once, caught hold of Harriet and Angelina's arms and pulled them to the front row. She made them sit down, then smiled sweetly at the lecturer. She'd never seen this one before and was determined not to let him get the better of her. Just because they were women, she was not going to let them be pushed out of sight.

'I said the *back*.'

Rose smiled again. 'We can't sit there, sir. We're so excited about hearing your lecture that we don't want to miss a word.'

Angelina stifled a laugh, Harriet gasped and Rose kept smiling. She knew she'd hit the right note when he said, albeit grudgingly, 'Very well, you may stay there.'

As it turned out, he was very good and Rose enjoyed every minute of his talk.

They had finished classes for the day and Rose was making her way to the library when she met Sir George. She saw at once that he was furious.

'Where have you been?' he snapped. 'I sent a message for you to come and see me this morning, and I waited an hour. Didn't the girl tell you?'

'Yes, but I couldn't spare the time.'

He caught her arm and pulled her into an empty room, then kicked the door shut behind them. 'Don't be insolent, my girl! I'll have you expelled if I have any trouble with you.'

'And if *I* have any trouble with *you*, I'll go to the Board of Education and tell them what an unprincipled, immoral and thoroughly untrustworthy man you are.' She glanced at his hand around her arm, then gave him a withering look. 'Let go of me, or I'll scream the place down.'

He released her and stepped away. 'My God!' he muttered. 'You really do hate me, don't you?'

'Why does that surprise you? My mother was disgraced by you and took the only option available to her, which was to marry the first man who offered her help and shelter.'

'What happened between your mother and me was a long time ago. I'm sorry now that I was so unfeeling at the time, but you would be astounded at what the staff, especially the young girls, get up to to try and improve their position in life.'

Rose snorted inelegantly. 'So you seduce them then throw them on the streets. Oh, I feel so sorry for you.'

'Don't be sarcastic, girl.'

'Stop calling me girl,' she said tartly. 'My name is Rose.'

'You're going to have to learn to control that temper.'

He had a nerve to say that! 'Like you do, you mean?'

Amusement replaced anger. 'It doesn't matter with me. I'm a man.'

'Really?' She looked him up and down. 'Are you sure? I'd never have guessed it.'

A hint of a smile curled his lips. 'Oh, yes. And I was man enough to father a fiery child like you.'

Rose didn't like the way this encounter was going. The last thing she wanted was for him to think he had any claim on her. 'It's a shame you didn't think of that when you condemned my mother to a life of poverty in a place like Garrett Street.'

He looked shocked. 'Is that where you live?'

'Yes.' She cursed herself for giving away that piece of information – but he would never come across the river, she told herself. 'When you turned her out, my mother had the choice between that or the workhouse.'

'I'm sorry.'

He actually looked it, and that made her even angrier. 'Save your pity. We don't need it.' She looked at the clock in the corner of the room. 'I've got studying to do. What do you want, anyway?'

'My mother wants to see you.'

'What on earth for?' She was astonished.

'She likes you.'

Rose looked away. She had to admit that she had taken to the elderly lady, but she had made it clear that she didn't want anything to do with the Gresham family. She looked back at Sir George. 'No.'

'She hasn't been well,' he went on, 'and your company would cheer her.'

'I'm sorry she's been ill – '

'Then come and see her, it would make her happy.' He gave her a searching look. 'You are so like her – in fact, you're the kind of grandchild she's always wanted.'

Rose bristled. 'I will not be thought of as her grandchild.'

Sir George held his hands up. 'I know you don't want to have anything to do with us, and I understand that, Rose, but my mother is old and she wants to see you.'

She chewed her bottom lip. Would it do any harm to humour an old lady?

'Just this once,' he persisted.

'I won't come to your house,' she told him firmly.

'My mother has a house in Bloomsbury. I'll take you there.'

'No, you won't, I'll go on my own. Give me the address.' She watched while he wrote it down, then took the piece of paper and slipped it into her pocket. 'Tell her I'll be there tomorrow evening after lectures.'

'Thank you.' He gave a brief smile, then opened the door and walked away.

Rose watched him go, angry with herself for giving in. She must be mad.

19

December 1919

'Come in, miss. Her ladyship is expecting you.'

Rose followed the footman, and gasped as she saw the hall. It was bigger than her whole house. It had electric light and the huge chandelier was breathtaking, sparkling with a rainbow of colours. The walls were covered with red and gold wallpaper. She had never seen anything so beautiful.

'Miss Webster,' the footman announced, then stepped aside to let her enter the drawing room.

If she had thought the entrance elegant, there was only one word to describe the room she had just stepped into: sumptuous. It was like entering another world, and for Rose, of course, it was. She had known the ruling classes lived in comfort but she was dumbstruck by the colour and beauty of her surroundings.

'Thank you for coming, Rose.' Lady Gresham beckoned to her from her chair by the fireplace. 'Sit here, next to me.'

Rose eyed the chair doubtfully. It was covered in gold satin – or was it silk? It hadn't been made to sit on, surely?

Lady Gresham patted the seat. 'Come, my dear, let me look at you.'

Rose gave the chair another uncertain look, then sat down. It was remarkably comfortable. When she looked up the elderly lady was studying her. Then she remembered why she was there and became defensive again. 'I'm not going to make a habit of this!' she declared.

'Of course not,' Lady Gresham said mildly, 'but thank you for coming this evening.' She watched Rose run her hand lightly over the arm of the chair. 'Do you resent the fact that we have so much?' she asked intuitively.

'I don't think that's the right word. When I think of the differences in the way we live, I feel angry. It isn't right, and I find it hard to understand how a society like ours can allow such deep divisions to exist.'

'You think everyone should be equal?'

'I'm not that naïve, Lady Gresham. I know there have always been the upper and lower classes, and I expect in my lifetime there always will be, but everyone's entitled to a decent standard of living, surely.' She straightened and held Lady Gresham's gaze. 'I don't mean we want riches like this. The wealth of the ruling classes has been handed down over generations, and we don't expect to own anything like it.'

'What *do* you expect?' Lady Gresham quizzed gently.

'Clean living conditions, jobs that pay a decent wage so that we can feed our families, and not have to live in constant fear of being turned out on to the streets because we can't pay the rent.'

'Is that all?'

'All?' Rose was indignant. 'Only someone who's never had to worry where the next meal was coming from would ask a daft question like that!' She was getting into her stride now, her surroundings forgotten. 'We don't expect jam on our bread every day, or to be surrounded by silks and satins, but we do have the right to live with dignity.'

'I agree with you. So, what are you going to do about it?'

Rose was startled. John had asked her the same question the first time she had met him, and she still didn't know the answer. She sighed. 'I don't know.'

'But you are going to try?'

'Yes.' She looked into Lady Gresham's shrewd eyes and asked boldly, 'What are *you* going to do about it?'

'I do charity work for the poor – '

Rose cut her off with a sound of disgust. 'The people trapped in the slums don't want charity. They need to be educated, shown how to improve themselves.'

'You're very passionate about education, aren't you?'

'Yes! It's the key that opens some closed doors.'

'Will that answer all the problems?'

'No, of course not,' Rose said sadly. 'But I feel it's very important for everyone to have a good education.' She leaned forward, the fervour of her speech showing how much she cared. 'Do you know what dirt, hunger and violence do to you?'

Lady Gresham shook her head.

'They grind you down until nothing seems worth bothering about. What's the use of applying for a better job when no one will employ you because you can't read or write?' She thumped the arm of the chair. 'They were good enough to die in the war, for heaven's sake!'

Rose stood up and started to prowl around the room, not seeing the expensive furniture, the exquisite pieces of porcelain, or the luxurious rugs. The bright light from the electric lamps was spilling out of the window, piercing the darkness with fingers of yellow, and she glimpsed well-tended gardens that stretched away into the distance.

'Have you seen those poor mutilated men standing on nearly every street corner begging?' Lady Gresham asked quietly.

'How could I miss them? They fought for their country and now they've been abandoned. Someone ought to help them.'

'I've set up a refuge in Mile End for them.'

'Oh?' Rose spun round, suddenly alert again. 'How many can you help?'

'About twenty-five.'

'It isn't enough. There are hundreds.'

'I know and I'm looking for a larger property, but in the meantime we can house twenty-five and feed about fifty a day.' Lady Gresham paused. 'Some of us do care, Rose.'

Rose turned to look out of the window again. She had misjudged this elegant, softly spoken lady. 'Is your son helping?' she asked.

'He's humouring me by trying to find another building for us,' she sighed, 'but I'm afraid he thinks it isn't any of our business, and that the authorities should deal with the problem.'

'But they don't, do they? They live in another world and haven't the slightest notion of what needs doing.' Rose came back and sat down again. 'How old are you?'

'Seventy.'

'That's a good age, but most people who live across the river never see fifty-five.'

'I know, my dear, but things must improve. The first step has already been taken by giving women the vote.'

'Thirty and over!' Rose grimaced in disgust.

'It's a start, and Lady Astor has taken her seat in Parliament. Change won't come overnight, you know.'

'I know.' Rose had given vent to her frustrations and felt better for it, but hearing what Lady Gresham was trying to do for the war wounded had burst her bubble of self-righteous indignation. 'I'm impatient,' she said, with a wry smile.

Lady Gresham laughed. 'It's a family trait.'

Rose grinned. She was feeling a little uncomfortable about her outburst. Who was she to lecture this wise woman on the injustices of society? 'I'm sorry. You didn't ask me here to listen to me rant on about the downtrodden masses.'

'You're wrong. That's exactly why I asked you to visit me. I now have some idea what kind of a person you have grown into.'

'An intolerant, angry one.' Rose gave a self-deprecating laugh. 'Do you know what they call me in Garrett Street?'

'No.'

'That black-eyed bitch. Pardon my language.'

Lady Gresham laughed, her eyes crinkling at the corners. 'I've been called worse in my time.' Then she became serious again. 'You admit you're angry, and that is obvious to anyone who talks with you for a while, but anger, when controlled and used properly, is a useful tool. However, you must be careful not to let it overwhelm you so that it clouds your judgement. You must be its master, and never let it run unchecked.'

Rose recognized some of her own passion glinting in Lady Gresham's dark eyes, and regarded her with new respect. 'Are you speaking from experience?'

'Yes. I caused a lot of upset and grief until I learned that lesson, but eventually I managed to turn my volatile temperament into useful channels.'

At that moment the door opened and Sir George strode in. 'Ah, she came.'

Rose was instantly on her feet, but Lady Gresham caught hold of her arm. 'What are you doing here, George? I don't remember inviting you.'

'I just came to see if she'd kept her word.'

'Her name is Rose, in case you've forgotten,' his mother reprimanded him, 'and of course she kept her word.'

He smiled, not a bit put out by his mother's sharp tongue. 'Good. I'll stay for dinner.'

'No, you won't, George. Rose and I are going to have a quiet meal together. We have a lot to discuss.'

He looked at them suspiciously. 'What are you up to?'

'We are merely getting to know each other. By your callous action all those years ago, you have deprived me of watching my granddaughter grow into a fine young woman, and I find that hard to forgive.'

He shrugged and walked towards the door. Then he stopped. 'Oh, by the way, I've found you the ideal property for your charitable scheme. It's down by the docks.'

When he'd gone Lady Gresham stood up. 'My son is an astute businessman, and it's only because of his careful management that I am able to help a few of these unfortunate men. Now, Rose, will you keep an old lady company over dinner?'

What could she say? It would have been churlish to refuse – and, anyway, much to her surprise, she was enjoying herself.

*

Rose surveyed the array of silver cutlery before her with a flutter of panic. What was it Grace had said? You start from the outside . . . or . . . was it the inside? She had thought at the time that it was useless information she would never need, but now she wished she had paid more attention.

'Sit down, Rose.' Lady Gresham took her place at the head of the table and a servant held out a chair for her, next to his mistress.

As each dish was served, Rose watched carefully to see what Lady Gresham did, then copied her. She quickly cottoned on that you started from the outside and worked your way in, and it was easy enough until she was faced with a strange-looking knife. If it was a knife. When the next dish was placed in front of her, she didn't know what it was. She gave a little sniff and decided it must be fish, but it was nothing like the fish she was used to – it didn't have batter on it.

'Try it. I think you'll like it.'

Lady Gresham hadn't picked up her cutlery for this dish, so she decided it must be the funny-shaped things because they were next in line. She held up the knife. 'Is it this one?'

'Yes.'

When she took the first bite a host of new flavours burst in her mouth. 'Oh, I've never tasted anything like this.'

'I knew you'd like it.'

Rose pushed away her quickly cleared plate. When the next dish arrived, she couldn't take her eyes off it. 'What's that?' she whispered.

'You'll see.' Lady Gresham looked as if she was enjoying the experience as much as her guest was.

A servant in splendid dark green livery started to carve, and she saw that it was a huge joint of beef covered with pastry. The smell and look of the succulent meat made Rose's mouth water. She watched as a large slice was put on to a plate, but before he served it to her, the man looked up. 'Would you like another slice, miss?'

'Yes, please.'

The whole meal was a revelation, and by the time they arrived at the pudding, she was glad she had only had small portions of the previous courses. She had lost count of how many different dishes they'd had. They finished with coffee in the drawing room, and that was a treat too – they only ever had tea at home.

'Did you enjoy the meal?' Lady Gresham asked.

'Oh, yes, Lady Gresham.' She grinned. 'I didn't know what some of it was, though.'

'There is no need to be so formal. You can call me Grandmother.'

Rose put her cup down with a clatter. 'I can't do that! I've only just met you and, anyway, it would cause a scandal.'

'I have survived worse,' Lady Gresham told her.

'No.' Rose shook her head vigorously.

'Why not?' Lady Gresham was unable to hide her disappointment.

'Because my mother will be upset. You might not mind the scandal, but she will. She's always kept this a secret and I won't have her shamed.'

'Of course, it was selfish of me not to think of that.'

She sighed. 'I'm afraid I speak my mind without thinking of the consequences.'

Rose drained her cup and stood up, alarmed now. 'I shouldn't have come tonight.'

'Please don't leave. Trust me, my dear, I will never do anything to harm you or your mother. If you don't want your connection with us to be known, I won't say a word to anyone.'

Strangely, Rose believed her and, with her suspicious nature, that was quite something. But she knew instinctively she could trust Lady Gresham.

'Are you ashamed of your parentage, Rose? You may speak frankly, my dear.'

Rose took a deep breath. 'Of course I am.'

'Even though you are connected to a noble family?'

'That doesn't make any difference. That your son is of high rank only makes things worse. If he had seduced one of his own, that would have been different, but he took advantage of an innocent servant girl.' Rose paused briefly. 'In my eyes that makes him lower than the tramp in the gutter.'

Rose saw Lady Gresham flinch, but carried on. She had asked for frankness, and she was going to get it. 'The fact that I'm a bastard doesn't worry me.' She gave a resigned shrug. 'That's just the way things are, but I'm ashamed to be your son's daughter. As far as I'm concerned, he's a cruel, selfish, unfeeling man, and no matter how high he is in society, I could never like or respect him.'

'And do you hate me, child?' Lady Gresham's voice cracked.

'You're a nice person, and I don't hold you responsible

for your son's behaviour . . .' Rose hesitated, hating to hurt her, but she couldn't let this family think they might interfere in her or her mother's life. 'But I don't think we should meet again.'

Lady Gresham nodded sadly, reached across to a small table, picked up something and handed it to Rose. 'I would like you to have this.'

It was a delicate miniature painting, set in a gold mount studded with gems. The picture was of a young girl with blue-black hair and large dark eyes. The resemblance to herself was remarkable. 'I can't take this,' Rose gasped. 'It must be worth a fortune!'

'I want you to have it.' There was a pleading note in Lady Gresham's voice.

'Is it you?'

'Yes, and if you won't do me the honour of letting me acknowledge you as my granddaughter, then at least take that so you won't forget me.'

Do her the honour? What was she talking about? Where was the honour of having a granddaughter born on the wrong side of the blanket?

Rose handed it back. 'I'm sorry, but this is far too valuable for me to accept. I'd worry about losing it – and it belongs to the Gresham family, not me.'

There was silence for a moment, then Lady Gresham took the miniature and placed it on the table again. 'I'll keep it in trust for you.'

Rose didn't know what that meant, but she was relieved she'd had the sense to refuse the gift. Just think what Sir George would have thought if he had seen her with it – he'd have jumped to the conclusion that she'd stolen it.

Lady Gresham picked up a silver frame, removed a

photograph from it, then handed the picture to her. 'If you won't accept anything of value from me, will you take this photograph? It would make me happy for you to have it,' she added gently.

The picture made Rose smile. It was of a young, carefree Lady Gresham, standing in a cornfield. 'Thank you, I'd like to have this.'

The old woman stood up and kissed her cheek. 'You have made me very happy by coming here tonight, and I have enjoyed our talk. I'm proud to have found such an intelligent, lively member of the Gresham family.'

'I'm not a member of your family,' Rose said firmly, 'and I will not accept your son as my father. He's a stranger to me.' She held out her hand. 'Goodbye, Lady Gresham.'

As she left the room she heard the old lady whisper, 'You may deny it all you like, Rose Webster, but you are a Gresham.'

20

'It's bloody freezing out there.' Angelina tumbled into the small room clutching several packages. 'And it's not much warmer in here. You'd think the university could provide us with a fire, or something. Thank goodness I'm going home for the Christmas holidays.'

Rose looked up from her packing in amazement. Angelina had sworn. After one term the girl had changed a lot; the haughtiness had almost disappeared, and the three now got on well together.

Then Harriet appeared and collapsed on to her bed with a groan. 'I'm worn out, but I think I've managed to find all the presents.'

'What on earth have you two been buying?' Rose asked.

Angelina pulled a garment out of a box and held it up for the others to see. It was dark blue velvet with gold embroidery around the low neck, obviously the latest fashion.

'That's beautiful,' Rose told her, without a trace of envy. 'Let's see what it looks like on you.'

'Yes, do put it on.' Harriet had jumped off the bed to get a better look. 'Where are you going to wear that?'

'Daddy has to go to a big party and he wants me to accompany him.' Angelina undressed hastily in the cold room and slipped the dress over her head.

'He'll be proud of you in that,' Rose told her, then

turned to Harriet, who was no longer so frightened of other people. She still harboured the opinion that she was not as clever as everyone else, but Rose intended to change that. 'Have you bought yourself a new frock too?'

'Yes, but not as grand as Angel's.' She showed them a pale green dress with a delicate lace insert at the neck and more lace around the short sleeves.

Rose took hold of it and held it up against Harriet. 'That will suit you beautifully. You've made an excellent choice.'

Angelina agreed.

Harriet smiled at the compliments, but then she became serious. 'I'm not sure I'm coming back next term. I don't think I'm good enough.'

'Of course you are.' Rose folded her one decent frock carefully and put it into her bag. 'You'll feel better when you've had a holiday.'

'No, I won't. I'm just not clever enough.'

'Don't be daft, Harriet.' Rose laughed. 'It isn't that difficult.'

'You might not think so – you're cleverer than most of the boys – but I'm finding it a struggle to keep up.'

'You're doing all right.' Angelina tossed some books on to a shelf. 'That lot can stay until we come back. I'm going to make sure this is the best Christmas I've ever had. I've earned it. And we shall expect to see you again, Harriet. You're as clever as anyone else.'

Angelina had changed too, Rose thought. Without the snooty veneer, she was a nice girl.

'Isn't that right, Rose?'

'You're brighter than some of the boys,' Rose agreed.

'Ooh, don't let them hear you say that.' Harriet

giggled. 'They don't like us being here and you've made them hopping mad, Rose.'

'Have I?' Rose feigned surprise.

The girls roared with laughter. 'She doesn't even know!' Angelina gasped.

Rose put her hands on her hips and grinned. 'What should I know?'

'Well . . .' Harriet tried to compose herself. 'You've got more brains than them, you're stronger and you don't take any notice of their nasty remarks – '

'Or their amorous advances,' Angelina interrupted. 'Though, come to think of it, not many of them are brave enough to tangle with Rose.'

'You make me sound like an ogre.'

The girls broke into another fit of the giggles.

Rose held up her hands. 'All right, I admit I'm difficult.'

Angelina began to roll around on her bed, thumping the pillow in glee. '*Difficult* is hardly the word I'd use. I'll never forget the look on Bradshaw's face when you threatened to flatten him if he didn't stop following you around. I've never seen anyone scuttle for safety as quickly as he did.'

'Yes, well, he asked for that.' Rose joined in the laughter. Once some of the boys had accepted their presence at the university, they had become quite friendly. Too friendly in some cases.

'And what about that time old Harrison refused to let us into his lecture.' Angelina turned to Harriet. 'Do you remember?'

'I do. What's that expression you use, Rose?'

Rose shrugged, warmed by the camaraderie that existed between them now.

213

'I remember.' Harriet had another fit of the giggles. 'You were "madder than a wet hen".'

'Oh, yes, I must remember to tell my family that one.' Angelina held her aching sides.

'By the time you'd finished with him, he looked as if he'd just gone five rounds with a prize-fighter.' Harriet looked at her admiringly. 'I don't know how we'd have got through the last few months without you.'

'Rubbish! You must both be pretty strong or you'd never have got this far.'

Harriet squared her shoulders. 'You're right. Perhaps I will come back next year.'

'You'd better,' Rose and Angelina chorused.

'Are you spending Christmas with your family?' Harriet asked Rose.

'Yes, Christmas Day and Boxing Day certainly, but the rest of the time I'll be working.'

'Working!'

'Don't look so horrified, Angelina. I'm nearly broke and I've got to earn enough to get me through next term.'

'It must be hard for you,' Harriet said gently.

'I'm used to it.' Rose gave them a bright smile to show them it didn't bother her, but in truth, it had been a nightmare trying to survive. If it hadn't been for Harold, she would never have been able to stay at university.

Angelina started to pack her bag. 'Who are you going to work for, Rose?'

'Professor Steadman's writing a book and I'm helping him with it. I've also managed to get a job in the grocer's where my sister works for a couple of days before Christmas.'

'Two jobs? But you need a rest as much as we do.'

'I'm all right, Harriet. I'm no stranger to hard work.'

'Good job you're strong.' Harriet picked up her bag. 'Well, I'm off. I'll see you next year.'

'Me too.' Angelina followed Harriet out.

Rose sighed. They were both looking forward to the holiday, but she couldn't say she was. She did feel as if she needed a rest, but she had to work.

Deep in thought she walked along the corridor and cannoned into a solid object. It was Sir George. 'What are you doing here?' she demanded.

'As gracious as ever, I see.'

Since her visit to Lady Gresham, she hadn't seen or heard anything from them, and that was the way she wanted it. She started to walk away.

'Wait!' he ordered.

She turned her head. 'Whatever you want, you're wasting your time.'

In a couple of quick strides he was in front of her, blocking her path. 'I want to ask a favour of you.'

'The answer's no.'

'Now, now, girl, don't be too hasty.'

'How many more times do I – '

He held his hand up in surrender. 'I'm sorry, Rose.'

She gave a grunt of satisfaction, then tried to elbow him aside, but he wouldn't budge. 'Will you please go away?'

'Not until I've asked the favour.'

Since she couldn't go on until he decided to let her, she growled, 'Make it quick, then.'

'Don't they teach you manners here?' he asked, raising an eyebrow in amusement.

'What do you want?' she snapped. 'I've got a bus to catch.'

'Will you visit my mother?'

Her hesitation was for the briefest of moments. 'No!'

'Rose, she likes you. Have a little compassion.'

'I haven't much time,' she told him, trying to ignore a prickle of conscience. 'I'm working all over the holiday.'

'Why?'

'Because I need the money,' she said, in a tone she might have used with an idiot.

'Why don't you let us help you?'

'I don't want your money,' she told him, with a sigh. 'I can manage without your help.'

'My God, you've got more pride than all the aristocracy put together.'

His words made her feel uncomfortable. What was it his mother had said? Ah, yes. 'Be the master of your anger.' Well, she certainly hadn't learned that lesson – *yet*.

'Try to find an hour or two to visit my mother,' he coaxed.

'Oh, all right – but I'm not promising anything.'

'Thank you. Just to know you're considering it will make her happy.'

She was shocked when he bent and kissed her cheek. 'Happy Christmas, Rose. We would have liked to give you a present, but we didn't think you would accept it.'

'You were right,' she said.

On the Saturday morning, Annie came up to Rose, a pleading look in her eyes. 'Can I come to the professor's with you, Rosie?'

'I don't know if he'd like that, Toots, and we'll be working on his book all day.'

'I know that, but I'll be very good, and I can make the tea.' She pulled a notebook from behind her back. 'You can work on his book and I can work on mine.'

'What are you writing?'

'It's a secret until I've finished it, but the professor can have a look, if he likes.' She looked up coyly from under long lashes.

Rose still couldn't deny Annie anything. And she was looking rather pale, so perhaps an outing would do her good.

'And who is this?'

'I'm Annie and Rose is my sister,' Annie told Harold Steadman proudly, 'and I won't be any trouble. Rosie takes me everywhere with her 'cos I'm good.'

The little devil, Rose thought, trying to keep a straight face. Perhaps she herself should take a leaf out of her sister's book: Annie was an expert at getting her own way.

'I see.' Harold stepped aside. 'In that case you had better come in out of the cold wind.'

The library he worked in was a mess, just as the office at the school had been when Rose had first met him. There were books overflowing from the shelves, and papers in great heaps all over the floor, chairs and windowsills – in fact anywhere there was a flat surface.

'Where shall I sit?' Annie whispered.

Rose noticed she was shivering with the cold, so she cleared a chair by the fire and put a small table in front of her so she could put her book and pencil on it. 'You all right, Annie?' she asked, frowning in concern.

'It was cold on the bus.'

Harold's housekeeper bustled in and smiled at Annie. Everyone smiled when they saw her, Rose thought.

'Would you like a nice hot drink?' the housekeeper asked, taking one of Annie's hands and chafing it gently.

'Yes, please.'

'A nice pot of tea for you and Rose, Professor?'

'Thank you, Mrs Stubbs, and some of your excellent fruit cake, if you please.'

'Certainly, sir.'

'Now, let's get down to work,' he said eagerly.

The time passed quickly and Rose was deep in concentration when Harold touched her arm. 'What is she doing?' He nodded towards Annie.

'Writing a story.'

'What's it about?'

'I don't know, she won't tell me.' She looked at Harold and raised her eyebrows. 'But I think she'd let you have a look.'

He winked. 'Very well. I'll read it at lunchtime.'

Rose had been working for about another hour when she heard a rasping sound. One look at her sister had her leaping to her feet. 'Annie!'

'What's wrong?' Harold looked concerned.

Rose picked Annie up, sat on the settee and cradled her in her arms. 'What's wrong, Toots?'

'I'm not feeling well, Rosie,' she croaked.

'Why didn't you tell me? I wouldn't have brought you out if I'd known.'

'I didn't feel too bad when we left home.' Annie closed her eyes and settled against her big sister. 'I'm sorry – I'm a nuisance.'

'You can't help being ill.' She smoothed the hair away from Annie's flushed face. 'I'll have to take her home.'

'Of course.' Harold felt Annie's brow and rang the bell for his housekeeper. 'She's burning up.'

'Whatever is the matter?' Mrs Stubbs rushed over to them.

'She has a fever,' Harold informed her. 'Will you get a blanket to put round her?'

'Want to go home, Rosie,' Annie moaned.

'You can both stay here. It's a long journey for Annie in that condition.'

'Home,' Annie said again.

'Thank you, but we'd better do as she wants.' Rose wrapped the child in the blanket the housekeeper had produced.

'All right, but I'm coming with you.' Harold started to put on his coat.

The journey was a nightmare and Rose had to admit that it was comforting to have Harold's help, but once she was on the last bus, she made him go back. He was not a young man and she didn't want to make him ill too. When they reached their stop, she carried Annie the rest of the way. She was not a baby any more and at eight was a heavy burden, but Rose didn't notice the strain: her concern for her precious sister overrode all other considerations.

With a sigh of relief she reached their house and took Annie straight up to her bed. By this time the child was almost delirious with the fever.

'What's the matter?' Their mother rushed into the room and gave a moan of despair. 'Oh, no! Is it influenza?'

'It looks like it.'

'But she never even got a sniffle when the house was full of it,' her mother said, wringing out a damp cloth to mop her daughter's face. 'Let's pray this isn't as bad as the last epidemic.'

Rose looked at Annie and worry gnawed at her. Even if this wasn't as bad, was Annie strong enough to survive? 'Where's Flo?' she asked.

'I'm here.' Flo came up to the bed and looked at Annie with a frown.

'I want you to go and fetch Dr Trenchard, Flo. You know where he lives.'

'I'll need the bus fare.'

Rose hadn't taken off her coat yet so she searched it, hoping she had enough money left to give her sister. When she found ten shillings, she realized that Harold must have slipped it into her pocket during the journey home and her heart went out to him: there would be enough to pay the doctor. It was much more than she had earned today, but she would make up the time as soon as she could.

She thrust twopence into Flo's hand, and pushed her out of the door. 'Hurry.'

It seemed an age before Rose heard heavy footsteps coming up the stairs, but in fact it was only about half an hour.

With a brief acknowledgement, Edward went straight to Annie. 'Hello, little one,' he said gently. 'What have you been up to?'

Annie didn't answer.

'Get me a bowl of cold water, Rose,' he ordered, 'and a large cloth. We must get this fever down quickly.'

They all worked on Annie until, finally, Edward stood

220

up. 'That's all we can do at the moment, Mrs Webster. Give her plenty to drink and sponge her down if she starts getting too hot again.' He took a vial out of his bag. 'Give her two drops of this every four hours until the fever breaks and I'll be back tomorrow to see how she is.'

'Thank you, Doctor. What's wrong with her?'

'It's influenza, I'm afraid, Mrs Webster.'

Marj's eyes filled with tears. 'I've lost two children already.'

He patted her shoulder kindly. 'You're not going to lose Annie. She's stronger than she looks.'

Rose knew he was trying to ease their fear, but she was terrified Annie would die.

She followed him downstairs. 'Thank you for coming, Edward. How much do I owe you?'

'Nothing,' he said firmly.

'But you must be paid.'

'Rose,' he said, 'I love that little girl as if she were my own and I won't take money from you. Do you remember what I said about learning to take as well as give?'

Rose nodded. 'All I seem to be doing lately is taking.'

'Good. You'll need all the help you can get until you graduate, and your friends are more than willing to support you.' He looked at her thoughtfully. 'Accept it graciously, Rose, because your day for giving will come.'

He was right, of course, but it was difficult – her pride kept getting in the way.

What a dreadful Christmas it had been. A tear trickled down Rose's face. The house had been hushed and they hadn't known if Annie was going to live or die – they still didn't. And, to add to their worries, they hadn't received any word from Bob since he had run away to sea. The little devil might at least have sent a note to say he was all right. Mr Pearce had gone home to his sister's for a few days, and her mother seemed to miss him.

A little hand touched her face. 'Don't cry, Rosie.'

'Annie!' It was the first time she had spoken since they'd come home from Harold's. 'Are you feeling better?'

She nodded. 'I've been a nuisance, haven't I?'

'No, Toots, never that,' Rose reassured her. 'Are you hungry?'

'Yes. Did I miss Christmas dinner?'

'I'm afraid so, but we've got some chicken stew. Would you like that?'

'Yes, please.'

Rose hurtled down the stairs and into the scullery. 'Annie's awake and she's hungry!'

'Oh, thank God.' Marj Webster wiped her eyes. 'I really thought we were going to lose her this time.'

Rose started to get the food ready. 'She's nice and cool now, and the dreadful cough has almost gone.'

'Is this good news I'm hearing?' Edward Trenchard had walked into the scullery.

'You go and have a look at her,' Rose said happily.

When she took the stew up, Edward was sitting on Annie's bed and the child was giggling.

'Is it all over?' Rose asked him, hardly able to believe her eyes. One minute her sister had looked like death, and now she was sitting up, smiling.

'The worst has passed, but you'll need to feed her well and keep her warm. In a few days you can let her get up for a couple of hours. But,' he gave Annie a stern look, 'you mustn't try to do too much, and you must listen to your sister.' He took the tray from Rose and picked up a spoon. 'And I'm not leaving until I see you eat all this.'

'I will,' Annie promised, and let him spoon the stew into her.

When the plate was empty, Edward turned his attention to Rose. 'You must get some rest now, you look worn out.'

Annie moved over in the bed. 'Rosie can sleep next to me.'

'Well? What are you waiting for?' Edward asked her.

With a yawn, she lay down beside her sister, and was instantly asleep.

21

'Happy New Year!'

It was good to hear laughter in the house. Rose sipped her beer and looked at the smiling faces. With Annie's recovery, 1920 had arrived on a tide of relief. Mr Pearce, or Wally, as her mother now called him, had arrived back from Kent yesterday, and had been determined that they should see the New Year in with music and laughter. He had pushed the furniture back in his room and produced an accordion, which he played with more enthusiasm than skill.

Good Lord, Rose thought as she watched the scene, I've had my nose stuck in books, and haven't noticed how they're all growing up. She studied each one in turn: Flo was sixteen, quite pretty and very sure of herself, Nancy at thirteen had not outgrown her timidity, and Will was twelve, growing into a handsome young man. There was a gap where Bert should have been. For a moment Rose's mind strayed back to the epidemic – what a dreadful time that had been. Nine-year-old Charlie laughed and she glanced at him with affection but then her gaze rested on Annie, who had always been her favourite, and at eight she was showing signs of becoming a real beauty. David would have been nearly six, had he lived.

How things had changed for them over the last few years. They were still living in this deplorable house, of course, but it was cleaner now and not quite so crowded. Her mother had more time and energy to look after the house and the children. Her mind drifted back to those awful times before the war – how had they survived?

A burst of singing brought Rose out of her reverie, and she slid down the wall until she was sitting on the floor and closed her eyes to listen. She wished she could forget the world outside for a while and relax, but however hard she tried, her brain would not let her rest. At such times she wondered if it was a blessing or a *curse* to have a mind like hers; there was always something churning through it.

The year ahead was going to be tough. Annie's illness had stopped Rose working and she had needed money to get through the next term. She couldn't ask her mother to help because despite Mr Pearce's presence in the house she had still had trouble in making ends meet.

More than a year after the Armistice, all the talk about a better life had come to nothing. After fighting and winning the war, everyone had expected improved pay and conditions, but things had slipped back into the old ways.

'You sing, Rosie.' Will jumped on her and tried to pull her to her feet.

'What?' she exclaimed in mock horror. 'You know I'm tone deaf.'

'That's right.' Flo giggled. 'We had a choir at school and the teacher always told her to stop singing. It was nice to know there was something she couldn't do.'

Rose remembered how much she'd wanted to be in the choir, but it was no use, she couldn't stay in tune. At least, that's what everyone told her, but her voice sounded all right to her.

'Oh, well, in that case, don't bother,' Will said, with a grimace.

'I think it's time for bed, anyway,' Marj Webster put in, 'but let's help Mr Pearce get his room straight first.'

The children had all been allowed to stay up as a special treat, but they were tired now and didn't make any bones about packing up. Annie was sleepy, but flushed with pleasure at being allowed to see in the New Year.

When the tidying was done and the children were in bed, Rose wandered into the scullery, too wound up to sleep. Wally stood up as soon as she came in, drained his cup and went out, leaving mother and daughter alone.

'Want a cup of tea?'

'Thanks, Mum.' She sat down. 'Wally didn't have to run away like that.'

'He was tired I expect. It was good to see everyone happy, wasn't it?'

Rose nodded, but didn't reply.

'Nancy leaves school in the spring, and she's already got a job,' Marj went on.

'Oh?'

'She's going to work in an orphanage. She's always liked children,' her mother added, stirring her tea thoughtfully. 'She's going to live in too, so that will be another flown the nest.'

Rose couldn't think of anything worse than looking after dozens of children. Still, her mother was right, it would suit Nancy.

'Er . . . Rose? Do you like Wally?'

'He seems to be a good sort, and he's turned out a respectable and reliable lodger.'

'Yes, he's a good man. We've been walking out, Rose.' Her mother hesitated. 'Do you mind?'

'Of course I don't. It's none of my business, and if you're happy, that's all that matters.'

'When Wally got back after Christmas he told me his sister has found herself a young man and is getting married, and her husband-to-be is willing to help support their mother, so that will take the worry away from him.'

'That must be a relief for him.' Rose waited, feeling that there was more to come.

'He's asked me to marry him.'

'And are you going to?'

Her mother nodded. 'I never had much of a life with the old man, as you know, but Wally's just the opposite, and I think we could be happy together.'

Rose looked at her mother in a new light. When she had been growing up, she had been disgusted by her mother's endless pregnancies, and by the way they lived. She had assumed Marj had been too weak to fight for something better, but she didn't believe that now: her mother had been trapped in a situation she tolerated only for the sake of her children. It had been this or the workhouse, and as horrible as this was, it was certainly better than that institution. For the first time Rose saw that her mother had done the best she could for her children in impossible circumstances, and was sorry she'd misjudged her.

She smiled. 'I hope you'll be happy, Mum, it's about time.' But it was a mystery to Rose why any woman would want to become a man's property. 'When are you going to wed?'

'In the summer. Nancy will have left by then and I

don't think Flo will stay much longer. That will only leave Annie, Charlie and Will, and they all like Wally.'

'The kids are nearly all off your hands.'

Her mother sighed. 'The house seems quiet when everyone's out.'

To Rose, marriage meant only one thing: squalling babies. 'You might have some more,' she remarked.

'No, my childbearing days are over, thank goodness.'

'I'll congratulate Wally in the morning.' Rose smiled, then asked, 'Does he know about me?'

'I've told him, but he doesn't know who your real father is. That's our secret, Rosie.'

The word 'secret' reminded her of something she hadn't told her mother. She took a deep breath. 'Mum, I've had dinner with Lady Gresham.'

'When was this?' Her mother frowned.

'Not long after I started at the university. She sent for me.'

'I hope they're not making trouble for you.'

'No, we just talked and I liked her,' Rose admitted.

'From what I remember of her, she was fierce but fair. Have you seen her again?' her mother asked.

'No.'

'What about your . . . Sir George?'

'I've had several arguments with him.' Rose pulled a face. 'What a self-opinionated ba– rogue he is!'

'Does that mean you've had a fight?'

Rose started to laugh. 'He said I've got an acid tongue, but it's no worse than his.'

'Do you like him?' her mother asked softly.

'Certainly not,' Rose said scornfully. 'And I'd never forgive myself if I used my connection with him to get ahead. I want to be able to look back in years to come and know I did it all on my own.'

'You've got the pride of the Greshams.'

'Maybe – but I'm not one of them and never will be!'

The next morning, Rose caught Wally before he left the house. 'Congratulations.' She held out her hand and he clasped it. 'Mum told me.'

He beamed. 'Thank you. I know how lucky I am and I'll do my best to make her happy.'

'I'm sure you will.'

'She's very proud of you, and says you're going to do great things in your life. I'm inclined to agree with her.'

'I don't know about that.' Rose laughed. 'Just because I can read Latin she thinks I'm a genius, but I hope to make a difference in some way.' She grew serious again. 'The country's in such a mess and I doubt one person can make any impact.'

'Maybe not, but if people band together they might be able to change things,' Wally said.

'Like the unions, you mean?'

'And the borough councils.'

'Hmm, they don't seem to do much except talk.'

'Don't be impatient, Rose. Even the working man resists change if it comes too rapidly.'

She grinned. 'I've already been told I'm too impatient, but sometimes I just want to shake some sense into people.' He glanced at his pocket watch. 'I'm sorry, I'm making you late.'

She watched him hurry up the street, relieved that her mother had someone to look after her now – and that

Annie was fit again. Heaven knows, Rose wasn't going to be much use to her family for a while.

She chewed her bottom lip. Could she survive on buns for a year?

She was making her way along the corridor to her room when Sir George caught up with her. 'You didn't go to see her!'

'See who?' Rose was a few yards from her room and could hear Harriet and Angelina talking inside. The door was ajar so she stopped.

'My mother, of course.' He was blazing mad. 'She was looking out for you all over the holiday.'

Rose's hand flew to her mouth. She had forgotten Lady Gresham.

'You never intended to go, did you?' he accused.

'Don't you shout at me!' she told him indignantly. 'I forgot because my sister's been ill. We thought she was going to die.'

'Oh.' The fury drained from his face. 'I'm sorry. Is she all right now?'

'Yes, thank heavens.'

'I'll explain why you didn't come. She'll understand.' He put his head on one side and studied her carefully. 'You look tired.'

'I am. Now,' she tried to dodge past him but he didn't move, 'I've only got an hour before my first class and I want to unpack my bag first.'

'Shall I tell my mother you'll call during the next few days?'

'No. I didn't make any promises before Christmas, and I'm not making them now.'

'The weekend, then,' he persisted. 'Would that suit you better?'

'Will you please go away?'

He ignored her. 'Why don't you bring your sister to see Mother? She loves children.'

Rose could have screamed in frustration. Would nothing shift him? 'Nobody knows about you, except me and my mother, and that's the way we want it to stay.'

'Ah, I see. We're a secret, are we?'

'Yes, you bloody well are, and if you don't stop coming here the whole university will soon work out who you are.'

'We're not ashamed of it, Rose. Are you?' he asked mildly.

'I'm your bastard child,' she hissed, through clenched teeth.

He shrugged his huge shoulders. 'That isn't so terrible.'

That did it! 'It is to me!'

She stormed away, leaving a trail of bad language. Just as she reached her room Sir George called, 'Dear me, Rose, even I don't know some of those.'

She wrenched open the door, swept inside and kicked it shut.

'Rose!' someone squeaked.

When she looked across the room, Harriet was sitting on her bed with her hands over her ears, her eyes wide with shock. Angelina was grinning.

Harriet lowered her hands. 'Have you finished?'

Rose nodded.

'Thank goodness for that. Where did you learn such appalling language?'

'Garrett Street. You ought to come there with me

some time, it would broaden your education,' she teased, her anger disappearing.

'I'd rather not.' Harriet gave her a speculative look. 'Who were you swearing at, anyway?'

'Someone who made me angry.'

Rose threw down her bag and started to unpack. Thank the Lord she hadn't been seen with Sir George.

Then it was time for their class. The three girls grabbed whatever books were within reach and hurtled out of the door.

22

Winter turned to spring, and spring to summer, before Rose could think of anything except studying and surviving. She felt drained. The grind of studying day and night during the week, working for Harold on Saturdays, then trying to improve her Latin with John on Sundays had taken its toll. Harold lived in Holborn, only a short bus ride from the university, but Rose went home on Friday nights, and although it wasn't more than twenty minutes from there, it still took up her time: the buses didn't always arrive when they should. Her weekends at home should have been for relaxing, but they were anything but. It was no good grousing, though, she'd known what she was letting herself in for – but it was taking more out of her than she'd expected.

She enjoyed the lectures at the university, and was pleased with what she had achieved so far. Her results had been good, but it wasn't easy. The male undergraduates had finally accepted her and the other girls and, on the whole, they were a nice lot. Angelina and Harriet enjoyed mixing with them now and often went out with a crowd to the pictures, but Rose didn't feel she could spare the time. She liked to spend any free moments in the huge library, or wandering around the beautiful building. The university had been established around 1836, and Rose especially liked the spacious entrance hall. The whole place was impressive and seemed to smell of books, and to Rose, nothing could have been nicer than that.

She sighed, rubbed her tired eyes and tried to concentrate on the typing Harold had given her today. Her fatigue had crept up on her, increasing gradually over the weeks, and she realized now that she should have gone out with Angelina and Harriet. With her punishing workload, it would have been sensible to spend an evening away from studying. It was a blessing that the summer term had finished, because her temper was even more volatile than usual. Most sensible people had learned to give her a wide berth.

Harold had been busy over the last week, if the amount of work he'd put in front her was anything to go by, and she typed until she could hardly see. She was relieved when she could go home.

She had to wait ages for the bus, and by the time she reached home she was exhausted and ill-tempered. So when she walked into the scullery and saw Bill sitting there, resplendent in his naval uniform, her composure deserted her.

Her bag hit the floor with a thud. 'What are you doing here?'

'Rose!' her mother said sharply. 'If you can't keep a civil tongue in your head, you can go back where you came from.'

Marj had never spoken to her like that before, but Rose was too tired to care. Without a word, she picked up her bag and started to walk out.

'*Nooo!*' Annie left Bill's side, caught Rose's arm and glared at her mother. 'Don't you shout at my Rosie, like that!' She stamped her foot and tears welled in her eyes.

'It's all right, Annie,' Rose told her wearily. 'I'll go back to my digs. I'm not fit company for anyone at the moment.'

'No, no! Mum, don't let her go! She won't ever come back again,' Annie cried in panic.

Tension made Rose feel as if she would snap in half and, much as she loved her sister, a fuss was the last thing she wanted. Through the haze of exhaustion, she realized she couldn't carry on like this.

Annie tugged again, but she ignored her and kept walking. She had to be alone.

Before she had reached the door, someone much stronger than Annie stopped her, and the bag was taken from her. 'There's no need for this,' Bill said gently. 'Come and sit down. You're worn out.'

Rose didn't protest. The fight had gone out of her, leaving her bewildered and disoriented. She allowed him to lead her back to the table and sit her down. A sigh escaped her.

Annie rushed to get her a cup of tea, but she never drank it. She rested her arms on the table, laid her head on them, and fell asleep.

Bill looked at the dark head and frowned. What the devil had happened to her? The girl he had last seen had been lively, bursting with enthusiasm, and eager to learn; he could hardly believe the change in her.

'I'm sorry she was rude,' Marj Webster apologized. 'She's often short-tempered, but I've never seen her like this.'

'She's tired.' Annie stroked her sister's hair. 'And she's broke too.'

'But she can't be, she gives me money each week,' said Marj.

'That's why she's broke, and hungry too.'

Marj Webster's eyes turned to her eldest daughter. 'I never knew,' she muttered, anguished.

Annie started to cry in heartbroken sobs. 'My Rosie's ill.'

'Shush, sweetheart,' Bill said, soothingly. 'You'll make yourself sick if you carry on like this.'

'Wally should look after Mum,' she sobbed. 'They're going to get married next week.'

'He can't, Annie, he's lost his job,' her mother said. 'That's why I had to take the money Rosie offered me. She said she could spare it.'

'Tell me what's been going on, Annie.' Bill listened to the little girl's disjointed story and was appalled. If it was all true, no one could manage such a punishing workload.

'I don't believe it!' Marj said. 'She told me she had some money saved up.'

'So you see,' Annie continued, ignoring her mother's outburst, 'she's all grown-up now, and if Mum turns her out she won't come back.' She hiccuped and tears streamed down her face. 'And I'll never see her again!'

Ah, that's the trouble, Bill realized. Annie was afraid of losing her beloved sister.

'Don't be silly, Annie,' her mother said.

'I'm not being silly!' She slipped off Bill's lap and sat on a chair beside Rose, who was still fast asleep, oblivious to the row raging around her. Annie laid her head on her arms in an exact copy of Rose's posture.

As he looked at the sisters, Bill swallowed the lump in his throat. 'How did things get so bad?'

Marj bristled. 'Begging your pardon, Captain Freeman, but I don't think this is any of your business.'

'All she cares about is Wally,' Annie muttered.

'Quiet, Annie!' her mother ordered. 'You don't know what you're talking about.'

'Don't shout! You'll wake Rosie up.'

'I'm sorry my girls have been so rude,' Marj Webster said abruptly. 'Thank you for bringing me news of my son. It was kind of you to take the trouble.'

Bill knew he had been dismissed, but he hesitated. Then he asked bluntly, 'Do you have enough money to feed your family, Mrs Webster?'

'I can look after my own, thank you.'

'Humph!' That was Annie again.

Bill's heart ached. He stooped and touched Annie's hand. Her fingers closed around his.

'Was Mrs Webster pleased with the news of her son?' Grace asked, when Bill arrived back.

'What?' He glanced at her, distracted.

'What's the matter, Bill?'

'I'm not sure, Grace.' He rubbed the back of his neck. 'Is John at home?'

'He's in the sitting room.' She followed him.

'Hello, Bill.' John folded his newspaper and put it on the table. 'You look troubled.'

'Have you seen Rose?' Bill sat down and stretched his long legs in front of him.

John nodded. 'She still comes every Sunday. Why?'

'How does she seem?'

'Oh, the same as usual, preoccupied with her studies.'

237

He looked at his friend thoughtfully. 'Why all the questions?'

Bill told them what had happened.

'Is she all right?' Grace asked, alarmed.

'I think so, but she's obviously at the end of her strength.' He sighed. 'She looked so vulnerable.'

'*Vulnerable?*' John exclaimed. 'I'd never use that word to describe Rose.'

'You would if you'd seen her today.' He told them what Annie had said.

'Well, Rose is used to managing on very little.' John looked doubtful. 'I wouldn't put too much faith in Annie's story, Bill. She adores Rose and isn't used to her being anything but strong and in control. To see her like that must have frightened her badly.'

'Anyway,' Grace put in, 'Harold pays her more than he should. It's his way of helping her through university because she won't take money from anyone without working for it.'

'That's right,' John said sadly. He removed his spectacles, polished them, then slid them back on to his nose. 'She'll let us teach and guide her, but that's all.'

This conversation was not easing Bill's worry. 'You say Harold pays her well, but what if she's giving most of the money to her mother?'

'She wouldn't need to do that,' Grace said. 'Her mother has a lodger and she's going to marry him next week.'

'He's lost his job.'

'What?' John was on his feet. 'Why didn't Rose tell us?'

'Too proud?' Bill asked wryly.

'When she comes tomorrow, you must make her tell you what's going on,' Grace told her husband.

'I'm not sure she'll come,' Bill told them.

'Oh, she'll come,' Grace and John said together. 'Nothing has ever kept her away.'

Rose surfaced sluggishly. Every limb ached and her mind was fuzzy as she hovered between sleep and waking. A candle was flickering, making patterns on the table, and she watched it, marvelling at the multitude of colours, red, orange, yellow . . .

'Rosie?' Her sister's voice penetrated through the mist, and she felt Annie's hand grasp hers.

'Rosie! Are you awake?' Her mother's voice now. She sat up and took a couple of deep breaths in an effort to clear her head. 'About time, too,' her mother scolded. 'You've been asleep for three hours. What have you been doing to get into this state?'

'Leave her alone, Mum. She isn't properly awake yet.'

Suddenly, the addle-headed feeling disappeared and Rose snapped back to full awareness. She had been looking after Annie ever since she'd been born, but now the roles were reversed. 'I'm awake, Toots.'

'Are you hungry?' Annie asked.

'Starving.'

Annie glared accusingly at her mother. She jumped off her chair, took a plate off the top of a saucepan of boiling water and put it in front of Rose. 'We've kept it hot for you,' Annie told her, 'and you must eat it all up.'

Rose looked at the mound of sausage and mash with amusement, remembering the many times she had sat beside Annie, coaxing her to eat.

Her sister watched every mouthful disappear until the plate was empty, then whipped it away and put a cup of tea in front of her. Rose drank it slowly and obediently.

'Now,' demanded her mother, 'tell me what's the matter.'

'Oh, Lord!' The memory rushed in. 'I was rude to Bill.'

'Yes, you were, and I was ashamed. Captain Freeman had kindly come to tell me that he'd met Bob in Australia.'

'Australia?'

Marj Webster nodded and Rose saw tears in her eyes. 'It seems Bob likes it so much there he's going to stay. We won't be seeing him again.'

'I'm glad he's happy,' Rose said.

'Bill said he looks fit and well. He's working on a sheep farm.'

'Bit different from here,' Rose remarked drily.

'Yes, and he was never happy in these crowded streets, was he?' Marj mused.

That was true enough, Rose thought, and was probably why he had been such a difficult child. She had rebelled by reading; he'd got into trouble all the time.

'And where did you think you were going when you started to walk out of here?' Her mother changed the subject. 'You frightened the life out of Annie.'

'I was feeling awful and you told me to go.'

'I didn't mean it – I was just putting you in your place because you'd been downright rude.'

'I'm sorry, Mum, I wasn't thinking straight. I'd wanted to get home so I could rest and when I saw him sitting there I was furious.' She grimaced. 'There's something about him that brings out the worst in me.'

'So I saw.'

'You're not going to leave us, are you, Rosie?' Annie appealed.

'No, of course not, Toots. I was so tired I didn't know what I was doing.' She smiled. 'And what are you doing still up?'

'She was terrified you were going to leave us and wouldn't let you out of her sight, so I thought it best to let her stay with you,' Marj said.

'I thought you might wake up and go away,' Annie gulped, 'and I'd never see you again.'

'Oh, Annie!' Rosie hugged her. 'I'd never leave you.'

'Annie said you'd been giving me money and going hungry yourself. Is that true?' Marj asked.

Rose looked at her young sister in astonishment. 'Where did you get that idea from?'

'Well, you only work one day a week, so you can't be getting much money, and I know you've been giving Mum some of it since Wally lost his job.'

Good heavens, Rose thought. Annie's eagle eyes missed nothing. She'd better explain.

'It's true I've been helping over the last two months, but I haven't been going hungry.' She stood up. 'Have I got any thinner?'

Annie examined her carefully, then shook her head.

'I've had to be careful,' she continued, 'but I've managed all right.'

'But you didn't look well when you came in,' Annie said, unconvinced. 'And you're never sick.'

'So you decided I was starving myself?'

Annie nodded.

Understandable, Rose thought. They'd all grown up not knowing where the next meal was coming from. 'I've been working very hard because I want to do well, and there are some exams coming up soon. I've been overdoing it, that's all.'

'Will you be able to have a rest now?' Annie looked reassured.

'I've got two weeks off and I intend to sleep and sleep.' She laughed. 'And it's Mum's wedding next week, so we'll have a lovely party, won't we?'

Annie nodded, then turned to her mother. 'I'm sorry I said nasty things to you, but I was frightened.'

'That's all right, Annie.' Her mother paused. 'I should have noticed how tired Rose was getting, but I've been so wrapped up in the wedding, and hoping Wally would find another job.'

'Has he got anything yet?' Rose asked, noting her mother's worried face.

'I'm afraid not. Now, I think it's time we all went to bed, don't you?'

Annie took hold of Rose's hand and pulled her towards the stairs. 'You'll feel better in the morning,' she told her.

'Rose?'

'Yes, Mum?'

'You'll apologise to Captain Freeman when you see him. He looked a bit upset, and I wouldn't like him to think badly of us. He's a nice man.'

Bill paced up and down anxiously, stopping every so often to look at the clock. 'I was right, wasn't I? She isn't going to come.'

'The bus might be late,' John told him. 'Ah, here's another.'

They watched as its passengers alighted and Bill sighed

with relief when he saw Rose. She looked much better.

Grace hurried to open the door. Annie rushed in, threw her arms around John then hurled herself at Bill. 'You look happy today,' he said.

'I am because my Rosie's better.' Then she whispered, 'She's going to apologize for being rude. Mum told her to.' She giggled then turned and waved a notebook at Grace. 'I've done my lesson, Auntie Grace.'

'Let's go into the kitchen and have a look at it, shall we?'

Annie nodded, then said to John, 'She mustn't work too hard, today. She's still tired.'

Bill saw Rose's eyes roll with exasperation.

But Annie hadn't finished. 'I was wrong about Rosie not eating,' she told Bill 'because if she hadn't had enough food she'd have got thin, and she hasn't, has she?'

'I don't think so.'

Annie spun away from him, took her sister's arm and pulled it away from her side. 'Show him, Rosie. Look, Uncle Bill, she isn't thin, is she?'

He managed to keep a straight face, as he ran his gaze deliberately over her figure. God! She was beautiful. He felt his body stir in response.

'Well, Uncle Bill, what do you think?' Annie's voice cut through his thoughts. 'She isn't thin, is she?'

He shook his head. 'No, she isn't,' he managed.

The little girl smiled with relief, then hurried away with Grace.

John was busy polishing some imaginary spot off his spectacle lens. 'Bill told us you were exhausted last night.'

'Ah, yes.' Rose faced Bill with evident reluctance. 'I must apologize.'

She turned aside, but he wasn't going to let her get away with that feeble attempt. 'Go on, then, I'm waiting.'

'What for?'

'Your apology.'

'You've just had it,' she said sharply, her black eyes snapping.

'Not a very gracious one.'

'I'm not a very gracious person.'

He sighed theatrically. 'Ah, well, I suppose I must be grateful for small mercies.' He sat in an armchair and picked up a newspaper.

'Is he staying?' she demanded.

He glanced over the top of the paper. 'You won't know I'm here,' he told her, lifting the paper to hide his grin. He had been desperately worried about her yesterday, and it was a blessed relief to see her back to normal again. But if this tigress thought she could order him around, or get the better of him, he had a surprise in store for her.

Rose sat down and opened her books.

As he listened Bill was fascinated. It wasn't long before, clearly, she had forgotten he was in the room, and he realized she had a brilliant mind. University was the right place for her.

As the afternoon went by a feeling of unease crept over him. He wanted her more than he'd ever wanted anything in his life, but if he had any sense he would run for his life. Otherwise he would have to wait until she had finished her studies – maybe longer. He could see only heartache and frustration in front of him.

He glanced at the dark head bowed over the books,

and knew, with a clarity that shocked him, that he would wait for her, whatever the cost.

It was too late. He was hopelessly in love with her.

23

It was a perfect August day for a wedding, there wasn't a cloud in the sky and a soft breeze kept the heat at bay, but Rose couldn't seem to get into the swing of it. Wally was nice enough, and her mother seemed happy, but Rose couldn't understand why she wanted to saddle herself with another man. The first had made her pregnant then thrown her out on the street; the second had been a drunken brute. How could she trust another?

Marj came into the scullery, smiling. 'I've got some good news. Wally's found a job. The pay's a bit less than he was getting, but we'll manage.'

A burden fell off Rose's shoulders. At least she wouldn't have to worry about her family when she returned to university next term. This would be the start of her second year, and it was hard to believe that the time had passed so quickly.

When they were ready to leave for the church, Rose handed her mother a single red rose to carry. Annie had tied a large golden bow to it and left the ends trailing down. It looked pretty against the simple navy dress Marj was wearing.

A lot of the neighbours had come, Rose noticed, as she looked around the church. Her mother had insisted on a 'proper' wedding ceremony, and they had all made an effort to dress smartly. Flo had brought her young man with her, Nancy had grown quite pretty over the last year, and Will and Charlie were at that lanky stage. Only Bob was missing. And Bert and David, of course. Rose knew her mother still grieved for them.

When the ceremony was over, she had to admit that her mother and Wally seemed very happy. In fact, she had never seen her mother look so young and attractive.

As they made their way out of the church, she was astonished to see Grace, John, Bill and Harold standing at the back. Annie, of course, was beside herself with delight and chattered excitedly to them.

Later, when the bride and groom were having their photograph taken, Grace handed Rose a large tin. 'A wedding cake for your mother and her husband.'

'Mum!' Annie called. 'Auntie Grace has made you a cake.'

Rose pulled a face as she watched her sister scamper away to tell everyone the good news. 'Your brother has a lot to answer for,' she remarked to John. 'If he hadn't fixed her tongue we might have a bit of peace now and again.'

He laughed. 'Now, Rose, you know you wouldn't have it any other way.'

'You're right, I wouldn't,' she admitted. Then she gasped as the whirlwind returned, nearly knocking the cake tin out of her hands.

'Come on, we're going to have our picture took.' Annie tugged at her arm.

Wally strode over, a huge smile on his face. 'We'd like you all to join us.'

Grace gave Annie a loving look. 'If our child is a girl, I hope she's like Annie.'

'Are you expecting?' Rose asked, not sure she had heard correctly.

'Yes, and we're delighted. I'm four months now.'

After the photos had been taken, Marj and Wally insisted that Rose's friends joined their modest celebrations. They accepted with alacrity, which surprised Rose: Harold had never seemed the sociable type.

When they got back to the house, Rose spread their one and only tablecloth on the table and placed the cake in the middle. It had real icing and 'Congratulations' written across the top. She could see that her mother and Wally were delighted with the thoughtful gift.

Neighbours started to crowd in and, as if by magic, the table filled up with food. Mrs Jenks had brought a jelly and a blancmange and someone else a plate of sausage rolls; then cockles, shrimps, bread and butter appeared. Rose began to remember the many occasions when everyone had rallied round to help one of their own in trouble. When a baby was born, or illness struck, or a woman was badly beaten, someone turned up to offer help and support. Everyone here lived from hand to mouth, but they all pulled together – as they were doing now.

The food was demolished, the cake cut, and Wally got out his accordion. The noise was deafening and it was too much for Rose, so she wandered outside. She'd never forgotten the factory, and ever since those days noise had made her ears ring.

'Phew!' Bill grinned at her. 'That's better.'

'Mmm. Is the racket too much for you too?'

'Yes. I'm more used to the wide ocean and the quiet of a night-watch.'

'Is it peaceful?' Rose asked, trying to picture what it would be like to sail on the sea with no land in sight. Were the stars brighter, she wondered, when you didn't have to peer through London smoke to see them?

'Mostly, but there are times when the wind roars and mountainous waves toss the ship around like a twig . . . and there's nothing to compare with the noise of someone shooting at you.' He shook his head. 'That's like nothing else on earth.'

'How did you become a captain?'

He leaned against the wall of the house, silent for a few moments. Then he started to explain. 'My father has been in the navy since he was a lad, and I was sent to naval college, expecting to follow in his footsteps, but I didn't like it. I had an almighty row with my father, left, and went to Oxford to study architecture. He never forgave me.'

'But you joined up when the war started?'

'There wasn't any choice. Because of my background, I was called on immediately.'

'They made you a captain straight away?'

'Good Lord, no! I started as a gunnery officer, but at the battle of Jutland our captain was killed. As I was the only officer still alive I took command. They promoted me after that.'

He spoke calmly as if it was of no importance, but Rose could hardly begin to imagine the horrors he must have faced. She'd heard terrible stories about Jutland.

'When do you go back again?' she asked.

'I've left the navy.'

'Oh!' Rose was surprised. 'What are you going to do?'

'I haven't decided yet. When the war started I took

some hurried exams and qualified as an architect.' He straightened up and took her arm. 'Let's go for a walk.'

She tried to pull away, but he held her firmly. 'We're going to walk, I'm not about to molest you.'

'I don't like being touched.' Ever since the rape she had had an aversion to any man coming too close to her.

'You make that very obvious, but I'd never do anything to upset you.'

He gave her his gentle smile and she believed him – but, still, she didn't like being so close to him. It made her edgy.

It was a lovely evening. The sun had started to sink over the horizon and the heat had gone out of the day. As they walked in companionable silence, she started to relax. She had been making a fuss about nothing again; she really must stop being so proud and bloody-minded. And it was downright stupid to panic every time a man came near her. It was time she got over that.

After about half an hour, Rose realized where they were heading, and stopped abruptly. She hadn't been near that place since the attack.

'This is far enough.' She pulled away from Bill and started to walk back the way they had come.

He caught up with her in two easy strides. 'They won't miss us.'

'Maybe not, but I'm not going in there!' The words were out before she could stop them.

'Why?'

'I don't like that park.'

'But it isn't even dark yet, and you'll be quite safe with me.' Bill was clearly puzzled. 'Is it me you don't trust?'

'I trust *you*.' And she knew she spoke the truth.

'Something unpleasant happened to you in there, perhaps?'

'No.'

'Then what is it that frightens you?'

'It's none of your business – and I'm not frightened.'

He sighed, took her arm again, and they walked back to the party.

John collapsed into his chair. 'I'm exhausted. They certainly know how to throw a party.'

Grace smiled. 'You enjoyed every minute of it.'

'I did.' His eyes crinkled at the corners. 'Did you see Rose's face when she spotted us at the church? She didn't know we were coming.'

Bill laughed. 'And she wasn't too happy about it either, but Annie made up for that.'

'She's such a sweet child.' Grace sighed. 'She was so happy today because Wally has found another job, and Rose won't have to give her mother any more money.'

'I bet she still does,' John said.

Bill was puzzled.

Seeing his expression, John leaned forward to explain: 'To Rose, money is a commodity to be used, and has no value to her beyond providing the necessities in life. If you gave her a hundred pounds she wouldn't want it.'

'Why?'

'Because it would be more than she needed.' John laughed. 'That's hard to grasp, isn't it?'

'I still don't understand.'

Grace joined in the conversation. 'Although she has grown up in poverty, money for its own sake doesn't interest her. It's merely a tool to be used to feed, house and clothe them, and I believe she would give anyone her last penny if she thought they needed it more than she did.'

'But she wants reforms – to see the slums knocked down,' Bill protested. 'Surely money will help to bring that about?'

'You're underestimating her intelligence and her understanding of the situation,' John remarked wryly. 'I've had long discussions with her on the subject, and she's convinced that no amount of money will bring about lasting change unless the people themselves want it.'

'Then how does she think it can be achieved?' Bill frowned.

'Through education.' Grace and John spoke together.

Bill sat back, deep in thought. Then he exhaled. 'My God, John, I've led a privileged life and have never really thought about these things, but I do believe she's right. The people we've been with today were enjoying themselves, making the best of a break from the usual worry and hardship, but I doubt they've ever made much effort to improve themselves.'

'Yes, but they're not content, merely resigned to their lot in life, and that is what Rose believes needs to be changed first – their attitude.'

'And did you notice the difference between her and the rest of them?' Grace added. 'She hates the place, and her discomfort is evident – she does not, and never will, accept that that is a fit way of life for anyone. If you can understand that, Bill, you might have an idea of what drives her.'

'She's a complex woman,' John told him, 'and underneath that aloof façade a fire is raging that she finds it difficult to control.'

'Good heavens, John,' Bill exclaimed, 'you make her sound terrifying.'

'She is, and the older she gets, the more formidable she becomes.' He gave his friend a sympathetic look. 'Don't get too fond of her, Bill.'

'Your warning comes too late.'

'I was afraid of that. What are you going to do?'

'I don't know. I'll have to sleep on it.'

But sleep was impossible. Images of Rose, smiling, then withdrawn, ran through his mind. And what had happened when they'd approached that scrubby little park? He was sure she'd been frightened of going in there, but why? He knew she'd had a tough life, but instead of grinding her down it had made her strong and determined. He was sure she wasn't as hard as she appeared on the surface. He'd seen the little gestures of tenderness towards her family and those who had helped her along the way, like Grace, John and Harold. He was positive that Rose Webster was capable of deep love.

Bill sighed and closed his eyes, willing himself to sleep. But how did you find the loving girl beneath the strong barriers she had erected around herself?

24

In October Rose was back at her studies, eager to start her second year. It had been good to see Angelina and Harriet again. Of course, she didn't have a lot in common with the two girls, who led very different lives from hers, but they got on well together. They tried to include her in their outings to the shops or the theatre, but Rose never went with them. She didn't have money to waste, and she didn't like frittering away her study time.

When she'd been unpacking this morning, the picture of Lady Gresham had fallen out of her Bible. Harriet had asked if she was a family member. Rose had said no, and quickly put it back in the book. However, the picture had reminded her that she hadn't been to see the old lady for some time, and she felt guilty.

She shook her head, dismissing the vexing subject from her mind, and settled down to read of how the Ancient Greeks had introduced the world's first democracy . . .

'Rose,' Harriet whispered, 'someone's left you a message.' She laid it on the open book, then left as quietly as she had arrived.

As soon as Rose saw the envelope, she knew who it was from. So they hadn't forgotten about her. She opened it.

My dearest Rose,

I am delighted to hear that you are doing extremely well with your studies. That makes me very proud. I know this because George has been keeping an eye on you, at my request.

I hope you will forgive this intrusion on your precious time, but you are constantly in my thoughts and prayers.

I don't suppose you have heard, but my grandson was killed in a motoring accident two months ago. Such a waste of a young life. I think the modern motor vehicle is an abomination, but the boy loved them. We are devastated. My son is taking it stoically, but I know he is grieving for his son.

I won't take up any more of your time, my dear, but this contact has brought me some comfort. You will always be welcome in my home.

With affection, Lavinia Gresham.

Loneliness and grief showed through every carefully penned word, and Rose felt ashamed of herself. It was a year since they had last met.

And Sir George, how must he be feeling? The loss of his son must be hard to bear. She remembered the only time she had ever met the boy: she hadn't liked him, but in the circumstances that was understandable. However, it was clear that his father and grandmother had loved him, and she was sorry he had died so young.

Rose had been touched by the letter, and it was on her mind all afternoon. As soon as lessons were finished for the day she went to Bloomsbury.

'Rose!' Lady Gresham rose to her feet, arms outstretched. 'I'm so happy to see you.'

'I got your letter,' she said. 'I'm sorry about your grandson.'

'Come and sit down, my dear.' She waited until her guest was seated, then turned to the footman still waiting in the doorway. 'We will have tea, if you please, Parsons. The blue china.'

'Certainly, my lady.' He left the room.

'Now, I want to hear all your news. How are you finding life at university?'

'It's hard work,' Rose told her honestly.

'Are you happy there?'

'Oh, yes! I still can't believe I've been given such a chance.' Rose spent some time telling her about the things they did and how she and the other girls had dealt with prejudice from the boys and some lecturers.

Rose was pleased to see Lady Gresham laugh: when she had arrived she had noticed how much older she looked.

When the tea arrived the china was so fine you could see the tea through it, and Rose couldn't help wondering why it didn't break as the hot liquid was poured into it. She was almost afraid to touch the fragile cup.

'Do you like it?' Lady Gresham asked, watching Rose examine it carefully.

'It's beautiful,' she remarked in awe. She had never seen anything so lovely.

'It was my grandmother's, and it's only brought out on special occasions.'

Rose looked up sharply. 'Am I intruding? Are you expecting someone else?'

'No, my dear, I thought you would appreciate something of such beauty.' She held out a plate of bread and butter. 'There's strawberry jam, and you must try a piece of Mrs Phipps's fruit cake – it is delicious.'

It certainly looked it, and Rose tucked into a hearty slice, but she noticed that Lady Gresham had only a cup of tea. 'You must eat,' she said. 'My little sister's always on at me because she thinks I don't eat properly.'

Lady Gresham took a thin slice of bread and butter. 'And is she right?'

'No.' Rose laughed. 'She's imagining things.'

'Tell me about your sister.'

By the time Rose had finished telling her about Annie, they were both crying with laughter.

'Oh, Rose.' Lady Gresham dabbed her eyes with a lace handkerchief. 'I would love to meet her. Would you bring her one day?'

'I couldn't do that,' Rose said, suddenly serious. 'She'd tell everyone.'

'Yes, of course. It was foolish of me to suggest it.'

Oh, damn! Rose thought. The old lady was lonely and now she had upset her. 'It isn't that.' She held up the delicate cup and pulled a face. 'I'd be scared to take my eyes off her.'

Lady Gresham brightened immediately.

Just then, the door swung open and Sir George strode into the room. He kissed his mother and turned to Rose. 'You two are having quite a party, if the laughter is anything to go by.'

Rose wasn't sure if he was cross or not until he smiled at her. She was shocked at the change in him. There was more than a sprinkling of grey hairs now, and deep shadows under his eyes. His son might have had many faults, but his father was grieving for him.

'I'm pleased to see you here,' he said. 'Thank you for coming.'

There wasn't the slightest doubt in Rose's mind that he meant it, which made her defensive. He had lost his son – would he try to make some claim on her? After all, neither Sir George nor his mother seemed ashamed that she had been born on the wrong side of the blanket.

'We will not interfere in your life, Rose,' Lady Gresham said softly, as if sensing her concern. 'All we ask is that you come to see us from time to time.'

She nodded. It was a reasonable request. She relaxed again, and looked up at Sir George – dark eyes meeting dark eyes. 'I'm sorry about your son.'

'Thank you.' He gave a faint smile. 'That is gracious of you, considering the way he treated you.'

'Just a young man having a lark.' There was no point, Rose thought, in holding a grudge against him now.

Sir George sat down and poured himself some tea. 'He had a reckless streak, I'm afraid, rather like myself at his age, but I grew up eventually.' He gazed at her and sighed. 'Not soon enough.'

'I'm sure your son would have turned into a fine man,' Rose said, hearing the pain in his voice.

He drank his tea and stood up. 'I'll stay for a couple of days, Mother.'

'Of course, dear.'

He gave them a courteous bow, then left the room.

Lady Gresham watched the door close behind him. 'This has hit him hard, and it also means the end of the Gresham line.'

'But he's still a relatively young man,' Rose protested. 'He could marry again and have other children.'

'He won't do that, even to produce an heir. He had a most unhappy marriage. After producing a son, his wife felt she had done her duty and refused to have more children. The kind of life she led after that was not . . . Well, she caused us much grief and shame.'

'I'm sorry,' Rose said. Was that why he had chased the maids? But it was none of her business. However, Lady Gresham had not finished.

'She was selfish and did not have a kind word for her husband, but she ruined the boy by leading him to believe that because he was from a titled family, he could do as he wished. George was never able to trust another woman.' She looked at Rose pointedly. 'The Greshams do not forgive easily when they have been wronged.'

That sounded familiar, Rose thought wryly. She seemed to have inherited a lot of the Gresham traits.

Soon after that, when she was about to leave, Sir George met her in the hall. 'Your company has done my mother good. Would you visit her again? When you have time, of course.'

'I can't make any promises, but I will try.' What else could she say? He had asked so humbly.

'Thank you, Rose.' Then he kissed her gently, turned away and walked up the elegant staircase.

She watched him. He looked like a man of sixty, yet he couldn't be much more than forty-five. He took each step as if it was an effort, and his body was slumped with dejection.

Rose didn't try to stop the stirring of pity within her.

Even their wealth and position could not protect them from heartache and tragedy. With a sigh she walked through the front door and heard the soft click as it closed behind her. She was going to have to be firm with them. She could not become a substitute for his lost son.

When Rose walked through the main door of the university, she saw Bill's tall figure leaning against a wall. She stopped in surprise, and he came over to her.

'There you are. I've been waiting for over an hour.'

'Really?' Her eyes flashed annoyance.

'Yes.' He slipped her hand through his arm and started towards the door. 'Come for a walk.'

'Wait a minute!' She dug in her heels. 'I don't want to go for a walk. And will you let go of me?' she hissed, casting a glance at a group of interested spectators, 'You're causing a scene.'

'Me?' he asked calmly. 'Are you sure you're accusing the right person?'

Infuriating man! She tugged at her hand, but his grip tightened.

'It's no good protesting, because you *are* coming for a walk with me, whether you like it or not.'

Determination was written all over his face, and she knew it would be useless to argue. 'All right!' she snapped. 'But only a little way.'

It was a pleasant evening and the street outside the university was crowded. Bill wandered along as if he had all the time in the world, but did not say a word.

'Where are we going?' she demanded. 'I've got work to do.'

'I only want half an hour of your time,' he said quietly. 'Is that too much to ask?'

Rose felt reproached. Why did anyone bother with her? All she did was snap at them – especially this man. She muttered an apology.

He bent his head. 'I didn't hear that?'

'Too bad. I'm not repeating it.'

He grinned and patted her hand. 'That's more like my Rose.'

'I am *not* your Rose!'

He started to whistle a popular song and kept walking.

They had left the crowds and were now almost in Russell Square. If he didn't turn round soon she'd be back at Lady Gresham's. He was in a strange mood, she realized, and it was driving her mad, but at least he'd stopped whistling.

'Why did you come tonight?' she asked.

'I wanted to see you before I went away.'

'Oh.' Something like disappointment ran through her, but she dismissed it. This was ridiculous. She didn't care if Bill Freeman stayed or went. 'Where are you going?'

'I've got a job with a firm of architects in Cambridge.'

'That's nice.'

'Hmm.'

'When are you going?'

'Tomorrow.'

'Is it a good job?'

'Yes . . .'

'You don't sound very happy about it.'

'I'm ecstatic!'

'That's good. I hope you'll enjoy it.'

'I expect I shall.'

She stopped suddenly. 'Can we go back now?'

He glanced around then pulled her into a shaded doorway.

'What are you doing?' She was alarmed.

'Shush, don't be frightened. I'm not going to hurt you.'

Panic coursed through her. This was a deserted area, and he was a strong man. 'Let me go!' she quavered, and was disgusted by her cowardice.

'I've got to have something to remember you by.' He lowered his head and gently touched his lips to hers.

A sound of distress escaped her. 'Don't!'

He ran his hand over her hair as if he was trying to pacify an animal. 'Just a kiss, Rose, that's all.'

She didn't believe him. No man would stop at a kiss.

When his lips touched hers again, she froze. Then he murmured comforting words, and claimed her lips more firmly.

She felt the soft warmth of his mouth on hers; felt the gentleness, and remained still. This was nothing like the brutality of the rape, and some of her fear seeped out of her.

There wasn't anything threatening about Bill's embrace. He slipped his arms around her, holding her against him, but not too tightly. Eventually, after what seemed an age, he released her and stepped away.

She stared at him, bewildered and confused. 'Why did you do that?'

'Damned if I know. Come on, I'll take you back.'

Once in her room, Rose was relieved to find herself alone. Her emotions were in turmoil and it wasn't a feeling she was used to, or liked. When Bill had pulled her into that doorway, panic had ripped through her, but it was as if he had sensed her fear. Although he had insisted on kissing her, there hadn't been any force, just gentle persuasion. Her mind replayed the kiss and she smiled.

It hadn't been too bad . . . in fact, it had felt quite pleasant.

Rose sat cross-legged on her bed thoughtfully. Still, it was a good job he was going away because she didn't want him making a habit of it. She wasn't like Angelina and Harriet – she didn't have time for this silly romance business.

25

At the end of her first week back they were given the results of their exams. Rose couldn't wait for Sunday afternoon to tell John and Grace of her success. She was doubly pleased to find Harold with them.

'Don't keep us in suspense,' Grace said, as soon as she arrived with Annie.

'I got top marks,' Rose told them, unable to suppress a chuckle of delight. 'Harriet and Angelina passed as well. We put some of the boys to shame.'

'Well done, Rose! We knew you could do it.'

John and Harold were beaming with pleasure, and Rose knew that without their help she would not have got this far.

'She has justified all our faith in her, hasn't she, John?' Harold was clearly overjoyed.

'More than that – I'm so proud I could burst!'

'Don't do that, Uncle John.' Annie giggled. 'You'd make an awful mess.'

At that point, Grace went out, and returned carrying a tray with glasses, a bottle of sherry and some lemonade. 'This calls for a celebration.'

'Hold on.' Rose laughed. 'It's a bit soon to celebrate. I've still got to get through another two years.'

Harold dismissed her caution. 'You'll manage.' Then he started to laugh. 'I can't wait to see you out there with all the men. They're going to think an earthquake has hit.'

'And I won't be the only one,' Rose said.

'My Rosie's going to be the best, though,' Annie told them proudly.

'She certainly is.' Grace smiled affectionately at her, and handed her a glass of lemonade.

Annie watched intently as Grace passed round the drinks. 'Auntie Grace is getting big, like Mummy did,' she whispered.

'She's expecting a baby, Toots.'

Her face puckered. 'Won't she want to see us any more?'

'Of course I will, Annie.' Grace had heard the remark and came over to them. 'What makes you think I won't?'

Annie looked uncertainly at her. 'Well, Mummy didn't have time for us when the new baby came.'

'I'll always have time for you, sweetheart,' she assured her, and planted a kiss on her cheek. 'You know a lot more about babies than I do so I'll need your help.'

Annie's face cleared and she beamed.

'Right!' John stood up. 'Let's drink a toast to Rose and wish her success in the future. Hard work and determination have got her this far, and those qualities will take her through to graduation.'

'To Rose,' they all cried.

'I'd like to make a toast now.' Rose held up her glass. 'To Grace, John and Harold, I'd never have made it to university without your help and belief in me. Thank you.'

She took a sip of the sherry and decided she didn't like it.

Later on, when Harold had gone home and Annie was in the kitchen with Grace, Rose asked casually, 'Have you heard from Bill?'

'We had a letter from him yesterday.'

'Does he like his new job?'

'He's only been there a few days but he said it's very interesting.'

'Good.' Rose couldn't understand why she was asking these questions – she didn't care what he was doing.

John was silent for a moment. Then he said. 'When I write back, shall I tell him about your exams?'

She shrugged. 'If you like, but I don't suppose he'll be interested.'

'Hmm. I'll tell him anyway, shall I?'

'If you want to.'

They settled down to work, and as usual the time flew by. John drew her out, made her search hard for answers and reasons for her thinking. Nothing was ever set out in a rigid schedule for study: she was free to break off and argue any point with which she didn't agree – and argue was the right word, because sometimes they disagreed strongly. But as heated as their discussions became, they were always good-tempered, and it gave her a wonderful sense of freedom to vent her feelings and opinions.

At the end of the allotted two hours, John closed the books and sat back.

'Time to go, Rosie.' Annie had come into the room. 'Auntie Grace says I can see the baby as soon as it's born. I hope she doesn't keep having babies like Mummy did.'

'I don't think she will, Toots.'

Annie was still in a thoughtful mood when they walked into the scullery and found their mother flushed with excitement.

'I've had a letter from Bob. A sailor friend of his brought it back with him. He says he's happy in Australia. There's so much open space and a lot of opportunities for someone willing to work hard.' Then she looked sad. 'He says he won't be coming back, but he'll try to send us a message now and again. I'm glad he's found somewhere he likes.'

It took Rose some time to go to sleep that night. Things were changing. Her mother was married again and appeared happy; Flo was getting married next summer; Nancy was living and working at the orphanage; the others were growing up fast. She drifted, half awake, half asleep, and muttered when the figure of a tall sailor came striding towards her, a baby in his arms.

Rose became so engrossed in her studies that she was surprised to find it was nearly Christmas. Where had the term gone?

Angelina and Harriet had already left to go home for the holidays, and she was packing a bag to do the same, when there was a knock at the door.

'Come in,' she called, then wished she hadn't when Sir George walked in. 'Oh. It's you.'

'I've come to ask you a favour,' he announced, without preamble. 'Before you go home would you visit my mother?'

'I really don't have time.'

'Please, Rose, she would like to see you – just for an hour.' He picked up her Bible, which was on the bed,

267

and began to turn the pages, pausing now and again to read the many passages she had underlined. 'You've read this right through.'

'I have,' she said curtly.

As she reached out to take it away from him, the photograph of his mother fell out. He picked it up and nodded to himself. 'You are remarkably like her. Have you seen the portrait of her when she was about your age?'

'She showed me a miniature – she even tried to give it to me but I wouldn't have it.'

'Ask her to show you the big painting next time you visit.'

Ah, Rose thought, we're back to that again. She continued packing her bag.

'I'll carry that for you.' Sir George reached out to lift it off the bed.

'I can carry it myself – and I'm not walking out of here with you!'

'Oh, yes,' he said drily, 'I'd forgotten – you're ashamed of me.'

Suddenly, she saw the funny side of it. 'That must be a new experience for you. Fancy a girl from the slums being ashamed to be seen with you, the great Sir George Gresham!'

'No, Rose,' he said quietly. 'I'm just an ordinary man who has made too many mistakes in his life. Mistakes he is sorry about and finds it is too late to put right.'

'Hmm.' He was behaving quite out of character. 'I'm afraid the humble act isn't fooling me.'

'Oh, damn,' he muttered. 'I thought it was quite an accomplished performance.'

Rose couldn't help smiling. 'Do you know? if you weren't such a bastard, I could almost like you.'

'You ought to watch your language.' He winced. 'If you're going to work as a solicitor you'll need to curb that colourful vocabulary.'

'Why?' she wanted to know.

'Because no one will employ you.'

Rose gave a satisfied smile. 'The people I intend to work for will.'

He stared at her for a few moments, then rubbed his temple wearily. 'I don't think I want to find out what you mean by that. I can make sure that you find a post with a prestigious law firm in the City.'

'You will do no such thing!' she blazed at him. 'I've already told you not to interfere in my life.'

He held his hands up in surrender. 'Forgive my presumption.'

'Oh, come on! This is me you're talking to, remember, not some gullible girl blinded by your aristocratic charm.'

He sat on her bed and folded his arms. 'Charm, Rose?'

'Get off my bed.'

Instead he made himself more comfortable. 'I don't understand you. You've a brilliant mind, I'm told, and are receiving a first-class education. You could climb the ladder of success and never look back.'

'I could,' she agreed, 'but that isn't what I intend to do with my education.'

'No, I suppose you've got it all mapped out, but I wish you'd let us help you.'

'You never give up, do you? We might have the same blood in our veins, but I will *never* . . .' she paused to let the word sink in ' . . . be able to think of you as anything

269

but the man who treated my mother disgracefully. That will always be between us.'

He looked sad.

'Your mother told me that the Greshams do not forgive when they have been wronged,' Rose went on steadily. 'Well, in that way, I am a Gresham.'

'It's what I deserve,' he said. 'But my mother had no part in it so will you come and see her – as a friend?'

'Tell her I'll come after Christmas, before the new term begins.'

'Thank you. That will make her happy.'

He smiled and picked up her bag. 'What time's your bus to Bermondsey?' he asked.

'Any minute now.' Rose took the bag from him, ran out of her room and down the corridor.

'Happy Christmas, Rose,' Sir George called after her.

It was Boxing Day and Rose and her mother were just clearing up after dinner when John walked into the scullery.

'John! What are you doing here? Is Grace all right?' Rose was filled with anxiety.

'She's well.' He took her hands and squeezed them affectionately. 'And so is our son! He was a couple of weeks early and took us by surprise, but he's a healthy baby.'

'Oh, congratulations, I'm so happy for you both.' And Rose was: she knew how much they had wanted this baby.

'Can we see him? Can we see Auntie Grace?' Annie was pulling on John's sleeve, and bouncing around like a demented rabbit.

'That's why I'm here. Would you like to come tomorrow morning? Then you can stay and have lunch with us?'

'Oh, yes, please!' Annie bounded over to Rose. 'Is that all right, Rosie?'

'Of course.' She put her hand on her sister's shoulder to quell her.

The baby was much admired – out of politeness by Rose, who couldn't find anything to enthuse about in a newborn baby – and Grace was the picture of health. They stayed with her for half an hour and then, when the baby needed to be fed, the three of them went downstairs for lunch.

They left at about two o'clock, but when their bus arrived Rose made no move to get on to it. Annie watched it disappear into the distance.

'That was our bus, why did you let it go?' Annie stamped her feet and rubbed her cold hands together.

'Would you like to visit someone else?' Rose cursed herself as soon as the words were out.

Annie brightened. 'Yes, *please*, Rosie. I like meeting your friends. Where do they live?'

'Bloomsbury.' Rose made for the other bus stop.

The bus took them over London Bridge, on to Holborn, and then Russell Square. She could see that Annie was bubbling with curiosity as they arrived at the imposing house.

'I've never been here before,' Annie exclaimed. 'It's ever so posh.' She gasped when Rose walked up the steps and knocked on the door. 'Who lives in this big house?'

'You'll see.'

They were shown into the hall, and Annie nearly toppled over when she craned her neck to look up at the ornate ceiling. 'Rosie . . .?'

The drawing-room door opened and Sir George came towards them. He gave Rose a smile, then bent down to Annie, whose eyes were as wide as dinner plates. 'And who is this?' he asked.

'I'm Rose's sister,' she announced, returning his smile. 'My name's Annie.'

'Well, Annie, you must come and meet my mother.' He held out his hand. After only a moment's hesitation, Annie clasped it and allowed herself to be led away.

Rose rolled her eyes in exasperation. Her sister liked any man, even though she had continually warned her about them.

'Mother, this is Annie,' Sir George said.

Lady Gresham rose to her feet, a tall, impressive figure, despite her age. 'Welcome to my home.' Then she kissed the child. 'You must be cold. Come and sit by the fire. And you, my dear.' The look she gave Rose was one of undisguised affection.

Refreshments were called for and Rose was relieved to see it wasn't the paper-thin china they'd used the last time, but it was still lovely. Annie, however, was too excited to stay seated, and started to explore the room, looking intently at every exquisite ornament and the luxurious fabrics.

'Don't touch anything,' Rose warned nervously, as Annie's hand reached out towards a delicate shepherdess figurine.

The hand withdrew. 'I won't. You know I'm always good when you take me out.' Then she gave Lady

Gresham an appealing smile. 'You've got some very pretty things. I like the pictures ever so much, and,' she went to an alcove, 'this one looks like Rosie.'

Rose got up to have a look. Annie was right: it was remarkably like her. 'I didn't see this when I came before.'

'No, I've just had it brought into this room.'

After that they settled down to enjoy their tea. It was a pleasant hour, but Rose found it difficult to relax: Sir George had stayed, and Annie was chattering away, not at all intimidated by her surroundings. And, of course, she told the Greshams much more than Rose would have liked. But that serves me right for bringing her, she thought.

Later, when they left, she knew she would have to tell Annie who those people were. When the child paused for breath, Rose looked down at her. She was trotting along, her face alight with the wonder of it all, clutching a fine linen napkin the old lady had insisted she keep.

'You going to tell me who they are, Rosie?' Annie inquired.

Rose took a deep breath and started to explain, hoping she could persuade her sister to keep her mouth shut about the Greshams.

A forlorn hope, she suspected.

26

March 1921

For a moment Bill gazed up at the house, then jumped out of the car and hurried through the front door. His father was ill and had asked to see him, so he'd left his job and set off for Hampshire. That wasn't any hardship because he'd soon realized that he'd made a mistake in accepting the post – it was too far away from Rose.

He stopped in the hall briefly, then went upstairs. This was the first time he had seen his home in several years. It was large, ugly and full of memorabilia his father had collected during his years in the navy. Bill hated it.

'Ah, you're here at last,' his father grumbled, as Bill walked into his bedroom.

Bill looked at the frail, sick man, and felt sorry for him. 'I'd have come any time,' he told him. 'You had only to ask.'

'I know.' His father sighed. 'I was wrong to try to dictate to you what you should do with your life, but I loved the sea so much and I wanted my son to have the same pleasure.'

'Well, you had your wish,' Bill told him. 'The war came and left me with little choice in the matter.'

His father nodded. 'You distinguished yourself, and I'm proud of you.'

'But I didn't stay in the navy.'

'It doesn't matter.' His father lifted a shaking hand and grasped his son's. 'All I want is for you to be happy.'

Two days later, Bill's father died in his sleep. It was as if the reconciliation with his son had eased his mind, and he slipped away peacefully. Bill was sad that they had been separated for so long, but he took comfort from the healing of the rift between them. His father had had peace of mind at the end, he was sure.

When Bill started to wind up his father's affairs, he was staggered to find that he was now a wealthy man. He immediately put up the house for sale, and donated many of his father's possessions and medals to a naval museum. With that part of the business settled he sat down one evening to give his own future some thought.

He laid back his head, closed his eyes and took stock of his life. He could start up his own business as an architect. He had enough money to live on for some time, so a slow start wouldn't matter. He would never have a better opportunity than this to give it a try.

He opened his eyes and reached for the whisky bottle. He poured himself a small measure, then studied the golden liquid with deep concentration. That was the business side settled, but what about his personal life? Rose! He sipped the drink. It was impossible to think of a future without her. He was a fool, of course, because the chance of persuading her to marry him was remote.

Bill drained the glass and put it on the small table beside him. Common sense told him he should leave Rose alone, but he was too much in love to take any notice of that.

The house sold almost immediately, and then he started

to put his plans into action. The first thing he did was to look for business premises in London, and he had no sooner opened his office than the first commission came in. He was on his way, and could launch his pursuit of Rose.

He was considering how best to approach this when he received a letter from Grace and John. They started by wishing him every success in his new venture, but the last paragraph made him laugh: 'We would like you to be godfather to our son, and Rose will be godmother. She is taking a day off from her studies to do this for us. The christening will be on 28 April, and we hope you will accept.'

Bill picked up his pen. Of course he would.

'Uncle Bill!' Annie tore over to the tall man, who was talking to John and looking as unperturbed as ever.

Rose watched as he sank down so that Annie could throw her arms around his neck. Then he unwound himself and looked directly at Rose. He was wasting his time if he thought he was going to get another kiss! One had been quite enough. She held out her hand politely. 'Hello, Bill.'

He ignored the hand and kissed her cheek. 'Hello, Rose. As welcoming as ever, I see.'

A sharp reply hovered on the tip of her tongue, but she managed to stifle it. This was Grace and John's day: she was not about to spoil it for them.

Grace came over. 'Everyone's here so we can go in,' she told them, and handed the baby to Bill, who cradled him in his arms.

Rose couldn't help noticing how at ease he looked

holding the tiny baby, and something inside her jolted. He had filled out since she had last seen him, had lost that gaunt, troubled look. He was big and strong, but he looked right somehow with a child in his arms. He ought to marry and have children of his own – he'd make a wonderful father, she realized. She wondered why she felt so uncomfortable with the idea.

After the baby had been named Harold John William, he was handed to Rose. She took him with practised skill and looked down at him. He was gazing up at her trustingly, and she decided he was a nice baby.

'It suits you,' Bill murmured in her ear.

She clamped her teeth together and gave him a withering glance. She was *not* going to allow him to provoke her today.

They all went back to the house for refreshments and Rose busied herself helping Grace. Annie was in her element surrounded by all her favourite men. She was chattering away to Edward Trenchard, hanging on to Harold's hand, when suddenly she left them and came over to Rose. 'Rosie? Do you think that old lady would mind if I gave the napkin to little Harold?'

'I'm sure she wouldn't, Toots, but I've already given Grace a shawl from both of us.'

'I know, but I'd like to give him something of my own.' She pulled a brightly coloured parcel from her pocket. 'Look, I painted a special paper to wrap it in.'

Rose admired it, then said, 'In that case, you go and give it to Grace. I'm sure she will be pleased.' She marvelled that such an unselfish and loving child could have grown up in their harsh environment. It was as if the hunger and deprivation hadn't touched her. She knew that the napkin was a treasured possession, yet Annie was willing to give it away. Her little sister was special. But she had always known that, hadn't she?

'I'll tell the lady what I've done next time I see her.' Annie looked hopefully at her big sister. 'I liked her. You will take me to see her again, won't you?'

'Of course.'

Annie began to scamper off, then turned back. 'Do they know about your real daddy?'

'Grace, John and Harold do. You don't have to worry what you say.'

'I haven't told anyone. You sure it's all right to talk about it?'

Rose nodded – she knew what a struggle it must have been for Annie to keep a secret. 'Now, are you going to give Grace your present?'

Annie turned it over and over in her hands. 'Have you seen what Uncle Bill and the professor gave?'

'No.'

'Uncle Bill's is a baby's rattle, and the professor gave a cup, both *real silver*.'

Rose guessed at once what Annie was concerned about, so she sat down and drew the child close to her. 'Do you remember the Bible story I read to you about the widow who put the smallest coin in the collection when all the others were giving a lot more?'

'Yes,' Annie said. 'She gave everything she had, but the others still had plenty left because they were rich.'

'That's right. And what do you think the story means?'

Annie screwed up her face. 'It means that a gift doesn't have to cost a lot to be special?'

'Exactly. Some have given expensive presents because they could afford it, but ours are just as precious to Grace and John because they come with our love.'

Annie kissed her. 'Thank you, Rosie. You always explain things so I can understand.'

Bill watched the exchange between the sisters. From what he had been told, Rose had practically brought up the little girl from birth and she had certainly done a first class job. Annie was affectionate, polite, and altogether a delightful child; it was touching the way she always ran to Rose for advice and guidance. They were more like mother and daughter than sisters. What were they talking about so earnestly?

Annie came back to them with a parcel in her hands. Ah, Bill thought, so that's what it was all about.

'For the baby.' She handed the package to Grace and waited anxiously for it to be opened, hands behind her back.

'Why, thank you, sweetheart.' Grace opened it, trying not to tear the carefully painted paper. 'Oh, this is lovely,' she exclaimed.

Annie beamed. 'The lady gave it to me, but I want you to have it.'

Bill looked at the fine embroidery and frowned. It was a crest.

John took it from Grace and opened it up, examining it carefully. 'It's beautiful, Annie. Did you say someone gave it to you?'

'Rosie took me to see a nice lady and she told me I could keep it.' She gave a little self-conscious giggle. 'It was for when we had tea, but I didn't know how to use it. She showed me, but it was too nice to wipe my hands on.'

'Was it Lady Gresham you saw?' Grace asked.

Annie nodded and started to talk about the big house and all the lovely things she had seen, including the portrait. 'It looked ever so much like Rosie,' she told them all, 'and the house was big enough for ten families to live in.'

'Would you like to live in a house like that?' Bill asked, trying to contain his curiosity. Why would a portrait in some aristocratic woman's house look like Rose?

Annie bounced up and down. 'Don't be silly, Uncle Bill, we can't live in places like that – and I'd be frightened of breaking something. My sister couldn't take her eyes off me in case I did – but, of course, I'd never do anything to upset her.'

Annie had enjoyed her visit to a posh house, but Bill couldn't detect a thread of envy in her. Remarkable.

Then the child leaned forward. 'I met Rose's daddy. She asked me not to talk about it before, but she says it's all right now. She doesn't like him, but I thought he was nice.' Annie stood on tiptoe and was about to go into more detail when she stopped and listened. 'Baby's crying, Auntie Grace. Can I come with you?'

When they had left the room, Bill turned to John. 'What on earth was all that about? Rose's father is dead, surely?'

'No, that man wasn't her father, but it isn't my story to tell.'

'Don't worry, John.' Rose came and stood beside them. 'I'll explain. There's little point in trying to keep it secret and, with Mum happily married again, I don't think I need to. Wally's been told about me.'

Bill saw the defiant tilt of her head and wondered what she was going to say.

'I'm a bastard,' she announced, without a hint of shame. 'My mother was seduced by the master of the house when she was in service, and was thrown out on to the street to fend for herself when she became pregnant.'

Bill wanted to take her into his arms and tell her it didn't matter – she was the girl he loved and nothing would change that – but the dark eyes blazed.

'I met my father recently, and I hate him, but his mother is a kind lady.' She smiled then and glanced at John. 'I took Annie to see her because she asked me to, and you should have seen that child's face when she saw all the lovely things. She was given the napkin as a reminder of her visit.'

'And now she has given it to us.'

'She loves you and Grace very much. It was her most treasured possession.'

'And therefore a most precious gift,' John said softly.

Rose nodded. 'Now I'll go and help with the clearing up.'

Bill tried to follow her but John stopped him. 'Let her go, Bill, she's said all she's going to.'

'Who is her father?' he asked, once the shock of her revelation had receded.

'Rose didn't mention his name, so I don't feel I can tell you, but he is someone of rank.'

Bill had already worked that out for himself. 'No

wonder she doesn't seem to belong in that dreadful street.'

'That's what we always thought, but I've come to the conclusion that we were wrong.'

'What do you mean?'

'Garrett Street is a part of her, always will be, and I believe that is the cause of her anger. She feels it isn't right for any human being to live like that, and she won't rest until she has done something about it.'

27

September 1922

Rose looked around the room. Everyone was here, and although Grace's house was much larger than theirs in Garrett Street, it was packed. Grace and John had insisted on throwing this party, and Harold was bursting with pride, as was her mother. Her own mood was of elation, mixed with disbelief. Against all the odds, she had been to university, and had graduated with honours. The last year had passed in a blur of study and determination, but it had been worth it.

'Congratulations, Rose.' Bill smiled down at her. 'What are you going to do now?'

'I've got plans, but I'm not telling anyone yet.' Excitement rushed through her. She couldn't wait to get started.

'Rose.' Harold was edging through the throng to reach her. 'I thought you were going to ask Angelina and Harriet to pop in tonight?'

'I did, but they have parties of their own to attend,' Rose told him.

'Of course – they would have. Will you be keeping in touch with them?'

'Harriet took my address, but I don't expect to hear from either of them again, really.'

'Why not?' Bill asked.

Rose gave him a studied look. 'After a shaky start the

three of us got on quite well together, and we were glad of each other's company at the university, but we never had much in common. Once they return to their own lives, our three years together will be forgotten.'

'That's a shame,' Bill remarked.

Rose picked up a small cake, then smiled at him. 'That's the way things go. It would be nice to see them again, but I'm a realist – our lives are just too different.'

The evening had been a great success and Rose was touched that her friends and family were so happy for her. Parts of the last three years had been a nightmare with family problems and lack of money, but most of it had been a joy. When she thought back on her childhood and how she had craved for books and a decent education, it had been nothing short of paradise.

'That was a wonderful party,' her mother said, as soon as they got home. 'Let's get the younger ones to bed and then we can have a nice cup of tea and a chat.'

The children were soon upstairs, and Marj had the tea ready. 'I expect it's going to seem strange being back here again,' her mother remarked. 'I know how you hate Garrett Street.'

Rose grimaced. 'I'll soon get used to it, I expect.'

'What are your plans, Rosie?' Marj asked, when they were settled at the table.

'I've got an idea, but I don't want to say any more before I've looked into it.'

Her mother nodded. 'I know you'll make a success of whatever you plan to do.'

'I hope so.'

*

First thing next morning Rose headed for a row of dingy shops at the top of Garrett Street, a cobbler's, a greengrocer's, a butcher's, a baker's and one other. She ran her hand over the roughly painted sign on the door, and as the grime came away the words 'Joshua Braithwaite, Solicitor' were just visible.

The inside wasn't much better, but that could soon be put right, she thought, undaunted.

'Can I help you, miss?' A scruffy man of about fifty got to his feet. His suit had seen better days, the shirt had never been ironed, and he had a beaten look in his eyes. In fact he looked as downtrodden as the area.

She treated him to her most brilliant smile. 'No, but I can help you.'

The look he gave her was startled. 'I doubt that, Miss . . .?'

'Rose Webster.' She grasped his hand and shook it. 'You need help, Mr Braithwaite. Please sit down and I'll explain.'

'I beg your pardon?'

Rose dusted off a chair and sat down, then waited patiently until he had sunk into his own. When he was settled she started her campaign. 'As I've said, you need help, and the best way to start is by employing me.'

That caught his attention. 'Employing – Miss Webster, my firm is on the point of closing for lack of clients. What makes you think I can afford to give you a job?'

She gave the room a detailed inspection, then turned back to Mr Braithwaite. 'You can't afford not to.'

'I don't think taking you on as an office girl would increase my trade, despite the appealing picture you would make.'

Rose flashed him another dazzling smile. 'I'm not an office girl, I'm going to be a solicitor.' She got the proof out of her bag and passed it to him.

'Hmm,' he muttered. 'Very impressive. But even if I could afford to employ someone else, it would be a man.'

'That is very short-sighted of you,' she declared. 'The women around here won't talk to a man, but they will come to someone who has grown up here.'

'Good Lord!' he exclaimed. 'You're not telling me you live here?'

'Garrett Street.'

He looked at her qualifications again. 'How did you manage to get into university?'

'Help from friends and hard work.'

'It couldn't have been easy for you,' he said, with more respect.

'It wasn't, and I want to put my education to good use.'

'So where do I come into this plan of yours?' He sat back, folded his arms and waited.

She noticed the alert gleam in his eyes, and knew that she had his attention. All she had to do now was sell him her vision. She chose her words carefully. 'The first thing we have to do is transform this place – open it up. Take that awful paper off the windows so everyone can see in.'

'That won't make any difference,' he objected. 'The people around here are too suspicious, as I've found out to my cost.'

She waved aside his objections. 'If they see one of their own inside, someone they know and trust, they'll come, even if it's only to find out what's going on.'

'Someone like you, you mean?'

'No, I'm a misfit here, always have been.'

'That I can believe,' he said drily. 'Who do you suggest?'

'My mother.'

He stood up. 'I think this nonsense has gone far enough. You're now suggesting I employ two of you.' He gave a grim laugh. 'I'm already living on the bread-line.'

Rose felt a flutter of panic – she was losing him. She gave him another confident smile. 'I can change that.'

He seemed bemused. 'I'm a fool to ask, but how do you propose to do that?'

'Offer an advice service as well as legal. Many people who live here can't read or write,' she explained. 'They struggle through life not knowing that help is available to them. We could tell them how to get this help, and fill in any forms for them.' She hesitated – he didn't look convinced.

'And how do they pay, or are you suggesting we offer this service *free*?'

'That's a lovely idea, but not practical.'

Mr Braithwaite gave a discouraging snort.

'We could charge, say, a shilling a time?'

He tipped his head back and laughed. 'And you think that will solve my financial worries?'

She wasn't going to let him beat her. 'It isn't much, I know, but the number of people wanting help will make up for that. Come on, Mr Braithwaite, think about it. You're not doing very well on your own, are you?'

He studied her speculatively for a while, then he said, 'Two shillings.'

'Absolutely not!'

'One and sixpence . . . and that is as low as I'm prepared to go.'

She had him! 'You drive a hard bargain.'

'Huh! You mean you do. Now, how do you propose I pay you and your mother?'

'We won't take much until business picks up.'

'I wish I had your confidence that this crazy scheme will work,' he shrugged, 'but what have I got to lose?'

'Exactly, Mr Braithwaite.'

'When can you start?'

'Right now.' Rose took off her coat, rolled up her sleeves, pulled a pinny out of her bag and put it on. 'I'll need a bucket of water to get that paper off the windows.'

'My God! What *have* I let myself in for?' He looked her up and down. 'You were so sure of yourself that you came prepared?'

'Of course. I'm not one to waste time.'

'What do you think, Mum?' Rose asked later that day, after she had finished the story.

'Are you sure I could do the job?'

'Of course. All you've got to do is sit within full view of passers-by, then talk to them when they come in.'

'Wally!' Marj called her husband into the scullery. 'Rose has found me a job.'

He came in and Rose had to explain all over again.

'I think that's a fine idea,' he said. 'Once word gets around I'm sure you'll have them queuing up at the door. It's just the thing this area needs.'

'I hope so. Mr Braithwaite is still sceptical about it, but I've given this a lot of thought.' For a moment Rose looked doubtful, then the determination came back into her face.

'It'll be a great success,' Wally encouraged her, 'and thanks for getting your mother the job.'

'I shouldn't get too excited,' Rose said. 'The pay won't be much to start with.'

'Oh, I don't mind that.' Her mother's face was alight with excitement. 'It'll give me something to do. I've missed not working since the war ended.'

'You'll have plenty to keep you busy – the place is in a shocking state. I've made a start, but there's a lot still to do.'

'I'll come with you tomorrow.' Her mother put the kettle on. 'We'll soon lick it into shape.'

'Annie!' Rose called, as she caught sight of her sister disappearing up the stairs. 'Would you do something for me?'

Annie's face peered around the door and broke into a delighted grin. 'Of course. What is it?'

Rose told her about the job, then said, 'I want a notice made so I can stick it in the window.' She wrote on a sheet of paper 'Advice Centre – no problem too small – Consultation fee 1/6d'. 'Do you think you can do that? I want "Advice Centre" in bright red letters.'

'I can do it, but I don't think I've got any paper big enough.'

'I've brought some home with me.' Rose unrolled a large sheet of cream paper.

Annie fingered it appreciatively. 'This will be fine. It'll take me a couple of days – I'll want to make a good job of it. Can't have you putting any old thing up, can we?'

How quickly Annie was growing up, Rose thought, as

she watched her sister go up the stairs. At eleven she was quietening down a bit, and although she was not academically brilliant, she was doing well enough at school. Her writing and English were good, and she had a real aptitude for art. She was sure her sister would do well in life, because she also had plenty of determination.

'I feel like a goldfish in a bowl,' Joshua Braithwaite complained, as he stared out of the sparkling window. 'No one's going to come in when they can be seen by all and sundry.'

'I've thought of that.' Rose opened the door of a room that had been used for storage, and revealed a sparsely furnished but clean space. 'And if we get more than one client at a time we can take them into the kitchen. So stop moaning, and tell me how you got on in court this morning.'

'I lost,' he grumbled.

She tutted. 'You'll have to do better than that. Why don't you let me help with the next case?'

'Good heavens, woman, you've only just been awarded your degree and you think you can do better than me! I've had thirty years' experience. Anyway, I didn't stand a chance today, the man was guilty.'

'I'm not suggesting I can do any better,' she said, placating him, 'but fresh ideas . . .'

'All right, you can work with me on the next one – if there is a next one,' he remarked despondently. 'I'm still waiting for this rush of clients you promised me.'

She winked at her mother and held out seven and sixpence. 'Put that in your cash box.'

He looked at it in disbelief. 'You've had five customers this morning?'

'Yes, and word's spreading. We're on our way, Mr Braithwaite.'

'Well, I'll be blowed. I never thought this idea of yours had a chance.'

'Why did you agree to it, then?'

'Because of your enthusiasm. I used to be like that a long time ago, but I've lost heart over the years. I've been on a continual downward slide, and when I ended up here,' he shrugged, 'well, it seemed like the end of the line and I stopped trying.'

'There's only one way you're going now,' she told him confidently, 'and that's up.'

'Do you know? I almost believe you.' Joshua Braithwaite laughed. 'I'd like you to call me Josh, Miss Webster. I shall enjoy working with you.'

'And I'm Rose. We're not going to earn a fortune, but we could make a real difference to some people's lives.'

Her employer didn't answer. He was gaping out of the window. 'Who the . . .?'

The tall, elegant lady getting out of the smart car was unmistakable – Lady Gresham. Rose opened the door for her.

'Thank you, my dear.'

'What are you doing here, Lady Gresham?' Rose was immediately suspicious. She hadn't seen either her or her son for some time.

'Business. I've come to see Mr Braithwaite.' Then she turned and looked at Marj. 'You must be Rose's mother.'

She gave a little curtsy – old habits dying hard. 'Yes, my lady.'

'You've done a fine job in bringing up your daughter. I regret you were treated so harshly, but I do not regret Rose being born.'

'Neither do I, my lady.'

Rose watched the scene through narrowed eyes. This meeting had been bound to happen sometime, but she could sense her mother's unease.

'Nevertheless,' Lady Gresham continued, 'I wish you had come to me on my return. I would not have allowed you to be turned out like that.'

'That would have been a waste of time, my lady,' Marj told her. 'I would never have been allowed to see you, and your son denied everything. It would have been my word against his.'

'And he would have been believed, not you.' Lady Gresham looked sad.

Marj nodded. 'This all happened a long time ago, when I was young and foolish and, as you can see, we've survived.'

Lady Gresham bowed her head in acknowledgement. 'But your life has been unnecessarily harsh, I think. Will you accept my sincere apologies at this late date?'

Marj gave a slight smile. 'I will, my lady. It was a long time ago and best forgotten now.'

'That is gracious of you.' Lady Gresham then turned to Rose. 'Now, introduce me to Mr Braithwaite.'

When that was done Josh said, 'Would you like a private room, Lady Gresham?'

'No, no, this is perfectly adequate.' She sat down and wasted no time in stating her business. 'I run two shelters for ex-servicemen. Many are destitute, and I want you to represent them in the fight for a better life. An organization called the British Legion has been founded for the purpose of helping struggling ex-servicemen. I suggest you contact them.'

Josh surged into life, and Rose guessed that some of his old spirit was returning. He had strong views on this matter, as she had discovered when talking to him.

'I would be delighted to take it on, Lady Gresham.'

'Good, good.' She handed him a piece of paper. 'My homes are at these addresses. As you can see, they are not in the most salubrious areas, but that is where the need is most urgent.' She glanced out of the window and gave a brief smile to the many curious faces peering in at her. 'I shall, of course, cover all your expenses, and I shall expect you to start at once.' She beckoned Rose. 'You do not object to this arrangement, my dear?'

When Rose glanced at Josh, his face was a picture in the art of pleading without saying a word. 'You're employing Mr Braithwaite, not me, and I'm pleased you're willing to try and help these poor men further. I firmly believe you've chosen the right man.' Rose held the old lady's gaze. 'As long as you don't try to engineer work for me.'

'I wouldn't dream of it. You've made it clear that I'm not to interfere in your life, and I won't. You want to succeed on your own, and I respect that.'

She stood up, leaning heavily on her ebony stick. 'Please find time to come and see me again, Rose, and bring your delightful sister with you again.'

Although the request was issued in a casual way, Rose did not miss the appeal in Lady Gresham's eyes. 'We shall come on Saturday afternoon, if that is convenient?'

'I shall look forward to it.' Then, with a gracious nod, she walked out, leaving a stunned silence behind her.

Marj let out a ragged sigh and sank on to her chair. 'She hasn't changed much!'

'My God, Rose, I feel shell-shocked after that encounter.' Josh laughed with delight. 'I've just been given the biggest chance of my career.'

'I told you you wouldn't lose by taking me on,' she joked.

'Er . . . I know it isn't any of my business, but I couldn't help noticing that you appear to know her.'

'She's my grandmother.' Rose was shocked at herself. It was the first time she had acknowledged Lady Gresham as such.

'But you said you grew up here?'

'I did.'

'Oh.'

'I can see your mind working, Josh,' Marj put in. 'I was expecting Rose before I married Webster, and I gave her his name, but she's Lady Gresham's granddaughter. I was in service and too innocent to refuse the advances of the master of the house, but I'm proud of my daughter.'

'I should think you are. She's unique. I spotted that as soon as she breezed into this office, and I wondered what the devil had hit me when she told me her crazy ideas.'

'They're not crazy,' Rose protested.

'I'm beginning to realize that. Now,' – he gathered papers together – 'I think I'll go and start talking to the men. It'll be a hard fight,' he said, with relish, 'but if they won't listen I'll make some damned big waves.'

'That will please Lady Gresham,' Rose remarked drily. 'She loves a good fight almost as much as I do.'

'I don't doubt it.' He grinned boyishly, straightened his tie and brushed down his jacket.

He looks ten years younger, Rose thought.

'Thanks,' he said earnestly. 'For the first time in many years I have something useful to do.'

When Josh had left Rose went and sat beside her mother. 'You didn't mind telling Josh about me?'

'No. After I'd spoken to Lady Gresham, I realized I'd been worrying too much about it. I was never able to forgive them, you see, but now I'm happily married, it doesn't matter any more.'

'I'm glad, because although I've managed to keep them at arm's length, I think they'll become a part of my life whether I like it or not.'

'Don't carry a grudge for me,' her mother told her, 'because I can see now that I wasn't blameless – and very foolish too. I think it's time to put it all behind us.'

'I agree. Now, I want to go to the council offices. Will you be all right on your own for a while?'

'You run along.'

28

April 1923

Bill pulled his collar up as a chilly wind whistled around his neck. Spring was reluctant to come this year. The open space in front of him was nothing yet, but in his mind's eye he could see the two houses he had designed for himself. His desire to have a home outside London had prompted him to find a suitable place, but when he had started to draw the plans, Rose had crept into his mind and taken over. He thought of it now as her home too. The longing to share his life with her was overwhelming.

He hadn't seen her since her graduation party, but he had kept in touch with her progress through John. She was earning herself quite a reputation as the women's champion – in and out of court.

'Nice spot you've got here, Mr Freeman.'

He dragged his thoughts away from Rose to the contractor he'd brought out here with him. Then he unrolled the plans. 'When can you start?'

'Next month is the earliest.' The man pondered the plans. 'Nice houses. This will be a good investment. Roehampton is an excellent area, and it's easy to get to London from here.'

Bill nodded. 'Let me know when you're ready.'

*

'Rosie? Can we go and see Auntie Grace? We haven't been for a long time.'

'It's only two weeks, Toots, and I've been very busy.'

Annie looked at her thoughtfully. 'Why do you call me that?'

'What? Toots?'

'Yes.'

'I don't know. I started calling you that when you were little. Don't you like it any more?'

She pulled a face. 'It sounds like a baby's name.'

'Oh, well, in that case I'll call you Annie because you're certainly not a baby.' Rose hesitated. 'Or would you rather Ann?'

'No, Annie's all right.' For a moment she had sounded rather grown-up. 'Can we go to Auntie Grace's?'

Rose put her papers back into the folder, and stood up. 'We'll go now, shall we?'

When she saw Bill there she was annoyed – he never came on a Sunday – but, of course, her sister was thrilled. 'I'm so glad we came today,' she cried, 'but I had a job getting Rosie away from her work.'

'You don't have to wait for me,' Rose told her. 'You're old enough to come on your own.'

'I know, but I like to come out with you – it's more fun.'

'How old are you now?' Bill asked.

'I'm twelve,' she told him proudly, 'and Rosie will be twenty-one this year.'

'My goodness,' Grace sighed, 'where have the years gone?'

'When's your birthday?' Bill wanted to know.

'March the sixth, and Rosie's is September the eighteenth.' Then she spun away from Bill. 'Uncle John, there's a lovely motor-car outside your house, is it yours?'

'It belongs to Bill,' John responded.

Rose glanced outside at the gleaming vehicle, then nearly burst out laughing when she saw what Annie was up to.

Her sister had sidled up to Bill with an appealing expression on her face. 'It's very pretty, Uncle Bill. Does it go fast?'

'It does, but I don't drive too fast because it can be dangerous, and I wouldn't like to frighten my passengers.'

Annie smiled up at him. 'Do you take lots of people out in it?'

Rose saw that Bill was fighting to keep a straight face. He lost the battle and chuckled. 'Would you like to go for a ride?'

Annie clapped her hands. 'Yes, please! Can we go now?'

'Tell you what, why don't we all go out? It's a warm afternoon and I know a lovely spot – we could have tea out instead of Grace getting it for us.'

There was immediate agreement and Rose found herself swept along in their enthusiasm. It would make a change and she needed a break from work.

Little Harold was soon ready and they all spilled out on to the pavement. Annie rushed to the front of the car and read the name. 'It's a Sunbeam,' she announced. 'I like that name.' Then she scrambled into the back of the car.

'Grace, you go in the back with Annie,' Bill suggested.

'I'll sit in the back too,' John said, settling his family comfortably. 'Then Rose can go in the front with you.'

During the journey, Rose couldn't help admiring the

car. The seats were cream leather, and there was a panel of gleaming wood with lots of dials on it. And as for the driver . . . well, he seemed to be working with hands and feet, but in a smooth, unhurried, efficient way. She glanced down to see how many pedals there were and felt a jolt as she saw Bill's leg muscles tighten as he worked one of the pedals. The modern fashion for men's trousers was too tight, she thought waspishly.

She gazed out of the window as they drove through Notting Hill. She hadn't wanted to sit in the front in the first place, and Bill took up such a lot of room.

'Look at that, Rosie!' Annie caught her attention.

Bill pulled over.

'What they doing, Uncle Bill?'

'Putting up new houses.'

Rose's irritation disappeared and she opened the car door. 'I want to have a look.'

Grace stayed in the car with young Harold, but the rest of them made their way across the road. Rose left them all behind in her eagerness to see what was going on. 'How many houses are you building?' she asked a workman.

'Ten.'

'What was here before?'

'Slums, but they was in a disgusting state. Nothing for it but to pull them down and start again.'

'Why are you working on a Sunday?' Rose fired another question at him.

'I'm not, miss. I've only popped along to sort out what needs doing tomorrow . . . Oh, hello, Mr Freeman, come to see how things are going?'

Rose spun round. 'These are yours?'

'No, but I designed them.'

She surveyed him with new respect, then grabbed his arm. 'Show me one that's nearly finished.'

Fifteen minutes later there wasn't a corner, cupboard or piece of plumbing she hadn't inspected, and she was thrilled with what she'd seen. 'You've done well,' she told him. 'Bathrooms, running water and electricity all laid on, and best of all a small garden for each house.'

Her intense gaze swept over the whole site. 'Set out beautifully, not back-to-back like the old ones.'

'I'm pleased you like – '

'Are they for rent?' Rose was too intent on asking questions to bother with anything else he might say.

'No, they're for sale.'

'Pity. They ought to be available for people to rent.'

'That isn't anything to do with me,' he explained patiently. 'I only designed them.'

'Of course.' She gave him a brilliant smile. 'Thank you for showing them to me. I'll just go and have another look.'

Bill and John caught hold of her before she disappeared, and urged her back to the car.

Rose spent the rest of the journey deep in thought, not noticing where they were going. She had forgotten Bill was an irritating man. Perhaps she had misjudged him – after all, he had designed some lovely houses.

'You know of any more being built like that?' she asked after a while.

'No, that was a commission I received when I first started my own business.'

'They're good.'

'Thank you.' He cast her a sideways glance of amusement.

'We need to clear the slums and replace them with houses like that.' She bubbled with enthusiasm.

'Rose, we're on a pleasant trip out,' John reprimanded gently.

'Sorry.' She turned and grinned at Grace and John. 'You know how desperate I am to improve housing conditions. But I promise I won't mention it again this afternoon.'

'Where are we going?' Annie asked, putting a stop to their conversation.

'Richmond Park,' Bill told her.

'Oh, that sounds nice. Is it much further?'

'We're almost there, sweetheart.' Then, a few minutes later, he drove through a pair of tall gates.

Rose loved it immediately, and Grace brought their attention to a group of animals.

'Oooh, what are they?' Annie cried.

Bill stopped the car. 'Deer,' he told her. 'Would you like to go and see them?'

Annie was already out of the car and heading towards the animals before Rose and Bill caught her up.

'Don't go too close,' Bill warned her. 'You might frighten them.'

'Are they dangerous?' Annie whispered.

'Not if you don't annoy them.'

'I won't do that. I never annoy anyone,' she told them confidently.

Rose caught Bill's eye and they exchanged a smile. Grace and John joined them and they all stood still to watch the deer munching the grass. Young Harold was wide-eyed at the sight.

'Look.' Annie tugged at Rose. 'One of the little ones is coming over.'

'If you keep very still it might come right up to you,' Bill told her.

Annie waited patiently and was rewarded when the deer came within three feet of them. 'I wish I had something to give it to eat,' she whispered.

'You mustn't feed them,' he said. 'They live on grass.'

'Is that all?' Annie sighed in disbelief, then gave a little jiggle of excitement. 'It's close enough to touch . . . Can I touch it, Uncle Bill?'

'Better not,' he told her quietly. 'They're wild animals, you see.'

'Isn't it a pretty colour? Oh, it's going away!' Annie's voice rang with disappointment.

'I think it's time for tea,' Bill said, and led them back to the car. When they were all settled again, he drove slowly through the park, giving them all a chance to admire the scenery.

'This is a beautiful place,' Rose murmured. 'Look at the trees, they're magnificent. I bet it's a glorious sight in the autumn.'

'It will be.' Bill glanced at her quickly. 'I'll bring you again, if you'd like to see it?'

'I'd like that,' she admitted.

They went out through another set of gates and Bill stopped on the brow of a hill. The Thames shimmered below them and curved its majestic way through lush countryside.

'I've seen pictures of this,' Rose breathed in awe, 'but it's more beautiful than any picture. You forget that places like this exist when you're surrounded by houses, streets and people, day after day.'

'I know what you mean,' Bill said. 'I grew up in Hampshire and I often long for peace and quiet and open spaces.'

'What river is that?' Annie asked John.

'The Thames.' He helped her on to a low wall so she could get a better look.

'You mean it's our river? Does it come all the way from London to here?'

'Yes – and I'm hungry!' He helped her down.

Bill took them into a small tea-room with blue and white checked tablecloths and cream china with little blue flowers decorating the edges.

'Oh, this is lovely.' Grace sat down with little Harold, who was now fast asleep.

Rose looked at the scene with a half-smile. Usually her mind was churning, but today she had managed to put aside all her worries and enjoy the occasion. She was among friends and there was nothing to do but be happy. It was a new experience for her, and she realized that she didn't know what it was like to have time to herself. And she didn't know what *fun* was. It was a poor reflection on the way she had lived her life.

'You're very quiet, Rosie,' Annie said. 'Aren't you enjoying yourself?'

'I'm having a lovely time, and I was just thinking about all the things I've never done.'

'Like what?' John asked.

Rose recited a list of the things she'd never seen in London. 'I'd forgotten that there's a world outside studying and working.'

Grace handed round the plate of quickly disappearing cakes. 'The last few years have been hard for you, but it's time to think about yourself now.'

Annie leaned across the table and caught hold of her sister's hand. 'If you're going out more would you take me to see the lovely pictures? I've always wanted to go to the big art galleries, but I didn't like to ask because you're always so busy.'

'First free day I've got we'll go to the National Gallery.' Rose smiled at her sister, her mind made up. It was all very well having her nose forever stuck in books, but it was time she started to broaden her outlook on life.

It was late afternoon when they got back to the car, and they drove slowly back through the park so they could see the deer again, then out through another set of gates.

'Look, there's some more houses being put up,' Annie told them.

Bill slowed as they went past, but didn't stop.

Rose could see only two. 'Someone's going to be lucky,' she murmured. 'This is a lovely spot. Where are we?'

'Roehampton,' was all he said, and picked up speed again.

Bill felt pleased with himself as he drove back into town. The trip had been a good idea: he'd found a way to get closer to Rose, and he had been able to show her a glimpse of *their* house. She also liked the others he had designed, and he hoped she was beginning to see him in a more favourable light. He had seen a softer side of her today, which was encouraging.

'You can drop us here,' Rose interrupted his thoughts. 'Don't go down Garrett Street.'

'You mustn't take your lovely car down there, Uncle Bill. There's lots of ruffians living here,' Annie chimed in.

Seeing that he was about to ignore the good advice, Rose touched his arm. 'This will do, Bill. We've got little Harold with us, remember?'

He pulled up outside her office, and watched the girls until they were out of sight. He felt sad to see them back in such squalid conditions after the beauty of the afternoon. He knew how much Rose hated the place, and her loyalty to her family showed the depth of her love. She tried to be hard, and in a lot of ways she was, but he suspected that she protected the gentle, loving side of her nature with anger.

Young Harold gave a tired grumble as Bill got back into the car. 'I'd better get you home,' he said.

After he had delivered the rest of his passengers safely, he went back to Kensington where he had a flat above his office.

For the first time since meeting Rose, he had hope for the future. She had been relaxed and happy today, and after seeing the new houses, her waspishness had disappeared. She had even smiled at him as if she meant it, which had given him a hint of what she might be like, if she ever stopped fighting.

29

The next morning Rose was at the council offices as soon as they opened. She was lucky and caught the chairman just as he was going into a meeting. When she called him, he glowered at her – he had already met her on numerous occasions. She ignored his ill-humour. She knew he considered her a nuisance, but she didn't give a damn.

'What are you doing about slum clearance?' she demanded, blocking his exit route.

He sighed. 'As I've told you before, Miss Webster, it takes time and we haven't got the money.'

'That's no excuse,' she said accusingly. 'I saw ten houses being built, but they were for sale, not rent.'

'Where were they?' he asked, looking as if he didn't care.

'Notting Hill.'

'Ah, yes, I know the ones. However, that is a private development and nothing to do with the council.'

He tried to move away, but she stepped in front of him again. 'I know that! But it does show there's some possibility for the run-down areas and it's your job to start doing something about it. And I don't mean private houses. Any built in Bermondsey should be for rent and given to the people who have always lived here, not for the privileged few who can afford to buy them.'

'Private ownership is considered the way forward.'

'And what about those who can only afford to rent?' she demanded, 'are you just going to forget about them?'

'Of course not.' He was clearly exasperated by now. 'And that development you saw is nothing to do with us – it's not in our borough.'

'I'm aware of that, but you should at least be looking into the idea of doing something here. You're going into a meeting, so bring the subject up, please.' She had added the 'please' reluctantly: these people needed a good kick up the backside – if you didn't keep on at them, they sat in their comfortable offices and didn't do a damned thing, except decide how much they could squeeze out of the residents of Bermondsey.

'The plight of the poor is always on our agenda,' he told her loftily, 'but we have a great many things to consider. Unemployment is rising at an alarming rate –'

'Then put them to work building new houses.' Rose knew from bitter experience that this was as far as she was going to get with this man today, so she gave a grim smile and softened her tone. 'I know it's a daunting task, but would you bring it up at the meeting today? There is little evidence of anything being done in the area.'

'We do what we can.'

'It isn't enough. I've seen how things could be improved, and as a representative of the people, it is your duty to explore all – '

'I'm well aware of my duty, Miss Webster, and you are making me late for my meeting.' He stepped past her and strode away.

It was a good thing he was too far away to hear what she called him.

The next item on her agenda was to call on Grace.

'Can you tell me where I can find Bill?' she asked, as soon as she arrived.

'Yes, I've got his office address somewhere.' Grace looked at some papers tucked behind the clock on the mantelpiece. 'Here it is.'

Rose took the printed card from her. 'Kensington? I'll have to catch the train and that's going to take what's left of the morning.' She gave a resigned shrug. 'I won't get much done today.' With that she sped out of the door and headed for the nearest station.

Very nice, Rose thought, as she studied the impressive brass plate with his name on it. She found his office on the second floor and marched in, expecting to see him there. Instead she found a young man of about nineteen, picking out the letters on a typewriter with two fingers.

'Is that the best you can do?' she asked, making him jump. 'It'll take you all day like that.'

'I know, but our typist is away ill.'

'How much have you got to do?' Rose went to the other side of the desk and peered over his shoulder.

'Two letters.'

'In that case . . .' She hoisted him out of the seat and sat down. 'Go and tell Mr Freeman I'm here and I'll do these for you.' She ripped his work out of the machine, put in fresh paper and started to type.

The boy gasped in admiration. 'You're much faster than our usual girl.'

'The WAAC trained me well. Now, go and get Mr Freeman, will you?'

One letter was expertly done and she was working on

the other when a voice said, 'Have you come to work for me, Rose?'

'Do you know her, Mr Freeman?' the boy asked, sounding flustered. 'She didn't give me her name.'

'She didn't have to,' Bill told him drily. 'I knew who it was the minute you said she'd taken over the office.'

Rose ignored them until the second letter was finished. She laid it on top of the first and stood up. 'I want to talk to you.'

'I'm with a client at the moment.'

'I'll wait' – she sat down again – 'but don't be too long.'

'Have you got any more typing to be done, Sam?' Bill asked the boy, with an amused expression on his face.

'Yes, Mr Freeman, there's that long report.'

'Give it to her. If you don't keep her busy while she's waiting she might just tear the place apart.' Then, with a chuckle, he went back into his office and closed the door.

'Bloody man!' Rose exploded, and glared at the door. 'He's talking about me as if I'm a wild animal!'

The door opened again. 'Sam?'

'Yes, sir.'

'Keep your ears covered. Her language is atrocious.' The door closed again.

The corners of her mouth twitched. Cheeky devil. She couldn't help noticing that the boy thought his boss might be right. 'Don't worry, Sam, I don't bite – often,' she told him. 'Nevertheless, you'd better give me the typing, because if he does keep me waiting too long, I might lose my temper.'

The boy tripped over the chair in his hurry to find the work and get out of her way.

She was on the last page when Bill came out of his office and saw his client to the door. She didn't look up until she had finished and, with a flourish, pulled the paper out of the machine. 'You shouldn't frighten your staff like that, Bill Freeman. Poor Sam really believes I'm dangerous.'

'You are. Have you looked in the mirror lately? You're stronger than a lot of men, and a look from your black eyes could stop anyone in their tracks.'

'I don't see any of this affecting you,' she replied, fighting a grin.

'Ah, but I'm different.'

'How?'

He tucked her hand through his arm, and led her towards the door. 'I'll tell you one day. Now, let's have some lunch and you can explain why you're here.'

As soon as they walked into the café, the food smelt wonderful. Bill found an empty table and handed her a menu. He insisted they eat first, and it wasn't until they had a cup of tea in front of them that he sat back. 'Right, what can I do for you?'

'I want to know all about those houses we looked at. What it cost to clear the site, lay the water-pipes and the electricity, and what you estimate the workforce will earn while they're being built.'

There was silence for a moment, then he asked, 'Anything else?'

'Yes, how much are they going to be sold for?'

He stirred another spoonful of sugar into his tea. 'It'll take a couple of days to get all that information together. I don't have it. I'm only the designer, not the contractor.'

'Oh.' Rose had assumed he'd know everything. 'In

that case I'll come back in two days.' She opened her purse to pay for her lunch.

'Don't you dare insult me by insisting you pay for your food,' he reprimanded her softly.

She looked up, surprised by the tone of quiet strength in his voice. 'I'm not trying to insult you, but I can't let you pay for me.'

'Why?'

'Because it isn't right when I've enough money of my own.'

He reached across the table and took her hand. 'It isn't a question of money, Rose. I'm pleased to see you and have enjoyed spending this time with you, so don't spoil it by arguing with me.'

Put like that, all she could say was 'Thank you.'

Rose walked outside while he paid the bill, and told herself sternly that she must learn to be more gracious.

'Who was that lady?' the boy asked, when Bill walked back into his office.

'Rose Webster. She's a lawyer.' He patted the boy on the shoulder. 'And she's not a lady – she has a vocabulary that would put the lowest deck-hand to shame.'

'She's very pretty,' he said, blushing fiercely.

'No, Sam, she isn't pretty . . . she's beautiful, and she isn't much older than you.'

He gaped in amazement. 'But she's so sure of herself.'

'She's had a tough life. It was a case of be strong or crumble, and she didn't intend to let *that* happen.'

'She was a bit frightening, but I liked her,' Sam told him.

'I like her too.' He walked into his office, shut the

door, and only just managed to stop himself giving a shout of triumph.

She had come to him. True, she had only wanted information, but it was a start.

Two days later he arrived at her office and handed her the information she had asked for. As she read it her brow creased.

'It's an expensive business,' he pointed out gently.

'So I see. Do you mind if I mention some of this to the council?'

'The costing for the development is no secret.'

His heart thudded as she looked up and smiled. He was glad she didn't do that too often because he wouldn't be able to stand it. It transformed her completely.

'Thanks, you've been a big help,' she said.

He sat on the edge of the desk and swung one leg casually. 'Have you taken Annie to the National Gallery yet?'

'I haven't had time.'

'Then make time.' He paused. 'Tell you what, I'll take you both tomorrow.'

'But I've got work to do.'

'Take a day off. You promised her,' he pointed out. 'I'll pick you up here at ten o'clock. We can drive around some of the sights, have lunch, and spend the afternoon looking at pictures.'

He watched her as she thought about it, and kept quiet: if he pushed too hard, she would refuse. One thing he had discovered about Rose was that she hated being told what to do.

'All right,' she said, suddenly, 'Annie would like it . . . and I would too.'

He was glad she had added the last bit. 'Good, I'll see you tomorrow.'

'Rosie! Hurry up, we mustn't be late.' Annie tore up the stairs to see what her sister was doing. 'I can't wait to show Uncle Bill our new coats.' She twirled in front of the old broken mirror. 'It's the best thing I've ever had.' Then her face went serious. 'You haven't spent all your money, have you?'

'No, they weren't expensive, and you know I never buy anything unless I can afford to pay for it. I'm earning more money now,' Rose added truthfully.

Her sister's face cleared. 'Won't Uncle Bill be proud of us!'

He was already waiting, and Annie danced up to show him her new coat. When Rose got there he was telling her sister how smart she looked.

'You won't be ashamed to take us out now, will you?' Annie said.

Bill stooped down to her. 'Sweetheart, I wouldn't be ashamed to be seen with you and your sister if you were dressed in rags.'

'Rosie used to be,' Annie told him, 'but she's never let me wear rags.'

'If you two have finished talking about me, perhaps we can go.'

Annie clasped her arms around Bill's neck and whispered, loudly enough for Rose to hear, 'She doesn't like anyone to know she's kind.'

'I'm aware of that, so we'd better keep it a secret.' He stood up and winked, which sent Annie into a fit of the giggles.

They drove along to Buckingham Palace and watched the soldiers on guard, then they had lunch at a proper restaurant, and after that they went to the National Gallery.

'Are you enjoying yourself?' Bill asked, as they gazed at the pictures.

Rose nodded. 'It was very kind of you to bring us.'

'I can hear a "but" in your tone,' he said. 'And I think you're worried about me paying again.'

'Yes, well . . .' Rose looked into his eyes and decided she'd better explain. 'Business has picked up tremendously and I'm earning a respectable wage now. I like to pay my own way.'

He took her hand. 'I know you do, but don't deprive me of the pleasure of taking you and Annie out today.'

She really was going to have to do something about her damned pride, Rose mused.

Annie was insisting she must see everything, so they walked until Rose's feet hurt and she found herself a seat. Having fun was a damned exhausting business, she decided, but she was enjoying herself. Bill was easy company, and knowledgeable on lots of subjects. Of course, that was hardly surprising: he had been to Oxford University so he must be clever.

Bill looked at his pocket watch. 'I think it's time we had tea.'

'There's lots more to see, but it's too much for one day,' Annie sighed regretfully, 'and I think Rosie's tired now.'

'I'll bring you again, and we can start from where we've left off,' Bill told her.

'Oh, yes, please.' Happy with that promise, Annie caught hold of Rose's hand and pulled her up. 'You hold her other hand, Uncle Bill, then she won't be so tired.'

Rose sighed inwardly. Her sister was incorrigible, but she didn't protest. Her temper was holding out quite well today, she thought. She hadn't snapped at him once.

After much discussion, they decided to have fish and chips instead of a proper tea, as they were all starving. It rounded off a happy day.

When they arrived home, they were both given a kiss, Annie on the cheek, and Rose on the lips, just a brief touch, but she didn't mind which was a bit of a puzzle: normally, she'd have been spitting mad at him for taking such a liberty.

By the time they walked into the scullery, Annie looked tired. She gave Rose a sleepy smile. 'Uncle Bill's very nice, isn't he? Do you like him?'

'Yes, I do.' And Rose knew that was the truth.

After a good night's sleep and lunch with the family, Rose and Annie set off to visit Grace and John.

'Oh, look, Uncle Bill's here,' Annie cried, as soon as she saw the car. Then she was off at full speed and erupted through the front door like a tornado.

Rose followed at her usual sedate pace, and found not only Bill but Harold too. 'Are you having a party, Grace?' she asked.

'It looks like it.' She hoisted her child over her shoulder. 'My goodness, he's getting heavy.'

Tea was a lively affair, and Rose was feeling surprisingly

tranquil. It had been a pleasant weekend: doing something apart from work had been good for her. She sighed contentedly. She was becoming quite placid, she thought, with a wry smile. That would never do in court.

30

June 1923

It was nearly ten months since Rose had burst into Joshua Braithwaite's practice and turned his life upside-down. During that time the local people had come to trust them and the business was growing. Josh was a changed man and took on worthy cases with enthusiasm, and won more often than not. As for Rose, she had been able to help quite a few women, but it was not enough: there were still too many out there suffering from injustice and abuse.

'There's someone to see you, Rose,' her mother said, poking her head around the office kitchen door. 'Better put the kettle on to boil. She's very distressed.'

'Show her in, Mum.'

When the woman slid through the door – and that was the only way Rose could describe it – she felt anger, quickly followed by pity. 'Please sit down,' she urged, not sure that the woman could remain on her feet for much longer. 'Would you like some tea?'

The woman nodded, then sat down with a thud. 'I shouldn't have come,' she murmured, 'but I'm at my wits' end.'

Rose motioned to her mother to stay, then put the cup in front of the woman, and smiled encouragingly. 'Will you tell me your name?'

'It's Ethel Grant . . .'

'And how can I help you, Ethel?' Rose studied her carefully as Ethel tried to make up her mind to speak of her troubles, though part of it was evident: she.had been badly beaten.

'He's taken my kids away from me.' Ethel wrung her hands in anguish and tears flooded down her face. 'My little ones are frightened to death and – ' She started to sob uncontrollably.

Marj pulled up a chair and sat beside Ethel, holding her hand until she calmed down a little. 'Tell my daughter what's happened,' she suggested.

After another cup of tea and a little more coaxing, the story poured out. 'My hubby's a violent man when he's been at the drink, but just lately it's got worse. I can't do nothing to please him, and yesterday he near beat the life out of me, and I was scared and picked up a plate and hit him with it. I didn't hurt him none,' Ethel added hastily, 'but he chucked me out, and when I tried to take the little ones with me, he said I'd never see them again.' She began to wail once more.

Rose waited for a minute or two, then asked, gently, 'Do you mean he's going to divorce you?'

'Something like that – said he doesn't need me no more and he'd find himself a better woman.'

'Do you know if he's already got one?' By now Rose's blood was boiling. If she could have got hold of the man she would have thrashed him herself, but that wasn't the way to do it. It was time some of these brutes were taken to court to face their crimes.

Ethel leaned across the table and grabbed Rose's hand.

'He mustn't keep them! They're not safe with him – not without me to protect them.'

'Are you willing to take this to court? It will mean telling strangers how violent he is, and if he's committed adultery we can use that against him too. But it will be an ordeal for you.' Rose had had other cases like this, but none of the women had been willing to take things further. That had been frustrating because there had been little else she could do for them.

'Will it mean getting my kids back?'

'I can't promise that, but we'll have a bloody good try.'

Ethel looked up. There was a spark of defiance in her pale eyes. 'I'll do anything to get my babies away from him.'

That was what Rose had been longing to hear.

'How many have you got?' Marj asked.

'Six, and the youngest is only two.' Tears ran down her cheeks again.

'Where are you staying?' Rose prompted, trying to get more details.

'With my sister in Lambeth. She'd heard about you helping women, and told me to come and see you.' Ethel blew her nose. 'I didn't know if I should come because we ain't got much money, but I don't know where else to turn.'

'Don't worry about the money, Ethel.' Rose knew she would do this for nothing.

Once she had all the information she needed, she took Ethel to the hospital and, luckily, the first person she saw was Edward Trenchard. He came straight over to her. 'This is Ethel Grant,' she told him. 'Could you have someone examine her and give me a report of her injuries?'

'I'll do it myself.' Edward led the frightened woman away, and returned half an hour later with the written details she had asked for. 'Are you going to do something about this brutality?' he asked, clearly furious.

'Yes – at least, I'll have a damned good try.'

'You can call me as a witness, if you like.'

'Oh, Edward, that would be such a help.' Rose smiled at him in gratitude.

He patted her arm. 'You be careful. This could get nasty.'

The next few weeks were frantic for Rose, as the plight of Ethel and her children filled her life. She had pleaded, argued and even threatened, until at last she had a modest success. The youngest boy was allowed to live with his mother, but the father was flatly refusing to give up the others.

'You women ain't got no rights,' he'd bellowed at her, when she had confronted him.

After that she'd hired a private detective to watch him, and now had proof that he was committing adultery. With that and Edward's testimony she should be able to put forward a good case, and with a sympathetic judge they might stand a chance. She had hoped to save Ethel the ordeal of going to court, but now it was the only option left open to her.

Rose rested her head in her hands and closed her eyes.

'Tough case?' a voice asked.

She opened her eyes and saw that Bill had come into the office. She nodded.

'Can you spare a couple of hours? I've been told about another slum-clearance project, and they're having trouble getting the last family to move.'

Rose was on her feet and hurrying out of the door, her tiredness forgotten. 'Let's go.'

They were soon on their way and she sat back with a sigh of pleasure. What a useful thing a car was. 'Where is this new development?'

'Canning Town.'

'And the people who are refusing to move, have they been offered somewhere else to live?'

'Yes, the houses are a vast improvement on the ones they've been living in, and most of them have gone willingly enough but . . .'

'I know,' she sighed, 'there's always someone who doesn't want to move. I think they get frightened.'

Rose heard the shouting before they turned the corner, and was out of the car and running almost before it had stopped. 'What's going on here?' she demanded, elbowing her way through the crowd of men.

'Mind your own business,' one of the men growled belligerently.

'I'm a lawyer, and if you're threatening these people, then it *is* my business.' She planted herself in front of them, hands on hips. 'Now, who are you?'

'Bailiffs.' A man in a suit and a bowler hat stepped forward. 'We don't want trouble, but we've been given orders to get this family out today. They're holding up the work.'

This man seemed in charge and more approachable, Rose thought. She held out her hand. 'Can I see the eviction notice, please.'

He handed it to her and she studied it carefully, then gave it back. 'That's all in order. I'm Rose Webster,' she introduced herself, 'and if you would hold your men off for a while, I'll go in and talk to them. What's their name?'

'Perkins,' he said, 'and if you can persuade them to move, we'd be grateful. All our efforts have failed, but I'm reluctant to use force. There's children in there and I wouldn't like them to get hurt.'

With a nod, she walked up to the house and smiled reassuringly at the frightened faces looking out of the grimy window. 'Will you let me in?' she called. 'I want to talk to you.'

'We ain't opening the door to no one,' a man snarled.

'My name's Rose Webster, and I only want to talk to you.' She heard arguing going on inside and waited.

'You that lawyer from Garrett Street?' a woman called.

'That's right, Mrs Perkins.' There was more arguing. Then the door opened a crack, a hand came out and pulled her inside. The door slammed shut behind her.

The place was disgusting: the demolition work going on all around them had covered everything with a thick layer of brick dust, and the three children, in as bad a state as the house, were hanging on to their mother's skirt, their faces streaked with tearstains.

My God, Rose thought, they ought to be running out of here, eager to get into another place. Instead, they were holding on to the familiar, as if their lives depended on it.

'What you want?' the man demanded.

'Will you tell me why you won't move?'

'We've lived here all our lives. Why should we be

322

chucked out? We always pays our rent.' He stopped and looked at her suspiciously. 'We've heard about you. What you doing with that lot out there?'

'Persuading them not to come in here swinging hammers and pickaxes to break the door down.'

'They won't do that,' he sneered.

'Yes, they will, Mr Perkins.'

'Oh, we must go, Tom, please,' his wife begged. 'All our friends have gone – '

'Shut up, woman. I'm not leaving my home.'

Rose sighed in frustration. This was the kind of attitude that would delay a big slum-clearance operation in the future. 'Have you seen the houses they've offered you?'

'No, and I don't want to!'

'I have, Miss Webster. They're nice – much better than this dump.'

'What do you mean "dump"?'

Tom Perkins turned on his wife and the children howled in fear. Rose waded in and hauled the couple apart. Placing herself between them, she decided to get tough. The wife was willing to move, and it was only the man's stubbornness that was stopping them.

'Do you care for your wife and kids?' she asked him bluntly.

He was startled. 'Course I do.'

'Then why haven't you even been to have a look at the new place? Are you too scared to find out that you like it?' she challenged.

'I'm not scared of nothing,' he growled.

'Then go and see it.'

'How can I? If I leave, they'll be in 'ere like a shot.'

'Not if I stay with your wife and children.'

323

'Oh, please, Tom,' his wife implored. 'You can trust Miss Webster, you know what we was told about her. She grew up like us and look at her now – a famous lawyer.'

Rose smiled inwardly. 'Well?'

He was weakening and she moved in quickly, not giving him a chance to change his mind. 'I've got a friend outside. He'll take you in his car and bring you back. It won't take long.'

'Car, you say?'

Rose nodded. 'Let me out and I'll go and talk to him.'

'All right.'

'How's it going?' the bailiff asked, as she strode over to them.

'I've nearly persuaded them, but the man wants to look at the new place.' She turned to Bill. 'Would you drive Mr Perkins over there?'

'Of course,' he answered, without hesitation. 'I'll bring the car to the door.'

She clasped his hand in gratitude. 'Thanks.'

'Tell you what, miss, what if me and the lads go and have a bit of lunch? You might have sorted this out by then.'

She smiled at the bailiff. 'That's a good idea. If Mr Perkins sees you leave, it might relax him a little.'

'Come on, lads,' he called. 'Let's have a break and leave Miss Webster to see what she can do.'

They walked off through the rubble and she went back to the house.

'Where they going?' Mr Perkins asked.

'For something to eat while you have a look at the other house.'

'Blimey!' he exclaimed, rubbing a spot clean on the window so he could get a better view. 'That your fellow in that posh car?'

'Yes.' She pushed him out of the door. 'Don't keep him waiting.'

Rose watched Bill shake hands with him, always the perfect gentleman. The more she got to know him, the more she respected him. They drove away, Tom Perkins sitting proudly in the front passenger seat.

They were back within half an hour, and Tom Perkins came in looking quite different. 'Quite a toff, that man of yours, but not stuck-up nor nothing,' he said, with approval. 'Fought in the Great War, didn't he?'

'He was in the navy.'

'Jutland?'

'I believe so. What did you think of the house?' she asked, changing the subject. Time was running out.

'It's all right. Bill explained everything to me,' he told them importantly. 'Knows what he's talking about . . . He's an arch- arc- – '

'Architect,' Rose supplied.

'That's right. Anyway, I can see now it's much better than this.' He turned to his wife. 'It's got water what comes out of a tap in the kitchen, and a privy attached to the house.'

'I know, Tom. Can we go there?'

'Don't see why not. Bill says we'll be better off there.'

Rose saw the men coming back. 'Shall I get someone to help you move, Mr Perkins?'

'Thanks, miss.'

As she went out of the door, Mrs Perkins grabbed her hand. 'I don't know how to thank you.'

'Just be happy in your new home.' She left the squalid house and went over to the men. 'They've agreed to move.'

A cheer rang out from the workmen.

'But they will need some help.'

'We've got a cart ready, and we'll see they get everything over to the new place.' The bailiff looked at her with respect. 'Thank you, Miss Webster, you've saved us a deal of trouble today.'

Elated by the success of the afternoon, she went to Bill with a broad smile on her face. 'You really impressed Mr Perkins. "Bill explained everything to me,"' she mimicked, then burst out laughing. 'You're a real charmer, Mr Freeman. I think if you'd told him the moon was made of cheese, he'd have believed you.'

'I always thought it was,' he replied, straight-faced.

She giggled. 'Oh, this has lifted my spirits after the pressure of the last few weeks.'

'Feel like celebrating?' he asked, as he opened the car door for her. 'Come dancing with me tonight.'

'But I can't dance.'

'Time you learned, then.' He gave her a sideways smile.

Rose was in too good a mood to refuse. 'All right, but what shall I wear? I haven't got one of those new fancy dresses the girls are wearing these days.'

'Wear anything. You always look beautiful,' he said.

'Oh! I can't go.' She'd remembered something. 'I've promised to visit Lady Gresham tonight.'

He turned the car around. 'We'll go and see her now. I'm sure she'll understand.'

He drove straight to the house without her giving him any directions. 'How do you know where Lady Gresham lives?' she asked.

'John told me.'

'Oh.' She walked up the steps and he came with her. 'You don't have to come in with me, I won't be long.'

He ignored her and knocked on the door. He's good at that, she thought, as they were shown into the drawing room. He gets his own way without uttering a word.

'Rose! You're early.'

'That's my fault, Lady Gresham.' Bill stepped forward. 'I want to take Rose dancing, but she insists that she can't because she's visiting you tonight.'

'You must certainly go. I used to love dancing when I was a girl.' She made them sit down. 'What are you going to wear?'

'I've only got the navy blue frock.'

'No, no, my dear, that won't do at all.' Lady Gresham rang the bell and a servant appeared instantly. 'Ask Martha to get out my black crêpe-de-Chine.' She stood up. 'Come, my dear, let's see if it fits. We're much of a size,' she remarked.

The door opened before they reached it and Sir George strode in. 'George, entertain Mr Freeman while we sort out a dress for Rose. Her young man's taking her dancing and we can't have her wearing that severe dress she uses for her legal practice.'

Rose had only a moment to wish that everyone would stop referring to Bill as her young man, before she was hustled out of the room. She glanced back at him

327

anxiously, but he looked as relaxed and unperturbed as usual. Does anything ruffle that man? she wondered.

The dress was exquisite. The delicate material flowed around her legs, the back was low, and the bodice shimmered with jet beads as the light caught them. It was also a perfect fit and Rose turned round to see it properly in the mirror. 'It's beautiful,' she exclaimed.

'I knew you'd like it.' Lady Gresham straightened the skirt. 'It's lovely on you and I'll never wear it again.' She looked down at Rose's shoes. 'We'll have to do something about those. These might fit.'

Rose took the soft black leather shoes, slipped them on and fastened the strap across the instep. They were perfect, and so comfortable.

'Good.' Lady Gresham looked as if she was enjoying herself. 'Now let's put this on.'

Rose watched in the mirror as a thin bandeau, sparkling with the same jet beads as the dress, was put over her short hair and adjusted until it was across her forehead. 'My goodness.' She viewed herself in the long mirror. 'Is that me?'

Lady Gresham nodded. 'Of course it is. Now, let us go and show Mr Freeman how charming you look.'

Rose knew that protest was useless. Over the last few years she had become very fond of her grandmother and she didn't want to upset her. It was only a dress, after all, and from what she had seen, the old lady's wardrobe was crammed with them.

The men got to their feet as they entered the room, and Rose realized with a shock that she was enjoying the attention and admiring looks. In fact, she felt quite feminine.

'Doesn't she look beautiful?' Lady Gresham said.

There were murmurs of approval, and Rose received a kiss on the cheek from Sir George. 'Absolutely lovely,' he agreed.

Bill seemed lost for words.

'You will both stay for dinner,' Lady Gresham ordered. 'Then you can go straight to the dance. You are already smartly dressed, Mr Freeman, and have no need to change.'

During the meal the elderly lady seemed in her element, while Sir George was enjoying having another man to talk to. Rose noticed how well Bill fitted in with the Greshams: he was charming and his manners were impeccable.

'Mr Freeman?' Lady Gresham looked at him thought-fully. 'You remind me of someone, and the name is familiar. Where is your home?'

'I live in London now, but I was brought up near Portsmouth.'

'Ah! I have it,' she declared triumphantly. 'I should have recognized you sooner, you are so like your father. How is the Admiral?'

'He died a little while ago,' Bill told her.

'Oh, I'm so sorry.'

Rose's mouth dropped open in surprise. Admiral?

'Did you know my father?' he asked casually.

'Indeed I did. I was quite tempted by the handsome devil when I was a girl.' Her dark eyes shone and she clapped her hands. 'This is perfect. The son of my first love has found my granddaughter.'

'Admiral Freeman?' Rose asked, when they were back in the car. 'Why didn't you tell me?'

'You never asked.'

Suddenly she began to shake with laughter.

'What is so funny?'

'Oh,' she gasped, 'I asked the son of an admiral to take Mr Perkins in his car.'

He chuckled. 'Don't worry, I kept all the windows open.'

The dance was at the Hammersmith Palais de Danse. Rose had heard of it, but never been inside. It was a warm evening so she hadn't brought a coat with her, and Bill led her straight into the hall. She gazed around in wonder. The place was crowded, but the thing that made the most impression on her was the music.

'Do you like jazz?' Bill asked, watching her face intently.

'Oh, yes.' She laughed up at him. 'It makes me feel as if I want to dance, even though I don't know how to.'

'I know what you mean.' He took her arm and led her towards a staircase. 'Let's have a drink first and then I'll teach you the steps.'

They took their glasses on to a balcony overlooking the dance floor, and Rose studied the throng downstairs, fascinated. Some of the dresses were outrageous, others stylish, but the one she was wearing was elegant, and she felt wonderful in it.

Later they went down to join the other dancers and Bill began to show her how to do the Jog Trot.

Rose watched the antics of the dancers all around her in amazement. 'I can't do that.'

'Of course you can. Just relax and move,' Bill encouraged her.

330

The music changed then and she was even more bewildered. 'What on earth is this called?'

'The Shimmy.' Bill demonstrated with great expertise, and grinned. 'Come on, Rose, forget everything and just move to the music.'

She found it difficult to unwind enough to join in, but soon the exciting jazz music got to her.

'That's perfect,' Bill shouted above the band. 'I knew you could do it.'

She was thoroughly enjoying herself, and an hour later he led her back to the balcony for another drink. She had never felt so happy and exhilarated. In fact, she felt like an ordinary young woman out to enjoy herself. What a lot she had been missing.

They sipped their lemonade and hung over the balcony watching the dancers.

'Look at that couple,' she said. 'I don't think they've got any bones in their bodies.'

Bill chuckled. 'They're very good. With a bit of practice you could do that.'

She looked at him in astonishment, then laughed so much she had to sit down.

The evening ended too soon. As they walked towards the car, Rose said, 'That was wonderful, thank you for bringing me.'

He stopped, turned her into his arms and kissed her firmly. It seemed to go on for a long time, but she wasn't frightened this time. Eventually he drew away. 'I shall be working in Scotland for a while,' he told her.

'How long will you be there?'

'I'm not sure.' He took her into his arms again and

the kiss was not so gentle this time. 'But I'll be back, you can be sure of that.'

31

Autumn arrived without a sign of Bill. Rose thrust away her disappointment. She was far too busy to be concerned about his continued absence, she told herself firmly.

Ethel's case was being heard, and she had much higher hopes of winning now. A new law, the Matrimonial Causes Act, had been passed, allowing women to sue for divorce on the grounds of adultery alone, and the husband could only have access to the children if he was a desirable influence. Well, Ethel's husband wasn't *that*.

But even with the new law, it did not prove an easy task: the legal system was still dominated by men and old prejudices were still strong. Her case was sound, though, and Rose presented it with confidence and determination. The evidence of the detective proved adultery beyond any doubt, and Edward Trenchard gave a description of Ethel's injuries. At the end of three often unpleasant days, Ethel was granted her divorce and the father was ordered to hand over the children at once.

It was a sweet victory, and Rose hoped it would serve as a precedent for similar cases in the future. It was widely reported in the newspapers, and heralded as a huge step forward for women. She also took satisfaction from the knowledge that, since 1920, women had been allowed to read for the Bar. It had crossed Rose's mind to do that, but she still felt she could achieve more in the job she was doing.

The next day, she worked late to catch up with some neglected paperwork and it was dark when she locked the office.

She was about to put the keys in her purse when something hit her and rough hands grabbed her arms. Every tiny detail of the rape rushed into her mind and, with a snarl of rage, she spun round.

It was not going to happen to her again.

Her eyes had become accustomed to the gloom and she could now see the outlines of two men. She clenched her fist and threw a punch at the nearest, putting all of her strength behind it. He screamed and covered his face with his hands, blood running through his fingers. 'You bitch!' he groaned. 'You've broken my nose.'

Rose ignored him. He wasn't going to cause her any more trouble. But before she had a chance to do the same to the other man, he caught her a stinging blow across the face, quickly followed by another.

Rose knew she couldn't expect any help. Whenever there was trouble, the people who lived here went in, shut their doors and kept out of the way. She was on her own.

However, she was not a young girl now: she was strong, and she used that to her advantage. Her blow made him stagger back and while he was stunned she took her chance: she seized his arms and forced them behind him. A quick look round told her that the other man had disappeared.

'Walk!' she ordered, and pushed him up the street towards the police station. When he tried to resist, she tightened her grip.

'Let go of me, you bitch!' he swore.

Rose had been too occupied to take any notice of who her assailants were, but now she recognized the voice of Ethel's ex-husband. She had known the man would be a bad loser. 'Keep moving or I'll break your arms,' she threatened.

The police station was about half a mile away, and her captive struggled and cursed every inch of the way, but she held him. The building was a welcome sight, though, and she hauled him through the door with a sigh of relief.

The sergeant on duty looked at her in amazement. 'What have you got there, miss?'

'She attacked me!' the now frightened man accused. 'Broke my mate's nose.'

Rose shoved him into a chair as two policemen came to her aid. 'Sit there and keep your mouth shut!' She introduced herself and explained what had happened.

'You want to make a complaint?' the sergeant asked.

'Of course I do. Why do you think I dragged him here?' she said impatiently. 'You lock him up and I'll prosecute him myself.'

'There's no need for that,' the man babbled. 'We wasn't going to hurt you, just wanted to teach you a lesson, that's all.'

She touched her bruised cheek and the rapidly growing lump on the back of her head. Who did he think he was trying to kid? 'So you thought an iron bar wouldn't hurt me, did you?'

'It wasn't an iron bar,' he protested loudly.

'Really? What was it, then?'

'Lump of wood,' he muttered.

Rose pointed to the form the sergeant was filling in.

'Put that down, and the fact that he has admitted attacking me with a weapon.'

'Bloody woman's too smart for her own good,' Grant snarled.

She gave a menacing smile. 'You've got that the wrong way round. I'm too smart for *your* good.'

'Do you know who the other one was?'

'Just look for a man with a broken nose,' she told the officer who had just joined them.

'What about you? Are you all right?' he asked, looking at a trickle of blood coming from the corner of her mouth.

'Yes, but you'd better get a doctor to have a look at him. I hit him a few times.'

The officer grinned. 'I've heard about you, Miss Webster. I'll bet they're sorry they tried to attack you.'

'What do you mean, "tried"? They damned near slit my skull open.' Rose didn't know what he was grinning at. She could see nothing funny about it.

'We'll have him in court at ten o'clock in the morning,' the officer told her, still struggling to keep a smile at bay.

'Good.' She turned to Grant. 'I'll see you in court – again.' Then she strode out of the police station.

She heard the officer chuckle and swore under her breath.

Rose crept into the house, trying not disturb anyone, but Annie must have been awake and waiting for her because she appeared almost immediately.

'You're late . . .' Then she caught sight of her sister's face. 'Oh, Rosie, you haven't been fighting again, have you?'

'You make it sound as if I'm always in a brawl.' Rose

put her hand to her head. She had a thumping headache.

'Sit down, and I'll make you a cup of tea. Then you can tell me who hit you.'

Rose was glad of the tea. The attack had been nasty – but it could have been worse. 'Ethel Grant's former husband and one of his mates thought they'd have a go at me, but I fought them off. One ran away with a broken nose, and Mr Grant is in a police cell.'

Annie looked anxious. 'Why did you have to choose such a dangerous job, Rosie?'

'It isn't dangerous, it's just that men aren't used to being dragged before the law to answer for their crimes.'

'But they haven't got any right to attack you.'

'I know.' Rose smiled at her sister, trying to allay her concern. 'You should have seen the other one run, and by the time word of this gets round, I don't think anyone will attack me again.'

Her sister giggled then. 'I bet they never thought you were so strong.'

'They've underestimated women for too long.' Rose stood up. 'Let's get some sleep.'

Ethel's ex-husband got a year, and the other man who had been found by police at a hospital received six months for his part in the attack. Rose left the court well pleased with the morning's work.

When she reached her office, she went into the back room where she could be alone and sat down. The attack had shaken her up more than she liked to admit. She had always been used to violence, but as a child she had escaped into books and study, shutting out her surroundings. She rubbed her temple. There was little time for books now, and the nasty side of men's characters seemed to fill her life. She thought briefly of Bill and wished more men were like him.

Then she sat up and pounded the table with her fist. She was letting her emotions get in the way. It didn't take much effort to slam the door on her feelings, but she mentally turned the key for added security.

Bill walked into his office. He hadn't intended to be away for so long, but one job had led to another and he hadn't been able to leave Scotland. Later he took the stairs to his flat two at a time. It was good to be back. The journey had been long and tedious, but he hadn't minded because every mile had brought him closer to Rose.

At the thought of her, a spasm of anxiety ran through him. What if she'd found someone else while he had been away?

Without thinking about the lateness of the hour, he rushed out to his car. The traffic was light and he was soon knocking on John's door.

'Bill! When did you get back?'

'About an hour ago. Look, I'm sorry to call so late, but I'm not going to be able to sleep until I know how Rose is.'

As Grace and John told him what his dark-eyed stick of dynamite had been up to, he didn't know whether to laugh or cry. 'My God! She isn't safe to be out on her own. She needs someone to look after her.'

'It wouldn't do any good.' Grace sighed. 'I seriously doubt that she can be tamed. She has even joined the Labour Party, and is in the thick of the fight for reform.'

'I shouldn't have stayed so long,' Bill regretted. 'I was

just beginning to get through to her. When I took her dancing she was so happy and carefree.'

Grace looked at him sadly. 'I know you love her, Bill, but there's a demon inside her that controls her life. She is so involved in what she's doing that she has little time for anything else. She won't rest until she has done what she's set out to do.'

'And what exactly is that?'

'A better deal for women, and the destruction of places like Garrett Street,' John informed him.

He stood up, suddenly weary. 'I've just got to accept her as she is.'

There was quite a party going on when Bill pushed open the door of Rose's office and walked in.

'Uncle Bill!' Annie cried, seeing him immediately.

'Hello, sweetheart. My goodness, you've grown.' He stooped to be hugged.

'We're giving Rosie a twenty-first birthday party.' Her face took on a worried expression. 'She works too hard and needs cheering up. Have you brought her a present?'

'I've got something special for her.' He stood up and searched the crowded room. Everyone seemed to be here, all of Rose's family, the neighbours, many of whom he remembered from the wedding, Grace, John, Harold, Josh and even Lady Gresham.

When he saw Rose his heart contracted. She looked the same – and yet she didn't. The proud carriage and determined tilt of her head were still there, but as she turned to look at him, he saw something that almost tore him apart. There was a new toughness about her, and the effect of her battles showed: her eyes were cold and unyielding. The woman he saw in front of him had lost her softness, and in its place was ferocity. She was ready to do battle with anyone who opposed her.

Despair surged through him but it was quickly replaced with compassion and a steely determination. She needed some stability in her life and he was going to provide it.

'Hello.' She stood in front of him. 'John told me you were back.'

'Rose.' As he bent to kiss her she tried to move away, but he wouldn't allow her to and kissed her firmly on the lips, then gave her his present. It was something frivolous and he doubted that she'd ever had anything like it before. 'Happy birthday.'

'Scent?' Rose turned it over and over in her hands.

'Chanel No. 5, and it's the latest thing.' He took the bottle from her, opened it and held it out. 'Put some on your wrists, let it warm for a few seconds, then smell it.'

She did as instructed and her expression softened. 'Oh, that's lovely. Thank you.'

'Hmm. It certainly is.' He lifted her hand, smelt the perfume, then gently kissed her palm. Much to his delight she didn't pull away.

'I see you haven't changed,' she told him drily.

'No, and I'm not going to.' She walked away then and he mingled politely with everyone, but all the time he watched Rose.

'She needs your love, Mr Freeman.'

He turned and saw Lady Gresham standing next to him, her eyes fixed on Rose too.

'My granddaughter has suffered too many disappointments in her short life, and endured too many fights –

physical and mental. She is beginning to shut herself away from all feeling.' She glanced at him. 'That must not be allowed to happen.'

'I'll do what I can.'

'No, no.' The elderly lady shook her head vigorously. 'That's not good enough. I know you love her and you must make her yours. And don't take any of her nonsense – I am sure she cares for you, but will not admit to it. If she comes up against a will as strong as hers, she will respect and listen to you. She considers a loving nature weak, but you must show her that that is not the case.'

'You consider me man enough for such an arduous task?' he asked wryly.

'Yes. You have gentleness, patience and courage, and I believe you are the only man she will respect enough to marry. And she *must* marry before it's too late.' Lady Gresham kissed his cheek and walked out regally to her waiting car.

'You're a favourite.' Rose came over to him, and they watched Lady Gresham drive away.

'I like her. She has wisdom and a clear understanding of human nature.' He took Rose's hand and headed for the door.

'Where do you think you're taking me?' She wrenched her hand free.

'We're going for a ride,' he told her calmly, taking hold of her again.

'I can't leave my party. Everyone's gone to a lot of trouble.'

'Oh, you do care about other people, then?'

'Of course I do.' She gave him a penetrating look. 'What's the matter with you? You go away for months, then think you can sweep back and start ordering me about.'

'It's time somebody gave you a good talking-to.'

'Now just a minute – '

Before she could protest any more, he opened the door and pushed her out. 'Don't argue, Rose. You're coming for a short ride. I won't keep you long, but we need to talk.'

'We haven't got anything to talk – '

The look he gave her stopped the flow of words, and she sat silently beside him until he found a quiet spot by the river. He stopped the car, turned in his seat and took her face between his hands. 'I love you. Will you marry me?'

'*What?*' she exclaimed. 'Are you mad?'

The kiss he gave her was a mixture of love, hunger and frustration. 'Yes, I'm mad,' he told her huskily, as he pulled away. 'Loving you has made me like that, and the only cure is for you to marry me.'

'Don't be daft.' Rose gave him a disbelieving glance. 'I'm too busy for this nonsense and, anyway, I'm never going to marry.'

'Yes, you are. You've always been strong, but you're becoming hard now. Everyone's worried about you, and you no longer have time for the people who love you.' When she didn't speak, he drove the point home. 'Come on, tell me the last time you took Annie out? And when did you take the time to visit Grace, John, Harold and Lady Gresham?'

'I've been busy,' she muttered.

'That's no excuse. You're surrounded by people who care, but you shut yourself away, locking the doors against

342

any kind of personal involvement. Obsession has taken over and it's driving you – '

'All right, I know,' she shouted. 'But how on earth is marrying you going to help.'

'Because I'll be there to give you something else in your life and, most important of all, I love you and care what happens to you,' he added quietly. 'I know you have fears, but I would never hurt you, and never force you to do anything you didn't want to.'

She laughed derisively. 'I can't imagine you wanting a loveless marriage.'

'I don't, and it won't be.' He ran his fingers gently down her cheek. 'You can trust me.'

'Maybe, but I don't want to marry you – or anyone else.'

'I'm not going to give up, so will you think about it?'

'This is a waste of time,' she said, clearly becoming agitated. 'I don't know what love is.'

'Yes, you do, but you've pushed it to the back of your mind and you refuse to let it surface. I've seen the love you've always had for Annie.'

'That's different. She's my sister and she's needed me.'

'And doesn't the fact that I need you mean anything to you?'

Rose sighed. 'I don't know what on earth you're going on about. I think your visit to Scotland has turned your head. Take me back to the party.'

'Not until you've promised to consider my proposal.'

'All right, I'll think about it. Now can we go?'

Bill started the car. It would be best to give her time to think things over. But he would give her one more jolt, he thought. 'I suppose I'd better go and ask your father for permission to marry you.'

She turned in her seat and glared at him. 'Don't you dare!'

He smiled to himself. At least that had woken her up.

32

The door opened and Josh swept in with a huge smile on his face. 'Rose, the day you came here changed my life. You're an angel.'

'I've never been called that before,' she said. 'Most people believe I came from the other place.'

'Then they're wrong. Our business is a success and we've been able to help a lot of people.'

What he was saying was true. But why didn't she feel better about herself? This uncomfortable, guilty feeling had been with her ever since Bill had made that ridiculous proposal three weeks ago. Since then, she had noticed that everyone was tiptoeing around her as if she was a bomb ready to explode.

'Don't look so unhappy.' He sat down. 'What's the matter?'

'Oh, nothing.' She dredged up a smile. The change in Josh was amazing. When she'd first met him he'd been shabby, downtrodden and beaten-looking. Now he was smartly dressed, lively and enthusiastic about life and work. 'Too much work, I expect. But never mind about me, what are you so pleased about?'

'The British Legion have asked me to act as their legal adviser.'

'That's wonderful. They're turning out to be a very useful organization.'

'Although I've only had a modest success in getting

increased compensation for some of the more badly injured, they're pleased I've managed to stir things up a bit. And guess who we've got on our side now?'

'No idea.'

'Bill Freeman. He's designing some homes for those who have difficulty getting about.'

'Oh?' Rose looked up quickly. This was news to her. 'Who's going to build them?'

'A private contractor.'

'I might have guessed,' she muttered.

'They'll be for rent, Rose. Don't condemn the scheme until you've heard the whole story.'

'I'm sorry.' Good heavens, what was the matter with her?

'You're too quick to judge,' he told her.

'I know what you're saying is true, but I get so frustrated. It's almost five years since the war ended, and improvement is so slow.'

'Change will only come gradually, but we're making our voice heard in a small way. That must help.'

Before she had time to answer, the door opened again and Bill strode in. Josh rushed up to him and shook his hand. 'Good to see you again. I've just been telling Rose about the new homes. Is there something I can do for you?'

'No, thank you. I've come to see Rose.'

'Right, I'll be off, then.' Josh paused at the door. 'Can you cheer her up? She's looking far too miserable for a young woman.'

'I'll see what I can do.' When Josh went out and closed the door Bill turned and smiled. 'Get your coat,' he ordered. 'I'm taking you out to dinner, and then to the

346

Hippodrome, for an evening of entertainment. And don't think about it, just do as you're told for a change.'

Rose looked at him uncertainly. Was he spoiling for a fight? No, she couldn't imagine him losing his temper enough for that. In fact, she doubted that he had one. But if she went out with him would she have to listen to another marriage proposal?

'This is just going to be a friendly night out. I'm not about to propose again, and I won't even touch you.'

He'd read her mind.

'Are you coming, or do I have to carry you to the car?'

He'd do it too, Rose thought. Oh, what the hell! She stood up, let him help her on with her coat, then marched to the door. His only comment was a silent lifting of one eyebrow.

Once they were on their way, she spoke. 'Josh told me –'

Bill stopped her firmly. 'We're not going to talk business tonight. We're going to have a good dinner, see a lively show, and enjoy ourselves.'

'I'm not dressed for one of your posh restaurants.'

'You look fine.' He gave her a sideways glance. 'You always do.'

'No, I don't! I look bloody awful.'

'Oh dear, we are in a bad mood,' he remarked mildly.

'*I'm* in a bad mood, not *we*,' she snapped. 'You seem the same as usual. Calm and infuriating as ever.' For some daft reason she felt close to tears, and she never cried. At least, not when anyone could see her.

Bill stopped the car. 'What's the matter, Rose?'

'You! You're what's wrong. I was all right until you came back with your silly proposal. I was doing all right until then . . .' Her voice wavered. 'Why don't you leave me alone?'

'Because I can't,' he said simply.

'Oh, that's right, you love me.' Her tone was scornful. 'How can anyone love a cold-hearted, stubborn woman like me?'

'You judge yourself too harshly. Your problem is that you care too much, but you won't admit it to yourself.'

The threat of tears had gone now, and she was feeling more in control. Was he right? She'd never thought of it like that before.

'Shall we get something to eat?' he asked quietly.

The restaurant he took her to was small, but the food was excellent. When she looked back on her childhood and remembered the almost constant hunger, she could hardly believe the difference in her life now.

'What are you looking so pensive about?' Bill's voice broke through her thoughts.

'I was just remembering what it was like when I was growing up.' She smiled, more relaxed now. 'Only today I was complaining that change was taking place too slowly, but my life has altered beyond belief. There's always food on the table at home, I can come into places like this, and afford to buy myself a new frock every year. All undreamed-of luxuries.'

'You've earned a better life.'

'I suppose you're right, but it's been a struggle. I seem to have been hammering on closed doors all my life, and some of them still won't open.'

'They will. Give it time.'

'I wish I had your faith. I've been trying to get my family out of Garrett Street, but Mum and Wally won't budge. Wally's afraid that if he loses his job, they'll fall into debt.'

'I understand his concern.'

Rose sighed. 'So do I, but I'd love to get Annie and the rest of them out of that place.'

'I know you would, and it will happen one day.' He gazed into her eyes. 'You could always marry me and let me deal with the problem.'

Rose surged to her feet, bristling with fury. 'You said you weren't going to mention that.'

He didn't speak while he paid for their dinner, or when he helped her on with her coat, or as they walked towards the car. For some reason, his silence was unnerving. It was only when they were driving towards the theatre, that he said, 'Have you taken Annie to the National Gallery again?'

'I haven't had time.' Rose was glad he'd changed the subject.

'I see. Then I'll take her next Saturday.'

'I'm not letting her go out on her own with a man.' She gasped as he braked fiercely and stopped the car.

He turned to face her and, for the first time ever, she saw anger blazing in his eyes. 'What are you implying?' He still spoke softly, but there was a steely note to his voice.

'Well, she's only a young girl – '

'My God, woman,' he growled, through clenched teeth, 'do you think I would interfere with a child?'

'Well, all men – '

'Don't say another word! I think you've insulted me enough.' He started the car again and spun it round in the road, making other drivers swerve, then headed back the way they had come.

Ignoring the mayhem he had just caused, he increased his speed. 'Little girls are not to my taste,' he told her tightly. 'I like big ones, and that shows what a bloody fool I am.'

Rose was shocked by his reaction. After all, she was only protecting her sister, and you couldn't be too careful – as she well knew. 'Bill – '

'Don't say another word, or I might forget I'm a gentleman and dump you in the gutter.'

She lapsed into silence, knowing by his tone that she had really done it this time. If she tried to explain, it would only make things worse. She usually liked a fight, but not with this man.

The car screeched to a halt outside her house. 'Get out,' he ordered, when she didn't move.

She did so, and watched him speed away. What had she done? Oh, come on, Rose, an inner voice taunted, you've insulted him in the worst possible way. He's a decent man, you blind fool. Why can't you learn to keep your mouth shut, and your suspicions to yourself?

She must have stood on the pavement for some time, because she suddenly realized it was raining and she was wet. She walked into the scullery to find Annie waiting for her.

'Uncle Bill was in a hurry, has he got to go away again?'

'I don't think so.' The last thing she wanted was her sister asking questions and putting two and two together.

'You stood out there a long time, and now you're all wet.' Annie touched her coat sleeve.

'Yes, that was silly of me.' Her laugh sounded forced

even to her own ears. She took off her coat and hung it by the fire, but she knew she wasn't fooling Annie. 'We had a row, and he was angry,' she admitted at last.

'Uncle Bill never gets angry.'

'Well, he did tonight. I insulted him.'

'Oh, Rosie, why did you do that? He's such a nice man and he loves you so much.'

'What makes you say that?'

'He watches you all the time.'

Rose dismissed the suggestion. 'That doesn't mean a thing.'

'You're very clever,' Annie told her, 'but you don't know much about people.'

'I haven't got the faintest idea what makes anyone tick and I wish I did, but I can't seem to trust anyone.'

'That's because you've been hurt,' Annie told her.

Rose looked up quickly. 'What do you know about that?'

'Well, Dad hit you, then those men attacked you after Ethel's case was finished . . .' She tailed off, and looked at her sister anxiously. 'And there was that time you came home hurt. You told us you'd fallen over, but I don't think that was true.'

'Oh, and why do you think I was lying?' Rose frowned.

Annie handed her a cloth to dry her hair. 'You were different after, and then you ran off to join the WAACs. I think you were miserable and just wanted to get away.'

'How do you know such things?' Rose asked. 'I thought I'd fooled everyone.'

'I watch people. I can tell if they're happy or not. You're quite good at pretending, but I know you.'

'You're right. I didn't fall over – a man attacked me. He hurt me bad.'

Annie's eyes filled with tears and she took her sister's hand. 'Uncle Bill wouldn't hurt you.'

'I know, Toots.' She used the old endearment without thinking. 'And I was wrong to insult him like I did – but you know me, I often speak without thinking first.'

'Are you going to tell him you're sorry?'

Rose nodded gloomily. This was becoming a habit. 'Yes. I'll have to.'

Bill eased his foot off the pedal as the fury evaporated. Where the devil was he? He'd been driving like a lunatic, not taking any notice of where he was going. What was that girl doing to him?

He stopped in front of a large house and took several deep breaths, relieved to feel his usual calm reasserting itself, but the fury was replaced with sadness. How could she accuse him of something so hideous? What hurt most was to understand that she believed all men were animals. What could have happened to her to convince her of such a thing? He knew she'd had a hard life, but Annie lived in the same environment and she was different. The little girl was loving, happy and trusting . . .

'Mr Freeman.'

He looked up in surprise and saw a man in footman's uniform standing by the car.

'Her ladyship saw you drive up and wondered if you would join her for a drink.'

Her ladyship? Bill glanced at the house again. Why on earth had he come here? It was miles out of his way. 'Yes, thank you.' He hauled himself out of the car and followed the man. He could do with some company.

'Mr Freeman.' Lady Gresham held out her hand. 'So good of you to visit.'

'I didn't intend to,' he admitted honestly. 'I've been driving around in a fury and didn't notice I'd come in this direction.'

'And who has been able to ruffle your calm façade?' she asked, with a knowing smile.

'Well . . .'

'Aha! It sounds as if you've had trouble with my granddaughter.'

He grimaced and took the large brandy the servant handed him.

'Sit down, Bill. I may call you that?'

'Of course.' He sat opposite her and stared into the fire.

'Would you like to talk about it?'

Feeling warm and comfortable, with the brandy burning a fiery path to his stomach, he explained what had happened.

'I know she was badly treated by her stepfather, but to have such a mistrust of all men seems excessive.' Lady Gresham gave him a penetrating stare. 'Do you know why that should be? Have you done something to make her doubt your integrity?'

'I don't think it's anything I've done.' Bill looked hopefully at the elderly lady. 'I was hoping you might have some idea.'

'Rose tells me little about her life, but one doesn't have to be a genius to know that it has been harsher than she will admit. I have learned more from her delightful sister.'

Bill gave a faint smile. 'She's a talkative child, much to Rose's dismay. And seemingly untouched by the squalid conditions in which they live.'

'I believe that is because Rose has protected her.' Lady Gresham smiled at Bill. 'I love my granddaughter, but I am aware of her faults.'

Bill took a large swallow of his drink, then put down the glass. 'I was horrified that the woman I love could think so little of me. Male pride, I suppose.'

'Pride is an affliction from which we all suffer,' she told him. 'What are you going to do now?'

'I don't know.' He sighed. And he didn't. He loved Rose desperately, but what was the use? Life with her would become a battleground, and he wasn't so sure now that he could handle that . . .

'May I give you some advice?'

'I would welcome it, Lady Gresham.'

'Don't go after her. Wait for her to come to you and apologize.'

He gave her a startled look. 'Do you think she will?'

'I'm sure of it. Rose has an abundance of Gresham pride, but she has called your honour into question and that will not sit easy with her. She will feel obliged to put that right.' Suddenly she smiled. 'She is fierce in court. She has only to fix someone with her dark eyes and they turn to jelly. In her opinion, injustice is something to be wiped out, and she has been unjust to you.' Lady Gresham gazed into space, then nodded. 'Yes, she *will* come to you.'

'She won't like doing it, though,' he remarked drily.

The door opened and Sir George strode in. 'Mr Freeman! What brings you here tonight?'

'Your daughter has been causing trouble again,' Lady Gresham informed her son.

'Never!' He lifted his hands in mock disbelief. 'Who has she been fighting with this time?'

'Me.' Bill was amazed by the Greshams' attitude. Rose was the product of Sir George's lusty youth, yet they spoke of her with pride and love.

Sir George chuckled, poured himself a drink and sat down. 'Did you ever hear what happened when I met her for the first time?'

The next hour was full of laughter, and Bill learned a great deal about the woman he loved. Yes, he still felt like that, and he knew nothing would ever change it.

As he took his leave, Lady Gresham whispered, 'Don't forget. Let her come to you.'

33

Two days after the argument, Rose's conscience was bothering her. It disturbed her sleep and work. *Why* hadn't she kept her mouth shut? All she'd had to do was say she would come with them. But no, she'd had to go and malign his character in the worst possible way. It made her feel sick to think of it. No wonder he'd been furious. He was never going to want to see her again, and for some reason, she didn't like that idea . . .

Rose massaged her temple. This damned headache wasn't helping, and she suspected it wouldn't go away until she'd faced Bill and apologized. A glance at the clock told her it was nearly five o'clock. She hauled herself to her feet. She had better get this over with or she wouldn't get any sleep again tonight. He was a gentleman and didn't deserve to be thought of as a child molester.

Her mouth set in a determined line. She grabbed her coat and hurried to the door. 'I'm going, Josh,' she called out. 'I'll see you tomorrow.'

The bus stop was crowded, and she knew it would be a long wait. She cursed silently. Why hadn't she done this earlier? By the time she reached Kensington, Bill would have packed up for the night. Then she remembered that he had a flat above his offices so he might be there. Now that her mind was made up she had to try to see him.

Two buses came at once and she was able to push her

way on to the second. The journey didn't take as long as she'd anticipated, and soon she was walking towards his office.

Bill was just coming out of the door, and Rose stopped, suddenly uncertain. He was with another woman. She only came up to his shoulder, but she was quite young and dressed in the latest fashion. Rose watched as she looked up at him and laughed. She wished she hadn't come. He obviously didn't care whether she apologized or not. He had already found himself someone else. Or had he always had this girlfriend, and just been amusing himself by proposing to her? Rose started to seethe.

She was about to walk back the way she'd come when he caught sight of her. 'Rose.' He strode towards her. 'What are you doing here? Is anything wrong?'

'No.' Rose saw the other woman walk towards them and said hurriedly, 'I came to apologize, but I can see you're busy.'

Just then a smart car pulled up and a chauffeur got out, bowing to the lady who was with Bill.

'Don't go away,' Bill ordered Rose, and went back to the woman. He shook her hand and waited until they'd driven off before he returned. 'Now, you were saying?' he asked.

'You didn't have to send her away,' Rose told him, a little more sharply than she should have done.

Bill searched her face intently, then smiled. 'Mrs Warrington and her husband have commissioned me to design a house for them. She came to see the plans today.'

'Oh.' Rose could have kicked herself – she'd jumped to conclusions again. She took a deep breath, anxious to get this over with. 'I've come to apologize. I should never have accused you of such a terrible thing.'

'No, you shouldn't. I would never do anything to hurt you or your sister, and I had hoped you trusted me.'

'I'm so sorry.' Rose dropped her gaze. 'What I said to you was unforgivable and I regret it. I wanted you to know that.' Without looking at him, she turned and started to walk away, but was stopped by a firm grip on her arm.

'I accept your apology, Rose, and forgive you.'

'You do?' Rose was surprised. She had not expected that. She regarded him with new respect.

'Are you hungry?' Bill asked.

She nodded. 'I haven't had much to eat today.'

'In that case' – he started to walk her up the road – 'I know a nice restaurant in the high street. You'll like the food there.'

Rose was lost for words, which was rare for her. She'd expected to be told never to come near him again. That hadn't happened, and he was even taking her out for dinner. Bill Freeman was a most unusual man.

They reached the restaurant in silence, but when they'd been shown to a table, Bill looked at her and said, 'I can recommend the rump steak. It melts in your mouth.'

Rose's stomach growled in anticipation. 'I'll have that, then.'

'Would you like some wine?' he asked, after he'd given the waiter their order.

Rose was about to refuse, but changed her mind. 'Thank you.'

'Red or white?' He raised a brow in query.

'I leave that to you. I don't know anything about these things.'

'Then we'll have red.'

Bill watched her right through the meal, hardly able to take his eyes off her long enough to eat. She was so lovely. Her hair shone with a blue tint under the bright lights. Her dress was plain and practical, but its dark navy was softened with a little white lace around the collar – not real lace, of course, the dress was too cheap for that, but she was still the most beautiful woman in the room. He was positive she was unaware of her stunning looks. One day he would get her into colours and fine materials, he decided.

At the end of the meal she folded her napkin and sat back. 'That was lovely. Thank you very much.'

'I'm pleased you enjoyed it.'

'I did.' Rose gazed out of the window at the nearly empty street. 'It looks late, I'd better get my bus.'

'I'll take you home.' Bill stood up and helped her with her coat.

'You don't need to do that,' she protested.

'Rose, it's nearly midnight. I'm not letting you go home alone.'

He was determined, and it seemed Rose recognized the quiet note of steel in his voice. She didn't argue with him, merely smiled and accepted.

The next day Rose was in quite a mellow mood, and she smiled to herself when she thought of their dinner last night. Bill had been charming and as gracious as ever, never once mentioning their argument. She had been dreading seeing him, but it had been a lovely evening. And the wine hadn't been too bad, either, after the second glass.

She put away the file she'd been working on. Her mother was only here three days a week now, and this was one of her days off. Rose thought she might as well join her at home. It was a long time since they'd been able to have a proper chat. 'I'm going home now, Josh.'

He looked up in surprise. 'It's only four o'clock. Are you feeling all right?'

'Never better. I've decided to knock off early for a change, and you ought to do the same, Josh, we hardly have any time to ourselves.'

'I agree, and I was going to talk to you about that.' Josh put his papers away too. 'Now that the practice is running smoothly we should take time off to spend with our friends.'

Rose realized she knew little about Josh's private life. She had always thought him a solitary man, but he had been taking extra care with his appearance just lately, and was really quite attractive. And there was something else; he looked happy.

'Have you got a special friend, Josh?' she asked.

He gave her a rather shy smile. 'Her name's Mary and I met her four weeks ago. Her husband was killed in the war and she was helping out at one of Lady Gresham's houses for veterans. We hit it off straight away, and I hope to persuade her to marry me.'

'Oh, I'm so pleased for you, Josh. I hope it all works out.' She kissed his cheek.

'Thanks, Rose.' Josh blushed a little at this unusual show of affection. 'Now, off you go and have a rest.'

As soon as she walked into the scullery, her mother poured her a cup of tea, and Annie was pleased to see her home so early. They were just settling down to talk when there was a rap on the door.

Annie was out of her seat in a flash to see who it was. She came back immediately, looking very serious. 'There's some policemen here.'

Rose's mother beat her to the door. 'What's happened? It must be serious to bring you down here.'

Rose edged past Marj, had a quick look at the scene and knew they were in trouble. There were two coppers on the doorstep with truncheons in their hands. A third was facing a jeering crowd in the road and smacking his truncheon against his leg.

With a growl of exasperation, she pushed past the policemen and faced the crowd. 'Go home!' she shouted. 'Haven't you got anything better to do?'

After a bit of disgruntled swearing, a few drifted away, but some stayed, the nastiest people in the street, but they didn't frighten Rose. 'Well? What are you hanging about for?'

'We're going to teach these coppers not to come down here,' a belligerent man called Stan snarled.

'What are you afraid of?' They shuffled uncomfortably. She knew every crime they had ever committed, and she used that knowledge now. 'Frightened they're going to find out what you've been up to?'

'We don't want no coppers down 'ere,' another man shouted.

Rose was now flanked by the three policemen. 'They've come to see me. They're not interested in you, so you'd better go home while you still can.'

Another round of foul language assailed her, but she didn't flinch. Her unwavering black-eyed gaze finally made them back down, and they started to leave, but as she turned to go into the house a stone caught her on the temple.

She spun round, ran towards a boy, caught him by the collar and shook him.

'Leave my kid alone,' Stan bellowed, and made a rush for her.

Still keeping a firm hold on the boy, she pushed the father away, making him stumble. 'If you dare to touch me, I'll have you and your son charged with assault. In fact, I think I'll do that anyway.'

The man was obviously alarmed by her threat. She had quite a reputation, and everyone in Garrett Street knew she didn't make idle threats.

'You don't have to do that – he didn't mean it for you, it was for one of them.' He pointed to the uniformed men, who were now standing behind her.

'That's worse.' Rose gave the boy a shove towards his father. 'I'll forget it this time, but you'd better push off before I change my mind.'

They did.

'You'd better all come inside,' Rose told the policemen. 'You'll be safer.'

Annie rushed to her. 'Are you all right? I saw that boy throw a brick at you.'

Rose put her hand to her temple, but there was only a small bump. 'I'm fine, and it was a stone, not a brick.'

Their mother had tea waiting for them, and Rose couldn't help grinning at the sight of three burly policemen filling the scullery, but she still didn't know why they were there. 'You'd better tell us what brings you to this dangerous neck of the woods,' she said, while they were all drinking their tea.

'Do you know a Charlie Webster?' the one with a stripe on his sleeve asked.

'That's my son. What's happened to him?' Marj was alarmed.

'Got himself into bad company, I'm afraid, and we've got him at the station. He's asking for his sister.'

Rose was already on her feet. 'I'll come straight away.'

'You'll get him out, won't you?' Marj looked imploringly at her daughter. 'He's not a bad kid.'

'I know. Try not to worry too much.' Rose paused at the door, then looked back at the men and grinned. 'You'd better come, too, so I can escort you to safety.'

With roars of laughter they walked up the street. Knots of people were standing at their doors, hurling abuse, but Rose was more than capable of doing the same.

They escorted her to the station then left to continue working their beat.

'Can I see my brother alone?' she asked the sergeant.

'Certainly, miss.' He took her to one of the cells.

'Oh, Rosie!' Charlie looked at her with a tearstained face.

She sat beside him on the hard bench. 'Tell me what this is all about.'

'It's that gang from Nelson Street. They met me from school and forced me to go with them to rob a shop. I didn't want to do it, but there was six of them and they dragged me along.' He sniffed and gulped. 'They know you're my sister and they thought it would be funny to make me into a thief.'

Rose was appalled. Now her family were being picked on because of her. 'Did you steal anything?'

'No – honest. But when the police caught us the others shoved some things in my hands and told them I was the ring-leader. But I didn't do nothing.' He wrapped his arms around his body and rocked back and forth. 'And now I've been locked up.'

Rose slipped an arm around his shoulders. Her heart ached for her young brother. 'Don't be upset,' she told him. 'I'll get you out of here.'

When she explained to the sergeant what had happened, he nodded in agreement. 'That's how we see it, but we had to bring him in with the others. The Nelson Street gang are a bad lot and we know them well, but everybody's afraid to speak out against them.' He started to fill in a form. 'We'll release your brother into your care.'

'Thank you. Will he be charged?'

'No, he's only twelve and we're satisfied he's innocent.' Then he smiled. 'Would you like to see the others?'

'Yes, please, and all at once, if you don't mind.'

He showed her into a room and brought the six gang members to her. They laughed and jeered when they saw who was waiting for them.

'Hey, we're all right now,' the eldest sneered. 'The big lawyer's here.'

'You gonna defend us?' One of the others chortled as if it was a huge joke.

Rose looked from one to another in a leisurely way, a slight smile on her face. 'No, I'm going to prosecute you.'

There was a deathly silence as this unexpected news sank in. A couple even paled, such was her reputation.

The eldest boy recovered quickly. 'Don't take any notice of her,' he told his gang. 'You know everyone's too scared to talk against us.'

'Don't be too sure of that. I can be very persuasive, and I'm certain I can talk the shopkeeper and a few more into coming forward. And,' her gaze captured the eldest, 'I'm going to make you sorry you ever picked on one of my family.'

'It was a joke,' the youngest whimpered.

She treated this remark with the contempt it deserved, and turned to the policemen. 'You can put them back in the cells now.'

'Be our pleasure, Miss Webster.'

When she got back to the front desk, her brother was waiting for her. 'Come on, let's get you home,' she said.

'Just a minute!' The inspector hurried over to her. 'Are you serious about taking that gang on in court?'

'I never joke about such things.'

'Do you think you can make a case against them? Mention that lot and everyone closes their mouth in self-defence.'

'Not this time,' she told him. 'I'll get that shopkeeper to talk, and when he does, others will follow.' Then she walked out of the door.

For the first time she wished she was earning good money: then she would be able to get her family out of Garrett Street.

34

There was uproar in the court when the two eldest boys were sent to prison.

Bill watched Rose as she faced the angry crowd without a flicker of fear on her face. Lord, she had courage. All the time she had defended and fought for these people, they had regarded her as a heroine, but now some considered she had turned on her own. Not all, though, he was relieved to see. Some were cheering, almost drowning the jeers.

He left his seat and hurried to the door. She was going to need help when she came out, and he was damned if he'd let anything happen to her.

He needn't have worried. Rose had a policeman at either side of her, and she didn't look intimidated. 'What's all this racket?' she shouted. 'How many of you have had trouble with this gang?'

Bill held his breath as the noise died to a murmur.

'You know me, I've been working to help you, but there are some you *can't* help, however much you try.'

There were nods of agreement.

'Would any of you allow your family to be threatened?' She threw the question at them and waited. 'No, of course not, yet you think I should just sit back and see my brother hurt.'

'No, Rosie,' someone shouted from the back of the

crowd. 'That lot have got what was coming to them, and we'll all be better off without them.'

There was a chorus of approval now. Instead of running and hiding, she had faced her accusers and turned the tide with argument. Bill had always known she was something special, but today had shown him just how special – and he loved her even more. If that was possible.

Rose said something to the policemen, who nodded and walked away, then she saw him and came over grinning. 'Come to see the show?'

He looked at her in wonder: she was enjoying herself. 'You need someone to look after you.'

'I can look after myself.'

'But what about your family? You ought to get them out of Garrett Street.'

The smile vanished, replaced with a worried frown. 'Do you think I don't know that? Everywhere I turn I come up against a closed door. The landlords don't want anyone from Garrett Street – and many think I'm a trouble-maker. They price their accommodation out of our reach. Grace and John have offered to take Annie, but the stubborn miss won't leave everyone else.'

He tucked her hand through his arm. 'Let's go and get something to eat, see if we can find a solution.' He squeezed her hand. 'Aren't you going to say you're pleased to see me?'

'Well . . . yes, I am, actually.'

'Aha, progress!'

Later he drove out to Richmond Park again. 'I promised I'd bring you in the autumn.'

Bill stopped the car and they got out. The trees were a mass of orange, yellow, brown and gold, and the ground looked as if a multicoloured carpet had been spread on it. 'It's so peaceful after the court,' Rose murmured. 'I can't bear noise – not since I worked in a tin factory.'

'How old were you?'

'Eleven.'

The more Bill learned about Rose Webster, the more his respect for her grew. He could understand why she had grown up a fighter.

He took her shoulders and turned her to face him. He brushed his lips over hers, then sat back. 'Marry me, Rosie.'

'Why do you keep asking? I'd make a terrible wife.'

'That's a chance I'm willing to take.' His heart was beating uncomfortably hard – she hadn't refused him immediately this time.

'Then you must be mad. I'm hard, not affectionate, I hate kids and don't like being touched.' She grimaced. 'I'm also intolerant, stubborn and contrary-minded, and you should be running for your life.'

'You've left out a few,' he said. 'You're also loyal, caring, intelligent, and the most courageous woman I have ever met. And I love you with all my heart.'

'But I'm not sure I love you. I don't even know what the word means.'

'Tell me what you do feel for me.' He'd got her talking openly now and he wasn't going to let this chance slip away.

'Well, I like and respect you, you're kind, and honest. I feel I can talk to you.'

'Do you like being with me?'

'Yes, I do.' She laughed, then became pensive. 'But I

can't understand why you want to marry a woman who doesn't love you.'

'That will come.' She was actually considering it, he realized.

'It might not. I don't know if I could stand the physical side of marriage.'

She was silent again and he felt as if he was losing the advantage. He drew her into his arms and kissed her firmly. 'It won't be such an ordeal. You don't mind me touching you, do you?'

'I don't feel threatened by you.'

Why had she used that word? Bill knew about the beatings she'd received at home, and there had been the attack after Ethel's case, but was there more to it? He had to know – whatever it was.

'Tell me why you feel threatened by a man.' He watched her intently.

Rose lowered her head, deep in thought.

'Help me to understand, Rose,' he said.

Her head came up and the defiant gleam was back in her eyes. 'You'll never be able to understand how I feel about this, but you might as well know. Then we can forget about this whole silly business of you wanting to marry me.'

'Whatever you tell me, Rose, won't make any difference to my feelings for you.'

She gave a harsh laugh. 'This will. I was raped when I was fifteen.'

Bill felt as if he'd been hit, and for a few moments he was speechless. Why hadn't he guessed? It all added up: her dislike of being touched, her distrust of men . . . Oh, God. He groaned inside.

369

'Right, that's sorted *that* out. You can take me home now.'

The bitterness in Rose's voice jolted him back to life. She thought he was disgusted, but he wasn't: he was devastated that she should have suffered so much – and he wanted to marry her even more.

He reached out, caught her hands in his, then rested his forehead against hers. 'Rose, I love you so much. Will you marry me?'

She moved her head back to look him in the eyes. 'You still want to?'

'Yes.'

'I don't want kids yet.'

'I will be careful, until you change your mind – but you should know that I want children.'

'We could think about it in a year or so,' she conceded.

'Is that a promise?'

'You have my word.' Then she frowned. 'But it wouldn't work. I can't leave my family – they need me. Can I think about it?'

'No, Rose. I want your answer now. This is the last time I'm going to ask. If you refuse, I'll leave and never see you again.'

Mentally he crossed his fingers. He had probably sealed his fate with that ultimatum.

'I'd be sad not to see you again.'

'Then you know how to keep me.' He watched her expression carefully. That last unguarded remark gave him hope that she really did love him, even if she wasn't ready to admit it yet.

Her sigh was ragged. 'I won't give up my work.'

'I wouldn't ask you to. I know how important it is to you.' That had to be the last hurdle.

'I'll leave you if you start ordering me about.'

'I wouldn't dare!' he exclaimed.

The corners of her mouth twitched. 'All right, I'll marry you.'

He was elated, but he knew his problems were only just beginning. 'Thank you, my darling. You won't regret it.'

'When do you want to get married?' she asked.

'Christmas.'

'But that's only about six weeks away.' She spun away, and got back into the car.

'I know.' He followed, and started the engine before she could say anything else. He knew he must be crazy to make such a commitment on the terms she had set out. But he didn't have any choice: without her his life would be empty.

As they drove out of the park gates, Rose was wondering if she was in full control of her faculties. Whatever had possessed her to agree to marry him? She had decided long ago not to tie herself to a man, but the thought of never seeing him again had been painful, and she knew he had meant what he said. He would have walked out of her life and never come back. When had that begun to matter to her?

Her feelings had started to change on the night of the dance, and when he'd been in Scotland, she had missed him. Of course, she hadn't admitted it to herself at the time. She had just told him she didn't love him, but was that true? There must be some feeling deep inside her, or she would never have capitulated so easily.

371

And there was something else too. She had always been happy with her own company, but just lately she had wished she had someone to share her life with. Her mother was happy with Wally, and the children were growing up fast – even Annie didn't need her so much now. And she could see how happy Josh was with his Mary. It was quite a shock to realize that she was lonely.

Perhaps marrying wasn't such a crazy idea after all, she thought. And she would have to go a long way to find a man as kind, gentle and understanding as Bill.

Just then Bill pulled up outside a beautiful new house. 'We passed this the last time we came to Richmond,' she remarked, 'but it was just a building site then. Did you design it?'

'That's right. Would you like to see inside?'

'Oh, yes, please!'

He took a key out of his pocket, opened the door, and she peered in. 'Oh, it's furnished. Do you think the owner will mind us going into his house?'

'No, he won't mind at all. Come on.' He held open the door.

Half an hour later she was in raptures. 'It's beautiful, and you've thought of everything, loads of cupboards, and the bathroom . . .' Rose sighed wistfully. 'It must be lovely not to go to the public baths.'

'I'm glad you like it.'

'It's perfect.'

He held up another key. 'Do you want to see the one next door? It's almost identical to this, but three bedrooms instead of four.'

As they walked up the path, she gazed around in

wonder. 'They're not attached to each other. It looks strange after the rows of houses in London.'

'There's more space here,' he told her, as he unlocked the door.

'Yes, there is,' she said thoughtfully. 'Perhaps we should consider building on the outskirts of London.'

'I think it will be the only way to provide enough houses, but the government is slow to acknowledge this,' he remarked.

'I know – I've had enough arguments with the council about it.' She looked into the hallway, and smiled, her concern about slum clearance forgotten in the excitement of examining another house.

Rose wandered from room to room, with Bill following. That was another thing she liked about him – he knew when to keep quiet, and that was a rare quality.

At the last bedroom she stopped and gasped. 'Oh, how Annie would love this!' She rushed over to a small table and examined the notebooks, pencils and paints, all brand new. Then she laughed. 'She'd think she was in heaven.'

'So, you think she'll like her room?' he asked softly.

Rose spun round and searched his face, but he seemed serious. 'Would you repeat that?'

'Do you think Annie will like her room, then?'

He had been leaning casually against the windowsill, but now he pushed himself upright and came towards her. 'This house is for your family and the other one is ours.'

A lump formed in her throat. Her family would be safe!

Bill gathered her into his arms and held her until she

had got over the shock. 'Why didn't you tell me?' she mumbled, into his chest.

'The houses have been ready for some time, but I had to wait until you agreed to marry me.' He kissed her. 'I do have some pride, and I'd have hated to think you were marrying me to provide a home for your family.'

'I wouldn't have done that,' she protested, peeved that he should think she might only be out for what she could get. She had never been like that.

'I know you have high principles,' he assured her, 'but I couldn't take the chance. For my own peace of mind I had to be sure.'

She did understand – many women would have snapped him up for a decent home, without a pang of conscience. She looked at him earnestly. 'I could never do anything like that because I would lose my self-respect, which is very important to me.'

'I know.' He held her away from him and smiled. 'We'll move your family in tomorrow, shall we?'

Rose hugged him in a rare spontaneous show of affection. 'I can't wait to get them out of Garrett Street. Oh, but what about schools and Wally's job – '

'There's a very good school just down the road, and an excellent rail service into London. And as for Charlie and Will, the keepers at Richmond Park are looking for young boys to help with maintenance work. They might be able to get fixed up there.'

'They'd love that.'

'And if Wally can't find work locally, he can help me in the office.'

Rose felt as if her heart would burst with happiness. 'You've thought of everything.'

'I've tried,' he said simply. 'My biggest challenge has been getting you to like me enough to marry me.'

Her smile was cheeky. 'You're a persistent man, Bill Freeman, and you're growing in my estimation every minute.'

'Good!' The kiss he gave her this time was more passionate.

'You like doing that,' she gasped, as the embrace ended.

'I'd like to do a lot more,' he said.

She tipped her head to one side. 'Not until after the wedding.'

'God! I hope I don't die of frustration,' he moaned dramatically.

'It's only a few weeks.'

'You wouldn't consider making it the end of the month, I suppose?'

'You suppose right.' She grabbed his arm. 'Come on, let's go and tell Mum the good news.' She stopped suddenly.

'What is it?' he asked.

'I must have taken leave of my senses. I've been so excited about getting them out of London that I forgot to ask what the rent is. They won't be able to afford a place like this.' She gave him a tortured look. 'How much is it?'

'Nothing. If they'll pay the rates and electricity, I'll be happy.'

'You'll . . .?' Rose shook her head, trying to clear it. This was getting more confusing by the minute. 'Are you saying you *own* these?'

'Yes.'

She blew a strand of hair out of her eyes. She'd known he wasn't short of a bob or two, but this was a bit much to take in. 'Are you rich?'

'Not like the Greshams, but when my father died he left me some money and a large house, which I sold. I designed and had these built out of that money as an investment. What was left over went into my business, and that is doing well. We'll be comfortably off, you needn't worry about your family living here.'

'But you'd be able to make money from these,' she protested.

He spoke earnestly. 'I don't want to. All I want from life is to see you and your family settled and happy.'

Her eyes filled with tears again, and she brushed them away impatiently. What had she done to deserve a man like this? 'I'm becoming a real watering-can,' she complained.

'Don't be afraid to have feelings, my love. It isn't a sign of weakness.'

'I've always believed it was,' she told him honestly. 'If you have feelings, you can get hurt.'

When they walked into the scullery, the whole family was there, and Rose was troubled to see Will sporting a black eye. 'How did that happen?' she asked.

'I did it at work.'

'I want the truth.' She feared he had been picked on in revenge for what she had done to that gang.

'I did, honest. Some wooden boxes fell down and hit me.' He scowled. 'I hate that job. I've a good mind to go to sea like Bob did.'

'There's no need for that.' Rose gave Bill a nudge. 'Go on, tell them.'

He slipped an arm around her and smiled. 'I've asked Rose to marry me, and she's accepted.'

He didn't get any further because Annie hurled herself at him, nearly knocking him off-balance, then threw her arms around her sister.

'I knew you liked him,' she declared. 'Now Uncle Bill will be able to take care of you.'

He cleared his throat. 'I'd like to take care of you all, if you'd let me. I've got two houses in Roehampton, next to each other.' He smiled at Marj and Wally. 'One is for you and the children, the other for me and Rose.'

Wally looked concerned. 'What about the rent?'

They spent the next hour talking about it, drinking tea, and by the time everything was explained, Marj and Annie were crying with joy. Charlie and Will were enthusiastic about working in Richmond Park, and Rose couldn't believe all this was happening.

Had some of the closed doors started to spring open at last?

35

Christmas Day 1923. Her wedding day!

Rose sighed and laid back her head, luxuriating in the scented water. It felt as if a dozen elephants were stomping about inside her. With Bill's insistence that they marry at Christmas, it had been a terrible rush. He certainly hadn't given her time to change her mind – and anyway, how could she? Her family thought he was nothing short of an angel in disguise, and over the last few weeks she'd had to admit that she had never met anyone so completely unselfish. Everyone thought she was a very lucky girl – and she was, she kept telling herself. But one fact was inescapable: she was frightened of the step she was taking.

'Rose!' Grace called. 'It's time you were getting dressed.'

'All right. Just five more minutes.'

Rose closed her eyes, reluctant to move, and turned her mind back to the day they had all moved to Roehampton. What excitement there had been! When Annie had seen her room, she had thrown her arms around Bill and refused to let him go. Her mother and Wally had been speechless. The transformation in Rose's family had been remarkable. Her mother had never looked so happy and contented, Wally had managed to find a job in an office locally, and Charlie and Will were working at Richmond Park. They looked like different boys: their faces had filled out and they were always smiling and joking, loving every minute of their outdoor life, even in the freezing weather. Annie was going to a school where art was encouraged, and her talent was blossoming.

'Rose! If you don't come out soon I'm going to get John to break down the door,' Grace threatened.

'I'm coming.' Rose stepped out of the bath, dried herself quickly then put on her underclothes and a dressing-gown Grace had given her. They were getting married in London because all their friends were there, and Grace and John had put her up for the night, so she would be near the church.

'Thank goodness!' Grace exclaimed, when she opened the bathroom door. 'I thought we were going to have to drag you out. You're not having second thoughts, are you?'

'Of course I am,' Rose admitted. 'Didn't you?'

'No, but if you're going to back out, then for goodness' sake do it now. Don't let Bill get to the church before you tell him.'

'I wouldn't let him down,' Rose said, horrified at the idea that she might.

'I'm glad to hear it, because I've had doubts that you would go through with this. I know you've always been against marriage, but you don't have to be.' Grace smiled understandingly. 'The love between a man and a woman is wonderful if you've got the right man, and I'm certain you have.'

Rose nodded. 'I'm sure you're right, but I'm still a churning sea of worry and doubt.'

'You'll feel better when you get into your dress. Come on, you mustn't be late for the church.'

At the mention of the ceremony, her insides started to leap about again. 'I never wanted all this fuss,' she grumbled, allowing Grace to slip the frock over her head. Then her testiness faded as she gazed into the long mirror. It was the most beautiful thing she had ever had. The dropped waist was the latest fashion, and the hem came to just above her ankles. The lace veil was fastened, cap-like, to her head with a band of white flowers, and her shoes were delicate white satin. She couldn't stop smiling. How things had changed!

The door opened a crack and Annie peered in. 'Can I come in?' She opened the door just wide enough to slip through. She was in her lovely pink frock with flowers in her hair. Bill had insisted on paying for all this finery, and Rose had protested at first, happy to have a quiet wedding, but he wouldn't hear of it.

She took a deep breath. She was marrying a good man, for whom she had the highest respect. That was better than all this soppy love business.

'What a lovely frock.' Annie reached out to touch the lace. 'Uncle Bill's going to be so proud of you.'

Her insides gave another lurch at the thought of him waiting for her at the altar. Once she walked down the aisle her life would have changed for ever. She fought valiantly to push aside the anxiety. He was a passionate man, as the last few weeks had shown her, but he had held himself in check, respecting her wish to wait until the wedding night. Now it was nearly here and she was going to have to face her fears.

'There, you're ready now.' Grace stood back to get a full view of her. 'You look beautiful. Come downstairs and show John before he leaves to meet Bill at the church.'

John held her hands and grinned. 'What a vision.' He was about to say something else when there was a knock at the door.

'That will be Wally.' Grace hurried out of the room.

Rose couldn't believe her eyes when Sir George swept in, and she heard her mother draw breath sharply. 'I didn't invite him to the house, Mum,' she told her quietly.

'I knew he was going to be at the wedding,' Marj murmured, 'but I didn't realize what a shock it would be to see him.'

As her mother turned away, Rose faced her father, angry that he should barge in like this and upset her mother. 'What are you doing here?'

'I wanted to see you before you left for the church.' His gaze followed Marj as she walked over to Grace, then returned to Rose.

'Why?' she demanded. If he caused trouble today she'd kill him.

He didn't answer the question, but just stood gazing at her. 'I should be leading you down the aisle, not your stepfather.'

'Don't be ridiculous!' Rose gave an exasperated sigh.

'What's ridiculous about it?' He raised his voice. 'You're my daughter.'

'You've only been invited to the wedding because of your mother. And don't shout!'

'Will you two stop fighting?' John called them to order.

Sir George seemed to notice the room's other occupants for the first time. 'I apologize. It was very rude of me to walk into your house like this.'

'Why did you really come?' Rose demanded.

'My mother wants you to have this. She wore it on her wedding day.' He handed her a small velvet box.

When Rose saw the simple row of pearls with a diamond clasp, she shook her head. 'I can't.'

'Please accept it. You'll break her heart if you don't.'

'Take it, Rose.' Her mother had come up behind her. 'Lady Gresham wants you to have it.'

Rose turned and studied her mother's face, and was relieved to see that she was now composed and looking Sir George straight in the eyes. There was a card with the pearls. 'To my beloved granddaughter. Please accept this as a token of my love. I hope you will be as happy in your marriage as I was in mine.' At that moment Rose saw that she had been too harsh with the Greshams. They had shown her nothing but love and kindness, even Sir George in his strange way. She held out the necklace to him. 'Will you put it on for me?'

He stepped forward and fastened it around her neck, then stood back admiringly. 'They look perfect with the dress. Mother will be overjoyed,' he said. He looked at Marj and asked, 'May I speak to you privately?'

'You can say whatever you have to in front of *my* daughter.'

Rose slipped her hand through her mother's arm and felt her shaking slightly. She smiled down and squeezed her comfortingly. 'You don't have to talk to him if you don't want to, Mum.'

'It's time this was dealt with,' Marj said firmly. 'You owe me an apology, Sir George.'

He nodded, a gleam of respect in his eyes. 'I treated you disgracefully. I'm deeply ashamed and sorry for the suffering I've caused you. I know words can't right a dreadful wrong, but I hope you can find it in your heart to forgive me. I was wild and arrogant in my youth,' he added, with a grimace.

'In your youth?' Rose snorted.

'Now, don't fight again, you two,' Marj reprimanded her sharply, putting a stop to another quarrel erupting. 'You must give me time, Sir George, but this is a happy day, and you're welcome at the wedding of Rose and Bill.'

'That is gracious of you.'

Rose was proud of the way her mother had handled this awkward meeting with the man who had shamed her all those years ago.

'John!' Grace cried in alarm. 'Wally's here with the car. Bill will think we're not coming. We must all get to the church at once.'

As Rose walked down the aisle towards Bill, she thought how handsome and relieved he looked. She must have made the right responses, because the next thing she was aware of, they were signing the register. She was now Mrs Freeman.

They made their way outside to have photographs taken, and Rose couldn't for the life of her think how this had all come about. Had he cast some kind of a spell over her to make her change her long-held decision never to marry?

The reception was held in a local hotel, where they had a room to themselves. The buffet was excellent and the cake a masterpiece. Bill had insisted on paying for it all, knowing that the family couldn't afford such a spread. Her mother had felt it was her duty, but Bill's calm assurances had won her over.

Rose watched him as he mingled with the guests, talking and laughing. He was obviously happy, and so he ought to be, she thought. He had got his own way in everything without even raising his voice.

After the cake was cut, Wally got out his accordion and started to play. Bill led her on to the floor to dance and soon all the guests had joined them. Josh had brought Mary with him, and even Harold was beaming at everyone. Annie was dancing with all her favourite men, and Rose couldn't help comparing the laughing, happy girl with the sickly baby she had been. The change in her was tremendous, as it was with all her family. No one would ever believe they had grown up in Garrett Street.

'Will you honour me with a dance?' Sir George was standing in front of her. 'I promise I won't shout or argue with you.'

Rose held out her arms. It was time to forget the past.

Later, he took her over to his mother, who was sitting in state, surrounded by women. Rose suppressed a chuckle as she wondered what their guests thought about the Greshams being here. The family connection was obvious, but she didn't give a damn, and neither did Bill. He had insisted that they be invited and to hell with what anyone else thought.

Rose sat next to her grandmother. She had already thanked her for the pearls, but this was the first chance she'd had to talk to her properly. 'Are you enjoying yourself?' she asked.

'I am indeed, my dear. It's the best wedding I've ever attended.' Lady Gresham leaned forward to kiss her cheek. 'I'm proud to see my granddaughter marrying such a fine man, and honoured that you should have invited us.'

'I wanted you to come and so did Bill.'

Lady Gresham chuckled. 'That was brave of you. Our presence here is causing much speculation.'

'We don't care.' Rose kissed her grandmother's cheek.

'That,' said Sir George, standing tall and straight, 'is the greatest compliment you could have paid us.'

'Can we hope that you have accepted us at last?' her grandmother asked softly.

'I have – but that doesn't mean I'll let you interfere in my life,' she added.

'We wouldn't dare try!' Sir George laughed. 'And, anyway, you have a husband to look after you now.'

Rose felt all the old animosity drain away, and turned to the elderly lady. 'I will call you Grandmother from now on, but . . .' she looked up at Sir George ' . . . I'm not sure I'll be able to think of you as my father. Not yet, anyway.'

'That's no more than I deserve.' He sighed. 'I caused you and your mother great hardship. I will always regret that.'

Rose smiled at him warmly. 'It's all in the past now, and I think we should leave it there.'

'Thank you.' He looked quite overcome.

'Darling,' Bill was at her side, 'it's time we left our guests to party into the night.'

They slipped away without anyone noticing, much to Rose's relief. She'd had enough fuss for one day.

'Where are we going?' she asked, as he drove down the road.

'I want our first night together to be in our own home. Do you mind?'

'I would prefer it.'

'Good.' He reached across and touched her hands, which were clasped tightly in her lap. 'Don't worry, my love, I'm not going to rush you or force myself on you just because you are now my wife.'

She felt a little reassured. She had told Sir George that they should leave the past behind, and that was what she must do with the memory of the attack. It had happened long ago – in another life. Bill knew about it and it didn't worry him, so why should she let it concern her?

It was starting to snow again and Bill had to concentrate on the driving, so the rest of the journey continued in silence. Glad of a bit of peace, Rose closed her eyes.

When they reached the house it was snowing quite hard. Bill opened the front door quickly, but when she tried to step inside, he stopped her. 'I'm going to carry you over the threshold.'

'You can't!' she laughed. 'I'm much too heavy.'

He pretended to be hurt. 'Are you suggesting I'm a weakling?'

'No.' Rose couldn't contain her amusement.

'Then stop giggling, woman, and put your arms round my neck.'

He kicked the front door shut and carried her straight up to the bedroom. There was a fire burning in the grate and the whole house was lovely and warm.

He put her gently on her feet and kissed her long and passionately. She thought he had forgotten his promise not to rush her but she was wrong. 'Do you want to take a bath?' he asked, as he removed her headdress and veil.

'What about the hot water?'

'There's plenty. I've engaged a woman to do the house-work, and she came in today to see everything was ready for us.'

'A servant?' Rose's eyes opened wide.

'She'll come in twice a week to help, and don't look so shocked.' He grinned. 'We'll both be working and will have little time for polishing and cleaning.'

'Fancy having someone to help around the house.' Rose gave him a self-conscious kiss. 'You think of everything.'

'I try.' He urged her into the bathroom. 'Have your bath before I forget my promise and drag you off to bed immediately,' he teased.

Two baths in one day, Rose thought, as she sank into the hot water. How her life had changed, but such luxuries only made her more determined to rid London of places like Garrett Street. When she got back to work in the New Year, she would intensify her efforts to bring that about.

When she went back into the bedroom, there was no sign of Bill but she could hear him moving about downstairs. Glad of the chance to get into bed without him watching, she jumped in, and started. When she looked under the covers, she chuckled – there were four hot-water bottles.

She snuggled down and was soon drifting into sleep. This was unbelievable luxury.

Rose turned over and found herself up against a hard body.

'You're awake at last.' Bill pulled her close and kissed her gently.

'How long have I been asleep?'

'About two hours.'

'Oh, I'm sorry.'

'You're getting good at apologizing,' he told her, 'but you don't have to. You were tired.'

'I expect you are too,' she said, hopefully.

'Not a bit.' He rested on one elbow and gazed down at her. 'This marriage is going to be consummated tonight, my love. Any delay will only make you more apprehensive. Don't be afraid.'

She tried, she really did, but when he started running his hands over her body, she froze.

'It's all right,' he murmured gently. 'I won't hurt you.'

The trouble was, she didn't believe him.

'Let's have this nightdress off, it's getting in the way.' He sat up and eased it over her head. 'There, that's much better, isn't it?'

Was it? As flesh touched flesh, Rose realized that he wasn't wearing anything either, and there was a funny feeling low in her stomach.

The pain she had been expecting didn't come, and with a huge sigh of relief, she relaxed.

36

April 1925

Rose breathed in the spring air as she made her way to the station. It was more than a year since her marriage and she wouldn't have believed it possible that she could feel so content. When she looked back, which she did from time to time just to remind herself of how fortunate she was, it took her breath away to see how much their lives had changed.

Her mother and Wally were still happy together. Charlie and Will were both at the park and had made some friends. Flo had a decent council house, and seemed happy in her marriage; she had recently had a baby girl. Nancy was still at the orphanage and came home occasionally. They heard from Bob about twice a year, and Annie was leaving school at the end of term. Rose had tried to persuade her to go on to university, but Annie wanted time to think about it first.

Most importantly of all, Rose thought, she wasn't pregnant, which was nothing short of a miracle because Bill was a very physical man. He was also patient and had kept his promise: she was free to carry on her work without interference. And although he never hid the fact that he wanted children, he hadn't pestered her. She hoped he might forget about it.

The only fights she had now were for her clients and

with the council. She continually badgered them about clearing the slums, but they kept coming up with lame excuses. When she walked into her office, she found the girl they had employed in place of Marj waiting anxiously for her.

'Oh, Mrs Freeman, thank goodness you've arrived. Sir George Gresham sent a message asking you to go to his mother's house immediately.' Rose didn't wait to ask questions. Something serious must have happened.

As soon as she ran up the steps the door opened. 'Go straight upstairs,' the servant told her. 'Sir George is waiting for you in his mother's room.'

The curtains had been drawn but she could see Sir George by the bed, his head bowed. Without saying a word, she pulled up another chair, sat beside him and laid a hand on his arm. 'What is it?' she whispered.

He clasped her hand. 'Mother's had a stroke. A bad one, I'm afraid. The doctors say she won't last long.'

When she looked at her grandmother Rose's eyes filled with tears. She was so still and had the look of approaching death about her. Rose had seen it a few times, and her heart felt as if it would shatter. 'Can't they do something?'

He shook his head. 'All we can do is wait. Please stay.'

'Of course I will. May I use your telephone to cancel some appointments and let my family know where I am?'

Sir George nodded again, and she hurried down to his study. She would have to leave a message at Bill's office because her mother didn't have a telephone at home. Much to her relief, he picked the telephone up himself, so she explained what had happened.

'Oh, I'm so sorry, darling. Do you want me to come over?'

'There's no point. She doesn't know anyone.'

'Call if you need me,' Bill told her sympathetically. 'I'll stay in the flat tonight.'

'Thanks.' Rose put down the receiver and hurried back upstairs.

They waited into the night, never leaving the room for more than a couple of minutes at a time. Just before dawn, Lady Gresham opened her eyes, smiled at them both, sighed, then slipped peacefully away.

Rose was devastated. Her grandmother had always seemed so vital, so indestructible. Now she was gone, and she knew she would miss her dreadfully. She telephoned Bill with the news, and told him she would stay with her father for a couple of days. When she turned round, Sir George was standing behind her, a look of grief mingled with joy on his face. 'That's the first time you have ever referred to me as your father,' he told her.

'Well, you are,' Rose admitted. 'What's the use of denying it?' She knew he would be alone now, and if acknowledging him as her father gave him comfort, then that's what she would do.

He hugged her, his face wet with tears.

The funeral was a sad affair and Rose cried for the woman she had come to love. She clung to Bill's arm throughout the service and was grateful for his strong, steadying presence.

Back at the house when the will was read, she took little notice, not considering it had anything to do with her. Sir George inherited the bulk of the estate, which was right and proper; a generous donation went to the British Legion, and a small bequest to Josh to allow him to continue with his work for ex-servicemen. However, Rose's attention was caught when she heard Bill's name mentioned.

'"I leave to William Jackson Freeman my sixty per cent share in the building firm of Grant Phillips."'

Rose's mouth dropped open. 'That's the firm who built our houses, isn't it? I didn't know Grandmother was involved in them.'

Bill looked stunned. 'Neither did I.'

Sir George smiled. 'She asked me what would be an appropriate gift for you, and we decided on the building firm. We bought a few more shares so you will have control in the business.'

'May we continue?' the solicitor asked.

They stopped talking and nodded.

'"To my beloved granddaughter I leave the blue tea service . . ."'

Rose smiled, remembering the first time they had drunk tea from it together. That was a lovely gift.

'" . . . the portrait of myself, the miniature in the gold frame, and five thousand pounds . . ."'

Rose would have fallen off the chair if Bill hadn't caught her.

The solicitor was still speaking. '" . . . to use to make one of her wishes come true."' He paused. 'There is one more small bequest. "To Annie Webster I leave the figurine of the shepherdess."'

He closed the file. 'That is the end of Lady Gresham's last will and testament.'

*

Rose and Bill were so shocked by Lady Gresham's will that they went outside and started to walk around the streets, trying to grasp what this meant to their lives.

'My God!' Bill gasped. 'This means I can design the homes *and* build them. But why did she leave it to me?'

Rose put her arm around her stunned husband. 'Grandmother did say that your father was her first love, so perhaps she did it for old times' sake.'

'Maybe.' He was silent for a few moments. 'But now I've had time to digest this, I think it's probably because I married you. You know what she's done, don't you?'

'I'm not sure,' Rose said. 'I can't seem to take it in.'

'She has set us up for life. You would never take anything from her when she was alive, so she has provided for you now.'

Rose tipped her head back and grinned. 'Sixty per cent means you'll be the boss. Do you like that idea?'

'Oh, yes, it's an exciting challenge.' He hugged her in delight, ignoring the curious stares of people in the street. 'What are you going to do with your money?'

'I'm going to set up a school for people who can't read or write,' she told him excitedly. 'I've always wanted to do something like that.'

Bill felt as if someone had just thrown a bucket of cold water over him. He stopped and turned her towards him. 'Rose, you're working yourself silly already. How are you going to find the time to do something like that?'

'Oh, I'll manage it.'

He saw the gleam in her eyes and sighed inwardly. As it was he hardly saw her. She was so involved in her work that she was growing away from him, and her family. Her passion for reform had become an obsession, and he was worried. He had known that this wouldn't be an easy marriage, but now he was starting to wonder if it stood a chance of surviving. Rose showed no sign of settling down and having the family he so badly wanted. He'd gambled everything on her becoming mellow in a happy relationship, but quite the opposite was happening.

They started walking again. What was the use of agonizing over it? he thought. He had enormous respect for what she was trying to do, and he loved her.

'You've gone very quiet. Don't you think it's a good idea?'

'Yes, I do, and I'm sure Lady Gresham would approve.' He stopped again. 'But what about us, Rose? We're wealthy now, and you don't need to drive yourself like you're doing. I was hoping that after we'd been married a year, you'd cut down on your work, or even give it up.'

'I can't do that,' she protested.

Bill turned and walked them back to his car. He wouldn't get anywhere with her today – he could see that she was already planning her school. He was going to have to find another way to make her ease up, or they would drift even further apart.

The next day Rose was up early. Sir George had lent her some money until her grandmother's estate was settled and she was eager to start on her school. The cobbler's next door to her office was empty and would be ideal for the purpose. The first thing she needed to do was see the owners and strike a good deal for it with them. Five thousand pounds was a lot of money, but there would be renovations to do, teachers to pay, and other expenses she hadn't even thought of yet.

'Morning, my darling.' Bill kissed her lingeringly. 'You were up early.'

'I've got a lot to do today.' She cast him a quick, embarrassed glance and felt herself colour as she remembered last night. He had never made love to her like that before. She had always known he was a passionate man but, good Lord . . .!

She pushed away the embarrassing memories. He had caught her at a vulnerable moment, that was all.

'I'll drive you, if you're ready,' he suggested, putting his coat on.

'Thanks.' She gulped her tea and grabbed her bag. 'You going into the building firm today?' she asked, as they got into the car.

'No, I'll give them a few hours to get used to the idea of a new chairman, then call a board meeting for tomorrow.'

He dropped her off at her office, and she set straight to work. By the end of the morning, and after a lot of haggling, she had persuaded the shop-owner to let her have it at a reduced rent. She had also engaged three unemployed ex-servicemen, two to do the decorating and one to see about advertising, which would have to be done mostly by word of mouth: the people she was trying to attract wouldn't be able to read. All she had to do now was find teachers.

'You got enough men?' Josh asked, when she stopped long enough for him to catch her. 'I know dozens who are desperate for work.'

'I don't need more at the moment, unless they're teachers or have had a good education.'

He shook his head sadly. 'Most of the poor devils

are labourers with little proper education.' He paused. 'Actually, there's one man who had a secondary-school education, but he's disabled. Lost a foot and his left arm in the battle of the Somme.'

'Send him along to see me,' she said. 'If he can teach others to read and write, he's got the job.'

'I'll go straight away.' Josh gave her a hug.

Rose pushed him off, laughing. 'Go and get the man and ask if there's anyone else.'

Later he returned with three men, all of whom had lost limbs. Her smile was warm as they stood there looking hopeful. 'Thank you for coming. Josh has told you what I require?'

'Yes, Mrs Freeman. I'm Peter,' one introduced himself, 'and this is Andy and that's Jim. We've all had a secondary education and would be grateful for something useful to do.'

Rose had only intended to offer one pound five shillings a week, but looking at these poor devils . . . What the hell! 'The hours will be from nine to six, Monday to Friday, and I will pay each of you two pounds a week.' She thought one man was going to cry, but he pulled himself together. 'Is that agreeable to you?'

'Yes, Mrs Freeman,' they said in unison.

'Good. I hope to be up and running within a week.' She went to her bag and handed them each two pounds. 'I'll pay you a week in advance.'

They were speechless with gratitude.

With the question of teachers settled, she took Josh with her to a shop and bought armfuls of books suitable for beginners, a few more advanced ones, pencils and notebooks. They stacked them in one of the back rooms, and went to put the kettle on.

A lot had been accomplished in a day.

'This is a good thing you're doing.' Josh sat down and rested his elbows on his knees. 'But I haven't asked you if you're going to charge for these lessons?'

'Certainly not!' Rose was horrified. 'My grandmother left me the money to spend as I wish, and if I'm careful it should last a long time. The education system is improving slowly, but this generation needs help.'

Josh sat up straight again. 'Can I send some of the ex-servicemen to you? They'd stand a better chance of getting a job if they could read and write.'

'They're exactly the people the school is aiming to help.'

'It was damned generous of Lady Gresham to leave me that money so I can carry on with *my* work,' Josh remarked. 'She also set up a trust fund so that the two houses can be kept open.'

'She's thought of everyone.'

'I expect she's watching us now to see we use the money wisely.' Josh chuckled.

'I don't doubt it.' Rose felt her throat tighten as she tried to visualize her grandmother looking down on them, urging them on. 'I'm going to call it the Lavinia School.'

'Sounds appropriate.' Josh yawned. 'And I've had enough for one day. See you tomorrow.'

Rose hadn't finished: her next stop was Harold's. Now that he'd finished his book, this was just the challenge he needed.

She would never have time to run this school herself.

Harold was pleased to see her, and jumped at the chance to teach again. They spent a long time in discussion, and when Rose looked at the clock, she gasped. 'Oh, Lord, I've missed my train to Roehampton – I'll have to stay at the flat tonight.'

'Do you want to telephone Bill?' Harold asked.

'No, he'll realize I couldn't get back.' Rose grabbed her coat and rushed to the door. 'If I don't hurry I'll miss the bus to Kensington, too.'

It was a long journey as some of the buses had been cancelled, and by the time Rose reached the flat it was nearly twelve o'clock. As she walked in the lights were on and there was a lovely smell of cooking.

'At last!' Bill didn't kiss her, which was unusual, but she was too tired to mention it.

'I expect you're hungry.'

'Ravenous, but what are you doing here?'

'Harold telephoned and told me you were staying at the flat tonight, so I came back.'

'You drove all the way back to London?' she asked, astonished. 'What on earth for?'

'I see little enough of you,' he told her sharply, 'and I'm not going to let you stay here without me.'

'It's only for one night.'

'Why didn't you let me know what you were doing?' he demanded.

'I was too busy, and I didn't know I was going to be so late.' What was the matter with him?

He turned away and started to dish up the meal.

*

Rose hardly remembered getting into bed and she must have been asleep as soon as she closed her eyes, but it wasn't a restful sleep. She was running down a long passage towards a door that was standing wide open, and then, just as she reached it, it slammed in her face. She awoke with a start and stared into the darkness, reliving the dream. She had an uneasy feeling that she had been the cause of the door closing.

She turned over and dismissed it. She was being silly, it had only been a dream.

The next morning Bill seemed to be his normal, affable self, and she was relieved. It was unlike him to be ratty.

'Is that a new suit?' she asked, seeing him dressed in a smart dark grey three-piece.

'Yes, what do you think? Do I look like the chairman?'

'Oh, of course, you've got your board meeting today.' Rose felt a surge of pride and love as she looked at her handsome husband. He wouldn't have any trouble at the meeting today: he had a quiet air of command, and knew how to handle himself in public. He was a good man and she was lucky to be married to him.

Everything was in full swing when Rose arrived at the office. At ten when they stopped for tea, her mind went back to Bill. He would handle the situation in his usual calm, authoritative way. She need not be concerned about him, she thought.

Then she plunged back into her work again.

37

Bill hesitated outside the boardroom, straightened to his full height, opened the door and strode in. His years of command in the navy hadn't been wasted, he realized, when he saw them all jump to their feet.

For the next two hours he listened, studied facts and figures, discussed the work being undertaken, then went into the financial position of the business. It was only when he had all the information that he understood what Lady Gresham had given him. This was a highly successful business and he was now a wealthy man.

After two hours he drove away elated. Everything had gone better than he had expected, and he had encountered no hostility. He started to whistle. He would arrange something special for himself and Rose. They hadn't had a holiday, so he would take her somewhere peaceful, she would like that.

After her grandmother's funeral, she had been different, more open and affectionate. Their lovemaking that night had been incredible – she had responded with passion, which she hardly ever did. He was never denied her body, she gave it willingly enough, but he wanted more: he wanted her love, and he wasn't getting it. She rarely made a spontaneous gesture of affection towards him, he always had to make the first move, and he longed for her to turn to him in the night.

He sighed. Apart from the day of the funeral when

she had been vulnerable, she never touched him. The rape had left scars, but he could handle that, so why was he fretting about it now? She had married him and he should be content.

But he wasn't! She was so absorbed in her work that she appeared to forget she had a husband who would worry if she didn't come home at night, and that was hard to take. If it hadn't been for Harold, he would never have known where she was last night. When she had eventually come in she had chatted away about the school as if that was all that mattered to her, and never once asked what he had been doing. She was taking him for granted, and that frightened him. He didn't want to lose her.

A week away from work would be a good idea. They needed time to be together, to talk, and discuss their future. Perhaps he would bring up the subject of children.

When he arrived at the shop Rose was turning into the school, she was disappearing up the stairs, giving orders. He waited until she came down, and caught her arm as she was about to walk past him.

'Oh, hello.' She gave him a distracted smile. 'I didn't see you there.'

'Are you coming home tonight, or staying at the flat?' he asked, as levelly as his irritation would allow.

'I don't know yet. It depends how the day goes.'

'That isn't good enough,' he told her sternly.

She sighed. 'What's the time now?'

'Four o'clock.'

'I'll come home, but I might be late.'

She tried to walk away, but he tightened his grip. 'How late?'

'I don't know. You can see how busy I am.'

'Be home by eight at the latest,' he told her quietly, 'or I shall be very angry.'

She laughed. 'You never get angry. Now, go away and let me get on.' She gave him a quick peck on the cheek and hurried off.

He walked out and closed the door behind him. He had always known she was obsessive, but she was getting worse. She seemed even more driven.

'Josh!' Rose called. 'If anyone wants me, I'll be at the council offices for about an hour.'

'Poor sods,' she heard him mutter, as she opened the door.

She glared at him. 'Don't be sorry for them, they need to be shaken until their teeth rattle.'

'And you're just the one to do it, Rose. Go to it.'

With nothing more than a grunt of agreement, she was out of the door and running up the street to catch the bus.

She caught the chairman and two councillors just as they were going into a meeting. She ignored their groans of despair and pitched into them. 'Is the question of slum clearance on your agenda for today?'

'It's always on our agenda,' the chairman told her drily. 'You never let us forget it.'

'Well, I can't see any evidence of you doing anything about it.'

'The cost . . .' one of the councillors muttered, but she stopped him with a ferocious stare.

'I've heard that one too many times. Now, if you'll just listen to me . . .'

The chairman looked at his pocket watch. 'We're late for our meeting.'

As they walked away she swore furiously under her breath. As far back as 1890 the Housing of the Working Classes Act had given local councils the power to close insanitary houses and build new ones with the proceeds of the local rates. Since then, there had been several acts along the same lines, the most recent last year. The Wheatley Act had increased the state subsidy for houses built for rent at a controlled level. Provision had also been made for the expansion of the building trades.

Rose made her way back to the office, deep in thought. Some progress had been made, but not enough.

'Harold!' she exclaimed in surprise, as she walked in. 'What are you doing here?'

'I came to see how you're getting on. I wondered if you'd like me to have a word with your new teachers, perhaps give them a few tips about teaching people to read.'

'Oh, would you? I'm sure they'd be grateful for your advice.' Rose was enthusiastic about his offer: she knew she needed all the help she could get.

Josh got to his feet. 'I'll go and fetch them, shall I?'

'Yes, please.' When he had gone she made a pot of tea for herself and Harold.

'How did your encounter go at the council offices?' he asked, the corners of his mouth twitching.

'The same as usual,' she grumbled. 'I don't know how to get through to them. They could find the money if they reviewed their budget and made some adjustments.'

'Hmm. Why don't you stand as a candidate in the next elections? They're only two months away.'

Rose stared at him in astonishment.

'Don't look at me like that,' he chided. 'You're just the person for the job. They need people with drive and ideas. A lot of them have been councillors for years and are set in their ways. I'd be willing to sponsor you.'

'Good heavens! Why – why didn't I think of that?' she stammered. 'But I wouldn't stand a chance.'

'Yes, you would. Everyone around here knows you and would vote for you. I'll get the papers for you to complete, shall I?' His eyes were shining with excitement.

'Yes, why not? It would be worth a try. Even if I don't get elected, I could stir things up a bit.' She grinned.

He patted her hand. 'Good girl. Now I'll go to the baker's and get some buns for our new teachers to eat with their tea.'

Rose arrived home just before eight, and Bill was pleased to see she had taken notice of what he had said. He took her in his arms and kissed her, but she seemed preoccupied.

'Hungry?' he asked.

'I had something before I caught the train. I think I'll go and have a bath.'

'Come and sit down for a while. I want to talk to you.' He had to speak with determination to gain her attention.

'All right,' she agreed. 'What do you want to talk about?'

He bit back a weary sigh. 'Don't you want to know how I got on today? Your grandmother's bequest is for your benefit too.'

'Oh!' Rose clapped her hand over her mouth. 'I'm so

sorry, I forgot about the board meeting. I've got such a lot on my mind. Tell me about it.'

When he had finished his story, she gave a grunt of satisfaction. 'I knew you'd be all right. You might be quiet, but there's an air of command about you.'

'Is that a compliment?' he asked quizzically.

'Of course it is. I know I don't have to concern myself with the business because you're more than capable of dealing with it.' She started to stand up, but he stopped her.

'I haven't finished yet.' He was going to have to be firm with her.

She sat down again and waited.

'I've arranged for us to take a holiday.'

'Holiday?' She didn't look pleased. 'What on earth for?'

'Rose,' he said patiently, 'we've been married for over a year and all we've done is work. We need a break.'

'I can't. I've got too much to do. When did you think we could possibly go away?'

'In two weeks' time. The weather's warming up and – '

'It's out of the question. Perhaps next year.'

He took her by the shoulders and turned her to face him. 'I want us to spend some time together without work always getting in the way. We need to talk about the future,' he told her earnestly.

Rose turned away impatiently. 'I can't go, especially now. There's the school to get going, I've got a court case coming up, and the local elections are only two months away.'

The word 'election' caught his attention. 'What are you talking about?'

'The borough council elections. I'm going to stand as a candidate.'

He surged to his feet and glared at her. 'How do you think you can fit that in? You're already working non-stop!'

'You said you didn't mind me working,' she retaliated.

'I was referring to your work as a solicitor, but ever since we married you've been taking on more and more. Damn it, Rose, I hardly ever see you now – what's it going to be like if you become a councillor?'

'But it's the only way,' she explained. 'If I get elected, they're going to have to listen to me.'

'And what about us?' he asked, controlling himself with difficulty. 'Do you ever give a thought to what *I* want out of life?'

She looked taken aback. 'Of course I do.'

'No, you don't. You've got everything you want from our marriage, and given me precious little.'

'Well, it was your idea, remember? And I never deny – '

'No, you don't. You give me your body because you feel it's your duty, that's all.'

'Well, isn't that what you wanted?' Rose looked puzzled.

For the first time in his life he was ready to explode with fury. 'There's more to it than that,' he grated, through clenched teeth. 'I want . . . need,' he corrected, 'some indication that you care for me, some response, but you lie in my arms like a rag doll.'

'I don't!'

'Most of the time you do,' he told her plainly. 'I can count on one hand the times you have shown any interest in our lovemaking. I want some affection, a family – '

Rose shot to her feet. 'I told you I didn't want children for a while.'

'You said a year or so. I've respected your wishes and been careful, but we should start thinking about it now.'

'Don't you dare make me pregnant!' she threatened. 'I'll never forgive you if you do.'

'And you believe I'd do that?' He felt as if she'd hit him. He hadn't thought she could distrust him like this. The blinkers were certainly being torn from his eyes. 'Don't you know that I would never put you in that position without your agreement?'

When she didn't answer, he swore fluently under his breath. 'Is that your opinion of me, after all this time? Don't you know me better than that?'

'Of course I do, but you're making a fuss about nothing,' she told him. 'I've explained that it isn't possible at the moment. What's the matter with you tonight? You've always been so reasonable and understanding.'

'Yes,' he said sadly, 'and that's my mistake. And as to what is the matter with me – well, you are shutting me out of your life and I don't like it.'

'Of course I'm not.'

He held his hand up. 'Don't deny it. When you have a minute or two to spare some time, think about it.'

'All right, I'll admit I've been preoccupied lately, but you're busy with your work too.' Rose made an impatient gesture with her hands. 'I don't know what on earth has got into you.'

'No, you don't, do you? And that is what's so sad.'

'Oh, this is silly.' She started to leave the room.

'Don't take me for granted,' he warned, with an edge of steel in his voice. 'There is a limit to my patience.'

38

The next few weeks disappeared in a flurry of activity. The school was open, and six ex-servicemen had come on the first day. Rose had knocked on every door in Garrett Street and persuaded two women and one man to come for lessons. The third of the original ex-servicemen, who was spreading the word, had found another four people. It was going to be a success, she was sure of it.

In a court case last week, a woman had been granted a divorce on the grounds of her husband's adultery, and given custody of the children because of the man's brutality. Things didn't change, Rose thought wearily. Thank God she didn't have a violent husband.

Rose massaged between her eyes. Another headache. They were becoming more frequent, and she knew that her punishing workload was part of the problem. But she suspected it was more due to Bill's coolness towards her, and she couldn't blame him. Since their argument about the holiday and starting a family, he had been distant with her. She had tried to involve him in the election campaign, but he had shown no interest at all.

'Rose,' Harold called cheerfully, 'time to get to the town hall. Hope you've got your speech ready.'

She tapped her head. 'It's all in here.'

'Come on, then.' He rubbed his hands in gleeful anticipation. 'Let's get things rolling.'

The place was packed and she recognized many of the

people sitting there. Harold had been right: they knew her, and wanted to hear what she had to say.

She was a good, confident speaker – a talent she hadn't known she possessed – and she handled the many interruptions with skill and humour. The audience liked that and applauded loudly when she had finished.

'Told you, didn't I?' Harold grinned. 'You've got another meeting at the church hall tonight, then one on Saturday afternoon.'

'This is hard work,' she complained, as her headache intensified.

'I never said it would be easy,' Harold reminded her.

'Oh, don't take any notice of me. It's just this damned bad head. If I can only get rid of it, I'll be back to normal.'

'Bring Bill along to some of the meetings,' Harold suggested. 'His presence might persuade some of the more affluent among them to vote for you.'

'He's very busy.'

Harold gave her a searching look. 'Don't shut him out, involve him in what you're doing. He'd be a strong man to have at your side.'

Sadness swept through Rose. Ever since they had married, he had been there, listening to her plans and calming her down when things got difficult. But that had been in the beginning – they hadn't had much time to talk just lately.

Harold caught hold of her chin and turned her face towards him. She squinted in pain. 'Why don't you go to the flat and get a couple of hours' sleep?'

'I think I'll have to.'

'Off you go, then. I'll just pop back and see that

everything's going all right at the school.' He marched up the road with a spring in his step.

On the bus her head was thumping so hard that she felt desperate to lie down in a dark room. It would be quiet at the flat: Bill wouldn't be there at this time of the day.

Strong hands were pulling her into a sitting position.

'Rose! What's the matter?'

She opened one eye, expecting the light to hurt, but there was only a dull ache now, so she opened the other . . . carefully.

Bill was looking down at her with a deep frown of concern.

'I had a bad head and had to sleep for a couple of hours,' she explained, and struggled to get out of bed.

He eased her back. 'Stay there and I'll make you some tea.'

'You don't have to,' she told him hastily. He didn't look too pleased to see her. 'My head's better now, and I've got to get to my next meeting.'

'Electioneering, are you?'

She nodded, worried by his grim expression. 'Would . . . would you like to come? It's quite fun,' she told him. She hated the tension between them.

'I've got a client to see this evening.'

'Oh, perhaps another time.' Her disappointment at his refusal, yet again, was crushing, but she had set out on this course of action and would see it through. Harold was right: becoming a councillor was the only way she was going to get anything done.

'You'd better stay here tonight,' he told her. 'It will

save you a train journey.' Then he walked towards the door with rolls of drawings tucked under his arm.

She couldn't let him go like that. 'Bill.'

He looked back.

It was time to be honest. 'I don't like us being angry with each other.'

'Neither do I.' He dropped the papers, stepped forward, took her into his arms and kissed her with more than a hint of desperation. Then he picked up his things again and strode out of the room.

Funny . . . her headache had vanished.

Her election address that evening was a roaring success, and she enjoyed every minute of the boisterous meeting, feeling brighter than she had all week. At one point she'd rolled up her sleeves, jumped off the platform and threatened one trouble-maker with instant destruction, much to the delight of the rest of the audience.

By the time it was over it was late, and she was glad she didn't have to go back to Roehampton. That afternoon Harold had bought himself a car, so he drove her to the flat. When she crawled into bed, she was exhausted. One day she would ease up, she promised herself.

Something woke her, and for a moment she couldn't think what it was. Then she felt Bill's warmth beside her and smiled into the darkness. She reached out and put on the light. It was time they started to talk to each other properly again.

He was lying with his hands beneath his head and an unreadable expression on his face. He wasn't going to make it easy for her.

'I'm sorry I'm so difficult to live with. Can you forgive me?'

He nodded.

'Thank you.' She went to turn out the light.

'Leave it on.'

'Why?'

'I want to look at you.'

'Oh.' Rose pulled a face.

She settled down again. He hadn't moved, which was unusual, because whenever they were in bed together he couldn't keep his hands off her. She glanced across at him. He was staring up at the ceiling. She couldn't stand his silence.

'Er . . . do you want . . .? You know . . .' God! She was becoming a gibbering idiot. Not long ago she had been arguing with confidence and fluency, but now she couldn't even string three words together.

'Say it, Rose.'

Why did she find this so difficult to talk about? They were man and wife, for heaven's sake! She took a deep breath. 'Do you want to make love?'

'There,' he smiled, 'that wasn't so hard, was it?'

'Don't make me angry with you again,' she snapped, rattled. She propped herself up on one elbow. 'You know I find it hard to talk about.'

He raised an eyebrow in query.

'Sex!' she shouted at him. 'There! Are you satisfied now?'

'Far from it,' he replied, with a glint of mischief in his eyes.

'What are you waiting for then?'

'I'm waiting for you to make love to me,' he told her calmly.

Rose looked at him suspiciously. 'What are you up to?'

'I'm tired of making the moves. It's time you learned to take the initiative.'

'Rag dolls don't know how to,' she threw at him, and regretted it when she saw him wince. Would she never learn to curb her sharp tongue? 'I'm sorry. I shouldn't have said that.'

'No, my love. I shouldn't have said that.'

She fiddled with the sheet. 'You had every right. I know I'm no good in that department.'

'That isn't true,' he told her seriously. 'It's just that you've got your emotions under such tight control that you can't relax enough to respond. On the odd occasion when you have let go you've been . . . well . . . All you need is a little gentle tuition.'

He winked and she laughed.

'I never knew you were a liar, Mr Freeman.'

'It's the truth.' He removed one hand to make a cross over his heart, then resumed his position again. 'Come on, I'm waiting.'

'What for?'

His sigh was dramatic. 'You to make love to me.'

'You're not serious, are you?' She was scandalized. 'Women don't carry on like that!'

'We are married, my innocent beauty, and it's quite proper for a woman to make love to her husband.'

Rose wasn't convinced, but she had already upset him enough, so perhaps . . .? 'I don't know what to do.'

'You do whatever you like.' He smiled encouragingly. 'The same things I do when I make love to you.'

She frowned. She'd always been happy with the way things were.

He removed his hands from behind his head and pulled her towards him. 'You can't touch me from over there, and I've decided to teach you the art of lovemaking.'

'Well, if learning this art means I've got to do everything, then you can forget it, mate.' She turned away. He'd never acted strange like this before.

'I'll guide you,' he coaxed.

Rose cast him a suspicious glance.

'Come on. It's easy, you sit astride me . . .'

'You're joking?' She was shocked.

He shook his head and continued to draw her forward.

She slipped one leg tentatively across his body, then stopped, sat up and folded her arms mutinously. 'I can't. I'm sorry, I just can't do that.'

He groaned and pulled her down in the bed, then rolled over until he was looking into her face. 'A man could die of frustration waiting for you to make your mind up.'

Bill stood at the back of the hall, praying that Rose wouldn't be elected, but he had a nasty feeling he was hoping in vain. Since their reconciliation he had attended a few of her meetings and had to admit that she was good. She spoke with conviction and fire, and the voters had come to believe she was their salvation.

Over the last few weeks she had tried to be more considerate and responsive, but he knew that she was wrapped up in her fight for justice. At least she had more or less handed over the running of the school to Harold. He sighed inwardly. Being married to Rose was like trying to ride out a force nine gale in a rowing boat, but he still loved her desperately – and knew he always would. And as much as he wanted her to lose this contest, when he'd listened to her impassioned speeches over the last few weeks, he had been proud of her.

Harold, Grace, John, Josh and Mary came up to him as soon as they saw him at the back.

'Our Rose is going to win,' Josh told him, smiling excitedly.

Harold was almost bursting with pride. 'Of course she is.'

John said nothing, but Grace squeezed Bill's arm and smiled up at him. 'Everything will be all right,' she told him. 'Rose has to get this out of her system. You've always known that, Bill.'

He gave a tight smile. 'I know, but it's more difficult than I anticipated. I always thought I had enough patience to cope but I'm not so sure now.'

Grace looked up at him sadly. 'Rose might not admit or show it, but she needs you, Bill. You and her family are the stabilizing forces in her life, and if she loses any part of that, I dread to think what will happen to her.'

John, who had been talking to Harold and Josh, turned to Bill. 'I always knew Rose was special, but I never dreamed that the scruffy girl of eleven who came to me for lessons would turn out like this.' He looked at her on the stage and shook his head in amazement. 'She's magnificent, isn't she, Bill?'

Bill nodded. That was something he had never denied. Rose was indeed *special*, but was she going to remain his?

A booming voice from the platform broke through his troubled thoughts.

The man was announcing the results, and Bill's heart sank as his hopes for a normal family life, and children, crumbled at his feet.

She had won.

39

December 1925

Rose tore into the house. 'I'm sorry I'm late.' Then she looked around at the festive decorations. 'Oh, this is lovely.'

'Where have you been?' Annie asked. 'You promised to come shopping and help decorate the tree.'

Rose saw the disappointment in her sister's face and felt awful. Then she glanced at Bill. He was angry, and had every right to be, she acknowledged. This was Christmas Eve and she had assured her family that she wouldn't work this afternoon – but something had come up and she couldn't ignore it. As the newly elected chairman of the council, she had called an extra meeting, much to everyone's annoyance, but swift action had been essential.

'We had to have a special meeting,' she started to explain. 'It's very ex – '

'We are not going to have any business talk,' Bill interrupted. 'Let's forget the rest of the world for a few days, shall we?'

There was a chorus of agreement from the family, so Rose kept quiet, although she was bursting to tell them the news. If that was the way they wanted it, she would keep it to herself. And perhaps it was for the best: there wasn't anything definite yet. But she would have loved to share this unexpected development with them.

'Perhaps we can have dinner now you've finally arrived,' her mother scolded. 'Everyone's starving waiting for you.'

'Why didn't you go ahead without me?' It looked as if they were all cross with her.

'Because it's Christmas Eve and we wanted to sit down together,' Annie explained, in a hurt voice. 'You're so busy these days, we hardly ever see you.'

She didn't miss the note of sadness in her sister's voice, or the look of censure on Bill's face. They would understand if they'd only let her explain, but she had clearly upset everyone, and they were not in the mood to listen to excuses, however good.

'Well, I'm here now, and I've got two days off.' She sat down at the table.

'Two?' Bill looked up sharply. 'I thought you were going to take four.'

Oh, Lord, more trouble. 'I can't.'

'What are you up to, my girl?' Her mother looked furious. 'You promised you'd forget work for a while and spend the holiday with us. We've got Grace, John, Harold, Josh, Mary and your father coming on the twenty-seventh. You must be here!'

Rose felt worse. She had even forgotten that. 'What time are they arriving?'

'Before lunch. And don't think you can slope off in the morning, because we know only too well that that will be the last we see of you,' Marj was evidently exasperated with her eldest daughter.

Annie glared at her mother. 'Don't shout at Rosie like that. She's doing her best.'

Rose looked down at the beautifully decorated table.

419

How could her sister continue to defend her when all she ever did these days was let everyone down? 'I'll stay at home that day.' It was the only concession she could make.

Annie smiled broadly, sat on the chair next to her sister and touched her hand. 'It'll be nice to have you here for a while.'

Rose looked at Annie's happy face, then round at everyone else. Her young sister was the only one who seemed to have forgiven her. Suddenly she felt ashamed of missing the shopping trip. 'Where did you go shopping?' she asked.

'Bill took us to Richmond. There were some lovely shops, you would have enjoyed it,' her sister said wistfully.

'I'm sure I would. Perhaps we can go in the New Year.'

'Don't make promises you can't or won't keep,' Bill told her pointedly.

Annie jumped to her defence again. 'She doesn't mean to forget, she's just got too much on her mind. Don't be angry with her, Bill. It's Christmas, so can't we forget it and be happy together?'

He nodded, then smiled for the first time. 'You're quite right, but don't take your eyes off her or she'll disappear again,' he teased.

'I won't.' Annie laughed and held on to her sister's arm.

The atmosphere lifted considerably and Rose felt herself relax. When did her sister drop 'Uncle'? I suppose she feels too grown-up for that now, she thought. The years were flying by. And they were right: she was working too hard. But she couldn't ease up yet.

It was a lively evening, with all the family in high

spirits, and Rose was pleased to see that the earlier unpleasantness had been forgotten. She gazed at each of her family in turn. What a difference in them since she had married Bill! The last person she studied was her husband, and saw with a shock that he had lost weight and looked very tired. Why hadn't she noticed before?

They put the last touches to the tree, and when she saw the parcels being put around it, she galloped upstairs: she hadn't wrapped her presents yet.

'You did find time to buy some presents, then,' Bill remarked drily, as he followed her into the room a couple of minutes later.

'Yes, I got them two weeks ago.' She hastily pushed his out of the way so he couldn't see it.

'Here, let me give you a hand.' He sorted through the modest gifts and frowned. 'You could have bought better things than this.'

'I couldn't afford to spend more.' Rose tied a lopsided bow, but it was good enough, she decided. Annie was the artistic one, not her.

'What do you mean?'

She looked up and found him frowning at her. Now what had she done?

'Why couldn't you afford to spend more? I give you a good allowance every week.'

'Oh, I couldn't use that. That's only for the house and food.'

He looked as if he couldn't believe what he was hearing. 'But that would never take all the money, surely?'

'Oh, no, you give me far too much. Anything I don't use is in the drawer over there. You can have it back, if you want.' Rose continued wrapping her presents.

Without saying a word, he walked over to the dressing-table, took a small cardboard box out of the drawer and opened it. 'My God!' he muttered. 'This is full of money. Why haven't you spent it?'

'I've been earning enough to pay my own way. That's yours.'

Bill sat next to her on the bed and took her hands. 'When will you realize that what we have we share? This money is for you to spend in any way you like.'

'But it's rather a lot, and I don't need it.'

He shook his head in disbelief. 'Rose, your grandmother left us a thriving business. There's no need for you to scrimp and save. We are wealthy. You haven't taken the slightest notice of how we've prospered, have you?'

She shrugged.

'You really must try to leave Garrett Street behind. Those days are over,' he told her firmly.

'Not for the people who still live there,' she replied hotly. 'I see them, and dozens more like them, every day.'

'I know. But you are out of it now, and when I give you money, I want you to spend it on yourself or your family. Do you understand?'

Rose picked up the scarf she had bought at the market for her mother. What a blind fool she was. Her family had moved on, but she was still living in the past. In her daily life she confronted poverty all the time, and it still filled her mind. 'It's too late to get anything else. Do you think my presents aren't good enough?'

'No,' he assured her hastily. 'They'll love them because they come from you, but try to remember in future that you don't have to be careful with money any more.'

'I'll try.' She gave him a hesitant smile, but he didn't return it. Feeling the need to explain what had happened today, she tried again. 'I'm sorry I was late but something unexpected cropped up.'

His mouth set in a grim line. 'It always does.'

Her spirits sagged. He was still cross with her. 'I can explain.'

'I don't think anything can excuse you breaking your promises at this time of year. Your mother and Annie were bitterly disappointed.'

Rose watched him stand up and leave the room. I've got the best excuse in the world, she wanted to shout, but in the silence of the room, she lowered her head. She had wanted to share the exciting news, but what was the use? They didn't care.

She felt so alone.

Then she surged to her feet. What was the matter with her? She had always been alone. From the time she could talk, no one had understood her, except Annie perhaps. It had never bothered her before, so why should she fret about it now? She had set out to do something and she wouldn't rest until it was done. If she upset a few people on the way that was sad, but the demon driving her wouldn't let her give up.

She was just about to go downstairs, when Annie came tearing up.

'We're going to the midnight service,' she announced. 'Come on.'

Rose listened to the Christmas story being read in the beautiful language of the King James version of the Bible, and realized with sadness that she hadn't opened her own copy for some time.

Her thoughts wandered back to the day she had won it for being top of the school, and the many happy hours she had spent trying to grasp the meaning of the stories and Psalms. She must get it out again, because she had found great comfort in the words when her world had been in turmoil as a child. Perhaps it would help now, in this time of great change and tension in her life?

The next morning, as everyone was opening their presents, Bill laughed at their pleasure, and was pleased to see that Rose's gifts were received with equal enthusiasm. The leather case she had bought him would be useful, and he was pleased she had remembered to get something for everyone.

The floor was littered with paper and empty boxes and he smiled to himself, cherishing the moment. He loved this family, and he yearned for children of his own. After all, he wasn't getting any younger.

'Oh!' Rose gasped, and looked at him wide-eyed.

He went and stooped down in front of her. 'Do you like it?'

'It's beautiful, but it must have cost a fortune.'

He took the ruby and diamond ring out of the box and slipped it on to her left hand. Then he whispered in her ear, 'Happy second wedding anniversary, darling.'

Rose kissed his cheek, relieved that she'd had the sense to buy a special card for him. 'Thank you. I love it.'

He stood up and turned to face everyone. 'Rose and I have a special gift to hand out now,' he announced, taking an envelope out of his pocket and handing it to Marj and Wally.

'I don't understand what it means,' Marj said, after looking at the papers.

Wally seemed overcome, but eventually cleared his throat and spoke to his wife. 'Bill has given us the deeds to our house.'

'Does that mean it's ours?'

He nodded and Marj burst into tears. Then pandemonium broke out as they all surged around to thank them.

Rose was stunned at this act of selfless generosity. 'Why didn't you tell me?' she asked quietly.

'You're never around to talk to these days,' he told her, 'and when you do come home you're too tired to do anything but sleep.'

On the twenty-seventh, Grace, John, their son, Josh, Mary and Harold arrived with Rose's father. Sir George and Marj appeared at ease with each other now, the past forgotten, and he was happy to be included in the family. Rose couldn't help marvelling at the way her mother had forgiven him. Mary was proudly showing off a modest engagement ring, and Rose had never seen Josh look so happy. She was delighted that things were going so well for him.

After lunch they all sat around the fire and handed out more presents.

John stood up, looking very pleased with himself. 'I have an announcement to make. We are expecting another child in five months' time.'

After everyone had congratulated them, Rose's father

cleared his throat. 'And talking of children, I have a special gift for my daughter and her husband.' He handed Bill a large envelope tied with pink legal ribbon.

Intrigued, Rose watched Bill open it. When he didn't speak, she leaned forward to look at the papers, then she took them out of Bill's hand and jumped up. 'You can't do this!' she exploded.

'Yes, I can. You are my daughter and it's all legal. And there isn't a thing you can do about it.'

'What is it?' Harold was bursting with curiosity.

'I have made Rose my heir. The Gresham blood will continue through her, with my estate going to her eldest son.'

'Will you stop pacing up and down like an enraged lioness?' Bill demanded, when they were alone later that night.

Rose spun round. 'What the hell do you expect me to do? How dare he do this to me?'

'He's only made you his heir.'

'Only!' she raged. 'If we hadn't had visitors I'd have wrung his bloody neck.'

Bill sighed and looked up at the ceiling. 'You are his daughter, the only one left with Gresham blood. What he's done is right and sensible.'

'Don't you talk to me about what's right! I know you're on his side,' she shouted, completely out of control now. 'I bet you just loved that bit about our *eldest son* inheriting the estate. If the pair of you think you can put pressure on me . . .'

Bill stepped forward, but she stood her ground, too furious to curb her words.

'You're lucky I'm not a violent man,' he ground out, between clenched teeth. 'If you're accusing me of talking about our private life, then you're wrong. Our disagreement about having children is between us,' he continued. 'I have never discussed it with anyone else.'

'Huh!' She snorted.

'All right. Let's get this out into the open, shall we?' He gripped her arms. 'When we married you promised to have children in a year or so. Well, it's two years now, so tell me what you intend to do about it.'

'I don't want any!' she shouted. 'I've got too much to do to tie myself down to squalling brats.'

He looked at her for a few moments. 'Does this mean you'll never change your mind?'

'I don't think so. Bill, I'm just starting to get somewhere, but it might still take me years.'

'You can't leave Garrett Street, can you?' He stepped away from her and ran a hand tiredly over his eyes.

Rose started to pace again. 'I won't be able to let go of Garrett Street until I see it flattened. Do you know what it was like living with the dirt, vermin, violence, the life-sapping fight to find enough food, and the constant threat of being thrown into the street if you fell behind with the rent?' She shuddered. 'I hated that place, and I still do.'

'I saw it many times – '

'Yes,' she interrupted, before he could finish, 'but you could walk away, back to your comfortable, clean home. We couldn't escape the squalor, and neither can the poor buggers still living there.'

Rose held up her hand when he started to speak.

'Don't bother with meaningless words,' she growled. 'You wouldn't understand, not in a million years.'

'I never realized what a low opinion you had of me.' He spoke so quietly that the words were hardly audible. Then he walked over to the wardrobe, pulled out a couple of cases, threw them on to the bed and piled his clothes into them. 'A marriage without respect is dead. You want to be free of all family responsibilities, so from this moment you are.'

'Don't be silly!'

He didn't stop what he was doing. 'For the first time since I met you I'm being sensible. You are obsessed with your work, and I have been obsessed with you, making excuses for you all the time, but not any more. John told me once that you would destroy anyone who loved you, but I'm getting out before that happens to me.'

'John was talking rubbish, and so are you!'

Rose watched as he closed the cases. She had gone too far this time, she knew. 'I didn't mean to be nasty to you. I was angry.' It was feeble and she knew it.

'You always are, and I've come to the end of my patience.'

'Are you going to the flat?' She was frightened now. She'd never seen this shuttered expression on his face before.

'I've closed the office and no longer rent the flat.'

'Why didn't you tell me?'

'The changes I've made are because of increased business. Those premises are no longer adequate, and I would have told you if you'd been here long enough for us to talk.'

'Oh, we're back to that, are we?'

'You don't think it's a valid point?'

'This is ridiculous!' she shouted, as he walked towards the door.

He stopped and looked back over his shoulder. 'Rid yourself of whatever demon is driving you, Rose. Until you do that, you're never going to be happy.'

Bill drove towards London, and it wasn't until he arrived in the apartment on the top floor of Grant Phillips that he allowed himself to think.

Her accusations had hurt so much that the pain had been almost physical. He had relied on her softening once they were married, but that hadn't happened. He had watched her obsession gather strength and intensity over the last two years and shut his eyes to it, but he couldn't do that any longer. Her unreasonable fury at her father's action had stripped away the last of his illusions, and made him see how hopeless things were. And the most disturbing thing of all was that she had broken her word to him about having children. He had never believed she would do such a thing.

He poured himself a large whisky, and sank into a chair. He still loved her, but this was tearing him apart. Until she achieved her aims, nothing would stop her. She was like a runaway train, and the only thing he could do was get out of her way until she came to her senses – if she ever did.

He downed the whisky in one gulp. For a man who didn't believe in taking reckless chances, he had been incredibly stupid.

40

January 1926

Rose felt wretched and watched the cup of tea grow cold in front of her. She shouldn't be at home wasting her time like this, but Bill had been gone for a week now, and nothing seemed worthwhile any more.

'Where's Bill?' her mother asked, as she came into Rose's kitchen.

Rose shrugged. 'He's left me.' There wasn't any point denying it: her family were going to know sooner or later.

Her mother's expression was one of profound shock. 'Oh, you stupid girl. What have you done?'

'We had a blazing row after my father made that ludicrous announcement.'

'But why?'

'Bill wants children and I said no.'

Her mother shook her head in despair. 'I knew you'd agreed to wait for a while, but I didn't think you'd refused altogether.'

'I didn't when we married. I said we'd think about it in a year or so,' she admitted, but not without shame.

'So you led him to believe that you would eventually have children.'

'I suppose so, but I've told him now that I definitely don't want any.'

Marj thumped the table, making her daughter jump. 'You've broken your word! No wonder he's left you. That's unforgivable.'

'I can't have a baby,' Rose protested. 'There's too much to do.'

'What's happened to you?' her mother asked. 'Once upon a time if you made a promise nothing on earth would have made you break it. Now it seems to mean nothing to you.' Marj stood up and stormed out of the room.

'Oh, bugger!' Rose watched the bus disappear round the corner. It would be twenty minutes before another came. She needed to talk to someone and there was only one person to whom she could turn.

She set off across the park at a fast walk, and her flesh crept as she passed the bushes she had been dragged into. She made herself slow down and walk at a natural pace. With the kind of mood she was in, if anyone tried to assault her now, she would murder them.

Her temper was volatile without Bill's calm presence in her life. She missed him. She hardly ever went back to the house any more. Everything there reminded her of him, and her family were still angry with her. She wished her grandmother was alive: she could have poured out all her troubles to her. But Lady Gresham would probably have told her she had become a self-righteous bore, and she would be right.

Rose felt completely alone. It was only lately she had realized how much her family meant to her, and how much she had depended on Bill always being there when she needed him. But it was all her own fault, and she deserved to be abandoned. Grace and John had helped and guided her from the time she'd been thrown out of school at eleven years old, so it was natural for her to turn to them at this time of crisis.

She reached the house and knocked firmly.

'Look,' she said, when John opened the door, 'I know you're cross with me, but I need help and I don't know who else to turn to.'

He stepped aside. 'You'd better come in.'

Grace smiled when she walked into the front room. 'It's lovely to see you again, Rose. We'd begun to think you'd forgotten us.'

The greeting surprised her, but it was obviously sincere. 'I didn't think you wanted to see me again.'

'We're always pleased to see you,' John told her earnestly. 'Whatever problems you and Bill are having, you are still our friends.'

Rose felt a lump form in her throat. What a fool she was to have assumed that they wouldn't want her to visit. When was she ever going to learn not to think the worst of people? 'Thank you. I didn't think I had a friend left, except Harold, and he's too busy running the school for me. I don't think he even knows when I'm around.'

John laughed. 'I saw him the other day – he's having the time of his life.'

Rose smiled when she thought about the elderly man. 'I don't know what I would have done without him. He's running the school. Two of his pupils have already found jobs now they can read and write a bit.'

'He was here yesterday and he's overjoyed about their success,' Grace said.

When they were seated, John asked, 'How can we help you?'

Rose felt embarrassed. She was not used to baring her soul. 'I just need someone to talk to, John, and I thought of you – just like when I was a kid.'

John took off his spectacles, polished them, then sat back and waited.

She told him everything, pointing out her faults, especially her temper, and after several painful minutes she ground to a stop and looked at John with anguish. 'I've got worse, I'm afraid, without Bill to calm me down. Do you know if he's all right?'

'He's fine,' John told her.

'How's Annie?' Grace asked.

'All right, I think.' Rose felt her eyes cloud with tears. Lord, what a mess she was in.

John looked at her sharply. 'You think?'

'She hasn't spoken to me for weeks.' The friendly atmosphere had made her drop her guard and, to her shame, a tear trickled down her face.

Wiping her cheek with the back of her hand, she stood up. 'I'm sorry, I'm making an exhibition of myself.'

'No, you're not.' Grace was beside her, pushing her back into the chair.

'Aren't your family talking to you?' John asked gently.

'Oh, they're civil when they see me, but I don't go home very often now. I sleep at the office.'

'Well, you must,' Grace urged, taking hold of her hand. 'If they never see you, how can the breach be healed?'

*

Rose took Grace's advice and went home the following weekend, although she was uncertain how she would be received by her family. But Grace was right; if they never saw her, how could the breach be healed? She had never been on bad terms with her mother, and this was only adding to her distress.

'I'm in here, Mum,' Rose called, when she heard her mother's voice.

Marj came into Rose's comfortable front room. 'Why didn't you tell me you were coming? I'd have lit the fires for you.' She looked round hopefully. 'You on your own?'

'Yes,' Rose said sadly. 'I haven't seen or heard from Bill since Christmas. He's left for good.'

'Are you sorry?'

She turned on her mother, her fragile temper snapping. 'That's a stupid question to ask. Of course I'm sorry! I know you all think I've got a heart of stone, but that isn't true. I miss him and I'm a stupid fool . . .'

'Calm down,' her mother said.

Rose took a deep breath. 'I've been an idiot. I've lost him, and I've got to accept that. I wish I could take back the nasty words, but it's too late. I've just got to get on with my life as best I can.'

Her mother changed the subject. 'Your father came the other day.'

'What did he want?' Rose frowned, wondering why he was calling when she wasn't here.

'He said to tell you that he's back home again and would you go and see him.'

'Where's he been?' Rose wanted to know.

Marj sighed. 'He told you he was going to Scotland for New Year.'

Rose thought for a moment, then nodded. 'Oh, yes, I'd forgotten. I'll call in some time next week.'

'Make it earlier than that. He's a lonely man, Rose, and he loves you.'

She gave her mother a speculative glance. 'You sticking up for him now?'

Marj sighed. 'We've put aside all the past, as you know, and you'd have remembered that if you turned your attention away from work now and again.'

The reprimand stung because Rose knew her mother was right. Her desire for reform had become an obsession, and that wasn't healthy. What a fool she'd been.

'I'll go and see him the first chance I get.'

'Good. Don't make enemies of everyone. Sir George only did what he felt was right.'

'I know that now. For a supposedly intelligent woman, it's taken me a long time to acknowledge my faults and face them.'

'Are you facing them?' her mother asked quietly.

'I'm trying.'

'We'll see you for lunch tomorrow, then, shall we?'

'I'd like that.'

Fences were being mended. Her relationship with Grace and John was back to normal, and her brothers, who had just arrived, were acting as if nothing had happened. That left her father and Annie. If she could gain their forgiveness, perhaps life would have some meaning again.

Wally walked in, smiled and kissed her cheek. 'It's good to see you again. You shouldn't have stayed away so long, everyone's been worried about you. How are you managing?'

435

'I'm bearing up.' She tried to smile.

'Bill's been to see us a few times.'

'Where's he living?' she asked urgently.

Wally shook his head. 'Somewhere in London, but we don't know the address. If I knew where Bill was, I'd tell you. I believe you're both missing each other badly, and if you ask me, the pair of you need your heads banging together.'

'I'm sure we do,' she admitted.

Rose made up her mind, there and then, to try to put things right with her father and Annie. Bill was another matter, though. She couldn't go to him, but there was one place she could leave a message for him: Grant Phillips. It would have to be a letter, and that was unsatisfactory, but it was the only option she had. She *had* to make her peace with him, even if he never wanted to see her again. The thought of spending the rest of her life without him was agony, but Rose didn't think there was any choice. Bill wasn't going to forgive her this time.

The next day after breakfast Rose wandered out into the garden. The sky was clear, the sun had a touch of warmth in it and there were little clumps of snowdrops dotted about. Spring was not far away.

Part of her dream coming true was a distinct possibility now, but one success would be only the beginning, and she doubted she had the heart to continue fighting on her own.

Lost in thought, she bent down again to pull up a weed.

'Leave that, Rosie. It's a flower.'

She forced herself to look up at Annie, and was over-joyed to see her smiling at her. 'Is it?'

'Yes. Why did you stay away so long?' Annie asked.

'I didn't think you wanted to see me.'

'I was upset, but I didn't want you to go away too.' Annie looked at her imploringly. 'Are you going to tell him you're sorry?'

'Yes. I'll send him a letter because he doesn't want to see me.'

'Oh.' Annie looked down and kicked a pebble, then took Rose's hand. 'Lunch is ready.'

Rose went willingly, happy to be back with her family. It was a start.

Her father was delighted to see her and kissed her cheek when she arrived. She didn't waste any time. 'I'm sorry I was so rude to you at Christmas. It was unforgivable of me.'

'It was only what I expected – but I didn't want everything the Greshams have worked for to go to the government just because there isn't anyone to inherit.'

'You could have left it to any number of worthy causes,' she protested.

He swept a hand around the room. 'All this has been in Gresham hands for generations and I want it to remain that way. You are my daughter, but if you don't want it then it's only right that your children should inherit the estate.'

'You realize there might not be any children. Bill has left me.'

He patted her arm. 'Everything will turn out all right.'

'Don't patronize me.' She snorted, irritation rising in

437

spite of all her good intentions. 'If Bill divorces me, I'll never marry again.'

'I'm sure it won't come to that. Now, tell me truthfully, do you want him back?'

'Yes, but he isn't coming. He's had enough of me.' Rose dropped her head in a defeated gesture.

Sir George studied her thoughtfully. 'Lost your fire, have you?'

'Of course not,' she replied indignantly.

'Then stop feeling sorry for yourself and do something about it. Go and face him, or are you afraid to admit you were wrong?'

'I *was* wrong,' she shouted, 'and if I could find the bloody man, I'd tell him so.' She stopped when she realized they were facing each other like a couple of prize-fighters again, and he was grinning.

'What's so funny?' she demanded, glaring at him.

'That's more like my daughter, spitting fire.' He chuckled. 'I was worried for a moment.'

A smile tugged at the corners of her mouth. 'You're impossible, do you know that?'

His grin got broader. 'So are you.'

'Hmm. I must have inherited it from someone.'

They both roared with laughter.

'That's better,' her father remarked. 'Now go and tell that man of yours that you're sorry and miss him dreadfully.'

'There's a lawyer here to see you, Mr Freeman.'

'Oh.' Bill looked up from the report he was studying. 'Who is it?'

'Miss Webster, sir. She says it's urgent.'

He pulled his watch out of his pocket and flipped it open, more to give himself a chance to decide what to do than to check the time. What had brought her here? And why was she using her maiden name?

'Sir?' The secretary looked anxious. 'She was most insistent.'

'I have a meeting in ten minutes. Would you ask her to leave a message?' He smiled at the young woman who was looking rather apprehensive. 'She won't bite.'

She gave a nervous laugh. 'I'm not so sure. I've heard about her.'

He stood up. 'Where is she?'

'Downstairs, sir.'

When he got to Reception Rose had her back to him and was pacing up and down by the window. 'What can I do for you, Miss Webster?' he asked formally.

She spun round, and he was shocked to see how much weight she had lost. There were deep shadows under her eyes, and she looked . . . lost. He didn't know how else to describe it.

'What do you want, Rose?'

She glanced anxiously at the people coming and going. 'Can we go somewhere private?'

'I've only got five minutes. This will have to do.' God, he hated doing this to her, but he had set out on a course of action and he had to see it through. He knew he only had to hold on for a little longer and then it would be over, one way or the other.

'Very well.' Rose straightened up. 'I want to apologize. I know all those things I said to you are not true. I was angry and lashed out at the person nearest to me. You've never done anything to deserve being treated like that.

I deeply regret my unreasonable behaviour and I am thoroughly ashamed of myself. If you want to divorce me, I shall understand.'

Then she turned and strode out of the building.

He watched her hurry out with her head bowed. That worried him. He'd never seen her like that: her carriage was always proud and straight. And had that been a glimmer of tears he had seen as she'd walked away from him?

It took all of his self-control not to run after her.

'What a beautiful woman,' James, the firm's manager, remarked, gazing after the retreating figure of Rose. 'She looks familiar, who is she?'

'My wife.'

'Of course,' James exclaimed. 'I'd heard you were married to Sir George Gresham's ill – er, daughter. She's the image of him.'

Bill gave him an amused sideways glance. 'Illegitimate. You can say the word. She isn't ashamed of it, neither am I, and her father loves her. Though you'd never believe it if you saw them together – they fight as soon as they see each other.'

James chuckled. 'I can imagine, especially if she's inherited his fiery temper.'

'She has.'

'Good heavens, Bill, how do you manage her?'

'With difficulty,' he said drily. 'Now, is there any news about that contract we're interested in?'

'Yes. They've increased the area and there will now be room for forty houses.'

'When did this happen?'

440

'I got word yesterday when I had lunch with the minister in charge of the project.'

'When do they intend to start?'

'In two months.'

Bill tipped back his head and grinned at the ceiling, feeling rejuvenated. 'I want us to get that contract. What are the chances?'

'Nothing's confirmed but I believe it's as good as ours,' James assured him.

Bill took the stairs two at a time in elation.

Forty houses! These were going to be built for Rose.

41

April 1926

Rose massaged her temple as another headache threatened. She had had several since Bill left her four months ago. Was it really only that long? she thought, as the pain intensified. It seemed like a lifetime. She had filled every hour with work in an effort to get through the empty days, and at night she tossed restlessly until the bedclothes were in a tangle. Every time she won a case or made a dent in some injustice, the usual satisfaction wasn't there, and outside work she had nothing.

Rose needed to feel close to Bill, so she left the office and headed for their home.

An hour later she stepped through the door. His presence permeated every room in the house he had designed and built for them. It was all she had left of him now. The last few months had been agony: she had hoped all the time that Bill would come back to her, but he hadn't. She knew now that he never would and she felt like crying in despair every time she thought about life without him – without his love.

She walked into the drawing room and ran her hands over the back of his favourite chair, remembering the way he used to sit there reading or talking and laughing about something. Then she picked up the framed photograph of them after their wedding. As she looked at his smiling face, she started to cry. Great broken-hearted sobs racked her body. She'd had everything, but by her thoughtless, arrogant conduct she had lost it all. What a bloody fool.

'Rose.' Her mother had come in behind her. 'What's the matter?'

She put the photograph back on the shelf and blew her nose, but the tears wouldn't stop coming.

'Let's make you a nice cup of tea.' Her mother led her gently into the kitchen.

Rose knew there wasn't any cure for her distress: she was going to have to live with it for the rest of her life. Bill was the only man she'd ever loved, and there would never be another. She loved John, Harold and Josh, of course, as well as her family, but that was another kind of love. What she felt for Bill was different, the love of a woman for a man, and she'd thrown it away.

The tears flooded down her cheeks as she remembered the happy times they'd shared. The dances, the art galleries, the trips to Richmond Park, the laughter and his sense of humour . . .

'Want to talk about it?' her mother asked gently.

Rose shook her head. 'I can't. I need to be alone, Mum.'

'I understand.' Marj stood up. 'You staying?'

'No, I'm in court this afternoon.'

'Can't you cancel it?'

'I'm afraid not. If a case is scheduled for a certain time you have to be there.'

'Try to have a rest before you go back.' Her mother squeezed her shoulder and left.

Alone once more, Rose gazed into space. When she

recalled her visit to Bill, she moaned aloud. He had looked every inch the successful businessman, so strong and dependable. She had wanted to sink on to her knees and beg his forgiveness, but all she had managed was that stilted apology. He deserved better.

If only they'd had somewhere private to talk, she might have made a better job of it, but he'd only got five minutes, he'd said. That had hurt, but it had made her realize that that was exactly how she'd treated him. She'd never had enough time to be with him and talk properly.

He had loved her and she had taken from him, giving practically nothing in return. No man would put up with that indefinitely, not even one as patient and gentle as Bill. He had told her once that there was a limit to his patience, but she hadn't believed him – too wrapped up in her own activities to realize he was warning her. She had taken his love for granted, an unforgivable crime. She couldn't find a single thing to offer in her own defence.

Since that time she had gone about her business with determination, and never allowed herself to break down or let her feelings surface, but she couldn't do that any longer. She had lost him, and the realization was too terrible to bear. She started to sob again.

A hand clasped hers and she looked up to see Annie sitting beside her.

'Don't cry, Rosie. He still loves you.'

'I don't think so.' She blew her nose again and wiped her eyes. Normally, she wouldn't have let anyone see her like this, but she didn't care now. She'd had too much bloody pride all her life, and what was the good of that? 'Why aren't you at the shop?'

444

'Mum came and fetched me.'

'She shouldn't have done that. I'm all right.' Now she'd resorted to lying, Rose thought.

'It didn't matter, I'm leaving tomorrow, anyway,' Annie told her.

'Are you? What are you going to do? Are you going on to university?'

'No, I've got a job with a ladies' magazine.' She looked at her sister with concern. 'Do you want to be alone?'

Rose tried to smile. 'No, I'm glad you're here. Tell me about your new job.'

'Well, I expect I'll only be the tea-girl for a while, but they liked my drawings and said I wrote well.'

'That's wonderful, Annie.' This news lifted Rose's spirits.

'I'm really looking forward to starting.' Annie got up. 'Mum said you've got to go back this afternoon. Would you like me to get you something to eat?'

'I'm not hungry.'

'But you must eat,' Annie told her sternly. 'You don't look well.'

'All right. Just a sandwich or something.'

'We've got a pot of home-made soup at home. I'll go and get some for you.'

While Rose was waiting for her sister, she went into the bathroom and bathed her face with cold water. She was going to look a mess in court today, but she didn't care: the cry had done her good and seemed to have relieved some of her inner pressure. The deep sadness hadn't gone, of course, and she doubted that it ever would, but she felt more able to cope now. She had done her best to make peace with everyone she had offended, and that was all she could do.

'It's ready,' Annie called from the kitchen.

The soup was delicious. Rose hadn't realized how hungry she was, and her sister nodded approvingly as she polished off a second bowl.

They spent an hour talking about everyday things, and then, feeling much more herself, Rose picked up her bag to go back to work again.

Later that afternoon, Bill stood up, stretched, and turned to gaze thoughtfully out of the office window. The information he had been receiving from the family had told him that Rose was still driving herself. He picked up his coat and slipped it on. He didn't want to be on his own this evening: he would go and see Marj, Wally and the children. They were always pleased to see him and he hadn't been there for a few weeks.

When he arrived Annie met him. 'What's the matter?' he asked. It was unusual to see her anything but bubbly.

'Rose came home for a couple of hours today.'

He nodded, waiting for what she really wanted to say. 'Did she?'

Annie nodded. 'She was crying. I've never seen her cry like that before. In fact the only time I've ever seen her cry at all was after her first day in that awful tin factory.' She looked up at him. 'She promised me then that she'd never cry again, and I don't think she has until now.'

'I think everything's got too much for her,' Marj put in.

Bill felt as if he was being torn apart. Oh, God, he groaned inwardly, this was destroying them both, but he had had no choice. The course of action he'd embarked upon was distressing, but he couldn't see any other way. He wanted to rush straight to Rose, but he mustn't weaken now.

Marj poured him a cup of tea. 'Rose isn't an unkind person,' she said, 'but she's fought all her life and it's a habit with her now. She's always considered emotion a weakness, and it's hard for her to change. But if it hadn't been for her, I wouldn't have survived all those years in Garrett Street.'

'And I wouldn't be alive if she hadn't looked after me,' Annie told him.

'You don't have to remind me about how much she has done for you, I know she is strong, determined and kind,' Bill told them gently. 'But over the last couple of years the need to bring about change has taken her over. She has pushed aside everyone and everything else. She was impossible to live with, and my patience was finally exhausted. I did the only thing I could. We would have destroyed each other if I hadn't left,' he said softly.

'She's very unhappy,' Marj muttered.

'So am I, but one way or another this will soon be over, and we'll be able to get on with our lives.'

'I hope you're right.'

So did he! If he had misjudged her, he had caused them both a lot of suffering for nothing.

'Bill, what's going on?' Marj asked. 'What's Rose up to? And don't pretend you don't know because I'm sure you're keeping an eye on her.'

He toyed with the idea of telling her, but if Rose hadn't told her family, then he couldn't. They'd find out soon enough anyway.

Marj looked at him suspiciously. 'You've got the same look on your face as she has. You're both biding your time waiting for something to happen, aren't you? And don't try that innocent look with me, Bill Freeman, your eyes give you away.' She wagged a wooden spoon coated with flour at him. 'Rose may have lost her way for a while, but I know my daughter, and she'll come back fighting for what she wants – and that's you.'

He just sat there smiling and saw the moment when Marj finally realized what he'd been doing.

'That's what you've been banking on, isn't it?' There was a long pause. Then she shook her head. 'You've taken a terrible risk.'

'Bill came the other evening,' Annie told Rose, when she arrived for the weekend. 'I think he misses you. Why don't you go and see him again?'

'He wouldn't want to see me.' Rose sat down wearily.

'What's happened to you?' her mother demanded. 'I've *never* heard you admit defeat before. You've always fought for what you want.'

'I –'

'Don't make excuses. You're acting like a coward.'

'But he doesn't want me,' Rose protested.

'Then for heaven's sake *make* him want you.'

Her mother was right, Rose thought. She had never dodged a fight before. Why break the habit of a lifetime just because she was hurting more than she ever had?

'Just one more month,' she promised, her eyes flashing with determination. 'Then he won't know what's hit him.'

'That's more like it.' Marj looked at her speculatively.

'Er . . . why one more month? What's so special about that?'

Rose gave a tired smile. 'You'll see.'

42

Rose sat in the back office and rested her head in her hands. She was drained. One month had turned into two, with one delay after another, and she didn't know how much more she could take. It was the end of June and work should have started by now. Part of the plan had been put into operation, but the last part, the thing she most wanted, was still being resisted.

She gave a snort of disgust. The great reformer! How had she become conceited enough to think she could accomplish this? Who did she think she was?

'Rose!' Josh burst into the room just as a loud thud shook the building. 'They've started!'

Rose scrambled to her feet, shot through the door and ran the few yards to the top of Garrett Street. Then she ran past the workmen and the cheering groups of people, on and on, until she reached a rise in the ground where she would get a good view of the whole area. Gasping for breath, she turned and faced Garrett Street, derelict now as all the residents had been moved out a couple of months ago.

This was what she had worked so hard for and she wasn't going to miss a second of it. The racket was ear-splitting, but for once she didn't mind the noise as one wall came crashing down, then another and another. There was a shout from the workmen as rats ran for cover. Lord, how she and her mother had struggled to keep the vermin out of their house.

She stayed for ages, watching the army of men level each house. She had insisted on a huge workforce to get the job done quickly.

There was a crash as part of another house tumbled. It wasn't taking much to bring them down, she noted. They had probably been holding each other up, and when one prop was removed, the next building came down of its own accord.

Her thoughts drifted back to her childhood. All the pain, hardship, disappointment and struggle to survive were associated with this place.

Then, with a roar that shook the ground, the Websters' house collapsed in a cloud of dust.

'Bloody hell!' a man shouted. 'If these had been left much longer, they'd have come down on their own.'

Yes, Rose thought, killing the families packed into them. At least they were safe now, in their new council houses. As she looked at the piles of rubble, she felt the past drain out of her.

She had always believed that because she came from this dreadful place, all doors were closed to her unless she fought and struggled. But that hadn't been true. She remembered again the Bible verse, ' . . . behold, I have set before thee an open door, and no man can shut it: . . .'

Now she could understand what had happened. The door had never been closed, only pushed to, and the people she had met along the way had opened it with their love for her.

Her heart went out to Grace and John, who had helped

her continue with her studying. Then there was Harold: without his help she would never have gone to university. Josh had given her a job and become a firm friend. After a stormy start, her grandmother and father had given her love and understanding. And the day Bill had walked into her life had been the greatest blessing of all. He had swung the door wide open for her, but she had refused to walk through and leave her past behind.

She'd often wondered why she had married him, when she had always been adamant that she would never marry. She had capitulated so easily, and at the time it had been a mystery to her, but now she knew why: she loved him – always had – but she had been too blind and stubborn to recognize it.

There was another ear-splitting crash. Then, a quiet voice made her jump. 'Is it all over, Rose?'

It sounded like Bill, but was it?

She turned. He was standing just behind her, so tall and straight with the dust settling on the jacket of his dark business suit. He looked as weary as she felt, but she was faint with joy at the sight of him.

She wrapped her arms around him and let the tears of relief fall unchecked. 'Yes, it's all over.'

He held her close. 'Thank God!'

She reached up and kissed him. 'I love you.'

He smiled in his gentle way. 'I love you too. Can we go home now?'

'Yes, please. It's time we gave my father a grandson, don't you agree?'

'Not a moment to waste.'

Holding each other tightly, they walked through the rubble, but she no longer saw it.

She had stepped through the door and left Garrett Street at last.

AUTHOR'S NOTE

When the idea for this story came to me I knew I needed a strong character, someone with intelligence and determination. I thought immediately of my mother. She rarely spoke of her childhood, but I knew it had been tough. Born in London and the eldest of a large family, her mother had had great difficulty in feeding them and they were often hungry.

But my mother's hunger was not only for food. She had an insatiable appetite for knowledge. She was always in the public library and would bring home as many books as allowed. These would be devoured, returned, and her search would begin again for something she hadn't read, which would help her to understand what life was all about.

To the outside world she appeared tough, intolerant and hard, but anyone who knew her recognized this to be just a protective front. She could be hurt, upset, insecure and worried, just like anyone else, but was expert at hiding her feelings.

She was highly intelligent and loved school but, like Rose in this story, she was made to leave at eleven because they couldn't teach her any more. She won a copy of the Bible for coming top of the school and was given the opportunity to continue her education, but because of her circumstances it had not been possible. I know she regretted it all of her life.

Apart from that one incident, this is not the story of my mother's life, but of the fictional Rose Webster who has been endowed with my mother's strength, beauty, intelligence and forceful character.

My mother was not an easy person to know or understand, and it was only in the last few years of her life that I began to find out what she was really like. For the first time she started to talk to me about her life and her inner feelings, revealing a kind, caring woman. I am pleased to say that by the time she died at the age of ninety, we were friends.

My mother never did fulfil her full potential in life, but I made sure my fictional Rose did.

I hope you have laughed, cried, sympathized and even been exasperated with her at times. But I also hope you have found much to admire in her, and enjoyed following Rose's struggles as much as I have enjoyed writing about her.

B. M., 2002

The author's mother, 1923

WINGS OF
THE MORNING

With thanks for all the help and support I have received
from Carole Blake my agent, Harriet Evans my editor,
and the Forest Writers Group.

Whither shall I go from thy spirit?
Or whither shall I flee from thy presence?
If I ascend up into heaven, thou art there:
If I make my bed in hell, behold, thou art there.
If I take the wings of the morning, and dwell in the
uttermost parts of the sea;
Even there shall thy hand lead me, and thy right hand
shall hold me.

Psalm 139: 7–10

I

So it had started!

The months of speculation were over and they were at war again.

Annie Webster turned off the wireless and walked into the garden, needing to be alone for a few moments. The tension of waiting for this announcement, knowing it must surely come, had been unbearable. There wasn't a sound anywhere and the streets were empty. A lone dog gave one short bark and stopped, as if it too sensed the enormity of the news. It seemed as if the whole country was holding its breath, wondering what the future would bring. The silence was eerie and rather frightening.

She closed her eyes briefly in an attempt to stop the tears that were threatening to spill over. She had tried so hard to dismiss the talk and hold to the belief that this would never happen, but she couldn't do that any more. The war was a reality now and she would have to face up to it just like everyone else. An overwhelming feeling of sadness swept over her, and for a brief moment her shoulders slumped. Then she straightened up again. This was not the time to indulge in despair and self-pity, because if the last war was anything to go by then there was a long hard struggle in front of them.

She lifted her face to the warmth of the sun and felt it

caress her. The air was clear and almost sparkling without a cloud in the sky. How could this perfect day be marred by such terrible news? With a deep sigh, she opened her eyes again as she heard her family coming out of the house. No one spoke, they were each lost in their own thoughts.

An unearthly wailing cut through the stillness and made them look at each other in alarm.

'Air-raid sirens,' Bill, her brother-in-law, told them.

Still they didn't move, but everyone's face was tilted up towards the sky. Watching, waiting. They scanned the clear sky, looking and listening for any sight or sound of aeroplanes, but nothing happened. In a short time the all clear sounded.

'Just trying them out, I expect,' her mother said softly.

Then all was quiet again and Annie let her thoughts drift. How good life had been in the last sixteen years since they had moved out of the slums of London into these two lovely houses in Roehampton, designed by Bill. The hardship and poverty they had endured seemed like a bad dream now.

'Two wars in our lifetime,' her mother whispered. 'I never thought it would happen again.'

Those few spoken words, cutting through their thoughts, seemed to snap them out of their daze. Her sister Rose bent down and scooped up her youngest child; a beautiful little girl now three years old.

'Why does everyone look so sad, Mummy?' she asked, reaching out for the comforting arms of her father.

'Nothing for you to worry about, Kate.' Rose gave her daughter a kiss and handed her over to her husband, while their ten-year-old son, James, stood by his mother, silent for a change.

'Let's all go inside and have a nice cup of tea.' Her mother turned and walked briskly towards the kitchen.

Annie smiled for the first time that day. A cup of tea was her mother's remedy for all ills – the kettle was constantly on the boil. They trooped after her dutifully, knowing it was useless to refuse.

'Where's Paul these days?' Annie's mother asked her, obviously trying to steer the conversation on to normal lines. 'Have you broken up with him?'

'No, he's been away for the past couple of months.'

'What doing?' Bill asked.

'I've no idea. He was very secretive about it, but he said he'd be back soon.'

'Why don't you marry the poor bloke?' Charlie, her brother, asked.

'I don't want to. I know I'm twenty-eight, but I'm waiting for the right man.' She loved Will and Charlie, her two brothers, dearly, but they still considered her the baby of the family and were always trying to give her advice.

Rose laughed. 'You're a fine one to talk about marriage, Charlie. You're twenty-nine and Will's thirty-two, and neither of you is showing any signs of settling down yet. You like your freedom too much.' She looked pointedly at her two brothers and rolled her eyes, making everyone laugh.

It was a good sound on such a gloomy day.

Annie slipped her arm through her brother-in-law's, and grinned. 'I'm still looking for someone like Bill.'

'Ah, then you're out of luck. He's the only one in existence,' Rose said.

Annie watched the way her sister's dark eyes lingered on her husband. Rose and Bill had a blissful marriage, and Annie wanted one like it and wouldn't settle for anything less.

At that moment there was a brief knock on the kitchen door and Paul strode in. The shock of seeing him hit Annie with such force that she leapt to her feet with uncharacteristic clumsiness and nearly sent her cup flying. He was in air force uniform and sporting a pair of wings on his chest.

She opened her mouth but nothing came out.

Paul laughed. 'Not like you to be lost for words, Annie.'

'Well, what the blazes do you expect?' she managed to say at last. 'You might have told me what you were up to.'

'You haven't wasted any time, Paul,' Annie's mother remarked.

'Well, it was clear that the war was coming, and as I already had my commercial pilot's licence it seemed the sensible thing to do.'

'Sensible?' Annie couldn't believe she was hearing this. She'd met Paul at a dance in Richmond four years ago and she knew he could be impulsive, but she hadn't expected him to do this. 'Why couldn't you wait until war had actually been declared before joining up?'

'The country is going to need pilots and I want to be in at the beginning.' Paul ran his fingers gently down her face. 'I can't sit on the sidelines, you must see that.'

'I do,' she admitted, as the shock began to recede. This was typical of Paul and she should have expected it. He had been totally absorbed in his flying lessons over the last year, but she'd put that down to the fact that his older brother, Reid, was already a pilot. She had never met him but from the snippets of information she'd been given he appeared to be a steadying influence on Paul. She thought too about Paul's parents. They were a lovely couple and she knew it would upset them terribly to have him going to war. However, it was done now. She tipped her head on one side and studied the cut of his uniform. 'You look very dashing.'

He gave a self-conscious grin and shuffled uncomfortably at her compliment, then he turned his attention to Bill, who was still holding his daughter in his arms. 'You were in the navy last time, weren't you? A captain, I believe?'

Bill nodded grimly.

'They'll be after you – '

'No!' Rose said sharply. 'He's too old this time.'

Annie watched a rare moment of panic flit across her sister's face. She tried to propel Paul out of the kitchen but he wasn't going to move. It was not the time to discuss this. They all needed a few hours to let it sink in that they were at war again. Decisions had to be made, but not until they'd had time to adjust and absorb the implications. Over the last few weeks many people had declared that Germany didn't want war with Britain, and she'd tried to believe them, but if you looked at the turmoil in Europe it was hard to delude yourself.

'How old are you?' Paul persisted.

'Forty-seven in December.'

'That won't matter. They'll be desperate for men with your experience – '

Annie tugged at Paul's arm, anxious to get him away. She could almost hear the thoughts of the people sitting around the table – troubled thoughts – things they would rather not face at the moment. They were well aware that their lives were going to change dramatically, and seeing Paul in his uniform was bringing home to them what this war would mean for their family. Will and Charlie, her brothers, were young enough to fight, and Bill . . . well, he shouldn't have to go through that again. The Great War had claimed a generation of young men and she didn't dare think about the horrors this one would inflict on them.

'Come on, let's go out somewhere.' She dragged Paul through the door before he could stir things up any more. He was a charming but immature young man, and seemed quite oblivious of everyone's concern. The prospect of another conflict was not something to look forward to, and the awful thing was that men like her brother-in-law would be dragged in to fight for the second time in their lives.

'I wanted to talk to Bill,' he complained as she hustled him towards the car.

'Paul Lascells,' she said sharply, 'you were upsetting everyone, especially my sister, with all your talk about Bill going back in the navy.'

'Rose?' he exclaimed. 'You can't upset her; she'll be rolling up her sleeves and getting stuck in. She'll be in the thick of it.'

Annie shook her head sadly. She was very fond of Paul but he seemed more like ten years younger than her,

470

instead of two. Was it any wonder she knew she didn't want to marry him?

'My sister loves Bill very much,' she explained patiently as Paul started the car and headed for Richmond Park. 'Rose does have feelings, you know.'

'You two are more like mother and daughter instead of sisters,' Paul remarked drily. 'I've never been able to work out why you're so close.'

Annie thought back to their childhood; her sister, being the eldest, had shouldered the whole burden of the family. Rose was very intelligent and had been made to leave school at eleven because they couldn't teach her any more. Although she had won a scholarship to a secondary school, she hadn't been able to take it up because they were so poor. That was when her old teacher Grace Trenchard and her husband, John, had taken over the job of her education in their spare time. A smile of remembrance touched Annie's face as she thought of those two dear people. Thank heavens they had moved out of London to Yorkshire a short time ago. They should be safer there.

She turned her attention back to Paul, who was waiting patiently for her to speak. 'I was a very sickly baby, and Mum was too busy with a large family to be able to give me much time. I wouldn't be alive today if Rose hadn't looked after me,' she explained quietly. 'I owe her more than I could ever repay. We all do.'

Paul shot her a sideways glance. 'I didn't know that. I've obviously misjudged her.'

'Everyone does. On the surface she appears tough and emotionless, but that's merely a façade, she can be hurt just like anyone else.'

He reached across and took hold of her hand. 'I'm sorry. I know you had a tough time when you were a child but you've never told me much about it.'

That was true enough, she hadn't, and perhaps it was time she did. 'Well, we came from the roughest street in Bermondsey. As a child Rose fought and studied until she was able to get into university. It was a very hard time for her but she never gave up, and eventually qualified as a solicitor.'

'Ah, now I'm beginning to understand the love and respect you all have for her, but to be honest I find her rather frightening at times. She is a formidable character,' Paul said, as he drove through the gates of Richmond Park. He slowed down so they could enjoy the beauty of the open parkland.

'Good job she is like that,' Annie told him with a hint of sadness in her voice. Her sister hadn't had any doubt that there was going to be another war and was already training with the Women's Voluntary Service, ready to help when necessary. 'We're going to need people like her if we are to survive another war.'

'I'm sure you're right. What are you going to do?' he asked, changing the subject. 'There won't be much call for a fashion editor until this lot's over.'

'No, you're right.' She sighed deeply, hating the prospect of leaving the job she loved. She'd started on a popular women's magazine at the age of sixteen and had worked her way up over the years, and she found her work as fashion editor interesting and fulfilling. Rose had tried hard to persuade her to go to university but Annie hadn't wanted that. She didn't have her sister's passion for learning and had been more interested in going out to work. She had always been good at art, English and languages, so when her application for a job with the magazine had been successful, she'd jumped at the chance. Rose had argued that Annie should make the most of her talents by continuing her education; but she wouldn't be swayed, and she was glad she hadn't because her time with the magazine had been very happy. It was going to be an awful wrench if she had to leave all her friends, especially Chantal Dean. Chantal came from Paris and, after marrying an Englishman, had made her home in London; and when he'd died suddenly she had stayed on. Annie smiled when she thought about the friendship she'd formed with Chantal; they spoke French all the time, and Annie had spent her annual holidays in France with Chantal for the last five years. Now all that was going to change; like Paul she doubted if she could stand on the sidelines either.

'Join the WAAF,' he suggested. 'The school you went to in Roehampton was excellent, and with your aptitude for languages you should be able to get an interesting job. You never know, we might be able to wangle a posting to the same place.' He grinned boyishly. 'It could all be jolly good fun.'

He doesn't know what he's talking about, she thought wearily, but said nothing. Let him keep his enthusiasm for a while longer. Reality would catch up with him soon enough. But he was right and her grasp of French and German might be useful. Because of Chantal her French was fluent and she spoke it as easily as English; her German was quite good because she'd loved languages and her teacher had encouraged her enthusiasm, but she didn't speak it nearly as well as French. All she needed was some practice, though . . .

Paul stopped the car in a spot where the tranquil scene of Richmond Park was laid out before them, the magnificent trees casting shade for the deer to rest under or munch contentedly on the lush grass. He turned and took her face in his hands. 'Before we get swept up in this conflict, will you marry me?'

This was the third time he'd asked her, but her answer was always the same. 'No, I'm sorry.'

He looked crestfallen. 'I hoped you might change your mind now things are different.'

She took hold of one of his hands. 'I wouldn't marry you just because you're going to fight in this war. I like you and enjoy being with you, but in all honesty I can't say I'm madly in love with you. I've never let you believe I feel anything but friendship for you,' she reminded him.

'I know but I keep hoping you'll change your mind.'

'Please don't hold on to false hopes,' she told him gently. 'I wouldn't dream of marrying unless I felt sure it would last.'

He sighed sadly. 'You are the kindest, most gentle girl I've ever met and I love you very much, but I know you don't feel the same way about me.'

'I'm sorry, Paul.' Oh, Lord, how she hated hurting him like this, but she knew in her heart that it just wouldn't work. In fairness to him she had tried to finish their relationship several times, but he wouldn't hear of it and just kept coming back.

'Hey! Don't look so upset,' he exclaimed, kissing her on the nose. 'I understand, but I'm going to keep on trying. In the meantime will you still be my girl? I'll need a glamorous picture to stick up by my bunk,' he joked, obviously trying to hide his disappointment.

'I'll get our fashion photographer to do a special one for you.' He looked so pleased with that suggestion, and this was one small thing she could do for him.

'Great.' He started the car again and headed out of the park.

'What does your brother think about you joining the air force?' she asked, changing the subject.

'He wasn't too pleased. He's joined up himself and I think he was hoping I'd run the family engineering business while he's away.' He drove slowly through the gates and then accelerated towards London. 'But I'm not going to let him have all the fun!'

She wondered how it was possible for two people to look at the prospect of war so differently. She was sad, apprehensive and worried about the future. So apprehensive in fact that she'd rushed out still wearing the old blue cotton frock she wore around the house, but he sounded as if he was looking forward to it.

'You're back early.'

Wally, her stepfather, was alone in the kitchen, a cigarette smouldering in the ashtray and a newspaper spread out on the table. 'Where's Mum?' Annie asked as she came in.

'She's babysitting for Rose. Bill's taken her out for the evening. I think they want a bit of time alone together.' He folded the paper up and tossed it on to a spare chair.

'Do you think Bill will get called up again?' She didn't

know why she was asking that; he would be one of the first to go. Her insides clenched with worry. This family, like every other one in the country, was about to be torn apart.

'Well, he's in the reserves and I think he was contacted a few weeks ago, but he hasn't said anything to Rose. He was hoping this war would never happen, I expect.'

'So were we all, but we were fooling ourselves.' Annie sat down and shook her head sadly. 'Why did this have to happen again, Wally? We've been so happy but now our lives are going to be disrupted, and all because of one man's lust for power.'

'It's crazy, I know, but we're in it whether we like it or not.'

She smiled sadly and patted his hand. 'At least you'll be safe this time.'

'I'm not sure any of us are going to be safe, Annie. This is going to be a very different war.' He dredged up a smile. 'Anyway, why are you back so soon?'

'We ended up in London, and Paul's all excited, but I'm afraid I couldn't share his enthusiasm.' They'd gone to Piccadilly and it had been crowded with people discussing the outbreak of war. Paul had caused a great deal of interest in his uniform but she knew that very soon it would be a normal sight.

'Thought he might be.' Wally looked at her speculatively. 'You going to marry him?'

'No. He's asked me to again but I just don't feel it's right.'

Her stepfather lit another cigarette. 'He's a good boy, but I think you need a stronger man, otherwise you'll lead him a merry dance.'

Annie gave him a playful swipe. 'Are you saying I'm difficult to live with?'

'Not at all,' he laughed, ducking as she aimed another gentle blow at him. 'I just mean you wouldn't be happy with a man unless he was strong-willed and decisive. Any man you marry will have to have a firm hand.'

'Meaning?' She propped her elbows on the table, rested her chin in her hands and looked at him thoughtfully.

'Well, you've got more of Rose in you than you realize, and you know what trouble Bill had with her . . .' He stopped and began to chuckle.

'You're digging yourself into a hole, aren't you?'

'Don't look so innocent,' he said laughing, 'you know darned well what I'm talking about. Let's change the subject, before I get myself into real trouble.'

Annie laughed, reached across and gave him a hug. He'd been a good stepfather to all of them and she loved him very much.

'When's Paul going back?'

'Tonight.' Annie's smile was wry. That was the first time Paul had ever been eager to leave her. He hadn't been able to contain his impatience to get back to his beloved aeroplane – a Hurricane, she thought he'd said.

'He's got a brother, hasn't he?'

'Yes, Reid, he's about three years older than Paul.'

'What's he like?' Wally asked.

'I've never met him, but Paul seems to be in awe of him, and I suspect that's the reason he wanted to learn to fly.' Reid had always been out working or away when Annie had visited the Lascellses' home, so she couldn't help being a little curious about him.

'He's a pilot as well then, is he?'

'Yes. He's got his own aeroplane he uses for business. One of those Lysanders.'

'I feel sorry for his family having both sons as pilots. They'll be just like we were last time, eager to get into it, and convinced it won't last long.'

'And will it, do you think?' All the talk in London had been about a short war, but she didn't believe that. Gas masks had been issued, plans to evacuate children were well under way already, and the government wouldn't be doing that if they didn't believe there was danger.

'I'm not a fortune teller,' he grimaced, 'but Hitler's a powerful man and Germany has been rearming for years.'

'Are we prepared?' she asked.

'Nowhere near. When Chamberlain came back from his visit with Hitler and waved that bit of paper saying there wouldn't be a war, it lulled some into a false sense of security.'

'When you look back you can see that it was unwise to believe anything Hitler said, or signed, wasn't it?' She for one had held on to any slight indication of hope. She knew there were many like her.

'It's easy to be wise with hindsight but I think there are a few politicians who never trusted Hitler's word.'

'It wasn't worth the paper it was written on, was it?'

'No.' Her stepfather gave a tired smile. 'Let's hope they don't attack too soon. We need time to get ourselves sorted out.'

Her mother walked in just then and the expression on her face was troubled.

'Has Bill been recalled, Marj?' Wally asked his wife.

She merely nodded and poured herself a cup of tea. 'Bill has asked George to leave his London home and live with Rose and the children while he's away. He'll be happier knowing Rose's father is there to look after them.'

'That should liven things up having them both living in the same house.' Wally said and chuckled.

Annie couldn't hold back her own smile of amusement. Rose was George Gresham's illegitimate daughter and had inherited his explosive temper; he loved her and his grandchildren dearly. He wouldn't need much persuading to come and live here. Annie admired her mother so much for the way she had forgiven Sir George Gresham. She'd been in service to the Gresham family as a young girl and George had taken advantage of her. When Marj had become pregnant she had been thrown out and ended up in Garrett Street with Tom, the man who took her in. It must have been a terrible choice for her mother but the only alternative had been the workhouse. Tom was a brute and Rose took the brunt of his drunken rages in an effort to protect the younger children. When he'd been killed in the last war none of the children he'd had with Marj were very sorry, including herself. Then just after the war, Wally had moved in as a lodger, and about a year later Wally and her mother had married. It was a good marriage and they were still happy together.

Annie went to bed then, her mind churning away. What was this conflict going to mean to her and those she loved? Her two brothers Charlie and Will were bound to join up, but what about her sisters, Flo and Nancy? They didn't see them very often now as they had families of their own and had drifted away, but they were in London. There was also another brother, Bob, but Annie hardly remembered him. He'd run away to sea when she was little and ended up in Australia. They had a couple of letters a year from him, but she doubted she'd ever see him again.

Thoughts of the war crowded her mind again. What were Hitler's plans, and would this country be given the time it needed to mobilize and arm properly? These were all questions no one could answer at this time.

2

Annie shivered and pulled her collar up to shield herself against the cold wind. They had been at war for three months and nothing much was happening. Many were calling it the phoney war, but there wasn't anything *phoney* about it for the poor devils now under Nazi rule.

She shivered again, not caused by the cold this time, but because, as she turned the corner and saw the outline of their house in the gloom, she'd had a brief vision of Germans marching along the road. It was a frightening thought but it couldn't possibly happen, she told herself sternly; they had won the last war against all the odds and they would do the same again. They had to!

When she thought about the terrible losses suffered in the Great War it made her feel sick. Of course, she had only been little but she had still been aware of the grief and terrible loss of young lives. Pray God that this one would not be so bad.

The Germans seemed to be an unstoppable force, but they *had* to be stopped, and that was going to need a supreme effort from everyone, including herself, so she was going to have to make a decision soon.

She opened the back door, pushed aside the blackout curtain and stepped quickly inside. Then she stopped in surprise; it was empty. The kitchen was always alive with activity at this time in the evening, and her mother would normally have a cup of tea ready for her as soon as she walked through the door. This was an unusual break in the routine so it was obvious something had happened. Without a moment's hesitation she hurried into the garden and through the special gate in the fence. She knew where they would be.

Her mother, Wally, George and her brothers were in Rose and Bill's kitchen; when she saw their serious faces her insides clenched with apprehension. 'What's happened?'

Annie's mother handed her a cup of tea. 'Will has enlisted in the Fleet Air Arm.'

'And I'm going into the RAF,' Charlie told her proudly.

Annie gave her brothers a startled look. It wasn't like them to be parted, they were more like twins than brothers. 'Why aren't you going into the same service?'

'No way!' Charlie held his hands up in horror. 'I don't like the sea, I want to keep my feet firmly on solid ground. We're both going to be aircraft mechanics but I will be on an airfield while Will is tossing about on an aircraft carrier.'

'But why didn't you wait until you were called up, like Bill did?'

'If we'd done that, Annie,' Will explained patiently, 'we wouldn't have had a choice. You know how mad we've always been about engines, and by volunteering we've been able to go into the branch of the service we want. I wouldn't have been able to get into the navy if I'd left it much longer.'

They were right, of course, and it was time she made

her own mind up about what she was going to do. 'When are you leaving?'

'We're all going at the end of the week,' Bill told her quietly.

This was it, then. Bill and Will in the navy and Charlie in the air force. Nothing was ever going to be the same again. Annie went and slipped her arms around Bill's waist, gave him a hug, then did the same to her brothers. 'You all take care,' she whispered.

Bill smiled. 'We will, and you never know I might be given a nice desk somewhere.'

Annie looked up at him hopefully. 'Is there any chance of that?'

His smile was wry. 'There's always a chance.'

Annie sat down, not sure that her legs would hold her much longer. She knew, as well as Bill did, that the chances of him being given a shore job were remote. This was a triple blow. She had known it was going to happen but had clung on to the foolish hope that her family would be spared. She looked into Rose's eyes, but they told her nothing. Her sister would accept the inevitable and fight for her family, as she had done all her life, but she would not let anyone see her fears.

'Hey! Why the long faces,' Charlie reprimanded. 'The sooner we all get stuck into this war, the sooner it will be over.'

'Quite right.' Bill put his arm around his wife's shoulders and grinned. 'We don't know where any of us will be at Christmas, so I suggest we have one hell of a party before we leave.'

There was a chorus of approval and everyone roused themselves from their gloomy contemplation of the

483

future. By the time they'd finished their planning it was clear that this was going to be the best party they'd ever thrown, even if the reason behind it all was a sad one.

'Rosie.' Annie looked into the kitchen. It was two weeks since the men had joined up but Rose was obviously preparing for Christmas as if everyone was going to be there. 'Are you busy?'

'No, come in. I've just got to put the last two puddings on to boil.'

Annie sniffed appreciatively. 'It smells wonderful in here.'

'This will be the last chance to have proper Christmas puddings, I think.'

Rose adjusted the gas under the saucepan, and then sat down. 'Once our store cupboards are empty there won't be any more treats.'

'Have you heard from Bill?'

'Yes, had a letter this morning, but he didn't tell me what he was doing. I don't suppose it's allowed.' Rose gave a slight shrug and changed the subject. 'Have you heard from Paul?'

'Had three letters all at once, but I haven't a clue where he is. He might not even be in this country.' The letters had been unusually subdued for Paul, but that was probably because he knew they would be censored before they were sent on to their destination.

'Let's hope some of them can get home for Christmas.' Rose got up and put the kettle on. 'We'll have a cup of tea and some biscuits. You look as if you've got something on your mind.'

Annie laughed. 'You know me too well.'

'Right, tell me what's troubling you.' Rose placed a cup in front of Annie, opened the tin of biscuits, and then settled down again and waited.

'I've left my job.' It had been a wrench but Annie knew it had to be done. A lot of the people she'd worked with over the years had already joined the forces and the magazine was being produced with a skeleton staff. Chantal had already left to stay with her husband's relatives in Edinburgh.

Rose dunked a biscuit and nodded. 'I thought you would. What are you going to do?'

'That's what I want to talk about. I was thinking of joining the WAAF.' She stirred her tea thoughtfully; it wasn't an easy decision to make. 'What do you think?'

'If that's what you want to do, then go ahead, you don't have to get my approval, you know. You're a grown woman now, Annie.'

'I know,' she grinned at her sister, 'but it's hard to break the habit of a lifetime.'

'Why the WAAF? Are you hoping to stay near Paul?'

'No, now he's in the RAF I'm hoping he will meet someone else. He won't take no for an answer, but no amount of persistence will make me change my mind.'

'You're wise to wait, Annie, don't take second best.' Rose poured them another cup of tea. 'So tell me then, why the WAAF?'

'Well, I've been down to the recruitment office and they were very interested in my languages, and besides . . .' She cast Rose a sheepish glance. 'I like the colour of the uniform best. Air force blue is much nicer than khaki.'

'Ah, well, that settles it, then,' Rose joked, her eyes crinkling at the corners, obviously amused.

Annie knew it was a shallow reason, but she really hadn't known what to do. She'd agonized over it night after night, trying to decide what would be the right thing for her. She changed the subject. 'Are you going to evacuate the children, Rosie?'

'Not at the moment, things are pretty quiet and we're not in the heart of London this time. I'd rather wait and see what happens.'

'Bill told me to make sure you send the children to a safe place if things get rough.' Rose raised an eyebrow and Annie laughed. 'I know, you won't take any notice of me but think about Bill. You don't want him worrying while he's away, do you?'

'That's sneaky,' Rose scolded. 'But you're right, and I promise to take the children away if it becomes necessary. Dad's bought a house in Wales and he's there now getting it ready. Bill said it's got four bedrooms so we should be able to cram the lot of us in if necessary, and it should be out of the firing line.'

'Let's hope it is.' Annie thought of Rose's father, George Gresham, with affection. He would make sure Rose and his grandchildren were safe. After their first explosive meeting when Rose had been about sixteen, George had been welcomed into the family. Father and daughter were both strong characters and often clashed but the love and respect between them was obvious.

'Of course I've had a terrible row with Dad about it. He's been rushing around the country looking for a place for us to hide in!' Rose was clearly exasperated. 'We're not right in London, for heaven's sake, and he's very much mistaken if he thinks I'm leaving here!'

'George only wants you and the children to be safe,' Annie pointed out gently.

'I know, and I will want the kids out of danger if things turn nasty, but I've told him he's got to use it as a refuge for others and not just the family.' A slight smile touched Rose's mouth. 'He exploded and said he'd call it "The Haven", and did that suit me?'

'And does it?' Annie asked.

'It has to; he's already bought the bloody place. That father of mine's got more money than sense!'

Annie knew that her sister had never accepted a penny from her father, although he was a wealthy man. Money for money's sake had never interested Rose, it was a commodity to be used to make a better life for her family and others. She had never lost her desire to help those in need, and Annie knew that she would hate to think money was being wasted on something unnecessary.

They fell silent and each thoughtfully dunked another biscuit in their tea just as their neighbour Joyce looked in the kitchen door.

'Rose! The Seascape fishmonger's got fish!'

Annie watched in astonishment as Rose grabbed her purse and ran out of the door, leaving her tea untouched. She began to laugh at the absurdity of it all, but with shortages already beginning to be felt you had to be quick on your feet to get any treats. Her sister had told her that she'd been in a queue the other day and after about half an hour the woman behind her asked what they were queuing for. It seemed that people jumped on the end of any line they saw.

*

Reid Lascells wandered into his brother's room at Tangmere airfield. He'd had a few hours to kill before going to see his brother so he'd borrowed a truck and headed for Bognor. It had been bitterly cold but he'd enjoyed the invigorating tang of sea air before heading for the West Sussex airfield. He picked up a photograph and studied it intently. The girl was quite lovely but the artificial pose wasn't right, it didn't seem to suit her somehow. Not that he'd ever met her, of course.

'Hey! Big brother.' Paul strode into the room, shrugged out of his flying jacket and collapsed on to the bed. 'Keep your lecherous eyes off my girl.'

'It's a bloody awful picture. Who took it?'

Paul removed the photo from his brother's hand and frowned. 'What's wrong with it? I'll have you know that this was taken by one of the top photographers at her magazine.'

'The glamorous pose doesn't suit her. Who is she?'

'Annie, and I think she's beautiful.' Paul looked offended.

'Oh, she's lovely enough, I grant you that, but she'd look better in something more natural.'

Paul fished in his pocket and produced a dog-eared picture. 'Like this?'

'Hmm, that's much better.' Annie was sitting on a fallen tree and laughing as the wind whipped at her hair. Then Reid turned his attention to the other woman in the picture and whistled through his teeth in approval. 'Who's the impressive woman she's with?'

'That's her eldest sister, Rose.' Paul laughed. 'But the word I'd use to describe her is formidable.'

'Yes, I can see that from the photo, but what a beauty!'

'Forget it, Reid,' Paul chided. 'She's a happily married woman with two children.'

'Pity, I'd have made you introduce me.' He handed the picture back, wondering if Rose was as stunning in the flesh as she was in the picture. 'Annie doesn't look like her.'

'Different fathers, I understand. Rose is the eldest of nine children, and Annie's next to youngest.' Paul tucked the picture into his pocket again. 'What are you doing here, anyway?'

'Heard you were back and as I've got a weekend pass I thought I'd come and see you. How was France?'

Paul shrugged. 'All right, but I couldn't understand a word they said.'

'You should have paid more attention to your lessons at university.'

'Nah.' He grinned boyishly. 'I leave all that stuff to Annie, she speaks the language fluently.'

Reid didn't pursue the subject. His brother would never change, and with the situation they were in it didn't seem important any more. Things might be quiet enough at the moment but he had a very nasty feeling that wasn't going to last. 'Have you got time for a drink?'

'Sure.' Paul sprang to his feet. 'Where are you stationed now?'

'Kenley.' This was close to London; Reid knew that if things started to get rough they would be right in the thick of it.

'Hey, I'm going to Biggin Hill in Kent next week. They're not far from each other and we might be able to meet up now and again. I'll try and get Annie down here and then you can meet her.'

489

Reid noted his brother's jaunty stride and smiled to himself. 'Are you going to marry her?'

'Of course I am. The only trouble is, she doesn't know it yet.'

'Haven't you asked her?'

'Yes, three times, but it will be fourth time lucky,' Paul stated confidently.

Reid didn't comment but he couldn't help wondering about the two women in the photo. Annie was fair and delicate looking and Rose tall, dark and magnificent. He regretted not having taken much notice of Paul's babbling about his girl. They looked an intriguing pair.

'Can you get leave for Christmas, Reid?'

'No. What about you?'

'Yes, I've managed to wangle two days. I'll spend one with Mum and Dad and the other with Annie and her family.'

'Wish I could join you.' And he really meant that. Christmas at the base would be lively enough but he'd rather be with his parents. They were going to be lonely this year without both of them there, and it was tempting to tell his brother to spend the two days with them, but he didn't. Paul would naturally want to see his girl.

'Never mind.' Paul held open the door of the bar and grinned at his brother. 'It will be all over by next Christmas, and we'll get drunk for a week.'

Reid nodded, but said nothing again. There wasn't any point in squashing Paul's enthusiasm, but he was certain that this war was going to last a lot longer than anyone was prepared to admit. And, as fighter pilots, they were going to be in the thick of things when it really started.

He was glad he'd been given a Spitfire; it was fast and handled like a dream.

'Right, everyone sit down,' Rose ordered.

There was an excited scramble for the table, made festive with Annie's artistic flair. This was the first Christmas of the war and she was determined to make a real show this year to cheer the family up.

When they were all seated, Annie looked at the happy faces, and if a brief flash of sadness flitted across her face it was soon gone. There was much to be grateful about. Rose's children, James and Kate, were still at home, her brothers Will and Charlie had a two-day pass each, and Paul had turned up unexpectedly. George had tried to persuade them to spend the holiday in Wales, but Rose had insisted on staying at home. After much arguing Rose had managed to convince George that they should spend Christmas at Roehampton, and delay the move to Wales until they knew how things were going to work out. He'd agreed reluctantly, as he was clearly excited about the house he'd bought and was eager to get everyone there.

The only person missing was Bill, and Annie knew her sister was disappointed about that, although you would never know by looking at her. But she couldn't fool Annie; she never had been able to. She only had to look deep into Rose's eyes to glimpse her innermost feelings.

For a moment her mind went back to their years living in that disgusting hovel in London. She'd watched her big sister fight with grim tenacity to improve their lot. Rose had taken beatings from the old man and suffered all manner of abuse and bitter disappointment; she had never flinched in her determination to drag herself and her family out of Garrett Street.

'Annie?'

Rose's call snapped her out of her reverie.

'You were miles away. What were you thinking about?'

'Garrett Street,' she admitted.

Rose visibly shuddered, and without a word continued with the Christmas dinner. Annie didn't miss the flash of distress on George's face at the mention of that street; she knew that he still felt guilty about his daughter growing up in such squalor because of his callous action as a young man.

'Auntie Annie, where's Garrett Street?' James asked.

'It's where we used to live, but it doesn't exist any more because your mum got it knocked down.'

'Did you, Mum?' he asked, searching her face with enquiring dark eyes, so like her own.

Not for the first time, Annie marvelled at just how much James resembled his mother, in looks, intelligence and intolerance. He was only ten but he did not suffer fools gladly, and that didn't make him an easy child to deal with.

'She certainly did.' Wally started to explain to James how dreadful conditions had been, and the struggle his mother had had to get the council to demolish the place.

Annie was pleased that Wally didn't go into too much detail about the vermin, dirt and violence. It would be enough to put everyone off their Christmas dinner.

James's eyes glittered with pride as he listened. 'I'm going to be just like Mum when I grow up.'

Rose turned round from the stove and grinned at him. 'Don't be too much like me, my boy.'

'Why not? You've done lots of good things.'

'Maybe, but I've also been difficult to live with, and I hope and pray you've inherited some of your father's gentleness.'

'Where's Daddy?' Kate interrupted, her bottom lip quivering. 'Why isn't he here?'

'I am here, sweetheart,' a soft voice said from the doorway.

Ignoring the squeals of delight, Bill threw his bag down and reached for his wife, holding her in a rocking embrace, and giving a heartfelt sigh of relief. Then he released her and bent down to scoop his children into his arms.

Annie watched with tears of emotion clouding her vision. What an impressive man he was, and his gentleness did not detract from his masculinity. Of course, he'd needed both gentleness and strength to take on her sister.

Bill rose to his feet, standing more than six feet tall, and smiled at everyone. 'Is there room for one more?'

James dragged another chair up to the table so his father could sit next to him, and Kate, who was now standing on tip-toe gazing at him, said in a hushed whisper, 'Don't you look lovely.'

After a few moments' silence, Rose, Bill and Annie burst into laughter.

'That's exactly what Annie said when she saw him in uniform just after the last war,' Rose explained.

Annie grinned affectionately at her brother-in-law. 'But I do believe you've got more gold braid this time.'

'Yes, and the uniform's a better fit,' he joked. 'Now, how about this dinner, I'm starving.'

Bill had clearly changed the subject, so Annie helped

493

Rose serve everyone, and then they joined the family around the table.

The talk was lively and never once touched on the subject of the war but Annie could feel Paul's impatience to ask questions so she whispered in his ear, 'Don't you dare ask Bill what he's going to do, he won't say anything until he's had a chance to talk to Rose.'

'But I want to know,' he complained. 'They haven't given him all that decoration to sail a desk.'

Dear God! She hoped he was wrong. Bill had been at Jutland in the last war, and later had lost his ship and most of the crew; then spent days adrift in an open boat watching the remaining few die before his eyes. She could only guess how dreadful the prospect of facing something like that again might be.

'You've got to admit it, Annie; they are going to give him a ship. He's an experienced, professional sailor, and his father was an admiral, for heaven's sake. Do you think for one moment they are going to let talent and experience like that go to waste?'

'I'm not a fool, Paul.' He was so tactless and it irritated her. 'I know we need men like Bill but can't you let us enjoy our dinner in peace. And if you can't contain your curiosity you can leave right now.'

'What!' he exclaimed, 'and miss Rose's cooking?' He smiled and took hold of her hand. 'Stop worrying so much about everyone, by this time next year it will be all over.'

She gaped in disbelief and studied his face. He really believed that. But at least he dropped the subject then and allowed them all to enjoy the festive meal without any more talk of the war.

After they'd finished, Marj and Wally insisted on washing up, so the rest of them retired to the front room and handed out the presents. When the children were absorbed with their gifts, Annie watched Bill take hold of Rose's hand and lead her from the room. He was about to tell her if he was going back to sea or not. Please God, let it be not, she prayed, but deep in her heart she knew it was a hopeless plea.

Fifteen minutes later they were back and joining in the fun, but Annie couldn't glean anything from their expressions.

Wally came in carrying a tray of drinks, whisky for the men and sherry for the women. 'I think we ought to drink to the fact that we've all managed to have Christmas dinner together, don't you?'

There were nods of approval, and they took a glass and raised it to toast the occasion. Annie studied her stepfather with affection, and wondered how many precious bottles of drink he'd managed to squirrel away before the war, because he always managed to produce something for a celebration. He was quiet, even tempered, and not at all like her own father who'd been killed in the last war. Her mother had had a wretched time with him, and it was lovely to see her and Wally still happy after twenty years of marriage.

'How are things going, Bill?' Paul asked, and yelped when Annie kicked his shin. 'What did you do that for?' he whispered.

'I told you not to ask questions,' she hissed at him. It was such a job to stop him when he wanted to know something; she didn't want Bill pestered with questions just yet. He would tell them what was happening when he was ready.

'It's all right, Annie,' Bill laughed. 'I've told Rose now.'

James had been watching with curious eyes, taking in every small detail, and clearly picking up on the tensions. He left his train set and went and stood by his father, then asked the question everyone wanted to know and had been wary of asking. 'Have they given you a ship, Daddy?'

'Yes, James, I'm on active service.'

'Gosh!' The boy jumped up and down. 'What is it?'

'I'm afraid I can't tell you that.'

His eyes opened wide. 'When are you going to fight the Germans?'

'I haven't received my sailing orders yet but I expect I'll get them as soon as I've finished a spot of retraining.'

'Why have you got to do that?' his son asked, clearly puzzled. 'You're used to boats.'

'It's nearly twenty years since I took command of a ship and things have changed a bit in that time.'

'Oh, I wish I was old enough.'

James looked crestfallen and went back to play with his toys again, so he didn't hear his father murmur, 'I thank the Lord that you are too young.'

3

'What a day,' Ruth, one of the girls in Annie's hut, moaned. 'We've been marched here and there, stripped, examined, had needles stuck in us, then issued with these.' She held up a brassiere with one finger and grimaced in disgust.

'And what about these?' howled Kath, holding a pair of blue winter knickers in front of her.

Annie was crying with laughter. In her job as a fashion editor she'd dealt with elegant clothes and she hadn't been aware that such abominations existed. She'd never seen so many pretty faces with expressions of pure horror on them. Not only were the underclothes and lisle stockings dreadful, most of the uniforms were ill-fitting. Skirts were too big or too small around the waist; one girl couldn't even fasten her jacket without taking a deep breath in and holding it. They were going to have to find someone in their hut who could sew!

'We can't wear these,' wailed another girl. 'Even my granny's don't come past her knees with elastic in them.'

'They will keep us warm.' Annie put her hand on the stove and found it practically cold. The West Drayton camp in Middlesex was lacking all the home comforts they'd been used to. Some of the girls had been horrified to find they would be sleeping in huts, but it was only

497

what Annie had expected. 'It's freezing in here and that bucket of coke isn't going to last long.'

'We'll soon see about that!' Dora, a rough-and-ready Londoner, stated. 'I spotted a wooden fence just around the back, I'll get some of that.'

'Put your knickers on,' roared Kath, 'it's freezing out there, as well.'

'I'll come with you.' Annie stood up, put on her peaked hat at a jaunty angle – at least that fitted properly – struck a model-like pose and slowly lifted her skirt. 'I'm already prepared.'

There was uproar as the entire hut of girls started to stamp their feet and whistle, with varying degrees of success.

Dora came and stood beside her, copied her pose and also lifted her skirt. The noise was deafening as the two girls rushed out of the hut, doubled over with laughter, and headed for the fence Dora had seen.

'You're something to do with fashion, aren't you?' she asked, as they made their way over the icy ground.

Annie nodded. 'Yes, I was fashion editor for a women's magazine.'

'Where do you live, then?' Dora asked.

'Roehampton.'

'Ah, I thought you was posh.'

'I haven't always lived there,' Annie said. 'I grew up in Bermondsey, in Garrett Street.'

The girl stopped and spun to face her. 'Wow! I've heard about that place. My gran said it was a filthy hole and so rough that the police had to go down there in threes for safety.'

Dora started to walk again, but this time she slipped

Annie's hand through her arm in a gesture of respect and comradeship. 'If I remember rightly, some woman got the place condemned and knocked down. Can't remember her name though.'

'Rose Freeman,' Annie told her with pride. She never ceased to be amazed how much Rose was remembered after all these years. 'She's my eldest sister.'

'Bloody hell,' Dora gasped, 'I had you worked out all wrong. When I first saw you I thought you was some snooty bitch.' She gave an evil leer. 'Until you showed your knickers.'

'Where's your home?' Annie asked, wanting to know more about this friendly girl.

'I come from Stepney and it's a bit rough in our street, but not as bad as the one you came from, if my gran's stories are right.' Dora rubbed her hands together and grinned at Annie. 'I'm glad to be out of there though, and even if it is bloody cold here, this place is still better than Stepney. I hope I'm sent somewhere in the country when we've done our basic training. I'd love to be surrounded by open fields instead of concrete.'

Annie knew just how Dora was feeling. She remembered how she'd felt the first time Bill had taken her and Rose to Richmond Park and then on to the terraces with the River Thames winding its majestic way in the sunshine. It was hard to believe such places existed when all you saw were buildings day in and day out.

'You'll love the countryside in the spring,' Annie remarked.

'Can't wait. I'm going to find myself a bluebell field and run through it with bare feet.' Dora chuckled at the thought.

499

By this time they'd reached the fence. It was just the other side of the camp's perimeter and already broken down in places, so they reached through the wire to collect all the loose bits, then hurried back to the hut. They didn't want to be accused of stealing on their first day.

The girls fell on the wood as soon as they staggered in, and started feeding it into the stove. It soon made a lovely blaze. Two other girls had been foraging while they'd been out. One had cadged some bread and margarine from the cookhouse, and another produced a tin of cocoa and some powdered milk. They were obviously going to be an enterprising bunch.

The water was just coming to the boil when Kath erupted through the door clutching a jar of jam.

'Where'd you get that?' Ruth wanted to know.

'From the NAAFI.' Kath waved the jar in triumph.

Ruth looked puzzled. 'What's that?'

'The Navy, Army and Air Force Institutes,' Dora explained. 'It's a shop, canteen and a place to meet and have fun.'

It was a happy feast of toast and a welcome hot drink, and if the cocoa was rather watery no one complained. They had survived the first day and were happy.

At lights out, Annie slipped into her bunk. It had been so hard to leave her job at the magazine, and even harder to leave her family. She'd felt that the only choice she had was in deciding which branch of the services to join, but after today she felt this was the right one. She was going to miss her family dreadfully, of course, but everyone had to make sacrifices now. She smiled in the darkness; things were going to be all right. She'd had doubts about signing the final papers but now she was glad she had.

'What do you think this is all about?' Kath asked Annie, as they filed into the room.

'I haven't got a clue. Another lecture, I expect.'

'Whatever it is, it's better than square-bashing.' Dora collapsed on to a chair with a groan. 'I don't think my blasted feet can stand any more, the last three weeks have been purgatory.'

Annie ignored her friend's exaggeration. The basic training had been tough at times, but they'd had fun as well. They had been confined to camp most of the time, but they had been able to get out occasionally, and they'd been to a lively dance in the NAAFI canteen one night. Once she'd got used to living in a hut with lots of other girls Annie enjoyed the whole experience.

At that moment two RAF officers came in and the girls leapt to attention. They had soon discovered that it was wise to move sharply, and if in any doubt about the rank, to salute. They had made some blunders at first, much to the hilarity of the men, but it was better to be safe than sorry. You could be put on a charge for any small misdemeanour, regardless of how new you were.

'I've never seen those badges before,' Dora whispered. 'The design looks like lightning.'

'At ease, and be seated,' the most senior of the officers ordered. When they were settled he nodded to his fellow officer who uncovered a machine and started to tap out Morse code.

Annie was fascinated and sat forward in her seat, listening intently. When he had finished she looked up and found the officer watching her. She felt slightly uncomfortable under his piercing blue gaze, but refused to be the first to break the contact. A slight smile touched his mouth but was quickly controlled, and Annie was shocked at how much she felt drawn to him. Some people you took to immediately and some you disliked at once, but she had a strong feeling that this man was special. She gave a mental shrug; all that square-bashing must have gone to her head.

He looked away and turned his attention back to the whole room. 'You have now finished your basic training and will soon be shipped to new camps, but first we have to decide the best way to use your talents.' A snicker rippled round the room, which he ignored. 'You all know what you've been listening to, I presume?'

'Oh, yes,' Dora spoke up. 'Messages can be sent and received like that, though how anyone can understand that jumble of bleeps is a mystery to me.'

Dora always spoke her mind and Annie expected the officer to reprimand her, but much to her surprise he merely smiled. He looked a very calm man and not at all like some they'd met since they'd joined up. She'd never believed people could have such loud voices.

'Well, let's see just how many of you can distinguish between the dots and the dashes, shall we?'

Annie found the next hour intriguing. First they had a short lecture, then had to listen to each sound and note down what they thought it was. Right at the end they had to try to decipher a very short burst.

After that there was a fifteen-minute wait while the men went through the results.

'Ann Webster,' the officer said suddenly.

Annie sprang to her feet. 'Sir!'

He gave a satisfied smile. 'You stay, the rest of you can go.'

'Oh, oh.' Dora whispered in her ear. 'I knew he was after you; he's been staring at you ever since we came in. You know the golden rule – never volunteer for anything. Whatever he wants, say no.' She gave the tall, elegant man a studied glance. 'On second thoughts . . .'

Annie gave Dora a push to send her on her way and looked down to hide her smile. She was incorrigible, but they got on well together and had laughed a great deal during basic training. Even when they'd been tired and fed up Dora could still make the girls smile. She was a great asset.

As the door closed behind the others Annie looked up again, eager to know what this was all about.

The officer had perched himself casually on the edge of the desk and pointed to a chair in front of him. 'My name's Graham. Sit there, please.'

She obeyed, eyeing him surreptitiously. Dora was right; he was dishy but not as young as she had first thought. He must be like her brother-in-law and have some special qualifications.

'You had a pass rate of ninety-five per cent in that test,' he told her.

Her eyes opened wide in surprise. She'd loved doing it but had no idea she'd got that much right.

'Don't look so startled,' he told her. 'It was the very result I was hoping for. I have been reading all the new recruits' records and decided that you were just what we were looking for, but we had to find out if you had an ear for Morse code.' He smiled warmly. 'And you most certainly do.'

He picked up a folder from the desk and started to read it. 'I see that you didn't go on to university but the grades from your secondary school are excellent, with art and languages your strong points.'

'Yes, I was lucky with my tutor. He said I had a good ear for languages, and he used to set me extra lessons.'

He continued reading her records and Annie waited patiently. When he spoke again it was in German, which threw her for a moment, but she quickly gathered herself together and answered in the same language. There was no doubt he was testing her for something and she became tense with excitement. What was this leading to?

He then reverted to English and started talking about films and books, and everyday things. When he switched to French, a language she was very much at home with, she talked for a while, and then could stand it no longer.

'Will you tell me what this grilling is for . . . sir?' It was always best to tack that word on the end.

He threw the folder down, folded his arms and grinned with pleasure. 'We need wireless operators, and your languages could be useful as well. Your concentration is good and your German, though a bit rusty, is adequate; but your French is excellent. Where did you learn to speak it so fluently?'

Annie explained about Chantal and watched him scribble notes in her file.

'We would like to train you for this, but I must warn you that it is a very secret occupation; the work will be arduous and the hours long at times.'

'I understand.' Annie couldn't contain her excitement. 'When do I start my training?'

'At once. We are in desperate need of operators. You will have to learn not only to receive and send in Morse code, but you will also have to be able to repair your machine should anything go wrong with it.'

'And how long will this take?' she asked.

'In normal times it's a lengthy process, but you will have to become proficient in just six months. Quite a daunting task, I admit, but I believe you are capable of doing it.'

'Where will I be going?' Annie was bursting with excitement and many questions. She had never imagined she would be asked to do anything like this.

'Your training will take place at Compton Bassett in Wiltshire.'

'And after that?'

'You will be told when the time is right and not before. There's a lot of hard work in front of you.' He smiled again and looked at his watch. 'You have thirty minutes to pack your kit and meet us outside.'

'Er . . . I thought we were due some leave now?'

'Not you, I'm afraid. We have to start your training immediately.'

Annie ran back to the hut and found all the girls waiting anxiously for her. She was too excited to be disappointed about having her leave cancelled.

'What happened?' Dora asked as soon as she was through the door. 'Does he want you for that tap tap stuff?'

'Yes, I've got six months' training ahead of me and I have to start at once.' She grabbed her bag and began stuffing her possessions in it without bothering to fold the clothes properly. 'I never thought I'd get such an exciting job.'

'How did you do in the test?' Kath wanted to know.

'Ninety-five per cent correct.'

'Wow! No wonder he wanted you.' Dora looked sad. 'This means we'll all be splitting up.'

'I'm afraid so, but it has been fun and we must try to keep in touch.' Annie would be sorry to lose Dora's companionship. 'What will you be doing, Dora?'

'I've signed on as a clerk because I thought it would help me get a better job after the war. I don't want to go back into a factory after this.'

'That's a good idea. My sister learnt to type in the WAAC during the last war, and it was very useful to her.'

'Ah, well, I've definitely done the right thing. Don't forget you promised to introduce me to her some time.'

'I won't forget.' Annie laughed at Dora's eagerness. 'What's everyone else doing?' she asked.

While Annie continued to pack, the girls spent the next half an hour talking about their various jobs and postings, then they said goodbye, and one or two tears were spilt. After that, Annie headed for the truck waiting to take her to her new posting.

Officer Graham was standing by the vehicle, talking quietly to another man, and when she hurried up he looked at his watch. 'Right on time.'

He threw her bag in the back of the lorry, then the three of them clambered in the front and set off. As the countryside sped by her Annie couldn't help wondering what she was heading into.

'Hello, Rose.' Annie popped her head around the kitchen door and grinned at her big sister, who was sitting at the kitchen table with a book in front of her, as usual. She'd been away from home for nearly four months and it was so lovely to see Rose again. She was wearing a dark red frock, which suited her beautifully; a shaft of the warm May sunshine was resting on her hair, making it shimmer blue-black.

Rose looked up from the book she was reading, smiled broadly and stood up to hug her young sister. 'When did you get home?'

'Just arrived. I've got a seven-day pass.' Annie did a graceful pirouette. 'What do you think?' She'd managed to have some alterations done to the tunic and now it fitted a treat; of course, the stockings and heavy shoes were unflattering, but with the complete uniform it wasn't too bad. The air force blue suited her as well.

'Very smart.' Her sister stood up and put the kettle on the stove. 'I'll make some tea and you can tell me how you're getting on.'

Annie sat down and picked up the book Rose had been reading. It was the Bible her sister had won at the age of eleven for coming top of the school.

'You still read it, then?' she asked, as Rose sat beside her.

'Oh, yes, and I'm still trying to understand it.'

'So I see,' Annie laughed, looking at the dog-eared, well-worn book in front of her. There was hardly a margin where Rose hadn't scribbled a comment or two. She remembered when she'd been very little finding her sister studying well into the night, with this book never far from her hand. The fact that she was reading it now alerted Annie. 'You're worried about something. Is Bill back at sea?'

'I'm afraid so. I knew it was going to happen, of course, but I couldn't help hoping the navy would change their mind and give him a shore job. He went through enough last time, and I've got a nasty feeling this could be even worse.'

Annie wanted to reach out and hug her big sister, but she knew Rose didn't like to be fussed over, so she picked up the Bible again. 'We'll pray for everyone's safety. What were you underlining when I came in?'

'That.' Rose pointed to a psalm.

Annie read the sections marked in red ink.

> Whither shall I go from thy spirit?
> Or whither shall I flee from thy presence?
> If I ascend up into heaven, thou art there:
> If I make my bed in hell, behold, thou art there.
> If I take the wings of the morning, and dwell in the uttermost parts of the sea;
> Even there shall thy hand lead me, and thy right hand shall hold me.

'Oh, that's lovely,' Annie said when she'd finished reading, 'and so appropriate.'

'Yes, it's one of my favourite passages. Now,' Rose settled back in her chair, 'tell me all your news; you haven't said much in your letters. We expected you home sooner than this.'

'I should have been, but when I'd finished my basic training I was posted immediately. I've hardly had time to draw breath since then.'

'What kind of a job have they given you?'

'Wireless operator.' Annie grinned and started to tap out Morse code on the table. 'Seems I've got an ear for it. I'm only halfway through my training, but when I start as a qualified operator I won't be able to talk about the work.'

'I understand. How are you finding things in general?'

'All right.' Annie then started to tell her sister about their first day at camp and the awful underclothes; the mess they'd got into when first on parade, all turning in different directions until the sergeant had been almost crying with frustration. She went through everything in great detail, and by the time she'd finished they were both roaring with laughter.

'Oh, you've cheered me up no end.' Rose wiped her eyes.

'I could hear you laughing from my kitchen.' Annie's mother walked in and kissed her, holding on as if she didn't want to let her go. 'It's so wonderful to see you. Sorry I wasn't here when you arrived. How long are you home for?'

'Seven days.'

'Oh, lovely, you look tired though. A few days relaxing in the garden will bring the colour back to your face.' Marj smiled happily at her daughter, sat down and poured herself a cup of tea. 'I had a letter from Charlie yesterday, and he seems happy enough in the air force, but I haven't heard from Will for some time. I wish he hadn't gone into the navy, but he was sure that was what he wanted.'

'They'll be all right, Mum,' Annie assured her.

Wally came in then. 'Annie!' he exclaimed. 'Good to see you again, we've missed you. Now, I don't suppose you've got a pitchfork or an old sword, or anything I can use as a weapon?'

'What on earth would we be doing with such things?' Marj asked her husband. 'What are you up to?'

'I'm going to join the Local Defence Volunteers, and they haven't got any guns yet, so we've got to improvise.'

'The LDV? You?'

Wally sat back with a huge grin on his face. 'You only have to be capable of free movement to join. And I'll have you know, my dear wife, that many of the men volunteering are a lot older than me, but as long as we hold our parades within easy walking distance of the pub we should be all right.'

Annie and Rose started to chuckle as their mother muttered, 'God help us!'

Just then James tumbled through the kitchen door, flushed with excitement.

'What are you doing home?' Rose asked. 'I thought you were spending the day on the river with John's father?'

'He's had to take the boat somewhere. It's been comm . . . comm . . . taken over by the navy. There's hundreds of them all going up the Thames!' He was jumping up and down with excitement.

'The word you're looking for is "commandeered",' his mother corrected, standing up quickly.

'What would the navy want with a load of small boats?' Wally asked with a worried frown.

'I don't know, but I'm going to find out.' Rose swept out of the house with a determined look on her face.

'John and me wanted to go with his dad but he wouldn't let us. He said he didn't know what it was all about and it might take some time.' James scowled in frustration. 'It's rotten being a kid, you get stopped from doing anything exciting, and no one tells you anything.'

Annie hid a smile and stood up. How like Rose her nephew was, always wanting to know, always looking for answers to his unstoppable questions. 'I'll just go and unpack my bag.'

She had no sooner reached her room than she heard Wally calling.

'Annie! Rose's back and she's got some news.'

She didn't like the tone of urgency in his voice. She had not been taking a great deal of notice of James's excitement, putting it down to childish exaggeration, but now she was worried. She ran across the garden and into Rose's house, looked at her grim expression and sat down, waiting for her sister to tell them what she'd found out.

'It's bad, I'm afraid.' Rose paced the room. 'I've had a hell of a job prising information out of people, but fortunately I've still got some good contacts. Our army is trapped on the beaches at Dunkirk. Mum, will you look after the children for me?'

'Of course, but where are you going?'

'Dover.' Rose was already pinning her WVS badge on to her coat. 'They're going to need all the help they can get when they start bringing the poor buggers home.'

Annie stood up, all thought of a leisurely few days disappearing. 'I'll come with you.'

4

Reid Lascells sat down and looked at the meal in front of him. He was so damned tired! He had been promoted to squadron leader only last week when Dan Holdsworth had been shot down and killed over France. It was a hell of a way to gain promotion, and it gave him no pleasure to try to fill that fine man's shoes in this way. He picked up his knife and fork just as the sound of the bell to scramble jangled through his head. He was on his feet and running, leaving his breakfast untouched on the table. They weren't even having time to eat, and he couldn't remember when he'd had more than three hours' sleep at a time, but the fatigue was forgotten as he hurtled towards his Spitfire. Those poor devils on the beaches were undoubtedly more tired than he was.

'All ready for you, sir.' The ground crew sprang into action as he reached the plane. 'We've repaired the damage and she's as good as new.'

'Thanks.' They strapped him in and he cast them a quick smile; he didn't know what they'd do without these men. They were totally dedicated to keeping the planes flying, and he knew they waited anxiously to see if *their* pilot returned after a sortie.

He climbed, and as tired as he was he felt the usual exhilaration as the sweet Merlin engine responded to his touch. After checking that the squadron was airborne, trying to ignore the blank spaces of those they'd lost, they banked and headed for the Calais–Dunkirk patrol.

'Hell! Look at that,' came through Reid's headset. The airways began to crackle with voices.

'They're not going to try and take them off the beaches in those, surely?'

'They're pleasure boats.'

'And barges.'

'Where's the navy?'

'On fire! Look to your left.'

'Oh, hell, what a mess.'

'Hey they're shooting at us!'

'Blue leader here, climb! climb!' Reid commanded.

When they had regrouped above the clouds, one pilot swore, 'Christ, don't they know the difference between us and the MEs?'

'I'd be shooting at everything if I was down there,' muttered another pilot understandingly.

'OK, shut up, everyone,' Reid ordered.

'Bandits! Three o'clock!'

In the mêlée that followed, Reid shot down two ME 109s, and saw one Spitfire blown apart and, just for a split second, he wondered where his brother was, but it was foolhardy to let your concentration wander when some swine was trying to kill you.

Kenley airfield was a welcome sight, and so were the ground crew who rushed up to help him out. 'How many missing?' he asked, as soon as his feet touched the ground.

'Three, sir, but there's always the chance they've landed somewhere else.'

He knew that for sure one of them was gone, and he

started to walk towards the debriefing hut, trying not to wonder who he wasn't going to see again.

'Sir, what's it like over there?' One of the ground crew looked at him anxiously. 'We'll be in a mess if we lose our army.'

Reid summoned up a smile; though he was so damned tired he wasn't sure if it came out as a grimace. 'You don't have to worry, lads, the navy will get them home.'

''Course they will.' The men gathered around him nodded in agreement.

'Did you make a kill today, sir?'

'Yes, two definite.'

The men cheered, and then started to clamber all over the plane to check for damage.

Reid walked across the grass deep in thought and cursing under his breath. He hoped they did manage to rescue the troops because they were losing quite a few planes in this operation, and worse still was the loss of the pilots. Many of them didn't look much more than kids. They hadn't had any experience of life before they were shot out of the skies.

They flew sortie after sortie that day, until they were exhausted. Their day started about three in the morning and continued until dusk, and he decided that if he survived this he was going to sleep for a week.

He was in the air again just as dawn was creeping over the horizon, and they were in battle as soon as they crossed the French coast.

'On your tail, Skip!'

Reid dived, then climbed and turned, trying to shake off the German fighter. The Spitfire didn't let him down and the position was soon reversed. He was just lining up for the kill when he heard a thud and the plane shuddered.

'You're trailing smoke!' someone yelled. 'Bail out!'

But Reid was too far inland so he banked and headed for the coast. He knew he was risking his life by staying in the air but the last thing he wanted was to land behind enemy lines and end up as a prisoner for the rest of the war. As soon as he saw the smoking ruins of Dunkirk in the distance he searched for a suitable landing place. He couldn't bail out now, he was too low, so he made for a small field just below him. The thought of dying never occurred to him, his main worry as he headed for the field was capture. That possibility made his insides clench in apprehension . . .

As he hit the ground his undercarriage collapsed; he crashed through a fence and came to rest on a dirt road. His head smacked against the side of the cockpit, knocking the breath out of him. For a split-second he didn't move, but as the smoke began to billow in front of him he shot back the canopy and slithered to the ground.

He stood there dazed and disorientated. The air was full of different smells, smoke, burning oil, and something else. He frowned and licked his lips, tasting blood, and then he turned his head and was staring straight into the eyes of a doleful-looking cow, busily chewing. In his befuddled state he thought its expression was accusing.

'I'm sorry,' he said, reaching out to stroke its velvet face. 'Have I made a mess of your field?'

The animal burped noisily and Reid started to laugh. 'I should have spoken in French.'

A strange noise coming from the Spitfire brought him

back to his senses. My God! He was standing here as if he was on a casual day out in the country, *and* talking to a cow.

At that moment three men came running through the gap in the fence waving their arms frantically and yelling at the tops of their voices. Two of them grabbed hold of the cow and started to tow it back into its field, the other one didn't stop running but caught hold of Reid and dragged him away from the plane. They had just made it when the Spitfire exploded and knocked them to the ground.

Reid was horrified. What was the matter with him? He should have been running for his life as soon as he'd got out of the plane, instead he'd been trying to have a conversation with a cow! That knock on the head must have scrambled his brains.

'You must get to Dunkirk,' he was urged. 'The Germans will be here soon.'

A young boy came hurtling towards him on a bike, and when he reached Reid he leapt off and thrust the bicycle at him. 'You go, quickly. That way.'

Reid was off and pedalling as fast as he could. It was an obstacle course, the road was littered with abandoned trucks, tanks, cars, dead bodies and animals, but he ignored the scenes of devastation, and pedalled like a man possessed. The irony of the situation did not escape him; he was going to end up on the beach they had been trying so desperately to protect. What chance of survival there? About fifty-fifty, he assessed, but it was his only hope, and he wanted to live so very much. Every time he went into battle, never knowing if he was going to survive had made him realize how precious life was.

He hadn't gone far when the bike had a puncture, but he kept riding, the rim of the wheel screeching as it spun on the road. It was either this or walk, and that would take him hours.

'That won't get you far,' a cultured English voice said.

Reid was gasping for breath by now, and looked up to see a motorbike idling along beside him. It contained an army officer and a bedraggled soldier of indistinguishable rank on the pillion.

'Hop on,' said the officer.

'But there isn't room.'

''Course there is, mate, I'll move up a bit.' The soldier patted a couple of spare inches behind him. 'You should be able to get your backside on there all right. I shouldn't hang about 'cos Jerry's right on our tail.'

He didn't argue; it would be better than the pedal bike, and quicker. Tucking his legs up, he hung on grimly to the man in front of him, and the bike sped off towards the clouds of billowing smoke that was the remains of Dunkirk.

An hour later he fell off the bike, thanked the unknown driver who had probably saved his life, and ran on to the beach. As he collapsed on the sand in exhaustion he became aware that his head was pounding and he could feel dried blood all over his face. Strange, but in the urgent dash to reach Dunkirk he hadn't been aware of his injuries.

'Blimey! The air force has arrived, at last,' a voice shouted scornfully. 'Where you been, mate?'

Reid dragged himself to his knees and stared at the sea

of hostile faces around him. He pointed to the sky. 'Up there, fighting like bloody maniacs.'

'You could have fooled us, mate,' another man jeered.

Reid was now on his feet, bristling with anger. 'I've lost half my squadron trying to protect you. Planes and pilots we're going to need to defend Britain since you couldn't bloody well keep the Germans out of France.'

'We did our best,' one soldier told him defensively.

Reid dropped wearily to his knees again; this was stupid. 'I know you did, and so have we.'

'Sorry, mate, we're just frustrated trying to get off this bleeding beach.' The man, who was a sergeant, knelt beside him. 'There's no need to take it out on you, though. That's a nasty gash you've got there. Dave!' he yelled, 'see if you can find a medic.'

'What did you do, bail out?' another soldier asked.

'No, I had to land in a field. The locals got me away just before she blew up.' There was no way he was going to tell them that they had found him talking to a cow!

'Christ!' the soldier muttered.

'Sorry, Sergeant.' The corporal returned. 'They're all busy.'

Reid waved his hand. 'It doesn't matter.'

'Here they come again!' the shout went up.

The two soldiers grabbed hold of Reid and dragged him towards a large crater. The next few minutes were sheer bedlam, screaming fighters strafing the beach, bombs falling, men shouting and cursing. And then, suddenly, it was all over and the only sound was an irate seagull screeching above their heads. Gradually Reid became aware of the moans and cries for help coming from the injured. If there was such a place as hell, then it must be like this. He lifted his head, looked at the sergeant and swore with ferocity, 'I'd rather be in a Spitfire, at least I can shoot back.'

The man held his hand out. 'My name's Ron.'

'Reid.' He shook his hand.

'Well, Squadron Leader, we'd better see if we can get you on a ship, because you're right, we are going to need you in the months to come.'

'Hey, Sergeant, that destroyer's coming back.'

The beach was suddenly alive with activity, and Reid was impressed with the way the men behaved. Every one of them must be frantic to get off the beach, but they were taking orders from their officers and forming orderly queues. The men started to walk into the sea and wait for the few remaining small boats to pick them up and ferry them to the large ship. It was an impressive sight but Reid didn't miss the anxious glances at the sky as they waited for the German planes to return again. Reid didn't rate his chances of getting on a boat very high.

'There's another small boat over there, Sergeant,' the corporal shouted. 'Let's get the Air Commodore on that.'

Reid grinned, but felt like weeping. These men had been here for God knows how long, but even in a situation as desperate as this, they could still joke.

He was hoisted into the boat and he reached out to give them a hand up.

'Not me, mate, I've still got some of my men on the beach, but the corp will come with you.'

'I'm staying.' The corporal grabbed hold of another man and tossed him into the boat.

Ron nodded, as if this was only what he'd expected,

and then they began to help others into the small vessel until it was dangerously overloaded. The sea was only inches from the top and one more passenger would have made it pour in and sink them.

As they headed towards the destroyer, Reid swallowed a lump in his throat as he wondered if those men would survive. He hoped to God they did. And what was going to happen to Britain now with only the strip of Channel between them and the might of the Germans?

The destroyer was in a dreadful state. She had obviously taken a real pounding, and he wondered how many trips she had made. It was quite a few by the look of the damage.

The men scrambling aboard were a mixture of British, French, civilians and sailors from ships that had been sunk, but as far as he could see he was the only pilot.

When she was full to capacity, the vessel headed out to sea, and all eyes were fixed on the horizon, waiting for the first glimpse of Dover.

'Sir?'

Reid turned to the sailor who had appeared beside him.

'The captain asks if you would like to come to the bridge?'

They pushed their way through the crowds of men and up a flight of steps. The man who greeted him was above average height, greying slightly at the temples, with deep lines of fatigue etched on his face. But there was a calmness about him that was balm to Reid's jangled nerves. As dangerous as flying was, he would rather be up there than down in this hell.

'You looked out of place with all the khaki.'

Reid grinned, taking an instant liking to the tall, impressive man. 'I'm surprised I wasn't thrown overboard. Some of them seem to think the RAF hasn't done much to protect them.'

'That's just their anger talking. Any fool knows that you couldn't provide continuous air cover. Do you know what the losses are to date?'

'I don't know the exact figures, but it's far too many.'

The captain grimaced. 'We've lost ships as well, but thank God we've been able to get a lot of the troops off the beach.'

'The soldiers seemed to recognize you. How many trips have you made?'

'Four, but we were damaged on the last run . . .'

'Captain Freeman!'

The sailor who had just come on the bridge was covered in oil and dirt, and dripping wet, but he still had a wry smile on his face.

'We've sprung another leak, sir. The pumps are coping but we'll need a repair crew as soon as we dock, or we won't be able to do another run.'

The captain nodded. 'I'll see that it's arranged. In the meantime, can you make a temporary repair?'

'Yes, sir.' The dripping sailor's face broke into a grin. 'We'll stick our fingers in the holes if necessary.'

'Have you got enough men for that?' the captain asked drily.

'Oh, I expect we could persuade the army to help us. We ain't got enough lifeboats for this lot, and I'm damned sure they won't want to swim home.'

Reid watched this light-hearted exchange and had a

vivid picture of the pilots diving into action, the courage of the soldiers on the beach, and now the crew of this battered destroyer. He was seeing a different side to his fellow man, and it was awe-inspiring. And at that moment he knew that no matter how desperate the plight of the country there was no way they could lose this war. A lot of them wouldn't see the end, of course, but they would win!

He walked forward and gazed out to sea for a while, then turned and watched Captain Freeman issuing orders in a quiet, unruffled manner. That his crew respected him was very clear, and his placid nature by no means hid the strength of the man.

'I'm sorry we can't offer you something stronger.'

A sailor carrying a tray of steaming cups thrust a mug of tea into his hand. Reid curled his fingers around it gratefully. 'Thanks. This will do just fine.'

'Why don't you sit down?' The captain pointed to his own chair. 'You look just about done in.'

'I am. God what a day!' Reid sat and rubbed his hand over his eyes, then started to gently probe the injury to his temple.

'There will be nurses to take care of you when we dock.' Captain Freeman turned away to deal with the business of getting his ship back to Dover.

Reid watched the captain and officers on the bridge spring into action as another crisis erupted. But he took little notice of it as reaction was beginning to set in, and his mind started to shut down. He had survived and was going home, that's all that mattered at the moment. And the ship wasn't going to sink, the captain had said so, and he believed him.

He wasn't aware of the passing of time as he sat there, the mug was replaced with a fresh one every so often, and the activity all around him was just so much background noise. He watched the sea, noting the different colours and shades, his mind drifting and thinking of nothing in particular . . .

He was roused out of his stupor when the destroyer's guns shattered the quiet. Rushing to the front of the bridge, he looked up into the sky and eagerly grabbed the binoculars being held out to him. It took him only a few seconds to identify the planes as German, but there, just above them . . . 'Stop shooting,' he yelled, 'those are our fighters coming to intercept them.'

Orders were quickly given and the guns fell silent. Reid breathed a sigh of relief, walked back to the chair and almost collapsed on to it. 'Bloody hell,' he muttered, 'we're going to have to do better at identification than this.'

'I agree,' the captain said. 'And I can assure you, Squadron Leader, that my men will get a refresher course as a matter of urgency.'

'It wasn't their fault,' Reid admitted. 'If our planes were there they would be high and coming out of the sun, so I knew where to look.'

Captain Freeman nodded. 'I'm glad you were here, and your planes, of course, have just saved us from serious damage. This poor old ship can't take much more.'

And neither can the crew, Reid thought, as he saw the strain on their faces. But he said nothing and sat back to wait out the rest of the journey. He was filled with a sense of gratitude for the courage of these men around

523

him. Without the soldiers on the beach and the crew of this ship he would still be stuck in France.

It didn't seem any time at all after that when he heard cheering, and there in front of him was Dover. It was the most beautiful sight he'd ever seen! The injured were taken off first, followed by the relieved soldiers. Reid thanked the captain and his officers, and then made his way ashore.

The quay was crowded with doctors, nurses and civilians, all helping the returning troops. He stood there for a while, wondering how he could get a lift back to Kenley, when he saw Captain Freeman striding along, then stopping in front of a woman and holding her close for a few moments, then kissing another girl on the cheek. He couldn't see who they were because of the crowds milling around them, but he was glad the captain had someone waiting for him.

'Let me see to your head, sir.' A military nurse began to lead him towards a building.

After he was cleaned up, had stitches and a dressing put on the gash, and been given something to eat he went outside again looking for any kind of transport heading towards his airfield. There was a blast on a ship's horn, and he saw the destroyer making her way out to sea. Dear God, they were going back again already. He prayed that they had been able to stop the leaks.

The journey back to Kenley was long and tiring. He'd spent more time looking for lifts than he had actually travelling. He'd had umpteen modes of transport and all equally uncomfortable, but the help had been willingly given. He finally reached the airfield at four in the morning.

He was greeted enthusiastically by everyone, and after a short debriefing he staggered into his hut.

'Reid! Where the blazes have you been? Couldn't you have let us know you were all right?'

He glanced at his brother's angry and worried expression, and then gave a lopsided grin. Paul must have driven over from Biggin Hill. 'It's good to see you, as well, little brother.'

Then he threw himself on his bed and was instantly asleep.

5

Annie rushed through the gate at Compton Bassett and sighed in relief; she'd only just made it in time after spending longer than she should have with Rose. Her sister had refused to leave Dover until she saw Bill come back again, so she'd stayed with her. Annie smiled to herself. How wonderful it had been to see him return, and now he had some leave while repairs were carried out to his ship.

As an officer approached she saluted smartly. She remembered the pilot she had caught a glimpse of on the dock. For a brief moment she had thought it was Paul but he had been taller and his hair darker. She hadn't been able to see all of his face for caked blood down one side, but there had been something about him that had drawn her. Before she could go over and offer him some help a nurse had led him away. Rose had put her WVS training to good use and Annie had taken her orders from her sister. It had been a relief to see the ships come in and the men pouring off them. At least they had managed to rescue a lot of men . . .

'Hey! Annie,' someone called. 'Show us your knickers!'

She spun round, a smile of delight on her face. 'Dora!'

They hugged each other, laughing.

'What are you doing here?'

'I've been posted here and I'm working in the office.'

Dora grinned. 'It's better than that awful factory I was in, and I'm getting to mix with some smashing blokes. I'm hoping to get promotion when I've finished my training.'

Annie fought back a smile. 'So I hope you're not going to get me into trouble while you're here.'

'Who me, now would I do that?' Dora put on an offended expression.

Both girls burst into laughter, remembering the escapades they'd been involved in while doing their basic training.

'Anyway . . .' Dora composed herself. 'Where have you been, I arrived three days ago and not a sign of you.'

'I've been with my sister, helping with the troops coming back from Dunkirk, but they're nearly all home now, thank heavens.' Annie shuddered inwardly when she thought of the perilous situation this country was now in. Getting the troops off the beaches had been a massive operation by the navy and a flotilla of little boats all manned by civilians. These men had shown remarkable bravery and disregard for their own lives in their determination to rescue the soldiers. The army had been plucked off the beaches, but all the military equipment – trucks, guns, tanks – had been left behind. What a mess! This was Hitler's chance to walk right in . . .

She glanced at her watch and gasped. 'I must drop off my kit and report back for duty.'

'There's a dance at the NAAFI this evening.' Dora grabbed Annie's arm to stop her running away. 'Can you come?'

'Wouldn't miss it.'

'Smashing. I'll see you later then.'

Annie hurried away. It would be fun to relax and have a laugh tonight, and that was always guaranteed when Dora was around. It might help to dull the distress of Dunkirk and the worries about the future. This country was alone now and vulnerable!

The afternoon was exam time to see how much they had learned in the last three months, so Annie grabbed a cup of tea and skimmed through her notes. There wasn't time to do more than that, but she felt confident of passing. Then it would be into the last three months of training, and she was determined to do well because she couldn't wait to start doing the job for real. She could already send and receive messages quite well with few mistakes, but the next stage would be learning to maintain their wireless sets and doing their own repairs. She smiled to herself; the work as a fashion editor had not prepared her for using soldering irons, or whatever it was they were going to have to do, but she loved the idea of it.

'Would you like to dance?'

Annie smiled at Officer Graham who was standing in front of her and felt the same surge of empathy she'd experienced when she'd first met him. 'I'd love to.'

He was an excellent dancer and Annie relaxed, lost in the floating music and the smooth movements of her partner.

The floor was crowded and as he marked time when they were surrounded and unable to move forward he smiled down at her. 'And how have you been getting on, Ann Webster?'

'Fine, thank you, sir. I love what I'm doing.'

'Good. And we're off duty now, so my name is Jack.'

'And everyone calls me Annie.'

He swept her off again as a space appeared. 'What do you like to do in your spare time, Annie?'

'Well, now that the weather is warming up, I like to get out in the countryside and just walk. I love the peace and quiet, and Wiltshire is a beautiful county.'

'So do I. Perhaps we could spend some time together? There are some good walks around here and I know of a very nice tearoom.'

'Oh, I'd like that.' Annie had taken to this man from the moment they'd met. He was so like her brother-in-law. But no, that wasn't true; her feelings for Jack Graham were different from those she felt for Bill. It was amazing that this was only the second time they'd met, and yet it seemed as if she'd always known him . . .

'Before you accept so readily,' his deep voice interrupted her thoughts, 'I must tell you that I'm married and have two children. I'm looking for companionship, that's all.' He shook his head. 'That sounds insulting. It isn't that I don't find you attractive. I do, but I'll behave myself.'

'Do you think that's possible at the moment when everything's so uncertain?' she asked drily, knowing instinctively that it was all right to joke with him.

'Difficult, I agree.' He held her away from him and looked down into her upturned face. 'Will you still come out with me?'

'I'd love to.'

'Thank you, Annie. I shall be stationed here for a while, so just let me know when you have some free time.'

The dance ended and he led her back to her seat, his fingers lingering on hers for slightly longer than necessary, before smiling again, and then leaving her.

'Ah!' Dora said with satisfaction as they watched him walk away. 'I thought he wouldn't be far away.'

'That's the first time I've seen him since he recruited me.'

'Go on?' Dora clearly didn't believe that.

The expression on her friend's face was too much for Annie and she dug her in the ribs. 'And what have you been up to since I last saw you?'

'Having fun. And if you think I'm going to tell you all about my sordid past, then you're in for a big disappointment.'

'I don't think I want to know.' Annie feigned a look of horror. 'I don't think my chaste little ears could stand it.'

Dora allowed herself to be dragged on to the dance floor by an exuberant sergeant before she'd had a chance to reply, but from the expression on her face it was clear she'd had a snappy answer ready for Annie.

Annie didn't see Jack again until the last waltz, which he claimed, and then walked her back to her billet. He kissed her hand gallantly, sighed deeply, and walked away.

There was no sign of Dora.

'Don't you ever get any time off?' Dora complained, a week later.

'Not much,' Annie admitted. 'I've got less than three months of training to go and I must be expert by then.'

'Do you know where they're sending you after that?'

'No.' Annie stirred her tea thoughtfully. 'About time off, I have got tomorrow afternoon free, but – '

'Oh, that's no good, I'm on duty until the weekend.'

'Never mind. If we can fiddle a couple of days together I could take you home to meet my family.'

'Wow! Annie, would you?'

'Of course.' She laughed. Dora had such an open expression and didn't try to hide her pleasure at the idea of meeting Annie's family. They would like her, she was sure.

Her friend started to flip through a diary. 'I'll go and make eyes at the sergeant in the office. So, what are you going to do on your own?'

'I won't be on my own. I'm going out with Jack.'

'Who's Jack?' Dora looked intrigued. 'I didn't know you'd found yourself another bloke, you've got this pilot, Paul, haven't you?'

Annie sighed. 'Yes, he thinks so.'

'Ah.' Dora pulled her chair closer so they wouldn't be overheard in the crowded mess. 'Tell me all.'

Realizing that she wasn't going to get any peace until Dora knew the facts, Annie bowed to the inevitable and explained about Paul.

'Why don't you just tell him that you don't want to see him any more?' Dora said when she'd finished the story.

'I can't do that, he's a nice boy and I wouldn't want to hurt him. Especially now.'

'Annie, you're too soft,' Dora told her gently. 'Have you got a picture of him?'

'Yes.' Annie took a letter out of her pocket and removed the photo Paul had sent her the other day.

Dora took it and whistled. 'Nice-looking bloke.'

'He is, and at the moment he needs me. I think he's

531

realized that being a fighter pilot isn't the fun he thought it was going to be.'

'Bloody dangerous, if you ask me.'

Annie agreed with that! 'So you see, I don't like it, but I don't see what else I can do at the moment.'

'Don't worry, it will all work out. Right, now you haven't answered my first question. Who's Jack?'

'He was the one who recruited me. He was at the dance, don't you remember?'

'What, you mean, *Sir*?' Dora squeaked. 'But . . . hold on a minute, mate, he must be about forty, and that means he's most likely married.'

'He is, but we're just going to be friends. He only wants some companionship.' Annie was well aware how ridiculous that sounded, yet somehow she believed Jack Graham. She knew she was being naive but he didn't appear to be a man who would lie to her. She trusted him.

Dora's mouth opened in disbelief. 'Oh, come on, Annie, you don't believe that, surely?'

'Of course I do. He's been absolutely honest with me.'

'Worse and worse,' her friend groaned. 'Never trust a man who's being *honest*.'

'Why on earth not?'

'My God! We've got a babe in arms here. I know you look like an untouched angel but you can't be that green.' She leaned towards Annie urgently. 'When a man says, I want to be honest with you, then it's time to run for your life.'

'You're wrong.' Annie laughed. 'He's so like my brother-in-law.'

'And you sleep with him, do you?'

'No, I don't. I love Bill, but not in that way. Anyway, Rose would kill any woman who tried to take him from her, even me!'

Dora's grin was evil. 'I bet she would. So where are you going with *Sir*, then?'

'Just for a walk.'

'Any cornfields on the route,' she asked drily.

'Oh, you're impossible,' Annie said and laughed. 'You've got only one thing on your mind.'

'Is there something else, then?' Dora sat back and pretended she was puzzled.

Annie glanced at her watch and got hurriedly to her feet. 'I've got to get back. And you needn't worry about me, I know what I'm doing.'

She left Dora muttering fiercely, 'Too bloody innocent for her own good.'

It was a lovely June afternoon. The sky was clear, the sun warm, and just for a few hours they could relax and pretend that everything was well with their world. When Churchill had been made Prime Minister, and given his first speech to the House of Commons on the 13th of May, he'd said, 'I have nothing to offer but blood, toil, tears and sweat.' They all knew this was true as they waited for Hitler to invade – for he must surely come now.

Annie smiled at the man walking beside her. 'What do you do, Jack, apart from finding people with an ear for Morse code?'

'Whatever I'm asked to do. Oh, look, there's a green woodpecker!' He pointed towards a clump of trees. 'On that lower branch.'

'Yes, I see. Isn't he lovely? Oh, he's flown away now.'

Jack started to talk about the different kinds of birds, which was a subject he was very interested in, and Annie knew he wasn't going to tell her about his work. She'd been asking a question he obviously couldn't answer. Though that made her even more curious. There was an air of mystery about him and that intrigued her. The attraction between them was very strong so she must not forget that he was a married man!

'Sorry,' she apologized, 'I shouldn't be asking you questions about your work, should I?'

He wrapped his long fingers around her hand and sighed. 'Let's not spoil this afternoon with talk about the war.'

They walked down country lanes, admiring quaint little cottages and open farmlands, sometimes talking and at other times quiet. The war seemed a long way away in this tranquil setting, and Annie sensed that Jack needed to unwind. He held her hand. Every so often she could feel the tension in him, then it would go and he'd smile again.

After over an hour of strolling along they came to a tearoom where in normal times they would have been selling cream teas. The thought made Annie's mouth water, but she knew they would be lucky just to get a pot of tea now.

They sat at a table near the window overlooking a picture-postcard scene of sheep grazing contentedly in a field. Annie sighed at such a peaceful scene in these violent and troubled times.

'This is blissful,' she told Jack. 'You could almost believe we weren't at war.'

534

'Hello, my dears.' An elderly lady, with grey hair and a round smile, came up to them. 'What would you like?'

'A huge cream tea,' Annie said, laughing.

'Ah, I wish I could.' The lady joined in the joke and her smile became even broader. 'I can let you have a pot of tea and a piece of home-made carrot cake.'

'That would be lovely,' Jack said, and watched her bustle away with her smile still firmly in place.

'There's a dance at Chippenham Town Hall tonight, Annie. Would you like to go?'

'Oh, I'd love to!'

'That's right, my dears, you enjoy yourselves.' The woman was back with their tea and had obviously overheard their conversation. 'There now, you'll find that cake quite tasty, though nothing like the ones I used to make. Famous for my fruit cake, I was.'

'I'm sure it's lovely.' Annie smiled and watched her walk away, her spotless and highly starched apron rustling as she moved.

They spent an hour over their tea and then walked back. As soon as the Compton Bassett camp came into view they were back in the real world, but it had been a lovely interlude of peace.

'I'll meet you at the gate at seven,' Jack said, and strode off after giving her hand a gentle squeeze.

It was only when she was having dinner with Dora, and thought about the afternoon, that Annie realized she'd told Jack a great deal about herself but had learned practically nothing about him.

The dance at Chippenham was crowded with service personnel determined to have a good night out. Jack was a wonderful dancer, but the dance Annie liked most of all was the foxtrot, and they swept around the floor as if they'd been partners for years. That was why she was amazed when after being there for about two hours Jack stepped away from her in the middle of the dance floor and swore fiercely under his breath.

'What's the matter?' she asked, alarmed by his action. They'd been dancing and laughing, completely at ease in each other's company, and suddenly he looked angry.

'This wasn't a good idea!' He turned and walked out of the room.

Annie's mind was racing – what had she done? She'd never seen him so disturbed; he was such a quiet, controlled man. She ran after him and caught him up just as he stepped out into the fresh air. 'Jack?'

'I'll take you back to camp,' was all he said.

Now she was getting cross. 'Not until you've explained!'

'I'm sorry. I thought we could just be friends,' he grimaced, 'but I was wrong. Being close to you and not being able to make love to you is agony.'

Annie saw his jaw clench in frustration and understood, for she felt the same, but this relationship couldn't be anything but a friendship. And if that was all she could have from him then she didn't want to let it go. 'We won't come dancing again but we can still see each other, can't we? Still go for walks?'

'Do you think that's a good idea?' He looked angry. 'If I can't control what I feel for you, will you sleep with me?'

'Oh, Jack.' She was dismayed by this conversation;

how she wished she could say yes. 'If you were free . . . but you're married, Jack.'

'Exactly! And you're not the kind of girl who could ignore that.' He ran the back of his hand down her cheek in a gentle gesture. 'I really am sorry.'

She caught hold of his hand and held on firmly. The thought of losing him was upsetting, and she wondered how on earth she'd become so attached to a man after only meeting him about three times. 'Let's try and be friends, please.'

Jack sighed and gazed into space for a moment with a deep frown on his face, and then he looked back with a smile. 'OK, Annie, we'll see how it goes, shall we?'

Over the next couple of weeks they spent every spare moment together, and he behaved like the perfect gentleman. It was as if the incident at the dance had never happened; he was back in complete control of himself again. Yet Annie's feelings were in turmoil. The more time she spent with Jack the more she liked him – or was it love? He was a quietly spoken man, but there was a strength about him that was obvious to her. They had much in common, the same music, a love of the countryside whatever the season, and their outlook on life seemed to dovetail without any seams showing. He had every quality she loved in a man, and at the end of each outing she couldn't wait to see him again. The attraction between them was very strong and if this was love then she didn't allow herself to admit it; he was a married man and she would never let herself be the cause of a breakdown in anyone's marriage.

One day they were returning from another walk and

were a short distance from the camp when Jack led her towards a large oak tree. He turned her to face him. There was an expression on his face Annie had never seen before and it took her breath away. This was not the warm, affectionate Jack Graham she had come to know; it was as if he'd switched something off inside himself. But one thing she was sure of, he was about to tell her something she didn't want to hear.

'Annie, I won't be able to see you again, I'm going away.'

'Oh.' Dismay ran through her. She didn't want to lose him, even if they did have to keep a tight rein on their feelings for each other. It wasn't easy, of course . . . If only he wasn't married! 'Are you being posted somewhere else?'

He nodded.

'Then we can keep in touch,' she suggested.

'I'm sorry but I won't be able to do that.'

She looked away from his face, sad that he was ending their time together like this. They got on so well and she would never have made any demands on him.

He kissed her gently on the lips. 'I would stay here for ever with you if I could but I have to go away. I shall be leaving tonight. I'll write if I can, but I can't promise anything.'

'I'm going to miss you, Jack.' It was difficult to keep her voice steady; this had come as a shock. He hadn't given the slightest hint that he was being moved and she was upset that he hadn't mentioned it before. 'Will you be coming back here after this posting?'

'Not before you've been sent somewhere else.' He brought her fingers up to his lips and kissed each one in turn. 'Thank you for this lovely couple of weeks; it has meant a great deal to me.'

She hugged him and knew that he was saying goodbye. That realization hurt very much, but she wasn't going to make a fuss, even if she couldn't understand why this sounded so final. When she was moved to another post he would still be able to contact her, surely? But from the shuttered expression on his face she knew he was cutting her out of his life.

'I hope we meet again.' Annie struggled to keep her tone bright.

He didn't comment on that. 'You take care of yourself, Annie Webster. You are a very special person.'

Then he turned and strode away, walking out of her life, she was sure.

6

August 1940

The need to refuel and rearm was urgent. Reid had already stayed up longer than he should have done, but the fight had been desperate so he'd left it to the very last minute before breaking off. Now he had to get down, and quickly. He cast an anxious glance at his gauges and put the Spitfire into a steep dive. He was close to Biggin Hill and headed for that, determined to make the airfield. He didn't want to land in some farmer's field as that would put his plane out of the fight and every single aircraft was badly needed.

He made it and the plane spluttered her way towards the hangars. 'Can you refuel and rearm her?' he asked, as he hauled himself out of the cockpit.

The ground crew sprang into action just as a truck skidded to a halt beside him.

'Hop in, sir. I'll take you to the mess so you can get a cuppa.'

'Thanks.' Reid got in and the driver hurtled towards a group of buildings at great speed. 'My brother's stationed here,' he told the sergeant, hanging on grimly and wondering if this was a frustrated would-be fighter pilot. 'I'm hoping I'll be able to see him.'

'Ah, well, they're all up, sir. It's a busy day.' He cast a quick sideways glance towards Reid, 'Not that I need to tell you that. It's turning out to be a bugger of an August, isn't it?'

'It certainly is.' He couldn't argue with that! By nightfall each day he was surprised to be still alive.

'Here you are, sir.' The airman disgorged his passenger and sped off in a cloud of dust.

Reid got himself a mug of tea, then wandered outside where there was an assortment of chairs. He sat down, closed his eyes and turned his face to the warm summer sun. Over the last few weeks he had learned to grab any quiet moment for a catnap, but any call to scramble and he was instantly awake and alert. He'd always been good at athletics during his days at university but he was sure his sprinting speed had improved lately.

The sound of aircraft had him on his feet and scanning the sky. Hurricanes and Spitfires were returning, and he watched each pilot as he jumped out of the plane. Then he saw Paul and, smiling, went to meet him.

'Reid!' He greeted his brother with enthusiasm. 'What are you doing here?'

'Ran out of fuel and ammo.'

'Well, we've chased them off for a while; so let me report in and then we'll get something to eat. I'm starving.'

Reid laughed. 'You always are. I'll wait inside for you.'

Fifteen minutes later they were both tucking into a large plate of sausage and mash. The wartime sausages had more bread in them than anything else, and just for a moment Reid remembered the succulent bangers his mother used to cook for them, but immediately dismissed the mouth-watering thought.

541

The brothers were ravenous after their time in the air and finished their meal in silence.

'Have you managed to get that girl of yours to agree to marry you?' Reid asked as they enjoyed a cup of tea after their meal.

Paul stirred another spoon of sugar into his tea and then smiled at his brother. 'No, she's busy training as a wireless operator and we are forever chasing the Luftwaffe, but I talk to her on the phone now and again.'

Reid studied his brother intently. Paul seemed to have a strange relationship with this girl and he hadn't been able to work it out yet. 'Have you changed your mind?'

'No, I'll never do that. I love her very much, but she's a very kind person, Reid, and I could probably persuade her to marry me, given the circumstances we find ourselves in, but it wouldn't be right to put that kind of pressure on her.' He sat back and sighed. 'And anyway, I wouldn't like to make her a widow so young.'

Reid didn't like to hear his brother voice his fear of leaving Annie a widow if they married, though he knew every pilot wondered if they were going to survive this fight. Of course they all believed it wouldn't happen to them but reality had a knack of creeping under your mental guard now and again.

'She's always been honest with me, and I know she doesn't love me the way I do her, but I can't seem to let her go.' Paul grimaced. 'I keep hoping she will change her mind but I know it's a forlorn hope.'

'I should leave it until the war's over; she might feel differently by then. This isn't the time to make serious commitments, just keep in touch and enjoy the friendship,' Reid told him.

'Sound advice as usual, Reid, and I do know a very accommodating girl in the village, so I'm not being deprived of comfort.' He winked at his brother then became serious again. 'But it's Annie I want for my wife, and always will.'

'Squadron Leader?' A WAAF was standing beside their table. 'Your plane's ready for you now.'

Reid hauled himself to his feet. Paul walked out with him, and when they reached his plane Reid clasped his brother to him for a brief moment. How he wished this brother of his hadn't followed in his footsteps and become a pilot, but there was no point in agonizing over it now. It was done and they had to make the best of things. 'Take care, and watch your tail, Paul.'

'And you do the same.'

Reid slid into the cockpit. He was glad he'd landed here, it had given him a chance to see Paul and get some idea of how he was coping, but he clearly hadn't needed to worry – his brother was handling the situation very well by the look of him.

'Hey!' Paul called. 'That's the first time you haven't called me "little brother".'

'Doesn't apply any more. All I can see is a man.' With a last wave to his proud-looking brother, Reid took off.

Annie put the last stitch in the badge and examined it with pride. She was now a fully trained wireless operator. It had been six months of hard and intensive training but she'd come through and was now qualified to start doing some proper work. When Jack had picked her out for this work August had seemed a long way off, but the time had flown by. The thought of Jack Graham caused the usual pain. Where was he now; what was he doing? How she would love to let him see that she hadn't let him down . . .

Dora came in and threw her bag on the floor and admired the badge. 'Very impressive. You ready? Don't want to miss our train.'

Annie grinned at her friend who was having a job to contain her excitement. She had been talking for days about going home with her.

'You sure your family won't mind me coming?' Dora looked uncertain.

'Of course they won't. We've got plenty of spare room now the boys are away.'

They managed to get a lift to the station and were soon on the train heading home. Annie's sigh was one of contentment. It was heaven to get away for a while and just relax.

'You heard anything from Sir?' Dora asked when they were settled in their seats.

'Not a word.'

'That's not very kind. You'd think he could write.'

Annie shrugged, trying to make light of her disappointment. 'Well, I don't suppose I'll hear from him again. It was just a pleasant interlude for him, I expect.'

'Men!'

'One of these days you're going to meet a man who will knock you sideways, and you won't have a cynical thought in your head,' Annie told her with a grin.

'Huh! That'll be the day.'

When they reached the station there was an RAF lorry outside, and with very little persuasion they managed to get a lift to Annie's house. The vehicle was crowded, and they laughed all the way to Roehampton. The men were discussing William Joyce, or Lord Haw-Haw as he'd been nicknamed. His broadcasts beginning with 'Germany calling, Germany calling' were the cause of much hilarity. Although a lot of the information was accurate, much of it was absolute nonsense, and his upper-class British accent made him sound ridiculous.

After waving goodbye to the truckload of airmen, and knowing where everyone would be, Annie took Dora round the back and into the kitchen.

'Annie,' her mother said in delight. 'What a lovely surprise.'

'Hello, Mum, I hope you don't mind but I've brought Dora home with me.'

Marj smiled at the girl standing uncertainly in the doorway. 'You're very welcome, Dora. Come on in, and I'll make us all a nice cup of tea. Wally's out with his Home Guard lot, but should be back soon.'

'I'm already here.' Wally gave Annie a hug. 'Oh, it's good to see you, the house seems empty these days.'

She kissed his cheek. 'Well, I've brought someone with me this time. Dora, this is Wally, my stepfather.'

'And I'm her brother,' said another voice from behind her.

Annie spun round and squeaked in delight. 'Will, I didn't know you were home.'

'Arrived yesterday. Aren't you going to introduce me to your friend?'

'Sorry. Dora, this is my brother Will.'

'I'm pleased to meet you, Dora. Are you girls staying long?'

'Three days,' Annie told him.

'Good. Don't arrange anything for tomorrow night, we can all go dancing in Richmond.'

When they were settled down with cups of Marj's famous tea in front of them, Annie studied her brother. He really was a very attractive man, and he looked smashing in his navy uniform. She also noticed Dora gazing at him with a very interested expression on her face.

After spending some time swapping stories about their service experiences, Will glanced at his watch and stood up. 'I've got to go, I'm meeting some mates at four.'

When he'd gone, Marj said, 'Dora can share your room. I keep the beds made up in case any of you turn up unexpectedly.'

'Thanks, Mum. Come on, Dora, we can stow our gear later. I'll take you to meet Rose.'

Annie opened the kitchen door of Rose's house and found her in a tussle with her daughter. It wasn't unusual, as Kate had a stubborn streak and mother and daughter often clashed.

'You'll do as you're told, my girl.'

'Won't go!'

Rose sighed and looked up. 'Come in, Annie.'

'This is Dora,' she introduced.

'Hello, Dora, welcome to bedlam.'

'What's all this about?' Annie asked her sister.

'I want Kate and James to go and stay with Dad in Wales. James is happy enough, but this little miss refuses to leave home.'

'Why?' Annie asked the little girl. 'You like Grandpa George, don't you?'

Kate nodded and a large tear trickled down her chin.

546

'I can't go. What if Daddy comes home and I'm not here? I'll never see him!'

'I've told you umpteen times that we'll come to Wales.' Rose was clearly exasperated.

'No, you won't.' Kate hiccuped and wailed in earnest. 'Daddy's gone away. I don't want him gone away. He don't love me any more.'

'Oh, that isn't true.' Dora was on her knees in front of the distraught child. 'How could he not love a beautiful daughter like you?'

Kate hiccuped again and stared at her with interest. 'Why's he gone away, then?'

'There's a nasty man who wants to come and take over our country,' Dora explained, wiping Kate's tears with her own hanky. 'Your daddy's gone to stop him.'

Kate thought about this for a while, and then gave a watery smile. 'He'll do it.'

'Of course he will.'

'Can't go away, though.' Kate obviously wasn't going to give way on this important point and her mouth settled in a determined line.

'Why not, sweetheart?' George Gresham strolled in and tossed his bag down. 'I've just come back from Wales and the house is all ready now. I've had to have a lot done to it because it's old, but everything's cosy now.'

Rose stood with her hands on her hips and sighed again. 'Thank goodness you're here, Dad, try and talk some sense into her, will you?'

George sat down and pulled Kate on to his knees. 'It's a pretty house and there's a farm next door with lots of animals. It's near a place called Pontypool and we won't get any bombs there.'

Kate looked unimpressed. 'No bombs here.'

'Not yet, but they're getting terribly close, my precious, and London is bound to be attacked soon.'

'We've got a shelter in the garden. Daddy dug it,' the girl pointed out.

Rose was about to say something but George silenced her with a look.

'You and James will be much safer with me. One of the farm dogs has just had puppies. You can choose one for your own.'

This caused a spark of interest, and although the little girl was fighting it, the mention of animals was too much for her. 'How many puppies?'

'Six, and they've got two donkeys as well. The farmer's very nice and he said you can help to look after them if you want to.'

Kate shoved her thumb into her mouth and sucked on it thoughtfully.

Annie and Dora walked over to Rose, who was shaking her head in disbelief.

'My God, look at her; she's weighing the whole thing up. That girl will never make a hasty decision in her life.'

The three of them watched the scene being played out, with the little girl firmly in charge.

Kate's thumb slipped out of her mouth and she looked up at her grandfather. 'What colour are these puppies?'

'Black and white, they're sheepdogs.'

'Hmm.' The thumb shot back and two feet waved about in concentration. 'You got pussy cats, as well?'

'Yes, one, and she likes to sit on my lap in the evening.'

The little girl screwed her face up as she imagined

548

that, and ran her hand over her knees as if there was an imaginary cat there.

'Come on, Kate,' Rose muttered. 'You're not going to get a better offer than that.'

The girl had now moved her hand away from her mouth and was studying the sucked thumb carefully. 'My Daddy won't be able to find me.'

'Yes, he will, sweetheart, he came with me when I bought the house. We got it so that you could come and live there with me and be safe from the bombs.'

Annie watched George with great interest. He was not a man known for his tolerance, but he showed infinite patience with the children. He loved them very much and nothing was too much trouble where they were concerned.

'Hmm.' Kate squirmed around and looked at her mother. 'You bring Daddy to see me?'

'I promise, Kate.'

She wriggled back and looked at her grandpa. 'Can I choose my own puppy?'

George nodded, struggling to hide a smile of triumph.

'All right,' she said on a sigh, 'I'll go,' then slid down and trotted out into the garden, leaving them all convulsed with laughter.

'I hope you can deliver on your promises, Dad,' Rose exclaimed, 'because if you can't she'll have you bringing her back straight away.'

George chuckled proudly. 'I know my granddaughter, Rose, she'll remember every word of that conversation and check it all out before she even unpacks her bag.'

'Dora,' Rose said, 'thank you for talking to Kate like

549

that. She idolizes her father and just can't understand why he isn't here.'

'Oh, I love kids, and she's adorable. She's got your lovely black hair, and those huge brown eyes . . .' Dora chortled. 'What a beauty she's going to be.'

Suddenly there was a loud squeal and they all rushed into the garden. Rose was running to the side gate where Kate was frantically pounding on it with her small hands and trying to climb over the securely locked gate. There was a tall sailor there in a captain's uniform. Bill!

Annie watched as Bill plucked his daughter off the gate and comforted her as she cried for joy on his shoulder. She blew her brother-in-law a kiss and told him she'd see him later, then turned to Dora. 'We'll leave them alone for a while.'

'Wow,' Dora exclaimed, when they were in Annie's bedroom. 'This is some family you've got here.'

'Special, eh?'

'I'll say! And I know you said that Sir reminds you of your brother-in-law, but' – she gave Annie a wide-eyed look – 'that man over there is stunning. No wonder Kate adores him.'

'We all do, and if anything happens to him this family will be devastated.'

Dora nodded, then smiled sheepishly. 'I pray every night that all my friends and family will survive this mess. I'll add yours to the list if you like?'

'Thanks, Dora.' Annie's respect for her was growing all the time. There was a lot more to her than the brash, worldly wise girl you saw on the surface. She was beginning to suspect that that was only a front. 'What did you think of Rose?'

550

'She's wonderful, and so beautiful. I never expected her to look like that.' Dora hesitated. 'There's something I don't understand, though. Rose called George, father, but didn't your dad die in the last war?'

'Yes, but he wasn't Rose's father. That's why she's so dark and me and my brothers are fair.' The contrast in their colouring was always being talked about, but when you saw Rose and George together there could be no doubt whose daughter she was.

'Your mother was married to George?' Dora looked puzzled.

'No. Mum was seduced when she was in service with the Greshams and so Rose is Sir George's daughter.'

'Sir George?' Dora asked, her eyes wide with astonishment.

'That's right. It was a stormy relationship, but they eventually became friends. It's a long story and when we've got a week to spare I'll tell you all about it.'

'But doesn't your mother mind him being part of the family now?' Dora was still having trouble grasping the situation.

'No, once she was happily married to Wally and George apologized for his disgraceful conduct towards her – he blamed it on his wild youth – she forgave him. They made their peace with each other a long time ago, and Rose is his pride and joy. He hasn't any other family so he's become a loved member of ours.'

Dora gazed at her friend in wonder. 'Doesn't Wally object to him being here?'

Annie smiled at the thought of her stepfather being angry about anything. 'He's accepted the situation and he really likes George. There isn't any conflict or jealousy between them.'

'My God, what a family!'

'And you haven't met all of them, yet,' Annie pointed out, laughing.

7

Annie was getting ready to go dancing with Will and Dora when Marj called up the stairs that there was someone to see her.

Annie was surprised to see Paul. 'Have you managed to get some time off?'

He kissed her gently and shook his head. 'No, I'm on stand-down for a few hours, that's all. When I phoned I was told you were on leave, so I came on the off-chance that we could spend a little time together.'

At that moment Will and Dora came into the room wearing their best uniforms.

'Paul, it's good to see you.' Will shook his hand and Annie introduced Dora.

'Ah.' Paul looked crestfallen. 'You look as if you're all going out.'

'Dancing,' Will told him. 'Why don't you come with us?'

'Well, I was hoping for some time alone with Annie,' he admitted.

Annie had been looking forward to going out with her brother and Dora, but Paul had driven to see her when he could have been resting, and he appeared strained. She didn't hesitate. 'We'll go for a quiet drink somewhere, shall we?'

Paul smiled happily at her. 'That would be lovely.'

553

'Do you mind if I don't come dancing?' she asked her friend.

'Of course I don't, I'm sure I'll be safe with Will.' Dora cast him an amused look.

'I can't promise that,' he joked, 'but we'll have a good time.'

Dora slipped her hand through his arm and raised her eyebrows. 'What more can I ask?'

Then, both laughing, they left.

'They look happy together,' Paul remarked.

'Yes, they do, don't they? Now, where do you want to go?'

'The nearest pub is only a couple of miles down the road, so we'll go there.' He held the door open for her. 'I've borrowed a car from another pilot because I haven't got much time.'

The pub was busy when they arrived so they went into the saloon bar where it was less crowded. Paul bought them both a half pint of beer then sat back, closing his eyes for a brief moment before opening them again and smiling affectionately at her.

'This is nice.' He reached out and took her hand in his. 'You look lovely in your uniform, Annie, and I hope I haven't spoilt your evening by turning up like this?'

'You haven't.' She squeezed his hand; she was glad he'd come tonight. He really did looked drained and a few hours relaxing and talking would do him good. 'I'm very pleased to see you.'

'I'm sorry it can't be for longer.' He consulted his watch. 'I'll have to leave in about three hours, I'm afraid. It seems they can't do without me,' he joked.

She was dismayed. On the surface Paul looked the

same as always but there was something different about him, and she couldn't work out what it was. Then, when she looked deep into his eyes, she knew – he had grown up. But dear Lord, what a way to do it. Dunkirk was behind them, and the pilots were now fighting fiercely to stop the Luftwaffe from gaining superiority in the air. It was a desperate battle with these tired, overstretched men in the air from dawn until dusk. The responsibility on them was enormous, because they knew, only too well, that if they failed then the Germans would be pouring across the Channel. She was sure each pilot was fully aware of the awesome task, and she often wondered how they felt each time they took to the air, knowing that it could be the end of their lives. Paul never mentioned it and nor, she suspected, did the others, but each one of them must have their own inner battle to win.

'I'm glad you came,' she told him brightly, and knew that if he asked her to marry him again she would agree this time. She was aware that couples were falling into hasty marriages; with the future so uncertain people were grabbing at happiness with little thought of the consequences. She had vowed not to do that but . . .

'So am I. Now, do you think the landlord would rustle us up something to eat. I'm starving.'

'You always are,' she teased, glad to see the boyish grin back in place.

'That's what Reid says.'

'How is your brother?' she asked. She guessed he was still alive because Paul would have told her immediately if anything had happened to him.

'He's a squadron leader now,' he told her with pride, 'and gaining quite a reputation as an ace.'

'I expect you both are.' She put her head on one side and looked at him. 'With both Lascells brothers in the fight, I shouldn't think Hitler stands a chance.'

'He doesn't. Believe me, we won't let him win.'

A man with a mission, Annie thought, as she watched him walk over to the bar. There had been a look of cold determination in his eyes, and she guessed that all the fighter pilots were like that.

When he returned, she launched into a few funny stories about the girls, and a while later the landlady put two steaming plates of food in front of them.

'My goodness,' Annie exclaimed. 'How did you manage that?'

The landlady smiled. 'You'll find more veg than meat in the pie but it's tasty and filling.'

Paul picked up his knife and fork. 'It looks smashing.'

'Well, nothing's too good for our pilots.' The woman patted his shoulder affectionately, and then walked away.

Paul looked up and winked at Annie. 'Wear a pair of wings and you can get almost anything.'

She laughed at his expression. 'And I see you're not too proud to take advantage of that.'

'Of course not; just lately we've hardly had time to grab a sandwich, so this is a real treat.'

After they had cleared their plates, Paul sat back and gave a contented smile. 'It's lovely to be able to relax like this, even if it is only for a few hours. Do you know where you're going now you've finished your training?'

'Yes, I have been told.'

'Can you tell me where?'

'No, but send your letters to Compton Bassett as usual

and they will reach me. I'll get out and phone you as soon as I can.'

'I hope it isn't in London.'

'It's near Stoke-on-Trent, and that's all I'm allowed to say.'

'Ah, Cheadle, the RAF intercept station.' He gave a knowing wink and laughed when Annie grimaced.

'It's supposed to be a secret place,' she told him, glancing round to make sure no one had heard them.

He laughed again. 'Annie, we're pilots and there isn't much we don't know.'

'Paul, you're in the front line,' she said, changing the subject, 'so how bad do you think things are going to get?'

'Very bad, Annie.' He took her hand in his again, his face suddenly serious. 'The Luftwaffe expected to break us in a few weeks after Dunkirk, but they haven't managed to do it. We think it won't be long before he starts to attack civilian targets, especially London, in an effort to demoralize the population.'

'He won't do that.' Annie spoke with conviction. 'No matter what he throws at us, I can't see anyone – man or woman – allowing the Germans to take over our country. They'll have to get past the Home Guard first.' A smile flashed across her face as she remembered some of the hilarious tales Wally had told them.

Paul chuckled. 'Don't put the Home Guard down, Annie. They're doing a grand job picking up German pilots who have been shot down. They even charged up to one of my mates as he parachuted down and tried to arrest him.'

'What happened?'

'Once they knew who he was they insisted on taking him back to the airfield, after he'd been escorted to the pub for a pint of beer first.'

'Oh, I can just picture the scene,' she said laughing.

At that moment a crowd of soldiers came into the saloon bar, putting an end to their quiet chat.

Paul glanced at his watch. 'I'd better make a move. Come on, my darling, I'll take you home.'

They were quiet on their way back. Paul didn't seem to want to talk any more and she left him in peace. He stopped outside her house and walked her to the door. 'I won't come in, Annie; I've got to get back. I shall be flying again at dawn.'

'You take care,' she told him gently.

'I will.' He turned her face up so he could gaze into her eyes. 'Hey! Don't look so glum. I know our survival rate isn't too hot but I'm an experienced pilot and that increases my chances.'

His kiss was nothing like the ones he had given her in the past; this one was full of passion, love and need, and she gasped when he pulled away.

'I expect you're wondering why I haven't asked you to marry me,' he joked.

She put her head on one side. 'You've changed your mind?'

'No, I'll never do that, but this is not the time.' He held her away from him. 'But as soon as this bloody war's over, I'm not going to take no for an answer. Is that clear?'

Annie saluted smartly. 'Yes, sir!'

'Good.' He kissed her again, then turned on his heel and walked away.

There wasn't anyone around when she went indoors, and she guessed that they were all with Rose and Bill. It was eleven o'clock and she was tired, so she went to bed. Her mind went over every moment of her evening with Paul. He wasn't the same person who had first joined up, and she liked this more mature man. But liking wasn't love! She sighed deeply and drifted off to sleep.

It was about one in the morning when Annie was woken by a giggle and some whispering going on outside her door. She smiled to herself; it sounded as if Will and Dora had enjoyed themselves. Will was tall and slim and he looked really good in his bell-bottom trousers; she knew her friend had noticed that as well. She was just dozing off again when there was a gentle knock on her door and it opened a crack.

'Annie, are you awake?'

'Of course.' She sat up and blinked when the light went on, and her friend came and sat on the other bed. 'Did you have a good time?' she asked, plumping up a pillow behind her so she could sit up.

'Smashing. How did your evening go with Paul?'

'Very enjoyable.'

'Did he ask you to marry him again?' Dora asked.

'No, he said he wouldn't until the war is over, but do you know, Dora, if he had asked me tonight I would have accepted.' Annie sighed. 'But I'm glad he didn't because it wouldn't have been right. He's such a nice man but I don't feel any passion for him.' Annie rubbed her temple. 'I wish I could feel more, I would love to make him happy.'

'Why didn't you just go to bed with him, then? I'm sure that would have made him happy.'

'He didn't have time, but I think I would even have done that tonight if he'd asked.' Annie laid her head back and closed her eyes. 'I'm confused. This flaming war has a lot to answer for.'

'I know this is none of my business, and you can tell me to sod off, but have you ever slept with him?' Dora raised an eyebrow in query.

'No.'

'Anyone?'

'No.'

'Ah, just as I always thought, an innocent babe.'

Annie sat up. 'How many have you been to bed with?'

'Only one, and don't look so surprised. I might be a flirt but that doesn't mean they get more than a goodnight kiss. Well, not much more. If the groping gets out of hand, I put a stop to it.'

'Did Will's groping get too urgent?' Annie asked with a grin.

'You can mind your own bloody business, that's between me and Will.' Dora rolled her eyes and began to undress for the night.

Annie held her hands up in mock surrender. 'All right, tell me what happened to your boyfriend. Do you still see him?'

'No, he got killed in an accident at the docks before the war started.'

'Oh, I'm so sorry.'

'Yes, it was a shame. We'd known each other since kids and it was taken for granted that we'd marry some day.' Dora slipped into her bed. 'It was a long time ago. Now, I'd better let you get some sleep.'

'Night.' Dora's hand hovered on the bedside light

before switching it off. 'Er . . . Annie, Will's asked me to write to him; do you mind?'

'Of course I don't, I think that's lovely. You seem to get on well together.'

'We do. Thanks, Annie.'

After their leave Annie and Dora returned to camp. It was two days later when Annie collected the details of her new posting and went in search of Dora to say goodbye. They were both sad to be splitting up again, but this was a fact of war.

Annie hugged Dora. 'You keep in touch now, and behave yourself.'

'I'll write every week, but I'm not sure about behaving myself,' her friend joked. 'Without your steadying influence, there's no telling what I'll get up to.'

'It's been fun,' Annie told her, 'and I really hope we'll meet up again at some time in the future.'

'Bound to, you're not getting rid of me that easy.'

They hugged each other again and Annie headed back to her hut, packed her bag and hitched a lift to the railway station. All she knew was that she had to go to Stoke-on-Trent, where someone would be waiting to take her to her new posting in Cheadle.

She had plenty of time to think during the journey and was excited at the prospect of doing the work for real, but also apprehensive, hoping she was good enough. Six months had been a very short time to learn everything about being a wireless operator, and mastering Morse code, and she hoped she wouldn't make any blunders. It was going to be strange not having Dora around, but she'd soon make friends with the girls already at Cheadle.

And there was another good thing about her posting; the journey from Cheadle to Wales should be fairly easy. She hadn't seen the house yet, but it sounded cosy.

As promised there was a truck waiting for her at the station. Annie was too excited to take much notice where they were going but she'd studied a map beforehand and she knew there was moorland not far away. As she loved walking there would be plenty of interesting places to discover in her spare time. Papers were checked as they arrived at the camp, and she was escorted to a hut. She unpacked her bag and looked around. It was rather spartan like most of the billets but it would be comfortable enough.

She had stowed away her things in a tall cupboard by the bed, and was wondering what she should do next when a pretty WAAF walked into the hut, checked Annie's badge, and held her hand out.

'I'm Jean. Welcome to Cheadle Intercept Station. If you're ready, I'll take you to the ops room. I've been ordered to take you there as soon as you arrive.' Jean gave Annie a curious look. 'They've been waiting for you. Are you someone special?'

'Me?' Annie was surprised. 'You must be mistaken.'

'No, they've been anxious for you to get here.' Jean led her to the operations room and Annie gazed around wide-eyed with excitement. It was a large room and filled with men and women, headphones clamped over their ears. No one looked up as Annie came in; they were all concentrating on the job they were doing. The officer-in-charge introduced himself as Group Captain Jones, and then led Annie to an empty place.

She looked up at him, awaiting instructions.

'Each day you will be given a certain frequency to work on.' He wrote something down on the pad in front of her. 'This is yours for today. Take down any Morse code messages you hear, then ring the bell and someone will take it from you to be deciphered.'

She took a deep breath. 'I understand, sir.'

He held out the headset to her. 'We have received good reports about your abilities, and I hope to God that's correct because we badly need you.'

'I won't let you down,' she said quietly. Praying that she was right to sound so confident. This was her first time doing the job for real; her heart was fluttering badly. She told herself that she must remember her training and concentrate as hard as she could.

He nodded grimly and strode away.

It wasn't until Annie was relieved four hours later that she realized just how hungry she was. She took the headphones off and smiled, feeling elated. She had managed to pick up several messages. She had no idea what was in them, of course, as everything was in code, but it was interesting work, and there was always the excitement of wondering if it was something really important.

Jean was waiting outside the door for her. 'I'll take you to the mess.'

'Thanks.' Annie smiled at the girl. 'Are you a wireless operator as well?'

'No,' she said and laughed. 'I'm not clever enough for that; my job's in the office and running errands.'

Annie fell into step beside her. 'Do you know a cipher officer by the name of Graham?'

Jean shook her head. 'The name's familiar, but I don't think he's here.'

Annie was disappointed; she had thought there was a good chance of Jack being stationed here, and she would love to see him again. She'd missed him dreadfully; the fact that she hadn't had a letter or phone call from him had been upsetting. He'd said he wouldn't be able to contact her, but that was hard to believe. It was obvious that he had cut her out of his life, and that hurt.

'Hello, Sam,' Jean said, as they sat opposite him. 'This is Annie, and she's asking about a cipher officer called Graham.'

Sam shook hands with her. He was a striking-looking man; around thirty or more, she guessed. His hair was a sandy colour and eyes a deep grey.

'What's his first name?'

'Jack, Jack Graham.'

His gaze held hers but it was hooded, blank. 'Sorry, never heard of him.'

He was lying, but why? However, a lot of these people were engaged in very secret work, so she didn't probe any further. She knew there was another place called Bletchley because they'd considered sending her there, but changed their minds at the last minute. She'd heard it referred to as Station X. Very cryptic, but Jack was most likely there.

'Never mind.' She smiled. 'He recruited me, that's all, and I thought he might be here.'

'She's special.' Jean winked at Sam. 'They've been on tenterhooks waiting for her to arrive.'

Sam's cup clattered back into the saucer and he

straightened up. 'Of course, you must be Ann Webster, I should have realized . . .'

'I wish someone would tell me what this is all about.' She was becoming rattled by now. What was going on?

The man on the other side of the table studied her intently, and then gave a very slight shake of his head. 'You look too delicate – '

'I'm stronger than I look, but what's that got to do with my job? And you haven't answered my question.' She understood the need for secrecy but someone should tell her what this was all about!

'Ah, yes, why have we been waiting for you? Well, the answer to that is simple. You speak French and German, and you are a good operator; we are short of people with your qualifications. We are delighted to have you here, Ann Webster.' He smiled, stood up and walked away, effectively putting an end to the conversation.

Annie watched him in disbelief. The man wasn't telling the truth, of that she was sure. However, half an hour later she was back on duty with no time to ponder the mystery, and it was midnight before she finished. They were on eight-hour shifts and they'd put her to work as soon as she'd arrived, not giving her a chance to settle in. Good job Jean had been there to show her around or she would have been wandering about lost. As she crawled into bed she was exhausted but quite pleased with herself. She felt as if she was doing something positive at last.

Her mind raced around for a while, denying her much needed sleep, but eventually she began to relax, listening to the other nine girls in the hut fidgeting. One right down the other end was snoring, but the sounds didn't disturb her. It was surprising how quickly she had become used to sharing a barren hut with lots of girls she'd never met before. She often remembered the fun they'd had on their first day in the WAAF when she had met Dora. What a good friend she had turned out to be.

As she drifted off to sleep, her thoughts lingered on her family, as they always did at the end of each day, and she prayed silently for Bill, Charlie, Will, Paul and all the pilots, not forgetting every other member of her family. Her loved ones were scattered around fighting for their freedom. It was clear now that Germany hadn't invaded because they were trying to destroy the air defences first. If they succeeded then God knows what awaited this country and its people.

In the seconds before sleep claimed her she thought about the man she'd met today. He was strange and she had been shocked when Jean had spoken to him in that casual way. You salute a group captain, not plonk yourself down at his table and call him Sam! It was unbelievable, but he hadn't seemed at all perturbed. He was clearly right when he'd told her they needed operators, so perhaps she had made more of their conversation than she should have.

She smiled to herself as she remembered her silly suspicions. Sam, whoever he was, had no reason to lie to her.

8

'Look at that, do you see them?'

'There's hundreds of the sods!'

'I see them,' Reid said, estimating that they were outnumbered by at least ten to one, and there wasn't anything in the manual to cover this situation.

Someone gave a tight laugh. 'Where do we start?'

Reid took a deep breath. Oh what the hell! 'They're all yours, lads,' he called, then shot through the middle of the formation, firing all the time. He hit one Dornier, then banked, missing another by feet, and hurtled out the other side. Turning, he saw one going down, two more on fire, and a Spitfire with smoke pouring out of it; the pilot was already floating down. The planes of his squadron were buzzing in and out of the German bombers like pesky flies; ones with a deadly sting.

It was a wild battle, the third one that day. Reid, like the rest of his squadron, was numb with fatigue but determined to inflict as much damage as they could, whatever the cost.

His ground crew were waiting for him as usual when he landed, and set to work immediately to get the Spitfire ready to fly again.

Reid watched the planes straggle back. One was coming in without the undercarriage down, and a gaping hole in the fuselage. It shaved the trees, leapfrogged over a fuel truck and hit the field, tearing along sideways. He jumped on to a lorry heading for the plane. When they reached it he leapt on the wing before it had even stopped. Another man joined him and they wrenched open the canopy, dragging the pilot free.

Reid swore fluently. 'Bouncer! I might have known it was you.'

His friend grinned. 'Wow! That was what you'd call a bumpy landing,' he exclaimed, wiping oil and dirt from his streaked face.

'You crazy bastard, why didn't you bail out?'

'Wanted to save something of the plane if I could.' He pointed to the fitters now swarming over it. 'See, they're already after it for spares.'

'You're more valuable than a few spare parts,' he exploded.

'That's jolly decent of you to say so, Reid, but you know how I feel about throwing myself out of a plane with only a scrap of silk between me and the ground.' He shuddered.

'You're going to get yourself killed one day,' Reid muttered.

Bouncer shrugged and looked totally unconcerned. 'If Jerry keeps this up for too long, I think we all will.'

Someone shouted and Reid looked up to see one plane coming in on fire, and they watched helplessly as it exploded before it hit the ground. Neither man said anything; they would find out soon enough who it had been. There was now another gap in their ranks, and another family to mourn the loss of a son or husband. Dear God, he prayed, please don't let this misery be in vain. Make something good come out of the sacrifices.

They hardly had time to grab a cup of tea before they

were scrambled again. Two hours later, Reid slumped on his bed.

'I've brought you a sandwich and a mug of tea, sir.' The orderly was standing beside the bed.

'Put it on the table,' he muttered, and closed his eyes.

'Take your boots off, sir. You'll be more comfortable.'

'Might have to scramble again.'

'That's unlikely, sir. It's nine o'clock and the light's failing.'

'Good Lord, is it?' Reid opened one eye. 'What's the date today?'

'August 15th, sir.'

'Ah, one to remember, eh?' Then he was asleep.

Annie stepped out into the night air and took a deep breath.

'Hard day?' asked someone beside her.

She started. 'Oh, I didn't see you there, Sam?'

'Just come out for a breath myself.'

'I've been so busy I haven't heard any news today, though I know something has been going on.' The airwaves had been buzzing all day. 'Do you have any details?'

'Jerry's been coming over in waves, but he's suffered heavy losses.'

'What about us?' she asked anxiously.

'Quite a few fighters have been shot down. I don't have the exact figure yet, but it isn't nearly as bad as the Germans. So they tell us.' Sam sounded sceptical.

Annie's insides tightened at this news. Everyone was doubtful about the figures announced every night on the nine o'clock news. Our losses were always less than the Germans, but how accurate were they? 'I've got a friend who's a fighter pilot,' she told him. 'I hope he's all right.'

'What's his name and where is he stationed?'

'Pilot Officer Paul Lascells, and he's stationed at Biggin Hill.'

Sam ground out his cigarette with the toe of his shoe. 'Stay here, I'll go and see what I can find out. Won't be long.'

As he disappeared back inside she couldn't help wondering, once again, who this man was? He was clearly a man with secrets, and expert at keeping them. He had a quiet air of authority about him and he was indeed an officer. But she hadn't found out what he did or how he fitted into the set-up here. His attitude to everyone was very informal and friendly.

He soon returned, but didn't speak until he had lit another fag, then he drew deeply on it and smiled at her. 'You can stop worrying; he's all right.'

'Thank heavens for that!' She felt herself relax. 'Thank you for checking.'

'No trouble.' He gave her a studied look, his eyes glinting in the gloom. 'Means a lot to you, does he?'

'Yes, I've known him a long time and he's a nice man.'

'Nice? That doesn't sound like a lover talking.'

'We're friends, Sam,' she said, surprised. It wasn't like him to start asking personal questions.

'Ah, no big romance, then?'

'Not on my part.' Annie tried to see his expression but his face was in shadow, and his voice gave nothing away. The questions were being thrown at her in a casual way, but she had the feeling that this wasn't idle conversation.

In fact, she was certain that Sam never did or said anything unless he had a good reason for it.

He nodded as if satisfied with her answer. 'I was told there are two Lascellses, and one is a squadron leader.'

'That's Paul's elder brother, Reid. Is he all right?' she asked quickly, feeling guilty for not enquiring about him sooner. She didn't know him but he was loved and respected by Paul.

'Yes, he's survived this day as well, but they've had a tough time, and I fear this is only the build up for a more intensified attack on the country.'

'A prelude to invasion?' she asked.

'Hard to say, but if the air force can hold out . . .' He shrugged. 'Who knows?'

'And can they, do you think?' She didn't know why but she felt she could talk to Sam; the fact that he was an officer didn't seem to matter. She wouldn't dream of being this familiar with any of the others, men or women. This man was an enigma and she was deeply curious about him.

He drew on his cigarette again, watching the smoke curling past his face. 'I believe they can if this kind of intensive attack doesn't last too long.'

Annie's heart reached out to all the pilots. They were in a frantic fight but they were giving the army time to regroup and rearm after Dunkirk. All the heavy equipment had been left behind on the beaches. All that stood between this country and the Germans were the exhausted pilots. 'They must be so weary.'

'No doubt.'

'I heard that Croydon was bombed today; is that true?'

'Yes, quite a few casualties, I believe.'

'Do you think London will be next?' It was her turn to quiz him; he was obviously well informed.

'Yes, I think it will.' Sam stubbed out his fag. 'What time are you on duty again?'

'Six hundred hours.'

'Then I suggest you grab a few hours' sleep, because I don't think any of us are going to get much rest during the next few weeks.'

Annie yawned. 'You're right. Goodnight, Sam, thank you for checking on the Lascellses for me.'

A light flared briefly as he lit another cigarette. 'Night. And by the way, you are doing a good job.'

'Thank you.' She started to walk away, then stopped and turned to face him. 'Why does everyone call you Sam?'

'That's my name.'

She gave an exasperated sigh. 'I know that, but I've never heard anyone call you sir, and yet you are an officer. And you seem to know a great deal, so just who are you?'

'No one you need be concerned about, Ann Webster. Yet.'

Information was a precious commodity, and in a quiet way the wireless operators were in the front line as well. Annie's hours on duty were long, and although she was fully aware of the seriousness of the war she was rather insulated in her operations room. There hadn't been time for leave or even a night out at the local pub. When she did finally get to leave her post all she wanted to do was sleep. She'd hardly had time to see Jean, who had become a firm friend, but they did manage to grab a meal together now and again.

Annie decided to make one more sweep of her frequency for that day when something came through her headset. It was very faint and interference from a radio station made it even more difficult, so she pressed her headset close to her ears in an effort to hear. The message started to come through but she could only get part of it. Damn!

Sitting back, she snatched off the headset and rang the bell. 'I couldn't get it all, there was too much interference,' she apologized to the officer who collected it from her, ready to be sent with the next despatch rider to the deciphering unit.

Annie put the headphones back on and settled down again, hoping she was going to be relieved soon. She was dying for a cup of tea and her ears were ringing. Even when she took the headphones off she could still hear the bleeping of Morse code in her head.

It was lunchtime the next day when Sam came and sat beside her. 'We want you to see if you can pick up another message from the sender you found last night. Do you think you can find him again?'

'Yes, if he transmits, I'm sure I can. Was it something important?'

'Maybe. We can only wait until he sends again, and then, hopefully, we can find out who it is.'

Annie knew she wouldn't be told anything else. It was frustrating not to know what the messages said when they picked them up, but everything was in code, and that was the job. 'That sounds exciting.'

'You like a bit of excitement, do you?' Sam asked.

'I've never thought about it, but I suppose I must.' She was beginning to uncover emotions in herself she hadn't known were there.

'Hmm.' Sam stood up. 'Well, you've earned a break, so do you think a meal in the mess with me would be exciting enough for the moment?'

She placed a hand over her heart. 'I don't know if I could stand that much excitement.'

'Come on then,' he chuckled, 'I'll catch you if you faint.'

'Er . . .?' She looked around for Group Captain Jones. 'I'm not sure if I can leave my post.'

'Yes, you can.' He signalled to the group captain. 'We're going to get something to eat.'

He simply nodded his agreement and went back to what he was doing.

Annie walked beside Sam, puzzled. 'You act as if you outrank the other officers.'

'Well, I don't. I have a special expertise, and can help them out quite often.'

'Can I ask what it is?'

He bent his head and whispered in her ear. 'I'm a spy.'

'Ours or theirs?' she asked drily, not believing a word he said. He was more relaxed with her now, and she felt able to joke with him.

'Ours, of course.' He looked offended, but the twitch at the corners of his mouth showed he was teasing her.

Annie searched in vain for the rest of the day but the mystery sender never came through. 'I'm sorry, Sam, I don't think he is going to transmit.'

'Never mind, you've done well. Now all we can do is leave it and hope he tries again.'

'Who do you think it was?'

He gave an expressive shrug. 'We're not sure, but we've managed to decipher a part of the message and whoever he is we need to catch him.'

She knew she couldn't ask any more questions, so she nodded and returned to her work.

It was the early hours of the 18th of August when Annie was summoned to the ops room. Sam was waiting for her, a huge smile on his face.

'We've got lucky. A concerned neighbour reported some strange sounds coming from next door, and it turned out to be our mystery sender. He was working for the Germans.'

'Oh, that's wonderful.' She was elated.

'It's even better than that. He was careless and so confident he hadn't even made an attempt to hide anything.'

Annie looked at him and laughed. 'Now I know what you do.'

'And what's that?' he asked.

'You're a spy catcher.'

'Ah, my cover has been blown,' he said in mock despair. 'Now I shall have to retire and go back to tending my chickens.'

She didn't believe him but joined in the fun anyway. 'And where are your chickens?'

'I expect the Germans have eaten them by now.'

Her mouth dropped open as realization dawned. Why hadn't she guessed?

'That's right, Ann Webster, I'm French.'

'But you haven't a trace of an accent,' she gasped, 'and you don't wear that on your uniform.'

'It's on my dress uniform only and I seldom wear that. And I speak English well because I was educated in this country,' he told her in French.

He asked her many questions about her life, making her answer him in French. He kept her there for about half an hour; she didn't mind though, he was an intriguing man to talk to. He probed deeply into her family life, but did it in such a way that she found herself answering his questions without hesitation. When she'd joined up they had been interested in her languages, but she hadn't used them at all, and that was rather disappointing. She'd had visions of being asked to translate captured German documents. She smiled inwardly at her fanciful notions.

Eventually Sam sat back and reverted to English. 'You have a slight accent but it's hardly noticeable. Where did you learn to speak so fluently?'

'I studied it hard at school, because I loved the language, and then when I went to work on a women's magazine I made friends with Chantal who came from Paris. She was the chief editor and more than ten years older than me, but we became firm friends. We used to speak French all the time we were together, and I often went home with her for my holidays.'

'What about the German?'

'That was only at school. I was lucky enough to have a teacher who took an interest in me. He said I had a natural ability with languages, and to be honest I found it quite easy and great fun.'

Sam rubbed his chin thoughtfully. 'What kind of training did you have when you joined up?'

'The usual basic training of square-bashing and PT. Why?' More questions. It was almost as if he was gradually building up a picture of her.

'I have an insatiable curiosity. Go and get some breakfast now, you're not on duty until eleven. And thank you for helping us to catch a spy.'

'I wish I could have got more of the message.'

He picked up a pile of papers and began to look through them. She had clearly been dismissed.

After she had eaten she went for a walk in the grounds. It was a beautiful day and she lifted her face to the sun, feeling its rays warm and relax her. This was just the kind of weather the Germans liked to launch an attack in; she prayed that they would stay away for a while, allowing pilots and ground crew a rest. She strode out, giving her legs a chance to stretch and move, knowing that she would be sitting at her desk for most of the day. She was enjoying this beautiful weather, but the pilots must view it with misgiving . . .

'Annie!' Jean came running towards her, puffing badly. 'I've been searching for you everywhere.'

'Why? What's the matter?' Annie asked.

'Don't know, but something's happening, and you're to report for duty immediately.'

Annie didn't even say goodbye as she started running.

9

The Kenley airfield had taken the most terrible pounding. Reid propped himself up with two hands on the tail of his Spitfire and gazed at the devastation around him. He bowed his head, took a deep breath and wondered how many of them were going to survive this day. It would surely go down as the day the Luftwaffe tried to crush their air defences once and for all.

'Don't worry, sir, we'll get her operational again.'

He dragged his eyes open and saw his ground crew were as battered as his Spitfire. Ted had a filthy bandage around his head and John could hardly walk but they were working like men possessed.

Standing up straight, he ran a shaking hand through his tangled hair. Thank God the sun was going down. If he went up one more time he would be asleep at the controls.

'The mess has been flattened,' Ted told him in a matter-of-fact tone of voice, 'but there's a mobile canteen over by the ops room. Why don't you go and get yourself a mug of hot, sweet tea, sir. We'll have her ready to go again in no time at all.'

'Thanks.' Reid picked his way through the rubble and looked at the row of bodies covered with blankets. Some were obviously female and he hoped that Paul's girl was safe somewhere. And the thing that was worrying him the most was, had his brother survived this horrendous day?

'Reid.'

He looked up and saw the station commander with two young boys, no more than nineteen or twenty, he assessed.

'Two new pilots for you, Barrett and Johnson, and we've put you all in the house just outside the gates. The accommodation took a direct hit, I'm afraid, but the people in the village are offering beds until we can sort something out.' He gave his squadron leader a sympathetic look. 'Debriefing won't take long, then go and get some rest.'

'You've had a bloody awful time down here,' Reid remarked wearily.

'Yes, but we managed to get the airfield operational again in time for you to be able to get down,' he stated proudly.

'Do you know what state Biggin Hill is in?'

'They've taken a pasting as well, but I don't have the details yet.' The officer smiled grimly. 'The Germans were attacked so fiercely by you lads that they eventually split up and ran for home.'

Reid nodded towards the destroyed hangar. 'Have we got any planes left?'

'Replacements are already on their way.'

'What about pilots?' he asked quietly, knowing that the loss of experienced men was high.

'We've pinched some from the Fleet Air Arm, and a few Canadians arrived yesterday.' He sighed and walked away.

There was a wealth of meaning in that heartfelt sigh. Reid knew he was saying that things were bad. And there wasn't a pilot who didn't know that to be true.

Reid made the recruits wait for him while he went to report in, then took them to the house just outside the gates that was serving as makeshift accommodation. He chatted away to them on the walk over, trying to put them at their ease, but they were clearly nervous.

When they walked in they were greeted with the cry, 'They've blown the bloody roof off the pub, the bastards!'

Reid grinned at the outraged expression on Timber Woods's face. 'Has the cellar survived intact?'

'It has.' The landlord of the Crown staggered in carrying a tray loaded with pints of beer. 'Here you are, lads, have these on the house – what's left of it.'

Hands shot out and whipped glasses from the tray. Reid did the same and downed the liquid almost without it touching the sides of his mouth. The two new boys watched wide-eyed as the glasses were emptied in one swallow and placed back on the tray.

Timber slapped the landlord on the back. 'By God, we needed that, Harry.'

'Thought you might. Er . . .' He looked anxiously around the room. 'Where's Lofty?'

'Bought it,' was the only comment from one of the pilots.

'I'm sorry about that.' His sigh was one of deep regret. 'The wife will be upset, she liked that boy.'

Just then the door opened and a dishevelled pilot came in, reeking of fuel and smoke.

Reid peered at him, trying to see through the thick layer of oil and soot. 'Bouncer?'

'That's right.' He pounced on the last remaining pint, and all that could be seen was his bobbing Adam's apple as the glass emptied.

'Hey!' Timber shouted, thumping the sleeve of Bouncer's flying jacket, 'you're still smouldering, you silly sod.'

'I know,' Reid said in a resigned voice, 'you thought you'd save the plane instead of bailing out.'

White teeth shone through the grime. 'That was the idea but she went up as soon as I landed.'

'What did you do, then?' asked one of the new boys, staring in disbelief at the apparition in front of him.

'Ran, old boy, what else would one do?' Bouncer asked innocently, not appearing at all perturbed by his narrow escape.

'You're a maniac, do you know that?' Reid told him.

Bouncer shrugged. 'It helps.' Then he looked around the room, counting under his breath. 'Have any of the others returned?'

'Not unless they've landed at other airfields or bailed out,' Reid told him, knowing there wasn't much chance for the other three. He'd seen two go down himself and there hadn't been a sign of parachutes.

There was a brief moment of silence, as they each remembered their friends who were no longer with them. It was something the survivors faced every day but they kept their emotions to themselves, knowing they would be up there again the next day, and it might well be them missing or killed. But of course it wouldn't happen to *them*.

Bouncer turned his attention to the new boys who were clutching their untouched glasses of beer. 'Are you going to drink those or make love to them?' he wanted to know.

One of them held his out with a slight tremor of the hand.

'Thanks.' It disappeared in a few seconds, and Bouncer looked pointedly at the other glass. This was also thrust at him and suffered the same fate.

'Ah, that's better, I feel almost human now.'

Timber snorted. 'You could have fooled me. You look as if you've just risen from the fiery depths of the earth.'

The white teeth flashed again. 'Just as hot up there today, old boy.'

'Are you injured under all that mess?' Reid asked.

'Nah.' Bouncer examined his ruined jacket. 'Just scorched around the edges, that's all. Now,' he turned to the two boys, 'are you our replacements?'

They nodded, clearly speechless by now, and someone in the background muttered, 'Christ!'

'Well, welcome to Kenley, though you're not seeing it at its best,' Bouncer joked.

Reid introduced the boys as Barrett and Johnson to the rest of the exhausted pilots, then asked, 'How many hours have you flown in Spits?'

'Ten, sir,' Johnson said.

'Ei . . . ght, sir,' Barrett informed him.

There was another muttered expletive in the background.

Reid tried not to let his dismay show. 'When we've had something to eat, and Bouncer has cleaned himself up, you are going to be given some lessons on how to fight, then if Jerry will give us an hour's peace at dawn we're going to take you up and put you through your paces.'

'Thank you, sir,' they said, a spark of enthusiasm in their eyes at last.

At that moment the cooks arrived and everything stopped while they demolished the food.

Reid stood up when they'd finished and headed for the door. 'I'm just going to see if I can contact my brother. I won't be long.'

'That might be difficult,' Timber told him. 'The last I heard all the land lines were down.'

'I know. I tried as soon as I landed, but I'll have another go.'

Then the door opened and Paul limped in, leaning heavily on a stick. 'Ah,' Reid smiled in relief, 'I was just going to have a go at phoning you again.'

'Hi, Paul,' Bouncer called. 'I'm afraid we've drunk all the beer.'

'I'll bet you have,' he laughed. 'What happened to you?'

'Well, there was this bloody-minded German, and he insisted on shooting at me.' Bouncer looked scandalized.

Paul tutted. 'Do you know they did the same to me? One bullet went straight through my leg. Can't think what we've done to upset them,' he added drily.

'We keep hurtling towards them with guns firing and spoiling their fun,' Timber chortled.

'Come into the other room, Paul,' Reid said, 'and we can talk in peace there.'

Both men slumped into armchairs and Reid asked, 'How badly are you hurt?'

'Oh, it's only a scratch and I'll be flying again in a

583

couple of days.' Paul held the leg out in front of him and flexed it. 'See, no problem.'

Reid looked at his brother's tired face and was pleased that he would have a short break. 'Are you going to see your girl now you've got time off?'

'No, she can't get any leave at the moment.' He leant forward and smiled. 'Guess what? I was so badly shot up that I had to land at Tangmere and Annie's brother Charlie is there. He's a mechanic, and a good one, I was told. Will and Charlie always were a whizz with engines.'

Reid stifled a yawn, not really interested in this family his brother seemed to think the world of. 'How did you get back here?'

'After the medic had bandaged me up, I hitched a lift.' He grinned. 'A female ferry pilot was delivering a trainer, so she dropped me off here.'

'Did you enjoy the ride?' he grinned.

'Not much, but she was quite competent. I offered to sit on her lap and fly the thing myself,' he joked, 'but she wouldn't hear of it.'

'I don't blame her,' Reid remarked wryly. 'So, will you go home for a couple of days?'

'No, I'm going to stay on the base. I want to get back in the air as soon as possible.' Paul gazed thoughtfully into space, then back at his brother. 'This has been the hardest day, hasn't it?'

'Yes.' Reid didn't add anything else, they were only too aware of the gravity of the situation, but he knew every pilot was determined to keep fighting. The thought of losing this battle was not something they were prepared to consider.

'Reid, can I ask a favour? If anything happens to me, will you look after Annie for me?'

'What makes you think I'm going to survive and you're not?' Reid asked, studying his brother intently, rather alarmed at the strange request.

He shrugged. 'I don't know what's going to happen, or if either of us will come out of this alive . . .'

'Good God!' Reid exclaimed, in horror. 'Don't even give that a thought. If that happens the parents will never forgive us.'

They both laughed, then Paul became serious again. 'I mean it about Annie.'

'Surely she's old enough to look after herself?' Reid didn't like the way this conversation was going. If his brother began to believe he wasn't going to make it, then he could start getting careless. He *mustn't* do that!

'I know what you're thinking, big brother, and you're wrong. Today has made me take stock of my life and I'll be happier if I know Annie is going to be all right should the worst happen.'

'What makes you think she needs a protector?' Reid asked, not willing to commit himself to such a promise. 'She's got a large family, you told me, and I'm sure she wouldn't want a stranger interfering in her life,' he pointed out.

Paul sighed. 'You don't understand. She's special, and if I'm not here to watch over her then I want you to do it. Is that too much to ask, Reid?'

There was such an intense look of concern on Paul's face that he knew he couldn't refuse. At least he could put his brother's mind at rest. He would never have to carry out this task, anyway, so there wasn't any harm in agreeing. 'No, it isn't too much to ask. If that's what you want, I'll see that Annie is all right.'

'Thanks.' Paul smiled and relaxed. 'That makes me feel a whole lot better. Have you got anyone special?'

'No.' Reid grinned, relieved his brother had dropped the subject of Annie. 'So that lets you off, you won't have to go looking after a girl for me.'

'Damn!' Paul remarked in mock dismay.

The brothers started to reminisce, laughing at the fun they'd had while growing up. They'd always been close and the three years between them had never made any difference to their friendship. Paul had always followed Reid's girlfriends around with wide-eyed admiration for his brother's pulling power.

'Seriously, though, Reid,' Paul said after a couple of minutes, 'you ought to have a special girl. You're not getting any younger,' he mocked, and then his look became dreamy. 'You find yourself someone like Annie. In fact, if I don't make it you can marry her yourself. I'd like that.'

Reid tipped his head back and laughed at the ridiculous notion. 'I don't think that will be necessary. I'll be very happy with her as a sister-in-law.'

'Yes.' Paul brightened up, his earlier gloom disappearing. 'We'll get married as soon as possible. In fact I think I'll ask her next time I see her, and you can be best man.'

'That's a date.' Reid stood up, pleased to see his brother back to his normal self. 'Let's go and get a pint. They've only blown the roof off the pub.'

★

When Paul had left and the rest of the pilots were flaked out, Reid and Bouncer, now somewhat cleaner, gave the new boys a lecture on how to attack and, hopefully, stay alive.

After snatching a few hours' sleep they went to the airfield just as dawn was breaking. Reid was determined that these young men were going to survive. Too many of them were dying within the first two weeks of combat, and that was terrible.

'Try to remember everything we told you last night,' he said. 'Once we're airborne we'll take you through a mock battle sequence.'

Barrett and Johnson nodded eagerly.

'And just one more piece of advice. Fly and fight like Bouncer, but whatever you do, don't land like him.'

They looked puzzled.

'He isn't called Bouncer for nothing,' Reid added drily. 'If you get into any trouble, for heaven's sake bale out.'

Bouncer shuddered and Reid despaired of his friend. He was a fearless pilot and fought like a tiger, but the thought of jumping out of an aeroplane sent him into a panic. Reid knew he wouldn't hesitate, especially if the damned thing was on fire.

'Sir?' Barrett, the younger, asked, 'we've heard that the Germans shoot at pilots on parachutes.'

'Some do, the bastards,' Bouncer growled. 'They know that if we land safely we will live to fight another day.'

'Nevertheless, you are a valuable asset,' Reid pointed out firmly, 'and we need you alive. The planes can be replaced, but experienced pilots are a necessity, and the only way you can become experienced is to stay alive.'

*

And they did. Reid watched over them for the next few days, and saw them quickly change from nervous boys into confident, efficient pilots. And whenever they received more new recruits he and Bouncer tried to find the time to give them some training before they actually had to face the enemy. It wasn't always possible and there were always some who didn't survive for long. Reid found that hard to take but he continued to nurture and instruct his pilots whenever he had the chance.

10

September 1940

'Have you heard the awful news?' Jean sat opposite Annie in the mess and wiped tears from her eyes.

'I've only just come off duty.' She reached out and took hold of her friend's hand in concern. 'What's happened?'

'The Germans have sunk a ship carrying children.' She looked up, her face stricken. 'How could they do a thing like that?'

Annie's heart lurched. Thank goodness Bill had vetoed the idea of James joining that scheme to evacuate children to Canada and elsewhere. His son had been keen to go but Bill and Rose wouldn't hear of it.

Jean blew her nose. 'The thought of all those terrified little ones in the sea is too dreadful for words. There's been an awful loss of life.'

'When did this happen?' Annie was surprised she hadn't heard about it earlier, but then she'd hardly left her post over the last few days.

'Two days ago, the 17th of September.' Jean grimaced and wiped away another tear. 'The *City of Benares*, I think it was called, and they sailed on Friday the thirteenth. How's that for a bad omen? This isn't a war of armies, is it?' Jean remarked with sadness. 'Innocent civilians are in the thick of it now. Look at poor old London, being bombed night after night.'

'Yes, it's terrible, and I'm relieved that my family are in Wales with George for a while, all except Rose, and she refuses to leave. She's working with the Women's Voluntary Service in London, and it's damned dangerous. I'm worried sick about her but she insists on doing something now the children are safe.' Annie gave a little dry laugh. 'Bill will be furious when he comes home and discovers what she's been doing. If anyone can send her packing to Wales, then it's him.'

'Annie?'

She looked up at the tall figure standing beside their table and leapt to her feet, nearly knocking over the chair in her haste. 'Jack!' It was four months since he'd walked away from her, but she was so pleased to see him. Her smile faded as she took in his appearance. He had deep lines across his forehead and around his mouth, and dark smudges under his eyes, which looked sunken in and haunted. There was also a lot more grey hair than she remembered. He had aged almost beyond recognition.

'Dear God!' she breathed. 'What have you been up to?'

'I need to see you, Annie. Have you got some spare time?' he asked, touching her arm.

'Yes, I'm off duty until six in the morning.' She'd planned to go to the pub with Jean, so she gave her friend an apologetic look, and nodded in relief when Jean indicated that she could forget their outing.

They walked out of the mess in silence, and Annie could hear Jack drawing in deep breaths of the early evening air, as if trying to revive himself. He was clasping her hand tightly; she knew that something traumatic must have happened to him but she didn't speak, sensing that he needed time to gather his thoughts together.

He stopped just outside the camp and leaned against a tree, pulling her into his arms and burying his face in her hair. 'I hope you don't mind me coming to you, Annie? I didn't know where else to go.'

'What is it, Jack?' she asked.

'You've heard about the ship with the children on it?' he rasped as if in pain. 'My two boys were on it.'

'Oh, Jack!' She hugged him in sympathy. No wonder he looked devastated. 'I'm so sorry. Do you know if they're safe?'

'Both missing.' He swore in anger. 'I was against this scheme, but my wife went ahead and made all the arrangements while I was away.'

'You mean you didn't know they were going?' she asked in disbelief. How could a father not know that his children were being sent abroad? What kind of a woman would keep that from her husband?

He nodded grimly. 'Alice knew I'd stop her if I found out. When she brought up the subject a while ago, I opposed it, but she didn't listen . . .' His voice broke.

'She shouldn't have done that, Jack, but she must be grief-stricken now.' Annie looked at him with tears in her eyes. 'You should be with her, not here pouring out your sorrow to me.'

'I've been home for the last two days, and she's all right; she's with her family, and I needed to be with you.' He kissed the top of her head. 'Our marriage was rocky before this happened but we stayed together for the children, now there's nothing to hold us together.'

'Oh, please don't feel like that,' Annie pleaded, frightened by the tone of utter despair in his voice. 'They might still be found.'

'Please God they are, but I don't think I can ever forgive her. And I couldn't stay any longer, I have to get back.'

Annie frowned. What could be more urgent than Jack staying with his family at a time like this? 'Back where?'

'France.'

The breath caught in her throat as she realized, for the first time, what he did. What an idiot not to have guessed it before. She'd known that his work must be secret but it had never entered her head that he might be doing something so dangerous. 'You're working behind enemy lines?'

'Didn't you guess that when I left so suddenly and said I wouldn't be able to keep in touch?' he asked.

'No, fool that I am, I thought you didn't want to see me any more.'

'Quite the opposite,' he said, summoning up a ghost of a smile. 'That couple of weeks we spent walking, talking and laughing, was like heaven. I had just returned from a mission and your relaxing company was a godsend to me.'

'Jack?' Annie chewed her lip, deep in thought. 'Are there many people doing what you do?'

'A few, yes.' His tone was guarded.

'Men and women?'

'No, Annie!' He held her at arm's length, his expression fierce. 'I admit that was what I had in mind when I recruited you, but it's out of the question.'

'Why?' she answered with determination. 'My French is fluent.'

'No.' He gave her a gentle shake. 'You're too fragile and far too beautiful. Do you know what the Germans would do to you if they caught you?'

'Shoot me?' she asked.

'Worse than that, and after they'd finished with you they might shoot you, if you were lucky.'

Annie's mouth set in a determined line. 'I still think – '

'Forget it, Annie! I've told Sam that if he tries to persuade you to do this, I'll come back and kill him myself.'

'Sam?' Annie studied his angry expression. 'So that's what he's involved in.'

'Of course, and he's got his eye on you, so if he offers to teach you unarmed combat you tell him to go to hell.'

So many puzzling things were now becoming clear, and her mind began to whirl when she thought about what Jack and others like him were doing.

'Annie,' he growled. 'I don't like the silence. I can practically hear your mind working. Don't even consider it,' he pleaded. 'We need you here – I need you here.'

She looked up sharply. 'What do you mean?'

'I have persuaded Sam to let you become my contact here. I transmit regularly and I need someone I can trust.'

'I'd like to do that,' she agreed eagerly.

'Thank you.' He breathed a sigh of relief. 'Tomorrow you will be given my code name and call sign.'

'Tomorrow? But when are you going back to France?'

He glanced at his watch. 'I'm leaving in six hours.'

Annie almost reeled in shock. He couldn't go at a time like this, and he didn't look fit enough. This was madness!

'But Jack, what about your children? Suppose they're found and they need you?'

'If there is any news you will be told and can transmit it to me, and if I need to come back they will send a plane for me, if they can.'

'I understand.' Her heart ached for this brave man who was still doing his job, even though he was burdened with a dreadful personal tragedy.

'There's one more thing I would ask of you,' he said softly. 'One of the officers is letting me use his room tonight and I need to get some sleep . . .' – he paused – 'would you . . .' He tailed off.

'What?' Annie wasn't sure what he wanted.

'Stay with me tonight. I'm not going to make love to you, I'm too damned tired, but I can't be alone tonight. If I could just hold you for one night I might be able to get some rest.' He grimaced. 'That sounds ridiculous, and if things were different I would want to love you very much, but a sexual relationship between us would be wrong for you.'

'Because you're married?'

'Among other things, yes.' He kissed her eyes gently. 'I'm too old for you and my life is in a mess. You deserve better and I would never do anything to hurt you, Annie.'

'Oh, Jack.' The tears began to flow down her cheeks. 'If you really wanted me – '

'Shush, don't cry for me, Annie. I don't want your love out of pity.'

'It wouldn't be for that,' she protested, but deep down, she knew he was right. She was desperately sorry for this lovely man and she absolutely adored him. She had never felt so in tune with anyone in her life, and she longed to reach out to comfort and take some of his pain away. 'I do care for you very much.'

'I'm too damned tired to take advantage of your generosity, and I'm glad, because I can leave in a few hours knowing that I haven't done something that will weigh heavily on my mind in the future. Do you understand?'

'Yes,' she whispered, 'and I'll stay with you tonight, Jack.'

When they reached his room, he sat on the bed, kicked his shoes off and held his arms out to her. She also removed her shoes and he pulled her down, nestling her into his arms with a ragged sigh of utter exhaustion. And he was instantly asleep.

Annie listened to his steady breathing for a while, and just before slipping into sleep herself thought, Dora would never believe this!

A movement in the room snapped Annie awake and she sat up, disorientated for the moment, wondering why she wasn't in her own bed.

Jack was in civilian clothes and standing by the window, looking up at the night sky. He turned when he heard her move.

'Are you leaving now?' she whispered.

He nodded. 'The truck has just arrived to take me to the plane.'

'Take care, Jack.' She stood up and wrapped her arms around him. 'I'll be waiting for your messages, and any word about your children will be sent to you as soon as possible.'

He smiled down at her. 'Thank you for staying with me, Annie.'

'Did it help?'

'Oh, yes.' He gave a crooked smile. 'I must be getting old if I can sleep with a beautiful girl and not make love to her.'

She chuckled. 'You're not old, you just needed some rest.'

'And I do feel rested,' he told her with a wry grin. 'It's a shame I've got to leave at this very minute.'

'Do you jump out of the plane?' she asked.

'Yes, but that's not my favourite part of the trip.' He turned her face to the window so he could see her expression clearly. 'And it is something you are never going to do, isn't it?'

'I promise,' she told him, wondering why the thought of parachuting out of a plane was so exciting to her. 'If you need me here, then this is where I'll stay.'

'That makes me feel easier. Now, Annie, I don't want to ruin your reputation, so try not to be seen when you go back to your own hut.'

She gave him an impish smile. 'You haven't done anything to ruin my reputation. I'm sure that sleeping on a bed, fully clothed, doesn't count as a reputation-ruining pastime.'

He groaned. 'Don't remind me. Nevertheless, I don't want people believing that I've taken your virginity.'

'How do you know I am still a virgin?' she asked.

'I just do; you are not worldly wise, and it shows. I believe you will only give yourself to a man you truly love.'

'You're making me sound deadly dull,' she protested.

She felt uncomfortable about the conversation. She knew that the danger and uncertainty of the war was making a lot of people's moral code slip, but she had resolved not to let that happen to her. However, she had been willing to make an exception tonight, but that had been out of pity and compassion for this man she admired so much. All the wrong reasons, in fact, and he had been right to refuse her.

'You are anything but dull, Annie, so you be careful going back.'

'Don't worry. If I'm seen people will just think I've been working late. We are often called out in the night.'

He hugged her again and whispered, 'I must go. Goodbye, Annie.' Then he turned abruptly and left the room.

She waited for about ten minutes after he'd gone, pondering that goodbye. It had sounded as if he was saying that he would never see her again. Then with a sigh she made her way back to her own hut. No one saw her and the other girls were fast asleep so she slipped out of her clothes and crawled into bed, her heart troubled. She could only guess at the things Jack would have to face.

Sam was waiting for her in the ops room at six o'clock that morning. Jack hadn't left Annie until three o'clock and sleep had been impossible through worrying about him. Their meeting had been too brief but it had answered a lot of her questions. She now understood why he had left her so abruptly four months ago. He was such a brave man and if she could have gone in the plane with him then she would have done so.

597

'Jack explained what you will be doing?' he asked.

'Yes, is there any news of the children?'

'Not yet, I'm afraid.' He sighed. 'Terrible business!'

Annie was desperately disappointed. 'I was hoping to be able to give him some good news. What time will he transmit?'

'Not until twelve hundred hours, but you'll have plenty to do until then. You will still be monitoring other calls for us.'

Annie settled herself down and picked up the headphones.

Sam put his head on one side and studied her face. 'Are you and Jack lovers?'

'No. Not that it's any of your business, Sam,' she told him, annoyed at his blunt question.

'That's where you're wrong. I like Jack, he's a very good agent, and I wouldn't like to see him get careless because of some slip of a girl.'

Annie bristled. 'I object to your tone of voice, and I certainly don't like being referred to in that rude way.'

Sam held his hands up in surrender. 'I'm sorry, my English has let me down. I should have said "young woman".'

She couldn't decide if she liked this man or not. One minute he was friendly and easygoing, and the next probing and insulting. 'You're a liar, Sam whatever your name is, because your English is as good as mine.'

He sat down again, his expression grim. 'This is a very dangerous business, and I don't like any of my operatives to be distracted by personal problems.'

She looked at him in amazement. 'If that's true, then why did you send Jack back when his two children are missing? That is a monumental personal problem, surely?'

'I didn't have any choice, I believe Jack is man enough to handle the situation and not let it interfere with the task he has to do.' He ran a hand through his hair in an agitated manner. 'I didn't want to send him, but he's the only one who can carry out this mission. Jack understood that.'

'But you didn't want him involved in a romantic attachment outside of his marriage?' she asked, not prepared to let the subject drop.

'That's right. Jack's marriage was finished a long time ago, and I didn't want him to fall in love with you.' Sam pulled a rueful face. 'Love scrambles the thinking process and that can have dire consequences when you're behind enemy lines.'

'I assure you that there is nothing romantic or sexual between us, and I know it sounds corny, but we really are only friends.'

Sam stood up again. 'That's what he told me. I think he could fall in love with you quite easily, but he's got too much self-discipline to let that happen. However, I did agree to you becoming his primary contact because I believe it will give him some comfort at this difficult time to know you are here for him.'

'Thank you, Sam.' Annie felt slightly better now. At least Sam had explained, and she could see what a difficult decision it had been for him to send Jack back to France. This was the first time she'd seen uncertainty in Sam's eyes. If anything happened to Jack he wasn't going to be able to forgive himself.

★

It was a week later when Sam called her into his office. Before each contact with Jack she'd been praying to have some news for him about his children, but nothing had come through and hope was now fading.

'I've got some good news and some bad news,' he told her. 'They've just found a lifeboat and Jack's elder son, Steven, is alive, but the younger, Peter, has been confirmed dead.'

Annie put a hand over her heart and gave a ragged sigh. 'Well, at least one has survived; that is bound to give Jack some comfort. Is the boy all right?'

'He's been in that small boat for many days but I'm told he has come through the ordeal well.'

'He has some of his father's strength of character, I expect,' she remarked sadly. Annie glanced at her watch. 'He'll be transmitting in half an hour. I'll tell him then.'

'Keep it short,' Sam warned. 'You know he mustn't stay on too long. Don't let him chatter or ask questions.'

'I won't, I know the danger.'

In fact, they needn't have worried. Jack was a trained professional and took the brief news without comment, except for two extra words at the end of his message – *thank you*.

II

December 1940

Annie sat cross-legged on the bunk and eagerly opened the first letter. It was from Paul.

> '*My darling, I'm being moved to the Midlands for a while to give our squadron a rest. I was hoping for a spot of leave over Christmas so I could see you, but couldn't wangle it, I'm afraid. Still, I'm sure you'll have a great time with your family, and Reid's lot are also being rested, so no doubt we'll be able to amuse ourselves!*'

Annie could almost hear his infectious laugh as she read the rest of the letter and put it back in the envelope. She was glad the two of them were being given a break because they had been in the front line for weeks without a rest. Paul never told her anything about the fighting, of course, but she heard stories and worried.

The next letter was from her mother and Wally, and his account of the exploits of the Home Guard had her in fits of laughter. Rose had added a footnote giving her all the news about the children, and how George was having the time of his life with them in Wales. Her sister Rose wasn't very forthcoming about her own activities but Annie knew she was in London almost every night. It frightened her to think what danger she was in. However, when her strong-minded sister made up her mind to do something then no one could sway her, not even George, who was doing his best to get her out of the firing line. Their rows were explosive, her mother and Wally had told her. Annie gave a sigh and looked at her other letters. There were hastily scribbled notes from her brothers Charlie and Will. Charlie didn't say much, except to rave about how much he loved being an air mechanic. She knew he was at Tangmere and the airfields had taken a pounding during the summer but he had come through it unscathed, much to their relief. Will's letter had been written weeks ago; with the strict censorship there was nothing to say where he was. The only one who wasn't mentioned was Bill, and that was because they had no idea where he was. News coming from those at sea was sketchy, and letters few and far between. Separation from loved ones was a fact of life all families were dealing with. With a sigh she put the letters in her bag, hoping she would be lucky enough to see some of them over the holiday.

Jean came in the hut then, all ready for her leave. 'See you in the new year, Annie.'

Annie gave her a hug, knowing she was going to London. 'You dodge those bombs.'

Jean pulled a face. 'I expect we'll spend quite a bit of time down the tube stations. Mum says it's quite lively there.'

After Jean had left Annie finished packing, sped over to Sam's office, and knocked on the door.

'Come.'

'I'm just about to go,' she told him. 'Thank you for arranging ten days' leave for me.'

'You've earned it.' He smiled. 'Have a happy Christmas, Annie, and don't worry about Jack, I'll look after him for you.'

She nodded, her expression sad. 'I wish it had been possible to bring him home so he could see his son.'

'So do I.' Sam twirled a pen around in his fingers. 'But it would have been too dangerous to move him at the moment.'

Annie was well aware of the peril Jack Graham was in, and wished with all her heart that he were back in this country.

'Don't look so sad,' he reprimanded. 'Jack knows what he's doing. Now, forget everything and enjoy yourself.'

It had been a cold journey as the trains were not heated, and Annie was grateful to get a lift from Pontypool station from a friendly local vicar. When he dropped her by the gate with the words The Haven painted on it, she stood looking at the house. George and Bill had certainly picked a beautiful place. There was a gravel path leading up to a solid two-storey house, built in a warm beige stone. It had four bedrooms, she'd been told, with room downstairs to fit in extra beds when needed. On the left was the neighbour's farm with a paddock between. A couple of donkeys munched hay in the doorway of their stable. They looked up briefly as she walked by, then went back to their food. At the back was a fairly large garden where the flowerbeds had been taken over and were now used for growing vegetables. Wally and George were turning into enthusiastic gardeners and were already producing a good supply of things to eat.

There was a chicken run at the end of the garden, next to a derelict brick building that had probably been a stable at some time. She stood for a moment savouring the peace; she was going to enjoy coming here now and again.

'Auntie Annie!' Kate hurtled towards her as soon as she arrived. 'Come and see my puppy.'

She allowed herself to be towed towards the kitchen by her excited niece, only having time to toss her kit into the corner of the hall.

Kate opened the door and peered in, then whispered, 'Is he still asleep, Mummy?'

'Yes.' Rose saw Annie and smiled. 'You found us all right, then.'

'Managed to get a lift from the station,' she told her sister, trying to control a chuckle. 'The Reverend Jenkins, he said his name was, and he seems to know you.'

'Ah, yes.' Rose filled the kettle and put it on the stove. 'We've had a couple of lively discussions.'

Annie burst out laughing, knowing her sister's *discussions* well. 'I'll bet you have. Does he know the Bible as well as you?'

'Just about, but like a lot of people, he takes it far too literally.'

'You mean you disagree on interpretation?'

Rose's grin spread. 'Of course, I've always believed that there's a golden thread running through the Bible, but like all things of value you have to dig for it.'

Annie felt a tug at her sleeve, and looked down at Kate, who had her finger to her lips.

'You'll wake Pirate,' she scolded.

'Sorry.' Annie knelt down to examine the bundle curled

up in a box by the old black-leaded cooking range. 'He's beautiful,' she whispered, 'but why do you call him Pirate?'

'Because he's got a black patch over one eye.' Kate carefully lifted his tail out of the way so Annie could see the animal's face.

The puppy opened one eye, then two, and fastened his gaze on the object of his undying love, and then he clambered to his feet, tail wagging frantically, and jumped on to Kate's lap. The little girl giggled in delight as she tried to ward off an enthusiastic wet tongue. Then she tore out of the kitchen with the puppy in hot pursuit.

'How long have you got?' Rose asked when they were alone.

'Ten days. I don't have to report back until the 2nd of January.'

'That's wonderful. We've seen so little of you,' Rose remarked.

'And I understand from George that the family hasn't seen much of you either,' Annie pointed out.

'Ah, been telling tales, has he?' Rose didn't seem at all worried by this.

'Tell me what it's like in London, Rose.' Annie settled down at the kitchen table and waited. If she could find out exactly what her sister was involved in, then perhaps she might not worry quite so much about her.

'It's terrible.' Rose shook her head in despair. 'The tube stations are packed with families, all sleeping on the platforms, but at least they're fairly safe down there. Up in the streets it's bedlam. I've never seen such fires and those firemen are bloody brave.'

'And what exactly do you do?' Annie prompted when

her sister looked as if she wasn't going to say anything else.

'Anything I can, but most of the time I drive an ambulance taking the injured to hospital or the dead to mortuaries. Quite often we can't get the vehicles through the rubble and when that happens I get out and start digging for survivors or help to clear the road. It's dangerous, but at least I feel as if I'm doing something useful.'

Annie felt cold when she pictured the scenes her sister had described, and knew that the 'something useful' was an understatement.

Their conversation was brought to a halt when the kitchen door burst open and James rushed in, throwing his school bag on to a chair in the corner.

'Auntie Annie,' he exclaimed in delight, 'are you staying for Christmas?'

She nodded and hugged her nephew, much to his discomfort. 'My goodness, you've grown.'

'I'm going to be as tall as Dad.' He straightened up proudly, and then left them to go up to his room.

'They've really changed since I saw them last. Are they happy here?'

'Very, and Dad loves having them,' Rose told her.

'Oh where is George, by the way?'

'Gone to get a Christmas tree and he's taken Mum and Wally with him.'

'Do you know if Bill can get home over Christmas?' Annie asked, knowing there was probably little hope of that happening.

'I doubt it, I haven't heard from him.' Rose began to peel the potatoes for dinner. 'We don't know if Will or

Charlie will manage to get here, either, but we are so pleased you could make it.'

At that moment, there was a commotion in the hall, and they went out to investigate. George and Wally were struggling to get a huge tree through the door with Marj giving them the benefit of her advice. It had become stuck and there was much cursing and swearing going on.

'Good heavens, Dad, couldn't you find one smaller than that?' Rose reprimanded as she pitched in to help release one of the branches and haul it into the lounge.

'There!' George stood back and admired it when it was safely in the corner of the room. 'That's perfect.'

Kate and James had arrived as they were struggling with the enormous tree, and were waiting patiently with the box of decorations. Everyone joined in the fun of dressing the tree, even the puppy and the cat.

An hour later, Rose called out, 'Leave that now. Dinner's ready.'

They all tumbled into the dining room, chatting and laughing, already in the holiday mood, in spite of the war. Rose was a master at producing meals out of very little and her cooking was always a treat. Tonight it was slices of spam fried in a light batter, and served with fresh vegetables grown in their own garden. The chickens provided a few precious eggs but these were mostly given to the children.

Annie was listening to James regaling them with tales about his school, which he seemed to love. In the background she could hear George trying, vigorously, to persuade Rose that her place was with the children and she shouldn't go back to London after the holiday.

'The children are safe and happy with you here, Dad,' she told him. 'I've got to do something to help the poor old Londoners. I was born and bred there and I still care what happens to it.'

George's sigh was resigned. 'I know, Rose, but I worry about you.'

The discussion ended when Charlie strode in the room and threw his kitbag on the floor so he could greet everyone. Marj and Wally were overjoyed to have one of their sons home for Christmas. Although Wally was their stepfather the Webster children now all looked upon him as a father. A place was made for Charlie at the table, and a plate heaped with food was quickly placed in front of him.

'How long have you got?' Rose asked her brother, smiling in delight.

'A whole week.' Charlie attacked his meal with obvious pleasure. 'I've managed to scrounge a few tins of food and I'm looking forward to some good home cooking for a change.'

'I only had a letter from you this morning,' Annie told him. 'I thought you couldn't have any leave?'

'Some of the pilots are being given a well-earned rest; the poor blighters are exhausted. The station commander said I was overdue for some leave, so here I am.'

After dinner George produced a precious bottle of whisky to toast Charlie's unexpected and very welcome arrival. Charlie savoured a mouthful of whisky, then smiled in amusement as he watched the children opening his kitbag.

'We'll do your unpacking for you, Uncle Charlie,' James told him, smothering a giggle as Kate let out a whoop of delight and held up two oranges. Their Uncle Charlie was a great favourite and he always managed to bring a few treats with him.

'Good Lord, Charlie, where did you get those?' Wally asked. They were a very rare luxury indeed.

'I won them in a game of cards.' He smiled at the children. 'They're for you.'

Kate handed one to James and said seriously, 'I think we should save them for Christmas Day and we can all have a bit.'

'That's a good idea,' Marj told them with approval.

'Do you want an egg for breakfast, Kate?' Rose asked her daughter the next morning.

The little girl looked up from her task of feeding the animals and nodded. 'Boiled please, Mummy, with a nice runny middle.'

'Aren't we lucky to have our own chickens,' George said, buttering a slice of bread and cutting it into thin strips. 'With soldiers, sweetheart?'

Kate nodded, washed her hands, and then sat at the table. She tackled her egg with obvious enjoyment, dipping the bread soldiers into the yolk, then scraping it out and tipping the shell upside down in the egg cup, making it look like a whole egg again. Then she pushed it towards her grandfather.

'You can have my egg, Grandpa,' she told him with a straight face, then laughed in delight as he tapped the top and it crumbled. 'Fooled you! Did you finish the tree?'

He nodded. 'And we've put the presents round it.'

The girl slipped off her chair and headed for the lounge.

Rose and Annie went with her, followed by the rest of the family.

They watched as Kate checked all the names on the parcels. It wasn't easy to find presents these days for there was so little in the shops. Most of the gifts for this Christmas had been hand-made.

Annie knew that George had been clearing out his storeroom in the London house and had found a train set for James; Wally had been working away in the shed making a doll's cot for Kate.

'No peeking,' George teased, but she didn't take any notice.

'There aren't enough here for Daddy,' she told them with an outraged expression, as she ran over to the bureau and collected her piggy bank.

Annie watched her niece with fascination as she tipped some coins on the floor and started to count them.

'How much have I got, Mummy?' she asked, chewing her lip in concentration.

'Three and sixpence.'

'Hmm. That's not much.'

'What do you want it for?' Rose asked.

'I'm going to get a present for Daddy. He hasn't got enough parcels.' She gave everyone an accusing look, and then counted her money again.

'That's because we've sent them on to him,' Rose pointed out patiently. 'They'll be delivered to his ship.'

Kate stood up and gave everyone a beatific smile. 'He might come home and I want to buy him something special.'

'Ever the optimist.' George gazed at his granddaughter with pride.

Annie marvelled at the tenderness in George where his grandchildren were concerned, and Wally was nearly as bad. The two men would spoil the children if Rose and Marj didn't keep a sharp eye on them.

Kate looked at the money again, and then she looked up. 'Have I got enough for a present?'

'Yes, plenty,' Rose said.

Annie saw George and Wally both put their hands in their pockets, but Rose stopped them with a fierce glare. Although George was wealthy and the Freemans very well off, Rose would never allow the children to be spoilt, and made sure they knew the value of money.

'Good. Can we go shopping now, Mummy?'

They all decided to have a family outing, so they put on coats and gloves against the cold wind and headed for the bus stop to take them to Pontypool.

Annie relaxed, determined to enjoy this time with her family. The worry about Jack was pushed to the back of her mind, knowing that Sam would contact her if she were needed.

12

New Year 1941

Doubled over with laughter, Reid watched the lanky Timber Woods trying to do the tango with a broom for a partner and a drooping chrysanthemum between his teeth. Some of them had been transferred to a Midlands sector station for a short rest, and he was determined the men would have a good time. They'd pushed the tables back in the mess to make a dance floor. Reid had a surprise lined up for them.

'That's disgusting!' Paul roared. 'He took that out of the vase and the water's green with slime.'

'You don't have to worry about that,' Bouncer told them, 'with the amount of booze he's downed he must be well anaesthetized by now.'

'Why don't you speak English?' another pilot chided. 'You mean he's drunk!'

'I thought that was what I said, dear chap?' Bouncer gave a puzzled frown.

At that moment the door of the mess burst open and girls poured in. They were a varied selection – tall, short, blonde, dark and even a redhead or two, and none of them above the age of twenty-two. They had obviously spent a lot of time on their appearance, all were wearing colourful dresses. These were civilians, and it was a treat to see red, green, yellow and pink, instead of the dull colours of uniforms. Some girls appeared hesitant and others quite bold, but they were all gazing at the group of pilots with great interest.

'Wow! Comforts for the weary pilots.' Bouncer rubbed his hands together and grinned at Reid. 'Who managed to get that bevy of lovelies here?'

'I did,' Reid told the wide-eyed pilots, and laughed. 'I paid a visit to a local factory and asked if any of the girls would like to celebrate the new year with us if I sent trucks to transport them back and forth. As you can see I had plenty of volunteers. Well, don't just stand there drooling, take your pick, lads.'

There was a stampede then, and even Timber threw his broom into the corner of the room, spat out the flower, wiped his mouth and joined in the mêlée. It did Reid good to see his men relaxed and enjoying themselves. The horrors of this summer could be forgotten for a while.

Reid watched the scramble with amusement. It was funny how sober they all appeared now, even Timber, who had chosen the shortest girl he could find. The top of her head only reached the wings on his chest.

He waited until the crowd thinned out then walked over to a girl who was standing by the door and looking as if she was going to bolt at any minute. He wasn't surprised. These crazy pilots were enough to frighten any timid girl.

He touched her arm. 'Not thinking of leaving, are you?'

She started, and looked at him with large green eyes, almost the same colour as her dress. 'I . . . I thought . . .'

'I'm Reid.' He smiled, trying to put her at ease. She was

obviously doubtful about the evening, and he couldn't blame her for that. 'What's your name?'

'Hazel.'

'I'm pleased to meet you, Hazel. Would you like a drink?'

She smiled for the first time. 'Yes, please.'

He led her over to the bar and thought he hadn't done too badly. She was no beauty, but she had nice eyes, and a refined air about her. It could turn out to be a pleasant New Year's Eve.

As he handed her a drink, he couldn't help wondering what 1941 would be like. He hoped that it wasn't as frantic as the last few months had been, but he didn't entertain the thought for long. This was a time for enjoyment, and whatever they had to face in the coming year would be dealt with then.

The holiday had flown by for Annie but it had been wonderful to have some time with her family. The house in Wales was a lovely place to relax, and The Haven was an apt name. Her mother, Wally, George and the children were there all the time now as Kate and James had settled into new schools; it was an open house for anyone who wanted to get away from the war for a while. Wally had transferred to another Home Guard unit, and he often had members of his squad lodging there when they were on duty in the area. Rose wouldn't stay though and spent most of her time in London. But that was Rose, and no one expected her to do anything else. George was still very vocal in his objections to her activities but it was a waste of time.

A car pulled up and Annie glanced out of the window.

If that was her lift then he was far too early, she had another two hours yet before her train left. She was about to turn away from the window when the front door burst open and the children erupted through it, giving wild screams of delight.

Annie watched the tall man get out and gasped in delight. Bill! She hurtled down the stairs and joined in the excitement, waiting patiently for her turn to give Bill a hug. He looked very tired and moved slowly, but was laughing and joking with the children, obviously delighted to see them and everyone again, especially Rose, whom he loved deeply. The gentle smile he gave her spoke volumes.

'Dad?' James was studying his father anxiously as he sat wearily on the settee. 'You are limping. Are you all right?'

Bill patted the seat beside him for James to sit down and pulled Kate on to his lap. 'It's nothing. My ship was torpedoed and we spent a few hours in a lifeboat, but someone soon found us.'

Bill gazed over the top of his daughter's head for a few moments as a look of pain crossed his face, then he smiled. 'I can stay here until they find me another ship; hopefully that might take a while.'

Annie was pleased to see the tension gradually leave Bill's face. A few days at home relaxing with his family was just what he needed.

Marj bustled in with a tray of tea and Wally snorted in disgust. 'Good Lord, Bill needs something stronger than that!'

'It's only eleven o'clock in the morning.' Marj was obviously scandalized.

'Tea will do fine.' Bill winked at Wally. 'You can save the stronger stuff for later. Now, tell me what you've all been up to?'

They were chatting away and Annie lost track of time. When she heard a toot on a horn outside she glanced at her watch. 'Oh, I've got to leave.'

After saying goodbye to them all she picked up her bag and hurried out to the waiting car, wishing she could stay for a few more days, but content that Bill was safe for a while.

'Group Captain André Riniou wants to see you urgently,' a WAAF Annie had never seen before told her as soon as she arrived back at Cheadle.

She frowned. 'Who's he?'

'Er . . . I think everyone calls him Sam.'

'Oh, why didn't you say so?' She tossed her bag through the door and watched as it thudded on to her bunk. 'I've never heard his proper name before.'

Without wasting any time she hurried to his office, eager to hear the news about Jack. After knocking on the door, she stepped in and saluted smartly. 'Reporting as ordered, Group Captain Riniou.' The corners of her mouth twitched as he scowled. 'That's a nice name,' she told him. 'Why do they call you Sam?'

'It was chosen for me because it's short and easily identifiable by all the operatives. And I prefer to be called Sam,' he told her sharply.

She curbed her amusement, wondering why addressing him by his real name should have put him in this tense mood.

'Sit down, please.' He gestured to a chair and waited until she was settled.

It was only then she realized that his worried frown had nothing to do with her knowing his name. Something had happened!

'What's wrong?' she asked, feeling her whole body tense as she anticipated bad news.

He threw his pen down, sat back and surveyed her intently. 'Did you enjoy your leave?'

She nodded and waited patiently for him to speak again. He wasn't the slightest bit interested in her time at home. Whatever his news was it was something he didn't want to tell her. She braced herself for something very unpleasant.

'We've lost contact with Jack,' he said suddenly.

The breath caught in her throat and she leant forward. 'When? And what are you doing about it?'

'We've got to find him first, then if he's still alive we'll try and get him out.' He studied her intently for a few moments, and then seemed to come to a decision. 'How well do you know France?'

'Not all that well,' she admitted. 'My friend came from Paris, but she had a holiday home at Dinard in Brittany, and I spent most of my time there.' Annie willed her hands to stay relaxed in her lap, guessing where this was leading, and not wanting to show any sign of agitation. 'I can read a map.'

Sam held her gaze with thoughtful eyes. 'You are familiar with Brittany, though?'

'Yes.' Her heart was thudding, but she spoke clearly and without any nervous haste. 'It's an interesting coastline, and we used to explore along there all the time.'

He stood up, went over to a large map pinned on the wall and stabbed at it with his finger. 'The last message we had from Jack was from here.'

Annie joined him and studied the map. 'That's only about twenty kilometres from Saint-Brieuc. What's he doing there?'

'No idea, but if he's still in that area . . .' – he began to pace the room – 'and we can locate him, we might be able to get him to the coast. We could then send in a motor torpedo boat to pick him up.'

'Suppose they've caught him, Sam?' she asked quietly. It was the question uppermost in her mind, and the thought of Jack Graham in Gestapo hands frightened her.

'I don't think they have. From the little information I've been able to glean there's been some trouble and he might just have gone to ground, afraid to use his wireless . . .' His words tailed off and he shrugged.

'But you're not sure?' They obviously didn't have much information and that was very worrying. Someone should know where he was!

Sam hit the wall with the flat of his hand in frustration. 'No, I can't be sure about anything, but I don't like this continued silence. It isn't like him, and if he's still alive then we've got to get him out.'

'Can you tell me what Jack's mission was in France?'

'He was there to help the Resistance destroy a certain factory. I can't tell you any more than that, but he shouldn't have been anywhere near Saint-Brieuc.'

'Did he succeed?' she asked quietly.

'Reports are coming in that it's been badly damaged.'

Sam ran his hand through his hair. 'We've got to find him, Annie. I've been told that his son is pining to see him, and that poor kid has been through enough.'

Annie held her tongue. Sam was experienced and would make a decision when he'd weighed up all the options, but he was obviously reluctant to abandon Jack to his fate. Something she was in complete agreement with.

'I wish I could do this myself but I'd be picked up as soon as I set foot in France.' He continued his restless prowling.

'Why, Sam?'

'Because my picture is plastered all over the place, offering a hefty reward for my capture.' He grimaced. 'I caused havoc with their communication lines and killed quite a few of them. They eventually caught me, but I threw myself off a lorry when we were going over a bridge and leapt into the river. I'm a good swimmer and managed to escape, but they'd love to get hold of me again.'

'Then you can't possibly go back,' she told him sternly. 'It would be far too dangerous!'

He sighed wearily. 'I know. And the added problem is that I've got the whole Resistance network in my head and those animals are experts at squeezing information out of their victims. I couldn't guarantee that I wouldn't talk – no one can.'

'It's out of the question, Sam,' she said gently, touched by his distress. 'You've got to find someone else.' She paused for a fraction of a second. 'I know Jack, and I'm familiar with that area of Brittany – you've got to send me.'

He sat down again and ran a hand over his eyes. 'You are the logical choice, but my God, Annie, Jack will kill me if I send you into such danger.'

'It's my decision and I'm willing to go,' she told him determinedly. 'I'm not a fool, Sam, I know the dangers.'

'Do you think you could jump out of a plane?' he asked.

'I won't know that unless I try, will I?'

He looked at her with renewed respect, hesitated for a few moments, and then surged to his feet. 'Come on, then, let's see what you're really made of, Ann Webster.'

This was the culmination of her brief training, and the part she was dreading the most. She was back at West Drayton where she'd done her basic training just after joining up; instead of square-bashing, she was swaying about in a basket under a balloon! If she could do this then they would fly her out from Croydon airfield. Annie took a deep breath, peered over the edge of the basket and her stomach heaved in terror. It was a long way down. She'd been all bravado when she'd volunteered for this mission, now she was not so sure. This last week had been hell and every limb ached, but this was the end of her very brief training. She drew in large gulps of cold air in an effort to calm herself. All she had to do was keep her mind focused on Jack. He was out there somewhere and obviously in trouble. She had to do this! She was the only one available who knew Jack, except Sam, of course, but that was out of the question. They couldn't waste any more time. Every hour of delay meant it would be harder to find Jack.

Sam eased himself beside her in the cramped conditions and she glanced at him, forcing herself not to show her fear.

'If you can't jump then I'll have to go in your place,' he told her grimly.

She couldn't let that happen. She knew he had already been frantically trying to find another operative to send instead of her but without success. If he went himself he could be signing his own death warrant, and maybe those of many more.

The instructor checked her parachute again, and then smiled encouragingly. 'I'll be right behind you. Come on, sit on the edge and close your eyes if you must, but you'll be missing a marvellous view,' he told her with a wink.

Annie gave him a withering look. This was not the time or place to make smart remarks. She glanced through the hole she was about to launch herself from, sat down and dangled her legs through the gap.

His grin broadened. 'Once you've done this then jumping out of a plane will be easy. Honest, everyone says that throwing yourself out of a balloon basket is the hardest.'

'Now that I do believe!' She was praying that she wasn't going to be sick and disgrace herself.

'When you're ready, jump.'

Forcing herself to keep her eyes open, for she was sure it would be much worse if she shut them, she gritted her teeth and dropped through the hole . . .

'You blasted fool!' she screamed into the empty air. 'You're going to die!'

Then there was a jerk, her world of terror steadied and she laughed, albeit with more than a touch of hysteria. She'd done it. Gazing up she saw the balloon and two more parachutes coming down – it was a beautiful sight.

But the moment of elation was short-lived as she saw the ground coming towards her with surprising speed. Concentrate on landing safely, she told herself sternly. If you break anything then you'll never be able to go on this mission.

Detached from the earth like this, everything was very clear, she knew that this was something she had to do. She had to find Jack. She would regret it for the rest of her life if she didn't try.

Sam checked Annie's parachute again, his face lined with worry. 'I've managed to get a wireless message through to a Resistance group and they will be waiting for you.'

Annie certainly hoped they were. With a brief nod of her head she walked towards the DC3, its engines already running. It was a cold but clear night, and moonlight was shining on the camouflage colours, giving it an almost ghostly appearance. She forced her legs to keep moving towards the airman waiting by the door for her; this was no time to let her silly imagination run riot.

'My name's Healey,' he told her, 'and the pilot is Group Captain Andrews, one of the best in the business. He'll get you safely to your destination.'

Annie's stomach did an unpleasant somersault. Dear Lord, she hoped so!

He helped her in, and as soon as the door was closed they were hurtling along the runway. Once they were airborne, Annie closed her eyes and laid her head back. It was too late to change her mind now; she would have to deal with her fears. It was too noisy to be able to talk above the roar of the engines and she was glad about that. She found the motion of the plane rather soothing and her mind drifted. Sam had given her every opportunity to chicken out of this mission but she had refused. She wondered what her family would say if they knew she was on her way to parachute into France. They'd be worried sick, just as she was herself.

The time passed without her noticing and she was startled when someone tapped her on the shoulder.

Healey held up five fingers to let her know it was nearly time. She stood up and was horrified to find her legs shaking badly. She had to clench her mouth to stop her teeth chattering. Heavens, she was in a state, and this wouldn't do!

The door had been opened now and she could feel the cold air rushing in. And then a strange thing happened – suddenly she was calm and focused on the task ahead of her. She made her way to the open door, and when Healey shouted 'Go!' she stepped out into space.

Once the chute opened she peered into the gloom and wished the moon would come out again just for a moment so she could see her landing site. The instructor had been wrong – this was much more terrifying than jumping from the balloon in daylight. At least she'd been able to see what was beneath her then, but the moon had chosen this moment to go behind a cloud and it looked just like an empty dark pit beneath her . . .

As she hit the ground every bone in her body was jarred and the breath knocked out of her, but she hadn't injured herself – that had been her greatest fear. Thank heavens she'd missed the trees. It had been a close thing and one part of her parachute was snagged on a lower branch. The plane she had come in had already disappeared and there was darkness and silence everywhere. The drop zone was as close to Saint-Brieuc as possible. She hoped the pilot had found the right field because she couldn't see a damned thing.

Two men and a woman appeared out of the trees and ran towards her, quickly freeing her and rolling the chute into a bundle. They already had a hole dug and it was soon expertly hidden.

'Come, come!' the woman whispered, 'we must hurry.'

The men were barking out orders, and Annie was glad her French was fluent as they were speaking hurriedly and in hushed tones.

Annie didn't have time to ask questions until they reached a secluded farmhouse, then they introduced themselves. The man who was obviously the leader shook her hand.

'My name is Pierre, and this is Marcel and Christine.'

She shook their hands. 'Annie.' It had been decided that she should use her own name because if she couldn't find Jack then he might hear it and come to her.

'Welcome, Annie, you must be hungry. Sit down and Christine will give us some food.'

Annie sat at the large kitchen table and hoped she could eat. That jump into the darkness had been terrifying and hadn't done her stomach any good, but common sense made her pick up the spoon and start eating as if she was starving. It wouldn't do to show any sign of weakness. These brave people lived with the danger every day but she would only be here for a short time if all went well.

'You know why I'm here?' she asked.

Pierre nodded. 'We were told you are looking for someone.'

At that moment the door opened and a small man slipped into the room.

'Ah, Pascal, have you had any luck?'

'Maybe.' He eyed Annie suspiciously.

'This is Annie,' Pierre told him. 'She has just arrived. Now tell us what you've found out.'

The man sat down next to Annie, and she instinctively wanted to edge away from him. He wasn't very tall but he looked tough and not at all happy to see her. She couldn't blame him for his caution because she knew that her presence here was a danger to them all. He kept glancing at her and shaking his head as if he couldn't believe what he was seeing. It was obvious from his attitude that he didn't think she was going to be much use, but she was determined to prove him wrong.

'There is a man being hidden in a church not too far from here, but nobody knows who he is or if he is French or English.'

'Why?' Annie asked sharply.

Pascal glared at her. 'He is badly injured and has not been able to speak.'

'What does he look like?' she demanded. This surly man was not going to intimidate her. She was determined to find Jack and would follow up any lead, however tenuous. Sam had only given her a week to find Jack; if she weren't successful in that time she would have to return. Going back without him was something she was not prepared to consider.

'I do not know.' He started to tuck into the bowl of stew Christine had placed before him. 'The place is swarming with SS and I didn't stop to ask questions.'

Annie stood up. 'Tell me where this place is and I'll go there now.'

Pierre placed a hand firmly on her shoulder. 'No, Annie, it is curfew until dawn. You and Christine can go and pray in this church tomorrow. No one will think that suspicious and the priest knows her.'

Annie sat down again. Of course, that was sensible. She mustn't allow her anxiety about Jack to make her careless. These Resistance workers knew what they were doing, and would make sure she didn't do anything stupid. And what good would she be to Jack if she was captured or killed before she found him? The silence from him made it clear that he was in great trouble and she had to find out what had happened.

She held her bowl out for another helping of stew. 'Very well, we will go in the morning.'

It was going to be a long, anxious night.

13

It was eleven o'clock before Annie and Christine reached the church the next morning. It was in a tiny village about twelve kilometres from Saint-Brieuc and, according to Annie's map, another five more kilometres from the coast. The journey had been nerve-racking for her, as she expected a hand on her shoulder at any moment. Annie and Christine were on bicycles and it took every ounce of her willpower not to pedal faster when they passed German soldiers. She became even more worried when she realized they were heading inland all the time, because the man they had come to see was badly injured, and if it was Jack then the journey back to the coast was going to be a long one for a sick man.

They slipped into a pew and Annie bowed her head in prayer. There were two Waffen SS soldiers in the old church and they weren't there to pray. They were standing at the back and watching everyone as they came in and went out. It was frightening, but Annie copied everything her companion did, and pulled the headscarf forward so it covered more of her face.

After about half an hour Christine whispered that if the SS men didn't go soon they would have to abandon any action for today. If they stayed there bowed in prayer for much longer then it would look suspicious.

Annie rested her forehead in her hands, certain that the Germans must be able to hear the thump of her heart, but she was reluctant to leave until she'd found out if it was Jack in the crypt. If it wasn't him then she would have to start searching. She had a rough idea of where his last message came from and that would be the place to start.

She prayed that it wasn't Jack being hidden here, because this church was about twenty kilometres from the coast; that was a long way when you had to move with stealth.

Christine made Annie jump when she touched her arm a few minutes later. 'They've gone. Quickly.'

Annie followed her as she lifted aside a curtain and opened a heavy oak door. This led to a flight of worn stone steps. At the bottom was a dark, bleak room. A makeshift bed had been made up behind a large marble tomb, and the priest, who was bathing a man's face, looked up anxiously.

'You must move him,' he said. 'It is getting too dangerous to keep him here. Two men of the Resistance brought him here; they could do no more for him, and left immediately because they were being hunted. I'm sure the SS are suspicious.'

Annie rushed to the bed and knelt down beside the injured man. It was hard to see his face in the gloom. He had a couple of weeks' growth of beard. She pushed his hair away from his forehead and felt like crying out in panic. She didn't know if it was Jack or not.

'Is it your friend?' Christine asked.

She was about to say that she didn't know when the man opened his eyes and looked directly at her. They glittered with fever and pain but she would have recognized the bright blue anywhere. It *was* Jack Graham.

She bent over and kissed his cheek. He muttered something. He was delirious and clearly didn't know who she was but she whispered, 'I'll get you home, Jack.'

'Come.' Christine pulled her to her feet. 'We will tell the men and they will move him today.'

'But how?'

'We will leave that to them, but now I will take you to the first safe house on the route and they will bring him to you.'

Annie never asked how Pierre and the others managed to spirit Jack out of the crypt right under the noses of the Germans, she was only too relieved they succeeded. Over the next three days they moved from one safe house to another, all the time getting nearer to the coast, but progress was slow and she was *so* afraid Jack was going to die. She prayed, talked to him and held his hand, refusing to leave his side for more than a couple of minutes at a time. If only he could know she was with him it might give him some comfort; but he didn't appear to know her, and when he did occasionally open his eyes she saw no sign of recognition in them. The only response from him was a moan every time they moved him. He was suffering and it nearly broke Annie's heart but she controlled her distress. These brave Resistance workers were risking their lives to help and she was not going to add to their problems by causing a fuss. As she nursed Jack she felt like screaming – *he's dying*, we must move faster than this. But she didn't.

Annie was heaping more straw around Jack to try to keep him warm when she heard voices – German voices! Her heart crashed against her ribs when the barn door opened and the soldiers came in. Annie lay beside Jack and pulled his head on to her shoulder. She was so frightened. If they came up to the loft then that would be the end for them.

Annie prayed as never before. Jack, she silently urged, be quiet or we shall be discovered. His arm moved around her waist and he became absolutely still, just as if he had picked up her urgent plea. She bit back a sob of relief. Through his delirious pain, did he know she was here? Was he aware of what was happening? She pressed her lips to his hot brow, and listened to the Germans below, hardly daring to breath. Were they looking for them?

The barn door scraped open again and Annie heard the farmer urging the soldiers to come into the house for food and a warm fire. He sounded so friendly and accommodating but Annie knew the Frenchman was only trying to get them away from the barn. The Germans didn't need much persuading and abandoned their search. As they all left, she allowed her rigid, tense body to relax, and sat up. That had been close. They just had to get away from here. But how?

'Annie,' Jack called.

She bent over him, her hope rising that he was coming round. 'I'm here, Jack.' But her hopes were immediately dashed when she saw that he was still delirious. She clasped his hand in hers and could have wept but she couldn't allow herself to fall apart. It was bitterly cold so she lay full length beside him, trying to keep him warm. Jack seemed to settle then and quieten down, so she stayed like that for an hour, until she couldn't stand the waiting any longer.

Scrambling down the rickety ladder in the barn she

peered through a small hole. There was no sign of the German soldiers. Annie had always considered herself to have infinite patience but there was little of that in evidence in this situation. Anxiety was making her want to take chances, and that was dangerous. Not only for herself but also for everyone who was helping her. The Resistance workers were too experienced at dodging the Germans to allow her to put this operation in jeopardy.

Annie sat on the floor and tried to calm her agitation, but it was useless. Where was Pierre? It was going to take days to reach the coast at this rate, but she knew she couldn't do this on her own – she needed their help. Then she heard a cart being brought into the yard and breathed a sigh of relief. At last!

With Pascal was a man she didn't know; he hurried in, shinned up the ladder and carried Jack down as if he were nothing more than a child.

'Quickly! The soldiers are relaxed and enjoying a good glass of wine, so we are taking you to the next safe house,' the farmer told her.

'And how far is that?' she asked.

'Five kilometres,' Pascal informed her.

'Is that all! We've got to make better progress than this,' she exploded, forgetting all her good intentions to remain calm.

'It is too dangerous, Annie.' Pierre had arrived. 'We have to go past a checkpoint as it is, so you will have to keep Jack quiet.'

'Can't we go another way?' Annie knew how difficult that was going to be; Jack was delirious and he groaned frequently.

Pierre shook his head. 'The farmer has to deliver the

631

hay to the next farm and it would be suspicious if he made a longer journey. Be patient.'

Annie bowed her head. She had no right to question the wisdom of these moves, but she was frantic with worry for Jack. He had been badly shot up in the sabotage operation, and although someone had done a good job in patching him up, each day that passed lessened his chances of surviving. He couldn't die like this, far away from his home and family. She wanted him to live so much.

The journey to the next safe house had been dangerous but they'd got through the checkpoint without being challenged. The farmer made this trip several times a week and was known to the guards, so as far as they were concerned it was simply routine.

Annie was relieved to find Christine there when they carried Jack into the house. The elderly woman with her had fresh bandages and some kind of ointment; without a word she set about tending to Jack's injuries. He had at least four gunshot wounds, two of which were obviously not serious, but despair ripped through Annie when she saw the other two. They were infected, and it was no wonder he was delirious.

She spun round, fists clenched, to face Pascal. 'How much longer before we reach the coast?'

'Not long,' he told her. 'You had better send a message now.'

Annie hurried upstairs, set up her wireless and tapped out the signal to Sam. It had been arranged before she'd left England and was only four words – *Wish you were here*. She waited, counting the seconds, because every one that passed put them all in danger. The reply came through quickly, and after deciphering it she went back downstairs.

'A boat will pick us up in two days' time, at two in the morning from a bay ten kilometres north of Saint-Brieuc. Can we make it?' Annie asked anxiously.

'We'll get there in time,' Pierre assured her.

When they reached the coast two days later, Annie was just about at the end of her strength. When the sea came into view and she heard the gentle sound of waves caressing the beach she nearly wept in relief. The sound and smell of the sea was the most wonderful thing in the world to her at that moment. They'd made it, and Jack was still alive, but only just. How he had survived the journey was a miracle.

They scrambled on to the beach and laid Jack in a sheltered spot to protect him from the biting wind. Annie shone the torch on her watch. They'd arrived with half an hour to spare. She walked forward until the water was lapping at her feet and then scanned the sea for any sign of the signal.

An hour later she was still standing in the same place and watching. Had she got the time wrong? Would they be able to come? Was this the right place? Oh, God, suppose she had come to the wrong beach? Doubts assailed her.

'Annie,' Pierre called softly. 'Over to your left.'

There was the flashing light she'd been waiting for. She let out a pent-up breath, returned the signal, then turned to the men who had helped her, and silently hugged them in turn. It was impossible to put her gratitude into words. 'You go now,' she whispered. 'You mustn't get caught here.'

They slipped into the darkness and she was left alone, watching a small rowing boat make its way towards her.

Two men leapt out. 'Where is he, Annie?'

'Over there,' she answered in surprise. 'You shouldn't be here, Sam.'

'Get in the boat,' he ordered. 'We'll argue about it later.'

The motor torpedo boat was a welcome sight and she groaned in relief as Sam tossed her aboard. Willing hands lifted Jack on to the deck and he cried out at the rough handling.

'There's a doctor with us,' Sam told her.

She tried to soothe Jack's pain, talking quietly to him, as she had done throughout this dreadful journey. The boat purred its way out to sea, moving as quietly as it could.

'Let's get him inside,' the doctor ordered.

Annie followed them and watched as they went to work on the dying man.

'How badly hurt is he?' Sam asked the doctor, after they had managed to strip the clothes from their patient.

'He has been shot several times, but someone has made a reasonable job of tending his wounds before he lost too much blood, and that has obviously kept him alive. However, I will need to get him to an operating theatre as soon as possible.'

The boat picked up speed as it left the Brittany coast behind, and Annie knew that England was going to be a very welcome sight. She closed her eyes as utter exhaustion swept through her and didn't protest as someone picked her up and put her on a bunk. Then, with all her responsibilities taken from her, she slept for the first time in days.

There was an ambulance waiting for them at Dover and they sped to the nearest hospital. When they arrived Jack was rushed straight into the operating theatre.

'Drink this.' Sam handed her a mug of black coffee, made by a kindly ward sister.

'Any news yet?' she asked, sipping the piping hot liquid. They'd been here for two hours; what was taking so long?

'No, they are still operating.' Sam sat next to her, studying her pinched and weary face. 'Is it any good telling you to leave?'

She shook her head.

At that moment the doctor came striding down the passage and she jumped to her feet. 'How is he?'

'I've done the best I could but his injuries are severe. If we'd been able to treat him as soon as it happened he *might* have stood a chance.'

Annie's head began to swim and she swayed as the floor seemed to be coming up to meet her. 'What are you saying?'

Sam had a firm grip on her and nodded to the doctor. 'Tell her the truth.'

'Well, he's survived the operation but I'm afraid he will not live more than a few hours.' He gave them a sympathetic look. 'I'm so sorry, but we've done everything we can for him.'

Annie gripped Sam's hand and took deep breaths to

635

clear her head, determined not to fall apart now. 'Go and get his son; I'll sit with him until you get back.'

The doctor showed them to a side room and when she saw Jack she knew the doctor had been right; he was not going to live. His breathing was distressed and he already had the look of death about him.

'Go! Go!' she told Sam urgently.

He left immediately and Annie settled beside the bed and took hold of Jack's hand. 'Sam's gone to fetch your son, so you've got to hold on a while longer,' she told him firmly. Then she began to tell him about their journey and all the people they'd met along the way who had been willing to risk their lives to get him to safety.

She had just finished telling him what a welcome sight the boat had been, when he squeezed her hand.

'Jack?' She stood up and leaned over him.

'Hello, my lovely,' he whispered. 'Thank you for getting me home.'

'Did you know it was me, then?'

He tried to smile. 'I knew it was you talking to me and soothing my pain. Having you there kept me alive, Annie.'

'So I should think.' She smiled and kissed him gently on the cheek. 'I wouldn't like to have made that trip for nothing, you know. I hope you're not going to kill Sam for sending me?'

'I'll let him off this time.' His voice faltered and he closed his eyes. 'I'm glad I shall be dying at home.'

'Oh, Jack, you're not – '

'Shush, Annie.' He squeezed her hand again. 'I'm not a fool . . .'

'Dad!' A young boy rushed in and Jack held up his arms to greet his son.

Annie stood up and quietly left the room. That gesture to his son had taken the last of Jack's strength, but it comforted her to know he'd been able to see at least one of his sons.

'Who are you?' a woman demanded, following her out into the passage.

Annie turned wearily and glanced at her. She was petite and had probably been quite a beauty, but now her face was lined with worry. This was obviously Jack's wife.

The woman opened her mouth to speak but Sam interrupted. 'This is Annie Webster, and it is only because of her bravery that your husband is still alive.'

It was then that Annie became conscious of the state she was in. She was dirty, smelled of various animals, and still wearing her filthy and torn civilian clothes. She brushed her hair out of her eyes. 'I'm pleased to meet you, Mrs Graham.'

The woman looked uncomfortable. 'Oh, I didn't realize . . .'

'Why don't you go and sit with your husband?' Sam told her firmly.

'He won't want to see me,' Mrs Graham told them miserably.

'Of course he will.' Annie stepped towards her and lied. 'He loves you very much.'

Mrs Graham hesitated for a moment, wiped a tear from her eyes and went in to her husband.

Sam touched Annie's arm. 'Nothing we can do here now. Why don't you let me take you back to base?'

'No, I won't leave him.' Annie sat down again and

dredged up a smile. 'I could do with a nice strong cup of tea.'

In fact, it was three cups of tea and a plate of sandwiches later when the door opened and mother and son came out. The boy came up to her and gave her a self-conscious hug.

'That's from Dad,' he told her seriously. 'He said you had rescued him and I was to thank you.'

'He's a fine man, and I was pleased to be able to do it.'

'He just died,' the boy blurted out, but was quite composed. 'I'm glad I got a chance to see him. My little brother got killed when the boat we were on was sunk and Dad's gone to join him now.'

Annie didn't know what to say, but one thing she knew for sure, it had been worth all the trauma to get Jack home.

'He forgave me in the end,' Mrs Graham told them, wiping tears from her face. 'Will you both come to the funeral?'

'We'll be there,' Sam told her and scribbled a telephone number on a piece of paper for her. 'You can contact me here when you have the date.'

They watched mother and son walk down the corridor and Annie turned to Sam, her mouth trembling: 'That boy was so composed.'

'Yes, he was, but remember, Annie, he must have seen plenty of people die as that ship went down, even his own brother.'

She nodded understandingly. 'What a terrible experience for such a young lad, and now to lose his father . . .'

Sam led her out of the hospital and into a waiting car.

'Time to get you cleaned up, a decent meal inside you and then you must rest.'

She nodded. 'I must look a sight.'

'No, you look beautiful.'

14

'And who are you?'

Annie hadn't expected anyone to be at the Roe-hampton house and was surprised to hear Rose's voice. She must have just arrived. The last she'd heard was that they were all in Wales to celebrate Wally's birthday. They'd just come from Jack's funeral and Sam had insisted that she take some leave, and made sure of it by driving her home. Coming downstairs, she hurried towards the kitchen as she heard her sister interrogating Sam.

'Group Captain André Riniou, madam,' he replied with a pronounced French accent. 'And may I ask who you are?'

'No, you may not!' Rose replied indignantly. 'What are you doing here?'

'Making tea.' He lifted a brow in query. 'Would you like some?'

Annie put her hand over her mouth to stifle a laugh and slid behind the door to listen. If Sam continued to act the polite Frenchman with Rose, then he could soon find himself in trouble. When her sister asked a question she expected a quick reply.

'I can see that, and if you don't give me a straight answer, then I'll box your ears, young man.'

Annie peered round the door. Rose could be very intimidating but Sam didn't look at all worried. He was carefully warming the pot before putting the hot water in.

Rose tapped his shoulder when he continued with his task. 'I still want to know what a Frenchman is doing in my mother's kitchen?'

'I've brought Annie home,' he said without a trace of accent.

'Well, why the devil didn't you say so? Where is she?'

Annie stepped out from behind the door and Rose touched her arm gently and smiled a welcome, but Annie knew her sister had noticed just how exhausted she was.

'Right,' Rose said lightly, 'as the tea's made we might as well all have a cup. Sit down, young man, you're making the place look untidy.'

Sam looked hurt. 'I'll have you know, madam, that this is my best dress uniform.'

'Oh, very pretty.' Rose put enough cups on the table. 'Do you take sugar, André?'

'No, thank you, and the name is Sam.'

'And that's as phoney as the fake accent,' Rose declared. He grinned.

Annie was seeing a different side to this enigmatic man, and he was clearly enjoying sparring with Rose.

As the first cup of tea was poured, Rose tutted in disgust. 'That looks like gnats.'

Sam placed elbows on the table and studied the tea for a moment. 'What's gnats?' he asked mildly.

'You know very well what I mean,' Rose scolded. 'That tea is too weak to struggle out of the pot.' She stirred it vigorously, poured another cup and shook her head in disgust.

'Ah, well,' Sam said, his accent reappearing, 'you can't expect a Frenchman to know how to make a proper cup of tea, can you?'

641

Rose's expression didn't change as she emptied the pot and started again.

'We didn't expect anyone to be here,' Annie said, changing the subject. 'I thought you were all in Wales at the moment.'

'Oh?' Rose popped the cosy on the pot, and gave Sam a questioning look. 'Wanted to be alone, did you?'

'Not for the reason you are implying,' he told her, holding the dark, accusing stare unflinchingly. 'Your sister has had a difficult time and needs rest. I shall be leaving within the hour.'

'I see. Well, I live next door and you're welcome to stay if you wish,' Rose informed him, clearly backing down, which was unusual for her.

And Annie knew that was as close to an apology as he was going to get.

'Thank you, but I have to get back.' His grin broadened. 'Are you not afraid to have a lecherous Frenchman in your house, madam?'

Rose controlled a smile, stirred the pot until the tea was a respectable colour, poured two cups and handed them to Annie and Sam. 'I'm sure I could keep you in line, young man.'

'I don't doubt it.' Sam gave a deep chuckle of amusement.

Sam was at ease with Rose, and her sister had clearly taken to him. Annie couldn't help wondering if he had lost more than his home when the Germans had invaded France. He wasn't much older than her, but he might have had a wife and children.

'And what is your job?' Rose asked, eyeing Sam's uniform with interest.

He shrugged expressively. 'Oh, this and that, but my main task is making a nuisance of myself. I'm very good at it.'

'That I can believe,' Rose replied with feeling, and then spoilt the serious expression by grinning.

Annie started to laugh at their antics, but something happened, tears began to stream down her face and she found herself crying in earnest. All the worry, fear, danger and distress had been enclosed within a strongly erected dam, but now it broke. She sobbed as if her heart was breaking.

'I'd like to know what's going on, Sam?' Rose demanded, placing an arm around her sister.

'We have been to a funeral,' he told her. 'It was a much loved and respected colleague.'

Annie gulped and wiped her eyes, thoroughly ashamed of herself for breaking down. 'I'm so sorry.'

'There is no need to be.' Sam reached out and took hold of her hand. 'It is right that we should shed tears for Jack.'

'Have you?' she asked.

'Of course.' He gave a gentle smile. 'We French do not believe in the stiff upper lip; if we need to cry then we do. There is no shame in it, Annie.'

The tears began to flow again and she forgot there was anyone else in the room. This was the first time she had allowed her true feelings to surface and it was painful. She had loved and admired Jack Graham, feeling a closeness to him that she had known with very few outside her own family. It was almost as if she had lost a part of herself. 'I feel as if I failed him, Sam.'

'No, no, it was because of you he died in peace with

his family around him, and in his own country. That was not a failure – it was a triumph.'

Annie blew her nose and nodded. 'Yes, of course. I'm sorry, I'm just being silly.'

He squeezed her hand affectionately. 'You are a very brave girl, Ann Webster, and I'm proud to know you.'

'I suppose it's no good asking you what this is all about, is it?' Rose asked again, and looked enquiringly at Sam.

He shook his head. 'I'm afraid not, but I will tell you one thing, your sister has great courage, and when the story can be told you will be as proud of her as we are.'

'We've always been proud of her,' Rose told him. 'Would you like to stay for dinner?'

'No, thank you.' He stood up. 'I must be going.'

He bowed to Rose, and then he lifted Annie's chin. 'You rest now, do you understand?'

'I promise,' she said, and then he was gone.

'Where on earth did you find him?' Rose asked.

Annie felt much better after her bout of tears. 'He just turned up one day.'

Rose sat back, clearly intrigued. 'Tell me about him.'

'All I know is that he was in France when the Germans invaded; he caused a lot of trouble and had to leave quickly. I don't know anything else about him. He never talks about his private life.'

'Hmm, there's a lot of fury simmering behind those eyes.' Rose gazed at her young sister and frowned. 'Do you want to go to bed?'

'Not yet.' Annie sat up straight again. 'It's nice sitting here talking to you like this. And I need to chat about normal, everyday things.'

Rose poured them another cup of tea and produced some biscuits. They had spent many hours in the past talking over tea and biscuits, and Annie found it very comforting at this moment.

'Why aren't you in Wales, Rose?'

'I can't stay there all the time, Annie, not when there's so much to do here. You know I love London, and it's taken such a pounding.' She grimaced. 'Talk about a drastic way to clear the slums.'

Annie knew her sister was remembering her battles for better housing when she'd been a young woman.

'You in love with this Sam?' Rose asked her bluntly, changing the subject.

'No.'

'What about this man you've buried today?'

'Jack.' Annie pondered for a few moments. 'We all loved him, he was a fine and brave man.'

Rose stood up. 'You going to have dinner with me?'

'Thanks, that would be nice.'

Rose slipped her coat on. 'Come over at six, then.'

'I'll be there if I can stay awake.' Annie yawned, feeling absolutely drained of energy by now. Jack's funeral had been held in a church near his Kensington home. It had been very emotional for her, and far too ordinary for such a brave man. She'd wanted to tell everyone what a special person he'd been, but of course that hadn't been possible. It was doubtful if anyone there, apart from Sam and herself, had known what he did, or how he had been killed. Even his wife would not have known anything for sure, though she may have had her suspicions.

'This man Jack,' Rose hesitated by the door, 'Sam said

645

he had been able to die in his own country because of you. You taken a holiday just lately?'

'I took a little trip.' Annie held her sister's gaze and knew she'd worked out what had been going on. She would love to tell her the whole story but knew she couldn't. Perhaps one day . . .

'Thinking of going again?'

'I really don't know.'

'You be careful, Toots,' Rose said gently, using the affectionate nickname she had called Annie when she'd been a tiny child.

'Tea, Annie?'

She dragged her eyes open and sat up in bed. 'Thanks, Rose. How long have I been asleep?'

'You haven't been aware of anything for the last four-teen hours. You missed dinner but you were so tired I didn't bother to wake you.'

Annie stretched, enjoying the comfort of her own bed, then picked up her cup and sipped the steaming brew. When she remembered the uncomfortable places she'd tried to rest on her journey to the Brittany coast, this was pure luxury.

'Paul phoned me yesterday but I told him you couldn't be disturbed. He wasn't best pleased but he knew better than to argue with me.' Rose sat on the edge of the bed. 'You've been crying in your sleep. Do you feel better now?'

'Yes.' Annie rested her head against the headboard and closed her eyes. So her sister had been watching over her during the night; that was just the sort of thing she would do.

646

'Are you going to get up for lunch?'

Annie opened her eyes and smiled at her sister and nodded. 'It's time I got up and tucked into one of your hefty meals.'

'It'll be that,' she laughed. 'I've made a huge suet pudding just for the two of us, as you need something to line your stomach by the look of you.'

'Lovely, I shall enjoy that.' This was a great favourite with all her family, and it was a mystery how Rose was finding enough suet to make it these days. She might have found a substitute for suet; everyone was very inventive with their ingredients in these days of shortages, but if she had, then it wouldn't spoil the taste of the pudding.

'I'll leave you to get up then.' Rose stood up.

Annie watched her sister leave the room and felt like a child again having Rose look after her like this. It was a secure and comforting feeling. She had come back to Roehampton because she'd felt the need for solitude to come to terms with what had happened. Sam hadn't agreed with her about being alone, and he had been right, she was glad her sister was here instead of in Wales.

She went into the bathroom and ran a bath, filling it past the regulation five-inch mark without a pang of guilt. After the deprivation of the French trip she'd earned a little luxury.

As she eased herself into the water her mind replayed the sequence of events. After Jack died Sam had wanted her to take some leave, but she'd refused, feeling that she would cope better if she kept busy. They'd had quite a row about it but once the funeral was over he had insisted, and she'd been too exhausted to argue any more.

After a relaxing soak she dried herself and got dressed. When she was brushing her hair she sent up a silent prayer that there was a heaven, and Jack had been reunited with the young son who had been killed in that ship.

She gazed at herself in the mirror, saw the gaunt face with dark shadows under her eyes, and didn't give a damn about her appearance. She had done her very best to get Jack back alive, and she'd succeeded. The fact that he had died afterwards was beyond her control . . .

'Annie!' Rose called up the stairs. 'Lunch is ready.'

'I'm coming.' She turned away from the mirror with a resolute expression on her face. It was time to put the episode behind her. There would be more challenges to face before this war was over, and although she would never forget Jack Graham it was time she got on with her life. He would have wanted that.

They were in the middle of their lunch when there was a sharp knock on the kitchen door and Paul strode in, fixing his eyes on Annie and ignoring Rose.

'Where the blazes have you been?' he demanded. 'I couldn't get hold of you while I was in the Midlands, and when I rejoined my squadron a week ago there wasn't any sign of you.'

'It's good to see you, too,' Annie replied with a touch of sarcasm.

He studied her face and drew in a deep breath. 'Are you ill, my darling?'

'No, I'm fine.'

'You don't look it, you're so thin and – '

'Stop badgering the girl,' Rose ordered sharply. 'All she needs is rest and plenty of good food.'

He looked up quickly. 'Oh, hello, Rose,' he said belatedly. 'I've been so worried about my Annie.'

Annie clicked her tongue in exasperation, and realized in that instant that she had changed. The danger and grief had made her tougher and not quite so ready to put up with this nonsense.

'You don't own me, Paul.'

'Not yet.' He smiled affectionately. 'But I will one day.'

She was about to say something about this when Rose interrupted.

'Sit down, Paul. Do you want some suet pudding and treacle?'

'Yes, please!' He pulled up a chair, his good humour back in place.

Annie raised her eyebrows to her sister, who winked back, piling a plate high with pudding.

Paul would never get over this obsession with her and Annie knew that she was going to have to deal with it one day – but not just at the moment.

15

'The CO wants to see you, sir.'

Reid eased himself out of the cockpit and jumped down. 'Thanks. I'll just report in first.'

'No, sir, he said you were to go as soon as you landed.' The WAAF smiled, not trying to hide her admiration for the handsome man standing in front of her. 'He was insistent.'

'All right.' Reid sighed, removing his jacket and draping it over his shoulder, then headed for the office. He wondered what the hell could be so urgent. All he wanted to do at the moment was report in and then find himself a large beer.

The office door was wide open in an effort to catch any breath of air. It was unusually hot for September.

'Ah, Reid, come in and shut the door.'

The officer indicated a chair and he sat down, not taking his eyes off the man on the other side of the desk. He was shuffling papers around for no apparent reason and Reid wished he'd get on with it. This was unusual for the commanding officer; he was a brisk, decisive man and he never wasted time. Reid couldn't help wondering what had made him so ill at ease.

Suddenly he looked up. 'I've received some bad news. I'm afraid your brother, Paul, was killed today.'

650

Reid felt as if he'd been punched in the stomach and his mind started racing. He must be talking about someone else. Paul couldn't be dead. They must be mistaken . . .

'I'm so sorry.'

Slowly Reid's mind began to clear and he looked at the officer, who was obviously unhappy about telling him this terrible news, and took a deep breath. Pilots died every day and they accepted it, but he had never thought his brother wouldn't make it through to the end of the war. A vivid picture of Paul laughing flashed through his mind, and he only just managed to stop himself from doubling over in agony.

'There's no mistake? He hasn't bailed out somewhere?' he asked, clutching at a last thread of hope.

The officer shook his head. 'No, he crashed in a field just after crossing the coast. His body has been recovered and it looks as if he might have been dead before he hit the ground – he was badly shot up.'

Reid felt paralysed with shock. Paul really was dead. It was impossible to grasp; he'd had such enthusiasm for life. And at that moment he would gladly have swapped his life for Paul's.

'I've given you leave,' the officer told him. 'Your family will need you.'

'Do they know?' It didn't sound like his voice as he struggled for control. His parents were going to be beside themselves with grief.

'Yes, and you needn't return until after the funeral. You've earned a rest.'

At least they would be able to give him a proper burial, and Reid knew this would be some comfort to his parents, but it was a small consolation. They'd lost a dearly loved son and he'd lost a brother he'd thought the world of. He stood up, but it was an effort, and a feeling of the utter futility of war swept over him. At that moment he hated Hitler with every fibre of his being. The madman was causing anguish and pain to untold millions of people. He had to be stopped!

'One more thing before you go, I do have some good news for you.'

Reid wondered how anything could be considered good on a day his young brother had died.

'You've been awarded the DFC and promoted to the position of Station Commander at Tangmere. That's if you want it?'

Reid nodded, not really taking in the implications of this change. 'Yes, I do.'

'Good. You take up the post as soon as you return from your leave.' The officer smiled for the first time. 'You deserve this decoration and promotion.'

Reid felt sick. It seemed obscene to be standing here talking about medals and promotion, but somehow he controlled his emotions. The only thing on his mind now was to get home as quickly as possible.

Reid's journey to his parents' house in Thatcham, in Berkshire, was a blur of pain and disbelief. It was so difficult to grasp that he would never see Paul again that he expected him to be in the lounge, with his usual easy smile, as he walked in the house. But that feeling was shattered when he saw his mother prostrate with grief and his father struggling valiantly to hold himself together.

'Oh, it's good to have you home.' He clasped Reid in relief, gazing at his elder son as if he couldn't take his eyes off him in case he too disappeared from their lives.

Reid's mother was on the settee and he went and sat beside her, taking her hands in his.

'Did he suffer?' she asked hoarsely. 'You hear such terrible things . . . fire . . .'

'No,' he said. 'They believe he died at the controls and that was why he crashed.'

She nodded, seeming to draw a little comfort from that news. Then the tears began to flow again as she looked at him with frightened eyes. 'Are we going to lose you as well, darling?' she asked.

'I've just been given a station commander's job,' he told her, relieved that he could at least put her mind at rest in this way. Suddenly it hit him what this was going to mean – he would be leaving his squadron – and that was going to be damned difficult. He'd been too numb when the job was offered to realize this . . .

'Does that mean you won't be flying any more?'

'I expect I'll be too busy.'

'Thank God!' His mother laid her head back and closed her eyes.

'We'll go into the garden,' his father said quietly, 'and let her rest. The mind's a strange thing, you always believe that these things only happen to other people, don't you, and it comes as a terrible shock when it's one of your own.'

Reid agreed, knowing exactly how his parents were feeling, and followed his father. It was a pleasant evening, and they walked in silence, each lost in memories of the boy they had loved so much. After a while they stopped in the rose garden and sat down on an old wooden seat. Reid closed his eyes as the heady perfume from the flowers acted as a balm to his grief. He took in a deep breath.

'Beautiful evening, isn't it?'

'Yes.' Reid knew what his father was thinking; that his younger son would never sit here like this again. He opened his eyes and looked around. He could almost see his brother as a ten-year-old, running wildly across the lawn, and their mother calling for him to mind her precious flowers. Paul had always done everything with such enthusiasm.

His smile was bittersweet as the happy memories flooded in. How they'd loved this old house with its huge gardens. There was also a wooded area with a small stream on the boundary, and many times they'd had a severe telling-off for coming home soaking wet and covered in mud. It had been a happy childhood, and it was sad to know that any children Paul might have had wouldn't –

Reid shot to his feet and cursed fluently.

'What's the matter?' his father asked in alarm.

He swore again. 'Paul's girl, Annie something or other . . .'

'Annie Webster.'

'That's right.' Reid raked his hand through his hair. 'Have you ever met her?'

'Yes, a few times. She's a very nice girl, and Paul adored her.'

'I know he did, and he made me promise that I'd look after her if anything happened to him.' He started to prowl along the rows of bushes, touching one colourful

654

rose after another. Damn, damn! he raged inwardly; he could do without this.

'She seemed a very capable girl, Reid, but Paul always did fuss over her too much. I think that's why she wouldn't marry him.' His father came and stood beside him when he stopped in front of a pale apricot bloom. 'But she must be told, and I'm ashamed to admit that in our shock we never gave her a thought.'

'Neither did I, but I must tell her. I did promise Paul, but I never believed for a moment that I would have to carry out his wishes.' Out of respect for his father, he cursed quietly under his breath. He should never have let Paul talk him into this stupid promise, but he must honour it now.

'Do you know where she is?' His mother had joined them looking much more composed.

'All I know is that she's a wireless operator in the WAAF, so I should be able to track her down all right.'

'Do that as soon as you can.' His mother came up to him and slipped her hand through her son's arm. 'They've been friends for a long time and I expect she'll want to come to the funeral.'

It was the next afternoon before he managed to find out where she was stationed. He decided to go at once. He had no wish to meet this girl his brother had been besotted with but it had to be done.

'Have you got any petrol in your car?' he asked his father.

'Yes, the tank's nearly full and there's a spare gallon in a can.'

'That should be enough to get me to Cheadle and

back. Can I borrow it? I'll try to replace the petrol for you.'

'Of course, and you might as well take the car back to base with you. I won't be using it.' The keys were handed over. 'You've found her?'

'Yes, but I had to pull in a couple of favours. This place she's at is very hush-hush, evidently.'

'Ah,' his father said knowingly. 'She always did strike me as a very bright girl. Paul told us she spoke French and German fluently.'

Reid raised his eyebrows and sighed. He was sick and tired of hearing about this paragon of virtue, and as soon as he'd seen her he wouldn't bother with her again. Promise or no promise!

'What's the matter, Reid?' his mother asked, not missing his exasperated expression. 'Don't you like Annie?'

'I've never met her, but from the way Paul went on about her I shall expect to see someone with wings and a halo.'

'He loved her,' his mother reprimanded gently. 'I wish they had married and then we might have had a grandchild to remember him by.'

Her eyes filled with tears and Reid was immediately sorry for his sarcasm. 'I apologize. I'm sure she's a charming girl, and I must tell her before she hears it from someone else.'

'Yes, that wouldn't be right.' His father picked up his son's bag. 'I'll help you get the car started; she hasn't been used for a while and might need a bit of persuasion.'

'When will you be back?' his mother asked anxiously.

'I'll get back tonight if I possibly can. I've been given

permission to go into this place so it shouldn't take long.'

'You will be kind to her, won't you?' she asked. 'It will come as a great shock.'

He bent and kissed her cheek. 'I will do my best.'

At Cheadle his papers were checked carefully before he was allowed to enter.

'I'll wait for her here,' he told the sergeant who was escorting him. When the man looked doubtful Reid said, 'I have some bad news for her and I'd rather see her alone.'

'Very well, sir, but I must ask you not to wander around.'

'I understand.' As the man hurried away, Reid lit a cigarette. He wasn't looking forward to this and felt it might be easier to talk to her in the open. He hoped she wouldn't be long because he wanted this unpleasant task out of the way.

The cigarette was nearly finished when he saw a slim, fair girl come out of a building and head towards him. He ground the cigarette under his foot and waited.

'Annie Webster?'

She saluted. 'Yes, sir.'

She looked puzzled; he knew he bore a slight resemblance to Paul but not enough for people to immediately identify them as brothers. But one thing was abundantly clear – she was quite lovely in a delicate way, and he began to understand Paul's protective feelings towards her. However, there was something his brother had missed – this girl was no weakling. He could see it in her eyes, in the way she stood, and he could feel strength coming from her and touching him. It was almost tan-

657

gible and he couldn't help wondering why Paul had never seen it.

'You wanted to see me?' she asked, breaking the silence between them.

'Yes.' He pulled in a deep, silent breath, steeling himself for this. 'I'm Reid Lascells.'

Surprise flashed across her face and the colour drained from it, but she remained silent, and he guessed she knew what he was going to say. It wasn't very hard to figure out, because there could only be one reason for him being there.

'It is my sad task to tell you that Paul was killed yesterday.' He heard the words as if spoken by someone else, and he cursed himself for breaking the news in this stilted way.

He watched her sway slightly and close her eyes as the shock hit her, then she opened them again and he caught a glimpse of the gentleness and compassion in her.

'I'm so sorry. How did it happen?'

'He was on convoy protection and got shot up badly; he crashed as he crossed the coast. He was nearly home but they think he was dead before he hit the ground.'

She nodded and reached out to touch his sleeve in a gesture of sympathy. 'It's a terrible loss, he was a lovely man.'

Reid narrowed his eyes, perplexed by her composed demeanour. He had the strong feeling that this was not the first loss she had suffered in her life. But he could feel anger building inside him. Apart from that first moment of shock, there wasn't a sign of a tear, and surely his brother warranted some display of grief from the woman he had worshipped? If she was such a caring creature, as he'd been told many times, then where was her sorrow?

He took a note from his pocket and handed it to her. 'The funeral is being held here next Thursday and you'll be welcome, if you want to come?'

Her eyes locked on to his and blazed with anger. 'Of course I want to come. Paul was my friend and I loved him.'

'Not enough to marry him, though,' he snapped.

'You are wrong. I loved him too much to condemn him to a marriage that couldn't last.'

'Well, it wouldn't have lasted, would it?' He was boiling now. The death of Paul had finally sunk in, and he was consumed with a raging anger. Just what did his brother see in this heartless creature? 'He died, didn't he?'

She took a step towards him, hesitated, and then moved back again.

My God, he thought, she was going to hit me. He knew he should back away as well, but some devil was driving him and he couldn't move. He was going to let this little madam know exactly what he thought of her.

'Don't pretend you cared for him. He spent his time fretting about you and you couldn't even be bothered to write or answer his calls.'

'That's not true!'

'Oh?' His laugh was humourless. 'What about January? He was beside himself with worry because he couldn't contact you.' He could remember Paul's frantic efforts to phone her when they'd been in the Midlands for a rest from combat, and being fobbed off with the excuse that she couldn't be contacted.

He noted the change in her expression. 'I see that hit home.'

'I wasn't in the country then.'

'You don't expect me to believe that, surely? There's a war on, so where would you go?' His voice was laced with contempt. What a ridiculous excuse!

'That's none of your business, and I object to the tone of your voice, Squadron Leader.' She lifted her head defiantly. 'I am not a liar.'

Whatever modicum of decency he had left was telling him to stop this, but he couldn't stem the tide of bitterness from pouring out. 'If you couldn't marry him, why didn't you at least sleep with him?'

She held his gaze firmly, and then spoke softly. 'Because he never asked me.' She turned and walked away.

Those few words made everything clear about Paul and Annie. His brother had put her on such a high pedestal that marriage between them would have been impossible, and this sensitive girl had had the sense to recognize that fact.

'Miss Webster,' he called. 'Annie.' But she didn't look back and soon disappeared from sight.

Reid lit another cigarette and drew on it deeply, trying to calm himself down. Why had he treated her like that? She hadn't deserved to be attacked by him, but there was something about her that riled him. Still, that was no excuse, his conduct had been inexcusable and he was thoroughly ashamed of himself. He would have some apologizing to do next time they met.

'I'm sorry, Paul,' he muttered, as he made his way back to the car. 'I made a terrible mess of that.'

Annie managed to reach her quarters before breaking down. She had been determined not to blubber all over that swine. She would mourn for Paul in her own way – in private.

This was turning out to be a terrible year. First the loss of Jack, and now, eight months later, Paul had been killed. Two men she had loved dearly, in different ways, and they were both gone. It was hard to believe, and there was now a big empty gap in her life. But it was fast being filled with dislike for Reid Lascells. How dare he stand there with that accusing look in his eyes? What had she done to deserve such treatment? How could brothers be so different?

Thankfully the hut was empty and Annie sat on her bunk and allowed the tears to flow unchecked. Perhaps she should have married Paul at the beginning of the war and given him a short time of happiness? But it was useless to agonize over that now – he was dead and nothing could change that. She pulled his photograph out of her bag, clutched it to her and wept.

After about an hour Annie blew her nose and splashed cold water on her face, once more back in control. She had work to do and her sorrow would have to be controlled, then she would write a letter to Paul's parents. They must be devastated.

She sat on the edge of the bed again, giving herself a few more moments before returning to the ops room. So that had been Reid, the arrogant devil. And that wasn't the first time she had seen him. He had been the airman she'd seen during the evacuation of Dunkirk. She hadn't been sure until she'd got close enough to see the scar on his forehead, and that had confirmed he was the same man.

Annie remembered how she had seen him looking

hurt and slightly bewildered on the quay, and had wanted to go and help him, but now she was glad she hadn't.

The objectionable man didn't deserve any help or sympathy.

16

Annie dropped a golden rose on to the coffin as it was being lowered and said a silent, heartbreaking farewell to Paul. It was almost impossible to grasp that she wouldn't see him again. She was going to miss him dreadfully. She felt so guilty that she hadn't been able to love him in the way he'd wanted.

Annie shivered; it was early October and felt more like the middle of winter, with overcast skies and a nasty wind whipping around the graveside. It seemed to have changed from summer to winter in one week, almost as if the weather was as angry and distressed as she felt at the terrible waste of young lives. Paul had loved life . . .

His mother touched her arm. 'Will you come back to the house with us?'

'I'm sorry, Mrs Lascells, but I have to get back and my train leaves in an hour.'

The woman smiled sadly. 'I understand, but thank you for coming, and for the lovely letter you sent us. We drew great comfort from it.'

Annie was relieved to hear that because it had been the most difficult thing she had ever tried to write. It had taken four attempts before she'd felt able to post it, and even then it had seemed so inadequate.

'Yes, we did.' Mr Lascells kissed her on the cheek. 'If you can't stay then let me drive you to the station.'

'No, you have a lot of people to ferry back to the

663

house, and I can walk.' She dredged up a smile. 'The exercise will do me good.'

Paul's mother seemed reluctant to let her go. 'You will come and see us now and again, won't you, Annie?'

'Of course.' She shook hands with everyone she knew and then stopped in front of Reid. 'Goodbye, Squadron Leader.' She didn't offer her hand or look into his eyes, she just turned and walked out of the churchyard making it clear that she never wanted to see him again. It was puzzling why he should have hurt her so much. She would normally have put such conduct down to grief, but his rudeness and sarcasm had cut deep. It had been totally unwarranted and she didn't know why he'd acted like that towards her. She could understand the anger he must have been feeling caused by the death of his brother, but where had his compassion been for her sorrow? Was he incapable of seeing past his own loss? But no, that didn't sound like the man Paul had loved and respected. Reid Lascells was a fighter pilot and, therefore, no stranger to death and grief. However, his hostile attitude towards her was puzzling. What had she ever done to hurt him?

She hadn't been walking for more than fifteen minutes when it started to rain, that heavy kind of drizzle that can soak you to the skin in no time at all. Blast, she thought as she turned up her collar, a rotten end to an upsetting day.

A car came along beside her and the passenger door was thrown open.

'Get in.'

After glaring at Reid, she put her head down and ignored him.

'You're going to get drowned,' he told her sharply. 'It's another mile to the station.'

She walked up to the car and slammed the passenger door with a thud, then continued walking. If he thought she was going to get into a car with *him*, he was very much mistaken. She'd been on the receiving end of his sharp tongue before, and had no intention of repeating the experience. Her emotions were too fragile at the moment and she would either hit him or sob uncontrollably. It was better to be wet than to have to endure another moment of his company.

The car disappeared from her sight and she breathed a sigh of relief; he'd got the message at last. But her satisfaction was short-lived. A door closed and footsteps crunched on the gravel road behind her, then Reid caught her up, shoved his hands in his pockets and started to walk with her, not saying a word.

Annie endured this for some ten minutes and then couldn't stand it any longer. She stopped and spun to face him. 'What the blazes do you think you're doing?'

'I'm walking to the station with you,' he replied mildly.

'What on earth for?'

'Well, this is a very lonely road, so I'm going to make sure you're safe.'

She was incensed. How dare he play the gallant knight after his heartless treatment! 'I'm perfectly safe. I've been trained in unarmed combat, and if you don't go away it will give me a great deal of pleasure to show you just how proficient I am.'

'Now come on, Annie Webster, you don't expect me to believe that, do you? Why would the RAF teach a fragile little thing like you to kill with her bare hands?'

'Believe what you like.' She realized that she shouldn't have given him that piece of information, but he made her fighting mad. He hadn't taken it seriously so it was all right. Anyway, she'd only had one week of intensive training, so she'd have been hard pushed to make good her claim if he challenged her. He was a tall, well-built man and she would have had to take him completely by surprise if she'd wanted to throw him. But, by heavens, she'd like to try!

She started to step out again, and still he came with her. 'Will you please go away?'

He shook his head and the water ran down his face. 'Can't do that. I promised I'd look after you.'

'Are you taking the bloody rise out of me?' Her voice had risen now, and if he wasn't very careful she really would belt him one. At the funeral she'd watched the coffin being lowered and felt as if Paul's death was all her fault. But, of course, that was ridiculous . . .

'Such language from a well-educated girl.' He gave her a disapproving look, but the corner of his mouth twitched.

'Oh, I know a lot worse than that, mate. I grew up in the roughest street in Bermondsey.'

'Well, well, you learn something new every day, don't you? Paul never told me that.' There was softness to his voice as he spoke his brother's name.

At the mention of Paul she stopped again. Her anger melted, leaving a lingering sadness. She pleaded, 'Will you leave me alone?'

'Can't do that.' Reid glanced at his watch. 'And if you don't keep moving you're going to miss your train.'

He was right, damn him. The only thing to do was ignore him.

They walked in silence until the station came in sight, then he stopped and turned her to face him. 'I want to apologize for the way I treated you when we first met. I was hurting badly from losing Paul, but I shouldn't have taken it out on you.'

'No, you shouldn't, but I forgive you. *Now* will you leave me alone?'

'I'll see you on the train.'

Annie tried to wipe the rain away from her face with her sleeve. It was like a soggy sponge; she was going to have a devil of a job getting it dry, and she was in for an uncomfortable journey back to Cheadle. Reid was in the same state. 'Why did you come with me? You could have stayed in the car and kept dry.'

He shrugged. 'I guess I can be as bloody-minded as you.'

A fleeting grin crossed her face. 'That I can believe.'

The train was delayed, which was nothing unusual. Annie was regretting her stubbornness; she was soaked to the skin.

'Ah, there's a mobile canteen over there.' Reid steered her over to it, and as they were both in uniform got them two cups of steaming hot tea.

'You know,' he said as he sipped his drink, 'you don't look a bit like the immaculate WAAF I met for the first time. You resemble a cat who's just been thrown in the river.'

'Thanks! You don't look any better yourself.' She put her head on one side and studied the scar on his temple. 'Anyway, we've seen each other before.'

He frowned and looked at her for a few moments, then shook his head. 'No, I'd have remembered.'

'It was when Dunkirk was being evacuated,' Annie said. 'I saw you on the dock and I was just going to come over and see if I could help you when a very pretty nurse led you away.'

'You were there?' he asked in disbelief.

'Yes, I was on leave and went with my sister, Rose, to see if we could be of any help.'

'Really?' He sat on a platform seat and pulled the wet trousers away from his knees with a grimace. 'What a day that was, I got shot down in France and managed to get on a ship. That captain was bloody brave, in fact all the crew were, but he was a very impressive man. Freeman, his name was.'

'That's my brother-in-law,' she told him proudly. 'He's married to Rose.'

'Good Lord!' Reid's eyes opened wide. 'Were you the two Captain Freeman hugged when he came ashore?'

She nodded.

His gaze was intense. 'I think I've badly misjudged you, Annie Webster.'

'You have, and you hurt me very much,' Annie said. 'I was devastated to hear Paul had been killed, and I could have done without a tongue-lashing from you.'

He tried to take hold of her hand, but she pulled away. 'Ah, here's my train, at last. Goodbye, Reid.'

He closed the carriage door and leant through the window. 'Can I see you again?'

'I don't think that would be a good idea.' Definitely not a good idea, she told herself firmly. There was something about this man she couldn't fathom. He appeared to be

668

the complete opposite to his brother. Though perhaps he wasn't as hard and unfeeling as she'd first thought. She'd glimpsed real pain in his eyes during the funeral, and on the way to the station he'd shown a dry sense of humour. She liked that, but one redeeming trait didn't mean he was someone she wanted to get to know.

The train pulled away and she gave him one more glance, then shut the window and sat down. She didn't want any more to do with him, even though she'd had a different view of him today. He was strong, could be aggressive and not the type of man she liked at all. He didn't appear to have any of his brother's gentleness.

When she arrived back at camp it was a relief to get out of her damp clothes, have a bath and put on a dry uniform. She wasn't due back on duty until six hundred hours tomorrow so she headed for the mess and had something to eat.

Sam was sitting on his own reading a newspaper, so she joined him. He looked up and smiled when she sat down. 'How did your day go?'

'Distressing.' Her voice was husky when she spoke.

'Take the day off tomorrow, Annie,' Sam ordered. 'Go for one of those long walks you love so much and clear your head.'

'Thanks, Sam,' she agreed gratefully. 'I'll do that.'

The sun was shining the next morning and Annie cadged sandwiches from the cook, put them with a bottle of water in her bag and set off. She caught a bus for the short ride to open country where she knew there would be some lovely walks. She needed to be alone and Sam had recognized that as soon as he'd seen her. She would find a quiet place, and while she walked she would ease the sorrow by filling her thoughts with memories of the two men she had lost. Happy memories!

17

March 1942

The last year had been sad for Annie as she'd tried to come to terms with the deaths of Jack and Paul, but slowly the pain was easing. There seemed to be no end to the war in sight, but spring was just around the corner and with the lengthening days the sorrow lifted. She had thrown herself into her work, not wanting to go out or socialize. Jean had despaired of her and had dragged her out to a couple of dances or the local pub whenever they could make it. She had been right not to let her brood, and Annie was grateful for her friendship and understanding. She loved her work, though, and the anticipation of finding messages that might be of use to the war effort never diminished. Three weeks ago she'd had seven days' leave and had spent it in Wales. Her family were very supportive, without asking questions, and Wally's quiet love for her had been particularly healing. Her stepfather was not a demonstrative man but he'd always made it clear that he loved them all. She was feeling more like her old self now.

The mess was in uproar. Annie couldn't help grinning as she put her hands over her ears. This birthday party was getting out of hand. In fact there had been a few parties over the last few months. Pearl Harbor on 7 December 1941 had been a dreadful affair, but at least the

Americans were now in the war and Britain was not alone any more. It was nothing short of a miracle that the country had survived. And a complete mystery why Hitler hadn't invaded after Dunkirk when the country had been so vulnerable, but he hadn't, and the brave battle by the RAF had given Britain a chance to regroup. With the Americans now involved, he was going to live to regret that decision.

Sam came to her table, spun a chair round and straddled it, then he reached out and pulled her hands away from her ears so he could talk to her.

He said something she couldn't hear, but at that moment the noise died down as quite a few of them left to go back to their duties, making conversation easier.

'We ought to celebrate the fact that the Americans are in the war with us, and now over here.'

She laughed. 'It's a bit late, Sam, they've been here since the end of January.'

Sam rested his arms on the back of the chair and smiled. 'I know but we were so busy we hardly noticed 1942 arriving. Would you come out with me tonight?'

'I'd love to,' she agreed at once. Jean was on leave and she felt like having a good time.

'Good, I'll borrow some kind of transport and meet you at seven.' He raised a brow in query. 'Will that suit you?'

'Perfectly, thanks, Sam.'

He stood up and swung the chair back into place. 'We'll have fun, Annie Webster, and it's wonderful to hear you laugh again.'

She watched him walk away and nodded to herself.

Last year had been a swine and she had been glad to see the back of it. At one point she had felt so wretched that she'd begged Sam to send her on another mission, but he had refused, and looking back she knew he had been right to veto the idea. He had stayed in the background, watching, waiting, and leaving her to recover in her own time.

He was a wise man, she realized, and she had come to like and respect him.

Glancing at her watch she gulped her tea down and headed for the ops room. She was on duty for another two hours but that would leave her plenty of time. A quick bath and change of uniform and she would be ready. She thought wistfully of the pretty dresses and shoes she had in her wardrobe at home and wondered how long it was going to be before she wore them again. Quite some time, she guessed, as this war still had a long way to go. She sighed as she pictured one of her favourite outfits: a turquoise dress and jacket she'd bought on her last holiday with Chantal in France. Those carefree days seemed like a dream now. She pushed the thoughts away.

Sam had commandeered a truck. When she got to where it was parked outside the mess hall it was full of service men and women. He shrugged and grinned. 'They all want to come.'

'That's fine.' She waved to the boisterous group and climbed in the front with Sam. 'Where are we going?'

'The Jolly Sailor's the nearest pub,' someone shouted from the back.

'I know the place.' Sam headed out the gate at a reckless speed.

Annie grabbed on to the dashboard and gasped. 'Who taught you to drive?'

'No one.' He crashed the gears and looked down, muttering under his breath.

'Sam!' she shouted at him. 'Have you ever driven one of these before?'

'No' – he shot her a sideways grin – 'but I'll soon get the hang of it.'

There was another ominous screeching and a head appeared through the gap at the back of them. 'I say, Sam, it's not a good idea to engage reverse when you're going forward.'

'Ah, is that what I was doing?'

Sam turned round to speak to the man and Annie grabbed the wheel in terror. 'Will you please keep your eyes on the road.'

He grinned again, thoroughly enjoying himself, then after some more crashing and pumping with his feet, he settled back. 'I've figured it out now.'

Annie groaned. 'Thank God! And I hope this pub isn't far because I'm going to walk back.'

Sam tutted. 'I never had you down for a coward, Annie.' He squeezed her hand. 'We're going to have fun tonight, things are on the turn and France will be liberated now we have the troops to do it.'

'You just missed the pub!' came a shout from the back.

Sam jammed on the brakes. 'Where?'

The head came through the gap again. 'You can put her into reverse now, old boy, the Jolly Sailor's about a hundred yards back.'

There wasn't room to turn the big truck around, so

he slapped it into the correct gear and shot back, narrowly missing an American car parked in front of the place.

Annie found that her legs were shaking as they all tumbled into the hostelry. Sam's driving was almost as bad as jumping out of an aeroplane. She hadn't realized he had such a reckless streak.

The place was crowded with British, American, Polish and Australian military personnel; in fact, there seemed to be just about every accent you could think of.

Sam kept Annie firmly in his sights, and made it clear from the moment they walked in that she was with him. Any amorous approach to her, and there were many, was quickly rebuffed; it amused her that he was being so possessive.

The table was soon littered with drinks, the French accent had appeared, and she had never laughed so much in her life. It was wonderful, and after the last traumatic year she revelled in feeling light-hearted and normal.

'You ought to be on the stage,' she chided, after listening to him having a ridiculous conversation with a group of Americans. He had pretended that he couldn't understand what they were saying, and in the end had them completely confused.

'If I didn't know you, I would really believe you couldn't speak English properly.'

He grinned again. 'Ah, would you deny a man a bit of fun with these allies of ours?'

'No,' she giggled, 'but they were trying to be polite and ask you where you lived in France and how you came to be over here, but you tied them up in knots and didn't say a thing they could understand.'

He leant forward until his mouth was touching her

ear. 'You think we should tell them that we are spies?'

Of course not!' She thumped him playfully as he nibbled her ear. 'Anyway, you might be, but I'm not.'

'Oh, yes you are.' He sat back and pulled a tatty sheet of paper out of his top pocket, then read it thoughtfully. 'I have your name on my list. ACW Webster, it says here . . . spy.'

She roared with laughter and made a grab for the paper, but wasn't quick enough. He stuffed it back in his pocket before she could get her hands on it. 'Group Captain André Riniou, you are incorrigible.'

He frowned. 'What does that mean?'

'Don't you start that with me,' she threatened. 'And my glass is empty; what kind of an escort are you?'

'I don't think I can drink much of this warm English beer,' he complained, and sighed. 'Oh, to have a bottle of exquisite French wine . . .'

One of their group tottered up with a tray loaded with pints. 'Come on, drink up, those Yanks are miles ahead of us, they've been here for hours.'

Annie smiled as Sam downed a pint in two gulps. He didn't seem to be having any trouble making do with the English beer after all. Suddenly she remembered something. 'I wonder if they've got any chocolate with them?'

'Oh, no, you don't,' Sam grabbed her as she stood up. 'Do you know what they want for a bar of chocolate?'

'I've no idea,' she told him, trying to look innocent. Tales were rife about these young men who were pouring into this country. A lot of the British servicemen resented them because they had more money, and attracted the girls with gifts of nylon stockings and chocolate. Over-

676

paid, oversexed and over here, was the common grumble, but no one could deny that this country was relieved to welcome them into the fight.

'A quick grope around the back of the pub, and more if they can get it.' Sam pulled her back into her seat again. 'What do you want sweets for?'

'I want some for James and Kate.'

Sam's expression softened. 'Ah, Rose's children. Would they like some, do you think?'

'They'd love it.' There was a sweets allowance on the ration, but it was hard to get even that, and usually involved a lot of queuing. When she'd been a child sweets had been a luxury they couldn't afford, but this generation of children just couldn't get them, or very few anyway.

'In that case,' he stood up, 'they shall have some.'

Annie watched him talking animatedly with a group of American soldiers, and after a while he came back and handed her two small bars of chocolate. 'Goodness. How did you manage that?' she asked.

He put his head on one side and studied her intently. 'I can be very persuasive when I need to be.'

She was beginning to believe that was true. If Sam wanted something bad enough he wouldn't be averse to putting on the French charm to get it.

At that moment all conversation was made impossible as a British soldier started thumping out all the favourite tunes on the piano, and everyone started to sing at the tops of their voices. Even the Americans, who appeared to love the pubs and enjoy the beer!

18

September 1942

Annie was about to go on duty when she was told to report to Sam. Jean was also waiting to see him when she arrived.

'Do you know what this is about?' Jean asked.

'No.' Annie could understand why Jean looked so puzzled because it wasn't like Sam to be so formal. If he wanted to see you he usually ambled up, said what he had to say, and then strolled away again. To be summoned to his office was very unusual, and intriguing.

The office door opened and Sam looked out. 'Good, you're both here. Come in and shut the door behind you.'

Annie and Jean cast each other amused glances. Sam's door was never closed!

They did as ordered and stood to attention in front of his desk. The corners of his mouth twitched at their military bearing.

'Sit down, I have something to tell you.' He waited until they'd settled. 'You've been given new postings and I want you ready to leave within the hour.'

Annie gasped in surprise, while Jean appeared to be speechless. This was very sudden.

'There's an RAF intercept station called Chicksands Priory, in Bedfordshire,' Sam explained. 'Men have staffed it until now, but they're moving out and WAAF wireless operators are replacing them. I've volunteered the two of you to accompany me.'

'Is this place special?' Annie asked.

'It's going to play an important part in the war effort. And you, Annie, are the most talented operator I've come across. You pick up messages others miss, and you also recognize individual operators by the way they key the Morse transmissions. You're just what they need there.'

Annie was stunned, but pleased with the praise, as she knew Sam didn't say anything unless he meant it.

'But I'm not a wireless operator,' Jean pointed out.

'They need clerical staff as well, and I'm going to need you to handle the paperwork.' He stood up and glanced at his watch. 'I'll meet you outside in forty-five minutes.'

They didn't even have time to say goodbye to everyone as Sam hustled them into a truck to take them to the station. Much to Annie's relief Sam wasn't driving.

There was one thing about being in the forces, Annie thought as the train chugged its way through the country-side, you certainly travelled around. The train was crowded as usual, making conversation impossible, so she gazed out of the window. She was sorry in a way to leave Cheadle as there had been some breathtaking walks in the area, but from the little Sam had told her the new posting sounded exciting.

Annie was shaken from her reverie when the train stopped and women from the Women's Voluntary Service came round with welcome refreshments. She smiled her thanks at the woman who handed her a cup of hot tea and a sandwich. Then they were on their way again. Everyone had the greatest respect for the women of the WVS. They worked tirelessly and often in very dangerous situations, like during the Blitz, but they always had a cheery smile and a joke when you met them. She could understand why Rose had joined them.

The rhythmic clatter of the train lulled Annie into sleep and she wasn't aware of the journey until Jean shook her awake at Bedford station. There was a truck waiting to take them the rest of the way. They drove through the town towards Shefford, and then turned right into a country lane, and another right turn brought them to some gates with a guardroom just inside.

Sam had obviously been there before, because, after their papers were checked, he pointed to some Nissen huts set under trees. 'Annie, you're in the first one, and Jean's in the one next to it. Jean, once you've stowed your gear, report to the offices and I'll meet Annie here in half an hour.'

They hurried off, eager to find out what their new posting was going to be like.

There were sixteen beds in Annie's hut and several were obviously empty, so she chose one about halfway down the hut. It looked as if there were a few girls to come yet, and she hoped they were going to be as nice as most of the others she'd met. Her mouth turned up in a smile as she remembered the first crowd she'd met back in February 1940. She wondered where they all were now. She unpacked her washing things and then looked around. The hut had beds, and that was all, so where on earth was she going to put her clothes? There weren't any cupboards.

'You'll have to keep your knickers in a box under the bed, I'm afraid.'

Annie recognized the voice, spun around and let out a squeal of delight. 'Dora, what are you doing here?'

Her friend grinned at her and tossed a cardboard box on to Annie's bed. 'That's your wardrobe.' She hugged Annie and danced her around the hut. 'Oh, I'm so happy to see you. I got fed up with Compton Bassett, it wasn't so much fun after you left, and when I heard they needed clerical staff for this place I volunteered.'

Annie was so delighted by this unexpected turn of events that she hugged Dora warmly. 'I'm so pleased.'

'Me too. I've been here three weeks, and when I saw all these girls fiddling with wireless sets I hoped they might send you here.'

Annie stuffed her clothes into the box and shoved it under the bed; she'd sort that out later. 'I must introduce you to Jean. She comes from Stepney as well.'

'If she's the bubbly WAAF with blonde hair and baby-blue eyes, then I've already met her. She's in my hut.' Dora glanced at her watch. 'I've promised to show her where the offices are so I must fly. See you later, Annie.'

Annie watched her friend hurtle out the door and then went in search of Sam. He was waiting outside smoking a cigarette, which he stubbed out as she walked towards him.

'Good, that didn't take you long. Now I'll show you where we are going to work.'

She fell into step beside him. 'You obviously know this place, Sam.'

'I've been here quite often, Annie, and when they asked me to transfer, I wanted to bring you with me.'

He gave her a sideways glance. 'I hope you don't mind?'

'Not at all, I liked Cheadle but it does hold some painful memories for me, and once I'd got used to the idea I wasn't too sorry to leave.' Annie knew that a change of location was probably a good thing at this point. The memories of Paul and Jack would always be with her, and she was glad about that, but it was time to move on. There was still a war to be won.

Sam stopped in front of a door, opened it and then they walked down some steps into the operations room. Annie looked around eagerly. There were rows of desks, each one partitioned off into small cubby-holes, and most occupied with WAAFs concentrating on their wireless sets.

'Annie,' Sam said, touching her arm, 'this is Wing Commander Felshaw.'

The wing commander was of medium height with brown hair sprinkled with grey; but the thing that struck her most about him was the shadows of tiredness beneath his brown eyes. The gathering of information was vital, and although they worked quietly in the background the demands on their time and concentration were immense.

'Glad you're here,' he told her. 'Sam's given us a glowing report of your abilities and we badly need experienced operators.'

Sam gave Annie a sly wink and sauntered off, leaving her to settle into her new post.

The wing commander showed her to a vacant desk and sat down beside her. 'I'm sure I don't have to explain the job to you, but I'll run through it anyway. You will be given a radio frequency to work on each day. Write down any messages you pick up, ring the bell and someone will take it to be deciphered.'

'I understand, sir.'

With a brief nod, he hauled himself to his feet. 'I'll leave you to it, then.'

Annie finished her shift by seven that evening, and as there was no sign of Sam she asked directions to the mess and headed there. She heard Dora's laugh as soon as she walked through the door, and found her sitting at a table with Jean. If the laughter was anything to go by, then the two girls were getting along well. She made her way over to them, feeling her spirits rise; it was going to be lovely having both Dora and Jean here.

'Ah, you're free at last.' Dora grabbed a chair from another table for her. 'Get yourself something to eat. They're giving a concert in the old house here, and we're going.'

'What kind of a concert?' she asked. She'd seen some of the ones put on by the troops at Cheadle, and although great fun Annie wasn't sure she wanted to watch amateurs tonight. It had been a long, tiring day.

Dora laughed at her doubtful expression. 'You'll like this; it's classical music. I've seen them before and they're good.'

'In that case I'd love to come.' Annie loved classical music and decided that an evening in the company of friends would be a lovely way to spend her first night.

The airman playing the piano was excellent and his repertoire extensive, from Beethoven to Gershwin. A

WAAF sang some Vera Lynn songs, and a squadron leader thrilled them with music from *Madame Butterfly.* The forces were crammed with talent and this intercept station was clearly no exception.

When the concert ended at eleven o'clock, Annie was ready for bed, but Dora wouldn't hear of it, declaring that they had far too much catching up to do. Although Annie had kept in touch with Dora through letters, they hadn't seen each other since Compton Bassett, so she stifled a yawn and agreed.

The hut Jean and Dora were in was in darkness but Annie's still had lights on, and it sounded as if there was a party going on. So they headed for that, not wanting to disturb the other girls if they were asleep. When they walked in Dora started to chuckle. 'Ah, Annie, this brings back memories, doesn't it?'

It certainly did. More girls had obviously arrived during the evening, and they were all sitting on the bunks, cups in their hands and eating sandwiches.

One tall girl stood and held out her hand. 'I'm Gladys, welcome to Chicksands. Would you like a drink?'

'Thanks.' Annie recognized Gladys as one of the wireless operators she'd seen in the ops room.

There was a scramble to introduce themselves, and then they all sat down again. Cups were thrust into their hands. Annie took a sip, gasped, and everyone in the hut collapsed with roars of laughter.

'What is this?' Annie said hoarsely. She looked across at Dora who was licking her lips in obvious enjoyment.

'Just a dash of bourbon,' Gladys explained.

'What's that?' Annie had recovered a little by now but her voice was husky and her eyes were watering.

'It's the Yanks' idea of whisky.' Gladys sat back and crossed her long legs in a provocative pose that reminded Annie of her time as a fashion editor. 'I'm going out with one and they can get anything.'

'Great!' Dora held out her mug. 'I'll have another one of those.'

After that they talked for a couple of hours, and by the time they packed up for the night Annie knew the life history of everyone in the hut. She went to bed late, but happy, and glowing from two slugs of bourbon. It wasn't too bad as long as you tossed it back quickly. She smiled to herself as she settled down for the night; this was going to be a good posting, she was sure.

Two days later Annie was delighted to receive some letters that had been redirected. She had thought it might take a few more days before the post caught up with her, and letters were so important to everyone in these times of long separations. There was one from Rose, with carefully penned notes from James and Kate thanking her for the chocolate that Sam had cadged from the Americans. There was another from her mother and Wally giving her news received from Will somewhere at sea. The last was in a bold hand. Reid! Blast the man, he was turning out to be as stubborn as his brother had been. It must be a family trait.

She searched through her bag and found the pen she was looking for. Perhaps this would get the message through!

19

October 1942

Oh, dear, Annie Webster, you're going the wrong way about getting rid of me, Reid thought. As he read the note again he laughed.

'What's amused you?' Bouncer sat beside him and peered at the letter.

Reid held it up. It was written by him, but had been returned with the words *Go away* written in green ink at the bottom. He chuckled again.

'Are you making a nuisance of yourself with someone?' his friend asked, rubbing his left arm.

'Hmm. Is that arm still bothering you?'

'Yes. It's taking too long to heal and this damp autumn weather doesn't help. I hate being grounded.' He glanced at Reid's expression and held up his good hand. 'I know, I should have bailed out.'

'Yes,' Reid told him. 'You've tried that trick once too often.'

Bouncer sighed. 'I really thought I could get down safely.'

'With no rudder control and only one wheel down, not to mention a bloody great hole in the wing?' Reid shook his head in despair. His friend was lucky he hadn't blown himself to bits.

'Underestimated the damage, eh?' Bouncer sat back and grinned.

'Anyway, thanks for getting me transferred to Tangmere. I'd have gone mad at Kenley with nothing to do.'

'I needed someone to help me with the job of station commander, and you are just the man.' Reid managed to keep a straight face, but with considerable difficulty. Bouncer was next to useless on the ground but he was glad to have him around. He found the station commander's job lonely after the camaraderie of the squadron, and it made Bouncer feel useful. And it was keeping his friend out of the air, which was much more important. How Bouncer had survived so far was nothing short of a miracle, as he took unimaginable risks.

'I'm glad to be here, but I can't believe you really need anyone. You're as organized and efficient on the ground as you are in the air. Tangmere is running like clockwork because of you.' Bouncer nodded towards the note. 'You still haven't told me who you're pestering.'

'Annie Webster.'

Bouncer's eyebrows nearly disappeared into his hair. 'Paul's girl?'

'That's the one.' Reid gave a gleeful grin. He didn't completely understand why he kept pursuing her, but in a strange way he was thoroughly enjoying the chase.

'Well, if the vivid green ink is anything to go by I'd say you've really upset her. What did you do?'

'I was rude and shouted at her,' he admitted honestly. 'I was shattered by Paul's death and her composure irritated me.' Reid grimaced in disgust. 'But that's no excuse for the way I treated her.'

'Have you thought about apologizing?' his friend asked with a wry smile.

'I did that after the funeral, and got soaking wet for my trouble. She wouldn't get into the car with me and it was pouring.' That walk in the rain amused Reid whenever he thought about it. Annie Webster was a spirited little thing, but he still didn't understand why he hadn't stayed in the car and left her to it. He just hadn't been able to leave the stubborn girl.

A deep chuckle came from Bouncer. 'I'm beginning to like the sound of her, and it doesn't look as if your usual charm had any effect.'

'Oh, she said she forgave me, then more or less told me to get lost.' The corners of Reid's eyes crinkled in amusement. From his brother's description, he'd gained a completely different impression of her but Paul had got it wrong, Annie Webster was not a timid, dependent woman. Behind the gentle façade there was a fire burning, and he'd love to get close enough to feel the heat.

'Then why are you still writing to her?'

'Bugger if I know.'

His friend struggled to strike a match with one hand, and when he had succeeded lit a cigarette and drew on it, his eyes never leaving Reid's face. 'Pretty, is she?'

He opened a drawer and took out the framed photograph Paul had always kept beside his bed. It hurt to look at it when he remembered just how much his brother had adored this girl, and he couldn't understand why he was holding on to it. 'I ought to give this back, I suppose?'

Bouncer took the picture out of his hand and whistled. 'No wonder Paul was crazy about her. I'd like to meet her. Tell you what, let's go and return this now.'

688

'I've only got a few hours free and, anyway, I've just found out she's been transferred to this hush-hush place, and I don't suppose we could get in.'

'Oh?' Bouncer was clearly intrigued. 'What does she do, for heaven's sake?'

'Wireless operator, and speaks French and German.'

'Does she now?' Bouncer prowled over to the window to watch the planes taking off, then turned and sat on the windowsill. 'I heard about these agents . . . do you think she's one of them?'

Reid tipped his head back and laughed at the ludicrous idea. 'Where on earth did you get that daft notion from?'

'Just a thought.' Bouncer grinned. 'Well, are you going to take me to meet her?'

'I've told you, there isn't time.'

'Reid, I know you've got your Lysander here doing nothing, and the weather isn't too bad, so can't you find somewhere you need to visit urgently – with your second in command?' he added.

'Well . . .' Reid only hesitated for a few moments because the expression on his friend's face decided him. Being grounded was purgatory for Bouncer. Reid knew that every time the Spitfires took off his friend's soul went with them. He stood up and shoved the photo into his pocket. 'Come on then, I've promised to pop in and see the station commander at Duxford to discuss a meeting of top brass we've been ordered to attend.'

'Ah.' Bouncer's eyes gleamed with amusement. 'Want to get your story straight beforehand, do you?'

'We're not sure what it's about but we don't want to be caught out with questions we can't answer. Once that's done with I'm sure he'll let us borrow a car. This place Annie's in is only about an hour or so from there, I think.'

Bouncer wasn't as nimble on his feet as he had been but he beat Reid to the door, and waited impatiently for Reid to obtain permission from Duxford and file his flight plan. 'Where is this place?' he asked when they reached the plane.

'In Bedford, near a place called Shefford.' Reid helped Bouncer into the plane and snapped his harness into place. As well as having badly injured his arm, he had also made a mess of one hip, which made manoeuvring into small places difficult.

'I'll fly,' Bouncer announced, his expression animated.

'No, you won't,' Reid told him. 'You're grounded, remember?'

'Oh, come on, you rotten blighter,' he growled. 'Who's going to know?'

'I'll make a bargain with you.' Reid eased his tall frame into the pilot's seat, well aware that his friend was desperate to get his hands on the controls of any plane again. 'You can fly her, but I insist on landing.'

'You've got yourself a deal.'

It was not the smoothest take-off Reid had ever experienced, and he breathed a sigh of relief as they levelled out. Once they were flying in a straight line he relaxed and listened to Bouncer singing at the top of his voice.

He was only doing this trip for his friend's sake, he told himself. It certainly wasn't because he wanted to see Annie again; he had promised his brother he would see she was all right, hadn't he? He couldn't just abandon her, even if she was more or less telling him to bale out without a parachute. His quiet chuckle of amusement was drowned out by the sound of the engine and Bouncer's happiness.

It didn't take Reid more than thirty minutes to talk over the forthcoming meeting with the station commander at Duxford, Simon Stratton, and he was only too happy to put an air force car at their disposal.

When they arrived at Chicksands their papers were scrutinized, and permission to enter took a while. Bouncer pulled his collar up and shoved his hands into his pockets in an effort to protect himself from the cold wind.

'Good Lord,' he complained. 'What is this place?'

'I told you it was going to be difficult to see her, didn't I?' Reid stamped his feet and blew on his fingers, wishing he were back at base. It had turned much colder since they'd left and he was concerned for Bouncer. This was a crazy idea.

'I thought that uniform you're sporting would get you in anywhere,' his friend muttered.

A sergeant came up to them and saluted. 'Would you follow me, please?'

He led them to a small, sparsely furnished room, which was like an icebox, then left them, closing the door firmly behind him.

'We've been arrested!' Bouncer roared. 'I bet he's locked the door.'

Reid laughed, opened the door and looked out. 'It isn't locked but there is a guard outside.'

'What do they think we're going to do, blow the place up?'

Reid paced the small room. 'I should never have let

you talk me into this crazy scheme. She won't see us, anyway.'

His friend looked astonished. 'So, it's my fault now, is it?'

'I've got to blame someone.' Reid grinned. 'And I'm flying the plane back.'

The stream of colourful language was cut off sharply as the door opened and Annie came in.

She saluted in front of Reid. 'You sent for me, sir?'

He ignored Bouncer's smothered laugh. If that was the way she wanted to play, then he'd go along with it. He took the photo out of his pocket. 'Yes, Webster. Paul always kept this beside his bed and I thought you might like it back.' He handed it to her and moved away. 'But if I'd known you were going to greet his brother so rudely I wouldn't have bothered. You do know how to hold a grudge, don't you?'

As she looked at the photo her military bearing sagged, he saw tears clouding her eyes and she was fighting for control of her emotions. This was the first glimpse he'd seen of how much she had cared for Paul, and seeing the special photograph again had caught her off guard. He had been, and still was, treating this woman in a disgraceful way but he couldn't seem to help himself. There was something about her . . .

'Thank you,' she said quietly.

He reached out to comfort her, but Bouncer stepped in front of him and blocked the gesture.

'It's a beautiful picture,' he told her kindly. 'Paul was always very proud of it, and you.'

She smiled at him. 'He was a good man.'

'And a brave fighter pilot.'

'You all are,' she told him with obvious respect.

Bouncer nodded towards Reid, who was sitting on the edge of the table watching his friend turn on the charm. 'And Paul's brother, over there, is one of the finest you could ever know.'

'I'm sure he is.' Annie ran her fingers round the edge of the frame, but didn't look up.

Bouncer tilted her chin up. 'I can hear a "but" there.'

'I don't like him very much,' she admitted, talking to Bouncer as if he was the only one in the room.

'Ah, well, I agree he can be an awkward devil, but he grows on you, if you give him a chance.'

'Will you two stop talking about me as if I wasn't here,' Reid demanded, getting to his feet. 'I don't need you to fight my corner for me, Bouncer.'

'Oh, oh.' Bouncer winked at Annie. 'That's torn it. Is there a pub where we can buy him something to eat and a large beer?' He rubbed his left arm. 'And a huge fire. I swear I'm frozen to the marrow.'

Annie looked at his left arm hanging useless by his side. 'I'm so sorry, they should have found you somewhere warmer to wait.'

Bouncer gave her one of his most beguiling smiles. 'I thought they'd arrested us when they put us in this cell-like room.'

Annie laughed. 'The Red Lion pub always has a log fire, but it's about three miles from here.'

'That's all right, the station commander here has borrowed a car.'

'In that case I'll explain how you get there.'

'I suppose you couldn't come with us, could you?'

Bouncer asked, giving a plaintive sigh. 'I was a friend of Paul's and have always wanted to meet his girl. It would be nice to have a chat. Somewhere warmer than this,' he added, rubbing his hip this time.

'Lying sod,' Reid muttered quietly under his breath. His friend had left a string of broken hearts, and goodness knows what else, he thought wryly, and he was damned if he was going to let him get Annie in his clutches.

'Well' – she looked at her watch – 'I do have a couple of hours, so let me tell them I'm leaving the base, and I'll meet you outside.'

Bouncer treated her to the full smile.

When she'd left, Reid turned on his friend. 'And what the hell do you think you're doing?'

'Digging you out of a hole, old chap. That was about to turn into a slanging match and the poor girl was already upset.'

'I know she was, and I was about to apologize until you stepped in with your phoney charm.'

Bouncer shook his head. 'You don't get it, do you? She can't stand you, and if you'd dared to touch her she'd have floored you.'

'You're exaggerating.' Reid opened the door and waited for his friend to follow.

'What about the unarmed combat you told me she can do?'

Reid laughed. 'You don't believe that nonsense, do you? I don't think she could do me much harm.'

Bouncer's limp was more pronounced now he was cold. 'I think, my friend, that she could do you a great deal of harm.'

'And I think the cold wind has seeped into your brain,'

Reid chided as he opened the door of the car. 'Get in before you turn into a gibbering idiot.'

'Ah, here she comes.' Bouncer eased himself into the back of the car. 'She really is very beautiful. I think I might make a play for her myself.'

'Don't you dare,' Reid warned.

When Annie reached them he held open the front passenger door for her, but she ignored him and got in the back with Bouncer. She really knew how to snub a man, he thought, highly amused by her continued hostility. She was wasting her time because it only made him more determined to break through her defences.

On the short journey, Reid decided that he wasn't going to let her get away with this for much longer. Her anger at him was understandable, but he'd apologized, damn it. He thought about his brother and a lump came into his throat. I've made a right mess of my promise to look after your girl, Paul, he said to himself.

The pub had a blazing log fire in the grate so they pulled up a table and chairs and settled down with a drink.

Bouncer held his leg out to the warmth and groaned in relief. 'Oh, that's heaven.'

How did you tell a man like him that he would probably never fly in combat again? Reid thought, his heart aching for his friend. Bouncer was like a fish out of water when he was on the ground and he made no secret that he was determined to get back into the fight.

'Rest your leg on here.' Annie dragged another chair over. 'You might find it more comfortable.'

'Thank you.' Bouncer gave her an approving smile. 'You'd make a good nurse.'

A brief moment of sadness flashed across her face. Reid was curious to know why a casual remark like that should have caused such a reaction. He was beginning to wish he knew more about her.

Bouncer had put a cigarette in his mouth and was trying to light a match with one hand. Annie took it from him, struck the match and held it up so he could light his fag. He nodded his thanks, drew deeply, and blew the smoke up to the ceiling.

Reid was highly amused, because if he'd offered to help he would have been put very firmly in his place with 'I'm not a bloody invalid'. But his friend was certainly playing for full effect now, the crafty devil. Bouncer had a real way with women when he set his mind to it.

He was brought out of his musing when Bouncer asked a question.

'That's right, isn't it, Reid?'

'Sorry. What were you saying?'

'I was telling Annie that I should have baled out.'

'It would have been wise,' he remarked drily.

'The thing is,' Bouncer turned his attention back to Annie again, 'the thought of trusting my life to a flimsy bit of silk terrifies me.'

'Many pilots are alive today because they did just that,' Reid pointed out. He'd lost count of how many times he'd said this to Bouncer. On one occasion he'd even managed to get him up in a DC3 and promised to jump with him, but no amount of urging had made his friend take that step into thin air. He found it quite exhilarating himself, and had even made a couple of jumps before the war. He was sure Bouncer only needed to jump once and then he wouldn't mind doing it again, but persuading him had proved an impossible task.

'I know, but they're braver than me.' Bouncer grimaced in self-disgust.

'I don't believe that,' Annie told him. 'Everyone is scared of something and yours just happens to be jumping out of planes.'

'You're right, of course. Have you ever jumped?' Bouncer asked, his face a picture of innocence.

There was a slight hesitation before she spoke, then, 'I jumped out of a balloon once.'

Reid frowned. Was this another tall tale, like the one about being expert in unarmed combat? 'Why would you do that?'

She gave him a cool look. 'To see what it was like, of course.' Then she turned back to Bouncer and smiled. 'It was frightening but I would do it again.'

Reid listened to her telling his friend all about it, heard her soft laugh, and started to reverse his opinion of her.

First impressions were definitely misleading. He narrowed his eyes and tried to see beyond Annie's apparent delicate façade. This was no weakling; there was a formidable strength of character radiating from her. Before the war she had probably been that rare creature, a career woman, or else she would have married before now. And she was clearly intelligent. He also doubted that she would be swayed by anyone else's opinions, and that was why Paul had never been able to persuade her to marry him. She would make her own decisions in life.

He sipped his beer thoughtfully, feeling a stirring of interest.

He liked her!

20

Annie removed the headphones and stretched her arms above her head, giving a groan of relief. It seemed as if she'd been sitting there for days.

'Come on.' Sam pulled her out of the chair. 'Let's see if they've got any food left in the mess.'

'I jolly well hope they have because I'm starving.' They walked outside and she breathed in deeply, enjoying the cold evening air.

'Looking forward to your leave?' he asked.

'Oh yes, it's an age since I've seen my family. Things have been so hectic we seem to have gone from winter to summer and back to winter without me noticing.'

'Do you even know what year it is?' he asked with obvious amusement.

'I think it's 1942, but the way I'm feeling at the moment, you'd better confirm that,' she joked.

'November 1942, to be exact.' He chuckled at her confusion and opened the mess door for her. 'You've been shut away for too long, Annie, and that's what you get for being so good at your job.'

'Oh, I enjoy it, but I just wish they wouldn't keep dragging me out of bed whenever there's a flap on, except for last night, of course.'

'Yes.' He rubbed his hands together in excitement. 'Montgomery's victory at El Alamein is a real boost to the spirit. This is the turning point, Annie, you can be certain of that.'

'I'm sure you're right.' She yawned. Everyone was so excited by the news that the Germans had been ousted from El Alamein. It was a tremendous boost to morale. 'But I'm so tired, Sam.'

'Well, from tomorrow you can forget everything for seven days and sleep the clock round.'

She sat down, leaving Sam to see what they could get to eat.

He was soon back. 'Spam and chips, all right?'

She grimaced and he chuckled. 'Sorry, they didn't have any rump steak. It'll be about ten minutes.'

'Have they got anything for pudding?' she asked, dreaming of a succulent steak and some of Rose's gorgeous trifle with real cream. Those days of plenty seemed like a dream now.

'Rice, made with powdered milk, of course.'

'Oh, well,' she said in a resigned voice, 'that will fill me up a bit.'

'I don't know how you do it, Annie, there's nothing of you and yet you can eat more than me.'

'Blame it on a deprived childhood,' she told him, moving her arms from the table so that the plate could be put in front of her.

'I don't believe that!' he told her, pinching one of her chips and popping it in his mouth.

She gestured with her knife. 'Get your hands off my chips, you've got more than me, anyway.'

He nicked another one and laughed when she scowled at him.

'You can have my rice pudding, I can't stand the stuff,' he said.

'In that case' – she speared a piece of spam with her fork and held it out to him – 'you can have a bit of this.'

Sam was tremendously cheered by the news lately, and Annie knew he was longing for the day when France would be liberated. Every defeat the Germans suffered made him more animated.

'Oh, no!' he told her in mock horror, 'I couldn't take that, you've had a *deprived* childhood.'

'You don't believe me?' Annie ate the piece of spam, tipped her head to one side and studied the man sitting opposite her. They had an easy rapport with each other now and she enjoyed fighting with him in this light-hearted way. 'Well, next time you see my Rosie, you ask her, she'll tell you what our childhood was like.'

'Are you going to see the magnificent Rose on your leave?' Sam asked.

'Yes.' Annie laughed at his description of her sister. 'They're all back at Roehampton at the moment.'

'I'll drive you there, if you like.'

She gave him a horrified look, remembering the last time she'd been in a truck with him.

'I've been having lessons,' he assured her, his eyes gleaming with mischief.

'Er . . . how many?'

'A couple.'

'No thanks!' She went back to her food. 'I think it would be safer on the train.'

He watched in disbelief as she polished off her spam and two plates of rice pudding.

Annie sat back with a sigh. 'Will you go home when

700

the war's over, or stay in this country?' she asked. She had come to know him quite well, and although he controlled his feelings well she knew he loved his own country. But what would he have to go back to?

'I don't suppose my home is still standing, but yes, I will try to rebuild my life there.'

'What about your family?' He'd never mentioned anyone but Annie was used to having a large and boisterous family, and was curious.

His expression changed to one of simmering anger. 'They were shot. All except my sister. I shall try to find her, if she's still alive.'

'I'm so sorry.' Annie placed her hand over his clenched fist. This was the first indication he'd given about the trauma of his escape from France, and she instinctively reached out to comfort him.

His fingers uncurled and wrapped around hers, the fury leaving his face, and he smiled. 'I can understand something of why Jack found you so comforting. There's an inner peace about you that reaches out and touches other people.'

Annie pulled a face. 'You make me sound more like Florence Nightingale than an ordinary woman.'

'Oh, no, that is not true. You are very beautiful and desirable, and I will not try to fool you, Annie, if I could take you back with me once my country is free, then I would.'

She hadn't missed the sadness in his voice when he spoke about his home. 'What will be waiting for you when you get back?'

'Very little, I suspect, but the land will still be there and I shall enjoy building myself a new home in a free

France. There is much to look forward to. And when I believe that the invasion is imminent, I shall return home' – he gave a boyish grin, his earlier fury gone – 'and cause some mayhem of my own.'

'You'll need a good wireless operator,' she suggested.

'Hmm.' He narrowed his eyes as he looked at her. 'We shall have to see, Ann Webster. Anyway, that is all in the future,' he told her, clearly dismissing the subject. 'I have managed to get more chocolate for the children; you can take it with you. They will be pleased, hmm?'

'Very.' She grinned. 'I had to send the other through the post, but I received the most enthusiastic thanks from both of them.'

Annie hesitated for a moment, and then decided. This man had lost everything, so surely she could share her family with him? 'You must have leave due you.'

'I have, but there seems little point in taking it.'

'Why don't you come home with me, and then you can give the children the chocolate yourself? There's plenty of spare room,' she told him quickly.

'Oh, I would like that very much, but are you sure it would be all right?' he asked, looking eager but doubtful.

'Positive. My friend Dora's coming as well, but we'll go on the train,' she added, the tone of her voice daring him to argue. 'There's one at nine-thirty in the morning, so be ready.'

Dora came over to their table, flushed with excitement. 'Annie, the Americans are having a dance at their base tonight and are sending trucks to collect us. Put your make-up on because we're going.'

Sam sat back and grinned. 'That should be interesting.'

'You can't come,' Dora told him. 'They only want the girls.'

'Now why doesn't that surprise me?' He stood up. 'Behave yourselves, and I'll see you in the morning.'

Jean rushed over looking as excited as Dora. 'Hurry up. The trucks will be here in an hour.'

'I've heard about this base, but how far is it away from here?' Annie asked.

Dora pulled a face. 'My God, I don't think you know what's going on in the outside world. I think all that Morse code bleeping in your ears is scrambling your brains. It's less than fifteen minutes in the truck, especially the way the Yanks drive.'

Annie laughed at her friends as they towed her out of the mess to get ready for the evening.

Annie couldn't believe her eyes. The tables at the end of the room were laden with food, ham, chicken, salmon and all manner of cakes. Things they hadn't seen for the duration of the war. 'Wow! Is that real cream?'

'It certainly is, ma'am,' an American pilot told them. 'Why don't you just tuck in and enjoy yourselves.'

They didn't need any more urging, and nor did the rest of the girls from Chicksands, as they all grabbed a plate. It was a difficult choice but most of them took just a small portion of everything, not wishing to appear greedy.

'Better take it easy,' Dora cautioned. 'Our stomachs aren't used to rich food any more.'

'Quite right.' Annie bit into a pastry and groaned in ecstasy as cream oozed out. She licked her fingers, not wishing to waste a precious drop of this luxury. At that moment a big military band burst into life with Glenn Miller's 'In The Mood', and the dance floor became a seething mass of gyrating bodies. The music was so uplifting it made everyone in the room smile and determined to enjoy themselves. Gladys was here with her boyfriend, and that probably meant another bottle of bourbon for them to enjoy. It was always shared out between the sixteen in their hut, and Dora and Jean who had become honorary members of their group.

It was a glorious evening and Annie even managed to jive with some of the Americans. They had all been very polite, and seemed to have fun teaching them how to do their dance. At eleven o'clock they were all in the trucks again, tired but happy after such an unexpected treat, and on their way back to camp.

The next day, the two houses in Roehampton were already full when Annie, Dora and Sam arrived. There were Rose, Wally, Marj, James, Kate and George, who loved the children so much he wouldn't let them out of his sight. Charlie had made it as well, and was still wildly enthusiastic about being a mechanic in the air force. It would have been even better if Bill and Will could have been there but they were both at sea and you never knew when they might turn up. This was a fact of life for everyone now and it was accepted without comment.

'It is very good of you to let me stay,' Sam told Rose, dropping his bag on the floor with a thud. He stooped down to open it and produced tins of fruit, corned beef, powdered egg and milk, and a few other treats.

'Where did you get all that?' Rose gasped, as the food was put on to the table.

'While the girls were dancing at the American base I slipped into the kitchens, and they were very generous to a poor homeless Frenchman.' He gave a dramatic sigh.

'You crafty thing,' Annie chided. 'Why didn't you let us know you were there?'

'Oh, they wouldn't let me in the dance hall, they wanted to keep all the girls to themselves.' He made a pretence of searching the bag. 'Now what else have I got here?'

'I should think you've brought quite enough,' Marj told him, eyeing the row of tins and packets in wonder.

'No, no, I'm sure there's something else.' He was on his knees and rummaging in the bag. 'Ah!' he exclaimed, pulling out two bars of chocolate and handing one to each child.

'Wow!' James couldn't seem to believe his eyes, and turned the bar over and over in his hands. 'Thanks, Sam.'

Kate threw her arms around his neck and kissed him on the cheek.

'Don't eat it all at once,' Rose admonished her children.

'We won't, Mum. We'll put it away until tomorrow.' James looked at his sister who was clearly tempted to start on the chocolate at once. 'Come on, Kate, let's leave it in our bedrooms.'

They both headed up the stairs, clutching their precious gifts.

Sam started to help Rose put the tins in a cupboard. 'And what have you been doing with yourself since I last saw you, madam?' he asked with a strong French accent.

'Not as much mischief as you have, I'll be bound,' Rose teased.

'She was in London during the worst of the Blitz,'

George interrupted. 'When she couldn't get the ambulance through the rubble, she got out and started digging for survivors.' His tone was exasperated, but he couldn't hide the pride in his voice.

'Well, you don't need to worry any more, Dad,' she told him. 'The worst seems to be over, and I'm only an air raid warden now.'

'Only!' George threw his hands up in a gesture of defeat. 'The raids on London might have eased, but the Luftwaffe is picking on our historic cities now. Exeter, Bath, York, places like that, and when Jerry's finished with those he'll most likely start on London again.'

'Pessimist.' Rose grinned at her father. 'You worry too much, Dad.' She finished packing the food away and then spotted a packet of biscuits on the table. 'Where did those come from?'

'I brought them.' Dora held out two packets of tea and a bag of carrots. 'I thought you might like these as well. I went and made eyes at the cook.'

'Well done,' Marj complimented her and picked up a packet of tea. 'I think this calls for a nice cuppa, don't you? And while we drink it we can decide who is going to sleep where.'

It was eleven o'clock before Annie wandered downstairs the next day. The rain was pounding on the windows and she'd been so comfortable in her own bed that she had just turned over and gone back to sleep.

She stuck her head round the kitchen door and saw only her mother and Rose in there. 'Do you need any help?'

'Ah, you've surfaced at last, have you? What have you

706

been doing to get so worn out?' Her mother handed her a cup of tea.

'Working.' Annie walked in and leant on the sink. 'What can I do?'

'Nothing.' Rose hustled her towards the door. 'Go and join the others in the front room, we've got everything under control here.'

They clearly didn't need her so she went to find the rest of them.

Sam was sprawled on the floor playing snakes and ladders with Kate; Wally and George were immersed in a game of draughts and everyone else was reading. Pirate was standing on the back of an armchair watching the rain and giving a ratty grumble from time to time.

Annie was greeted when she came in, then they all went back to what they had been doing. She sat in an armchair, sipped her tea and gazed into the fire. This is lovely, she thought with a satisfied smile on her face. No straining to pick up Morse code under atmospherics, no jumping to attention, or rushed meals. It was only when she was away from the base that she realized how tiring the work was. It took total concentration, but she still loved it and wouldn't want to do anything else.

Suddenly Charlie surged to his feet. 'Come on, Dora, let's put our coats on and take Pirate to Barnes Common for a run.'

The dog's ears shot up at the mention of his name, and he jumped down straight away and started to tear around in excitement.

Dora tossed her book aside and stood up. 'That's a good idea. Do you want to come, Annie?'

She shook her head and yawned again. 'No thanks, I'll stay by the fire.'

Charlie ruffled her hair as he walked past. 'Try and wake up by tonight, because Sam and me are taking you girls out dancing in Richmond. We want to see if you can do the jive.'

'What's that?' Annie pretended she was puzzled. Charlie didn't know they'd been taught by the Yanks, and she did love to tease him.

Her brother frowned at Sam. 'Where do you keep her, in a cage?'

Sam shook the dice in his hand and grinned. 'Something like that.'

Pirate had obviously had enough of this delay and dropped his lead at Charlie's feet.

'Oops! We'd better go. We'll show you tonight, Annie.'

The next three days were the most relaxed Annie had spent for some time. It stopped raining, they took long walks in Richmond Park, went to a dance and the pictures.

They returned on the fourth day after an invigorating walk to find an air force truck parked outside the house.

'Looks like trouble,' Sam said, striding into the kitchen, where the driver was enjoying a cup of tea.

He jumped to his feet when he saw Sam, and handed him a sealed envelope.

Sam slit it open and read in silence for a while, then said, 'I have to leave.' He looked at Rose and Marj. 'I have enjoyed myself immensely.'

'You are welcome any time,' Rose told him.

He smiled and headed for the stairs. It only took

him five minutes to get his kit together, and after a quick goodbye to everyone, he hurried out to the truck.

'Sam!' Annie caught him at the gate. 'You're not going to do anything dangerous, are you?'

He bent and touched his lips to her cheek in a fleeting kiss. 'It is just another boat trip.'

She knew how dangerous that could be.

It was ten o'clock the next morning before Annie dragged herself out of bed, and as it was raining she played games with the children or read a book and dozed by the fire. Outwardly she was relaxed and enjoying her rest, but her mind was racing. Where was Sam now? But she wasn't allowed to dwell on this too much, as Kate and James dragged her into dealing the cards for a game of snap.

There was a knock on the front door, and James listened to the sound of voices, and then leapt to his feet. 'More visitors,' he exclaimed and shot out of the door, closely followed by his sister.

Annie, finding herself alone, stood up. She had better go and see who had arrived.

Her mother was making tea, as usual; James was standing in front of two tall airmen, gazing at them in worship, and Kate was surveying them from the other side of the table, a rapt expression on her face. And what Dora was thinking was anyone's guess, but Annie knew she would find out after their visitors had left. Her friend was studying the pilots and would no doubt have some comments to make.

'Hello, Bouncer.' Annie spoke quietly and waited for

him to turn, relieved to see he could move with more ease than the last time she'd seen him.

'Annie!' He reached out with his good arm and pulled her towards him for a kiss on the cheek. 'We didn't know you'd be here. Have they let you loose for a few days?'

'Yes, I'm on leave. They think they can do without me for a while,' she joked. Annie had only met Bouncer once but he seemed like an old friend. 'How are you?'

'I'm fine, but the station commander here still won't let me fly.' Bouncer glared at his friend. 'Says he can't do without my help, but he's lying, of course.'

These two men were obviously great friends and Annie suspected that Reid was concerned about Bouncer, and was trying to keep him out of combat as long as he could.

Reid, who hadn't taken his eyes off Annie, smiled. 'You're looking well, Webster.'

She snapped to attention and gave a sloppy salute, although she was out of uniform and wearing a pair of slacks and a jumper. Reid had an amused glint in his eyes and Annie had a job to keep a straight face. He really was quite handsome. 'Thank you, sir.'

'At ease.' Reid started to chuckle as he gazed at her casual outfit, his eyes lingering on her curves.

The look he'd just given her told her, quite plainly, that he liked what he saw. Reid Lascells was a vital, physical man and she was beginning to feel drawn to him. That was dangerous . . .

Bouncer groaned and raised his eyebrows, looking around at everyone. 'They haven't been in the same room for more than two minutes and they're at it again. As soon as they see each other they fight.'

Annie laughed with everyone else and pulled a chair

out for Bouncer. 'Sit down, both of you, and tell us what you're doing here.'

'Reid came to thank me for the letters I've been writing to his parents.' Marj said and poured them all a cup of tea. She smiled with pleasure as Bouncer slid her a packet of the precious brew. 'Oh, thank you so much, that was very thoughtful of you.' Bouncer received a kiss on the cheek for that.

'How are they?' Annie asked Reid. 'I meant to get over and see them, but I've been so busy.'

'They understand, and the letters they've received from you and your mother have been much appreciated. Losing Paul has been a terrible blow, but they're coming to terms with it, slowly.'

'I'm glad.' Annie knew it was going to take his parents a long time, and Paul would never be forgotten by any of them.

'Would you stay for lunch?' Marj asked them.

'Thank you, but we must get back.' Reid stood up. 'This was only a fleeting visit as we were in the area.'

After they'd gone, Annie went back to her reading, but couldn't concentrate. They'd only refused lunch because it wasn't the done thing to take other people's rations. If you knew you were going to eat at someone's house you took food with you, just as Sam and Dora had done. Still, she was glad they hadn't stayed as her nerves were too strung out from worrying about Sam, without having to put up with Reid's disturbing presence.

Dora came into the lounge and sat beside Annie. 'Well, well, so that was Reid Lascells. Wow!'

'I'm not denying that he's gorgeous' – Annie looked over the top of her book – 'but he's an awkward devil.'

'Yeah, I'll bet he is!'

Dora grinned at her, so Annie went back to her reading, feeling it was better to cut this conversation off right now!

21

'It was a shame Will couldn't get home,' Annie told Dora, when they were on the train going back to Chicksands. 'But did you enjoy yourself?'

'Of course I did, Annie. You know I adore your family.' Dora cast her friend a sideways glance. 'Fancy Paul's brother and his mate turning up like that.'

'Just fancy.' Annie gave a snort of disbelief. She'd managed to fend off Dora's talk about Reid for the rest of their leave, but now they were on the train there wouldn't be any escape from her opinions. 'Bouncer didn't know I would be there, his surprise was genuine, but I'll bet Reid did. He's always writing, and sometimes I get the feeling the blasted man is following me.'

'No.' Dora shook her head. 'I'm sure he didn't know – and anyway, what have you got against the poor man?'

Annie had never spoken about Reid's rudeness when he'd come to tell her about Paul. It had upset her too much at the time, and still did, she had to admit. She didn't normally harbour a grudge or take offence so easily, but the circumstances had been distressing, and she couldn't seem to let go of it. Taking a deep breath, she started to tell her friend what had happened, allowing the hurt to see the light of day for the first time. And she was surprised at the intensity of her feelings for him. It was a confusing mixture of dislike and admiration. He really was a most disturbing man!

'Oh, Annie.' Dora patted her arm in sympathy. 'That's no reason to be so hostile towards him. I expect he was devastated by his brother's death and lashed out at the nearest person he could. Everyone reacts to grief in a different way. He's obviously sorry for the way he acted, you ought to understand that and forgive him.'

'You're quite right, but there's something about him . . .'

'He's too handsome?' Dora asked.

'Hmm.' Annie's mouth turned up at the corners in amusement. 'He is a bit of a stunner, isn't he?'

'There's a very kind man lurking under that abrupt exterior, and I can't help thinking he would make you a gorgeous husband.'

Annie stared at her friend in astonishment. 'Now you're delving into the realms of fantasy.'

Dora roared with laughter, drawing curious stares from the packed train. 'You sounded just like Rose then.'

'I'll take that as a compliment,' she told her.

'It was meant as one.' Dora studied Annie carefully. 'Have you fallen for Sam?'

'I like him and he is attractive.' Annie stared out of the train window, trying to decide how she really felt. 'But I don't think it's more than that.'

'If you don't love him, Annie, then let him know, because I think he's attracted to you. He's had enough sorrow in his life, hasn't he?'

'Yes, he has, and it isn't going to be easy for him when he returns to France.' How would someone recover from being thrown out of their country and losing all their family? Britain had suffered death, destruction and a shortage of food, but they hadn't had to deal with a conquering force walking the streets.

'Then leave him alone, my friend.' Dora smiled. 'If you're not sure if you love him, then I can tell you that you *don't*.'

'Oh, how can you tell?' Annie frowned. She'd heard girls talking about being in love, and listened to their raptures as they explained that they couldn't live without a certain person, but quite honestly she'd never felt so bowled over. She was fond of a lot of men, but each time she'd asked herself if this was the one man for her she hadn't been able to give an affirmative answer. This being in love was a mystery to her.

'You just know when it's right. That's all I can tell you.'

Annie settled back in her seat. 'Do you know what you feel for Will?'

'I'm in love with him. Do you mind?'

'Not at all.' Annie grinned. 'Welcome to the Webster family, Dora.'

'Oh, don't be hasty.' She held her hands up in horror. 'Will hasn't said he loves me yet, but I'm hopeful.' Dora looked curiously at her friend. 'You've changed since we first met, do you know that?'

'So you told me once before, but a lot has happened, and I'm sure none of us will come out of this war unscathed.' Annie shrugged. 'I hope you don't think I've changed for the worse?'

'No, I think I like the new Annie Webster better, but be careful you keep your gentleness. I'm not sure exactly what you've been doing, but I know that it's something quite traumatic, and you're starting to bury your feelings.'

That remark, from someone she trusted so much, shook Annie. She had seen her sister Rose do exactly the same thing when she'd been about twenty-one and remembered how worried they'd all felt. She mustn't do the same thing. She'd send Reid a letter of apology – as soon as she had time.

'Hi, Annie,' Sam greeted her as she walked into his office. 'Did you enjoy the rest of your holiday?'

'Yes, thanks. How did your trip go?'

'Weather was rough, but we didn't have to swim back.' He grinned. 'But it was a successful exercise.'

She didn't ask what the emergency had been, knowing Sam wouldn't give her an answer. She was surrounded by secrecy in her job and you were only told what was necessary. She headed for her desk, feeling refreshed and ready to start work again after her leave.

She was soon totally absorbed in what she was doing and jumped when she was tapped on the shoulder.

'There's someone here to see you, so take an hour's break,' the officer told her. 'He's waiting outside.'

Annie was alarmed to see her brother Charlie waiting for her, and pacing up and down in a very agitated way. She'd only seen him this morning as they'd all prepared to return to their bases. It looked as if he'd thrown his air force uniform on in a hurry; if an officer saw him with buttons undone and tie badly knotted he would be put on a charge. A sense of dread gripped her.

'What's happened?' she asked, rushing up to him.

His face was ashen and he was close to tears, but he just gazed at her without speaking.

'Charlie! Tell me,' she exclaimed.

Her brother took a deep breath and blurted out, 'Will's missing.'

Stunned, Annie hugged her brother, and a strange thing happened. She was back in the scullery of the Garrett Street house during the First World War, the day they'd received the telegram saying that their father was missing. It was as if Rose was standing beside her again saying, '*Missing doesn't mean he's dead.*'

'When did the news arrive?' Her mind was racing, searching for some way to comfort him. The brothers had always been close, and she knew this would hit Charlie very hard, as it would every member of the Webster family.

'This morning, after you'd gone.' He gulped, trying to control his emotions. 'I rushed to the station to catch you but the train had already left.'

'How is everyone coping?'

He lifted his shoulders in a helpless gesture. 'We're all worried, of course, but Mum is holding up quite well, and Rose is being positive.' A brief smile flashed across his face at the mention of their sister. 'She's trying to get information out of the Admiralty with not much success at the moment.'

Annie was relieved to see her brother more in control. Worry and fear gnawed away at her but she was determined to hold herself together. If she broke down now it would upset Charlie even more.

'Thanks, Sis, I feel better for talking with you.' He gave her another hug.

'Are you going back home?' she asked.

'No, I've got to return to base at once.' A worried frown appeared. 'Tell Dora. I've gathered from Will's letters that they have a romance going, albeit from a distance.'

'I'll do it right away.' She watched her brother jump into a truck and drive away, and then she went to look for Dora. This wasn't going to be easy, and she wanted to get it over with.

Annie found her friend in the mess, taking a break.

'Ah, come up for air at last, have you?' Dora pushed her a cup of tea across the table. 'Here, you look as if you need this, I'll get another one.'

'Sit down again, Dora, I've something to tell you.'

'What is it?' Her friend touched her hand in sympathy. 'You look upset.'

'There isn't any easy way to do this.' Annie's eyes clouded with tears and she wiped them away with her hand. She now had an inkling of how Reid must have felt when he'd had to tell her about Paul.

'Tell it straight, Annie.' Dora's mouth set in a straight line.

'Will's been reported missing. His ship was torpedoed, but that's all we know at the moment.'

Annie's friend let out a ragged sigh. 'I thought you were going to tell me he was dead, but missing doesn't sound so final.'

'You're needed back on duty, Annie.' Sam was standing next to their table.

She squeezed Dora's hand, and then stood up, wishing she could stay a while longer, not only to help Dora but also to deal with her own emotions. However, they had all learned that you had to keep going, whatever was happening in your own life. 'I'll let you know the moment there's any news.'

As she headed for the door, Sam fell into step beside her. 'Trouble?'

'My brother Will is missing. Dora's been writing to him and I think they are serious about each other.'

Sam stopped suddenly and swore in two languages. 'If I'd known I wouldn't have dragged you back to work.'

'That's all right, I'd rather be busy.' She gave a tired smile. 'You know that's how I cope with grief. When is it all going to end?' she asked wearily.

'Not for a while yet, I'm afraid.'

Annie straightened up and marched along with a determined stride. Let's hope 1943 will be a better year, she thought.

Over the next three days Annie phoned her sister a couple of times a day, and after each call felt weighed down with worry and disappointment. On the fourth day after she'd heard about Will she tried again and prayed for some good news this time.

'Rose!' The line was bad and she had to shout down the phone. 'Have you heard anything yet?'

'Nothing yet, but it's only been a few days.'

'How's Mum bearing up?'

'She's all right, Annie. She's no stranger to trouble, as you know, and all we can do is wait.'

'It's hard though,' Annie grumbled. 'Anything else been happening?'

'We're all getting ready to go to Wales for Christmas, and Reid came round with some sweets for the children.'

Reid! Blast, she'd forgotten all about her apology. 'That was kind of him.'

Rose's laugh echoed down the distorted line. 'He's a handsome beast, isn't he?'

'I agree with . . .' Annie was talking to herself and it wasn't worth trying to get reconnected. She'd phoned for news of Will, but there wasn't any.

Annie wandered back to her hut and wrote to Reid, before it slipped her mind again.

'What are you looking so pensive about?' Bouncer eased himself into a chair.

Reid glanced up from the letter he was reading. 'Hmm?'

'I asked why the deep frown, old boy? Who's the letter from?' Bouncer leaned forward to get a closer look. 'It isn't in green ink, so it can't be Annie.'

'Yes, it is, but she only uses that when she's being rude to me.' Reid watched his friend light a cigarette, using both hands quite freely. 'It's a sort of an apology. She says she's sorry for insulting me whenever we've met.'

'That's nice.' Bouncer took a deep drag on his fag, watching his friend through a cloud of smoke.

'Then she ends by saying that she would appreciate it if I would stop pestering her with letters.'

'Ah, that sounds more like our Annie. I was getting worried there for a minute.'

'So was I.' Reid grimaced and fanned away the smoke drifting towards his face. 'What the blazes are you smoking?'

'Got them from a Yank.' Bouncer grinned as he waved the cigarette under Reid's nose. 'Do you want one, they're not bad.'

'No thanks.'

'So, why do you think Annie suddenly decided to apologize?'

Reid folded the letter and put it back in the envelope. 'She's probably feeling down at the moment; her brother Will has been reported missing.'

'Hell, I'm sorry about that. Air force, is he?'

'Fleet Air Arm, and I expect they're all worried sick.'

'Yeah.' Bouncer lit another American cigarette and fished in his pocket for a Players Navy Cut, then handed that to Reid. 'They're a nice family, and what do you think of Rose? If she wasn't a happily married woman, I'd like to take her on. What a beauty!'

Reid laughed at his friend's expression. 'You'd have a job in your state of health.'

'I'm nearly back to full strength, but you, my friend, are looking frayed around the edges. How long is it since you've had some fun? And more to the point, how long is it since you've bedded a woman?'

'Let me see.' Reid blew smoke rings in the air, his brow furrowed in thought. 'Bugger if I can remember.'

'Right! That settles it.' Bouncer dragged Reid out of the chair. 'We're going out on the town tonight to find ourselves a couple of girls.'

Reid opened a drawer and shunted the paperwork into it. He'd deal with that tomorrow.

'What do you think of those?' Bouncer nudged Reid so hard his beer slopped on to the table.

He peered through the smoke-filled bar. 'Too young.'

'Hmm. Perhaps you're right. Drink up and I'll get the next round in.'

Reid watched his friend weave towards the bar, and

then studied the dregs in the bottom of his glass. This hadn't been such a good idea. He was restless, unsettled and drinking himself senseless wasn't going to help.

A soldier started to pound on the piano and the bar erupted into 'Roll Out the Barrel'. The table Reid was leaning on actually shook as everyone sang at the tops of their voices.

Bouncer arrived back carrying a tray full of pints of beer. 'Thought I'd get a few reserves in, it was like a rugby scrum trying to reach the bar.' He shouted above the racket.

'Let's go in there,' Reid yelled, pointing to the door of the saloon bar.

They fought their way into the quieter room and closed the door behind them. They could still hear the noise from the other bar, but at least it was muffled now.

'Are you sober enough to have a serious talk?' Bouncer asked, when they'd settled themselves at a table in the corner of the bar.

Reid eyed the four pints lined up in front of him and tried to remember how many he had had already. 'You'd better talk now, because by the time I've polished off those, I'll be incapable of doing anything.'

'I've put in a request to return to my squadron,' Bouncer announced.

'Ah, I thought it wouldn't be long; you've made a remarkable recovery. And to tell you the truth, Bouncer, I've been considering the same thing myself.' He couldn't remember when he'd been so restless, and had wondered if flying regularly again would help. The only thing stopping him was the distress he knew it would cause his parents. They thought he was safe on the ground for the duration of the war, running the Tangmere airbase. If he took to the air again they would be in constant fear of him being killed, and after losing Paul he didn't want to put them through that.

'You mustn't do that, old boy. You're a first class administrator.' Bouncer emptied his glass and pulled another one towards him. 'You've been used to running the family business. What do you make?'

'Nut and bolts.'

'That's right, and very useful too. Well, as I was saying, you've been used to working for a living and you're making a damned good job of station commander . . .' Another pint vanished. 'But I've come from the idle rich and the only useful thing I've ever done in my life is fly, and being grounded is driving me round the bend.'

'I know how you feel.' Reid drank two pints in quick succession. He was a bit out of practice with this drinking lark, but he'd soon get back into it again . . . with Bouncer's help.

Bouncer watched and grinned. 'Now you're getting the hang of it. Have you had enough booze to make you forget the desirable Annie?'

'Who's she?' Reid finished off his last pint and heaved himself on to his feet. 'I don't think those two girls were that young, do you?'

'Nope.' Bouncer staggered upright. 'Perfect age, I would say.'

'Come on, then. Let's have some fun.' Reid draped an arm over Bouncer's shoulder and the pair of them lurched back into the public bar, singing 'White Cliffs of Dover'.

22

January 1943

Annie was so excited. What a way to start the new year! The last few weeks had been terrible as they'd waited for news of Will, and to make matters worse they hadn't heard from Bill for weeks. She knew Rose fretted in her own quiet way, but kept her fears to herself. However, George had finally won the battle he'd been having with Rose and had persuaded her that it was time she joined them in Wales. James and Kate were living there most of the time and they didn't see enough of her. She had agreed in the end to move there and was no doubt immersed in her beloved books again. Her sister had never lost her thirst for knowledge; it was part of her character. She was still in the WVS and had taken over the library books in a convalescent hospital for injured servicemen. Rose would enjoy that. Annie remembered how concerned her sister had been for the ex-servicemen after the last war. She had done all she could for them and would want to help again.

She walked into Dora's hut and found her sitting on the bunk gazing at a photo of a tall sailor.

'Get your coat,' Annie ordered, 'we're going down the pub for a drink.'

'Oh, I don't think – '

'It's no good you arguing. You're coming whether you

724

want to or not.' Annie's heart went out to her friend. The long wait without any news had been agonizing.

'Come on, Dora,' she coaxed. 'It will do us both good.'

'You're right.' The photo was tucked back into a bag and Dora sighed. 'Life goes on, eh?'

''Course it does. Everything's going to be all right, you'll see.'

She gave Annie a suspicious look. 'You seem very bright; have you been at the booze already?'

'No, but I'm certainly going to have a few tonight.'

'Well, if that's how you feel, what are we hanging around here for?' Dora shivered as a blast of cold wind hit them on the way to the gate. 'Damned cold tonight, have you got your knickers on?'

Annie stopped and lifted her skirt a little to show the hated air force issue.

Dora smirked. 'I can't help remembering when we saw these dreadful bloomers for the first time.'

'They're warm though, but I draw the line at wearing those awful brassieres.' Annie signalled the driver of a truck. 'You going near the Red Lion pub?'

'Sure. Jump in.'

The place was crowded as usual, and Annie stood in the doorway, searching the faces. At that moment she saw him and her face broke into a brilliant smile. 'Look over there,' she told her friend.

With a cry of joy, Dora shot across the room into the waiting arms of Will. He kissed Dora, then lifted his head and smiled at his sister, drawing her into his embrace.

'Annie!' Dora was crying. 'Why didn't you tell me?'

'He just walked in earlier. No one told us he was all right and on his way home.'

'I asked Annie to keep it a secret.' He kissed Dora again. 'I wanted to surprise you.'

'You've done that all right!'

'Hey, mate, that's a bit greedy, hugging two gorgeous women at once.'

Annie could just make out the figure of an Australian soldier through her tear-clouded vision.

Will laughed. 'This is Dora, and that's Annie.'

'Good grief!' the Australian exclaimed. 'That's never little Annie?'

Annie rubbed her eyes so she could see better, and studied the man. He was talking as if he knew her, but she was sure she'd never seen him before.

'Don't you recognize him, Annie?' Will asked, looking highly amused. 'This is Bob.'

'Bob?' She gazed at him in bewilderment. There was something vaguely familiar about the man.

'Take a closer look. It's our long lost brother.'

'Bob?' she cried, then threw her arms around him and received a bear hug in return. 'We didn't think we'd ever see you again. Have you seen Mum?'

'Yes, and Rose.' He grimaced. 'You should have heard what *she* called me.'

'I can imagine, and you deserve all you get from her,' Annie pointed out, as she remembered the upset Bob had caused when he'd run away to sea as a young boy. He'd been a rebellious child, nasty, bad-tempered, and always fighting with Rose who did her best to control him. It was only after he'd run away that they'd realized

726

how unhappy he had been, and how he'd hated life in Garrett Street.

'I know, and I'm sorry I hurt everyone, but I couldn't take it any more. I just had to get out of that dreadful hovel. Mum said she understands.'

Annie nodded. 'We all managed to get out eventually, and it's all thanks to Rose and Bill.'

Bob shook his head in disbelief. 'I've heard the whole story and it's hard to believe the things Rose has done, and without her our family would have ended up in the workhouse. I still remember that terrible beating she took from the old man as she tried to get the rent money back from him. She's still as fierce, though.' He gave a deep chuckle. 'When I saw her glaring at me with those black eyes, I nearly turned tail and got out of there quick. But I would have known her anywhere.'

'Sit down everyone.' Will pinched another chair from the next table. 'We've got a lot of catching up to do.'

'I'll get a round of drinks in first,' Bob said.

Annie watched him make his way through the crowd, absolutely astonished by this turn of events. There had been sporadic letters from him over the years, but they had been brief, giving little indication of his life in Australia, except to assure them that he was all right. When he'd written to let them know that he was getting married, their mother had been upset because she couldn't be there to see her son on his special day. 'He's an officer, Will.'

'Yeah, who'd have believed it, and he's attached to a British unit here. He's doing all right for himself, and when you look at him now it's hard to believe he was once a rebellious tearaway.'

Dora was holding on to Will's arm and appeared to be speechless with happiness. Annie had never seen her friend so quiet before.

'What happened to you?' Annie asked Will when Bob returned with the drinks.

'I was on my way back from America when the troopship I was on was so badly damaged by a U-boat attack that we had to take to the lifeboats. The weather was appalling and we were scattered all over the ocean so it took some time to find us.'

'What on earth were you doing in America?' Dora asked, finding her voice at last.

'I'd been working in one of their factories, learning about the American engines. A merchant ship eventually picked us up, which was a damned risky thing to do. Then we went straight into battle again, and the radio room was damaged. Fortunately for us a destroyer came back to look for the straggler and saved us from further damage.'

Annie understood why they hadn't had any news before. Her brother was making light of it but things must have been dangerous.

'When I turned up it caused quite a rumpus, but not as much as when Bob walked in an hour later.' He gave a deep chuckle. 'Mum didn't know whether to hit him or hug him.'

'Rose knew what she wanted to do, though,' said Bob grinning. 'She would have liked to shake me until my teeth rattled.'

'And she could do it,' Dora said and laughed.

'You don't have to remind me what she's capable of.' Bob took some photos out of his pocket and gave them to Annie. 'That's my wife and daughter, Sara, with baby Emma.'

'Ah, they're lovely, Bob.' She touched her brother's hand, pleased to see he had such a lovely family. 'Are you happy in Australia?'

'I was until this bloody war started. I've got a sheep farm and love the wide open spaces; after Bermondsey it's paradise.'

Now Dora had got over the shock of seeing Will again she was bursting with curiosity. 'Would someone tell me what's going on? I didn't know you had another brother, Annie?'

'Bob ran away to sea when I was only little,' Annie explained, 'and this is the first time we've seen him since he disappeared.'

'Wow! What a night this is turning out to be!' Dora smiled happily and clung on to Will's arm even tighter.

'Did you enjoy yourself in America?' Annie asked her brother.

'I'll say. But do you know they don't have a tea break in their factories?' He looked scandalized. 'They've got these machines and you can get drinks from them, but we weren't going to have that. We bought a small camping stove, a saucepan to boil the water in, tea, milk, sugar and biscuits, but we couldn't get a teapot anywhere so we had to use a coffee pot.'

Annie was laughing. She could just imagine a group of British sailors wanting their tea break, and she wondered if they put a tot of rum in it as well. She wouldn't put it past them. 'And what did you do then?'

'We sat on boxes, lit the stove and brewed up in

the middle of the factory floor.' He shook his head in amusement. 'The Yanks thought it was hilarious and used to call out "Having a tea party, boys?"'

There was so much news to catch up on that the evening flew by, and all the time they drank steadily. Annie didn't know how much she'd had, but she was too happy to keep count. This was a night to enjoy and blast the consequences!

As she reached out to pick up another glass, it was whipped out of her way. 'You're not going to be fit for anything in the morning.'

She peered at the man standing beside the table. 'Hello, Sam, I didn't know you were here.'

'I've been sitting no more than six feet from you all evening, watching you trying to get drunk.'

'I think I've made quite a good job of it,' Annie giggled. 'Sam, meet my brothers. Will has just been rescued from the sea, and the last time I saw Bob I was no taller than knee-high.'

'Ah.' Sam shook hands with the men. 'I see the reason for the celebration, but I'm afraid I need Annie sharp and alert tomorrow.'

'He's my boss,' Annie informed them from behind her hand, and then fell about laughing as if it was the funniest thing she'd ever said.

Bob was grinning. 'It's a bit late for that, mate. She's plastered; you'd better take her back now.'

Dora whispered in Annie's ear. 'Go back with Sam. I'm staying with Will tonight.'

'Right.' She managed to stand up by holding on to the table. 'What are you going to do now, Bob?'

'I've got a room here for the night, the same as Will,

and in the morning I'm going to Wales with Mum and Wally to meet Rose's kids.' He stood up and smiled ruefully. 'I'm told I'll also see Rose's real father, Sir George Gresham. That was a turn-up for the book, wasn't it?'

'You'll like him, Bob,' Will said. 'That's where Rose gets her fiery temperament from.'

'I can't wait.' Bob wiped his brow in mock fear.

Annie hugged both her brothers, and being in a very emotional state shed a few tears, before being helped out of the pub by Sam.

'Jush you and me, then, Sam.' The cold air had a strange effect on her and she gave a lopsided smile. 'I'm so happy.'

'I can see that.' He held her around the waist to keep her upright. 'Wish I'd brought the truck with me.'

Annie staggered as she shook her head. 'Noo, rather walk.'

He chuckled. 'Still don't trust my driving, then?'

'I'm not that drunk.' She tried to prove the point by pushing him away and walking in a straight line – without any success at all.

'Really? You could have fooled me.' He grabbed hold of her again as she staggered dangerously, then they headed up the road towards Chicksands.

They had almost reached her hut when she stopped and threw her arms around Sam's neck. 'Kiss me.'

He did, but it was a gentle, teasing embrace.

'You're not taking this seriously,' she complained. 'I think I could fall in love with you.'

'I don't want you to do that, Annie, but I wouldn't mind some uncontrollable lust.'

731

She leant against him and sighed. 'I think I can manage that.'

Annie opened one eye and groaned. She had to be on duty in an hour and she didn't think she could move.

'Here, drink this.' Dora thrust a glass of something fizzy at her.

Without asking what it was Annie emptied the glass and then shuddered. 'Hell, that is the first and last time I ever get drunk.'

Dora sat on the edge of the bed. 'You'll feel better when you get moving.'

'You sure?' Annie was finding that hard to believe. There was a notice on the wall opposite her and she could swear it was sliding up and down of its own accord.

Her friend nodded and grinned. 'You're not used to drinking and you really overdid it last night.'

'Well, I've learnt my lesson. Never again!' She looked at Dora's happy expression. 'You seem cheerful enough. Had a good night, did you?'

'Wonderful! Annie, me and Will are getting married.'

'Oh, that's marvellous,' Annie exclaimed, throwing her arms around Dora in delight. 'When?'

'As soon as we can.' Dora hugged her back, and then glanced at her watch. 'I'll tell you all about it later, but you'd better hurry or Sam will be furious with you.'

Sam! The way she had behaved last night came rushing into her thoughts, and she coloured in embarrassment. 'Oh, my God!'

'That look of horror tells me you've been up to something. What have you and the delectable Sam been doing?'

'I remember getting back here, and then I tried to seduce him.' Annie buried her head in her hands. 'After that my mind's a blank.'

'You've made it then.' Sam studied her face carefully. 'You look awful; are you all right?'

'That's what I need you to tell me.'

'Ah' – he was clearly fighting to keep a straight face – 'you can't remember our night of passion.'

She took a deep breath. 'Tell me what I missed.'

'After you threw yourself into my arms and begged me to make love to you . . .' He paused.

'Begged?' Lord, but she'd really made a fool of herself this time.

Sam nodded. 'Definitely *begged*.'

'What happened then?' she asked with a resigned air.

'You passed out.'

'And?' She had to know the whole sordid truth.

'Annie,' Sam laughed, 'I didn't want to make love to a senseless woman. I expect the girl I'm with to join in with enthusiasm, or it's no fun. I put you to bed – your bed. I had to do it myself because the place was deserted – not a damned female in sight when you need one,' he complained.

Annie sagged in relief. 'So nothing happened?'

'Well, I wouldn't say that.' He raised his eyebrows. 'I did have the pleasure of undressing you, but that's all.' He sighed. 'I managed to control myself, but it was damned frustrating. Still, those terrible military issue knickers did help to cool my ardour a little.'

Annie blushed. 'I was wearing them because it was so

733

cold. I'm sorry for my disgraceful conduct. And I'm never going to get drunk again.'

'It would be wise,' he told her. 'Drink obviously makes you amorous, and the next man you try that with might not have my self-control. Can you remember anything?'

'Yes.' Her head came up and her gaze locked on to his eyes. 'You told me you didn't want me to fall in love with you. Why?'

'I would find it impossible to place you in danger again, and I can't afford that kind of emotional baggage. It clouds the judgement, as you well know, and I don't know what awaits me when this war is finally over.'

'Are you going to send me to France again, Sam?' she asked quietly.

'Once the invasion is imminent, then I might not have any choice. We're going to need as many operatives as possible to help the Resistance disrupt German communications.'

The hangover was forgotten and she smiled. 'I wouldn't mind doing another parachute jump.'

'Hmm. You like a bit of excitement. Is that why you never married your pilot friend? Was he too tame for you?'

Annie chewed her lip, deep in thought. That had never occurred to her before. 'There's nothing like a war to make you realize what you really are, is there?'

'I agree, and our true nature comes as a shock, eh?'

She changed the subject. 'When the invasion does start, what are you going to do?'

'Go home and help to kick the bastards out of France.' There was a look of grim determination on his face.

Annie hoped she was there to see him get his revenge.

23

Dora and Will were married at Caxton Hall in London at the beginning of February; they were in uniform, but it was obvious that her friend didn't mind not having a grand wedding, for she was too much in love to care. And it didn't matter because Will looked splendid in his naval uniform and Dora radiant in air force blue. Annie tried not to cry as the ceremony came to a close. Will and Dora were now husband and wife. She was so happy for them.

There was a large turnout. Dora's family were there, and Charlie had managed to get home just in time to act as best man. Bob went as well, and had been welcomed back by the family as if he'd never been away. George seemed to have taken a great liking to him; they were talking and laughing outside the registry office like old friends. There wasn't a trace of the boy she'd remembered. Bob was mature, good looking, and obviously a happy man. The only one not there was Bill. That had upset Kate for a while, but her natural enthusiasm for life and any new experience had soon banished her gloom. James appeared quite disgusted with the whole sentimental affair, and Annie grinned to herself. It wouldn't be long before the boy changed his mind about girls and romance. He was at the lanky stage but it was clear that he was going to be a handsome man. As time passed, James was showing signs of his father's quiet temperament, and that was a relief to his mother. Rose had always said that she hoped her children didn't inherit her intolerant, explosive nature. And, as time passed, it looked as if neither of them had.

While the photographs were being taken Annie noticed that Rose was relaxed and clearly enjoying herself. Her sister might have been difficult in her youth, but time, Bill, and children of her own had certainly mellowed her.

'That was a very nice wedding,' Marj said, blowing her nose. 'I thought that son of mine was never going to marry, but he's found a fine girl in Dora. And I might get some more grandchildren now.'

Annie laughed. 'After having nine children I would have thought you'd had enough of babies.'

'Grandchildren are different. You can always hand them back to their mother when they get too much trouble.' Her eyes clouded for a moment. 'All except Bob's children, of course, I don't suppose I'll ever see them.'

Annie squeezed her mother's arm, knowing this was a source of sadness to her. 'I expect you'll have plenty of others.'

After the photos were taken, the boisterous wedding party made their way to Rose's place.

In spite of rationing, Rose and Marj, with help from Dora, had managed to put on quite a spread. The wedding cake looked splendid, until the cardboard replica was removed to reveal a simple sponge. This caused a lot of laughter, but the war had been going on for over three years now, and shortages were accepted without comment. Everyone just did the best they could.

736

'Annie!' Dora called over. 'Gran wants to have a chat with Rose but she won't stay in one place long enough for Gran to catch her.'

'Come with me.' Annie took hold of the elderly woman's hand and gently walked her over to Rose. 'Sit down for a while, Rose. Dora's grandmother wants to talk to you.'

Annie pushed her sister into a chair and pulled up another one for the old lady.

'My name's Maude,' she told Rose, 'and I've been itching to meet you. I saw you in action once and I've never forgotten it. You were standing for election to the local council, and at one of your public meetings you jumped off the stage, rolled up your sleeves and threatened to flatten one heckler.' Maude slapped her leg in glee. 'I've never seen a man so terrified. Hadn't laughed so much in years. You got my vote all right.'

'I remember the incident.' Rose looked highly amused. 'He couldn't have been much more than five feet.'

'That's right,' Maude chortled. 'You towered over him, and could easily have carried out your threat.'

They both roared with laughter, and Annie, seeing they were getting along well, left them to it.

When Annie returned to camp the next day there was a spring in her step. It had been a long time since she'd felt so light-hearted. It had been wonderful to see Will married to such a lovely girl as Dora. The traditional honeymoon was out of the question, but they had managed to grab a couple of days in a hotel by the sea. Annie smiled to herself. They hadn't said where they

737

were going but the happy couple had disappeared as soon as was polite. The future looked much more hopeful now, because after a fierce battle by the Russians the Germans had just surrendered at Stalingrad. The Germans didn't seem so invincible now and morale was high.

'I'm back, Sam,' she called, as she walked past his open door. A few steps further on she stopped. There hadn't been any response and she knew he was there; she'd caught a glimpse of him sitting at his desk.

Retracing her steps, she went and stood in front of him. She had never seen such a strange expression on his face and it was difficult to decide what kind of mood he was in.

'Is something wrong?' she asked him.

'Hmm?' He appeared preoccupied. 'Did the wedding go well?'

'Yes, it was lovely and we were all sorry you couldn't come. What's happened, Sam?' she asked again.

'I've just finished debriefing one of our operatives who's returned from France.' When he looked up, pain was visible in his eyes. 'He might have come across my sister and she's working for the Resistance.'

'Oh, that's wonderful,' Annie said, knowing just how worried Sam had been about the only remaining member of his family.

He looked ready to explode. 'I've got to find out if it really is her. We were sending someone in tonight, but I've managed to get permission to take his place. Once I've gathered the information we need then I'm going to try and find her.'

'You know you can't do that, Sam. Send someone

else.' The expression on his face was making shivers run through her. This was dangerous.

'No. This is something I must do myself.'

'Then take me with you.' Annie knew from his anguished expression that it would be suicide for him to go in this mood.

'No!' He thumped the desk to emphasize the rejection. 'This is none of your business.'

Annie recoiled as if she'd been struck. She had never seen him this volatile. He was usually a quiet, controlled man; she knew it would be useless to argue. And he'd obviously already cleared it with those in charge.

'Very well,' she told him. 'But if you get caught, then you and a lot of other people could be killed. And when you're knocking on the Pearly Gates, remember that I told you so.' She turned to walk out of the room.

'Wait!' He ran round his desk, caught her arm and turned her to face him. 'I'm sorry for shouting. I know you're only trying to help because you care, but there's more to this. I think there's someone else with my sister. Sit down and I'll explain.' He held a chair out for her.

When they were settled, she waited patiently for him to speak.

'As I listened to the operative talking about the people who had helped him in France, I became convinced he was talking about my sister. The description fitted, right down to the small heart-shaped birthmark on her right arm.'

Sam stopped and gazed into space for a few seconds, then continued. 'In the house with my sister was an elderly woman who was looking after a small boy of

739

about three years old. It was her grandson, she had told him.' His voice became husky with emotion.

Annie didn't interrupt. Sam obviously needed time to compose himself, for something had come as a great shock to him.

He took a deep breath and then cleared his throat. 'There was a girl I'd known from childhood, and as we grew up it was expected by both families that we would marry one day. And if the war hadn't come along that's what we would have done.' Sam stood up and started to pace the room. 'Maria was heavily pregnant, and we were going to be married in two weeks, but the wedding never took place. As soon as the Germans invaded I was off fighting.'

'Do you know if your girl is still alive?'

Sam shook his head in a forlorn gesture. 'I was away for about six weeks, and when I finally got back to my village I was told she had been killed by shellfire during the battle for our village. I got out of France then. If this woman is Maria's mother, then the boy she is looking after could be my son.'

He looked at Annie, searching her face, and there was a gleam of hope in his troubled eyes. 'Suppose Maria had the baby before she died?'

The look he gave her was enough to bring tears to her eyes. Annie knew Sam was building up for some unbearable grief if this turned out to be untrue. She hated saying this, but he shouldn't hope for too much. 'If you were told she had died, then that is probably what happened.'

'I know.' He sat down again and buried his head in his hands.

'Things are very confusing over there,' she felt she ought to point out, although he knew that better than anyone, 'and the grandmother might not be any relation to your Maria.'

'I've got to find out!'

Now Annie understood why he was willing to risk his life. She couldn't blame him for that. 'What are your plans?'

He sat back and sighed. 'I'm leaving tonight, and if it is my son then I'll try and bring him, Maria's mother and my sister back here.'

'That's quite a task,' she told him quietly.

'I know the odds against success are enormous. But what would you do, Annie, if you thought it might be one of your family?'

'Nothing would stop me from finding them,' she admitted with honesty. Sam shouldn't go back to France yet, but she knew that if she were in his shoes she wouldn't hesitate to take the same chances.

He glanced at his watch. 'I must get ready. I will send only two messages, one with the intelligence I've gathered, and the second for transport back here.'

'I understand. Take care, Sam.'

'I will.' He gave a tight smile, and then strode out of the room.

The next three weeks dragged by without a word from Sam and a feeling of gloom began to settle over the ops room.

Annie had remained hopeful for two weeks, but as the silence continued, she began to fear that he had been caught, or even killed. Every intercepted message was quickly decoded in case it gave an indication of arrests, either of Sam or any other operatives. But there was nothing, and the waiting was tearing everyone's nerves to shreds. Dora and Jean had given up trying to coax her away from the camp; even the promise of all that lovely food at the American dances wouldn't shift her. Only those closely connected with Sam knew what was happening, but the tense atmosphere alerted everyone that something was up.

'Get some rest,' Wing Commander Felshaw told Annie. 'If anything comes through, I'll let you know.'

It was two-thirty in the morning and Annie rubbed her tired eyes. 'OK, I'm too exhausted to concentrate, anyway.'

When she arrived back at her hut, Dora was waiting for her.

'It's about time too. If you don't get some sleep soon you'll make yourself ill.'

Annie dredged up a smile. 'Just because you're my sister-in-law doesn't mean you can boss me around.'

'Really?' Dora feigned surprise. 'I thought that was my job now.'

'Where on earth did you get that idea from?' Annie was too tired for the usual banter, and kicked off her shoes, then stretched out on the bed with a groan of relief.

'Have you had anything to eat?' Dora threw a blanket over her.

'Can't remember.'

'That means you haven't,' her friend declared. 'I'll go and cadge you a sandwich and a cup of tea.'

'I don't want anything, Dora, I just need to sleep for a few hours.'

'Don't argue with your new sister-in-law.'

Annie peered at Dora. 'Does Will know how bossy you are?'

'No, I'm keeping that as a surprise.'

'My poor brother,' Annie murmured. 'He doesn't know what he's let himself in for.'

Dora laughed. 'Oh, I think he does. We had a riotous honeymoon.'

'That's nice.' Then Annie was asleep.

'Wake up!'

Annie's reflexes surged into action and she sat up, although she was still half asleep. She peered at her watch and saw that it was five in the morning; she'd only had a couple of hours' rest.

Jean stopped shaking her. 'You're needed back on duty.'

'Right.' Annie took some deep breaths to try to clear her head.

'Hurry. They said it was urgent.' Jean was forcing Annie's feet into her shoes and tying the laces. 'Good job you're already dressed.'

Annie was out of the door of the hut and running, then tumbling down the steps to the ops room. There must be news, and she was praying that it was good.

'We've heard from Sam,' Wing Commander Felshaw told her as she erupted into the room. 'He wants transport for himself and two passengers, tonight, if possible.'

'Are you sending in a motor torpedo boat?' Annie asked.

743

'No. He can't reach the coast. We'll have to get them out by plane.'

Annie was dismayed. 'That's dangerous. Why are you taking such a chance?'

'No choice, I'm afraid. This hasn't just been a mission to find his family; Sam's gathered some vital information for us, and he's got to get out in a hurry. The message was too lengthy for him to send it through.'

Annie nodded, knowing how imperative it was to keep all transmissions short.

'He will be coming through again in thirty minutes and you are to give him these instructions.' He handed her a sheet of paper and studied her through narrowed eyes. 'You look a mess.'

'Sorry.' Annie tried to smooth the creases out of her skirt. 'I fell asleep in my clothes.'

He gave a wry smile. 'Well, when you've finished here, go and put on a clean uniform and meet us in the yard. I want you to meet the plane with the immigration official. Sam might need your help.'

Annie gazed through the window of the control tower and searched the sky. The small Tempsford airfield was only a short distance from Chicksands, and as dawn began to stain the sky with a silvery glow even the field seemed to be holding its breath. There was an eerie feel about the place, and the waiting was agony. Had the plane been able to get in and pick up its passengers?

'Here it comes,' someone said.

'At last!' Annie hurried down the steps and waited for the small plane to taxi towards them.

When it stopped she could see an elderly woman being

lifted out in obvious distress, and Annie stepped in to help. Then Sam eased himself to the ground carrying a small child.

No one spoke until they were inside. Welcome mugs of tea were provided, and Annie concentrated on trying to get the woman to drink some. When she had managed a few sips and seemed more composed, she turned her attention to Sam and the child.

The boy was staring at his grandmother in wild-eyed terror, and fighting to get away from Sam. The breath caught in Annie's throat as she looked at them. They *were* father and son; the likeness was unmistakable.

She knelt in front of Sam and reached for the struggling child. 'Let him go to his grandmother,' she told him as gently as possible.

As soon as the boy was free he threw himself at the elderly woman and buried his face in her skirt.

'Drink this,' Annie ordered, and thrust a mug into Sam's hand.

He gulped the tea down, and she was relieved to see some colour coming back into his face. 'Rough journey?' she asked.

He nodded, not taking his eyes off the child.

'Where's your sister?'

'She wouldn't come.' Sam looked as if he'd been to hell and was not sure if it was possible to get back from there.

'Your son's the image of you,' she told him, reaching out for his hand. When he looked at her the torment in his eyes nearly made her cry out. Whatever he'd discovered on this journey was clearly traumatic.

'He's terrified of me.' His words were barely audible.

It took less than an hour for the forms to be completed, and Sam's son and the boy's grandmother were officially classed as refugees. Then, to Annie's dismay, Sam was whisked off to a debriefing session even though he was obviously at the end of his strength.

Sam paused at the door, gave Annie a beseeching look, and asked, 'Will you stay with them for tonight, Annie?'

'Of course,' she replied giving him a reassuring smile. Then she picked up the child and followed a nurse, who was helping the grandmother to the waiting ambulance.

24

March 1943

Sam had rented a flat in Shefford for Jacques and his grandmother. It was close enough to Chicksands for him to pop round there every spare moment he had, but it was not a satisfactory arrangement, and Annie was losing patience with Sam. She'd walked into the tiny lounge and found him nearly out of his mind with worry.

'Stop pacing around and listen, Sam!' Annie ordered. 'You've been back two weeks now and little Jacques shows no sign of settling down. You can't keep him cooped up in this flat; he's used to the country.'

'I can't dump the problem on your family, Annie.'

'You won't be *dumping* anything on them. They've offered.' Annie smiled, hoping to coax him out of his stubbornness. She was extremely worried about the little boy and his grandmother. The elderly woman was very ill, and Jacques was becoming more withdrawn with each day that passed. She'd talked it through with her mother and Rose, and they'd felt it might help if Jacques lived with a family for a while.

He gave a weary sigh. 'I don't know what to do for the best. I'm out of my depth with this.'

'Sam!' Annie was getting cross with him now. 'Maria's mother is ill and needs looking after; she can't cope with a small, troubled boy at the moment.'

'I'm aware of that,' he growled, his expression a mirror of his irritation and worry.

'Rose said that if you refuse she's coming round here to knock some sense into your stupid head.' Annie adopted her sister's determined pose and placed her hands on her hips.

'Ah.' He gave a strained smile. 'I can't risk that.'

'You'd be wise not to. You've never seen my sister when she's made up her mind about something. She's an unstoppable force, believe me.'

'Oh, I do believe you.'

Annie sensed he was giving way so she pressed the point. 'George has managed to get enough petrol for the journey, so Maria's mother will not have to travel by train. Come on, Sam,' she coaxed. 'You know this will be best for your son, and Mum will take good care of his grandmother. If we place him in the middle of a large and loving family it will help him overcome his fears, and I've been given extended leave so I can stay with you.'

Sam nodded, ran a hand wearily over his eyes and conceded defeat. 'Thank you, Annie.'

The journey to Wales was hard on the grandmother, and to make matters worse the boy knew she was ill. He was clearly frightened and clung to the elderly lady for the whole trip. Any effort by Sam or Annie to comfort him was pushed away. Jacques allowed Annie to care for his grandmother during the journey and accepted food and drink from her, but he wouldn't have anything to do with his father. Annie was relieved that George was doing the driving and not Sam. Sam was not a good driver at the best of times, and the poor man was so distracted with concern they would surely have had an accident.

It was a relief when they arrived and Rose strode towards the car, taking charge of everything in her usual, no-nonsense manner. Once the old lady was settled in bed she fell asleep instantly, and the doctor was sent for.

'Come along, young man.' Rose scooped Jacques from the bed. 'Let your grandmother rest.'

He opened his mouth to scream, then looked into Rose's eyes, and the sound was cut to a whimper. Even he recognized that you didn't argue with Rose.

James, Kate, Pirate and Tibby were waiting in the lounge with a selection of toys scattered about the floor. When Rose put the boy next to them he scuttled on to the settee and hugged a cushion in front of him for protection.

'What's wrong with him?' James asked Sam.

'He has been taken from everything he was familiar with, and his grandmother is too ill to help him. He knows no one and is very frightened.'

James nodded in understanding, picked up a small toy train and handed it to the cowering boy. A hand sneaked out from behind the cushion and touched the desirable object.

'You can have it,' James told him, pushing the toy into his hand.

The little fingers curled around it and then it was pulled under the cushion and examined in secret.

Annie heard Sam's sharp intake of breath and she touched his arm. 'It will be all right. Just give it time.'

'What's his name?' Kate spoke for the first time.

'Jacques,' Sam told her.

'Hmm. I'll call him Jack.' Kate went and sat beside him, gave a wide smile, then began to ease the cushion away from him.

At that moment Marj arrived with tea, bread and jam, and even a home-made cake. 'Sit down all of you. We'll have our tea in here today. I've got milk for the youngsters.'

Kate had managed to get the cushion away from Jack, who was staring at her as if fascinated. But he was still huddled in the corner of the settee.

'Poor little sod!' Wally muttered. 'What kind of a life has he had?'

'Not good,' Sam told him, but did not elaborate further.

Rose, a glass of milk in her hand, went over and sat on the arm of the settee. 'Here you are, Jack, you drink this. You must be famished.'

The boy tore his eyes away from Kate to look at Rose, his gaze swinging from mother to daughter, and then back again to Rose.

Annie handed Sam a plate. 'It looks as if he's been renamed. Do you mind?'

'No. At least they're getting some response from him, and that's more than I've been able to do.'

'They'll soon have him laughing and running around.' Annie wasn't surprised to see tears well up in Sam's eyes. It was obvious he adored his newly found son, and the strain of rejection must be hard to take.

'I just had to get him out of France, Annie.' He sounded almost apologetic. 'But all I seem to have done is inflict more unhappiness on him.'

'It was the right thing to do.' Annie tried to put herself in Sam's place. She knew that if she'd found a member of her family in such terrible circumstances she'd have done the same thing. It might take time but Jacques would eventually adjust. She watched her sister, and sighed to release the tension in her chest. If anyone could ease his fear, it was Rose.

'There's a good boy.' Rose held up the empty glass and smiled at Jack. 'Would you like some bread and jam now?'

'He can't understand you,' George pointed out, as he came into the lounge after unloading the car.

'He soon will.' Rose cut a slice of bread into small squares and popped one piece at a time into Jack's mouth, waiting patiently for him to chew and swallow.

Annie remembered Rose doing that for her when she had been little.

They were all settling down to enjoy their tea when the door opened and a tall man strode in.

'Daddy!' Kate erupted off the seat and into her father's arms.

Everyone was milling around, greeting Bill and laughing, except Sam and Annie who had seen Jack's reaction to the tall sailor.

'Oh, my God!' Sam rushed over to the settee.

'What is it?' Bill was beside him at once.

Sam explained briefly about his son, then said, 'It's the uniform, he's terrified of them.'

Bill shrugged out of his jacket, ripped his tie off and bent down to look behind the settee. 'Hello, young man.' He spoke in French, his voice calm and gentle, as always. 'Aren't you going to come out and see me?'

Kate joined her father. 'You don't have to be frightened of my daddy, he's very kind.'

Annie listened to a scuffling sound from behind the settee, and then saw Bill surge to his feet holding Sam's son.

'My goodness, you are a handsome boy,' Bill told him as he sat down and settled the child on his knee. 'What's your name?'

'Jacques,' he whispered.

Kate climbed up beside her father. 'I'm going to call him Jack.'

'Really?' Bill ran a hand affectionately over his daughter's hair, and then smiled at the boy. 'Is that all right with you?'

The child nodded and said, 'Jack.'

'The doctor's here,' George announced.

Rose and Sam left the room, and returned twenty minutes later, their expressions grim.

'She's bad, isn't she?' Marj said.

Rose nodded. 'She refuses to go into hospital, so she'll stay here with us and we'll look after her.'

Sam cast Rose a grateful look, then spoke to them. 'She knew she was dying and agreed to come here so that my son could have a better life. But the journey and worry have weakened her.'

'I'm so sorry.' Annie's heart bled for Sam and his son. There were difficult times ahead of them.

During the next few days the March weather decided it was going to have a last winter fling; it was bitterly cold and trying to snow all the time. Jacques followed James and Kate everywhere and became agitated if he couldn't find them. But he still wouldn't go to his father, and it was obviously upsetting Sam.

Twice a day Jacques was taken to see his grandmother, who made a supreme effort to smile and joke with him. She told him each time that he was now with good people who would look after him. He listened solemnly, and clung to James and Kate even more after each visit.

Bill returned to his ship after three days, and a week later the elderly woman died peacefully in her sleep.

'How are you going to tell Jacques?' Rose asked Sam.

'I'm going to let him see her. If she suddenly disappears he will think I've sent her away, and God knows I have enough problems with him as it is.'

'Do you think he will understand if he sees her?' Annie asked him. 'She looks so peaceful, as if she's just fallen asleep.'

'It's the only thing I can do; I think he will understand what has happened to his grandmother.'

'I'll come with you.' Annie held out her hand to Jacques and he followed obediently.

The boy stood by the bed staring at the body of his grandmother. He was absolutely still and silent, the only movement was a single tear as it trickled down his cheek. Then he ran from the room, down the stairs and into the lounge, throwing himself on to the settee and huddling in the corner, as he'd done the day he arrived. He had made progress, but now it seemed as if that had been reversed.

Annie watched as Sam sat beside his son and tried to comfort him, but the boy screwed himself into a tight ball and ignored him, lost in his own misery.

Kate surveyed the scene for a while, then sat next to Sam and reached across him to take hold of Jacques's hand. She slipped her other hand through Sam's arm and leaned against him.

Annie was constantly amazed by her niece's ability to do the right thing at the right time. By her gestures she was clearly telling Jacques that his father could be trusted. The boy seemed to think about it for a while, then slid on to Sam's lap and gave way to his grief, sobbing into his chest.

Annie breathed a sigh of relief; he had turned to his father at last. There was a long way to go, of course, but it was an encouraging step. She was at the end of her special leave and had to get back to Chicksands, but at least she had the comfort of knowing that progress had been made with the boy.

'Blimey!' Dora exclaimed when Annie arrived back at camp. 'You look awful. What on earth have you been doing?'

'It was a rather harrowing leave.' Annie then explained about Jacques and his grandmother.

'Poor little bugger.'

'Yes. It's been a tragic business. Rose persuaded Sam to let Jacques come to the funeral so the boy could see and understand that his grandmother really had gone. I think it worked because he seems to have accepted it now.' Annie closed her eyes as tiredness swept through her. 'I feel wrung out, and would like to have stayed for a few more days, but Sam is on compassionate leave for another two weeks.'

Dora gave Annie a searching look. 'You ought to think about yourself for a change. You're always doing things for other people and you're not getting any younger. It's time you found yourself a husband.'

Annie tipped her head back and laughed. 'And that will solve all my problems, will it?'

'No, but life will be much more fun,' Dora told her. 'Don't you want a family of your own?'

'When the war's over, but I can't say I've given it much thought. Why all this talk about babies, anyway?' She gave her friend a suspicious glance; she appeared extra pleased with life.

Dora looked smug. 'I think I might be pregnant.'

'What! You and Will haven't wasted any time. Are you sure?'

'No, I'm not sure, it's too soon, but I'm hoping.'

If this turned out to be true, Annie knew her mother would be delighted to have another grandchild.

Dora grinned. 'Anyway, we're getting off the subject. You ought to keep your eyes open for a suitable husband and father of your children.'

As tired as she was, Annie couldn't help being amused. Her friend certainly was broody. She placed a hand on Dora's forehead. 'Are you feeling all right?'

'Of course I am, you daft date. I'm trying to be serious here and give you a little sisterly advice, but you're not taking it seriously.'

'And I'm not going to, I'm quite happy as I am.' When they reached the mess, Annie pushed Dora through the door. 'I'm not on duty for another hour, so let's get something to eat.'

'I suppose you could marry Sam,' Dora persisted, clearly changing her earlier opinion that Annie should not consider it. 'You'd have a ready-made family then.'

'That man's got enough problems without adding to them by taking on a wife.'

'I suppose you're right.' Dora sighed. 'You wouldn't make him a good wife anyway. You can be an awkward devil where men are concerned.'

Annie looked at her friend in astonishment. 'When have I been awkward? Come on, tell me!'

'Well, you kept Paul hanging on when you had no intention of marrying him.'

'Now just a minute! Paul hung on to me, not the other way around. I told him often enough, but he just wouldn't listen. And I was too soft-hearted to hurt him.'

'You're not now, though. There's a toughness about you that wasn't there before.'

'So you keep telling me.' They wandered up to the counter to see what was on offer. 'So what else am I supposed to have done?'

'From the sound of it, you've been bossing Sam around.'

'I have *not*.' Annie sighed. 'I like and respect Sam, but he was drowning in problems and I couldn't bear to see it. He just needed someone to push him in the right direction. The man's got a stubborn streak.'

'Hark who's talking!'

Annie went to clout her friend but Dora ducked out of the way. 'Hey, no hitting a pregnant woman.'

They both burst into laughter while they collected a cup of tea and a sandwich, and then sat down. The mess wasn't very busy so they were able to find a table to themselves. All Annie wanted to do was rest her head on her arms and sleep but if she did that then she'd never wake up in time to report back for duty. She sat up straight again and tried to shake off the fatigue. She hoped to goodness that Dora and Jean didn't want her to go out this evening, because she just wasn't up to it. Losing Jacques's grandmother had been distressing for all of them, but at least the boy was talking to his father now.

Annie dragged her attention back to Dora. 'Now you've started to pull my character to shreds, you might as well continue. What else am I supposed to have done?'

'Well, there's the way you've treated Reid. You're being unreasonable, and that isn't like you at all.'

Annie stirred her tea aimlessly. She wasn't too happy about Reid being brought into the conversation, but Dora had a point, things had become rather muddled just lately and it was time she sorted her life out.

'When we were on leave and I met him at your house I had a real good look at him.' Dora sat up straight, clearly warming to her subject. 'I'm good at summing people up, and Reid Lascells is something special, believe me.'

Annie sighed.

'And it's no good you looking like that. You're like a horse with blinkers on, so I'll tell you what he's like. Reid's a strong man, I admit, but he's not uncaring; just look at the way he's keeping an eye on Bouncer. And if you took the trouble to look into his eyes a bit more you'd see he's got a good sense of humour. He's witty, brave, handsome, and so damned gorgeous that I'll bet the girls fall at his feet and beg to be taken to his bed.'

'I'll bet they do!' Annie muttered darkly.

'There, you're jealous!' Dora grinned in triumph. 'I

knew you couldn't be as uninterested as you pretend, and he fancies you as well.'

'I think you've flipped,' Annie told Dora, in disgust. 'We can't stand each other, but you are right about one thing: I have been rude to him.'

'Then do something about it,' Dora persisted, serious once again. 'Don't harbour resentment, it will hurt you more than him.'

'When did you suddenly become so wise?' Annie gave a faint smile.

'Since I fell in love with your wonderful brother. And I'm so proud to be a part of the Webster family.'

'Even if one of them is turning into a bitch?' Annie couldn't help asking.

'I never said that,' Dora protested. 'You're still the same kind girl I met when we joined up, but you've just lost your way a bit. You should go and see Paul's parents the first chance you get.'

'You're right, I do feel guilty about that . . . as well,' Annie added, and then looked at her friend. 'Is that the end of the list of things to do?'

'Of course.' Dora grinned. 'I didn't mean it when I said you'd become hard-hearted. You've got a centre like marshmallow, but you ought to put things right with Paul's family – and that includes his brother.'

'I've already sent him a letter.' Annie was getting fed up with this now. Dora was always going on about her and Reid, and she was too damned tired for another lecture.

'That's no good. Arrange to meet him and look him in the eyes when you tell him you're sorry.'

That was the last thing she wanted to do. The thought

of facing Reid again was rather unsettling, and she couldn't for the life of her understand why she felt like that. He would probably laugh in her face if she tried to apologize.

Dora drank her tea, watching her friend closely over the rim of her cup. 'He's a good man, and just the type you need.'

'Reid!' Annie roared at the ludicrous idea. All they ever did when they met was snipe at each other.

Dora gave a dramatic sigh. 'Well, if he won't do, then I'll just have to find you someone else.'

'Don't you dare!'

25

August 1943

As the Spitfire came to a stop Reid eased out of the cockpit and jumped to the ground. He didn't fly as often as he would like to these days, but when he did find the time it was exhilarating. He gave the aeroplane an affectionate pat and examined a small oil leak coming from the engine. 'You're running a bit rough, old girl.'

As he strode towards his office he called one of the ground crew over. 'Get someone to have a look at that plane, please.'

'Yes, sir, Webster will deal with it, he's just finished the job he's on.'

'Right.' Reid continued walking. Webster? Of course, he'd forgotten that Annie's brother was stationed here at Tangmere. He should have taken the trouble to speak to him before now, but his days were so busy, and the mountain of paperwork seemed to grow by the minute, not to mention the interminable meetings.

An hour later he prowled over to the window. The Spitfire had been taken into the hangar. He'd just go and see how they were getting on with it.

He had met Charlie when he'd visited his mother's house and he recognized him at once. 'Anything serious?' he asked.

Charlie scrambled down. 'No, sir, we'll soon have it fixed and you can take her up again in an hour, if you want to.'

'Wish I could.' Reid grimaced. 'But I've got a meeting to attend in a couple of hours.'

'Bit boring after flying, sir.' Charlie wiped his greasy hands on a rag and smiled. 'But safer.'

'True.' Reid looked at him carefully. The family resemblance was clear to see. Charlie had the same colouring as Annie. 'I was pleased to hear that your brother was safe.'

'So were we,' Charlie told him. 'He got married in February to one of Annie's friends.'

'How is your sister?' Reid knew that question had come out with a hint of eagerness when he saw Charlie's speculative glance.

'Fine, as far as I know.'

Reid was pleased to hear he had dropped the 'sir' and was chatting quite normally with him. 'What does she do, *exactly*?'

'She's a wireless operator but she never talks about her work. We've even tried to find out from Sam, but he doesn't talk either. Of course, with her languages she's probably involved in some secret work,' Charlie said, obviously proud of his sister.

'Who's Sam?'

'He's French and Annie works with him sometimes. He's a nice bloke,' Charlie added, looking back at the engine he'd been working on.

Reid could see he was eager to get on with it, and he had wasted enough of Charlie's time. 'Remember me to your mother when you see her again.'

'I'll do that.' Charlie was already climbing on the plane.

It was a lovely summer day, and Reid wandered back to his office deep in thought. Annie had obviously taken this Sam home, because Charlie seemed to know him quite well.

He stopped suddenly, surprised by the depth of feeling running through him, and at that moment he wanted the hostility between himself and Annie to be at an end. He was in a strange mood and the thought of all that paperwork waiting for him made him change direction, so instead of returning to work he headed out of the gate; he had a bit of time before the meeting. Once outside he walked along a small lane, deep in thought. When he'd been listening to Charlie talking about Annie he'd wanted to ask what she had been like as a child, what did she like and dislike? In fact, he'd wanted to hear all about her – all the small and large things that made her the woman she was today. Had she had any lovers?

He paused and gazed across a field, watching the birds pinching the farmer's soft fruits and treating the scarecrow with contempt. He was experiencing a feeling quite alien to him – jealousy! He remembered her smile, the way her eyes glowed when she was angry, and how good she looked in her uniform. Her slender figure and shapely legs even the awful stockings couldn't hide. But it wasn't just her outward loveliness; there were hidden depths to Annie Webster that it could take a lifetime to discover . . .

A gust of wind blew the hair into his eyes; he brushed it away and gave a sardonic laugh. Of course, it was obvious. He had fallen in love with her, and that was a damned stupid thing to do!

★

The next morning Reid tossed his bag in the car. The sun was shining and there were seven peaceful days ahead of him. He needed this break. Being station commander was not an easy job, but Bouncer was right, he was well suited to it, and most of the time he enjoyed the work, but he did miss flying and the friends he'd made in his old squadron. Bouncer was back with them now, and if his letters were anything to go by he was thrilled to be flying again.

The drive to his home in Berkshire was relaxing and Reid used the time to analyse his feelings for Annie. There had been other women in his life but he'd never felt like this about any of them; they had been there for a while and then gone, and he could hardly remember any of them now. But Annie Webster was different; he wanted to be with her all the time, to touch her, hold her, laugh and even argue with her, just so long as they were together. When they'd first met he'd been determined to dislike her, but that hadn't been possible, and he had a sneaking suspicion that he'd fallen for her the moment he'd set eyes on her. He'd fought it, of course, but it was no use denying that he was in love with her. Yet she showed no liking for him. However, he'd never been one to back away from a challenge and by the time he reached home he knew what he was going to do about her.

His mother hugged him as soon as he got out of the car. 'How long have you got?'

'Seven days.' He kissed her cheek. 'Where's Dad?'

'He's at the factory; some sort of crisis. They are struggling to get out an order of nuts and bolts, I think.'

'Shall I pop down there and see if I can help?' he asked.

'Would you? Father would be so relieved. He's always saying that you are twice the businessman he is. Have a cup of tea before you go, though.'

They went inside and she put the kettle on to boil. 'Are you going to stay in the air force after the war, Reid?'

'No. I'll get out as soon as possible.' That was something he was clear about. Paul would probably have considered a career in the air force after the war, but not him, he would be out as soon as he could.

'Oh, that's a relief. Your father isn't finding it easy managing the engineering business again and said that if you decided to stay in the air force then he would sell the factory.'

'There's no need for that.' He stirred his tea and smiled at his mother. 'By the time this lot's over, I'll have had all the excitement I can handle. It will be a pleasure to take over the business again.'

His mother looked at him hopefully. 'Time you settled down.'

That's what he wanted as well, but he was going to have a fight on his hands if he wanted to win Annie.

Reid walked into the factory and found it strangely quiet; one of the machines was standing idle. A middle-aged man came up to him, all smiles, and shook his hand.

'It's good to see you again,' the worker told him.

'And you, Tom. How's the family?'

'We lost our son-in-law, but our daughter's a sensible lass and she's pulling her life together again.' Tom looked sad. 'Damned shame about Paul, he was a nice boy.'

'Yes, it was a shock. I'm sorry to hear about your loss as well, Tom.'

'Bloody war. Still, it looks as if things are on the turn now.'

Reid nodded. 'Let's hope so. Now, what's going on here?'

'The machine has broken down and we can't repair it. Your dad's at his wits' end; we've got a shipment of nuts and bolts to deliver in three days, and this has to happen. It's old, of course, and needs replacing.' He gave a helpless shrug.

'Let me have a look.' Reid removed his jacket, rolled up his sleeves and started to examine the machine.

'Hello, son, when did you arrive?'

'Just got here, Dad.' Reid noticed how tired his father looked, and smiled in encouragement. 'This always was a temperamental brute, but it knows better than to argue with me.'

It took him the best part of an hour, but he finally stepped back with a grunt of satisfaction. 'Try it now, Tom.'

The machine coughed, shook, and sounded as if it wasn't going to start properly, but when Reid aimed a kick in the region of the motor it sprang into life with a roar.

His father slapped him on the back and grinned in relief. 'Haven't lost your touch, I see.'

Reid washed his hands in the sink to remove the worst of the grime, said goodbye to Tom and led his father out of the factory. 'I'll be here for a week, so you needn't worry if she goes wrong again.'

'But it's your leave,' his father protested. 'It isn't right to have you working when you need a break. And just wait until your mother sees you. You're covered in oil.'

When they arrived back his mother was sitting in the garden under the old oak tree talking to a girl in uniform.

'Annie!' His father walked across the lawn to greet her. 'How lovely to see you.'

'And you, Mr Lascells. I'm sorry I haven't been able to come sooner.'

'We understand, my dear.' He kissed her cheek. 'How long have you got? Can you stay a while?'

Reid saw Annie glance at him, and as she hesitated he stepped forward, smiled and also kissed her cheek. Though he would like to have done more. She was so lovely and he wanted to keep her here for as long as possible.

'Please stay,' he said.

'Well . . .' She was obviously surprised by his greeting. 'I've only got a forty-eight-hour pass, and I haven't brought any overnight things with me.'

'Don't worry about that,' Mrs Lascells said. 'I have spare toothbrushes and everything else you could need.'

'In that case I'd love to stay tonight.'

'Wonderful! I'll start dinner at once.'

'Can I help?' Annie asked politely.

'No, my dear, you stay here and talk to the men.' Mrs Lascells examined her son. 'What on earth have you been doing? That shirt's covered in grease.'

'He's repaired one of our machines,' her husband told her. 'I swear he's the only one who understands the temperamental beast.'

'You'd better change out of that shirt before dinner and I'll soak it overnight.'

Reid nodded and sat on the grass, leaving the garden

766

seat for Annie and his father. 'I was talking to your brother Charlie yesterday,' he told Annie.

Her smile was animated at the mention of her brother. 'How is he?'

'Fine. He was working on a Spitfire I had just landed.' As soon as the words were out he knew he shouldn't have said that.

'Are you still flying?' his father asked, concern showing on his face.

'Whenever I can,' Reid admitted.

'Whatever you do, don't tell your mother. She thinks you are permanently grounded now.'

'I won't say anything to worry her, but I love flying, Dad.'

Just then his mother came back and there was silence for a moment as they stopped speaking. Reid hoped she hadn't heard their conversation because the last thing he wanted to do was upset her. But she was smiling.

'Only an hour to dinner,' she told them.

Annie moved up to make room for her on the seat. 'There's something I'm curious about, Mrs Lascells. Reid is an unusual name; where did it come from?'

'My maiden name was Reidmont, and I wanted to keep something of it, so when our first son was born we named him Reid.'

'I'm glad you didn't call me Reidmont,' he remarked with a slight grimace.

'I was tempted,' she laughed, 'but your father wouldn't let me.'

'Thank heavens for that!' Reid caught sight of his shirt and hauled himself on to his feet. 'If you will excuse me, I'll go and change.'

767

Once in his room he stood by the window gazing at the garden below. His parents were talking to Annie and they were all laughing. What a bit of luck her turning up like this; it would give him a chance to put things right between them. He felt optimistic about being successful because he hadn't sensed the usual hostility. Of course, she might just be appearing polite for his parents' sake, but he didn't think so. She had very expressive eyes, and they hadn't been glaring at him in contempt.

He whistled as he washed and changed his clothes. Time to put his plans into action.

'Fancy going dancing?' Reid asked Annie later when they'd finished their meal.

She hesitated for a moment. 'I don't think I can do that. I came to see your parents.'

'Don't stay in because of us.' Mrs Lascells smiled at them both. 'You go and enjoy yourselves.'

'Of course you must,' her husband agreed. 'We shall have the pleasure of seeing Annie tomorrow.'

'Well, if you're sure? It would be nice, I haven't been dancing for some time.'

'Then you must go,' they said together.

Reid stood up and held out a hand to Annie. 'Come on then, let's jive the night away.'

'Can station commanders jive?' she asked, looking highly amused.

He put on a hurt expression. 'I'll have you know that I was the squadron expert.'

'This I've got to see.' She laughed and placed her hand in his.

He closed his long fingers around her delicate hand

768

with a feeling of elation. She had clearly changed her opinion of him and was prepared to be friendly. But he wanted more than *friendly*.

He took her to Newbury Corn Exchange which was situated in the historic market place. Reid told her that the building had opened for trade in 1861 but was now being used as a community venue. The place was crowded when they arrived, and a big band was in full swing. Dancing was a favourite pastime for everyone, but especially young service people. It gave everyone a chance to relax, mix with a crowd and enjoy glorious music.

Reid towed Annie into the middle of the throng and was delighted to see that she was an excellent dancer, and obviously loved it.

'You're good.' He shouted above the sound of the orchestra, as he spun her round.

'So are you,' she told him.

He pulled her back into his arms. 'Something we agree on at last.'

Annie smiled up into his face. 'It took a while, didn't it?'

The music had now changed to a foxtrot so he wrapped his arms around her, and as there was hardly room to move he marked time, enjoying the feel of her close to him. He wanted to bury his face in her silky hair, but resisted the urge. He mustn't move too fast.

'I'm sorry I've been so rude to you, Reid,' she told him.

He held her away from him so he could look into her upturned face. 'I'm the one at fault, Annie. I had no right to shout at you.'

'Why did you?' she wanted to know.

'I was devastated about losing Paul and your composure angered me.'

'That was the second time in about eight months I'd lost someone close to me and I was still hurting,' Annie explained. 'The blow of Paul's death hit me hard, but I wanted to grieve in private. Can you understand that?'

Reid nodded. 'Who was this other person? Not one of your family, I hope?'

'No, he was a dear man and everything possible was done to save him but to no avail.' She smiled up at him. 'This is a very gloomy subject when we are supposed to be forgetting our problems and enjoying ourselves.'

'You're right.' The tempo changed to a quickstep and he swung her round and back into his arms again. 'Now we've both apologized, do you think we can be friends?'

'I'd like that.' Her laugh was exuberant as they started to jive along with all the others on the dance floor. The American dance had soon caught on, and people were finding it a wonderful way to relieve the stress of wartime life.

That was one hurdle over but he was determined to deepen the relationship. It was going to be difficult since they could only meet occasionally; he would have to make the most of every opportunity.

During the interval they took their drinks and went outside for a breath of fresh air.

Annie sighed and leaned against a wall. 'Phew! That's better. It's like an oven in there.'

Reid finished his beer and put the glass down. 'Who's Sam?'

Annie looked startled by his sudden question. 'Someone I work with. Why?'

'No reason, I was just making conversation.'

'Well, I think you'd better change the subject because you know I can't talk about my work or anyone connected with it.'

'Of course. Careless talk costs lives,' he added rather flippantly. 'I should have known better. Would you like another drink?'

'Yes, please.'

He picked up the empty glasses and headed for the bar. He was curious about this man and he would have to see what he could find out about him.

He was soon back with two more drinks. 'How's Captain Freeman?'

'Bill? He's fine as far as we know.' Annie sipped her drink. 'How long is this blasted war going to last?'

'Fascism in Italy is finished, and there's a good chance they will surrender now Mussolini's been ousted.' He took the glass out of Annie's hand, put both their drinks down, and pulled her towards him. 'It's another step in the defeat of Germany but there's a long, hard fight ahead of us still.'

She didn't protest as he wrapped his arms around her, so he lowered his head and sought her lips. When she relaxed in his arms he deepened the kiss, ignoring the whistles he could hear coming from others enjoying the night air.

Suddenly, and with surprising strength, she pushed at his chest. He released her at once and stepped back. If they hadn't been in such a public place he might have been able to find out how much she really did like him, for he felt that her whole attitude had changed, and it was exciting. After taking a deep breath to steady himself, he said, 'I thought we were friends?'

'Not *that* friendly.' She straightened her jacket and glanced at the interested spectators.

'How friendly do you want to be, Annie?' He placed his hands on either side of her face, bringing her attention back to him. He knew he was pushing his luck, but after tomorrow she would return to her post and it might be months before he saw her again. It wasn't any surprise that there were so many hasty marriages these days. There wasn't time for long courtships when you weren't sure if you'd ever see each other again.

'I don't know. You confuse me,' she admitted, ducking away from him. 'The dancing's started again.'

He led her back into the hall. Confused was she? Well, he would settle for that tonight, and he had the satisfaction of knowing that she hadn't pushed him away immediately. In fact it had taken her quite a long time.

As they swung into an energetic dance routine, she was soon laughing again. Reid spun her round and round, feeling light-hearted. One thing he was certain about – *he* wasn't at all confused!

26

October 1943

Annie smiled to herself as she walked along the country lane, feeling the leaves crunch under her feet. She loved to walk whenever she had some spare time, and autumn was her favourite time of the year, with its riot of colour and nip in the air. She breathed in deeply; the war seemed a million miles away on a day like this.

Dora and Will's baby was due in a month's time. Much to Dora's disappointment she hadn't been pregnant soon after the wedding, but she certainly was after Will's next leave! Annie's family were scattered around at the moment. Her mother and Wally were looking after Dora, Bill and Will were at sea and goodness knows where, Charlie was still at Tangmere, and Rose was staying in Wales with George and the children. Her sister had taken over the responsibility for Jacques, and according to her letters the boy was settling in quite well. Bob was attached to a British unit and was still in this country, managing to see their mother now and again, which made Marj very happy. George was also delighted to have his daughter out of the firing line. Annie knew he had fretted all the time that Rose was in London, for he knew she would be in the most dangerous place she could find.

Annie hadn't seen Reid since the summer, but he wrote often and she looked forward to receiving his letters. She was not sorry to be away from him though, because she found his strong, dominant presence disturbing . . .

Annie carried on walking, lost in thought and enjoying the quiet of the countryside. She only heard the roar of the motorbike for a second –

There were half a dozen requests from the men for special leave on his desk and Reid shuffled through them. Some of the men were quite inventive with their reasons, and he was about to toss them aside to be dealt with later when a name caught his attention. As he read, a cold chill rippled down his spine.

'Jenkins!' he thundered.

'Sir!' The man almost fell into the room in his haste.

'Bring Webster here – at once!'

Charlie arrived out of breath and stood to attention.

'Which sister?' Reid demanded without preamble.

'Annie, sir. An American on a motorbike knocked her down.' Charlie's voice wavered. 'Mum says she's hurt bad, got a broken ankle, broken arm and a gash on her head. The doctors are checking now to see if there are any internal injuries.'

'Where is she?' Reid was already putting on his hat as fear gripped him like an iron band.

'They are worried about the head injuries and they've taken her to Bart's in London.' Charlie's voice shook. 'She's still unconscious, sir.'

'Stop calling me, sir,' Reid growled, as he looked at the address. 'The bloody name's Reid to you and your family.'

'I want to go and see her.' Charlie was clearly agitated

and an erupting commanding officer was not helping his composure.

'I'll take you.' Reid headed for the door with Annie's brother close on his heels.

It took just under two hours to reach the hospital, and every mile was agony to Reid as he pushed the accelerator pedal to the floor of the car and held it there.

The hospital was busy but Reid pushed to the front of the queue at the information desk, ignoring the rumble of protest coming from the other people waiting. To jump a queue was considered a grave sin when standing in line for every small item was the way of life. You waited patiently for your turn, but Reid was not in the mood to obey the rules this time. 'Ann Webster,' he demanded.

The nurse looked down a list of names. 'Ward D4, sir, but you can't . . .'

The two men didn't wait for her to finish speaking; they headed for the stairs, taking them at a run.

Marj and Wally were sitting one side of the bed, and a man Reid didn't know was on the other side holding Annie's hand. He was talking very quietly to her in French.

Reid's whole attention was focused on the girl in the bed and fear gripped him. She was unconscious, there were lacerations and bruises on her face, her left arm was in plaster and there was a cage over her legs. Even in the desperate days of 1940 he had never felt as scared as he was at this moment.

'Charlie, Reid,' Marj greeted them. 'I'm so glad you're here.'

'How is she, Mum?' Charlie asked in a hushed voice.

'The doctor thinks she will be all right, but he'll know more when she regains consciousness.'

'And when will that be?'

'We don't know, Charlie, but the longer it goes on, the more worried I am,' his mother told him, looking at her daughter anxiously. 'There has been some movement and a couple of times we thought she was going to open her eyes, but it seemed too much effort for her.'

Wally squeezed his wife's hand in encouragement. 'I don't think she's far away from regaining consciousness now.'

'What exactly are Annie's injuries?' Reid asked.

'Bad cut on her head, concussion, arm broken in two places and a smashed ankle, but they said there aren't any internal injuries,' Wally explained.

'Thank God for that!' Reid turned his attention back to Annie. The immediate need was to bring her round and the Frenchman would never get through to her like that! His tone was soft and coaxing. He guessed that this must be Sam.

The words began to penetrate Reid's mind and he frowned. His French wasn't fluent but he could understand some of what was being said.

'It will be a long time before you jump out of aeroplanes again. That ankle will never take the strain, but your right hand is uninjured, so you will still be the best wireless operator we've got.' Sam waited to see if there was any response, then sighed and stood up. 'She's still out, I'm afraid. I'll see if I can get us all some tea.'

When Sam moved away from the bed Reid took his place, but he didn't sit down; instead he bent over the inert figure. 'If you die on me, Webster, I'll never forgive you!'

His deep voice, raw with emotion, echoed around the ward, and all eyes turned in their direction.

A nurse hurried over. 'There should only be two visitors at a time, so some of you will have to leave. Miss Webster needs rest.'

Reid tore his attention away from the girl in the bed and fixed on the nurse, who backed down, looking uncomfortable caught in his penetrating gaze. 'She can rest when she's fully conscious again. And see she's moved to a private room,' he ordered.

'Very well, I'll make the arrangements, and you may all stay if you keep quiet,' she conceded, then left to attend to her other patients.

With that interruption out of the way, Reid leaned over Annie. 'Are you bloody well listening to me?'

Suddenly, Annie's eyelids flickered and her mouth twitched at the corners. 'Language, Squadron Leader,' she said faintly.

'Oh, she's awake,' Marj said in relief.

Reid sat down then. This was one time he didn't mind being demoted; it showed that Annie was in full command of her faculties.

'The voice of authority,' Charlie told his mother, smiling for the first time. 'She wouldn't dare disobey him.'

Reid ignored the remarks, took hold of Annie's hand and watched her fingers curl around his. 'Open your eyes,' he ordered. He'd known he loved her but until this moment he hadn't realized just how much. If he lost her the pain would be intolerable.

Annie's eyelids lifted and she gave a tired smile to everyone around the bed, then she closed them again.

'Thank the Lord she's regained consciousness.' Sam had returned with a tray of tea and biscuits.

As soon as Annie had responded to Reid, Wally went in search of a doctor, who examined her. 'Good. She is sleeping naturally. You must all leave now.'

They found a small waiting room and settled in there to enjoy the much-needed refreshments Sam had scrounged for them.

'Now, can someone tell me exactly what happened?' Reid asked.

'I'm afraid it was my fault, sir.' A very young American soldier slunk into the room and shuffled anxiously as he looked at them. 'My name's Warren. I borrowed this motorbike, you see, and took it along a country lane to see what it could do. I came round a bend and there she was . . .' His words tailed off.

Reid managed to resist the temptation to throttle the young idiot, but only because the boy was close to tears and obviously upset.

'I'll never ride a bike again,' he choked. 'I thought I'd killed her.'

Marj took the boy by the arm and made him sit down. 'The doctor said she is going to be all right, Warren. You have a cup of tea, it will make you feel better.'

He took the cup she offered, looked at the pale liquid with distaste and then drank it politely.

Marj patted his arm in approval. 'It was an unfortunate accident, Warren. Were you hurt?'

'No, ma'am, but the bike is a heap of junk now.'

Wally joined in the conversation with the American,

so Reid turned his attention to Sam. 'What did you mean when you said she wouldn't be jumping out of aeroplanes again,' he asked quietly, not wanting any of Annie's family to hear.

'Ah, you speak French.'

'Enough to understand what you were saying in there.'

Sam thought for a moment. 'She did a parachute jump once and I think she enjoyed it.'

'Why did she do that?' Reid remembered Annie and Bouncer talking about jumping out of a balloon, but he didn't know she'd jumped from an aeroplane as well. Did that delicate façade conceal a daredevil?

'Because she wanted to. What other reason could there be?' Sam asked in a dismissive tone.

Reid bit back a sharp retort. The man was being evasive, but he knew from his demeanour that that was the only answer he was going to be given. And anyway, this was not the place to cross-examine him. Though his curiosity deepened about Sam. What did he do in this war, and how closely was Annie associated with him and his work? Reid knew they were questions he wouldn't get answers to. His own part in this war was simple – you got your plane off the ground and fought the enemy almost face to face – but there were people in the background doing things no one would know about until this conflict ended . . .

Sam studied him carefully. 'I watched you with Annie. Are you in love with her?'

'Yes.' Reid didn't hesitate with the answer.

'That's a change of heart, isn't it?' Sam gave a wry smile. 'I thought you couldn't stand the sight of each other?'

779

'We got off to a bad start, that's all. Are you in love with her as well?'

'There are different shades of love,' Sam replied. 'Annie has my love and respect, and the rest of her wonderful family have my undying gratitude.'

'And what *shade* is your love for Annie?' Reid asked.

'Not bright red like yours, it's more of a glowing yellow, but . . .' Sam paused for a moment. 'When this war's over I'm going to need a wife, and I can't think of anyone more suitable than Annie.'

'You'll have to get past me first.' Reid's attitude couldn't possibly leave Sam in any doubt about his determination.

'You could be right because it was you she opened her eyes for, not me. But I shall not give up until she tells me that she loves you with all her heart. The last thing I would want is for her to be unhappy.'

Reid nodded. Now he knew where he stood, and he had no intention of losing her to this Frenchman, or anyone else.

The doctor put his head around the door. 'You might as well all go home. She's sleeping soundly and we don't expect her to wake up until tomorrow morning. She will be in the private room next door when you return.'

'Thank you.' Marj stood up and said goodbye to the American soldier who hurried away with obvious relief.

Charlie came over to Reid. 'Can I stay for the night? I'd like to see my sister in the morning.'

'Of course.'

'If you need a bed for the night, we have plenty of room,' Wally told Reid.

'Thanks.' He looked at his watch. 'It's too late to go

back now, and I would like to visit in the morning as well. We can go back together, Charlie.'

Annie groaned as she woke up, and found a doctor bending over her.

'Are you in pain?' he asked.

'Yes,' she gasped. 'What happened? I feel as if a tank ran over me.'

The man smiled. 'No, it was only a motorbike. Do you remember anything?'

Annie tried to think back but it felt as if she was struggling to recall a dream. 'I was walking along a country lane, there was no one around, and then I heard a roar. After that, nothing.'

'Good, that's excellent,' the doctor told her. 'An American soldier was on a motorbike and hit you when he came round a corner.'

'Good job he wasn't driving a truck.' Annie lifted the sheet with her good hand. 'How badly hurt am I?'

'You have a broken arm and ankle, lacerations and concussion.'

'Oh, Lord, what a mess!' Annie fought back a groan, but she wasn't going to let self-pity swamp her. She was alive and her injuries would heal in time.

'What about the soldier?' she asked.

'He escaped with a few cuts and bruises.' The doctor took her pulse and examined her, then gave a satisfied smile. 'You are going to be just fine, and you remember everything, so the concussion will not be a problem. Plenty of rest and you'll be as good as new.'

As he strode away Annie tried to move and fell back with a gasp. 'Nurse, can you sit me up, please?'

Two of them came over, pillows were placed behind her, and they lifted her up.

'Oh, thank you,' she sighed, 'that's much more comfortable.'

'Your mother's here,' the ward sister told her. 'Shall I send her in?'

'Please.'

Marj hurried in looking anxious until she saw her daughter sitting up and wide awake. 'That's better. You gave us all a scare yesterday.'

'Hello, Mum.' Annie held out her hand and pulled her mother towards her for a kiss. 'I'm sorry I frightened you. Are you on your own?'

'The others are coming later. We got told off yesterday so we thought we'd better stagger the visits. There were too many of us here, and when Reid shouted at you they asked us to be quiet, or leave.'

Annie frowned. 'Reid? What was he doing here?'

'He brought Charlie home. Don't you remember?'

There was a hazy recollection at the back of her mind of a deep, firm voice giving her orders, and after thinking about it for a while she gave a wry smile. 'Ah, yes, he swore at me.'

'That's right, but it did the trick because you opened your eyes then.'

'I expect I did,' she admitted. 'That man has an air of command about him, doesn't he?'

'He's certainly very forceful.' Marj eyed her daughter with interest. 'Not a bit like his brother, is he?'

Annie nearly choked on a laugh. 'Complete opposites! Paul was such a gentle and considerate man, but Reid is tough. He speaks his mind.'

She didn't want to dwell on the man who was causing her so much confusion. She had been able to deal with him when they'd met on bad terms previously, but after the dance he'd taken her to she was no longer sure about her feelings. They seemed to have done an about-face, and that didn't appear to be a good idea to her. He was turning out to be far too charming for her peace of mind. She had been receiving letters, phone calls, gifts of items like scented soap, an unheard of luxury in these austere times, and even a bunch of flowers on her last birthday. The man was showing signs of being a romantic at heart . . . She dragged her thoughts away from Reid. 'Does Sam know about the accident?'

'Yes. He spent some time here yesterday, but he's had to return to duty today. He said to tell you that he will visit as soon as he can.'

Wally walked in. 'Hello, sweetheart, you're looking better.'

'Flatterer.' Annie grinned as much as her sore face would allow. 'I must be a real sight.'

'A bit bruised and battered maybe, but you're still as beautiful as ever.' Wally placed a hand on his wife's shoulder. 'Charlie and Reid are outside and would like to see Annie. They've got to return to camp this morning. I think Reid has stretched the rules by allowing Charlie to stay this long, but it was damned good of him.'

'He's a kind man.' Marj stood up and smiled at her daughter. 'We'll go and see if we can find a cup of tea, then come back after Charlie and Reid have seen you. Mustn't have too many people round the bed or we'll upset the ward sister. Rose and George wanted to rush back from Wales but we told them that you were out of danger, and there wasn't anything they could do. George has insisted that you come to Wales to convalesce.'

When they'd left Annie closed her eyes for a moment. She was feeling very tired, but so grateful for and touched by the love of her family. She was an extremely lucky girl.

'Not going to sleep again, are you?'

'I wouldn't dare!' she muttered, and looked up at the tall figure of Reid standing by the bed. 'He must be one hell of a commanding officer,' she told Charlie.

Her brother grinned. 'Oh, he isn't too bad as long as you stay out of his way.'

'That must be difficult.'

Reid chuckled. 'I thought we were friends now, Annie?'

'Is that what we agreed?' she asked in mock horror. 'You must have caught me in a weak moment.'

'That sounds more like our Annie.' Charlie bent over and kissed her cheek, obviously relieved to hear his sister joking like this.

For the next half an hour they talked, and the men did their best to make her laugh and raise her spirits, but Annie secretly found it very tiring. She ached from head to toe and felt completely drained of energy.

Reid glanced at his watch. 'We had better be going, Charlie. I phoned in to say that we would be back by twelve.'

Charlie stood up and squeezed Annie's hand. 'Being with the commanding officer does have its advantages. At least I won't be put on a charge if I'm late reporting in.'

'You want to bet?' Reid joked.

'Oops! Must go, Sis. You hurry up and get better.'

'You make sure you do!' Reid told her. 'As soon as you're on your feet again I'll take you dancing.'

Annie looked at the cage over her legs and grimaced. 'That might take some time.'

'I can wait.' He leaned over, gave her a lingering kiss, and spoke softly, 'I can be very patient when I have to.'

'Really?' Annie opened her eyes wide in mock surprise. 'You could have fooled me.'

Charlie clearly didn't believe that either. 'That will be news to the boys back at base.'

'Really?' Reid feigned surprise. 'I thought I was a most tolerant officer.' Then he kissed Annie again.

Charlie cleared his throat. 'It's getting late . . . and I thought you and my sister were just friends?'

Reid stood up. 'We are, but I'm working on it.'

Annie didn't miss the look of amusement on her brother's face.

27

Annie had been in hospital for nearly four weeks and was bored to tears. The first couple of weeks had been painful and she'd felt too ill to take much notice of what was going on around her, but now she felt fine. As her health had improved the restrictions forced on her by the broken ankle and arm were enough to drive her mad! She had been told not to attempt to move without the nurses' help; she was considering having another go at standing up, when a visitor walked in.

'Will!' Annie exclaimed in pleasure. 'When did you arrive home?'

'Last night. Our ship's in dock to have some new equipment fitted.' Her brother sat on the bed next to her chair. 'And just in time too. Dora had a girl in the early hours of this morning.'

'Oh, how wonderful!' She clasped his hand. 'Congratulations. Are they both all right?'

He smiled proudly. 'They're just fine.'

Annie was sitting in a chair beside the bed and stamped her uninjured foot in frustration. 'When am I going to get out of this place? I'm missing everything, and I want to get back to work.'

Suddenly Sam walked into her room. 'You won't be fit enough for duty until the new year.' He sat beside her.

'Why not?' Annie waved her right hand at him. If she had to endure much more of this idleness she'd go crazy!

'Look, there's nothing wrong with this, I can still operate a wireless.'

'The injury to your ankle is very bad and you can't walk yet,' Sam pointed out. 'And you won't be able to use crutches with a broken left arm.'

Annie felt like screaming, but he was right, blast him. She'd tried walking with a stick and would have fallen if a nurse hadn't been holding on to her.

'You've got to be patient,' Will told her. 'You've had a serious accident and recovery is bound to be a slow business.'

'I'm trying to be patient.' She sighed, laid her head back and closed her eyes. 'What are you going to call your daughter?'

'We haven't decided yet. Dora wants to call her Rose, but I'm not sure about that.'

Annie opened her eyes. 'Why not? It's a nice name and Dora admires Rose very much.'

'I know.' Will frowned. 'But Rose is a unique woman, and I'm not too keen on giving our little daughter the same name. She might be constantly compared with our Rose and that wouldn't be right for her.'

'Hmm.' Annie could see Will's point and it would seem strange having another Rose in the family. 'What about Emily, Rose's other name?'

'What a good idea.' Will beamed at his sister. 'I'll suggest it to Dora when I see her this afternoon. I'm sure she'll like that.'

'I wish I could see her as well.' Annie's mood plummeted into gloom. It was terribly difficult to keep depression at bay when she felt so helpless. 'Give Dora my love and kiss little Emily for me.'

'I think Emily's a lovely name,' Sam told Will in approval. 'What did she weigh at birth?'

'Seven pounds exactly.'

Annie watched Sam's face as he talked to Will about the birth and wondered what he was thinking. He'd never seen Jacques as a baby, or taking his first steps, or heard his first words . . .

She felt it was time to change the subject. 'Tell me what's going on in the outside world, Sam.'

'Well, you know that Italy declared war on Germany three weeks ago.' Sam couldn't contain his excitement. 'And this country is filling up with troops and equipment . . .'

'Ready to launch an invasion?' Annie asked.

He nodded. 'Next year! It *must* be next year.'

'Oh, damn, damn!' Annie moaned. 'I've got to get out of here, Sam.'

'How does next week sound?' A doctor strolled up to her. 'You've made an excellent recovery and we'll be able to remove the plaster from your arm in a few days' time. However, you will still have to keep it in a sling for another couple of weeks.'

'What about my ankle?' she asked. She could manage with one arm but the ankle was causing her concern.

'That will have to wait a while longer. We want you to come back on January the 3rd and we'll have a look at it then.'

'Thank you, doctor.' Annie's sigh was heartfelt. 'I'm going round the bend being cut off from everything.'

He laughed. 'So I've noticed but you'll still have to take things very easy for a few more weeks.'

As the doctor walked away Will said, 'You can go down to Wales and spend Christmas there.'

'That would be lovely. George has written several times insisting that I come home and be looked after properly.' Then her smile faded. When she thought of the journey on a crowded and cold train, she wasn't at all sure she had the strength to cope with it. She was feeling shaky and weak. 'But how on earth am I going to get there? I'll never manage on the train.'

'I'll fly you there.' Reid strode into the room.

She looked at him in disbelief, and then closed her eyes for a moment. He really was a stunning man: tall, straight, with his dark hair and eyes almost the same colour as his uniform. 'You're joking?'

'No, I'm not. I've still got my own plane and I'm sure I can get permission to use it on this occasion. There's a small airfield near Pontypool.' He shook hands with Will and Sam. 'I can squeeze another one in, if anyone wants to come.'

'Not me, I'm afraid,' Will told him with obvious regret. 'I'd love to see everyone but I've only got a three-day pass, and I want to spend as much time as possible with Dora and the baby. God knows where I'll be at Christmas.'

'I'd like to take you up on the offer,' Sam said. 'I could help with Annie and it would give me a chance to see my son.'

'Son?'

Sam explained briefly and Reid listened, a deep frown furrowing his brow.

'Of course you must come,' he said when Sam had finished talking. 'I'll bring you back as well, if that would help?'

'It certainly would, but I'd like to stay for a couple of days.'

'I think I can wangle some leave,' Reid told him with confidence.

Annie looked at the three men as they made arrangements without consulting her. 'Just hold on a minute. Don't I have any say in this? And what are you doing here, don't you ever do any work, Squadron Leader?'

'Now and again,' he replied, a slight smile on his face at the demotion again. 'I've left Tangmere in the hands of my deputy for a few days.'

'If you don't want to fly,' Sam said with a mischievous grin, 'I could always take you down by truck.'

Annie held up her hand in horror. 'Oh, no, I'd rather fly than risk you behind the wheel again.'

'Good, that's settled then.' Reid noticed the sweets on her bedside table. 'Where did all those come from?'

'I've had a constant stream of American soldiers bringing me treats. Warren said his buddies wanted to cheer me up and let me know how sorry they were that one of them had hurt me so badly.' She gave a delighted grin. 'I've even been given two pairs of nylons.'

Sam glanced at Reid and pulled a face. 'We must definitely get her out of here or we won't be able to get in the door for American soldiers.'

Reid spun on his heel. 'I'll go and find out when we can move her.'

Four days later Reid carried Annie into The Haven and laid her on the settee. She rested her head back and closed her eyes. Although Sam and Reid had done everything they could to make the journey to Wales as quick and comfortable as possible, it had taken a lot out of her. It was a blessed relief to be there.

Rose pulled a stool over and lifted Annie's injured leg on to it. 'We've made up a bed for you downstairs, and there's a toilet and washroom right next door.'

'Thank you, Rosie.' Annie smiled. 'How are the children?'

'They're fine.' Rose turned to Sam. 'Jacques is settling in very well. He's having his afternoon nap at the moment.'

Just then the door was pushed open and Jacques trotted in carrying a toy rabbit by the ear. He stopped suddenly when he noticed Reid, then looked at Sam.

'Daddy?' He spoke the word exactly as Kate did, and it was clear he'd been listening to her very carefully.

Sam knelt down and hugged his son, and Annie was delighted to see that the child did not pull away. Progress was being made.

Annie smiled, holding out her hand to him. 'Hello, Jacques, do you remember me?'

'You're Auntie Annie,' he said in clear English.

He sidled past Reid and stopped by the stool, reaching out to touch the plaster on her ankle. 'What's that?' he asked.

'I've broken my ankle and have to keep that on until it's healed,' Annie told him.

Annie was surprised at how well Jack had picked up the language. 'You speak English very well now.'

'Auntie Rose 'elped me,' he told her as he climbed on to the settee beside her, still clutching his toy.

'That's a nice rabbit,' she said.

'Kate give me.' He squirmed about until he pulled a

small toy soldier from his pocket and showed it to Annie. 'James got lots of these and 'e let me play.'

Sam knelt down in front of his son. 'Are you happy living here, Jacques?'

He nodded. 'Auntie Rose is nice. Grandpa Wally and Grandpa George play with me, and Grandma Marj read me stories. Kate and James say I can be their brother.' He gave his father an uncertain look, then tugged at the ear of his rabbit as a glimmer of tears shone in his eyes.

Sam and Annie were talking to Jacques in his own language now, and Reid watched the scene with narrowed eyes. He could see why Sam wanted Annie for his wife; she would be perfect for him and his son. The boy was obviously still troubled and was holding on to Annie with one hand and gazing at his father anxiously.

Reid's heart ached with pity for this poor little boy; he was so clearly confused and troubled.

Not being able to stand seeing the three of them together any longer, Reid walked out of the room, through the kitchen and into the garden. He leant against the house and lit a cigarette, ignoring the cold wind.

Now he understood how his brother had felt about Annie. Paul had been clinging on to an elusive dream – a dream out of reach. He drew in deeply and blew the smoke out, watching the wind snatch it away. Was he doing the same thing? It had taken him a long time to really fall in love, and now he felt as if his hopes were as insubstantial as the smoke. Oh hell!

'Don't give up.' Rose came and stood beside him, pulling her coat close around her. 'Sam and Annie have been through a lot together, but quite what, only they know. They like and respect each other but I don't think it would be right for them to marry.'

Reid offered her a cigarette, and when she refused he said, 'They look happy together, so why do you say that?'

'Haven't you noticed that Sam hardly ever touches her? Annie wouldn't like that; she's always been very tactile. But there's more to it than physical attraction,' Rose said. 'I believe he only sees her as a suitable mother for his son.'

Reid was angry at the thought of a man using Annie like that. She deserved better. You couldn't just label her as a suitable mother; she had feelings and needs of her own. She was a complex and adorable woman . . .

Rose gave him a speculative glance. 'I've seen the expression in your eyes when you look at her, so don't give up. It took Bill ages to persuade me to marry him, but he won in the end, in his usual quiet way.'

'How did he manage it?' Reid asked. It was unusual for Rose to open up like this and he was hoping she would keep on talking. He wanted to know all about this family Annie loved so much.

'He kept going away, leaving me to get mad with him, then he would return and pick up where we'd left off, as if it had been only yesterday.' Rose gave a quiet chuckle.

Reid grinned, remembering the tall captain who had the respect of all his crew without ever raising his voice. 'He knew what he was doing.'

'Bill always does.' Rose smiled back at Reid. 'But I'm glad he never took "no" for an answer.'

'Why hasn't Annie ever married?'

793

Rose shoved her hands in her pockets and frowned. 'I've always assumed it was because she had a career she enjoyed and didn't want to be tied down with a family of her own just yet, but I believe the real reason is that she hasn't met anyone she could love with passion.'

'And you believe that's important to her, do you?' Reid asked.

'Yes. As a small child she was always outgoing and affectionate, loving people in a way I could never understand.' She laughed softly. 'As soon as I turned my back she would be sidling up to the men I knew, giving them an appealing smile until they lifted her up. I know she would never marry unless she felt absolutely sure it was right, and in the absence of that special man in her life she has showered her family with love.'

Reid tried to imagine Annie as a small child and it wasn't difficult to do; she must have been a real charmer. And although she was a grown woman now, she had retained an air of innocence that was damned appealing. Whenever they were together he found himself watching the way she responded to people; the ready smile and gentleness he often glimpsed in her eyes. His brother had been right – Annie Webster was a very special woman and he wanted her! He looked at Rose and smiled, dragging his mind away from the girl who was starting to fill his every waking moment. 'Charlie told me that you have another brother who ran away to sea as a boy and ended up in Australia.'

'Yes, Bob.' Rose grimaced. 'He was difficult as a child and he did the right thing by leaving. He's made a good life for himself out there; but at the moment he's in this country with the Australians. We've got two more sisters:

Nancy and Flo. They are settled with their own families and we hardly ever see them now, which makes Mum sad, but that's the way with families, isn't it?'

'Yes.' Reid looked at the tall, beautiful woman beside him, and could understand why Bill had pursued her with such determination. Suddenly he felt better; Rose knew Annie better than anyone else, because she had practically brought her up during those tough years in Garrett Street. He didn't know the whole story but he'd gathered that Annie could have died very young if it hadn't been for Rose's care. If she believed that Annie and Sam weren't in love with each other, then that was good to know. 'Thanks for talking to me, Rose.'

'It was my pleasure.' She walked towards the kitchen door. 'Are you coming in now? It's cold out here and tea will be ready soon.'

Reid followed her into the warmth of the kitchen with its tantalizing smell of freshly baked bread, then on through to the lounge again. The cold air and the talk with Rose had cleared his mind.

Jacques gave Reid a doubtful look when he back came in but Sam told his son, 'He's a pilot and flew us here today.'

The little boy's eyes opened wide and he fired rapid questions at his father in their own language.

'He wants to know if he can see your plane?' Sam told Reid.

'I'll take him tomorrow.'

At that moment there was the sound of children's voices and Jack scrambled off the settee. 'Kate and James home from school.' Then he was off as fast as his legs would carry him.

No sooner had the boy left the room when he was back again, trailing after Rose's two children.

'Auntie Annie.' Kate came and kissed her gently, making sure she didn't knock her arm or leg.

'Can you walk?' James asked as he examined the bulky plaster on her foot and ankle.

'It's difficult, but I can manage.' Annie put her foot to the floor and stood up. 'See, they've put something on the bottom of the plaster so I can stand on it.'

'Tea's ready!' Rose looked into the room. 'I'll bring yours in here, Annie.'

'No, you won't. I'll eat with the rest of you.'

Reid stepped forward as she tried a step, but she waved him away. 'I've got to do this myself. I can't be forever calling for help.'

When Annie reached the table she collapsed on to a chair and gave a triumphant grin. 'Made it! I knew I could do it. And it's no good you looking so disapproving, Squadron Leader, because I'm determined to fend for myself while I'm here.'

'I've been demoted again, have I?' Reid asked, smiling at her dangerously.

'Well,' said George, changing the subject quickly to avoid a row erupting, 'it looks as if we'll soon be ready to invade France. Will you go home after the war's over, Sam?'

Jacques stopped chewing and fixed anxious eyes on his father. 'Home?'

'Yes, Jacques, but not until all the Germans have left,' Sam told him.

The boy swallowed. 'We find *ma mère*?'

'What does that mean?' James whispered to Annie.

'His mother,' she told him, anxious that the little boy should have asked such a question.

Jacques looked at his father. 'I want nice mummy, like James and Kate 'ave got.'

'I promise you shall have one.' Sam's voice was husky with emotion.

'Don't make promises you might not be able to keep, Sam,' Rose reprimanded firmly. 'It isn't right to give the boy false hopes.'

'I'll keep my promise, Rose.' Sam had a look of sheer determination on his face. 'I'll do anything to make my son happy.'

Reid could feel Annie slipping away from him with every word from the grim-looking man sitting opposite him.

The next morning was a Saturday so the three children, Sam, Wally, George and Reid, crammed themselves into George's car and went to the airfield to see the plane. Before the war it had been a private airfield and there were still a good many small planes parked there for the duration. Because of his rank, it hadn't been difficult for Reid to obtain permission for this brief visit. James was soon inside Reid's Lysander asking a stream of questions, but Kate and Jacques didn't seem too keen and only wanted to view it from the field. Reid studied the two children and couldn't help noticing that Kate, at seven years old, was beginning to show a hint of her mother's dark beauty, and Jacques, only three years old, appeared frightened to be out in the open. Poor little devil!

Reid left James in the cockpit and jumped down. The little boy had asked to see the plane, but now he was hanging back, looking rather unsure of himself. He was hanging on to George's hand and glancing nervously around the field. 'Don't you want to have a look inside?' he asked Jacques.

It took some persuading but he eventually managed to entice the two reluctant children inside. Kate was clearly uneasy, but after a couple of minutes Jacques was looking around with interest and chattering excitedly in his own language. Reid couldn't follow the rapid flow of words, and he doubted that the children could either, but they didn't take any notice, and kept talking to him as if they understood every word. He smiled at their antics. It was refreshing to see how they all got along together even if they couldn't always understand the words. Mankind could take a lesson from children, he thought.

Jacques began to shiver with the cold, so Reid scooped him up and put him in the back of the car, tucking a blanket around his little legs, and then everyone else clambered in. He started the car and they made their way back to the house, the children chattering away all the time.

'Are you still flying in combat?' George asked as they pulled up in front of the house.

'No, and I do miss it,' Reid admitted to George and Wally, 'but my mother's relieved. After Paul was killed she was terrified the same thing would happen to me.'

Wally helped Jacques from the car and then looked at Reid. 'You stay on the ground, my boy. Losing one son is enough for any family.'

That was something Reid couldn't argue with. The loss of Paul was still an open wound for them all, and he wondered how many years it was going to take before the pain eased.

As soon as they arrived back everyone went into the lounge and huddled around the log fire. One good thing about living in the country like this was that there was always a plentiful supply of firewood, and fresh food from their kitchen garden.

Marj bustled in with mugs of cocoa. 'I saw the car pull up and thought you would need this. It's perishing cold out there today.'

Reid took one with a smile of thanks. Annie's mother was looking tired and that was hardly surprising; this house was always full.

'Gosh, that was great!' James rubbed his hands and held them out to the fire in an effort to get them warm again. 'I'm going to learn to fly when I'm old enough. Will you teach me?' he asked Reid.

'If you still want to in six years' time when you're twenty.' Reid looked at the silent little boy. 'Would you like to learn when you're grown up?'

Jacques gave this careful thought, and then shook his head. 'You fly us.'

Marj handed round the hot drinks and Reid settled in an armchair. He couldn't help feeling troubled. The more time he spent in Jacques's company, the more obvious one thing was. The child never smiled!

28

The journey from Pontypool to London had been long, tiring and cold. Annie felt it had all been worth it, though, as she watched her cast being removed, and gave a groan of sheer pleasure. Thank heavens for that! She had hated the restrictions the plaster had imposed on her life.

The doctor examined her ankle and nodded approval. 'That's healed well. How's the head, no bad headaches or dizzy spells?'

'No, none.' She put her foot to the floor, stood up very carefully and grimaced.

'No jiving for a while,' he joked.

'I promise.' After the doctor had left, the nurse helped her on with her stockings and shoes, and then handed her a walking stick. 'Use this for a couple of weeks.'

'Thanks for everything.' Annie hobbled to the main waiting area and nearly bumped into Reid, who was charging along with a scowl on his face.

'Sorry I didn't meet the train,' he apologized. 'I was delayed and the roads are treacherous.'

'That's all right. I got a lift from the station, and I wasn't expecting you, anyway.' And if his thunderous expression was an indication of his mood, she thought, then he needn't have bothered coming.

Reid glanced around. 'Where are Wally and George?'

'They both have bad colds and I wouldn't let them come.' Annie was glad of the stick as she made her way along the corridor. The ankle did not feel at all secure now the support had been removed.

'What?' Reid stopped her. 'Are you telling me you made that journey on your own?'

'Of course I did. People were very kind and helped me all the way.' She continued walking, wondering why he was making such a fuss. It hadn't been a pleasant or easy journey but she'd managed quite well considering the bulky plaster had made movement difficult.

'Why the hell didn't you let me know?' he exploded. 'The weather was too bad to fly you back, but I could have come and collected you.'

'Reid, I am not helpless.' She cast him an exasperated glance. 'My arm is completely healed and I could walk reasonably well, if slowly.'

'Where are you going now?' he asked with a resigned sigh.

'There isn't a train for Bedford today so I'm staying at Roehampton for the night. I'm fit to return to duty as from tomorrow.' She couldn't wait to get back and stuck into the job again. Although Dora wasn't there any more, Jean still was, and the rest of the girls were a lively bunch. Before, when she had spare time, which wasn't often, they had gone in a group to the pub, or dancing. Although dancing would be out of the question for some time, she thought, as she limped along.

'Well, if we get any more snow you'll have a job reporting back on time.' Reid held a door open for her and they made their way to the main entrance.

'I'll worry about that in the morning,' she told him

sharply, suddenly feeling very tired. She could do without this kind of pessimism. 'But I'll get there all right.'

'Can't wait to get back to Sam?' he snapped.

Annie gave him a withering look. 'What's that supposed to mean?'

Reid's sigh was weary and he massaged between his eyes. 'Sorry. I'm in a foul mood. I was concerned about you when the weather closed in, but I thought Wally and George would be with you.'

'I couldn't let them come, Reid,' Annie explained. 'They were both too ill to sit in a freezing train for hours.'

'Couldn't Rose have come with you for support?'

'There's Dora, the baby and her family down there, and with two sick men to look after as well, she couldn't leave.'

Annie stopped when they stepped outside and she saw the air force truck parked right outside the door. 'Did you come in that?'

'My car wouldn't start,' he grumbled.

The expression of disgust on his face was too much for Annie, and she began to laugh. 'Oh, dear, you have had a rotten day, haven't you?'

'I'm glad you find it funny, because I bloody well don't!' He opened the truck door and lifted Annie into the passenger seat, then jumped in himself. 'Is there anyone at home?' he asked as they drove out of the hospital gates.

'No, our houses have been empty since early November.'

'Oh God! I hope the blasted pipes aren't frozen.'

Annie hit him on the arm. 'Will you stop being so gloomy? Of course they won't be. Bill made sure everything was properly lagged. Are you coming down with the flu or something?'

'Nope. I'm disgustingly healthy.'

Annie decided it was useless talking to him, so she settled back and the rest of the journey was silent. Something had upset the big, scowling man, and she didn't think she wanted to know what it was.

When they got to Roehampton it was colder in the house than outside, and that was clearly too much for Reid's fragile temper.

'You can't stay here,' he exploded. 'It's like the Arctic.'

She rummaged in the kitchen drawer for a box of matches, fed up and with her patience evaporating. 'It will soon warm up when I get the fires going. They are already laid and I've only got to put a match to them.'

He took the matches out of her hand, struck one, and lit the paper in the large black-leaded kitchen fire. 'If you insist on staying, then you'll need hot water.'

Annie was pleased to see that he sounded a bit more reasonable now. 'It won't take long, that fire is very efficient.'

Reid blew on the flames and gave a grunt of satisfaction as the fire caught. Then he disappeared to light the lounge one.

Annie shook her head, bemused by his strange mood, and put the kettle on to make some tea. While the water was boiling she unpacked her bag. Thank goodness she'd brought enough food to feed Reid as well. She dreaded to think what he would be like if he had to go hungry this evening.

'It's snowing again,' he said, as he came back into the kitchen.

'I'll get you something to eat, then you'd better be on your way before it gets too bad,' she told him.

'I'm not leaving you here on your own,' he said in astonishment. 'How the hell are you going to get back to camp in the morning?'

'On the train, of course.'

'Oh, fine!' he said, throwing his hands up in disgust. 'What do you want to do, break the other leg?'

She spun to face him, hands on hips. 'What the blazes is wrong with you? You're treating me as if I was some brainless idiot. I've taken care of myself in worse conditions than this and survived.'

'Oh, when?' Reid was studying her through narrowed eyes.

Blast! Annie thought, that was careless of me, but the man was infuriating, and he was also curious. But what she'd said was true. That trip to France had been cold, arduous and frightening, but it had certainly made her tougher and more able to cope with difficult situations. She busied herself with making the tea and putting soup on to heat, hoping he wouldn't pursue the subject. She must watch her tongue more carefully in the future. Not that she considered Reid a security risk, but her mission to rescue Jack Graham was top secret, and she wouldn't want to put the brave people who had helped her in danger.

'So, why the foul mood?' she asked, changing the subject.

Reid shrugged. 'It's nothing. I'll get over it.'

Annie put two bowls of steaming vegetable soup on the table with chunks of Rose's home-made bread. 'Do you want to talk about it?'

804

'No.' He sat down and started to eat. 'What's Will and Dora's baby like?'

'Just beautiful, she's got masses of silver-blonde hair, and is a contented little tot. Mind you, she was spoilt rotten by everyone.' Seeing baby Emily had been wonderful. Her mother had fussed over her new grandchild, clearly delighted with the little girl.

'The house must have been packed over the holiday.' Reid finished off his soup and spread margarine on another piece of bread.

'All room was taken up, with camp beds crammed in every space,' Annie said and laughed, 'and because of the bad weather they are all still there.'

'Except you,' he remarked, picking up his knife and fork to tuck into the vegetable pie Annie had brought back from Wales with her.

'I had to return,' she told him, a defensive note in her voice. 'I've been out of action for long enough and can't wait to get back to normal again. I believe 1944 is going to be an exciting year, and I want to be in the thick of it.'

'I know, Annie.' He reached out and placed his large hand over hers. 'I'm sorry I took my bad temper out on you.' He grimaced. 'I'd promised myself I wouldn't do that to you again but when I thought about you struggling on your own I was furious with myself. I should have come for you.'

'I am a grown woman, Reid. I don't need a nursemaid.'

'I have noticed,' he remarked drily.

Annie pulled her hand away from his. Arguing with him made her feel sad. 'Can we go back to being friends again?'

He laughed then, a deep amused sound that Annie found rather disturbing. 'We do seem to antagonize each other, don't we?'

She looked closely at the handsome man, and couldn't help wondering why she always felt so defensive around him. But she couldn't come up with an answer.

He helped clear away their dishes, refusing to let her stand up for too long. After everything was put away Annie opened the airing cupboard and felt the tank. 'Good, there will soon be enough hot water for a bath.' The sooner she could soak her ankle the better, for it was aching badly now. In spite of all her bravado about being fit for work again it wasn't going to be easy.

'It'll be cold up there,' Reid pointed out. 'Have you got an electric fire?'

'There's one in my bedroom but it's only a single bar.'

'I'll put that in there for a while, it will take the chill off.' He headed for the stairs, taking them two at a time.

While he was upstairs, Annie checked to see if there were fresh sheets and blankets in the airing cupboard, but to be honest she didn't feel like shivering in a cold bedroom. The warmth of the fire was seeping through her now and she felt dreadfully tired. She yawned.

'Come on, you look exhausted.' Reid came back and took her by the hand. 'The lounge is warm enough now.'

She didn't protest when he led her to the other room. The settee was pulled up to the fire and she sat down with a sigh of relief.

'You've had a long hard day,' Reid said. He put some more logs on the fire then joined her, gathering her into his arms. 'Rest now.'

Annie tucked her legs up and rested her head on his chest. He was such a thoughtful man when he wasn't snapping and snarling, she mused as she drifted off to sleep.

'Annie!'

She didn't want to wake up. She was so warm and comfortable . . .

'The fires will go out if I don't see to them soon.'

'Hmm?' She sat up and yawned. 'How long have I been asleep?'

'Over an hour.' He stood up, stretched, and then started to build the fire up again. 'The bathroom will be nice and warm by now. I'll remove the electric fire when you're ready.'

Annie flexed her foot and ankle; it was feeling rather sore. Perhaps she had overdone things today.

'A hot bath will ease that.' Reid smiled down at her.

She hoped he was right. 'I think I'll sleep down here tonight, in the warm.'

'I was going to suggest that,' he agreed. 'The beds will need airing before they can be used. You take the settee and I'll sleep in one of the armchairs.'

'Will you be comfortable enough?' she asked. He looked much too large to rest in a chair for the night.

'Sure. When we were flying several times a day I learned to snatch sleep wherever I could, and so did the rest of the squadron.' He gave a wry smile. 'We were so damned tired.'

'They were desperate times, weren't they?'

He nodded, a faraway look in his eyes, and Annie knew he was reliving the struggle they'd had. No one was going to come out of this war the same person they'd been before it started.

'You don't have to worry about me. I could sleep on a clothes line if I had to.' Reid poked the fire into a good blaze again, and then sat on the floor staring into the flames, obviously lost in a world of his own.

Annie stood up and stretched. 'I'll go and have my bath now.'

Half an hour later she was back, dressed in her flannel pyjamas, dressing gown and a pair of Wally's long hand-knitted socks. She threw the pillows and blankets she was carrying on one of the armchairs.

Reid had a glass of whisky in his hand and he held it up to her. 'I found this in the sideboard, do you think Wally will mind?'

'Of course not.' Annie studied Reid's downcast expression. 'I wish you'd tell me what's worrying you.'

He swallowed the drink down and grimaced. 'Well, there's this girl I'm crazy about . . .'

For some daft reason the thought of Reid with another woman disturbed her, but she managed to laugh. This was the last thing she would have expected. Reid didn't seem the type to let a woman trouble him.

Annie sat on the settee. 'Come and tell me about her.'

Reid settled next to her and put his arm around her shoulder. 'She's lovely, intelligent, infuriating and she's got another man after her.'

'You're not going to let that stop you, surely?' She couldn't believe he would step aside and let someone else have what he wanted without a struggle. His character was too determined for that.

'It's complicated.' He shrugged.

'What's complicated about it? You want her, don't you?' It was hard to understand why she found this so difficult to talk about. After all, if he was in love with some woman, then what was that to her? She was just feeling a bit emotional after finally having that damned plaster removed, she thought, that's all it was. Once she got back to work, she would feel more like herself.

'More than anything I've ever wanted in my life,' he admitted.

'Then go after her, you fool,' she told him. 'If you don't, you'll regret it for the rest of your days.'

'I'm glad you feel like that.' He reached across and started to unfasten her pyjama jacket. First one button, then the second . . .

'Just a minute!' Annie caught hold of his hand. 'What do you think you're doing?'

He gave her a searing look. 'You told me to go after her, so I'm trying to see if making love to her will win her over.'

Annie pushed him away and scrambled to her feet, the sore ankle forgotten. She was deeply wounded by his attitude. 'I will not be used by you to relieve your frustration. I am not a substitute for the woman you love.'

'You've got it all wrong, Annie. You're not a substitute. The only one I'm thinking about is you. It's you I'm in love with!'

Annie was incensed by what she considered a blatant lie. 'Don't you make fun of me, Reid Lascells. And don't try to excuse your conduct by lying to me. I know you're only looking after me to keep the promise you made to

Paul. Your mother told me all about it. All I can say is that you can't love this girl very much if you are willing to put someone else in her place for one night. I would not have expected you to take advantage of our situation.'

Reid gave a ragged sigh. 'I'm telling you the truth.'

Annie had had enough of this. If she didn't get rid of him soon she would burst into tears, and she was damned if she'd do that in front of him. The lying devil! She picked up a pillow and a blanket and tossed them to him. 'You can sleep in the kitchen. There's an old armchair in there by the fire.'

It had been a long and sleepless night. Annie had found it difficult to stop her mind from racing. The fact that Reid had tried to make love to her after telling her he was crazy about some other woman was beyond belief, and had hurt dreadfully. Not that *she* loved him, of course, but she objected to being taken advantage of like that. Although they always seemed to fight when they met, she respected him, and to think he would stoop to doing something like this was upsetting – and disappointing.

Reid was already in the kitchen making tea and toast for their breakfast. He gave her a hard stare as she walked in. 'Did you sleep well?'

'No,' she admitted. 'Did you?'

He didn't answer as he spread margarine on the bread and placed it in front of her. 'The weather's cleared a bit so I can drive you back to Bedfordshire as soon as you're ready.'

'I can catch the ten o'clock train.' She bit into the toast and ignored the look of fury racing across his face.

'Don't you argue with me, Miss Webster,' he growled,

'because I'm not in any mood to put up with your nonsense this morning.'

She decided it would be best if they didn't speak to each other if they couldn't be civil, and they certainly didn't seem to be able to this morning! The atmosphere between them was positively explosive. They drank their tea and ate the toast in silence. Within half an hour they were on their way.

Annie slept most of the journey, making up for the hours of tossing and turning last night. It was the safest thing to do because if they argued any more she'd start to crumble, as her emotions were raw at the moment. She'd never known anyone who could upset her like this man.

'We're here.' Reid shook her awake and got down to help her out. He lifted her out of the truck and handed her the kit bag. He looked her straight in the eyes for a few moments. His expression was intense and strained. 'I'm not a liar, Annie,' he said quietly, and then jumped back into the vehicle and sped off up the lane.

She stood there for a while as she wrestled with a deep sense of hurt. She was convinced that Reid was only paying her all this attention because of the promise he'd made to his brother. How she wished his parents had never told her about it.

'I'm back, Sam.' She looked into his office and wiggled her foot. 'Look, no plaster.'

'Good. I didn't think you'd make it,' Sam said. 'Are the trains running?'

'Reid brought me back in an air force truck.'

'Did he now?'

'Yes. He collected me from hospital yesterday and we stayed overnight at my house.' Annie wondered why Sam was frowning.

'But your family are still in Wales, aren't they?' he asked. 'Were you alone with him all night?'

'I could hardly send him out on a terrible night like that, could I?' Annie had had enough! What was the matter with these men? She'd had to put up with Reid in a foul mood, and now Sam.

She stormed out and headed for the ops room. Sam and Reid were as bad as each other. She wasn't daft. It was obvious that Sam was looking in her direction as a mother for his adorable son, so he might not like to think there was another man on the scene to spoil his plans, but what was Reid up to? And what right did any man have to make plans regarding her future without finding out if she was agreeable or not?

Annie had always considered that she understood men reasonably well but not any longer. She had been wise to remain single. They were a blasted mystery!

29

April 1944

The watery spring sunshine filtered through the high cloud and bathed Tangmere airfield in a golden glow. Reid shaded his eyes as he scanned the sky. The invasion of France couldn't be far away now and troops were being moved to various places along the coast. He'd been overjoyed when he'd heard that his old squadron was being transferred here for the next few months. This was just the lift he needed. Since that disastrous night in January, he had stayed away from Annie, hoping this tactic would work as Rose had suggested, but he doubted it. It was his own fault, of course; he should have convinced her, but the truth was he had bungled it. He had been thrown by her disbelief that he could love her, and dismayed to find she knew about the promise he'd made to Paul. It was clouding their relationship and the way she thought about him. He might be a good pilot but he had a hell of a lot to learn about women.

One Spitfire roared over their heads and spun into a victory roll. Reid chuckled, his worries forgotten for a moment. Bouncer. He was tempted to put his reckless friend on a charge for that.

Some of the pilots now landing had been involved in the Battle of Britain, as Churchill called it, and although that phase of the war was over, life was still dangerous for them. One of their many tasks was to escort bombers across the channel, and that meant they were fighting over France. If they had to bale out there, then they were taken prisoner. Reid felt his insides clench when he remembered how close he'd been to that when Dunkirk was being evacuated. He'd have hated to have been locked up and unable to take any further part in the war.

'Hi, skip.' Timber Woods sauntered over to him.

Reid slapped the tall pilot on the shoulder, then he was surrounded by the men of his old squadron. Some he knew; some he didn't; many he missed. 'It's good to see you all.'

They fell silent as they watched Bouncer land. It was always a breathtaking moment.

'Ye Gods!' Reid exclaimed. 'He doesn't get any better, does he?'

'No,' Timber agreed, 'but once he's airborne he's a real demon.'

'I remember. He's always a good man to have with you.' Reid walked over to his friend who was clambering out of the plane. His mobility was still slightly impaired, but nothing to speak of considering how badly he'd been injured. It was five months since he'd seen Bouncer but instead of slapping him on the back in delight Reid kept his expression serious.

'Patterson! You're on a charge for that fancy bit of flying.' Reid used his best command voice.

Bouncer sprang to attention. 'I realized the undercarriage wasn't down so I had to go round again. Took a bit of shaking loose.'

'Is that the best excuse you can come up with?' Reid asked, raising a brow in query.

His friend rubbed his chin. 'It worked in the past.'

'Not this time, you're talking to me now.'

'Ah, well.' Bouncer gave a resigned sigh. 'What's the punishment, then?'

'You've got to get the first round of drinks in tonight.'

A cheer rang out from the rest of the pilots. They were in full agreement with that kind of reprimand.

The ground crews were waiting to get their hands on the new planes, and Reid called Charlie over.

'Bouncer, Charlie, Annie's brother, will look after your Spit for you.'

The pilot beamed and shook Charlie's hand vigorously. 'How is the delightful Annie, now?'

'Completely recovered from her accident and back to normal,' Charlie told him.

Reid made a sound that sounded suspiciously like a snort of disgust, and Bouncer eyed his friend.

'Don't tell me you're still fighting with each other?'

Reid's only answer was a wry smile.

'I think you need your head examined, old boy.' Bouncer turned back to Charlie. 'Give her my regards next time you talk to her, and tell her I'll be writing shortly.'

Charlie nodded and hurried off to check over his new charge.

'What are you writing to Annie for?' Reid asked.

'It's nothing to concern you, old chap. I've got a bit of news for her, that's all.' Bouncer watched Charlie clambering over his plane. 'Good, is he?'

'The best we've got,' Reid assured him. 'He'll look after you well.'

His friend nodded. 'Thanks. Wouldn't like to cop it now the end is in sight.'

Reid looked at Bouncer in astonishment. 'When did you start worrying about your safety?'

'Things change.' He punched Reid on the arm and grinned. 'Things change.'

Bouncer *had* changed, though in what way Reid couldn't quite fathom. There was something different about him. The strained, rather cynical look about him wasn't there any more, and his friend seemed alive with happiness, but what could have caused this transformation wasn't clear. He'd have to get to the bottom of the mystery later.

Reid shot back his cuff and checked his watch, then looked at the group of pilots. 'I shall expect you all to be in the Fox and Hounds by twenty hundred hours.'

'Yes, sir!' they chorused.

Reid watched them amble off to stow their gear and settle in, and he felt more uplifted than he had done for many a long week. It was going to be wonderful having them stationed here. How he'd missed the camaraderie, the flying, the exhilaration of touching down after a hard fight, and even the danger. That was when he'd felt truly alive – every moment had been precious and to be lived to the full.

He marched back to his office with a purposeful air to his stride. Now they were stationed here he was going back up with them at the first opportunity, and damn his responsibilities on the ground. When the invasion began he was going to be a part of it!

★

The pub was in uproar by the time Reid arrived.

'You're late,' Bouncer scolded and pushed two pints towards him. 'Get those down you at the double; the next round's on its way.'

Reid complied, then sat back as the table was quickly filled with full glasses again. Timber held one of the glasses aloft.

'Here's to Bouncer. Congratulations, mate.'

'What's all this about?' Reid glanced round at the smiling faces and took a mouthful of beer.

'I'm getting married,' Bouncer told him.

Reid choked on the drink and received thumps on the back from the men. 'You're *what*?' he asked hoarsely.

'I'm getting married in two weeks,' his friend repeated.

'Good God! I never thought I'd see the day.'

Bouncer gave a smug grin. 'I told you things change. Will you be my best man?'

'Of course I will. When did you meet her?'

'It was soon after I returned to Kenley. Jenny's so lovely and kind, Reid, she really bowled me over.'

'I'm very happy for you,' Reid told him with sincerity. He had recovered from the shock now and surged to his feet. 'This calls for a real drink. I wonder if the landlord's got a bottle of good whisky tucked away somewhere?'

'If anyone can get him to part with it, it's you,' Timber encouraged.

The barman was only too happy to help the pilots celebrate and Reid was soon back with double whiskies and beer chasers.

'Oh, well done!' Bouncer complimented. 'That officer's uniform does have its uses sometimes.'

'I should hope so.' Reid held up his glass of whisky.

'Let's all drink to Bouncer and his bride. May they grow old together in happiness and peace.'

'That was a fine toast, my friend.' Bouncer looked quite overcome for a moment. 'I'd like as many of you to come to the wedding as possible.'

'We'll *all* be there,' Reid announced. 'I'll fix it. We can't have one of our squadron getting married without a guard of honour.' Although he was no longer a part of this group he still felt as if he belonged, and after the Battle of Britain he doubted that the link would ever be broken.

'Jenny would like that.' Bouncer drained his whisky, quickly followed by the beer. 'My round again, I believe.'

By now they were a very *happy* crowd, and although Reid had drunk as much as anyone else his mind felt surprisingly clear. He had allowed himself to become bogged down with responsibilities and cares. The job he was doing wasn't always easy or smooth running. Then there was Annie. She had tied him up in knots and he was a fool to have allowed that to happen. It would be best if he just accepted that she couldn't stand the sight of him, and that she would eventually marry Sam.

He downed another pint. Yes, that's what he'd do. Much better for both of them, and that decision might help to improve his temper. He would still keep an eye on her, of course. After all, he'd promised his brother, hadn't he?

Annie loved receiving letters and she had four today. The first one was from her mother and Rose, giving her all the family news, the second was from Dora, and that had her in fits of laughter; motherhood certainly hadn't dimmed her sense of humour. The next was from Charlie and she gave a wry smile as she read the account of Reid's old squadron arriving, and the party they'd had in the pub that night. 'You should have seen them, Annie,' he wrote. 'Those men certainly know how to have a good time.'

She could just imagine.

The last letter was in a hand she didn't recognize, and after slitting it open she gasped in pleasure. It was from Bouncer inviting her to his wedding in six days' time. She had taken a great liking to Bouncer and she was very happy for him. She would go, if it were possible.

Annie went immediately to see if she could have the leave. She didn't think there would be any problem because she was always willing to work extra hours, and often didn't even take the time off she was allowed.

'I can let you have twenty-hour hours only,' the wing commander told her. 'And make the most of it because it might be the last for some time.'

'Thanks.' She stopped on her way out and turned back. 'Do you think the invasion is imminent?'

He shrugged. 'Couldn't say, but if any more troops and equipment arrive this island will sink into the sea from the weight of it all.'

Annie laughed at the thought and went back to her post. The tension and anticipation were building, and Sam was becoming more restless as each week passed. If there was an invasion of France this summer, then she knew that Sam would be right behind the first wave of troops.

*

Annie had managed to catch a train to Chichester all right, but she'd had to wait ages for a bus to Boxgrove where Bouncer and Jenny were getting married. It was a beautiful spring day, just perfect for a wedding; Annie was looking forward to this very much. Bouncer was a fine man and deserved to be happy. She reached the church just in time; the bride's car was arriving as she hurried inside. Bouncer was in the front pew, laughing at something the man next to him was saying. Of course, Reid would be the best man, Annie thought, as she studied them. An impressive pair, they were great friends who had been through hell together.

The organ burst into tune and the large congregation stood to watch the bride walk along the aisle. She was quite lovely, with chestnut hair, and wearing a flowing gown made of parachute silk. Annie couldn't help smiling to herself: it looked as if Bouncer had made good use of his parachute at last.

It was a touching ceremony but there was a slight ripple of amusement as Charles Algernon Patterson took his vows. Bouncer was going to take some ragging for that, Annie realized, and fought back a chuckle. It was probably the first time any of them had heard his real names. While the register was being signed, the ushers urged everyone outside.

'Charlie!' Annie cried in delight when she saw her brother. 'I didn't know you'd be here.'

'Didn't know myself until the last minute, but Reid fixed it for me. They've chosen this church because it's not much more than half a mile from the Tangmere airfield. Friends can pop along to the wedding, even if they can only stay for a hour or so.'

'It's good to see you.' She hugged him, and then stood back. 'Why have they made us come out of the church?'

'You'll see in a minute.'

Reid strode out, gave an order, and two lines of pilots formed a guard of honour. When Bouncer and his bride stepped through the door they made an archway of swords for the newly-weds to walk under.

'That's wonderful,' Annie sighed. 'And a fitting tribute to a brave man, but where on earth did they get the swords from?'

'Those crazy men can get anything if they set their minds to it. But they're all special, Annie. I watched them through the battles; never knowing if they were going to die that day, and waiting in vain for friends who never returned. They may seem crazy at times but it's just their way of coping with the danger.'

'I agree, Charlie, and there are others working quietly in the background who have that kind of courage as well.'

Her brother gave her a studied look. 'Yes, you would know about that, wouldn't you, little sister?'

Annie merely smiled and watched Reid. Wearing full dress uniform he was enough to take her breath away. How could the girl he was crazy about not fall into his arms? His temper and sarcastic tongue were disturbing, of course, but he had seen and done things beyond the imagination. And now he had a lot of responsibility. She had judged him too harshly.

Bouncer called them over for the photographs. 'Annie, thank you for coming; this is Jenny.'

Annie smiled at the radiant girl. 'I'm delighted to meet you. And you look absolutely beautiful.'

'Thank you.' Jenny smoothed her hand over the gown. 'It made a lovely wedding dress, didn't it?'

Her new husband laughed. 'Much better use for it than jumping out of aeroplanes.'

It was a pleasant late April day and the photographer took his time, ordering them into special groups and different poses.

Once the photos were finished and the bride and groom were on their way to the reception, Reid came over to Annie and Charlie.

'Glad you could make it, Webster.'

Annie, being in uniform, saluted him. 'Wouldn't have missed it for anything, Squadron Leader.'

'Oh God!' Charlie muttered, and beat a hasty retreat.

She watched her brother for a few moments then started to laugh. 'He's afraid you might put him on a charge if he associates with me.'

'Not because of his sister's insubordination, I wouldn't.'

Annie looked up at the man in front of her, saw the amused glint in his eyes, and grinned. It seemed as if their argument in January had been forgotten, and she was pleased about that.

'Is the girl you're crazy about here?' she asked, scanning the crowd for a likely candidate.

'I'm afraid you'll have to look in a mirror if you want to see her,' he told her.

It took a few moments for that to sink in, and when it did she shook her head. 'Reid. You really do say the most outrageous things. Are you ever serious?'

'Yes, I'm really serious now.' He gave a long, resigned sigh. 'But of course you still won't believe me.'

'You'd hardly expect me to, would you?'

'Why do you find the notion so ludicrous, Annie? I'd like to know.'

'Well, from the moment we met we've fought, except for a couple of tranquil meetings, and the idea of spending the rest of our lives together is too dreadful to contemplate. We wouldn't have a piece of china left.'

Reid's face broke into a grin. 'Life wouldn't be dull, though, would it?'

'No, it wouldn't.' Annie looked earnestly into his eyes. 'I know you find me physically attractive, and I feel the same way about you, but that isn't enough to build a lasting relationship on.'

He fell silent for a few seconds, and then nodded. 'You're quite right, we've got to stop fighting with each other. I'll work on it and see if I can improve my temperament.'

'You're impossible, do you know that?' Annie couldn't help smiling.

He bent and kissed her fleetingly on the lips. 'Don't marry Sam, he isn't right for you.'

Annie watched him stride away, and felt a mixture of indignation, amusement and confusion. What right did he have to tell her what to do with her life?

'I've cadged us a lift, Annie.' Charlie ushered her towards a car. 'Why do you and Reid always treat each other like that?'

'Oh, it comes quite naturally,' she told her brother.

Charlie watched his commanding officer for a moment then shook his head in amusement. 'He would make one heck of a brother-in-law.'

Her brother ducked as Annie took a swipe at him.

'Don't you start. I thought it was only women who got soppy at weddings.'

He gave her a curious look. 'What has the big man been saying to you?'

'A load of nonsense, if you must know,' she retorted. 'Anyway, you're the one who should be thinking of marriage.'

'Well, I must admit it does seem like a good idea . . .'

'Have you found someone?' Annie asked eagerly. She adored her brothers, and now Will was married to Dora, she would love to see Charlie settled with a family of his own.

'I might have,' he hedged.

'What's her name?'

'Patricia – Pat, but don't go saying anything yet,' he warned. 'We only met a few weeks ago.'

Annie almost danced in delight. 'I won't say a word, and I do hope it works out for you, Charlie.'

'What about you, Sis, are you thinking of marrying Sam?'

'He hasn't asked me, but I know he's thinking about it.' Her sigh was deep and thoughtful, and then she shook her head. 'It might seem like a good solution to young Jacques's future, and I do love the little boy, but we would probably end up regretting it after a while. I'll only marry for one thing, Charlie, and that's love.'

Her brother gave her a speculative glance. 'You're a real romantic at heart, aren't you?'

'Have you only just found that out?' She smiled and walked over to the car, but her brother's remark had given her pause for thought. Had her romantic streak stopped her from finding happiness with a man? Was she looking for the impossible? She'd always joked that she was waiting for another man like Bill, her brother-in-law, but she doubted that another man like him existed.

The reception was being held in a village hall about a mile from the church. Considering the wartime rationing the buffet was quite sumptuous.

'It looks as if someone has been dealing on the black market,' Annie remarked to her brother as they helped themselves to the food.

'Maybe, but I'll bet the squadron had a hand in this spread.' Charlie chuckled. 'Those pilots are an enter-prising bunch.'

Reid's speech had the guests roaring with laughter as he related some of Bouncer's funniest exploits. The groom took this all in his stride and sat there with a wicked grin on his face, as if to say, I'll get you later for this, my friend.

A small air force band arrived and everyone began to dance. It was a joyful occasion, and for a short time the war was forgotten.

'Is the ankle strong enough to dance?' Reid stood in front of Annie and held his hand out.

'It's as good as new.' She let him lead her on to the dance floor. The band was playing a slow foxtrot and Annie relaxed in his arms. He really was a wonderful dancer, and this was the only time they never argued. Her smile was mischievous.

'What's amusing you?' Reid asked.

'I was just thinking that the only time we are in harmony with each other is when we're dancing.' She looked up into his face and laughed. 'Perhaps if we danced every time we met we might not fight.'

Reid pulled her closer. 'Now there's a tempting idea.'

'Did you enjoy the wedding?' Jean asked Annie the next day.

'It was lovely, but I think I danced too much.' She massaged her ankle and foot before easing her shoes on and smiling at Jean. 'Back to work now, though.'

Annie hurried to Sam's office. It was empty. 'Where's Sam?' she asked Wing Commander Felshaw.

'He's taken a few days' leave to go and see his son while he's got the chance.'

Annie sensed the excitement in his voice. 'Is the invasion close?'

'Not far off,' he told her. 'We're going to be busy. The enemy mustn't get wind of this until it's too late.'

'Let's pray the preparations stay hidden.' Annie wasn't sure how the huge build-up of troops could be kept secret, but the whole operation depended on taking the Germans by surprise. It seemed like an impossible task because this small island was bursting at the seams with men and equipment. Hitler must know!

30

June 1944

It must be on! The orders were that no one could leave the base or make contact with anyone outside. The skies had been black with bombers making their way over to Germany and elsewhere. No one had ever seen such massive formations, and Annie couldn't help sparing a thought for the people who were going to be on the receiving end of these bombardments. Tanks had been rumbling out of their hiding places in wooded areas, and were now heading for Portsmouth and other parts of the coast. Troops and vehicles were trundling through the villages, clogging roads, and all heading in the same direction.

All it needed was one reconnaissance plane to spot them . . . but everyone was holding their breath, hoping that wouldn't happen.

Annie had been at her post for hours but didn't feel tired. The feeling of anticipation was keeping everyone wide awake.

'Take half an hour and get something to eat,' the officer told her.

'I'm not hungry.' Annie didn't want to take a break in case something happened while she was away. She felt a moment of sadness. How sorry she was that Jack Graham wouldn't see this day . . .

'That was an order,' she was told sternly.

She removed her headphones and another operator stepped into her place.

Annie found Sam outside glaring up at the leaden sky. 'Your blasted English weather. What a time for it to close in. They can't go in this. The longer this operation is held up the more chance there is of discovery.'

'Maybe not, Sam,' she told him. 'They won't be expecting us to launch an attack across the Channel in these bad conditions.' Annie touched his arm. 'Come and have a meal with me, Sam. You're getting soaked out here and worrying won't change the weather.'

'All right,' he agreed. 'There isn't anything else I can do at the moment.'

Annie didn't even know what she was eating and she was certain that Sam didn't care. They were just clearing their plates because it was the sensible thing to do, but it wasn't surprising because everyone was on edge. Although the mess was busy it was strangely quiet. Men and women were toying with the food, unable to eat, or letting cups of steaming tea grow cold. Waiting, waiting . . .

'I thought you were going to France before the invasion,' she said, breaking the tense atmosphere.

'I wanted to, but it was considered unwise, and I had to agree. We didn't want to take the chance of arousing the suspicions of the Germans. I'm going in as soon as the troops start to move inland.'

'I assume you don't want me with you? I'm completely recovered now, and I wouldn't have to jump out of a plane this time.' She knew it was a forlorn hope, but she would dearly have loved to follow the troops in as France was liberated.

'No, Annie, I will be able to move much faster if I'm on my own. But I'll take a wireless and keep in touch.' He smiled to soften the refusal. 'There won't be any need for a covert operation and this trip of mine will be more personal than military.'

'I understand. The Germans must know we're coming, though, mustn't they?' She watched the distracted man stirring his tea. The tension was so great Annie found it hard to even take a breath.

'They know, but let's hope and pray they haven't guessed when or where the landings will be.'

Annie looked at her watch, knowing that that prayer was uppermost in everyone's thoughts. 'I've got to get back. You won't disappear without telling me, will you?'

The deep worry lines smoothed out for a moment and he smiled. 'No, I'll let you know. Rose has promised me that if I get killed she will adopt Jacques and bring him up as her own son.'

'She's a good mother and Bill adores children, so you need have no fears for him.' Annie smiled and touched his hand. 'But nothing is going to happen to you, Sam.'

'I know, it's just a precaution, that's all.'

June the 6th and the news they'd all been waiting for came. Troops and equipment were pouring on to the Normandy beaches. Annie and many others shed a few tears of relief but there was a great deal of worry as well. Where were the sailors in her family, and was Bob among the first wave of troops to hit the beaches? Would this be the decisive move and the end of the German aggression? How many more lives was this going to cost?

The news coming through over the following couple of days was optimistic, but it was frustrating trying to glean information. They guessed that everything coming over the wireless was carefully edited before it was given out. Annie knew only too well that they couldn't give away vital information that might help the enemy. But some troops were moving inland already and there was cause for hope that this was the beginning of the end.

Three days later, Sam found Annie at breakfast.

'I'm leaving for Portsmouth now,' he told her. 'I've got permission to go across at last.'

'You take care, and please keep in touch. Try to stay behind the Allied lines, and I hope you find your sister again,' she said. Sam was kitted out in combat gear with French badges on his shoulders. He had hardly worn them since Annie had met him, as the nature of his job made him keep a low profile, but now he was a determined man going back to his own country to see it liberated.

'That will be my first task, and then I'll try to see if any of Maria's family have survived.' He smiled at her and then hurried on his way, obviously eager to get going.

Annie realized, for the first time, that Sam was still in love with the girl he'd been about to marry when the war started, and she found that incredibly sad. Not only for the brave, complex man, but also for Jacques, who would never know his real mother. Damn the war, she muttered under her breath as her eyes clouded with unshed tears. It had already caused so much suffering, and there was more to come as the troops poured into France.

She sighed and returned to her work. It was obvious that Sam couldn't wait to return to France, and she wondered what he was going to find when he saw his home again. Annie's heart ached for him and everyone who had been torn from their homes by this madness.

What a night! Reid scanned the sky over Tangmere airfield. Dawn was just beginning to stain the sky with a glimmer of light; they would be able to get airborne soon. One week after the invasion and Hitler had unleashed his latest weapon against them.

'They're not bombers. What are they?' Bouncer tumbled into Reid's office having slept through the night. He was still buttoning his shirt. His hair stood on end and he needed a shave.

'Unmanned aircraft – flying bombs,' Reid told his friend. 'They've been coming over all night.'

'Why didn't you sound the alarm?' Bouncer ran a hand through his hair, but it immediately sprang up again.

'There isn't anything we can do until it's light,' Reid said, and flinched at Bouncer's colourful language.

'I don't like this, Reid, from what I've heard they're dropping all over the place. Doesn't that blasted man know when he's beaten?'

'He's making one last desperate effort to stop us, I expect,' Reid said.

They waited anxiously until light filtered through the clouds; Reid donned his flying gear, then walked out with Bouncer to meet the rest of the pilots. There was no way he was keeping out of this! 'We've got orders to try and shoot some of those things down before they reach our coast.'

They did their best and were reasonably successful, but the flying bombs were difficult to shoot down, and far too many still managed to cross the coast. Once again London and the surrounding areas were suffering death and destruction. The invasion was progressing with parts of France already liberated, and this onslaught of the flying bombs had come as an unwelcome shock.

'There's someone at the gate to see you,' Wing Commander Felshaw told Annie. 'Says she's your sister and it's urgent.'

Annie ran. If Rose had left the children and come here to see her, then it must be something very serious. The last time she'd been called out like this Will had been missing. Was it Bill? No, her sister would not leave the children if that were the case, she reasoned.

'Rose!' Annie stopped and struggled to catch her breath. 'What's happened?'

'I'm on my way to London, Annie, and I thought I'd stop off here and try to see you.'

Her sister's expression gave little away, but Annie knew her too well. Anxiety showed in her eyes. 'What is it?'

'As soon as the D-Day landings were under way, Dad was convinced the war was as good as over and he headed for London to open up his house again.'

Annie's heart thudded. The doodlebugs!

'It's been four days now,' Rose continued, 'without a word from him, and he'd never do that. I wanted to let you know before I go and search for him.'

832

Annie didn't want her sister doing this on her own. Rose's relationship with her father hadn't been easy, but over the years a deep and abiding affection had grown between them. If anything had happened to George then her sister was going to be devastated. 'I've got some leave coming up; I'll see if I can bring it forward. I've been on duty practically non-stop since the invasion began.'

Rose looked relieved. 'Thanks, Annie.'

Fifteen minutes later, Annie was back with a two-day pass and an air force lorry. 'I've cadged a lift with Flight Sergeant Hargreaves. He's going to London,' she told her sister. 'Hop in.'

They were dropped off about a mile from Bloomsbury and continued on foot.

'I told him not to go,' Rose said as she strode along. 'But the stubborn old fool wouldn't listen, as usual.'

'We'll probably find him in the local pub drinking with his friends.' Annie tried to soothe her sister. It wasn't often anyone saw Rose as worried as this, and the closer they got to their destination, the faster she walked.

'I expect you're right.' Rose scowled. 'And if he is, then it will give me great pleasure to hit him for causing us all this worry.'

Annie grinned in spite of her concern. 'You've done that before, haven't you?'

'The first time we met.' Rose's eyes gleamed at the memory. 'What a fight we had. It was a shock meeting my real father at the age of sixteen, and I hated his guts!'

'But his mother was a lovely lady, wasn't she?'

A smile touched Rose's mouth. 'She was a fine woman, and it was really because of her that I eventually became friends with George.'

'Do you remember when you took me to see her?' Annie asked. 'You were frightened to death I was going to break something.'

'We'd never seen such beautiful things in our lives, had we?' Rose gave Annie an affectionate glance. 'You loved looking at everything, and weren't at all jealous about someone having so much and us so little. I could never understand why you weren't bitter. The conditions we lived in were inhuman.'

'I didn't have anything to be bitter about, Rose. You looked after me and shielded me from as much of the squalor as you could.' Annie smiled at her big sister, remembering those difficult years when the whole family had relied on Rose. What a burden they'd placed on her.

They walked in silence for some time, and then Annie heard a strange swishing sound. She looked up and gasped in horror. Following them along the road was a doodlebug with its engines cut, and it was gliding down.

Rose spun her to face the way they had just come. 'Run!'

They hurtled back up the road and were thrown to the ground as the bomb exploded.

'Are you all right?' Rose scrambled to her feet and helped Annie up.

'Yes. I thought those things were supposed to cut their engines and then nose dive.'

'So did I, but evidently they don't always do that.' Rose brushed off the dust and swore fluently under her breath as she looked at the devastation at the end of the road.

The street was suddenly alive with people running to see if they could rescue anyone. Annie watched Rose hesitate and knew that her sister's instinct would be to pitch in and help, but concern for George was uppermost in her mind, so she spun around and walked away.

'We'll have to go around that. Let's try and find that father of mine.'

When they turned into the street, Annie gave a cry of anguish, but Rose remained silent, not moving. The house wasn't there. All that remained was a huge pile of rubble.

Rose's mouth was set in a grim line and she grabbed a policeman who was hurrying past her. 'When did this happen?' she demanded.

'About two nights ago.'

'Anyone killed?'

'I don't know. You'll have to enquire at the Town Hall. They've set up an information desk there.'

'Not much left, is there.' Annie's voice was husky with tears as the two sisters stood looking at the place where a grand house had once stood – a house with so many memories for both of them. 'If he was in there . . .'

'He wouldn't have stood a chance.' Rose finished Annie's sentence, then strode away, her face a mask as she headed for the information centre.

Annie hurried to catch her up, too upset to face the facts. 'Perhaps he wasn't there?'

'Of course he was. We'd have heard from him otherwise.' Rose's tone was brisk but she couldn't hide the inner pain she was feeling.

It didn't take long to discover the truth. There had been several people killed that night. They were sent to identify the body.

Annie couldn't bear to go in but Rose took on the unpleasant task without flinching. 'At least we can have a funeral,' Rose told her, after she'd confirmed that one of the dead was Sir George Gresham.

Rose's eyes were dry but Annie knew how her sister was suffering. Being so alike, father and daughter had often fought, but they had loved each other. When George had walked into her life for the first time the arguments had been fierce but he'd accepted her as his daughter, and made no secret of how much he loved and admired her. He had become a loved member of the family and his loss would be deeply felt.

'London was his home,' Rose said, her voice softening, 'so we'll bury him here.'

It was a simple ceremony with only the two sisters present. Rose had chosen the Bible readings herself and Annie felt that George would have approved of the arrangements. His beloved daughter was there and that would have been all he'd have wanted.

'I wish I could come back to Wales with you,' Annie said to her sister. 'But I have to report back now.'

'I know, and thanks for being here, Annie. It has helped a lot.'

'Are you going to try and salvage anything from the rubble?' Annie asked.

'No, Dad moved the most valuable pieces down to Wales, and anyway, I don't suppose much has survived. It looked as if it took a direct hit.'

Annie thought about the lovely house. It had been George's pride and joy, but now it was gone, like so many homes. 'It was supposed to have been part of James's inheritance, wasn't it?'

'Yes.' Rose gazed into space for a moment. 'But

material things can be replaced; it's the loss of loved ones that's hard to take. They are irreplaceable.'

'We've got our memories, though, Rose, haven't we?' Annie lingered to take a last look at the simple grave before they turned away.

Her sister looked grim as they walked out of the churchyard. 'I'll get a nice headstone when the war's over. Though why the silly old fool had to go and get himself killed when we're nearing the end . . .'

For the first time, Rose allowed herself a few tears, and Annie joined in, for the man they had all come to love. It was going to be difficult telling the rest of the family that George was dead, and she didn't envy her sister the task.

'Any news from Sam?' Annie asked as soon as she arrived back at Chicksands. The tragic loss of George had pushed Sam from her mind for a while but now the worry was back in full force. Ten days and not a word from him!

The officer shook his head. 'Nothing.'

'Where is he, and why didn't he contact us as soon as he landed?'

'Perhaps his wireless set isn't working, or he's lost it.'

Annie couldn't accept that. If that were the case then he would have found another way to let them know he was all right. France was swarming with Allied troops and any of them would have relayed a message for him. Her nerves were frayed. What with losing George so unexpectedly, and now Sam disappearing, she was feeling more than a little edgy. 'He ought to have more consideration! My sister told me his son keeps asking when he's coming to see him.'

'All we can do is wait.' The officer walked away.

Annie jammed the headphones on and gave a weary sigh. She wished she'd gone with Sam. At least she'd know what was going on. It was damned frustrating sitting on the sidelines and waiting . . .

31

'Anything?' Annie asked the same question every time she reported for duty, but she already knew the answer. It was the beginning of September and still no word from Sam. She feared the worst by now and her heart ached for his little son. Jacques had settled in well with Rose and the children, but he was constantly asking for his father. He was in a strange country, speaking a strange language, and he'd lost the one woman he'd clung to – his grandmother. Was it any wonder the boy didn't know how to smile? Even James and Kate had been unable to coax a laugh out of him.

Annie sat down, muttering under her breath. When this war was over there would be a lot of adjusting to do, and many families were going to have empty spaces in their lives. There was talk that the war would soon be over, but she had her doubts about that. It was true that Paris had been liberated on August 25th, and this had been the cause of great rejoicing, but now there was a new threat of v2 rockets. These weren't like the doodle-bugs; you couldn't see or hear them, and there wasn't any defence against them. The first anyone knew about them was when they exploded, and then it was too late. How she longed for this dreadful war to be over.

Annie tried to shut off the jumble of disturbing thoughts. She still had work to do but her mind constantly wandered back to Sam. Was he alive or dead? Worry gnawed away at her insides. Was she fated to lose all the men she became fond of – Paul, Jack Graham, George, and now perhaps Sam? Thank heavens Reid was no longer flying.

She sat up straight and frowned. Where had *that* thought come from?

'Take a break,' she was ordered by the officer-in-charge.

Annie glanced at the clock and was surprised to see that she had been at her post for nearly four hours. She stood up, stretched and headed for the door.

The mess was busy but she managed to find a corner table on her own. She didn't feel like talking at the moment. How she missed Dora's cheerful company.

After eating, she cradled her cup of tea in her hands and bowed her head. She was so weary. 'Where the hell are you, Sam,' she muttered fiercely under her breath.

The tap on her shoulder made her jump and the tea slopped over the side of the cup.

'You're needed,' Jean told her.

'Right.' Annie drank what was left of the tea, and hurried back.

'We've had a message from Sam,' Wing Commander Felshaw said and handed her a sheet of paper.

Annie read it and gave a sigh of relief. It said: 'Returning immediately. Await my call.'

For some strange reason an uneasy feeling grew. 'Is this all he said?'

'Yes,' was the brisk reply.

What did he mean by – await my call? And when would he call? Why was the message so short? There wasn't any need for that restriction now. She stared at the paper in the forlorn hope that it might reveal some answers, but of course it didn't.

'I'm afraid we'll have to be patient.'

Annie studied the officer. 'What's going on, sir?'

'Nothing that need concern you at the moment.' His tone was dismissive.

Annie wasn't going to be so easily put off. 'I think it is, sir. My sister is looking after his son, and if something has happened to Sam then I have a right to know.'

'As far as we are aware he is OK.'

'I can hear a "but" in your voice.' Then something became clear. 'This isn't the first message you've had from him, is it?'

'No, we received one at three this morning.'

'What did it say?' she demanded, stung that the news should have been kept from her.

'All I can tell you is that he has been in trouble, but he's out now and coming back on the first available boat. The rest of the information is confidential.' He walked away, effectively putting an end to her questions.

Annie sat at her desk with a stubborn expression on her face. How the hell had he got into trouble? If he'd been behind the German lines she'd kill him herself! He ought to be thinking about Jacques, and trying to stay alive for his son, not chasing off on some mission of his own. She decided she wasn't moving from this spot until Sam's call came through.

It was sixteen hundred hours when she was summoned to the officer's room. 'Sam, he wants to talk to you.'

She reached out eagerly but he held on to the phone. 'Whatever help he needs, you are to give it. You can take all the time off necessary.' Then he released the phone to her and strode out of the room.

Annie's heart was thudding. Something was wrong. 'Sam, are you all right? Where are you?'

'I'm in Dover.' He spoke quickly, as if in a hurry. 'I need to get to Wales. Will you see if Reid can fly us there?'

'I don't know if that –'

Annie!' He almost shouted at her this time. 'I've got to get there. I've brought someone back with me and they can't travel by road or train. I need Reid's help.'

'Please don't upset yourself.' There was a note of desperation in Sam's voice and she didn't like it. 'Is he ill?'

'Yes, and Wales is the only answer. I've already contacted Rose and she has agreed we can go there.'

'I'll see what I can do. If Reid can't help then I'll find someone who can.' Though it was difficult to know how she was going to do that. This request was unusual and highly irregular. Still she had been told to give him all the help he needed . . . .

'We can't travel today; the journey has already taken its toll. Sometime tomorrow, if possible.'

'All right, Sam, where can I get in touch with you?'

'We're in a hotel.' He gave her the address, and a ragged sigh echoed down the line. 'I thank God for the day I met you and your wonderful family.'

Reid was on his way out the door on seven days' leave when he was called back.

'Urgent phone call for you, sir.'

'Yes,' he snapped into the receiver.

There was silence at the other end, and he tapped his fingers impatiently on the desk. He was looking forward to this leave and was eager to be on his way.

'Is this a bad time?' Annie asked hesitantly.

'No, no,' Reid assured her, regretting his sharp tone again. 'It's good to hear from you. I hope there isn't anything wrong?'

His brow creased into a deep frown as he listened. 'Give me the address,' he said when she'd finished talking. He scribbled it down.

'Sam said he needs you, Reid, but I'm sure he'll understand if you can't do this. It might be impossible to arrange, but he sounded desperate.'

'It's all right, Annie,' he soothed. She sounded sick with worry. 'As of this moment I'm on leave, and we must move Sam and this other man from Dover. You never know where these v2 rockets are going to land. How bad is this other person?' he asked.

'Pretty bad, I think. Sam said they couldn't travel today because the journey has taken its toll.'

'You go on down there and I'll come as soon as I can.' He picked up the slip of paper with the address on it and shoved it into his pocket. 'You tell Sam I'll be there sometime tomorrow.' Reid put the phone down, his mind already working out the details. He could take his own plane, of course, but by the sound of it they needed something larger for this trip. However, it wasn't going to be easy to arrange. If Sam was taking someone to Wales then this was a private matter. Still, he would see what he could fix up.

After three phone calls he was intrigued. Everyone was falling over themselves to give him anything he asked for. Who the hell was Sam, and who was his injured passenger?

He strode out to one of the hangars, intent on getting all the arrangements in place. Charlie was working on the very plane he wanted – a DC3. 'What's wrong with her?' he asked briskly.

Charlie scrambled down. 'We're changing an engine. It won't take more than another hour.'

Reid nodded. 'Good, I'm taking her tomorrow. Make sure there's a bunk for a sick passenger. I've just had a call from your sister Annie to say that Sam is back from France and has a sick man to take down to Wales.' Then Reid turned on his heel and hurried away, not giving Charlie a chance to ask questions. His mind was set on the task he'd been assigned. There were a lot of arrangements to make. His first stop was the mess where he found the man he was looking for.

'Hi, Reid.' Bouncer said grinning. 'Thought you were on leave. Can't you bear to leave the place?'

'Something's come up and I need a co-pilot. We'll be leaving at eight tomorrow morning.'

'Where are we going?' his friend asked.

'Hawkinge first, then pick up some passengers in Dover, and then on to Wales.'

'Great.' Bouncer's face broke into a wide grin. 'What's this all about?'

'I really don't know much.' He told Bouncer about the call. 'We'll have to see when we get there, but Annie sounded out of her mind with worry.'

'I expect she is.' Bouncer shook his head in concern. 'But can we do this? We can't just take the DC3 without permission.'

Reid picked up Bouncer's mug of tea and drank it in a distracted way. 'I had grave doubts so I made a few calls, and it looks as if someone has been oiling the wheels. Anything Group Captain André Riniou wants is to be granted.'

'That's interesting.' Bouncer picked up his mug, looked inside, then put it down again. 'His passenger must be important, but why take him to Wales?'

'Damned if I know. Rose and her family have taken in enough waifs and strays as it is. That house is aptly named The Haven; it's always packed.'

Bouncer smiled. 'Yes, they are a remarkable family. So, how ill is this person?'

'No idea, but I'm trying to get a military nurse to come with us just in case of an emergency.' Reid stood up. 'See you in the morning.'

'Reid!' Bouncer called him back. 'How long can we stay?'

He shrugged. 'As long as it takes, and as my co-pilot you'll have to wait until I'm ready to return. Could take a while and I do have seven days' leave to use up.'

'Right.' Bouncer rubbed his hands together with pleasure. 'A few days in the country will be just the ticket.'

They reached the Bartlett Hotel in Dover at ten o'clock the next morning, and the manager told them which room Sam was in. Reid gave a gentle rap on the door and Sam opened it at once. The first sight of him was a shock and he heard Bouncer suck in his breath. The man was gaunt with exhaustion.

'Reid.' Sam grasped his hand. 'Thank you for coming.'

'I've brought a nurse with me in case she's needed.'

The woman stepped forward. 'My name's Gloria Stevens, Group Captain Riniou, and I can stay with your patient as long as I'm needed.'

Sam stepped aside for them to enter the small room. 'I'm grateful. You are needed.'

For a moment, Reid thought Sam was going to collapse so he caught hold of his arm to steady him. 'You've had a rough time by the look of you.'

Sam glanced anxiously towards the bed. 'Not as rough as her.'

Her? It was only then that Reid noticed the other occupants of the room. Annie was sitting beside the bed, holding the patient's hand and talking gently in French. In the bed was a girl.

Annie stepped away from the bed to make room for the nurse to examine the patient. As the nurse pulled the sheet back Reid just managed to cut off a gasp of horror. He had never seen anyone so emaciated before.

'Oh my God!' Bouncer breathed, his words hardly audible.

'You can see why I need help,' Sam told them.

'I've come with a plane equipped with a bunk and medical supplies.' Reid was so relieved that he'd had the sense to arrange this.

Sam gave a ragged sigh. 'That will make the journey easier.'

'We thought the patient was a man,' Bouncer said.

'That was my fault.' Annie spoke for the first time. 'I assumed it was.'

'Who is she?' Reid asked.

Sam smiled at the girl in the bed and looked back at

846

Reid and Bouncer. 'This is Maria. Jacques's mother.' He put a finger to his lips to stop them asking questions. 'I'll tell you about it later.'

The nurse came over to them. 'She should be in hospital, sir.'

'No!' Maria's voice was weak but determined. 'I wish to be near my son.'

'You will be,' Reid said, disturbed by the anguish in the woman's voice. 'We'll be flying you to him today.'

'I do not wish Jacques to see me like this.' Maria lifted a skeletal arm with difficulty, and grimaced. 'But I want to be near to him.'

'My sister's suet pudding with treacle will soon have you on your feet again.' Annie grinned at Maria's puzzled expression.

'What is this suet treacle?' Maria asked Sam.

He bent over and kissed her. 'You'll soon find out. It's marvellous stuff.'

Reid touched Annie's arm to gain her attention. 'I thought she was dead?' he murmured.

The nurse, now firmly in charge of her patient, ordered them to be quiet. 'That is enough talking. She must rest now, and we shall need a light meal for her before she can travel.'

'I'll see what I can get.' Annie opened the door.

'A thin soup and perhaps a slice of bread will suffice.'

Annie nodded and left.

The nurse turned her attention to the men. 'Now, sirs, if you will leave us alone for half an hour I will prepare my patient for the journey.'

They left meekly and made their way downstairs to

the dining room, where the manager of the hotel supplied them with a pot of tea and toast.

Sam rubbed his eyes then sat back and smiled at Reid and Bouncer. 'I hope you didn't have too much trouble arranging this?'

'None at all.' Reid stirred sugar into his tea. 'Everyone was tripping over themselves to be helpful. Now why would that be, do you think?'

'I gathered some useful information on this trip. They sent someone along to collect it last night, and in return for that service they have given me everything I need.'

Reid nodded in understanding. So, he'd been behind enemy lines. 'What the hell happened, Sam?'

'Soon after the D-Day landings I hitched a ride and made straight for my home. While I was there a villager told me that he thought Maria had been shipped to Germany.' Sam paused, a look of utter pain showing in his eyes. 'I dismissed it at first because her mother had said Maria was dead, but then I met a man who'd escaped from a labour camp. He told me Maria was definitely alive but that she couldn't survive much longer. So I went after her.'

'Into Germany?' Reid asked.

'Yes. What had started out to be a visit to my home turned into a mission of great importance. I saw unimaginable things and was able to bring back a lot of useful information.'

'Hell, that was risky.' Bouncer shook his head in amazement.

'I didn't have any choice. If it was Maria, then I had to try and rescue her.'

'How did you manage to find her?' Reid asked. His

respect for this man was growing with every word he spoke. And for the first time he began to have an inkling of the things Annie had been involved in. The two of them had worked closely together, and Reid remembered the talk of parachute jumps. Dear Lord, what had she been doing? His love and respect for her grew.

'That was easy enough. The problem was rescuing her. Thank heavens the weather was still warm because I had to wait for three days before she came out with a working party. I remained hidden, and with only a loaf of bread and a bottle of water with me I was damned hungry, but I couldn't leave. If there was the slightest chance that Maria was there, then I had to stay, no matter how dangerous and uncomfortable the conditions.'

'How did you recognize her?' Reid couldn't help remembering the pitiful sight he had seen upstairs.

Sam gave a sad smile. 'We have known each other since children and were about to be married when the war tore us apart, and she is the mother of my son, so I would have known her whatever state she was in.'

'How did you get her away?' Bouncer was sitting forward in his chair, obviously riveted by the story.

'It was dusk when they returned, and as they passed by I shot out of some bushes, swept Maria up and ran like hell. Luck was on my side, the guards never saw me.'

'What about the other prisoners?' Bouncer asked. 'Didn't they make a noise when you dived out of the undergrowth?'

'They were too weak to respond, all except one girl who tumbled into the bushes with us.' Sam grimaced, obviously remembering the sight of those starving men and women. 'When the column was out of sight, we

849

supported Maria and got as far away from there as possible. We moved at night and hid during the day. I don't know what I'd have done without that girl, she was a wonder at finding food and shelter for us.'

'What was her name?' Reid asked.

Sam gave a dry laugh. 'I never found out. We didn't talk much. We were exhausted, and our situation was dangerous, so we focused all our attention on not getting caught. If the Germans had found us they would have shot us as spies for sure.'

Sam paused as if to gather his thoughts, then continued. 'We eventually crossed into France, but by that time we could hardly stand upright. It was too much for Maria and from then on I carried her. We still couldn't take a chance on there not being any Germans around, so we kept to the wooded areas and rough ground where we could move without being seen. Dear God, but it was hard going. Maria didn't weigh much, but I was getting weak by then.'

Bouncer handed Sam another cup of tea. 'There's a nip of brandy in that, it'll do you good.'

'What happened then?' prompted Reid, eager to hear more of this extraordinary story.

'We just kept walking until we met up with some British soldiers. They told us that Paris had been liberated and the girl took off. It was her home, evidently. Maria and I were transported to the coast and on to a ship returning to Dover.' Sam gave a tired smile. 'So here we are.'

Reid could only guess at the horrors of that journey, but it was clear from the condition they were in that it had taken a superhuman effort.

The nurse appeared and addressed Reid. 'We are ready

to leave now, sir. Maria cannot walk so I shall need help.'

Reid was immediately on his feet, placing a hand on Sam's shoulder to keep him in his seat. The man looked as if he could hardly stand up, let alone carry someone. 'I'll see to her.'

Nurse Stevens had wrapped the frail woman in a blanket and he lifted her carefully off the bed. She weighed practically nothing.

Reid had an ambulance waiting outside and once Maria was settled they headed for the airfield. When they reached the plane, and the nurse had made her patient comfortable and secure, Reid and Bouncer prepared for the flight.

Permission was given for immediate take-off, and they were all soon on their way to Wales.

32

Maria was fast asleep. Annie looked at Sam leaning over the bed. Rose had given them the cottage so they could have peace and privacy. Before George had died he'd had an extension put on the stable at the end of the garden and converted it into a two-bed cottage. When Rose had argued against it he'd told her that The Haven wasn't big enough for all the people she kept taking in. He'd won that battle, and now it was going to be very useful as there was room for Nurse Stevens to stay near her patient.

'Sam,' Annie said quietly. 'You'll come and see Jacques as soon as you're ready?'

'I do not want him to see his mother like this. It will frighten him.' Sam gave a lingering look at Maria, almost as if he was afraid that if he took his eyes off her she would disappear.

'We all understand,' Annie said. The last thing any of them wanted to do was heap more distress on the child. He would stay in the main house with Rose and Marj until it was right to move him in with his real mother and father. 'You need have no fears on that score.'

'Thank you.' He gazed at the woman in the bed and sighed. 'I have put her through hell dragging her across country like that. She wasn't strong enough.' His hand shook as he swept it across his eyes.

'You've given her a chance of life, young man.' Marj's voice was firm as she walked in with a tray of tea. 'She might not have lived much longer, and who knows what the Germans would have done when they knew defeat was staring them in the face. You have nothing to reproach yourself for.'

'You're right, of course. But I still feel guilty.'

'Now you know how I felt when Jack Graham died after getting him home,' Annie told him gently. 'The feeling passes, and when you look back you'll see you did the right thing.'

Sam merely nodded and sipped his tea.

Marj smiled and patted his arm. 'I'll bring dinner over for nurse and Maria, but you must join us. Jacques will be so pleased to see you.'

Annie and her mother walked back to the house. 'How is Jacques?' she asked her mother.

'He's been unhappy and fretful. He keeps asking if his father has left him.'

Annie could understand that. Jacques would feel very insecure, and his father disappearing must have thrown him into a panic, wondering if he'd been abandoned.

They walked into the kitchen. Wally was peeling potatoes and Rose was busy making pastry. The old black wood-burning cooker was covered in bubbling pans, and Annie breathed in the lovely aroma. This kitchen seemed to have retained the glorious smells of years gone by, and she always loved coming in here. George's presence was greatly missed in the house. The children had been very upset when Rose had arrived back with the news that he had been killed. They had spent most of their time with him since the outbreak of war, and like everyone else in the family had loved him very much.

'Hello, sweetheart.' Wally wiped his hands and gave

her a hug. 'It's good to see you again. Are our guests settled in?'

'Yes. It was a relief to get Maria here. She's in a poor way.' Annie smiled at her sister. 'But your cooking will soon have her on the mend.'

'Let's hope so.' Rose dusted the flour from her hands. 'Where's Reid?'

'He's still at the airfield with Bouncer.'

'Auntie Annie!' James rushed to greet her when she walked into the lounge.

'My goodness,' she laughed, 'you're nearly as tall as me.' He allowed her to kiss his cheek. At fifteen he was looking quite the young gentleman, and she could now see his grandfather in him.

He straightened up proudly and measured up against her. 'I'm taller than you now.'

'So you are, and by a good inch.' She smiled at Jacques who was sitting on the floor trying to fit a piece into a jigsaw puzzle.

'And how are you?' she asked gently.

'All right, thank you,' he answered politely, and then picked up the toy rabbit, which was looking quite bedraggled by now, and started to stroke one long ear.

James sat next to the child and helped him put the piece of jigsaw into the right place. 'He's worried about his dad.'

'He'll see him soon,' Annie told James very quietly. 'Where's Kate?'

'I'm here.' She came in carrying some more toys, and, when she'd put them down by Jacques, kissed Annie.

The children were obviously doing everything they could to amuse Jacques.

854

At that moment Reid and Bouncer strode in and said hello to everyone. Reid went over and swept Jacques off the floor. 'Hello, young man, I've got a really *big* aeroplane this time. Would you like to see it tomorrow?'

Jacques nodded and began to run his fingers over the wings on Reid's uniform.

'What's up?' he asked, obviously sensing the strained atmosphere.

Rose explained and he shook his head sadly. 'I expect he's been bewildered, poor little devil.'

Marj put down a tray loaded with cups of tea and Wally winked at Annie. 'Do you know that the first thing she did when we met was to give me a cup of tea, and she hasn't changed in all these years. Not even rationing has stopped her making her favourite brew. It's a bit weaker now, of course.'

The little boy had settled himself on Reid's lap and took a glass of milk from Kate. He started to drink, his troubled eyes searching all the faces in the room.

Suddenly Jacques squealed as Sam came into the room. He shot off Reid's lap – Reid deftly fielded the glass when it shot in the air – and threw himself at his father. The child was swung into the air and then hugged and kissed.

Jacques started to chatter in rapid French and wave his arms about.

'What's he saying?' Reid asked Annie. 'I can't keep up with that.'

'He's telling Sam how he thought he'd left him for good, and he likes everyone here but he wants to go home.'

It was then that the full import of Jacques's real mother

being found settled on Annie. There was no longer any question of Sam persuading her to marry him for his son's sake, and she was swamped with a feeling of intense relief. It would have been so wrong for all concerned, and when she looked at the little boy she was not sure she would have had the courage to refuse.

Maria had made remarkable progress in only four days, and Annie guessed that it was her desire to see her son again that had accelerated her recovery. Rose had a tape measure in her hand and Marj was pinning some of Annie's clothes on Maria. Annie, being the smallest, had given her a few garments but they all needed altering.

Sam touched Annie's arm. 'We must talk.'

They left the women to it and wandered outside. It was late September now, but the day was pleasant, and warm enough for them to walk around the garden in comfort. The singing of the birds was soothing, and Annie smiled at a thrush in the tree warbling out its tune. These little birds were quite oblivious of the drama unfolding all around them.

'Maria is looking so much stronger,' Annie remarked.

'Yes, it must be Rose's suet treacle.'

They both laughed at Maria's description. She spoke a little English but it often came out with words missing.

Sam turned his head and looked at Annie, a hint of regret in his eyes. 'I have been very selfish. I thought only of making a family for my son, and I was prepared to use you,' he admitted.

Annie's glance was quizzical. 'What makes you think I would have allowed you to do that?'

'I did not doubt it after you tried to seduce me.' He grinned then.

'I was drunk, Sam.'

'Yes, and very revealing it was too.' His smile faded. 'Nevertheless, I owe you an apology. I gave no thought for your happiness, I saw you as a suitable mother for my troubled son.' He was looking rather embarrassed and uncomfortable.

'Oh, Sam, you don't have to apologize for that. I would probably have done the same thing in your position.'

'I expect you would,' he agreed. 'Family is important to you, isn't it?'

'Yes, I grew up watching Rose fight to give us all a better life, and what we have now is very precious to all of us.'

'She's a very special woman.' Sam sighed. 'I don't know what would have become of Jacques if she hadn't taken care of him.'

They walked in silence for a while, then Annie asked, 'What are your plans now?'

'I won't be coming back with you. My work is finished and I have been discharged on compassionate grounds.'

'I'll miss you,' she told him. It was going to be strange without Sam around. She'd worked with him since 1940 after becoming a wireless operator, and he'd become a part of her life.

'We have shared much in the last few years, but we'll still be friends. Yes?' he asked.

'Of course.' Annie slipped her hand through his arm. 'I want to see Jacques grow up.'

'Rose has given us permission to stay at the cottage

for as long as we need it. I will marry Maria as soon as it can be arranged.'

'Good. That will make her very happy, and speed her recovery, I'm sure.' Annie stopped to cut a late pink rose with a pair of dressmaking scissors she had in her pocket. 'Give her this from me.'

Sam smelt the perfume and smiled. 'Thank you, she'll love it; there hasn't been much beauty in her life for a long time. My home is still standing, Annie. It will need a lot of work, but as soon as the war's over we shall return to France.'

'Oh, I'm so glad you have something to go back to. When are you going to take Jacques to meet his mother?'

'As soon as Marj and Rose have finished making her look nice.'

'Nice?' Annie laughed. 'Sam, she's lovely, and even in her frail state the beauty shines through.'

'Just wait until she has put on some weight and is in full health again.' Sam's eyes shone with love, and he swallowed back emotion. 'I never thought to see her again.'

Annie squeezed his arm. 'I'm so happy for you.'

Sam stopped and turned her to face him. 'I hope I haven't ruined things for you with Reid. I told him that I intended to make you mine, and I warned him off.'

'So? That wouldn't have bothered him.'

'You don't know, do you?' Sam gave a rueful shake of his head.

'I haven't the faintest idea what you're talking about.' Annie tipped her head to one side and frowned. 'I think you'd better explain.'

'The man is in love with you, Annie.'

Her mouth opened in astonishment. 'Where on earth did you get that idea from?'

'He told me.'

Annie gave him a disbelieving look. 'Oh, I've heard that tale before. He was pulling your leg.'

'No.' Sam was adamant. 'We were rivals for your love, but I was determined to win, even though I knew Reid loved you deeply. And for that act of selfishness I am very sorry.'

Annie was speechless. Reid had been telling the truth when he told her to look in the mirror to see the woman he loved. Dismay and shame swamped her. What a heartless fool she'd been, and how she must have hurt him by calling him a liar that night at Roehampton . . .

'Do you care nothing for him?' Sam asked.

'I'm not sure what I feel,' said Annie, confused. 'I find him attractive and I enjoy being with him, even though we argue most of the time.'

Sam waved a hand in a dismissive gesture. 'Take no notice of that. It is just Reid's defences surfacing. He did not want to fall in love, I think.' He gave Annie an earnest look. 'Give him a chance.'

She knew she would. Sam's revelation had been a shock, but now she came to consider it . . . well, the signs had all been there but she'd ignored them. And her own feelings!

'I expect Maria must be ready. I'll collect Jacques and take him to meet his mother.'

Reid stood by the window watching Sam and Annie talking. It was obviously a serious discussion. Were they deciding what to do about the unexpected turn of events?

859

He clenched his fists. He was certain Sam wouldn't marry Annie now the real mother of his son had been rescued, but if he was hoping to hold on to her in some way then the man would have a fight on his hands. He was damned if he was going to allow that to happen. He loved Annie so much, and if he'd believed that her happiness was with Sam then he would have slipped out of the picture, but things had changed. He would not let Sam ruin her life now!

'What do you think they're talking about, old boy?'

Reid jumped. 'Bouncer! I didn't hear you come in.'

'Bit edgy, aren't you?' his friend remarked.

'I was deep in thought, that's all.'

Bouncer looked enquiringly at him. 'How long can we stay, Reid?'

'Another day and then I must get back. I promised my parents I'd see them before my leave ends.'

'Ah, well,' Bouncer sighed, 'I'd better make the most of my time here. I'll see if Wally needs any help in the kitchen.'

Reid chuckled as his friend left the room. He wasn't sure Bouncer had ever seen a kitchen in his life. It was more likely he was after Wally's secret store of whisky. As the door closed he turned his attention back to the garden, but Sam and Annie were no longer there.

He was about to go in search of the children when Annie walked in.

'Hello,' she said. 'Where's everyone?'

'Most are in the kitchen, I think.' Reid studied her face. She didn't look upset, in fact she appeared to be very happy. 'I saw you talking to Sam. Do you know what his plans are now?'

Annie sat in one of the armchairs and waited until Reid was settled opposite her. 'He's out of the air force now, so he won't be coming back with us. Rose is letting them have the cottage for as long as they want it, and he and Maria will be married as soon as it can be arranged.'

'And how do you feel about that?' He watched her reaction carefully.

Her smile was one of genuine pleasure. 'I'm absolutely delighted. He's taking Jacques to see his mother now.'

'Good. I was preparing to fight him for you,' he declared with honesty. He was going to convince her of his feelings this time!

She laughed. 'Spitfires at dawn?'

'Something like that.' His eyes narrowed at her flippant response. 'You don't seem surprised.'

'I am actually. I was under the impression that I irritated you.'

'You do at times,' he admitted, 'but only because I like to be in control of my life, and I don't feel like that when I think about you. The first time we met I came to you to fulfil the promise I'd made Paul, but after that it was for myself. I wanted to be with you, touch you, see your eyes light up with a smile, or cloud with sadness. Whatever your mood I needed to be with you.'

'Now that's quite an admission!' Her eyes opened wide at his frankness.

He leant forward. 'It's cards on the table time, I think. I honestly believed that you would accept Sam.'

Annie looked thoughtful. 'I must admit that the idea was tempting, and I would have done everything I could to help, but I hope I would have had the strength to refuse him. I want love in a marriage, above children.'

Reid stood up and pulled her out of the chair. 'You can have both, right now.' He kissed her, releasing all the passion he'd kept under tight control. 'What do you say? There's an empty bedroom upstairs.'

Annie eased away from him looking flushed from the heated embrace. 'I'm not going to let you rush me. I won't make a decision until this war's over.'

He studied her expression intently. 'Will I stand a chance then?'

She smiled, stood on tiptoe and kissed his lips briefly. 'We'll see, Squadron Leader, we'll see.'

For that demotion, he kissed her again. From behind them came a voice.

'Whoops!'

Through the haze of his desire, Reid heard the exclamation and stepped back from Annie. James and Kate were standing in the room grinning.

'Shall we go away again?' James smirked.

'No need.' Reid drew in a deep breath. Annie had responded and that was the second time he'd felt her passionate nature come alive in his arms. She might back away from commitment now, but he was pretty sure she wouldn't for much longer.

Feeling more in control, he smiled at the children. 'What have you two been doing with yourselves?'

'We've been looking for Jack,' Kate told them.

'He's over at the cottage with his daddy,' Annie said.

'Ah, there you are.' Rose held open the door for Bouncer who was carrying a tray loaded with the ever-available cups of tea.

Soon the room was crowded as Marj and Wally came

in as well. The discussion quickly turned to the progress of the invasion.

'When do you think the war will be over?' James asked. He was growing up fast and taking an avid interest in developments.

'Well, I don't think it will be this year,' Reid said. 'Winter will soon be here, but if things go well then we might see the end around spring next year.' He looked pointedly at Annie. He wasn't going to let her dither that long.

Annie returned the look and her lips lifted at the corners. She'd clearly understood his meaning without him saying a word, and there was a look in her eyes that made his heart soar with hope.

Suddenly Jacques burst into the room, his face alive with excitement. 'Auntie Rose, can we move my things? I'm going to sleep in the other house.'

'I'll do it before your bedtime,' she told him, smiling down at his flushed face.

The little boy grabbed hold of Kate and tried to pull her to her feet. 'Come see!' When she stood up he launched himself at James. 'Come see!'

Reid had never seen the boy so animated and it was obvious the first meeting had gone well.

Rose's children looked surprised at the excited antics of Jacques. The little boy had just turned four, but to Reid he seemed much younger. The poor little devil had had a traumatic time since he'd been born, and it was wonderful to see him laughing.

'I've got a mummy!' He was leaping up and down. 'My real mummy!' He smiled and then turned and tore out of the room, the toy rabbit in danger of losing its ear.

Kate and James glanced at their mother, who nodded to them. 'Why don't you go with him?'

Without further hesitation they ran after Jacques.

'That's the first time I've seen the poor little thing smile.' Marj wiped her eyes.

Wally patted his wife's arm. 'He'll be all right now.'

Marj nodded. 'We did our best for him, but there's no substitute for his proper family is there?'

Maria and Nurse Stevens joined them that evening. The old house had a dining room but it had been turned into another bedroom, and the family loved to gather around the kitchen table. Annie and her mother had gone to great trouble to make it look lovely for a special occasion. The best linen had been brought out, the glasses sparkled under the lights, and a huge bowl of flowers adorned the centre of the table. Annie was pleased to see what a good job her mother and Rose had made of the clothes for Maria. The navy skirt was full and gathered at the waist, the pale blue blouse had long sleeves, and a silk scarf was tucked into the neck, effectively hiding her thin body.

Jacques had been allowed to stay up late to mark the occasion, and he kept close to his mother the whole time. He watched her shyly, and each time she smiled and stroked his hair he grinned and squirmed with pleasure.

Yes, Annie thought as she saw the little touches of love and affection between them, everything was going to be all right now. Jacques couldn't possibly remember his mother, but he'd clearly accepted her without reservation, which was more than he'd done with his father.

Her gaze strayed to Reid, who was laughing with Bouncer. What a fool she'd been not to recognize her feelings for him sooner, but their first meeting had not been a good one, and she had doubted that a relationship between them would work. She had also been too absorbed in her work with Sam and Jack Graham to give much thought to her own life, but now the end of the war was in sight she was starting to think about the future.

After the meal was over they all went into the lounge. A fire was burning in the grate to take the chill off the evening. Annie gazed into the flames, deep in thought.

'You look pensive.' Reid sat on the arm of her chair. 'What's causing that faraway look in your eyes?'

'I was wondering what I'll do when I'm demobbed,' she said. 'I don't think being a fashion editor again will hold enough excitement.'

'Ah.' He sighed dramatically. 'There was I hoping it was me making you look so dreamy.'

Annie smiled but said nothing. There was no way he was going to know that she'd really been thinking about him. Not yet, anyway.

'Have you found your job as wireless operator exciting then?'

'A lot of the time it's routine and a hard slog, but never dull.'

It was obvious from the way he'd asked the question that he was curious about what she did. And now Sam's activities had been revealed, he clearly wanted to find out how involved she'd been with his work.

'And at other times it's exciting?' He persisted in probing.

'It's had its moments.'

Nurse Stevens came over and Annie took the opportunity to change the subject. Perhaps one day she would tell Reid that she had been behind enemy lines, but not now.

'Hello.' Annie smiled. 'Your patient is making a good recovery.'

'Indeed she is.' The girl turned to Reid. 'I am no longer needed here, sir. When will you be returning to Tangmere?'

'Tomorrow. I have a flight time of eleven hundred hours.'

'If you will take me with you, sir, I will arrange for transport to take me back to the hospital in Aldershot.' The nurse returned to her seat and started talking to Rose, when the door swung open.

Bill was greeted with hugs and exclamations of pleasure when he came into the room. Then he saw Jacques and lifted him up.

'My word, you've grown since I last saw you,' Bill told him. 'Not frightened of me this time?'

Jacques shook his head and whispered in Bill's ear.

'Really?' He put the boy down and smiled at Maria. 'It's wonderful to meet you. No wonder your son is looking so much happier.'

Sam shook Bill's hand. 'How long are you home for?'

'Two weeks.' That announcement was greeted with whoops of delight from James and Kate.

Wally put down his cup. 'This calls for a proper celebration. I've got a drop of whisky and sherry put aside for Christmas, but we'll have it now.'

While the glasses were being filled Bill looked at Reid. 'Have we met before?'

Reid was immediately on his feet and shaking Bill's hand firmly. He very much wanted to meet this man again, but he'd stayed in the background while his family welcomed him home. 'You brought me back from Dunkirk after I'd been shot down.'

'Of course, I thought there was something familiar about you.' Bill grinned. 'You're a bit cleaner this time.'

Annie watched Reid laugh, and his admiration for her brother-in-law was evident.

'I saw you leave for another rescue trip,' Reid told him. 'How did you manage to repair the leaks so fast?'

Bill chuckled. 'They stuck something in the holes. I didn't ask what it was, but we could only do one more trip. We were shipping too much water after that.'

'Here we are.' Wally handed the women a sherry each, the men a whisky, and lemonade for the children.

'A toast.' Wally held up his glass. 'To Maria, Sam and Jacques, may the future hold much happiness for you.'

Everyone drank to that with pleasure.

'And now to Bill.' Wally lifted his glass again. 'Welcome home and we pray you will soon return to us for good.'

Agreement echoed around the room, but Bill frowned. 'Where's George?'

The silence was total, and Annie could feel the shock running through the room.

Rose was the first to recover. 'I sent you a letter, Bill. George was killed by a doodlebug when he went to London to get his house ready for the victory celebrations.'

'Oh, dear God.' Bill obviously knew nothing about it, and the news had come as a terrible blow. 'I never received your letter, my darling. I'm so dreadfully sorry; we will

867

miss him.' He held Rose in his arms and rocked her gently. 'What a dreadful thing to happen, I wish I'd been here to help you.'

Rose kissed his cheek. 'I wish you had been too, but we managed.'

Bill kept his arm around Rose and turned to face the room. He raised his glass. 'Let's drink to a fine man.'

Annie's eyes clouded as she watched Bill coping with his grief. Her brother-in-law had always had the utmost respect for George Gresham, and she knew he was going to miss him dreadfully – as they all did.

The glasses were soon emptied and Sam stood up, his hand on Maria's shoulder. 'Will you excuse us. Maria must rest now.'

Jacques caught hold of his mother's hand as soon as she stood up and smiled proudly at everyone in the room.

Annie watched them leave. Maria was leaning heavily on Sam. It had clearly been an exhausting evening, but it was a step back to normality for her.

'Annie?' Bill was puzzled. 'I thought Jacques's mother was dead.'

'That was what we all believed.' She then explained what had happened.

'Poor soul.' Bill was silent for a moment, and then nodded. 'But it's good to hear of a happy ending, eh?'

Annie sat back in the chair and silently agreed with that statement. This war had caused untold sorrow and heartbreak, but it had also produced acts of heroism, and a miracle or two.

33

'I'll land her.'

'Oh no, you won't.' Reid glanced at Bouncer and shook his head to emphasize his decision.

'Come on, Reid,' Bouncer complained. 'It isn't often we get the chance to fly something this big.' He gave an evil grin. 'I want to see if she bounces.'

'She won't.' Reid watched his co-pilot eagerly flexing his fingers, and smothered a chuckle. 'Don't forget we've got a passenger. You'll frighten the life out of her.'

Bouncer glanced back at the nurse. 'I don't think so, old boy, she looks calm enough.'

'That's ignorance,' Reid pointed out. 'She's never seen one of your landings.'

'I'll handle her like a new-born babe.' When his friend didn't answer, Bouncer said, 'I think you're the one who's scared.'

'Too right I'm terrified, look.' Reid held up a shaking hand.

'You liar,' Bouncer roared. 'You've never been terrified in your life and that's what made you such a good squadron leader. You haven't got any nerves.'

'You think I wasn't scared?' Reid asked, remembering how he'd been drenched in sweat, as he'd pushed himself and his Spitfire to the limit in those battles. God, but they were wonderful aeroplanes!

'Scared, yes, we all were, but you were never *terrified*.'

The two men were silent then, each with his personal memories of the struggle they'd been involved in. The only sound was the hum of the engines.

'I'll buy you a beer when we get down if you let me land her.' Bouncer had resorted to bribery.

'Huh! I'll need more than that. I might consider it for a double whisky.'

'You're on.' Bouncer turned his head and shouted to their passenger. 'Strap yourself in, we land in about fifteen minutes.'

'I must be mad,' Reid muttered to himself as he gave the controls over to his friend. Just to be on the safe side he tightened his harness as much as he could, then watched the airfield come into sight.

'I wonder what would happen if I tried a victory roll?' Bouncer asked gleefully.

'I expect the wings would fall off,' Reid sighed.

'Ah, not a good idea then.'

Reid's eyes narrowed as they made their approach and he watched every move the pilot made. His friend was one hell of a pilot, but somehow he'd never quite mastered the art of getting down without bouncing along the runway. He braced himself as the wheels touched the field, but the expected lurch never came. When they were taxiing towards the hangar, he gasped in astonishment. It was a perfect landing.

'Don't look so surprised, old boy. I'm not quite as crazy as I used to be, not now I've married Jenny.'

They jumped down, helped a relieved Nurse Stevens out and said goodbye to her. Then Bouncer slapped Reid on the back. 'Come to my room and I'll give you that drink.'

Reid followed him, sat in the only easy chair in the small room, watched Bouncer retrieve a bottle from behind a cupboard and pour generous measures into two mugs.

Bouncer held his mug up in salute. 'Sam and Maria are in good hands. Annie belongs to one hell of a family.'

'She certainly does.' Reid took a swig of the whisky and felt it burn a path down his insides. He couldn't help remembering the shock of everyone when they realized that Bill didn't know about George's death, but the post was very erratic and was often months late. For those at sea it was even worse, and in this case the important letter had never reached Bill . . .

'Pity Annie didn't come back with us.' Bouncer gave his friend a studied look. 'You could have whisked her away for a couple of days on your own. That house was so full it was a job to find any privacy.'

'It nearly always is. I understand that Rose won't turn anyone away who needs help.' Reid drained his glass.

'An extraordinary woman.' Bouncer examined his empty glass and held it up. 'Want another one?'

'No thanks, I'm heading for home right now to see my parents.'

'It would have been more exciting to take Annie away, eh?' Bouncer suggested with a waggle of his eyebrows.

'What makes you think she would have come?' Reid asked drily.

'Because she's crazy about you.' He gave a knowing wink. 'I don't think you're trying hard enough, old boy.'

Reid stood up. 'It's damned near impossible carrying on a courtship when you can only meet a couple of times a year, if you're lucky. Especially with someone as tricky as Annie.'

'Courtship!' Bouncer exploded. 'There isn't time for that kind of messing about. When you fix the target in your sights you've got to go in and conquer, or else she'll slip away to safety.'

'Is that how you pursued Jenny?' Reid asked, his eyes gleaming with amusement. He'd never heard such eloquence from his friend before.

'Of course, she never stood a chance, so stop mucking about, dear chap. Go and get her. Start writing letters and phoning her,' Bouncer advised. 'Show her your romantic side.'

Reid opened the door and glanced back over his shoulder, his mouth set in a determined line. 'I've been trying to do that, but don't worry, she won't get away without one hell of a fight.'

'Oh dear.' Marj's brow furrowed as she read the letter.

'What is it, Mum?' Annie asked. Her mother had been looking rather worn out just lately, which was hardly surprising considering the chaos this house was always in, with people coming and going all the time.

'Bob's been wounded and they've brought him back to a hospital in Folkestone. I must go and see him.'

'I'll go,' Annie said. She didn't want her mother making the long journey at the moment. 'I must return to camp now Sam and Maria are settled. I'll visit Bob first and let you know how he is.'

'Oh, would you, Annie?' Marj smiled gratefully at her daughter.

'Don't worry,' she advised her mother, 'if he was in a

bad way he wouldn't have been able to write the letter.'

'You're right, of course. I never thought of that, and it is his handwriting.' The frown left Marj's face and she smiled in relief.

Annie knew that her mother treasured the few letters she'd received from Bob over the years, and often took them out of her dressing-table drawer to read them again. He had been the most difficult and unruly of her children, but she'd always loved him.

A check on the train times showed there was one in two hours. Providing it was on time, of course. What a shame they hadn't known the day before; she could have returned with Reid and Bouncer. It didn't take Annie long to pack, and she headed for the cottage to tell Sam she was leaving.

Sam and Maria were taking a gentle stroll in the garden and Sam waved when he saw her. It was lovely to see him looking so relaxed and content, Annie thought, as she hurried over.

'I have to leave this morning,' she told them. 'Bob's been wounded and I'm going to see him before I return to camp.'

'Hope it isn't too bad, Annie.' Sam made Maria sit on a seat while they talked.

'I won't know until I get there. He didn't say much in his letter.'

'When will you come back?' Maria asked.

'Not for some time; I doubt if I'll be able to get any more leave until the war is over.'

'That is a shame.' Maria smiled at Sam. 'You will miss our wedding.'

'We are to be married in four weeks' time,' Sam said, 'and we shall be very sorry if you can't be there.'

'So will I, but I'm sure the rest of my family will make a real party of the occasion.'

'No doubt,' Sam said and smiled. 'Bill is going to try and return in time to give Maria away, and Wally will act as my best man.'

Maria became serious, stood up and reached out to kiss Annie on both cheeks. 'I have been told how kind you and your family have been to my son, and now also to me. I am deeply grateful.'

Annie hugged her. 'We are happy everything has turned out so well.' She glanced at her watch. 'I must hurry if I'm going to catch my train.'

'Mind you behave yourself when you get back,' Sam said with a grin.

Annie pretended to be hurt. 'I'm always good, and without your disruptive influence my life will be one of tranquillity.'

Sam tipped his head back and roared with laughter. 'That sounds deadly dull. It has been a pleasure working with you, Annie Webster.'

'And you.' She hugged him also. 'You be happy, Sam.'

'I shall,' he assured her.

The journey back to Roehampton had been interminable, with delay after delay. She'd been sorry to leave so soon after Bill had come on leave. He was over fifty now and she hoped he would soon be free of the navy. Her sister would be relieved as well. She never voiced her concerns but Annie knew she was worried about him – he looked so dreadfully tired.

She let herself into the house. It was too late to go on to Folkestone today, so she'd sleep in her own bed tonight and see Bob tomorrow.

Annie threw her bag on to the stairs. That could be taken upstairs later, but she needed a cup of tea now. Much to her surprise the kitchen wasn't empty, and the girl standing by the cooker turned and glared at her.

'Who are you?' the stranger demanded.

'I think that's my question.' Annie's gaze raked over the girl and certain things about her registered. She was average height, ample curves, very obvious in a tight-fitting red skirt and cream jumper. She had carefully tended blonde hair, eyes green and hostile.

The scrutiny was returned. 'You must be Annie,' she sneered. 'Well, you'll have to sleep next door because I'm spending a few days with Charles – *alone*.' She emphasized the last word.

'Pat!' Charlie was standing behind Annie. 'This is my sister's home and she has every right to be here.'

Annie turned and hugged her brother. 'Charles?' she murmured in his ear, and they both burst into laughter.

'I didn't mean to be rude.' Pat slipped her hand through Charlie's arm and gazed up at him. 'I was just disappointed we weren't going to be alone after all.'

The girl's attitude had changed completely and with imploring smiles she leaned against Charlie. 'You do forgive me, don't you?'

Her act didn't fool Annie for one minute. She might appear to be contrite but the coldness in her eyes could not be disguised. All that Annie had seen and done in the war, and the loss of Paul, Jack Graham and George had hardened some of the soft edges. She was no longer the trusting girl who thought everyone was inherently nice. This girl of her brother's was quite transparent, and Annie didn't like her – in fact her feelings were stronger than that.

Annie filled the kettle and put it on the stove. 'I'm dying for a cuppa. Anyone else want one?'

'Please.' Charlie sat at the kitchen table.

'Charles,' Pat said with a pout. 'You promised to take me out for a drink.'

'After I've had a chat with my sister.' He took the cup from Annie and smiled. 'Now tell me all the news.'

'We've had a letter saying Bob's been wounded and I'm going to see him tomorrow.'

'What!' Charlie exclaimed. 'Where is he?'

'Folkestone, and we only found out this morning. Mum wanted to come but she's a bit run-down at the moment.'

'Has she seen a doctor?' Charlie looked concerned.

'Yes. He said she's been overdoing things and needs to rest, that's all. It's nothing serious,' she assured him.

'That's a relief. How's Sam and his family now?'

'They're fine.' Annie wasn't prepared to discuss this in front of Pat. The girl looked as if she was eating every word.

Charlie drank his tea and dropped the subject. He'd clearly picked up Annie's reluctance to discuss things in front of Pat. 'You know I've only seen Bob once since he came back so I think I'll come with you tomorrow.'

'He'd like that.' Annie smiled.

'Oh, Charles,' Pat wailed. 'You were going to show me Richmond Park tomorrow.'

'It'll have to wait, I'm afraid.' He headed for the door.

'Let's leave Annie in peace, and go and have that drink.'

Annie watched them leave, and worry for Charlie gnawed at her. How on earth had her brother got involved with a girl like that?

Pat insisted on coming with them to Folkestone but refused to come in the hospital.

'I'll have a walk around and find a tearoom somewhere.' She smiled appealingly at Charlie.

With only a faint sigh, he pulled some money out of his pocket and handed it to her. After counting it she gave him a quick peck on the cheek and was off.

Charlie watched her for a moment then gave a rueful smile. 'She thinks I'm made of money.'

Annie didn't comment. 'Where did you meet her?'

'It was at an RAF dance. She's a Londoner, but they were bombed out and now she and her family are living near Bognor.'

'What are her family like?' Annie chose her questions carefully. After all, she had no right to interfere in her brother's relationships.

'I've never met them.' Charlie held the door of the hospital open for his sister. 'Grief, look at this place, it's crowded. Do you know which ward Bob's in?'

'No, we'll just have to queue up.' Annie resigned herself to a lengthy wait.

'You don't like her, do you, Annie,' Charlie remarked.

'My opinion isn't important,' she told him. 'You're a grown man and if she's your choice then I'll do my best to get along with her.'

'I know you will . . .' He hesitated. 'At first I was

absolutely besotted with her but now something worries me. I think she believes we're rich.'

Annie looked at her brother in amazement. He looked so handsome and a man of the world in his air force uniform, and she couldn't help laughing at his expression. 'But we are, Charlie. We have a great deal more than a lot of families.'

'I keep forgetting that.' He grimaced. 'The hunger, violence and poverty of our childhood made an indelible impression on me.'

'Does Pat know we originally came from Garrett Street, one of the roughest places in London?'

'I told her, yes, but she didn't seem interested. She's asked a lot of questions about Rose, Bill and George but I've been cagey about telling her too much.'

'Why is that?' Annie wanted to know.

'Dunno.' Charlie frowned. 'I suppose I don't quite trust her, and I believe our family business is our affair and nothing to do with outsiders.' He looked at his sister and pulled a face. 'When I first met her I believed she was the one I'd been waiting for but I have some doubts now.'

'Can I offer a little sisterly advice?' Annie asked.

Charlie nodded.

'Don't make any hasty decisions. Take your time getting to know her, and if you're serious insist on meeting her family.' Annie smiled. 'You can learn a lot from families.'

'Sound advice.' Charlie looked at his sister with renewed respect. 'You're tougher and a lot more cautious than you used to be.'

'So I've been told.'

They finally reached the information desk and asked where Bob was, then made their way along the corridor. Annie paused outside the ward. Her brother was in the mood to talk and she felt he needed to. He seemed to be having serious doubts about Pat and she found that reassuring. They were a close family and it would be awful if someone joined them that they couldn't stand. But that could happen, as it wasn't possible to like everyone you met in life. Look at the way she'd disliked Reid after their first meeting.

'Why have you never married, Annie?'

She thought about this for a moment. 'Perhaps I've been looking for the impossible, but to be honest I don't think I've ever really wanted to. I was quite happy with my life and career before this war started.'

'I know what you mean. Will and I felt the same but things are different now, aren't they?'

Annie sighed and pushed open the door. 'Yes, everything's changed.'

'Annie, Charlie!' Bob waved to them from his bed. 'What a marvellous surprise.'

'We've come to see how you are.' Annie kissed him. 'What happened to you?'

'I was caught in heavy shellfire and got peppered with shrapnel.' He grimaced. 'They've dug loads of the stuff out of my back and legs.'

'Will there be any permanent damage?' Charlie asked.

'They don't think so, but it will take some time before I make a full recovery.'

'Well, as soon as you're out of here you can go to Wales and rest.' Annie sat on the chair that Charlie had pulled up for her. 'Mum was worried about you.'

Bob looked gloomy. 'All I've ever caused Mum is worry. I was a swine of a kid, wasn't I?'

'That's all in the past.' Annie held his hand in comfort. She knew how easy it was to become depressed in hospital. 'And forgiven.'

'One good thing,' Charlie said, 'by the time you're fit the war will be over.'

'God, I hope so! I miss my wife and nippers something awful,' Bob exclaimed.

'You'll be on your way home to Australia before you know it.' Annie felt sad at that thought. Bob had fitted in as if he'd never left and Annie knew her mother was going to be very upset when he went back to his home so far away. She pushed the gloomy thought away, dived into her pocket and produced a small bar of chocolate. 'That's all I could manage to get, but I expect you could do with a treat.'

'Oh, thanks, I'll eat that when nurse isn't looking.' He popped it in the cupboard next to him. 'Now tell me all the news.'

It took quite a time to bring Bob up to date with all the happenings, and they overstayed their welcome and were ordered to leave by a stern nurse. But they came away happy, knowing that although their Australian brother had been quite badly injured he would make a full recovery. Though he'd been separated from them for many years Annie and Charlie felt they knew and loved him.

'Where have you been all this time?' Pat complained when she saw them. 'I've been waiting ages.'

'We had a lot to talk about,' Charlie told her.

'Can we get something to eat?' Pat moderated her

tone and smiled at Charlie. 'I've found a smashing café.'

'Good idea.' He took Annie's arm. 'Our train doesn't leave for another two hours, so we've plenty of time.'

As they made their way to the café Pat chatted away, but Annie noticed that she never once asked about Bob.

34

December 1944

The weeks dragged by. Annie was as busy as ever but felt strangely depressed. It was ridiculous, she told herself repeatedly. She still found her work as exciting and challenging as it had always been, but it had been a strange year with many ups and downs. There had been D-Day in June, the liberation of Paris in August, and the steady advance of Allied troops towards Germany. However, the vi flying bombs had caused damage, including the death of George, and also the v2 rockets that had followed them. But it was becoming clear that the end of the war could only be months away and she should be feeling ecstatic.

'Why the gloomy face?' asked Greg – a bomber pilot who had come to the end of his flying days due to injury – as he sat down at her table in the mess.

'I really don't know and I'm just berating myself for feeling so low.'

'Don't give yourself a hard time,' he advised. 'Waiting is always the worst, as I well know. Before a bombing raid I used to feel physically sick.'

Annie nodded in understanding. 'That's a bit how I feel now. Suppose the Germans launch an offensive and start to regain the upper hand?'

'They won't.' He spoke with confidence. 'They've

taken a severe pounding, and when Hitler's own generals tried to assassinate him, like they did in July, then they know they're beaten.'

'You're right, of course.' Annie sat up straight and smiled. When that bit of news had come through it had caused elation, and then disappointment that it hadn't succeeded. 'I expect I'm down in the dumps because I can't get home for Christmas.'

'Never mind. We'll have a good knees-up here.'

Annie watched him walk away, leaning heavily on a cane, and set about pulling herself together. She had never felt so unsettled in her life. Even if she couldn't spend the holiday with her family that was no reason to act like a sulky child. That was something she had never been.

Rose's last letter had told her that Bill would be on leave for a couple of days; Bob had arrived in Wales and would convalesce there; Sam and Maria were now married, and Jacques was a very happy little boy. Annie was dreadfully sorry she hadn't been able to get leave to go to Maria and Sam's wedding, but they'd sent her some lovely photographs. Charlie would also be in Wales, but they weren't sure about Will. Dora and her grandmother were arriving in a couple of days' time as well, so the house would be crammed full for Christmas. That was just the way the Webster family liked it.

Annie mentally shook herself. It was no good wishing she were somewhere else, she still had work to do. There was a lot to be grateful for and who knew what would happen next year.

Hopefully they would *all* be together.

*

'You can have twenty-four hours to celebrate New Year.' The duty officer handed Annie a pass. 'Go out and enjoy yourself.'

She looked at the pass and chewed her bottom lip. What was she going to do with this? It wasn't long enough to travel to Wales and back, and it wasn't any use going to the Roehampton house; she didn't want to see 1945 in on her own.

'You don't appear to be very pleased.'

'I am, sir,' she said hastily. This was unexpected and she didn't want to seem ungrateful. 'I was just trying to decide what to do.'

'I thought that was settled. Your fiancé is waiting at the gate for you.'

Her head came up in shock. 'My what?'

'Fiancé.' He sat back and folded his arms, looking amused. 'Don't you want to see him?'

'I might if I knew who it was.'

'Ah.' He started to chuckle. 'So he lied to get you time off, but there isn't anything I can do about that. He outranks me.'

'Reid!' Annie exploded.

'If his name's Lascells then that's the man, and I suggest you hurry because he outranks you as well.'

Annie left the room, the officer's laugh echoing along the corridor. I'll kill him, she fumed, as she collected her coat. This will be all round the base within the hour.

But her anger seeped away as she walked towards him. Her mouth turned up at the corners, amused now by his audacity. He was leaning against a car, his collar turned up against the cold wind, and a cigarette in his hand. He really was the most attractive man, she thought to herself. She might as well enjoy the evening.

Reid straightened up and ground out the fag with the toe of his shoe as she approached.

'Resorted to lying, Squadron Leader?' she asked.

He grinned and held the door of the car open for her. 'Whatever it takes, Webster.'

'Well, it worked. I've been given a twenty-four-hour pass.' She got into the car and ignored his muttered expletive.

'I asked for forty-eight hours, at least.' He started the car and headed up the road.

'What on earth would we do in each other's company for that long?'

He cast her a quick glance, and there was no mistaking the gleam in his eyes.

Annie sighed. 'Am I going to have trouble with you tonight?'

'Definitely.'

'Ah well, it's a good job I've only been given a short time off. Where are we going?'

'To a party at the Sterling Hotel, it isn't far from here. They've got a big band and I want to see if you can still jive.'

'And where you have, no doubt, booked rooms?' Annie turned in her seat so she could see his face clearly. There was something different about him.

Reid shook his head. 'Only one room.'

'Did you try for two?' Annie was suspicious of his innocent expression – and he was in such a good mood.

'Why would we want a room each?' he asked.

'Why indeed.' Annie managed to keep a straight face

with difficulty. It was going to be an interesting New Year's Eve. He had told her, quite plainly, what he wanted, and he was giving her the chance to object before the evening began. But she wasn't going to.

It was at that moment she knew that she had, at last, stopped running. It was time to take what life was offering – and if that was Reid then it was all she wanted in this world. The sudden realization of the depth of her feeling for him was a revelation to her.

On the stroke of midnight the party-goers erupted with cheers of joy. The ballroom was packed with every branch of the services, a sprinkling of civilians, and many nationalities. And they were all determined to make this the best New Year party of all time. There was so much hope expressed in the sound that it brought tears to Annie's eyes.

Reid wrapped her in a fierce embrace. 'This is going to be the year, Annie, 1945 is going to see the end of this bloody war.'

He kissed her with unrestrained need, and when he finally broke away he asked, 'Will you marry me, Annie Webster? I love you so very much.'

At that crucial moment she was whisked out of his arms by a crowd of exuberant soldiers and drawn into the snaking line of revellers. Reid quickly pushed in behind her. The noise was deafening and he had to shout to make himself heard.

'What's your answer?'

'*Aye, aye, conga!*' Everyone was singing with legs shooting out from the line in all directions.

'Annie,' he bellowed.

She glanced over her shoulder and mouthed the word *yes*, almost collapsing with laughter at the same time.

Reid grinned, squeezed her waist and threw himself into the revelry with abandon. This was a bizarre proposal, he thought to himself, but it didn't matter; she'd accepted and that was the only important thing. He'd show her how much he loved her later.

After they'd all snaked their way out of the hotel, up the road, returned and made a tour of the garden, then back into the ballroom again, everything quietened down a little.

'Not the kind of proposal I had planned.' Reid gave a rueful shake of his head. Bouncer had told him to be more romantic, and he'd planned to take her outside, go down on one knee, and give her the ring, but he hadn't been able to wait. The whole thing had turned into a farce.

Annie laughed and wrapped her arms around his neck. 'I think it was lovely.'

'So do I.' He kissed her, and then whispered in her ear, 'There's a nice double bed upstairs, or are you going to make me wait?'

'I think we've both waited long enough,' she told him. 'And we've wasted far too much time arguing with each other.'

The speed with which he led her to the stairs left her in no doubt that he heartily agreed.

Reid propped himself up on his elbow and looked down at Annie. She was fast asleep, her hair in disarray where he'd run his fingers through the silky strands, and his heart squeezed with emotion. She was so lovely and she was his now. He wouldn't have believed he could feel so possessive about a woman but she had changed all that. He'd had plenty of girlfriends but had never felt any sense of loss when they'd parted. The thought of losing Annie, though, brought him close to panic.

Annie muttered in her sleep and he slid down in the bed again, drawing her gently into his arms. Their loving had been wonderful. After her first nervous hesitation she had unleashed a passion that had literally taken his breath away. He was damned sure this had been her first time but how she had managed to stay out of some man's bed until now was a mystery. He seriously doubted that many women in their early thirties were still virgins. Not those as beautiful and loving as Annie, anyway.

He kissed her gently and then cradled her head on to his chest. A feeling of utter contentment swept through him. She obviously had a moral code, which meant she had waited for the right man to come along. It must have been difficult in the wartime atmosphere. The fact that she had come willingly to him tonight meant only one thing as far as he could see. She loved him.

There was a burst of raucous laughter from the party downstairs and Annie opened her eyes. 'Sounds like they're making a night of it,' she said with a yawn.

'Did they wake you up?' Reid cupped her face in his hands so he could look into her eyes.

She gave a slight nod and closed her eyes again.

'Look at me, Annie.'

She smiled up at him with an amused expression. 'Aren't you tired?'

'No. I want answers to three questions, then I *might* sleep,' he said, tucking a loose strand of her golden hair behind her ears. Propping himself up he gazed down at her. 'First. When can we get married?'

'When the war's over.'

'Good,' he agreed. 'That won't be long now, so we can start making plans.'

'Have you got a spare parachute?' she asked, and her grin spread. 'Or perhaps Bouncer's got one he isn't using.'

'I'll ask him, but he's a reformed maniac since he married Jenny.' Reid chuckled as he thought about the dramatic change in his friend. 'I'll get you one anyway.'

'Good, because my family are going to want a proper party.' She gave him an uncertain look. 'I hope you don't mind?'

'Not at all; my parents will expect the same.' He ran his hand over her warm body. 'Now that's settled . . .'

'Wait!' She laughingly caught hold of his wandering hand. 'You said you had three questions.'

'Did I?' He frowned. 'Ah, well, I'll think of them later.'

'No, you won't. I want to know what the questions are.' Annie tried to wriggle away from him but he wouldn't allow it.

He pulled her back into his arms. 'Stop squirming about or I'll never think of them. Now let me see . . . Ah, yes. The second question is, do you love me, Annie?'

'Yes,' she told him with a sigh of pleasure. 'I wouldn't be in this bed with you now if I didn't.'

'Do you want children?'

'Yes, please.'

That was just the answer he wanted and he couldn't stop himself from showing her how happy he was.

She gasped when he broke off the heated embrace. 'Not until we're married, of course.'

'I'll try to see that doesn't happen before our wedding, my darling,' he assured her. 'Why have you waited so long to commit yourself to a man?'

'That's four questions,' she pointed out, 'but I'll answer it anyway.' She snuggled closer. 'I wanted love, and I needed to be sure it was a relationship that had every chance of lasting. I couldn't bear to be in an unhappy marriage; it would destroy me. And I had to be convinced that whoever became my husband loved me as much as I loved him.'

'I do.' His voice was husky with desire.

'I know you do, but I don't mind being reminded again.' Her smile was provocative.

Reid was only too happy to oblige but he restrained himself long enough to slip a lovely diamond and sapphire ring on her finger.

'Oh, that's beautiful.' Annie held her hand towards the bedside light so she could have a proper look at the ring. 'You had this all planned.'

'Yes, all planned. Except the conga, of course.'

It had been a blissful twenty-four hours, Reid thought as he jumped out of the car at Tangmere. He'd reluctantly returned Annie to Chicksands, not knowing when they would be able to see each other again. Damn the war, he thought, he would be glad to see the end of it now. Trying to wangle leave at the same time was difficult, but he'd fix it somehow, as he didn't want to be away from Annie for too long – in fact he wanted her with him all the time! But at least he now knew that she was going to marry him! She loved him!

Before unpacking his bag he strolled into his office to see if there were any urgent messages.

'Sir.' Sergeant Jenkins rushed through the door. 'One of the returning fighters is in trouble.'

Reid surged to his feet. 'Who is it?'

'Don't know, sir.'

He left at a run and headed for the control tower. The atmosphere was tense and everyone was listening to the faint voice coming over the speaker.

'What's happening?' he asked the officer in charge.

'Spitfire with engine trouble, we think.'

'What do you mean – you think?' Reid glowered at the man.

'We can't pick up a clear message from the squadron. Something's wrong this end, we think.'

Reid ground his teeth. If he said 'think' once more he'd belt him one. 'Get it put right – at once!' he ordered. 'Now tell me what you *do* know.'

'Not much, I'm afraid, sir, but it sounds serious.' The man shuffled uncomfortably under the fierce glare of his commanding officer.

'If it's that bad why hasn't he baled out?'

'His canopy's stuck . . .'

Reid noted the hesitation and silently dared him to say 'I think', but the man obviously wasn't going to risk it again. However, that piece of information made his insides clench. Being trapped in a crippled plane was every pilot's nightmare. He didn't want to ask the next question but he knew he must. 'Any fire?'

'We don't know. He's been trying to tell us but there's

too much static for us to be able to understand what he's saying.'

The muttered expletive made everyone in the tower stare at Reid but he just ignored them and took over the radio. 'Tell me your situation,' he demanded.

The sound of static crackled through the silent room. 'Someone talk to me, damn you.'

A faint voice came over the speaker. 'Smoke everywhere . . .'

Reid tried to recognize who it was but it was no use, and to make matters worse the radio seemed to have packed up altogether. He knew every one of these men, had flown with some of them during the Battle of Britain and he didn't want to see one of them injured or killed at this stage of the war. It was nearly over.

At the sound of engines he rushed to the window and scanned the sky. Two planes roared low over the tower, banked and climbed into the clear, cold January sun. That was the signal to let the fire crews know the plane was arriving.

After taking a couple of deep breaths to try to ease the tightness in his chest Reid hurried down the stairs.

'His canopy's stuck,' he told the fire chief, and the man nodded grimly.

At that moment a Spitfire made a slow pass and wiggled its wings.

'Here he comes.' Reid shaded his eyes and watched the plane's erratic descent. Clouds of smoke were billowing out of the engine and staining the clear sky behind it.

The fire and ambulance teams hurtled off, taking up positions just behind the plane as it attempted to land.

The air was rent with the noise of sirens, some Spitfires landing and others screaming across the airfield in support of their colleague. And Reid knew that each of them was urging the pilot on to make it safely.

The Spitfire was now skidding along almost sideways, and Reid could stand it no longer. He jumped in a truck and headed for the plane. He knew the rescue teams were on the scene and expert at the job but he had to be there.

The pilot was being pulled free when he jumped from the truck. The man was coughing and retching but still very much alive if the stream of strong language was anything to go by.

'Stop swearing,' a medic ordered as he held an oxygen mask over the pilot's face, 'and get on the stretcher.'

The tall man pushed the medic away and swayed when his support was removed.

'Timber, take it easy.' Reid rushed to his side and held his arm. 'That was a close call. What happened?'

'God knows.' He ripped the mask off. 'The engine started to make a terrible noise and I couldn't see a damned thing when smoke started to fill the cockpit. If it hadn't been for the rest of the boys buzzing around and guiding me in I'd have crashed for sure.'

Two medics were now urging Timber towards the ambulance, and while this tussle was going on the rest of the squadron arrived.

'You all right, old boy?'

Reid dipped his head at the sound of his friend's voice, giving him a moment to control his emotions. He hadn't dared consider that it might have been Bouncer up there in that smoking plane. And the knowledge that he might

893

have had to tell Jenny her husband had died made him feel physically sick. He'd had to face many unpleasant tasks during the war but the thought of facing Jenny with news like that was too awful to contemplate.

Someone slapped him on the back and he turned to face Bouncer, completely in control again after that momentary lapse. Good job he hadn't been this emotional in 1940 or he'd never have survived. Watching Bouncer's happiness with Jenny and being in love himself had brought home to him just how precious life was.

His friend grinned. 'That was a landing I'd have been proud of.'

Reid surveyed the smoking, crumpled aircraft and grimaced. 'I would have expected this of you, but not Timber.'

Now the drama was over Reid's temper exploded. He strode towards the truck that was now full of pilots waiting for a lift. 'Heads are going to roll for this fiasco.'

Bouncer clambered in beside him. 'Oh, good, can I come and watch? You're ferocious in a rage.'

'By all means,' Reid said dangerously, 'but first we'll see how Timber is.'

The pilot had quietened down by the time they saw him, and had returned to his usual placid nature.

'I'm going to wring someone's neck over this, Timber,' Reid promised.

'Oh, these things happen, you know that.' Timber laid his head back and gave a tired smile. 'At least she didn't burst into flames, and apart from being badly shaken up I'm unhurt.'

'Thank heavens for that,' Reid said. Then he looked

at the men crowding around the bed. 'Drinks are on me tonight.'

A cheer rang out and the pilot sat up, looking suddenly very perky. 'Mine's a whisky, and what about some female company as well?'

'I'll see what I can arrange.' Reid strode out of the room, a smile of relief hovering on his lips. He remembered the last time he'd arranged a party for the men, and they deserved another one. Reid's mind went back to New Year 1941 when they'd been sent north for a rest and how they'd needed it after the battle to stop the Luftwaffe gaining superiority of the air. If they'd failed then Hitler would most certainly have invaded. He'd make sure they had one hell of a party tonight!

Bouncer looked around the room and raised an eyebrow at his friend. 'No girls for us?'

'Did you want one?' Reid asked.

'No, but I thought you might.' He drank half his beer in one go. 'Or dare I hope that you've snared Annie at last?'

Reid nodded. 'We're engaged.'

'About time too.' Bouncer grinned with pleasure. 'When did you propose?'

'New Year's Eve.'

'So that's where you disappeared to.' His friend gave a satisfied nod. 'Hope you were in bed at the time.'

'No.' Reid couldn't help laughing as he explained about the dance. It had been the most bizarre proposal.

Bouncer's mouth dropped open and he snorted in disgust. 'Dear me, old boy, couldn't you do better than that? I'm surprised she accepted you.'

'So am I.' Reid's attention was caught by Timber who was dancing. 'That man's all legs, but he's soon recovered from this morning's crash.'

'Thank God.' Bouncer sighed. 'That was dicey, Reid. We've been together a long time and it would have been tragic if he'd bought it now.'

'It certainly would.' Reid's expression was grim for a moment, and then it cleared. 'Annie won't marry until the war's over but I've managed to pin her down to early June by convincing her that it will be finished long before then.'

'I should think that's a safe enough bet.' Bouncer looked over the rim of his glass. 'Who's going to be your best man?'

'You, of course.' Reid sat back to allow more drinks to be put in front of them.

'Smashing party,' the tall pilot told them. 'Aren't you two going to join in? We'll let you dance with our girls.'

'We might take you up on that later,' Bouncer told him. 'We're busy planning Reid's wedding.'

That announcement was all it took for the pilots to stampede to the bar and order what they considered enough drinks to celebrate with. The table was soon crowded with glasses of beer; the squadron was hell-bent on toasting Reid's forthcoming wedding.

Bouncer roared with laughter at the chaos and his friend's look of dismay. 'That will teach you to try and keep this a secret, old boy.'

Reid winced as someone thumped him on the back but he took the boisterous congratulations with pleasure.

'Tell me all the details,' Bouncer asked, when things had quietened down a little.

Reid then related what had happened as he'd proposed to Annie on the stroke of midnight.

His friend was nearly crying with laughter. 'And what did you do then?'

'Mind your own business.'

Bouncer held up his hand. 'Don't worry; my imagination will fill in the details. Tell me what plans you have for the wedding.'

'Annie's asking Dora and Jenny to be maids of honour, Kate a bridesmaid, but James has flatly refused to be a page boy. He'll be sixteen later this year and he wasn't going to have anything to do with it.'

Bouncer choked on his beer and they both burst out laughing, trying to picture the rather serious boy in satin breeches. Reid couldn't help remembering the look of horror on James's face at the suggestion. When Annie had suggested that he be an usher he'd accepted with indecent haste.

'Why didn't Jenny tell me? I spoke to her only yesterday.'

'She'd been sworn to secrecy until I'd told you,' Reid explained. 'So don't go making her pregnant until after the wedding.'

His friend looked smug. 'Too late, old boy, she's three months now.'

Reid's grin spread. 'Congratulations. It's going to be an interesting wedding.'

'Specially if the bride's pregnant, as well.' Bouncer watched Reid's face carefully.

'She won't be,' he replied with confidence.

'Really? You sound so sure, and that makes me think . . .' He paused and frowned, then shook his head.

'No, you're trying to kid me you're waiting until the wedding night and I certainly don't believe that!'

'I can't control what you believe.' Reid's expression gave nothing away. What happened between him and Annie was private and nothing to do with anyone, not even this great friend of his.

'True,' Bouncer agreed, changing the subject smartly. 'Oh, by the way, I've managed to rent a house just down the road from the airfield and Jenny's moving in next week. I'm fed up with being parted from her. Where are you and Annie going to live?'

'Don't tell Annie any of this,' he admonished, 'but I own a piece of land in Berkshire not far from my family's factory in Thatcham, and I'm going to ask Bill to design and build a home for us.'

'I thought he was a professional sailor.'

'No, he's an architect really, and he'll be out of the navy as soon as this war ends, if he can arrange it.' Reid couldn't help remembering how tired Bill had looked last time he'd seen him. To make a man fight in two world wars was asking too much of him, and it had obviously taken its toll on his health. 'Rose and Bill own the building firm of Grant Phillips and they're going to be very busy when this lot's over. Rose told me he'd designed the Roehampton houses they live in.'

'Ah, well, then he knows his job if they are his.' Bouncer studied his friend thoughtfully. 'What do you think your brother would say about you marrying Annie?'

'He told me once that if he didn't make it through the war, then I could marry her.' Reid looked into the distance, remembering that time, and wondered when the pain of losing his young brother was going to heal. It would take a long time.

'Ah,' Bouncer nodded understandingly. 'He'd like to think you were looking after her, then.'

'Yes, he would. He only ever wanted Annie to be happy, and I *will* make her happy.'

35

May 1945

Annie closed her bag and glanced at her watch. Reid should be here any minute now. They had decided to make an early start and it wasn't even light yet. Reid had managed to get some petrol so they were going to take a leisurely drive to Wales, lasting most of the day, and snatching the chance of a few hours alone together. It had taken them until the beginning of May to arrange leave at the same time, and even this had not been certain until the very last minute. Things were happening so fast. Hitler had committed suicide a week ago on the 30th of April, and it was expected to be only a matter of days before Germany surrendered.

Annie gazed around the Nissen hut that had been her home for so long and let out a ragged sigh. It seemed as if she'd been shut away here for ever. Sleeping in this hut she shared with fifteen other girls whenever she could grab a few hours' rest, and working the rest of the time. Oh, it had been exciting at times, but mostly plain hard graft, except for the trip behind enemy lines to find Jack Graham. It still hurt her when she remembered how he had suffered on the journey to the Brittany coast, but at least he had died in his own country with his wife and a son by his side. She was glad she'd been able to do that for him. Jack had been a wonderful man and he would always hold a special place in her heart. Her thoughts drifted back to the winter of 1940 when she'd joined the WAAF, and she smiled as she remembered the laughter at their military issue underclothes. She wondered where most of those girls were now. Annie hoped they'd survived because they had been a good crowd. The one friendship that had remained from the start was with Dora, who was now happily married to Annie's own brother. She could never have imagined that one of the girls she'd met on her first day in the forces would end up as her sister-in-law. After she'd completed her training as a wireless operator she'd been transferred to Cheadle and then on to Chicksands, where she had remained, and it was during those years she had faced her most painful and challenging times: the loss of Paul, Jack Graham and George. But there had also been times of laughter and friendships made, like Jean and Sam, with his adorable son, Jacques.

After another quick check of the time Annie picked up her bag and walked towards the gate. Reid had been pulling strings to get them this leave. They'd been able to snatch a couple of days now and again, but at last they could go to Wales for seven whole days. Reid's parents were already there, so a belated engagement party had been organized. She smiled in anticipation at the thought of seeing everyone again. There had been regular reports from her mother and Rose, of course, so she knew that Jacques had blossomed now he had a *proper* family, as he called it, and Maria was almost back to full health. Sam doted on both of them, Rose had told her, and Annie was delighted. That family had suffered so much and they deserved to be happy now.

Reid was already there, leaning on the car in his usual relaxed manner. As soon as he saw her he came towards her and wrapped his arms around her with a groan of pleasure. 'Ah, I've missed you, my darling,' he told her before kissing her as if he'd never let her go.

Then he tossed her bag into the back of the car and they were soon on their way. Annie was looking forward to a leisurely drive, though she didn't know where he'd managed to get the petrol for such a long journey. But quite frankly she didn't care – she was with Reid and they were going home for a few days.

He gave her a quick sideways glance. 'I've managed to wangle Charlie leave as well, and he's making his way by train.'

'Oh, why didn't you bring him with you?' she asked. 'We could have all travelled together.'

His glance was smouldering. 'Hell, Annie, I've hardly seen you since New Year and I want you to myself for a while, you know that.'

Annie saw his point. She was just as frustrated with this long separation, and was yearning for the time when they could be together. How she wished this flaming war were over. 'That's a good idea because once we get to Wales any time alone will be hard to come by.'

'I'm glad you agree. Charlie's bringing his girlfriend, by the way.'

That news didn't please Annie. 'Oh, dear.'

'Ah,' Reid remarked, 'you don't sound as if you like her.'

'Well, I've only met her once but to be honest I didn't take to her. She tried to order me out of my own home.'

Annie gave a resigned shrug. 'Still it's Charlie's life and if he's happy then that's all that matters.'

A deep chuckle came from Reid. 'If she tries to do that with Rose, then she'll really be cut down.'

Annie grinned at him. 'That should be interesting. The house is going to be packed by the sound of it.'

'Hmm. I hope they've given me a room near yours.'

Annie smiled broadly. This was something he didn't know about. She was tempted to wait and let him find out when they arrived but decided against that. 'Rose wrote and asked me if we wanted a double bed.'

He pulled the car over on to a grass verge, stopped and then turned to face her. 'And what did you say?'

'I told her that as the house would be crowded one bed would do, even if it was in the shed!'

He hugged her. 'That's marvellous. At least I'll have you all to myself at night. I hate being away from you and can't wait until we're married.'

'I feel the same.'

Reid started the car and they resumed their journey. Annie laid her head back and closed her eyes.

'Are you all right?' he asked. 'You look tired.'

'I didn't get off duty until three o'clock this morning, so I haven't been to bed.' They'd been so busy and it was a relief to get away for a while. She'd always loved her job as a wireless operator, but now, with the war drawing to a close, she wanted to be free of the stress. She wanted to be married to Reid and have children.

'In that case you rest. I'll wake you when we stop for a break,' he said.

*

They drove at a sedate pace, stopping by the roadside to watch the dawn come up and eat the food they'd brought with them. They sat there for some time just talking and enjoying the solitude. They did this a couple more times as the day wore on, in no hurry to reach their destination, and each time they resumed their journey Annie slept.

But just after three o'clock Annie opened her eyes and sat up straight. The car had stopped near a pub and there was no sign of Reid. She was surprised to see the place surrounded with every kind of vehicle, including push-bikes. One hell of a racket was coming from the pub. A group of people came along the road, laughing and singing and waving flags, and then disappeared inside. What on earth was going on?

Just as Annie clambered out of the car to investigate Reid came through the door and ran towards her in long, loping strides. She watched his fluid movements and wondered how many times he'd hurtled towards his Spitfire like that? Several times a day in those terrible months of 1940, she guessed.

When he reached her she was swung off her feet as he danced her round and round in excitement.

'Reid!' she gasped. 'What's happened?'

'It's all over!' He kissed her, then said, 'Germany has surrendered. It's official. Churchill has just announced it on the wireless.'

Annie gave a squeal of delight and wrapped her arms around his neck.

'They won't need us any more, my darling, and we can get out of the air force as soon as possible.'

Before Annie had a chance to say anything a crowd erupted from the pub and towed them inside.

'Landlord,' an elderly man in ARP uniform called. 'Let's have some drinks for the pilot and his lady.'

Reid was wearing his best uniform, with its medal ribbons. It didn't take a genius to know what he'd been doing during the conflict; he was a highly decorated pilot, though she'd never once heard him talk about how he won his medals.

A whisky was thrust into her hand, and it was more than an hour before they could slip away and continue their journey. All Annie wanted to do now was celebrate with the family. All the way along their journey there were crowds of people hell-bent on celebrating; it was impossible to drive through some of the villages without stopping to join in. Everyone thrust drinks into their hands; it was obvious that some carefully hoarded bottles were being opened at last, having been saved for this very occasion.

Annie had lost track of where they were but it didn't really matter. No one cared about anything except that the war was over, and the country was one great big, cheering, laughing party. One man had dragged his wind-up gramophone out on to the street, and when the people started to line up for the conga Annie laughed at Reid. 'Oh no, not that again!'

'Come on,' Reid said and dragged her towards the snaking line of revellers. 'Let's join in and remember the night I proposed to you.'

They danced their way up the street, through people's gardens, and back again towards their car. As soon as they reached it Reid lifted Annie off her feet and dumped her in the front seat. 'Let's get out of here or we'll never see the family tonight!'

They were both laughing as they inched their way along the crowded street, and once they were clear Annie laid her head back. The conga would always remind them of Reid's proposal of marriage, and it was such a happy memory.

Reid grinned as another group cheered and thumped on the car as they went past. 'We're going to be a bit late, I'm afraid.'

'It doesn't matter.' Now the first feeling of euphoria was passing Annie began to grasp what this meant to her, Reid and their families. Bill, Will and Charlie had survived . . . A tear trickled down her face as she remembered those who wouldn't see this day. Paul, George, Jack Graham, and his younger son, lost when the ship had been torpedoed . . . And she couldn't even imagine how many friends Reid had seen die.

She felt Reid squeeze her hand and she gave him a tearful smile.

'I know, darling, it's a bitter sweet moment, isn't it?'

She was unable to speak. The pain of loss was heightened at that moment.

It was almost dark by the time they reached Wales, but the house was ablaze with lights, just the same as every place they'd passed and stopped at along the way. Obviously the first thing everyone had done was rip down the hated blackout curtains.

As soon as they drew up the front door opened and the children came running out with torches in their hands. They were flashing the beams up into the sky and screeching at the novelty of being able to show a light. After years of trying not to show even a small chink of light this was unbelievable fun for them. There wouldn't be any more need for the air-raid wardens to walk down the street shouting, 'Put that light out!'

Annie laughed and shielded her eyes as Jacques pointed the light straight in her face. Reid swept the small boy off his feet making him squeal in delight.

'The war's over!' Jacques shouted at the top of his voice. 'The Germans gone. We can go home now.'

'That's wonderful.' Reid put Jacques down and watched him hurtle towards Sam and Maria, who had come out of the house with everyone else.

'What a difference in the boy,' Reid said to Annie.

She nodded but didn't have time to say anything as Kate and James hugged them. It was an unusual gesture from James, but this was a special time – a time to let the emotions run riot. And when she saw the happiness of Sam, Maria and their small son it made her almost believe that the terrible struggle had been worth-while.

Once inside Annie looked around the crowded room and gasped. Will, Dora and her family were there; Reid's parents; Rose, Bill, Charlie and Bob. 'How did you all manage to get here at the same time?' she asked in wonder.

Bill smiled and kissed her cheek. 'This is your engagement party and we were determined to make it a real family affair. After all, we've had to wait a long time for you to make your mind up.'

Annie laughed and slipped her arm around Reid.

Wally arrived with a tray of drinks. 'We didn't expect the end of hostilities as well when we arranged this knees-up, so we're going to have a double celebration tonight.'

Annie raised her eyebrows at her sister. 'Where are you going to put everyone, Rose?'

'It'll be a tight squeeze,' Rose answered. 'James and Kate will be sleeping at the cottage with Jack, so we'll put at least two or three in every room. We've got some bunk beds to put up down here. But I don't think any of us will be sleeping tonight, do you?'

'I doubt it very much.' Annie gazed around at the sea of faces. 'I thought Charlie was bringing his girl.'

'He did. She's in the kitchen helping with the sandwiches.'

Annie gaped at Rose in amazement. 'You're joking.'

'No, I'm not. She seems a nice girl,' Rose said, 'and she pitched in as soon as she arrived.'

'Really?' Annie still couldn't believe what she was hearing. The girl she'd met would never have volunteered for kitchen work. 'That doesn't sound like Pat.'

Rose chuckled. 'Her name's Madge. Charlie must have changed her.'

'Oh, I do hope so.' Annie headed for her brother. 'Introduce me to your new girlfriend.'

'Sure, Annie.' Charlie headed for the kitchen. 'You'll like Madge.'

'What happened to the other one?' she asked him.

'Oh, she found someone with more money. American I believe.'

Annie regarded her brother and saw that he didn't look at all sad about this turn of events, so he couldn't really have loved her. 'Thank goodness for that. She'd have drained you dry, Charlie.'

'I know.' He stopped by the kitchen door and winked

at her. 'I'm not daft, Annie, and you needn't worry, I had a good time for a while.'

She thumped him playfully on the chest. 'I bet you did.'

Madge was petite with dark-brown hair and hazel eyes. She was a homely looking girl; Annie liked her at once and was happy to see that she obviously adored Charlie. Mum will be relieved to see all of her remaining children settled at last, Annie thought.

The youngsters were allowed to stay up; but around eleven Jacques was drooping from all the excitement, and James, now looking quite the young man, took Kate and Jacques to the cottage. He stayed with them, leaving the grown-ups to celebrate.

Bill had bought a gramophone and lots of records – Glenn Miller, Frank Sinatra, Artie Shaw, Vera Lynn and many more of the famous singers and big bands of the war. The furniture was moved back so they could dance and sing the night away.

The dawn was throwing golden fingers of light across the sky when Annie and Reid finally managed to slip away to bed.

'This is the first day of peace in Europe,' Reid told her as he gathered her into his arms, 'and our life together is just beginning.'

He made love to her until she was gasping with pleasure. Afterwards, as they drifted into sleep, it occurred to Annie that they hadn't bothered with any precautions this time. She smiled to herself. What did it matter? The war was over and they would be married in a month's time.

*

It was midday before anyone started to wander downstairs, much to the children's disgust. And it was a rather subdued gathering around the kitchen table. After the joy of knowing that the war was over at last there was a much more serious air about everyone, as they all began to think of the future. For five and a half years the only thing to occupy their minds had been surviving the war, but now everyone had to come to grips with picking up the threads of their lives.

Sam was the first one to announce his plans. 'We are going back to France on the first available boat,' he told them, holding Jacques in his arms and smiling down at his wife. 'We shall be leaving early tomorrow.'

'Then we'll be able to travel part of the way together,' Marj told him, 'because we're returning to Roehampton in the morning. I can't wait to get back to my house again.'

'Why don't you and Annie stay here for the rest of your leave,' Bill suggested to Reid.

Reid looked at Annie for her approval, and then nodded. 'We'll do that if you don't mind.'

'What are you going to do with the house now?' Annie asked Rose.

'That's up to James. George left it to James, so it belongs to him now.'

'Oh, that's right.' Annie remembered now. Rose had insisted that her father leave everything to the children, so James had inherited all the Gresham property, and Kate some money in trust as a nest egg for when she married or reached the age of twenty-five – whichever came first.

'We'll keep it for holidays,' James told them. 'Grandpa

George loved this place and I'm sure he would have wanted us to keep it.'

'Good decision,' Bill told his son. 'It's a fine, solid house and with our growing family it will be made good use of.'

James looked pleased with his father's approval and Annie could see that he was growing into a sensible boy. But with parents like Rose and Bill it was hardly surprising.

'We must take Tibby and Pirate with us,' Kate declared. 'They will be unhappy on their own here.'

'We wouldn't dream of leaving them behind.' Rose smiled at her daughter. 'I've already got a cat box for Tibby to travel in.'

So it was all decided. The rest of the day was spent packing as everyone prepared to return to their normal lives. After all these years it wasn't going to be easy; there was still Japan to be dealt with, but the threat to this country was over. The time had come to look forward, and not back.

It was chaos the next morning as everyone prepared to leave. Reid watched Jacques tearing around in a state of high excitement, the toy rabbit once again dangling from his hand by its ear. Although he was five years old now, today he looked like an excited baby. The little boy obviously had no intention of leaving the precious rabbit behind. Kate and James had given him more toys to take home with him and he was insisting that his father find room for them in their luggage. Kate was overseeing the packing of toys, looking very grown up and motherly for a nine-year-old.

Charlie had disappeared soon after breakfast, but he was back now, rumbling up in a large air force truck. When he stopped and jumped out he gave Reid a thumbs-up sign and winked.

'Where did Charlie get that?' Annie asked as the men started to load the cases into the back.

'I've no idea.' Reid's expression was one of innocence.

Annie laughed. 'Don't try to fool me. He couldn't have commandeered transport without proper authorization.'

Reid grinned at her. 'Just look at the number of cases everyone's got. We had to do something. Charlie's going to drive it back and that means the train journey will be more comfortable for the others.'

'But what about Sam's luggage; is that being loaded as well?'

'Bill has persuaded them to stay at Roehampton tonight and make their way back to France tomorrow.'

'Annie.' Maria came and kissed her on both cheeks. 'I thank you for all you have done for us. You must promise to visit soon and bring Kate and James with you. Jacques does not realize it yet but he is going to miss them very much.'

'We'll come to France as soon as we can,' Annie promised.

'Thank you.' Maria gave a sad smile. 'You will enjoy your next visit more. No Germans to hide from, eh?'

Annie gave her a startled look.

'Ah, yes, André has told me all about your brave action.' Maria turned to Reid and stood on tiptoe to kiss him also.

'You will bring everyone to see us?' she asked.

'Of course.' Reid hugged Maria but his mind was

racing. What the devil had she meant when she'd told Annie that there wouldn't be any need to hide from the Germans this time?

As everyone else came and said goodbye Reid watched Annie through narrowed eyes as she hugged Sam.

'Should I call you André now?' she asked, giving a little laugh of amusement. 'You were ratty the last time I tried to.'

'Of course, Sam is no longer needed. That part of my life is finished.'

'Well, André, you and your family be happy.' Annie kissed him on the cheek and then hugged Jacques.

Reid put his arm around Annie as they watched the truck drive away with everyone waving from the back. They would all be dropped off at the station, leaving Charlie and Madge to drive back with the luggage and the animals. He waited until they were out of sight, and then led her back indoors. The house was strangely silent now, and he was glad they were going to have a few quiet days on their own. But first there was something he had to find out.

'Tell me what Maria was talking about,' he said, making her sit on the settee.

'Sorry?'

Reid sat next to her and turned her to face him. 'What was that remark about dodging Germans?'

'It was nothing.' Annie tried to stand up. 'I'll make some tea, shall I?'

'No, not until you've explained, Annie.'

She sighed, reached out and ran her finger lightly over his lips. 'I suppose it's all right to talk about it now. After all, Sam . . . sorry, André, has obviously told Maria.'

Reid waited, giving Annie time to compose herself. Whatever this was, it was clearly difficult for her to talk about. He knew just how she felt because he had seen things he doubted he would ever be able to discuss.

Annie began hesitantly, and for the next half hour he never said a word as the story unfolded. He saw the pain in her eyes and watched the tears flow unchecked in rivers down her face. And he knew for certain that this was the first time she'd ever taken this experience out from the back of her mind, looked it square in the face, and relived each moment.

When she'd finished she dipped her head as if all energy and emotion was spent, and Reid wrapped her in his arms and held her. She didn't need words at this moment, just someone who loved her and understood.

If he felt a pang of jealousy for this man Jack Graham she had risked her life for, then he pushed it aside. He now knew how special she was and he loved her even more. If that were possible!

36

It was the middle of June before Annie and Reid could arrange a suitable date for their wedding. They wanted as many of their family and friends there as possible, and it had taken a lot of sorting out. In the end they'd had to settle for the 25th, otherwise Bob would have been on his way back to Australia. He had fitted in with the family as if he'd never left, although they had not seen him since he'd run away to sea as a boy. It would please her mother to have him at the wedding, and as he was leaving in two days' time it would give them a chance to include him in just one more family celebration. Once he left again for Australia it was unlikely they would ever see him again. There was another cause for celebration as well. Bill had been out of the navy for two weeks now and already appeared relaxed and much happier.

Annie looked over her shoulder to check the back of the dress and then turned around, admiring the way the parachute silk hung in elegant folds from a nipped-in waist. She had designed the dress and her mother and Rose had made a wonderful job of it, following her drawing with absolute accuracy.

'You look lovely,' Rose told her.

Annie smiled. It was a relief to be out of uniform for a change.

Marj tweaked the veil and gave a satisfied nod. 'Now,

have you got something old, something new, something borrowed and something blue?'

'I don't think so. Does it matter?'

Her mother looked horrified. 'Of course it does. You can't marry without those things.'

Annie shook her head. 'You're too superstitious, Mum.'

'That's as may be, but I'll not have my daughter walking up the aisle without proper preparation.'

'Humour her, Annie,' Rose laughed. 'I had to go through the same routine before I married Bill.'

'And a good job you did, my girl. You needed all the help you could get to make your marriage survive those first two years,' Marj accused her eldest daughter.

'It was Bill who saved us,' Rose pointed out. 'Not some meaningless material symbols.'

'I know.' Marj smiled at her two daughters. 'But let's not take any chances, eh?'

'Right.' Annie touched the veil. 'This was Rose's, so is that old enough?'

Marj agreed that it was, just about.

'Good. The dress is new and so is everything else I'm wearing, thanks to the family pitching in with their clothing coupons. So the next is something borrowed.'

'I know.' Rose disappeared upstairs and returned with a velvet box in her hands. 'Grandma Gresham gave me this to wear on my wedding day and you can borrow it for yours.'

Annie let Rose fasten the beautiful row of pearls around her neck.

'That's perfect.' Marj beamed with pleasure. 'That just leaves something blue.'

'Will this do?' Annie lifted the long skirt and revealed a saucy garter with a pattern of blue forget-me-nots on it.

Rose laughed and their mother gasped. 'Where did you get that?'

'Dora gave it to me. She wore it when she married Will.'

'Ah, well, that will do just fine,' Marj said. 'They are happy enough with one babe and another on the way.'

Rose winked at Annie. 'This is going to be some wedding with both the maids of honour pregnant. Let's hope Jenny doesn't decide to give birth during the ceremony.'

'She's promised me she won't,' Annie told them through her laughter.

'Auntie Annie.' Kate walked into the room, followed by Dora and Jenny. 'We're leaving now, the car's here to take us to the church.'

A lump came into Annie's throat as she saw how lovely her friends and niece looked. Their dresses were also made of parachute silk but they had been dyed a pale lilac, except for Kate's, and that was white with a large lilac sash. It was a truly stunning sight in these austere times.

Wally looked in. 'Come on, girls, the car's waiting.'

Marj bustled off to see that everyone left at the proper time and the two sisters were left alone.

'Nervous?' Rose asked.

'No.' Annie shook her head. 'I know I'm marrying the right man.'

'Good.' Rose stood silent for a while, and then spoke softly. 'Don't make the same mistakes I did, Annie. Reid's a good man – show him you love him.'

'I will.'

917

Rose nodded, and then did a surprising thing. She kissed her sister, smiled and walked out of the room.

Annie was touched by the unusual outward show of affection, but Rose had mellowed over the last few years. The tough young woman had disappeared, leaving hardly a trace of the anger and frustration that had driven her. The tight control on her emotions was still there, of course, and Annie doubted if that would ever change. Rose's young life had been too harsh for that last barrier to come down completely, but those who knew her recognized the deep love she had for family, friends and all who suffered injustice and deprivation . . .

'Time to go, Annie.' Wally handed her the flowers and they went out to the waiting car.

The church in Putney was crowded with family and friends. As Annie glanced at the smiling faces she couldn't remember when she'd felt so happy. Her brother Will was there; his ship had docked just the night before. Charlie was serving as an usher with some more of the ground crew from Tangmere. As she looked around at the sea of air force blue uniforms her grin broadened. That airfield must be empty today!

As the organ began to play Wally squeezed her arm to make her start the walk down the aisle. Everyone in the church faded from thought and vision as she concentrated on Reid. He was standing with Bouncer at his side and had turned round to face her as she walked towards him. He looked stunning in his uniform and Annie wondered how she could ever have believed that she didn't like him. It was only with hindsight that she realized she must have fallen in love with him when she'd glimpsed him on the quay during the evacuation of Dunkirk.

She reached his side and he smiled, leaning forward to kiss her gently on her cheek. 'I love you, Annie, and you look so beautiful,' he murmured for her ears only.

The ceremony passed all too quickly for her. After signing the register they walked down the aisle together, husband and wife. Annie felt so proud as she saw the guard of honour waiting for them outside the church. All the pilots were in their best uniforms, sporting rows of medals on their chests, with every buckle and button shining in the brilliant sunshine.

As they started their walk along the line Reid made a pretence of inspecting them. They stood fiercely to attention in true military style, until you looked into their faces and noticed the wide grins.

'You won't find anything wrong with us today,' Bouncer told them as they reached him, which caused a quiet ripple of amusement to rumble along the line.

'I'd better not.' Reid cast his glance over the pilots again and then gave a satisfied nod. 'You're certainly smarter and cleaner than I've ever seen you.'

They were all laughing now, including the man standing at the end of the line, holding up a pair of headphones.

'Sam!' Annie was ecstatic. 'I didn't think you'd be able to make it.'

He kissed her cheek and handed her the headphones. 'Here's a souvenir for you. I wouldn't have missed your wedding for anything.' He then shook hands with Reid. 'I wish you both a lifetime of happiness.'

'Thank you. How are Maria and Jacques?' Reid asked.

'They are both well. Maria is becoming stronger all the time, and although Jacques misses Kate and James he is settling down and making friends. He keeps asking when you are coming over to see him, though.'

'When can we go?' Annie looked at Reid imploringly.

'We'll go as soon as Kate and James are on their school holidays,' Reid promised.

Marj hurried up. 'They want to take the photos now.'

'We'll talk later,' Annie told Sam, as she was hustled away for the wedding photos.

After a great many were taken there was one Annie knew would be her favourite. Reid and Sam were on either side of her, and the pilots of Reid's old squadron surrounded them. It was obvious to Annie that through the perilous times they had formed a bond that would never be broken, just as she had with Sam, and Jack Graham, had he lived.

But this was not a time for sadness. She had just married the man she loved passionately and the future looked bright and inviting.

Annie moved in Reid's arms and he kissed the top of her head. He couldn't remember if he'd ever felt so contented and at peace with himself. Her delicate fingers traced a pattern over his back and he shuddered with pleasure.

'Are you awake?' he asked huskily.

'Yes.' She moved her head back on the pillow so she could look into his face and smiled. 'I've got a special present for you but I haven't had a chance to give it to you until now.'

Reid grinned. 'You mean I jumped you as soon as we reached the bedroom?'

A soft chuckle ran through her. 'You were in rather a hurry.'

'Hmm. Anyway what's this present? I thought I'd already been given it,' he added suggestively.

'Not this one; it's a gift of life.' She kissed him, then said, 'I'm pregnant, Reid.'

He thought she was joking until he gazed into her eyes; they were serious and slightly wary, as if she wasn't sure of his response. Then he grinned. 'I don't know how you can tell that so soon. This is the first time we haven't taken any precautions.'

'No, it isn't. Remember VE Day?'

That gave him a jolt. Good Lord, he'd forgotten that night, which was hardly surprising with the amount they'd all drunk. And in the euphoria of Germany's capitulation all caution had gone by the board. The shock of Annie's announcement was rapidly being replaced with one of utter joy. 'Are you sure? It's only about seven weeks.'

Annie nodded. 'The medical officer checked me over two days ago.'

'That's wonderful,' he groaned, rolling on to his back and pulling Annie on top of him. 'But I wish you'd told me before and I would have treated you with more care.'

Annie looked horrified. 'You're a strong, passionate man and that's the way you must stay. I'm feeling fine. So you're pleased about the baby?'

'Pleased? I'm ecstatic. Get out of the WAAF as soon as you can, Annie.' Reid started to make rapid plans in his head. This changed everything. 'I've got a piece of land in Thatcham near my parents' house, where we can have a house built. I'll find a place to rent until ours is ready. The plans are finished; Bill gave them to me yesterday and Grant Phillips can start the work immediately.'

Annie sat up. 'What's all this? Has Bill designed a house for us?'

Reid nodded. 'This was going to be my special wedding present to you – when I had time to give it to you, of course.'

'But when did Bill have time to do this?' she asked, astounded by the news.

'As soon as you agreed to marry me I got in touch with Bill and explained what I wanted. He was all for the idea and has been working on the design during any spare moment. It's fabulous, you'll love it.'

'I know I will.' She started to rain small kisses all over his face. 'Did anyone ever tell you what a wonderful, thoughtful man you are?'

Reid pretended to give this a lot of consideration. 'Not lately, but you can show me how pleased you are, if you like.'

'I like.'

It wasn't until the war with Japan was over in August that Annie was finally demobbed. The terrible force of the atomic bombs the Americans had dropped on Japan had appalled her, along with everyone else, but it was a blessed relief to know that the war was completely over now. She prayed that the world would never do this again; the weapons of destruction were too horrible to contemplate. She wanted their child, and all the others, to be able to grow up in peace.

She put the finishing touches to the table and went

back into the kitchen to check on her roast chicken. This was a luxury given to her by a local farmer, and she couldn't help wondering how long it would be before food was plentiful again. It would be wonderful to go into the shops and buy whatever you wanted but Annie guessed that it would be some time before that happened. This country was going to need time to recover.

She sang contentedly to herself. This was a pleasant house but she couldn't wait for their home to be finished. With luck the house should be ready for them to move into by Christmas. The baby wasn't due until early February, so that would give them plenty of time to furnish the nursery. She had already chosen which room to use and had it all planned.

'Annie.' Reid strode into the kitchen and kissed her like a desperate man. 'I've wangled fourteen days' leave,' he announced when he finally broke off the embrace. 'And I'll be demobbed by October.'

'That's marvellous.' She knew just how much he wanted out, but he was such an efficient officer that the RAF had been trying to hold on to him. However, Reid wouldn't be swayed, he was eager to get back to the family business and let his father take a well-earned retirement.

'I've also arranged with Rose and Bill for us to take the children over to France to see Jacques at the end of the week.' Reid ran his hand gently over her expanding waistline. 'We'll go by sea, and if you don't feel like tackling the journey, I'll take the children on my own.'

'There's no need for that,' she protested. 'I'm disgustingly fit, the doctor told me yesterday, and now the morning sickness has gone, I'm fine.'

'Good.' He looked relieved. 'James and Kate are excited about going, and we'll have a holiday while we're there.'

It was a glorious summer morning with the first faint rays of the sun giving a hint of the heat to come. Annie leaned on the rail and looked out over the calm sea. There was only a gentle swell and the boat seemed suspended in time. Her mind drifted back to the last time she'd been to France; the circumstances were very different this time. The fear and grief of that journey to find Jack Graham had faded now and she could remember him as the laughing, gentle and very brave man he had been. The horror of the experience no longer troubled her nights. She had done her best and he'd known that, and had been grateful to her for seeing that he survived long enough to see his son . . .

She felt Reid place an arm around her shoulder and she looked up and smiled at him.

'Memories?' he asked perceptively.

'Yes,' she told him, 'but they don't hurt like they used to.'

He nodded in understanding. 'We'll never forget, though, will we?'

Annie straightened up and shook her head. 'And we shouldn't. I just hope that the sacrifices of so many are remembered.'

'They will be.' He smiled and dropped a quick kiss on her nose. 'Fancy a cup of tea?'

'Please. And something to eat, I'm starving.'

A deep chuckle rumbled through him. 'You always are.'

'I think the baby takes all my food.'

'And how is my son enjoying the sea voyage?'

Annie gave Reid a quizzical glance. 'You're sure it's going to be a boy, aren't you?'

'Your mother told me it was.' He led her to the refreshments bar where James and Kate were already enjoying an early morning feast of tea and buns. 'We can have a girl next time.'

Annie laughed. 'Has my mother been reading the tea leaves again?'

'Something like that, I expect.'

'Auntie Annie,' Kate called. 'We've saved some for you.'

'Thanks.' She sat down.

'What's it going to be like where Jacques is?' James wanted to know.

'OK.' Reid helped himself to a bun. 'Sam said that the village is recovering and they've repaired a lot of the buildings now.'

'Must have been terrible to be occupied like they were,' James remarked.

'Yes, and thank heavens it never happened to us.' Reid cut his bun and put half on Annie's plate, giving her a secret smile.

'Only because men like you and Bouncer kept them out.' James gazed at Reid with undisguised admiration.

'Everyone played their part, James.' Reid was serious now. 'It's true the RAF held them off long enough for us to regroup after Dunkirk, but without the merchant navy and the ships which protected the convoys we'd have starved. And the way the army recovered after their defeat showed great courage and determination.'

'And there were all the ordinary people,' James reminded them. 'We mustn't forget them.'

'Yes, you're right.' Reid smiled at Annie. 'All unsung heroes and heroines.'

When they landed at Calais Reid managed to hire a car, after much haggling with the owner of a small garage. It was not in the best of condition and had a habit of burping then making a sound like fireworks going off. This sent James and Kate into hoots of laughter, but it was better than public transport, which was practically non-existent.

As they travelled the twenty-five kilometres inland to reach Sam's village, great swathes of the countryside appeared untouched until they came across ruined farm-houses here and there. Annie wondered where the owners were now? There were displaced persons all over Europe and it was going to be a mammoth task trying to get everyone back to their homes.

Reid broke through her sombre thoughts. 'This must be it.'

Jacques came running as soon as he saw them, shouting in excitement. 'You came! You came!'

Annie was thrilled to see the change in them. Jacques was noisy and boisterous, not at all like the frightened little boy who had cowered in silent misery. Maria had changed beyond recognition, and standing in front of Reid and Annie was the most stunning woman, vibrant and alive – and finally Sam. Annie studied him carefully and saw a man at peace with himself and content to be with the family he loved. The deep anger that had always lingered in his eyes was a mere shadow now.

When he came and embraced her she hugged him in delight knowing that she no longer had to worry about him. He had come home and was happy.

Reid and Annie spent two days with Sam and Maria, then, leaving the children with them, they snatched a belated honeymoon in Paris.

It was a wonderful time for them, and although stifling hot during the day, they walked beside the Seine during the cool of the evening. After three blissful days they returned to pick up the children. Before leaving for home they all visited a small memorial that had been set up by the villagers to record the names of those who had been killed during the occupation.

James and Kate solemnly placed flowers at the site, then they left, promising to return again soon.

37

Annie was spending the day with her mother and Rose. The October sun was casting shadows across the kitchen table as they sat amid the debris of their lunch, enjoying a good chat over a cup of tea.

'I expect Reid's looking forward to leaving the air force,' her mother remarked.

'Yes. Only one more week and he can't wait. Neither can his father who is eager to hand over the running of the business to him again.'

'He'll be glad to be rid of that responsibility.' Rose started to gather up the dishes.

'Here, let me help with that.' As Annie stood up a searing pain shot through her making her double up and gasp.

'What's the matter?' Marj grabbed hold of Annie.

'I don't know.' She groaned as another pain nearly made her pass out.

Her mother and Rose helped her into the other room and made her lie on the settee with her feet up. Annie was by now moaning in fright. 'The baby! I'm only five months. It's too soon to go into labour.'

Rose was already phoning for the doctor and an ambulance.

'Hold on,' her mother soothed. 'Help will soon be here. It'll be all right.'

But it wasn't going to be, Annie knew that, and the tears streamed down her face in speechless agony. She was bleeding. She was losing the baby!

'Sir!' An out-of-breath sergeant raced up to Reid. 'There's a phone call for you. Says she's your sister-in-law, and if I don't find you immediately she'll come here and break my bloody neck.' He stopped to gulp in a couple of quick breaths of air. 'She meant it. It's urgent.'

Reid was running for his office before the man had stopped speaking, his heart crashing against his ribs. Rose. No one else would threaten a stranger like that. And Annie was with her today. Oh God, what had happened?

He skidded through the door and lunged at the phone. 'Rose!'

Reid thought he knew all about the pain life could deal you at times, but as he listened his world of happiness crumbled around him.

'Is Annie all right?' As Rose told him he bowed his head in grief and tears burnt the back of his eyes. 'I'll come to the hospital at once.'

The phone crashed back on its cradle and Reid thought he must be paralysed. He couldn't move.

'Sir?' The sergeant was looking at him with concern. 'Shall I find you a car and driver?'

Reid dragged his screaming mind together and nodded. 'At once, please, Jenkins.'

When Reid saw Marj and Rose's strained expressions he knew things were bad. 'Where is she?'

929

Marj was speechless with grief, and it was Rose who nodded towards a door. 'In there, she's just come back from the operating theatre.'

There was a doctor and a nurse at Annie's bedside but Reid pushed past them to reach his wife. He hooked a chair over with his foot and sat down, cradling her hand in his. She was so still and silent, not at all like his lively, animated Annie.

'Is she going to be all right?' he asked, not taking his eyes from her face.

'She's lost the baby and a lot of blood,' the doctor told him as kindly as possible. 'But we don't think there's any permanent damage. She should make a full recovery in time.'

Reid let the tears overflow then, quite unashamed. She was going to live, and that was the only thing that mattered.

He lifted her hand to his lips and kissed her cold fingers. 'Don't you dare leave me, my darling,' he scolded. 'My life would be empty without you.'

It was about two hours before Annie stirred and opened her eyes. Her gaze fixed on Reid immediately and he saw the moment when realization dawned. Her hand was shaking as it moved down towards her stomach, but he caught it and held on tightly. He felt his own grief fighting to surface when he saw the pain in her eyes, but he mustn't let that happen. Annie was going to need him to be strong, and although she was no weakling herself this loss was going to devastate her. They had both been so excited about the baby.

Silent tears began to flow and she reached out for him.

He sat on the bed and gathered her gently into his arms. Her body shook as the sobs came in great heart-rending sounds.

'Why?' she moaned. 'Our baby was conceived at a time of such joy and I was healthy. Why?'

Reid had talked to the doctor while Annie had been asleep. He had the answers and he decided that it would be better if she knew. It might help the grieving.

'She had a heart defect.' He stroked Annie's hair in a soothing motion. 'And she died before you lost her. The doctor said that even if you'd gone full-term, she wouldn't have survived for long.'

'It was a girl?' she whispered.

'Yes.' Reid held her face away so he could look at her. He could give her some hope. 'The doctor told me that there isn't any reason why we shouldn't have healthy children in the future.'

Annie gave a ragged sigh of relief. 'I'm all right then?'

'Perfect.' He tried a smile, and was pleased to see her return it, even though the tears were still coursing down her face.

'I'm so sorry, my darling.' She held on to him tightly.

'It wasn't your fault, Annie. You mustn't believe it was for a moment.'

She nodded, closed her eyes, and sank into blessed sleep again.

Annie fought her way out of sleep but it was a struggle. She could hear muted voices – voices she recognized. Then her mind began to clear and icy fingers of despair clutched at her. She had lost the baby.

Through her whimper of distress she heard Reid call. 'Annie.'

She opened her eyes then. The private room she was in was only small but somehow most of her family had managed to squeeze in. There was Reid, her mother and Wally, Rose, Bill, Kate and James, Will and Charlie. And by the look of it they'd all brought flowers; the room was a profusion of blooms, the heady perfume overriding the antiseptic atmosphere. It was at that moment she knew just how lucky she was to be surrounded by so much love.

She gave Reid a tremulous smile. She was determined to put a brave face on things, not only for his sake but also for her own. They would get through this together, of that she was certain.

'Sit me up,' she asked, 'so I can see you all.' Reid lifted her and Rose arranged the pillows. 'Ah, that's better. You'll all get told off,' she said, trying to lighten the mood and remove their worried expressions.

'No we won't,' Will said and grinned. 'We've bribed Sister with a bar of chocolate. She said we can stay for an hour and not a moment longer.' Then he was serious again. 'We're all dreadfully sorry about the baby, Annie.'

She nodded, and dropped her head as the tears started to gather, but she fought them back. A small hand touched hers and she looked up to see Kate was sitting on the bed. At nine years old it was clear just how beautiful she was going to be.

'If you like I can be your *pretend* daughter – just until you have one of your own, of course.' Kate's dark gaze fixed on Reid. 'That's only if you want to, of course. Mummy and Daddy won't mind sharing me.'

'I think that's a wonderful idea, don't you, darling?'
Reid squeezed Annie's hand.

'We'd be honoured to have you as our *pretend* daughter.' Annie pulled Kate towards her so she could kiss her, and not for the first time she marvelled at her niece's insight. It was as if she knew just what to do in any crisis.

'Uncle Will, I know you've got another bar of chocolate, and I think we should share it now,' James suggested.

The chocolate was produced and as chatter increased Annie reached up to smooth the frown from Reid's face. 'Don't look so concerned, my darling,' she said softly. 'I'm all right now, and we'll have more children.'

She saw him relax, and the words from the Bible that she loved so much came clearly into her mind. 'If I take the wings of the morning.' Reid and his pilots had climbed into the sky not knowing what the future held for them, and that's what she must do. The pain of this loss would probably always be with her but she had learned to deal with grief over the last few years, and she was a stronger person now.

Her gaze swept over her family and lingered on Reid. He smiled at her and kissed her cheek gently, as if he understood her thoughts. The war had brought hardship and grief but it had also given her the greatest gift of all – the love of a wonderful man.

She would take *the wings of the morning*, and with that uplifting thought the future was full of promise.